A TEXT BOOK OF

BROADBAND COMMUNICATION SYSTEMS

FOR

SEMESTER - II

FINAL YEAR (BE) DEGREE COURSE IN ELECTRONICS AND TELECOMMUNICATION ENGINEERING

According to New Revised Syllabus of Savitribai Phule Pune University, Pune.

(2012 Pattern)

Mrs. DEEPA S. PANDIT

B.E. (E & TC), M. Tech (Embedded System)
Assistant Professor,
Electronics & Telecomm. Engg. Deptt.
Institute of Knowledge (IOK),
College of Engineering,
Pimple Jagtap, Pune.

N 3729

BROADBAND COMMUNICATION SYSTEMS (B.E. E&TC SEM. II)　　　　ISBN 978-93-5164-888-8**

Second Edition	:	**January 2017**
©	:	**Author**

Published By :　　　　　　　　　　　　　　　Polyplat

NIRALI PRAKASHAN

Abhyudaya Pragati, 1312, Shivaji Nagar,
Off J.M. Road, PUNE – 411005
Tel - (020) 25512336/37/39, Fax - (020) 25511379
Email : niralipune@pragationline.com

☞ **DISTRIBUTION CENTRES**

PUNE

Nirali Prakashan : 119, Budhwar Peth, Jogeshwari Mandir Lane, Pune 411002, Maharashtra
Tel : (020) 2445 2044, 66022708, Fax : (020) 2445 1538
Email : bookorder@pragationline.com, niralilocal@pragationline.com

Nirali Prakashan : S. No. 28/27, Dhyari, Near Pari Company, Pune 411041
Tel : (020) 24690204 Fax : (020) 24690316
Email : dhyari@pragationline.com, bookorder@pragationline.com

MUMBAI

Nirali Prakashan : 385, S.V.P. Road, Rasdhara Co-op. Hsg. Society Ltd.,
Girgaum, Mumbai 400004, Maharashtra
Tel : (022) 2385 6339 / 2386 9976, Fax : (022) 2386 9976
Email : niralimumbai@pragationline.com

☞ **DISTRIBUTION BRANCHES**

JALGAON

Nirali Prakashan : 34, V. V. Golani Market, Navi Peth, Jalgaon 425001,
Maharashtra, Tel : (0257) 222 0395, Mob : 94234 91860

KOLHAPUR

Nirali Prakashan : New Mahadvar Road, Kedar Plaza, 1st Floor Opp. IDBI Bank
Kolhapur 416 012, Maharashtra. Mob : 9850046155

NAGPUR

Pratibha Book Distributors : Above Maratha Mandir, Shop No. 3, First Floor,
Rani Jhanshi Square, Sitabuldi, Nagpur 440012, Maharashtra
Tel : (0712) 254 7129

DELHI

Nirali Prakashan : 4593/21, Basement, Aggarwal Lane 15, Ansari Road, Daryaganj
Near Times of India Building, New Delhi 110002
Mob : 08505972553

BENGALURU

Pragati Book House : House No. 1, Sanjeevappa Lane, Avenue Road Cross,
Opp. Rice Church, Bengaluru – 560002.
Tel : (080) 64513344, 64513355, Mob : 9880582331, 9845021552
Email:bharatsavla@yahoo.com

CHENNAI

Pragati Books : 9/1, Montieth Road, Behind Taas Mahal, Egmore,
Chennai 600008 Tamil Nadu, Tel : (044) 6518 3535,
Mob : 94440 01782 / 98450 21552 / 98805 82331,
Email : bharatsavla@yahoo.com

niralipune@pragationline.com | www.pragationline.com

Also find us on 🅕 www.facebook.com/niralibooks

1.6.2 Phase and Group Velocity

- Within all electromagnetic waves, whether plane or otherwise, there are points of constant phase.

- For plane waves these constant phase points form a surface which is referred to as a wavefront.

- As a monochromatic lightwave propagates along a waveguide in the Z-direction these points of constant phase travel at a phase velocity υ_p, which is given as,

$$\upsilon_p = \frac{n_2}{n_1} \qquad \ldots (1.6)$$

where ω is the angular frequency of the wave .

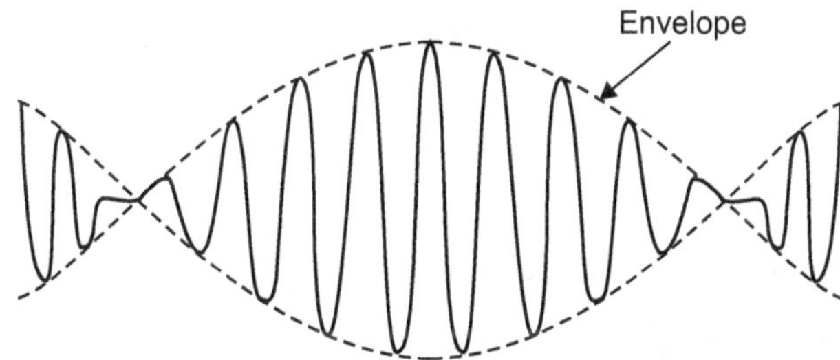

Fig. 1.8 : Formation of a wavepacket. The envelope of the wave package or group of waves travels of a group velocity υ_g

- Often the situation exists where a group of waves with closely similar frequencies propagate so that their resultant forms a packet of waves. This wavepacket does not travel at the phase velocity of the individual waves but is observed to move at a group velocity υ_g given by:

$$\upsilon_g = \frac{\delta\omega}{\delta\beta} \qquad \ldots (1.7)$$

- The group velocity is important in the study of the transmission characteristics of optical fibers as it relates to the propagation characteristics of observable wave groups or packets of light.

- If the propagation in an infinite medium of refractive index n_1 is considered, then the propagation constant may be written as:

$$\beta = n_1 \frac{2\pi}{\lambda} = \frac{n_1\omega}{c} \qquad \ldots (1.8)$$

where c is the velocity of light in free space.

- Equation (1.8) follows from equation $k = \dfrac{2\pi}{\lambda}$ and $\beta_z = n_1\, k \cos\theta.$ ... (1.9)

  where we assume propagation in the Z-direction only and hence $\cos\theta$ is equal to unity.

- Using equation (1.6) we can obtain the following relationship for the phase velocity

$$\upsilon_p \;=\; \frac{c}{n_1} \tag{... (1.10)}$$

- Similarly, employing equation (1.7) where in the limit $\delta\omega/\delta\beta$ becomes $d\omega/d\beta$, the group velocity:

$$\upsilon_g \;=\; \frac{d\lambda}{d\beta}\cdot\frac{d\omega}{d\lambda} \;=\; \frac{d}{d\lambda}\left(n_1\frac{2\pi}{\lambda}\right)^{-1}\left(\frac{-\omega}{\lambda}\right) \tag{... (1.11)}$$

$$=\; \frac{-\omega}{2\pi\lambda}\left(\frac{1}{\lambda}\frac{dn_1}{d\lambda}-\frac{n_1}{\lambda^2}\right)^{-1} \tag{... (1.12)}$$

$$=\; \frac{c}{\left(n_1-\lambda\dfrac{dn_1}{d\lambda}\right)} \tag{... (1.13)}$$

$$=\; \frac{c}{N_g} \tag{... (1.14)}$$

where, N_g is group index of the guide.

1.6.3 Cut-Off Wavelength

- Single mode operation of fibers occurs only above a theoretical cut-off wavelength λ_c which is given by

$$\lambda_c \;=\; \frac{2\pi a n_1}{v_c}\,(2\Delta)^{1/2} \tag{... (1.15)}$$

where v_c is the cut-off normalized frequency. Here λ_c is the wavelength above which a particular fiber becomes single-moded.

$$v \;=\; \frac{2\pi}{\lambda}\,a n_1\,(2\Delta)^{1/2} \tag{... (1.16)}$$

- Dividing equation (1.15) by the equation (1.16).

- For the same fiber we obtain the inverse relationship

$$\frac{\lambda_c}{\lambda} \;=\; \frac{v}{v_c} \tag{... (1.17)}$$

- For step index fiber where $v_c = 2.405$, the cut-off wavelength is given by

$$\lambda_c = \frac{v\lambda}{2.405} \qquad \dots (1.18)$$

- An effective cut-off wavelength has been defined by the ITU-T which is obtained from a 2m length of fiber containing a single 14 cm radius loop. This definition was produced because the first higher order LP_{11} mode is strongly affected by the fiber length and curvature near cut-off. Recommended cut-off wavelength values for primary coated fiber, range from 1.1 to 1.28 µm for single mode fiber designed for operation in the 1.3 µm wavelength region in order to avoid modal noise and dispersion problems.

Example 1.4 : *Determine the cut-off wavelength for a step index fiber to exhibit single mode operation when the core refractive index and radius are 1.46 and 4.5 µm respectively, with the relative index difference being 0.25%.*

Solution :

$$v_c = 2.405$$

$$\lambda_c = \frac{2\pi a n_1 (2\Delta)^{1/2}}{2.405}$$

$$= \frac{2\pi \times 4.5 \times 1.46 \, (2 \times 0.25)^{1/2}}{2.405} \ \mu m$$

$$= 1.214 \ \mu m$$

$$= 1214 \ nm$$

Hence, the fiber is single-moded to a wavelength of 1214 nm.

1.6.4 Group Delay

- The transit time or group delay τ_g for a light pulse propagating along a unit length of fiber is the inverse of group velocity υ_g.

  Hence,

$$\tau_g = \frac{1}{\upsilon_g} = \frac{d\beta}{d\omega} = \frac{1}{c}\frac{d\beta}{dk} \qquad \dots (1.19)$$

- The group index of a uniform plane wave propagating in a homogeneous medium has been determined as:

$$N_g = \frac{c}{\upsilon_g} \qquad \dots (1.20)$$

- However, for a single mode fiber, it is usual to define an effective group index N_{ge} by:

$$N_{ge} = \frac{c}{\upsilon_g} \qquad \dots (1.21)$$

where υ_g is considered to be the group velocity of the fundamental fiber mode. Hence, the specific delay of the fundamental fiber mode becomes:

$$\tau_g = \frac{N_{ge}}{c} \qquad \ldots (1.22)$$

- The effective group index may be written in terms of the effective refractive index n_{eff}.

$$N_{ge} = n_{eff} - \lambda \frac{dn_{eff}}{d\lambda} \qquad \ldots (1.23)$$

β may be expressed in terms of the relative index difference Δ and the normalized propagation constant b by the following approximate expression,

$$\beta = k\left[\left(n_1^2 - n_2^2\right) b + n_2^2\right] \simeq kn_2 [1 + b\Delta] \qquad \ldots (1.24)$$

- Approximating the relative refraction index difference as $(n_1 - n_2)/n_2$, for a weakly guided fiber where $\Delta << 1$, we can use the approximation.

$$\frac{n_1 - n_2}{n_2} \approx \frac{N_{g1} - N_{g2}}{N_{g2}} \qquad \ldots (1.25)$$

where N_{g1} and N_{g2} are the group indices for the fiber core and cladding regions respectively.

- We obtain the group velocity per unit distance by substituting equation for β into equation

$$\tau_g = \frac{1}{\upsilon_g}$$

$$\tau_g = \frac{1}{c}\left[N_{g2} + (N_{g1} - N_{g2})\frac{d(vb)}{dv}\right] \qquad \ldots (1.26)$$

- The dispersive properties of the fiber core and the cladding are often about the same and therefore the wavelength dependence of Δ can be ignored. Hence, the group delay can be written as:

$$\tau_g = \frac{1}{c}\left[N_{g2} + N_2\Delta \frac{d(vb)}{dv}\right] \qquad \ldots (1.27)$$

- The initial term in the above equation gives the dependence of the group delay on wavelength caused when a uniform plane wave is propagating in an infinitely extended medium with a refractive index which is equivalent to that of the fiber cladding.

- The second term results from the waveguiding properties of the fiber and is determined by the mode delay factor d(vb)/dv, which describes the change in group delay caused by the changes in power distribution between the fiber core and cladding.

1.7 CYLINDRICAL FIBERS

1.7.1 Modes

- In common with the plannar guide TE and TM modes are obtained with the dielectric cylinder. The cylindrical waveguide, however is bounded in two dimensions rather than one.

- Thus, two integers, l and m are necessary in order to specify the modes in contrast to the single integer (m) required for the plannar guide. For the cylindrical waveguide we therefore refer to TE_{lm} and TM_{lm} modes.

- These modes correspond to meridional rays travelling within the fiber.

- However, hybrid modes where E_z and H_z are non-zero also occur within the cylindrical waveguide.

- These modes which result from skew ray propagation within the fiber are designated HE_{lm} and EH_{lm} depending upon whether the component of H or E make the larger contribution to the transverse field.

- The analysis may be simplified when considering optical fibers for communication purposes. These fibers satisfy the weakly guiding approximation where the relative index difference $\Delta \ll 1$.

- In fact, Δ is usually less than 0.03 (3%) for optical communication fibers. The approximate solutions for the full set of HE, EH, TE and TM modes may be given by two linearly polarized components.

- These polarized modes are not exact modes of the fiber, except for the fundamental (lowest order) mode.

- However, Δ in weakly guiding fibers is very small therefore HE – EH mode pair occurs which have almost identical propagation constants. Such modes are said to be degenerate.

- The superpositions of these degenerating modes characterized by a common propagation constant correspond to particular LP modes regardless of their HE, EH, TE or TM field configurations.

- This linear combination of degenerate modes obtained from the exact solution produces a useful simplification in the analysis of weakly guiding fibers.

- The relationship between the traditional HE, EH, TE and TM mode designations of the LP_{lm} mode designations are shown in the Table 1.1. The mode subscripts l and m are related to the electric field intensity profile for a particular LP mode.

- There are in general $2l$ field maxima around the circumference of the fiber core and m field maxima along a radius vector.

Table 1.2

Linearly polarized	Exact
LP_{01}	HE_{11}
LP_{11}	$HE_{21}, TE_{01}, TM_{01}$
LP_{21}	HE_{31}, HE_{11}
LP_{02}	HE_{12}
LP_{31}	HE_{41}, EH_{21}
LP_{12}	$HE_{22}, TE_{02}, TM_{02}$
LP_{lm}	$HE_{2m}, TE_{0m}, TM_{0m}$
LP_{lm} ($l \neq 0$ or 1)	$HE_{l+1, m}\ EH_{l-1, m}$

- The subscript l in the LP notation now corresponds to HE and EH modes with labels $l + 1$ and $l - 1$ respectively.

1.8 OPTICAL FIBER MODES AND CONFIGURATIONS

1.8.1 Fiber Types According to Refractive Index Profiles

- According to refractive index profiles there are two types of fibers:

  (1) Step index fiber, (2) Graded index fiber.

1. Step Index Fiber:

- The optical fiber with a core of constant refractive index n_1 and a cladding of a slightly lower refractive index n_2 is known as a step index fiber.

- This is because the refractive index profile for this type of fiber makes a step change at the core-cladding interface as shown in Fig. 1.9 which illustrates the two major types of step index fiber.

- The refractive index profile may be defined as:

$$n(r) = \begin{cases} n_1 & r < a \text{ (core)} \\ n_2 & r \geq a \text{ (cladding) in both cases.} \end{cases} \qquad \ldots (1.28)$$

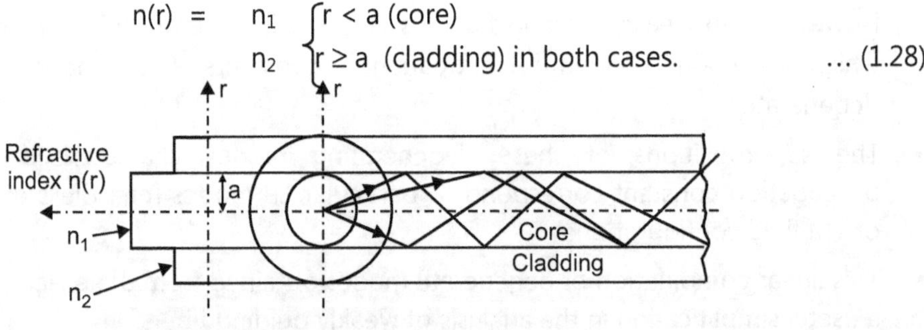

(a) Multimode step index fiber

- In practical step-index fibers the core of radius has a refractive index n_1 which is typically equal to 1.48. This surrounded by a cladding of slightly lower index n_2, where

$$n_2 = n_1 (1 - \Delta) \qquad \ldots (1.29)$$

- The parameter Δ is called the core-cladding index difference or simply the index difference. Values of n_2 chosen such that Δ is nominally 0.01. Typical values range from 1 to 3 percent for multimode fibers and form to 1.0 percent for single-mode fibers. Since the core refractive index is larger than the cladding in electromagnetic energy at optical frequencies is made to propagate along the fiber waveguide through inter reflection at the core-cladding interface.

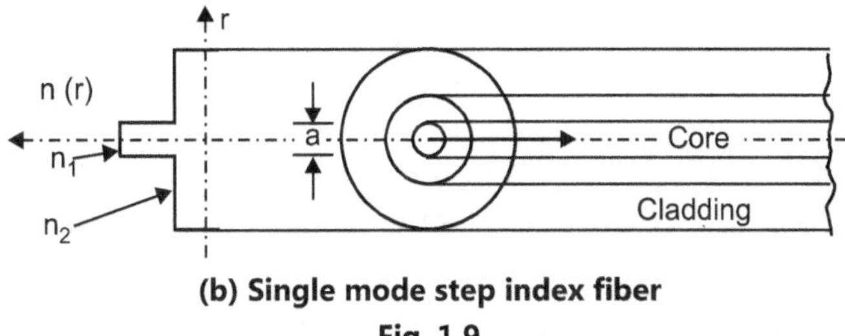

(b) Single mode step index fiber

Fig. 1.9

- Fig. 1.9 (a) show a multimode step index fiber with a core diameter of around 50 μm or greater, which is larger enough to allow the propagation of many modes within the fiber core.

- Fig. 1.9 (b) shows a single mode or mono-mode step index fiber which allows the propagation of only one transverse electromagnetic mode (typically HE_{11}) and hence the core diameter must be of the order of 2 to 10 μm.

- The single mode step index fiber has the distinct advantage of low intermodal dispersion (broadening of transmitted light pulses), as only one mode is transmitted, whereas with multimode step index fiber considerable dispersion may occur due to the differing group velocities of the propagating modes.

- This in turn restricts the maximum bandwidth attainable with multimode step index fibers, especially when compared with single mode fibers. However, for lower bandwidth applications multimode fibers have several advantages over single mode fibers.

- These are:

    (1) The use of spatially incoherent optical sources (e.g. most light emitting diodes) which cannot be efficiency coupled to single mode fibers.

    (2) Larger numerical apertures, as well as core diameters facilitating easier, coupling to optical sources.

    (3) Lower tolerance requirements on fiber connectors.

- Multimode step index fibers allow the propagation of a finite number of guided modes along the channel. The number of guided modes is depends upon the physical parameters (i.e. relative refractive index difference core radius) of the fiber and the wavelengths of the transmitted light, which are included in the normalized frequency v for the fiber.

- There is a cut-off value of normalized frequency v_c for guided modes below which they cannot exist. However, mode propagation does not entirely cease below cut-off.

- Modes may propagate as unguided or leaky modes which can travel considerable distances along the fiber.

- It can be shown that the total number of guided modes or mode volume M_s for a step index fiber is related to the value v for the fiber by the approximate expression.

$$M_s \simeq \frac{v^2}{2}$$

- Which allows an estimate of the number of guided modes propagating in a particular multi-mode step index fiber.

- In an ideal multimode step index fiber with properties (i.e. relative index difference, core diameter) which are independent of distance, there is no mode coupling and the optical power launched into a particular mode remains in that mode and travels independently of the power launched into the other guided modes.

- Also the majority of these guided modes operate far from cut-off and are well confined to the fiber core.

- Thus, most of the optical power is carried in the core region and not in the cladding.

- The properties of the cladding (i.e. thickness) do not therefore significantly affect the propagation of these modes.

Example 1.5 : *A multimode step index fiber with a core diameter of 80 μm and a relative index difference of 1.5% is operating at a wavelength of 0.85 μm. If the core refractive index is 1.48 estimate:*

(a) The normalized frequency for the fiber.

(b) The number of guided modes.

Solution :

The normalized frequency may be obtained as:

$$v = \frac{2\pi}{\lambda} \, an_1 \, (2\Delta)^{1/2}$$

$$= \frac{2\pi \times 40 \times 10^{-6} \times 1.48}{0.85 \times 10^{-6}} (2 \times 0.015)^{1/2} = 75.8$$

(b) Total number of guided modes is given as:

$$M_s = \frac{v^2}{2} = \frac{5745.6}{2} = 2873$$

Hence, this fiber has a v number of approximately 76, giving nearly 3000 guided modes.

Example 1.6 : *An optical fiber in air has an NA of 0.4. Compare the acceptance angle for meridional rays with that for skew rays which change direction by 100° at each reflection.*

Immunity to Interference and Crosstalk: Optical fibers form a dielectric waveguide and therefore they are free from electromagnetic interference (EMI), radio frequency interference (RFI) or switching transients giving electromagnetic pulses (EMPs). Therefore communication using optical fibers is unaffected by transmission through an electrically noisy environment and fiber cable does not require shielding from EMI. The fiber cable is also not susceptible to lightning strikes if used overhead rather than underground. Crosstalk is negligible, even when many fibers are bundled together.

Signal Security: The light from optical fibers does not radiate significantly and therefore they provide a high degree of signal security. Therefore, any attempt to acquire a message signal transmitted optically may be detected. This feature is attractive for military, banking and general data transmission applications.

Low Transmission Loss: The development of optical fibers has resulted in the production of optical fiber cables which exhibit very low attenuation or transmission losses as compared to copper cables.

Fibers are fabricated with losses as low as 0.15 dB km^{-1} and this feature becomes the major advantage of optical fiber communication. It provides the facility of implementation of communication links with extremely wide optical repeaters or amplifier spacing which reduces both, system cost and complexity.

Ruggedness and Flexibility: Even if the protective coatings are essential, optical cables may be manufactured with very high tensile strengths. The fibers may also be bent or twisted without damage. Optical cables have been developed which have proved flexible, compact and extremely rugged. Considering the size and weight advantage, optical cables are superior in terms of storage transportation, handling and installation in comparison to copper cables.

System Reliability and Ease of Maintenance: These features primarily stem from the low-loss property of optical fiber cables which reduce the requirement for intermediate repeaters or line amplifiers to boost the transmitted signal strength. Hence, with fewer optical repeaters or amplifiers, system reliability is generally enhanced in comparison with conventional electrical conductor systems.

Potential Low Cost: Optical fibers offer the potential for low-cost line communication. Overall system costs when utilizing optical fiber communication on long-haul links are substantially less than those for equivalent electrical line systems because of the low-loss and wideband properties of the optical transmission medium. The requirement for intermediate repeaters and the associated electronics is reduced, which gives a substantial cost advantage.

1.6 ELECTROMAGNETIC MODE THEORY FOR OPTICAL PROPAGATION

1.6.1 Modes in a Planar Guide

- The planar guide is the simplest form of optical waveguide. It is assumed that it consists of a slab of dielectric with refractive index n_1 sandwiched between two regions of lower refractive index n_2.

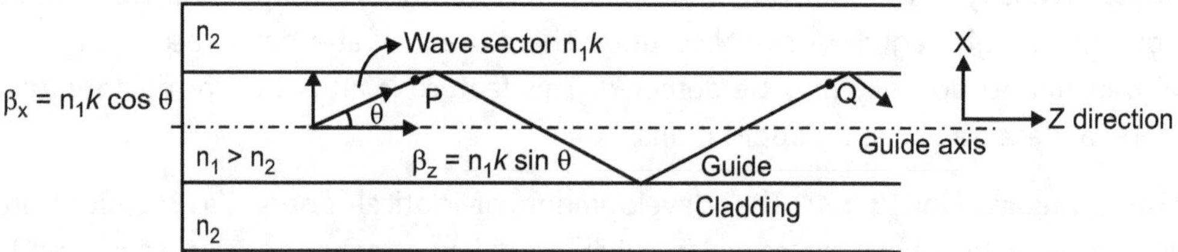

Fig. 1.7 : A plane wave propagating in the guide shown by it's wave vector or equivalent ray the wave vector is resolved into components in the Z and X directions

- As the refractive index within the guide is n_1, the optical wavelength in this region is reduced to λ/n_1, while the vacuum propagation constant is increased to $n_1 k$. When θ is the angle between the wave propagation.

- Vector of the equivalent ray and the guide axis, the plane wave can be resolved into two component plane waves propagating in the Z and X directions, as shown in the Fig. 1.7.

- The component of the phase propagation constant in the Z-direction β_z is given by

$$\beta_z = n_1 k \cos \theta \qquad \ldots (1.4)$$

- The component of the phase propagation constant in the X-direction β_x is:

$$\beta_x = n_1 k \sin \theta \qquad \ldots (1.5)$$

- When light is described as an electromagnetic wave it consists of a periodically varying electric field E and magnetic field H which are oriented at right angles to each other.

- When the electric field is perpendicular to the direction of propagation, $E_z = 0$, but a corresponding component of the magnetic field H is in the direction of the propagation. In this instance the modes are said to be Transverse Electric (TE).

- When a component of E field is in the direction of propagation but $H_z = 0$, the modes formed are called Transverse Magnetic (TM).

- When the total field lies in the transverse plane, Transverse Electromagnetic (TEM) waves exist where both E_z and H_z are zero. TEM waves occur in metallic conductors they are seldom found in optical wave guides.

* करविर निवासीनी महालक्ष्मी देवी, कोल्हापूर *

...चरणी अर्पण

PREFACE TO THE SECOND EDITION

I am very much glad and excited to announce that the First Edition of this book received an overwhelming response from the engineering student community, compelling me to release its **Second Edition** within a very short period of time.

This thoroughly revised **Second Edition** has been updated with additional matter, many solved problems, including **Solved University Examination Papers (In Sem. Feb. 2016 and End Sem. May 2016 and Nov. 2016)** and Numerous Exercises for practice.

Special care has been taken to maintain high degree of accuracy in the theory and numericals throughout the book.

I take this opportunity to express my sincere thanks to Dineshbhai Furia of Nirali Prakashan, a reputed pioneer in the publication field. My special thanks to Jignesh Furia and Mrs. Nirali Verma for their effective cooperation and great care in bringing out this revised edition. I also appreciate the efforts of M. P. Munde and the entire staff of Engineering Books Deptt. of Nirali Prakashan namely Mrs. Deepali Lachake (Co-ordinator) for bringing this book to the students in a timely manner.

I sincerely hope that this "**Second Edition**" will also be warmly received by all concerned as in the past.

Valuable suggestions from my esteemed readers to improve the book are most welcome and highly appreciated.

Pune **–Author**

PREFACE TO THE FIRST EDITION

It gives me great pleasure to bring out the book on **"Broadband Communication Systems"**. This book is strictly written as per the New Revised Syllabus of Savitribai Phule Pune University, (2012 Pattern) for the students of final year Degree Course in Electronics and Telecommunication Engineering.

The book is as per New Revised Examination Scheme which has been implemented from this academic year. According to this, In-Semester Examination carries 30 Marks over first three units and End-Semester Examination carries 70 Marks over entire syllabus of which the first three units will carry 20 Marks and units 4, 5 and 6 will carry 50 Marks.

I have given **Sample Question Papers of In-Semester University Examination (30 Marks) and End-Semester University Examination (70 Marks) in this book for the practice.**

I have tried to provide the best possible material in simple and lucid language to the students preparing for degree course. The subject is divided into Six Units and each unit is explained thoroughly with diagrams. So, I am sure that, this book will fulfill all needs of the subject. Sufficient number of questions are also included at the end of each unit for the revision of the subject.

I would like to express my gratitude to the many people who saw me through this book; to all those who provided support for this book.

Above all, I want to thank my family members and friends, who supported and encouraged me in spite of all the time it took me away from them. It was a long and difficult journey for them.

I am gratefully acknowledge co-operation from **Shri. Dineshbhai Furia, Shri. Jignesh Furia, Mrs. Nirali Verma**, **Shri. M.P. Munde** and **Mrs. Deepali Lachake** (Co-ordinator) of **Nirali Prakashan.**

Any suggestions and feedback for the improvement will be appreciated and acknowledged.

Pune   **Author**

SYLLABUS

Unit I : Light Wave System Components   6L

Key Elements of Optical Fiber Systems, Optical Fibers as a Communication Channel: Optical Fiber Modes and Configurations , Mode Theory for Circular Waveguides, Single-mode Fibers, Graded-index Fiber Structure, Signal Degradation in Optical Fibers. Optical Sources: Basic Concepts and characteristics of LEDs and LASERs. Photodetectors: Basic Concepts, Common Photodetectors.

Unit II: Lightwave Systems   6L

System Architectures, Point-to-Point Links: System Considerations, Design Guidelines: Optical Power Budget, Rise Time Budget, Long-Haul Systems.

Unit III: Multichannel Systems   6L

Overview of WDM, WDM Components: 2 x 2 Fiber Coupler, Optical Isolators and Circulators, Multiplexers and De-multiplexers, Fiber Bragg Grating, FBG applications for multiplexing and De-multiplexing function, Diffraction Gratings, Overview of Optical Amplifiers: SOA, EDFA and RFA in brief.

Unit IV: Orbital Mechanics and Launchers   6L

History of Satellite Communication, Orbital Mechanics, Look angle determination, Orbital perturbations, Orbital determination, Launchers and Launch Vehicles, Orbital effects i communication system performance.

Unit V: Satellites 6L

Satellite Subsystems, Attitude and control systems (AOCS), Telemetry, Tracking, Command and Monitoring, Power systems, Communication subsystems, Satellite antennas, Equipment Reliability and space qualification.

Uniy VI : Satellite Communication Link Design   6L

Introduction, Basic transmission Theory, System Noise Temperature and G/T Ratio, Design of Downlinks, Satellite Systems using Small Earth Stations, Uplink Design, Design of Specified C/N : Combining C/N and C/I values in Satellite Links, System Design Examples.

●●●

CONTENTS

Unit I

LIGHT WAVE SYSTEM COMPONENTS

- Communication is the method of message transfer or information transfer from one place to a distant place.

- Communication is the need of growth. The first use of optical transmission links was a fire-signal method used by the Greeks in the 18th century. It was used for sending alarms, call for help or certain announcements etc.

- In 1880, Alexander Graham Bell reported the transmission of speech using a light beam. Investigation of optical communication continued in the early part of the twentieth century, but it's use was limited to low capacity communication links.

- This limitation for links was due to the lack of suitable light sources and the other problems which limits the transmission.

- Light transmission in the atmosphere is restricted to the line of sight and is affected by disturbances such as rain, snow, fog, dust and atmospheric turbulence.

- Since Lower frequency means longer wavelength, electromagnetic waves proved suitable carriers for information transfer in the atmosphere.

- Depending on their wavelengths, these electromagnetic carriers can be transmitted over considerable distances but are limited in the information transfer which they can convey by their frequencies.

- The information carrying capacity is directly related to the bandwidth or frequency extent of the modulated carrier.

- In theory, the greater the carrier frequency the larger the available bandwidth and thus the information carrying capacity of the communication system is increased.

- Due to this reason, radio communication has been developed.

- A renewed interest in optical communication occurred in the early 1960s with the invention of the laser.

- Despite the problems, some modest free space optical communication links have been implemented for applications such as the linking of a television camera to a base vehicle and for data links of a few hundred metres between buildings.

1.2 ELECTROMAGNETIC SPECTRUM

- In parallel with the development of the fiber waveguide, attention was also focused on other optical components which would constitute the optical fiber communication system.

- Since optical frequencies are accompanied by extremely small wavelengths, the development of all these optical components essentially required a new technology.

- For this, semiconductor optical sources and detectors were designed and fabricated to enable successful implementation of the optical fiber system.

- These devices were originally fabricated from alloys of gallium arsenide (AlGaAs) which emitted in the near infrared between 0.8 and   0.9 μm.

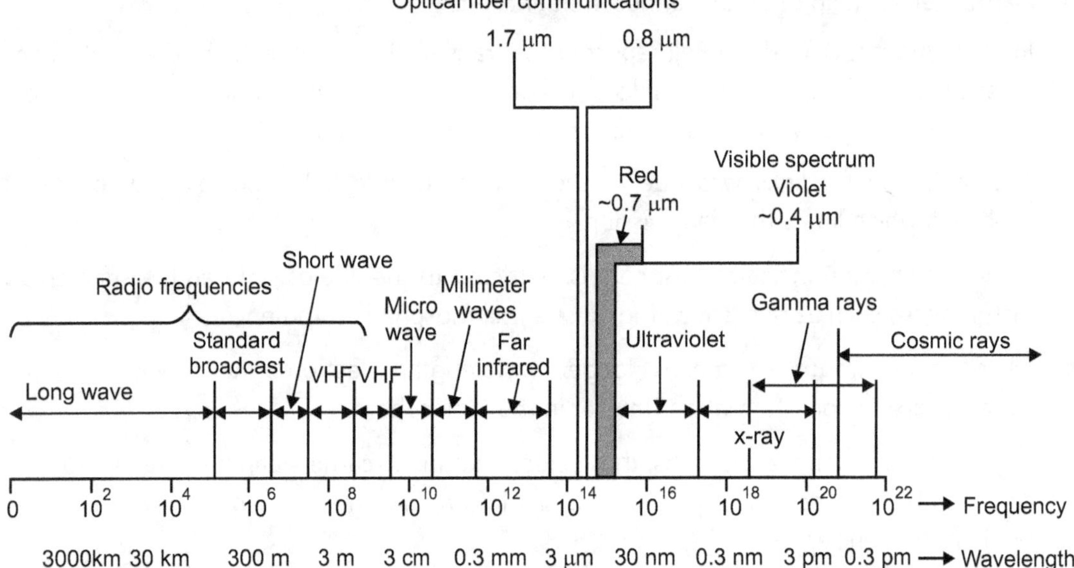

Fig. 1.1 : The electromagnetic spectrum showing the region used for optical fiber communications

- To take advantage of the enhanced performance characteristics displayed by optical fibers over this range, the above wavelength range was extended to include 1.1 to 1.6 μm region by the use of other semiconductor alloys.

- Hence material growth and fabrication technology has been developed specifically for telecommunication applications.

- For telecommunication applications such lasers are often provided with a thermoelectric cooler together with a monitoring photodiode in the device package in order to facilitate current and temperature control.

- Direct modulation of commercial semiconductor lasers at 2.5 Gbit s^{-1} over single-mode fiber transmission distances upto 200 km at a wavelength of 1.55 µm can be achieved and this may be extended upto 10 Gbit s^{-1} over shorter unrepeated fiber links.

- More recently, research and development has been focused on 40 Gbit s^{-1} transmission where, external laser modulation is required.

- The lowest silica glass fiber losses to data of 0.1484 dB km^{-1} were reported in 2002 for the longer wavelength window at 1.57 µm.

- There is a limitation for the maximum bandwidth use, due to chromatic dispersion at this wavelength.

- In the ensuing years an increasingly larger portion of the electromagnetic spectrum was utilized to develop and deploy progressively more sophisticated and reliable electrical communication systems with large capacities for conveying information from one place to another.

- Fig. 1.1 shows the electromagnetic spectral bands used for radio transmission. As the radio technologies move from lower to higher frequency bands, higher information transmission speeds can be employed to provide a higher link capacity.

1.3 OPTICAL SPECTRAL BANDS　　　　(May 2012)

- All telecommunication systems use electromagnetic energy to transmit signals. Electromagnetic energy is a combination of electric and magnetic fields and includes power, radio waves, microwaves, infrared visible light, ultraviolet light, X rays and gamma rays. Each discipline takes up a portion of the electromagnetic spectrum.

- The physical properties of the waves in different parts of the spectrum can be measured in several interrelated ways. These are length of one period of the wave, wavelength, photon energy or optical power.

- In vacuum the speed of light C is equal to the wavelength λ times the frequency f, so that

$$C = \lambda f \qquad \text{... (1.1)}$$

where f is the frequency measured in cycles per second or Hertz (Hz).

- The relation between the energy of a photon and it's frequency (or wavelength) is determined by the equation known as Plank's law,

$$E = hf \qquad \text{... (1.2)}$$

where, h = Planck's constant, h = 6.63×10^{-34} J.s = 4.14×10^{-15} eV-s

　　J = Joules, eV = electron volts

$$E\ (eV) = \frac{hC}{\lambda}$$

$$E\ (eV) = \frac{1.2406}{\lambda\ (\mu m)} \qquad \text{...(1.3)}$$

- The International Telecommunications Union (ITU) has designated six spectral bands for use in optical fiber communications within the 1260-to-1675 nm region. These long-wavelength band designations arose from the attenuation characteristics of optical fibers and the performance behaviour of an Erbium-Doped Fiber Amplifier (EDFA).

Table 1.1 : Spectral Band Designations Used in Optical Fiber Communications

Name	Designation	Spectrum (nm)
Original band	O-band	1260 to 1360
Extended band	E-band	1360 to 1460
Short band	S-band	1460 to 1530
Conventional band	C-band	1530 to 1565
Long band	L-band	1565 to 1625
Ultra-long band	U-band	1625 to 1675

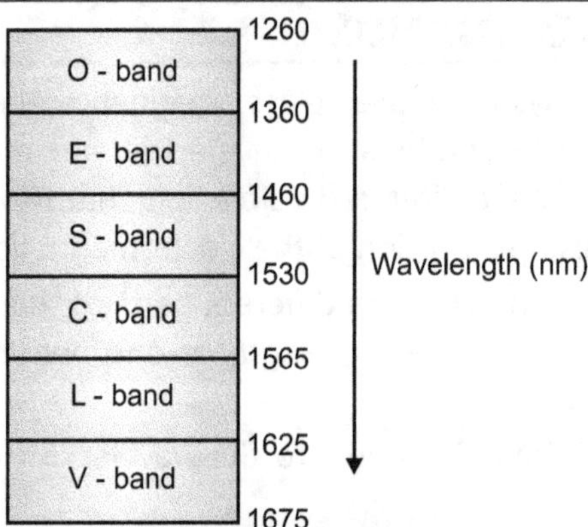

Fig. 1.2 : Designations of spectral bands used for optical fiber communications

- The 770-to-910 nm band is used for shorter wavelength multimode fiber systems. Thus, this region is designated as the short-wavelength or multimode fiber band.

1.4 KEY ELEMENTS OF FIBER OPTIC COMMUNICATION SYSTEM

(Dec. 2012, 2013)

- The basic function of an optical fiber link is to transport a signal from one location to another location with a high degree of reliability and accuracy. Fig. 1.3 shows the main constituents of an optical fiber communication link.

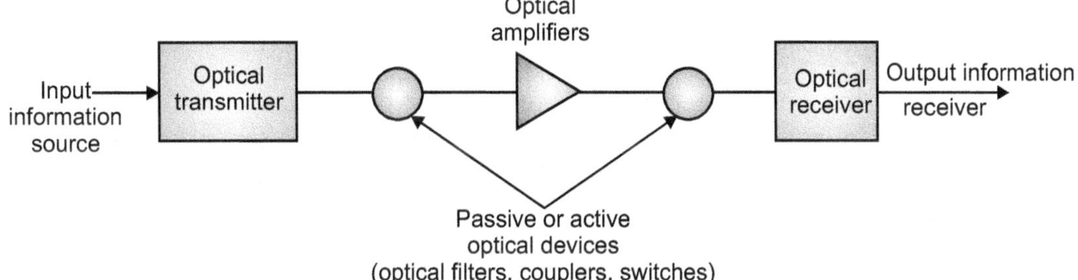

Fig. 1.3 : Optical fiber communication link

- The key components of an optical fiber communication link are a transmitter which consist of a light source and its associated drive circuitry, a cable offering mechanical and environmental protection, the fibers and a receiver consisting of a photodetector plus amplification and signal restoring circuitry.

- Additional components required are optical amplifiers, connectors, splices, couplers, regenerators and other active and passive components.

1.4.1 Overview of Element Applications

- Fiber cable is one of the most important element in an optical fiber link. In addition to protecting the glass fiber during installation and service, the cable may contain copper wires for powering optical amplifiers or signal regenerators, which are needed periodically in long-distance links for amplifying and reshaping the signal.

- To protect the glass fibers during installation and service there are many different cable configurations depending on where the cable is to be installed.

- Very low-loss optical connectors and splices are needed for joining cables and for attaching one fiber to another.

- Due to installation and manufacturing limitations, individual cable lengths will range from several hundred metres to several kilometres. Once the cable is installed a transmitter can be used to launch a light signal into the fiber.

- The transmitter consists of a light source that is dimensionally compatible with the fiber core and associated electronic control and modulation circuitry.

- Semiconductor light emitting diodes and laser diodes are used for this purpose.

- The functions of the associated transmitter electrons are to set and stabilize the source operating point and output power level.

- Once the optical signal is launched into the fiber, it becomes attenuated and distorted with increasing distance because of scattering absorption and dispersion mechanism in the glass material.

- At the destination of an optical fiber transmission line, there is a photodiode that defects the weakened and distorted optical signal and converts it to an electrical signal.

- The receiver also contains electronic amplification devices and circuitry to restore signal fidelity.

- The design of the optical receiver is more complex than that of the transmitter. The figure of merit for a receiver is the minimum optical power necessary at the desired data rate to attain either a given error probability for digital system or a specified S/N ratio for an analog system.

- The ability of the receiver to achieve a certain performance level depends on the photodetector type, the effects of noise in the system and the characteristics of the successive amplification stage in the receiver.

- Passive devices are optical components that require no electronic control for their operation. Optical filters select only a narrow spectrum of desired light.

- Optical splitters divide the power in an optical signal into a number of different branches.

- Optical multiplexers combines signals from two or more distinct wavelengths onto the same fiber, in multiple-wavelength optical fiber networks and couplers, which are used to tap off a certain percentage of light, usually for performance monitoring purposes.

- Modern sophisticated optical fiber networks contain a wide range of active optical components.

- They are, light signal modulators, tunable optical filters, reconfigurable elements for adding and dropping wavelengths at intermediate nodes, variable optical attenuators and optical switches.

- When the optical signal travels over a constant distance, it becomes weak due to power loss along the fiber.

- Hence, while setting up an optical link, engineers calculate a power budget and add amplifiers or repeaters when the path loss exceeds the available power margin.

- Optical amplification mechanisms for WDM links include the use of devices based on rare-earth doped lengths of fiber and distributed amplification by means of a stimulated Raman scattering effect.

- The installation and operation of an optical fiber communication system requires measurement techniques for verifying the specified performance characteristics of the components.

- System engineers must have knowledge of the characteristics of passive splitters, connectors and couplers and electro-optic components such as sources, photo detectors and optical amplifiers.

- When a link is being installed and tested, operational parameters that should be measured include bit error rate, timing jitter and signal to noise ratio indicated by the eye pattern.

- Measurements are needed for maintenance and monitoring functions to determine factors such as fault locations in fibers and the status of remotely located optical amplifiers.

1.4.2 Windows and Spectral Bands

- The optical fiber, light sources, photodetectors and optical amplifiers are four key components of a optical link.

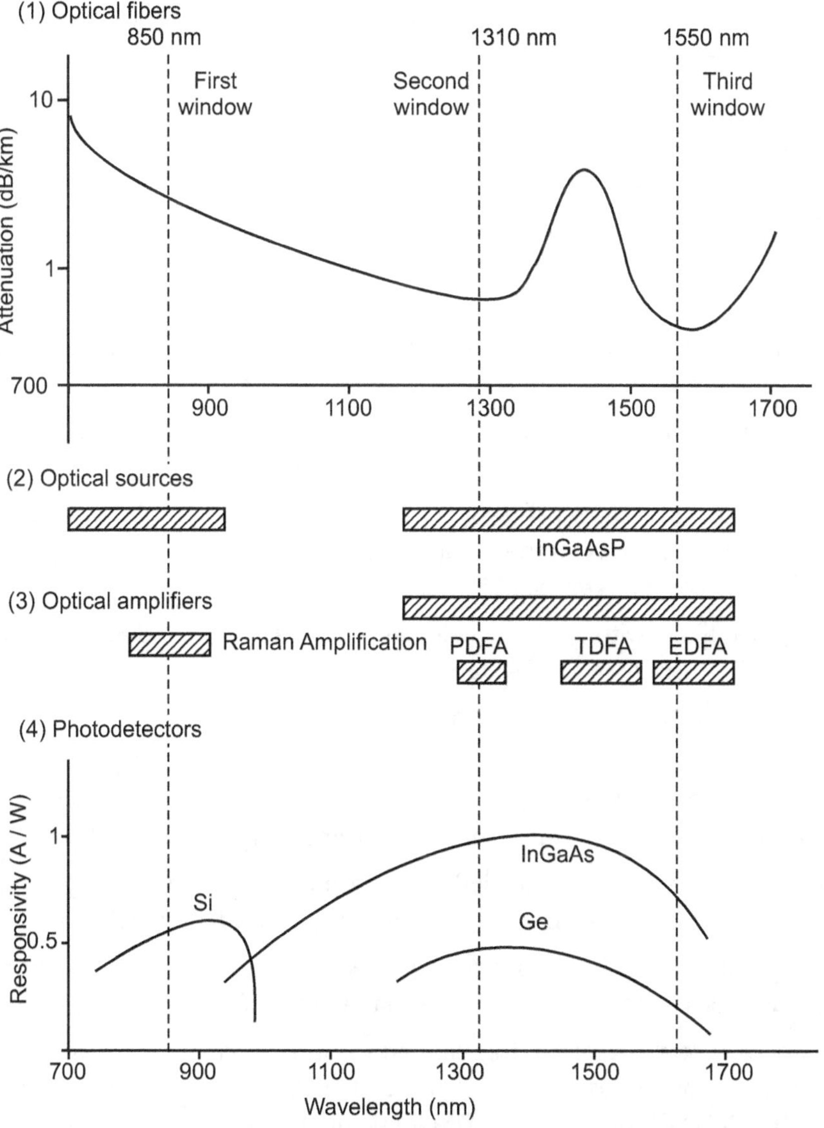

Fig. 1.4 : Characteristics and operating ranges of the four key optical fiber link components

- Fig. 1.4 shows the operating range and characteristics of the four key components. In the figure the dashed vertical lines indicate the centers of the three main traditional operating wavelength bands of optical fiber systems, which are the short-wavelength region, the O-band and the C-band.

- One of the principal characteristics of an optical fibers is it's attenuation as a function of wavelength.

- The late 1970s used the 770 to 910 nm wavelength band where there was a low-loss window and GaAlAs optical sources and silicon photodetectors operating at these wavelength were available.

- Around 1000 nm there was a range attenuation spike due to absorption by water molecules. As a result of this spike, early fibers exhibited a local minimum in the attenuation curve around 850 nm.

- In the 1980s manufacturers fabricated optical fibers with low losses in the 1260 to 1675 nm region by reducing the concentration of hydroxyl ions and metallic impurities in the fiber material.

- This spectral band is called the long-wavelength region. Since the glass still contained some water molecules, a third order absorption spike remained around 1400 nm.

- This spike defined two low-loss windows, these being the second window centered at 1310 nm and the third window centered at 1550 nm.

- These two windows are now called the O-band and C-band, respectively. InGaAsP-based light sources and InGaAs photodetectors which can operate at 1310 and 1550 nm can be used in the low-loss long-wavelength regions.

- Doping optical fibers with rare-earth elements such as Pr, Th and Er creates optical fiber amplifiers CPDFA, TDFA and EDFA devices.

- These devices and the use of Raman amplification give a further capacity to boost long-wavelength WDM systems.

- Special material purification processes can eliminate almost all water molecules from the glass fiber material, which reduces the water attenuation peak around 1400 nm.

- Due to this the E-band, 1360 to 1460 nm transmission region can be used around 100 nm to provide more spectral bandwidth in these specially fabricated fibers.

- Systems operating at 1550 nm provide the lowest attenuation, but the signal dispersion in a standard silica fiber is larger at 1550 nm than at 1310 nm.

- Fiber manufacturers overcame this limitation first by creating the dispersion-shifted fibers for single-wavelength operation and then by devising a Non-Zero Dispersion-Shifted Fiber (NZDSF) for use with WDM implementations.

- The latter fiber type has led to the widespread use of multiple-wavelength S-band and C-band systems for high capacity, long span terrestrial and undersea transmission links.

1.5 BLOCK DIAGRAM OF THE OPTICAL FIBER COMMUNICATION SYSTEM   (Dec. 2012, 2013)

- An optical fiber communication system is same as any type of communication system as far as the basic concepts are concerned.

- The general communication system consists of a transmitter or modulator which is linked to the information source, the transmission medium and a receiver or demodulator at the destination point.

- The general communication system has limited transmission distance between the transmitter and receiver beyond which the faithful communication does not occur.

- Due to this for long distance applications repeaters or line amplifiers are used at regular intervals, to remove signal distortion.

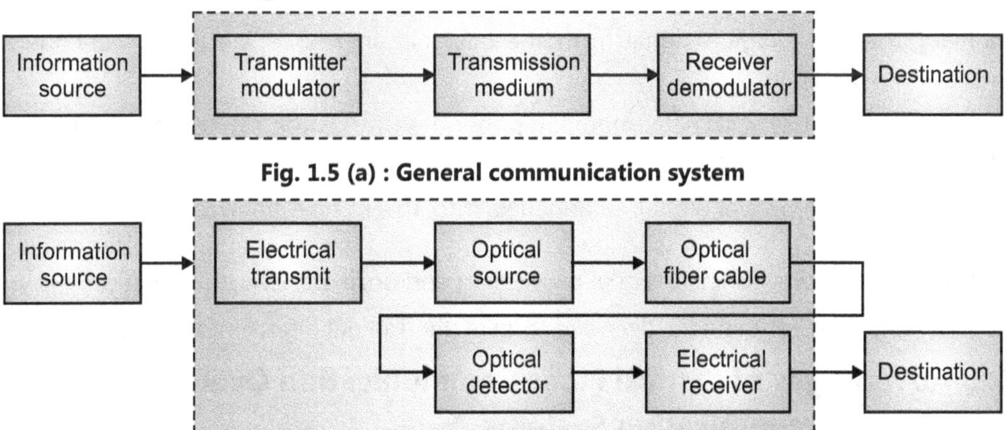

Fig. 1.5 (a) : General communication system

Fig. 1.5 (b) : The optical fiber communication system

- Fig. 1.5 (b) shows the block diagram of an optical fiber communication system. In this, information source provides an electrical signal to a transmitter comprising an electrical stage which derives an optical source to give a modulation of the light wave carrier.

- The optical source which provides the electrical-optical conversion may be either a semiconductor laser or Light Emitting Diode (LED).

- The transmission medium consists of an optical fiber cable and the receiver consists of an optical carrier.

- Photodiodes (p-n, pin or avalanche) or in some cases phototransistors and photoconductors are used for the detection of the optical signal and the optical-electrical conversion.

- The optical carrier may be modulated using either an analog or digital information signal.

- Even if it is simple to implement, analog modulation with an optical fiber communication system is less efficient, requires high S/N ratio at the receiver and the linearity needed for analog modulation is not always provided by semiconductor optical sources, specially at high frequencies.

- For this reason, analog optical fiber communication links are generally used for shorter distances and lower bandwidths.

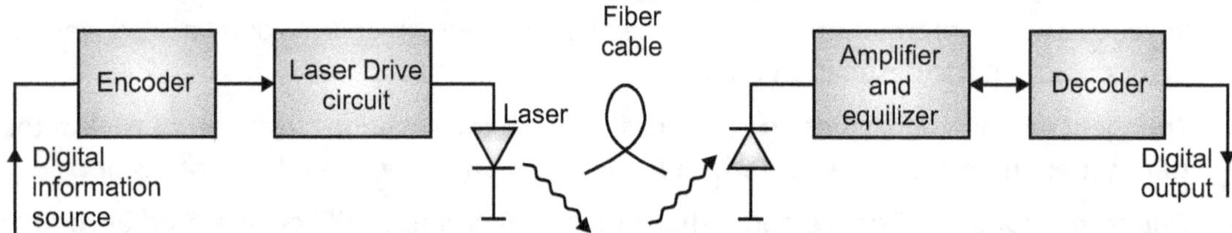

Fig. 1.6 : A digital fiber link

- Initially the input digital signal from the information source is suitably encoded for optical transmission.

- The laser drive circuit directly modulates the intensity of the semiconductor laser with the encoded digital signal.

- Hence, a digital optical signal is launched into the optical fiber cable. The Avalanche Photodiode (APD) detector is followed by a front-end amplifier and equalizer or filter to provide gain as well as linear signal processing and noise bandwidth reduction.

- Finally, the signal obtained is decoded to give the original digital information.

1.5.1 Advantages of Optical Fiber Communication Over Other Communication Systems   (May 2013)

Enormous Potential Bandwidth: The optical carrier frequency in the range 10^{13} to 10^{16} Hz yields a far greater potential transmission bandwidth than metallic cable systems (i.e. coaxial cables provides bandwidth 20 MHz over a maximum distance of 10 km). Even millimeter wave radio systems provide bandwidth of 700 MHz over a few hundreds of meters of 700 MHz over a few hundreds of meters. The fiber bandwidth can be extended further with the help of wavelength division multiplexing.

Small Size and Weight: Optical fibers have very small diameters, no greater than the diameter of a human hair. So even when such fibers are covered with protective coatings they are far smaller and much lighter than the corresponding copper cables.

Electrical Isolation: Optical fibers which are fabricated from glass or sometimes plastic polymers, are electrical insulators. Therefore they do not exhibit earth loop and interface problems. Hence, these optical fibers are suitable for communication in electrically hazardous environments.

Solution :

The acceptance angle for meridional rays is given by the equation below with $n_0 = 1$ as

$$\theta_a = \sin^{-1} NA$$

$$= \sin^{-1} 0.4$$

$$= 23.6°$$

The skew rays change direction by 100° at each reflection. Therefore, $\gamma = 50°$.

Hence, $$\theta_{as} = \sin^{-1}\left(\frac{NA}{\cos\gamma}\right)$$

$$= \sin^{-1}\left(\frac{0.4}{\cos 50}\right)$$

$$= 38.5°$$

2. Graded Index Fiber:

- Graded index fibers do not have a constant refractive index in the core but a decreasing core index n(r) with radial distance from a maximum value of n_1 at the axis to a constant value n_2 beyond the core radius a in the cladding.

- This index variation may be represented as:

$$n(r) = \begin{cases} n_1 [1 - 2\Delta (r/a)^\alpha]^{1/2} & (r < a) \\ n_1 (1 - 2\Delta)^{1/2} = n_2 & (r \geq a) \end{cases} \qquad \ldots (1.29)$$

where Δ is the relative refractive index and cladding α is the profile parameter which gives the characteristic refractive index profile of the fiber core.

- The above equation of n(r) which is a convient method of expressing the refractive index profile of the fiber core as a variation of α allows representation of the step index profile where $\alpha = \infty$, a parabolic profile when $\alpha = 2$ and a triangular profile $\alpha = 1$.

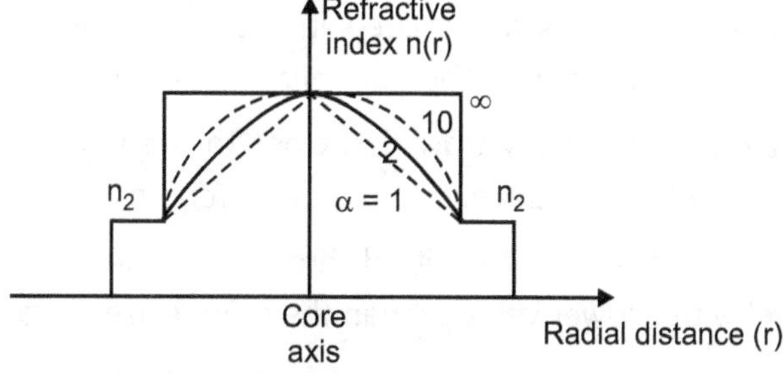

Fig. 1.10 : Possible fiber refractive index profiles for different values of α

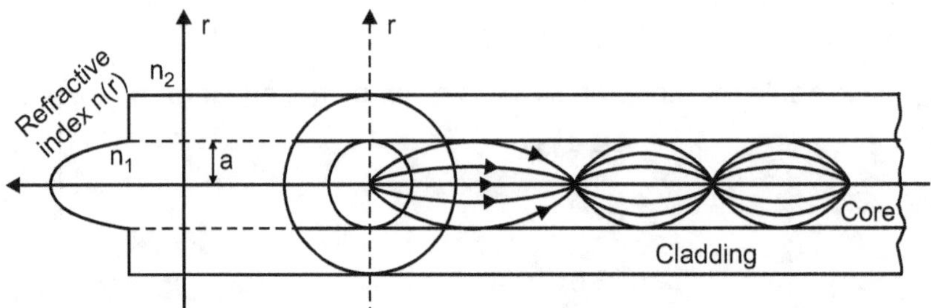

Fig. 1.11 : The refractive index profile and ray transmission in a multimode graded index fiber

- The graded index profiles which at present produce the best results for multimode optical propagation have a near parabolic refractive index profile core with $\alpha = 2$.

- A multimode graded index fiber with a parabolic index profile core is shown in Fig. 1.12. It may be observed that the meridional rays shown appear to follow curved paths through the fiber core using the concepts of geometric optics the gradual decrease in refractive index from the centre of the core creates many refractions of the rays as they are effectively incident on a large number of high to low index interfaces.

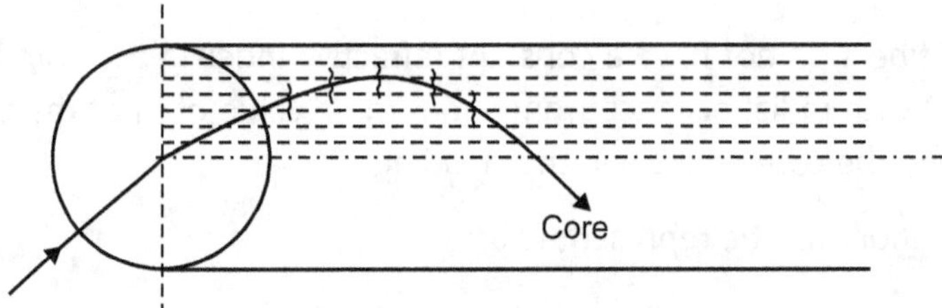

Fig. 1.12 : Refraction at various high or low index interfaces within a graded index fiber

- The mechanism is illustrated in Fig. 1.12, where a ray is shown to be gradually curved, with an ever-increasing angle of incidence, until the conditions for total internal reflection are met and the ray travels back towards the core axis, again being continuously refracted.

- Mutlimode graded index fibers exhibit far less intermodal dispersion than multimode step index fibers due to their refractive index profiles.

- Although many different modes are excited in the graded index fibers, the different group velocities of the modes tend to be normalized by the index grading.

- Considering the ray theory, the ray travelling close to the fiber axis have shorter paths when compared with rays which travel into the outer regions of the core.

- However, the near axial rays are transmitted through a region of higher refractive index and therefore travel with a lower velocity than the more extreme rays.

- This compensates for the shorter path lengths and reduces dispersion in the fiber. A similar situation exists for skew rays which follows longer helical paths.

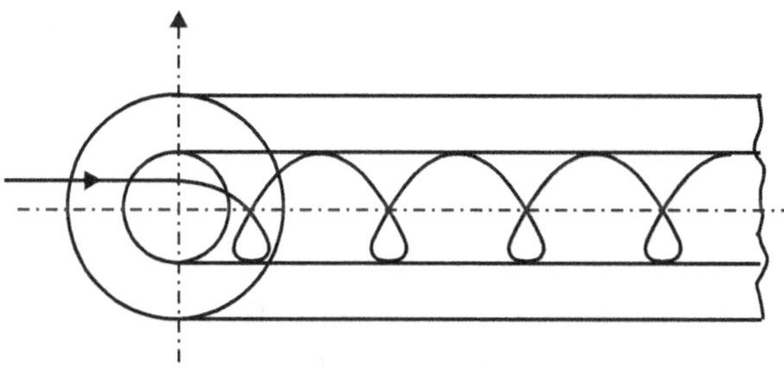

Fig. 1.13 : A helical skew ray path within a graded index fiber

- These travel for the most part in the lower index region at greater speeds, thus giving the same mechanism of mode transit time equalization.

- Hence, multimode graded index fibers with parabolic or near parabolic index profiles cores have transmission bandwidths which may be orders of magnitude greater than multimode step index fiber bandwidths.

Example 1.7 : *A graded index fiber has a core with a parabolic refractive index profile which has a diameter of 50 µm. The fiber has a numerical aperture of 0.2. Estimate the total number of guided modes propagating the fiber when it is operating at a wavelength of 1 µm.*

Solution :

$$v = \frac{2\pi}{\lambda} a \, (NA)$$

$$= \frac{2\pi \times 25 \times 10^{-6} \times 0.2}{1 \times 10^{-6}} = 31.4$$

The mode volume may be obtained from equation,

$$M_g \simeq \frac{v^2}{4} = \frac{986}{4} = 247$$

Hence, the fiber supports approximately 247 guided modes.

Difference between Single Mode Fibers and Multimode Fibers :

Single Mode Fibers	Multimode Fibers
1. Due to small core diameter it is not easy to launch optical power using LED.	1. Due to large core diameter it is easier to launch optical power into the fiber.
2. These are excited with laser diodes.	2. Light can be launched into a fiber using LED.
3. These type of fibers exhibit low inter-modal dispersion.	3. Exhibits comparatively large intermodal dispersion.
4. Bandwidth is fully utilized.	4. Cannot use the maximum bandwidth.

1.8.2 Another Category of Fiber Exists Depending on Mode of Propagation

(1) Single mode fibers.

(2) Multimode fibers.

1.8.2.1 Single Mode Fibers

- The advantages of the propagation of a single mode within an optical fiber is that the signal dispersion caused by the delay differences between different modes in a multimode fiber may be avoided.

- For transmission of a single mode, fiber must be designed to allow propagation of only one mode, whilst all other modes are attenuated by leakage or absorption. For single mode operation, only the fundamental LP_{01} mode can exist. Hence, the limit of single mode operation depends on the lower limit of guided propagation for the LP_{11} mode.

- The cut-off normalized frequency for the LP_{11} mode in step index fibers occurs at $v_c = 2.405$. Thus, single mode propagation of the LP_{01} mode in step index fibers is possible over the range:

$$0 \leq v_c < 2.405 \qquad \qquad \dots (1.31)$$

- In order to obtain single mode operation with a maximum v number of 2.4, the single mode fiber must have a much smaller diameter than the equivalent multimode step index fibers.

- It is possible to achieve single mode operation with a slightly larger core diameter by reducing the relative refractive index difference of the fiber.

- Both these factors create difficulties with single mode fibers.

- The small core diameters pose problems with launching light into the fiber and with field jointing and the reduced relative refractive index difference presents difficulties in the fiber fabrication process.

- The maximum v number which permits single mode operation can be increased still further when a graded index fiber with a triangular profile is employed.

- Hence, significantly larger core diameter single mode fibers may be produced utilizing this index profile.

- A further problem with single-mode fibers with low relative refractive index differences and low v values is that the electromagnetic field associated with the LP_{01} mode extends appreciably into the cladding.

- Another approach to single mode fiber design which allows the V value to be increased above 2.405 is the w-fiber.

- The refractive index profile of this fiber is explained in Fig. 1.14. where two cladding regions may be observed.

- Use of such two step cladding allows the loss threshold between the desirable and undesirable modes to be substantially increased.

- The fundamental mode will be fully supported with mall cladding loss when its propagation constant lies in the range.

$$kn_3 \; < \; \beta \; < \; kn_1 \qquad\qquad\qquad ...\,(1.32)$$

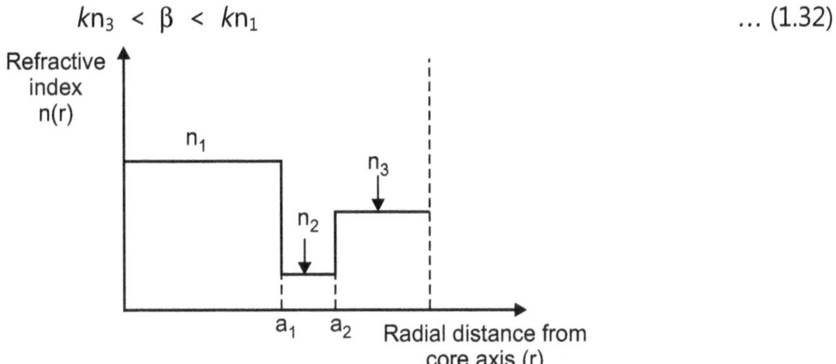

Fig. 1.14 : The refractive index profile for a single mode w fiber

- If the undesirable higher order modes which are excited or converted to have values of propagation constant, $\beta < n_3 k$, they will leak through the barrier layer between a_1 and a_2 into the outer cladding region n_3.

- Consequently these modes will lose power by radiation into the lossy surroundings. This design can provide single mode fibers with large core diameters than the conventional single cladding approach which proves useful for easier jointing difficulties, w-fiber also tend to give reduced losses at bends in comparison with conventional single-mode fibers.

1.8.2.2 Advantages of Single Mode Fibers

- They exhibit the greatest transmission bandwidths and the lowest losses of the fiber transmission media.

- They have a superior transmission quality over other fiber types because of the absence of modal noise.

- They offer a substantial upgrade capability for future wide bandwidth services using either faster optical transmitters and receivers or advanced transmission techniques.

- They are compatible with the developing integrated optics technology.

- The above advantages provides confidence that the installation of single-mode fiber will provide a transmission medium which will have adequate performance such that it will not require replacement over its anticipated lifetime of more than 20 years.

Example 1.8 : *A graded index fiber with a parabolic refractive index profile core has a refractive index at the core axis of 1.5 and a relative index difference of 1%. Estimate the maximum possible core diameter which allows single-mode operation at a wavelength of 1.3 μm.*

Solution :

The maximum value of normalized frequency for single-mode operation is:

$$v = 2.4 \, (1 + 2/\alpha)^{1/2}$$
$$= 2.4 \, (1 + 2/2)^{1/2}$$
$$= 2.4 \, \sqrt{2}$$

The maximum core radius may be obtained where:

$$a = \frac{v\,\lambda}{2\pi n_1 \, (2\Delta)^{1/2}}$$
$$= \frac{2.4\,\sqrt{2} \times 1.3 \times 10^{-6}}{2\pi \times 1.5 \times (0.02)^{1/2}}$$
$$= 3.3 \, \mu m$$

Example 1.9 : *Estimate the maximum core diameter for an optical fiber with the same relative refraction index difference (1.5%) and core refractive index (1.48) for the multimode step index fiber in order that it may be suitable for single-mode operation. It may be assumed that the fiber is operating at the same wavelength (0.85 μm). Further, estimate the new maximum core diameter. For the single operation when the relative refractive index difference is reduced by a factor of 10.*

Solution :

The maximum v value for a fiber which gives single-mode operation is 2.4.

Hence, the core radius a is:

$$a = \frac{v\,\lambda}{2\pi \, n_1 \, (2\Delta)^{1/2}}$$
$$= \frac{2.4 \times 0.85 \times 10^{-6}}{2\pi \times 1.48 \times (0.03)^{1/2}}$$
$$= 1.3 \, \mu m$$

Therefore, the maximum core diameter for single mode operation is approximately 2.6 μm.

Reducing the relative refractive index difference by a factor of 10.

$$a = \frac{2.4 \times 0.85 \times 10^{-6}}{2\pi \times 1.48 \times (0.003)^{1/2}}$$
$$= 4.0 \, \mu m$$

Hence, the maximum core diameter for the single-mode operation is now approximately 8 μm.

1.8.2.3 Effective Refractive Index

- The rate of change of phase of the fundamental LP_{01} mode propagating along a straight fiber is determined by the phase propagation constant β.

- It is directly related to the wavelength of the LP_{01} mode, λ_{01}, by the factor 2π, since β gives the increase in phase angle per unit length. Hence,

$$\beta\lambda_{01} = 2\pi \quad \text{or} \quad \lambda_{01} = \frac{2\pi}{\beta} \qquad \ldots(1.33)$$

- The effective refractive index is sometimes referred to as a phase index or normalized phase change coefficient η_{eff}, by the ratio of the propagation constant of the fundamental mode to that of the vacuum propagation constant.

$$\eta_{eff} = \frac{\beta}{k} \qquad \ldots (1.34)$$

- Hence, the wavelength of the fundamental mode λ_{01} is smaller than the vacuum wavelength λ by the factor $1/\eta_{eff}$ where:

$$\lambda_{01} = \frac{\lambda}{\eta_{eff}}$$

- It should be known that the fundamental mode propagates in a medium with a refractive index n(r) which is dependent on the distance r from the fiber axis.

- The effective refractive index can therefore be considered as an average over the refractive index of the medium.

- Relation between the effective refractive index and the normalized propagation constant b.

$$b = \frac{(\beta/k)^2 - n_2^2}{n_1^2 - n_2^2} = \frac{\beta^2 \quad n_2^2 k^2}{n_1 k^2 - n_2^2 k^2} \qquad \ldots (1.35)$$

Making use of the mathematical relation

$$A^2 - B^2 = (A + B)(A - B) \qquad \ldots (1.36)$$

$$b = \frac{(\beta + n_2 k)(\beta - n_2 k)}{(n_1 k + n_2 k)(n_1 k - n_2 k)} \qquad \ldots (1.37)$$

However, taking regard of the fact that $\beta \simeq n_1 K$ then the equation for b becomes:

$$b \simeq \frac{\beta - n_2 k}{n_1 k - n_2 k} = \frac{\beta/k - n_2}{n_1 - n_2} \qquad \ldots (1.38)$$

- Finally, η_{eff} is equal to B/K therefore,

$$b \simeq \frac{\eta_{eff} - n_2}{n_1 - n_2} \qquad \ldots (1.39)$$

b, the dimensionless parameter which varies between 0 and 1, is particularly useful in the theory of single-mode fibers because the relative refractive index difference is very small, giving only a small range for β.

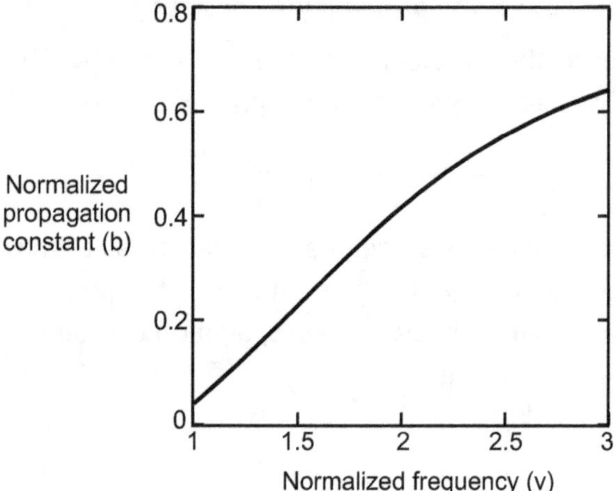

Fig. 1.15 : The normalized propagation constant (b) of the fundamental mode in a step index shown as a function of the normalized frequency (v)

1.8.3 Ray Optics Representation

- Since the core size of multimode fibers is much larger than the wavelength of the light we are interested in (which is approximately 1 µm), an intuitive picture of the propagation mechanism in an ideal multimode step-index optical waveguide is most easily seen by a simple ray (geometrical) optics representation. For simplicity, in this analysis we shall consider only a particular ray belonging to a ray congruence which represents a fiber mode. The two types of rays that can propagate in a fiber are meridional rays and skew rays. Meridional rays are confined to the meridian planes of the fiber, which are the planes that contain the axis of symmetry of the fiber (the core axis). Since a given meridional ray lies in a single plane, its path is easy to track as it travels along the fiber. Meridional rays can be divided into two general classes: bound rays that are trapped in the core and propagate along the fiber axis according to the laws of geometrical optics, and unbound rays that are refracted out of the fiber core.

- Skew rays are not confined to a single plane, but instead tend to follow a helical type path along the fiber as shown in fig. 1.15. These rays are more difficult to track as they travel along the fiber, since they do not lie in a single plane. Although skew rays constitute a major portion of the total number of guided rays, their analysis is not necessary to obtain a general picture of rays propagating in a fiber. The examination of meridional rays will suffice for this purpose. However, a detailed inclusion of skew rays will change such expressions as the light-acceptance ability of the fiber and power losses of light traveling along a waveguide.

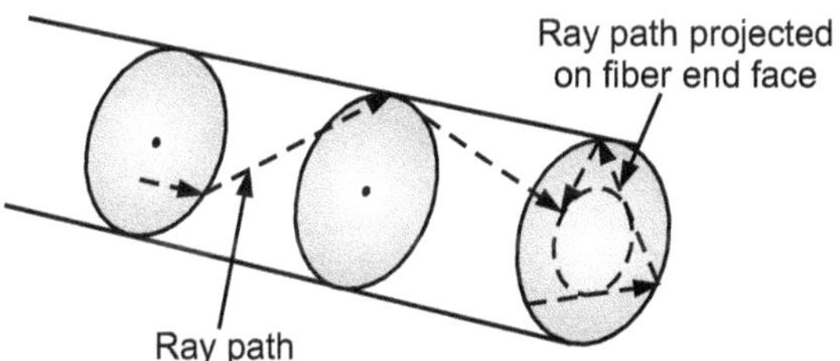

Fig. 1.16: Ray optics representations of skew rays traveling in a step-index optical fiber core

- A greater power loss arises when skew rays are included in the analyses, since many of the skew rays that geometric optics predicts to be trapped in the fiber are actually leaky rays. These leaky rays are only partially confined to the core of the circular optical fiber and attenuate as the light travels along the optical waveguide. This partial reflection of leaky rays cannot be described by pure ray theory alone. Instead, the analysis of radiation loss arising from these types of rays must be described by mode theory.

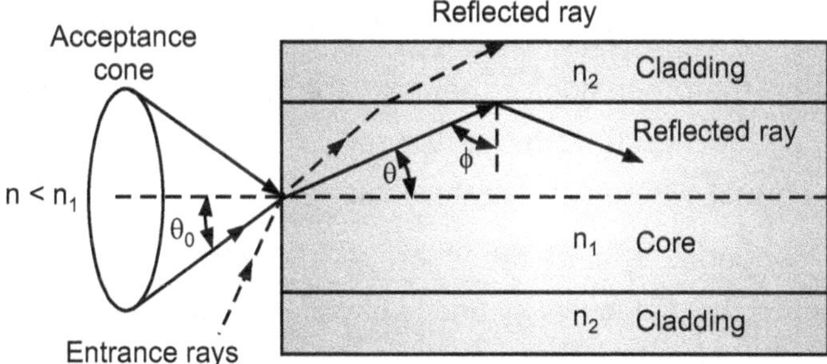

Fig. 1.17: Meridional ray optics representation of the propagation mechanism in an ideal step-index optical waveguide

- The meridional ray is shown in Fig. 1.17 for a step-index fiber. The light ray enters the fiber core from a medium of refractive index n at an angle θ_0 with respect to the fiber axis and strikes the core-cladding interface at a normal angle Φ. If it strikes this interface at such an angle that it is totally internally reflected, then the meridional ray follows a zigzag path along the fiber core, passing through the axis of the guide after each reflection.

1.8.3.1 Ray Theory Transmission

A) Total Internal Reflection (TIR)　　　　　　　　　　　　　(May 2014)

- To study the propagation of light within an optical fiber the ray theory model is used.
- The refractive index of a medium is defined as 'the ratio of the velocity of light in a vacuum to the velocity of light in the medium'.
- A ray of light travels more slowly in an optically dense medium than in one that is less dense and the refractive index gives a measure of this effect.
- When a ray is incident on the interface between two dielectrics of differing refractive indices (e.g. glass-air), refraction occurs as shown in Fig. 1.18 (a).

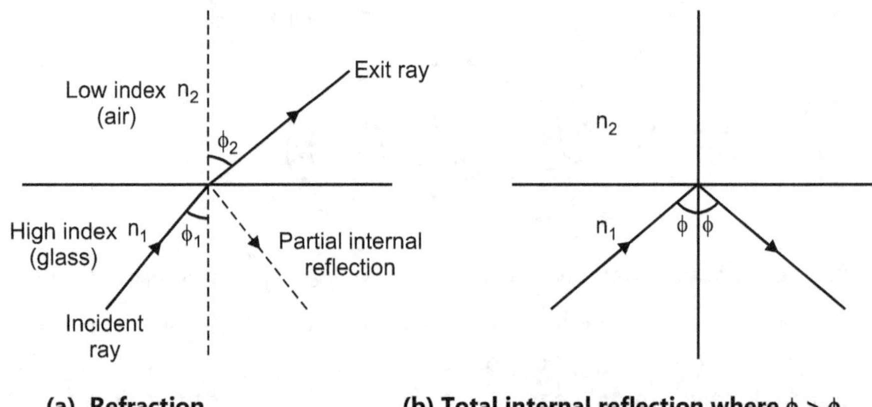

(a) Refraction　　　　　　　　**(b) Total internal reflection where $\phi > \phi_c$**

Fig. 1.18 : Light ray incident on a high to low refractive index interface (e.g. glass-air)

- It may be observed that the ray approaching the interface is propagating in a dielectric of refractive index n_1 and is at an angle ϕ_1 to the normal at the surface of the interface.

- If the dielectric on the other side of the interface has a refractive index n_2 which is less than n_1, then the refraction is such that the ray path in the lower index medium is at an angle ϕ_2 to the normal, where ϕ_2 is greater than ϕ_1.

- The angles of incidence ϕ_1 and refraction ϕ_2 are related to each other and to the refractive indices to the dielectrics by Snell's law of refraction, which states that:

$$n_1 \sin \phi_1 \;=\; n_2 \sin \phi_2 \qquad\qquad \ldots (1.40)$$

or

$$\frac{\sin \phi_1}{\sin \phi_2} \;=\; \frac{n_2}{n_1} \qquad\qquad \ldots (1.41)$$

- It may also be observed from Fig. 1.18 (a) that a small amount of light is reflected back into the originating dielectric medium (partial internal reflection).

- As n_1 is greater than n_2, the angle of refraction is always greater than the angle of incidence.

- Thus, when the angle of refraction is 90° and the refracted ray emerges parallel to the interface between the dielectrics, the angle of incidence must be less than 90°. This is the limiting case of refraction and the angle of incidence is now known as the critical angle ϕ_c.

$$\sin \phi_c \;=\; \frac{n_2}{n_1} \qquad\qquad \ldots (1.42)$$

- At angles of incidence greater than the critical angle the light is reflected back into the originating   dielectric medium (total internal reflection) with high efficiency (around 99.9%).

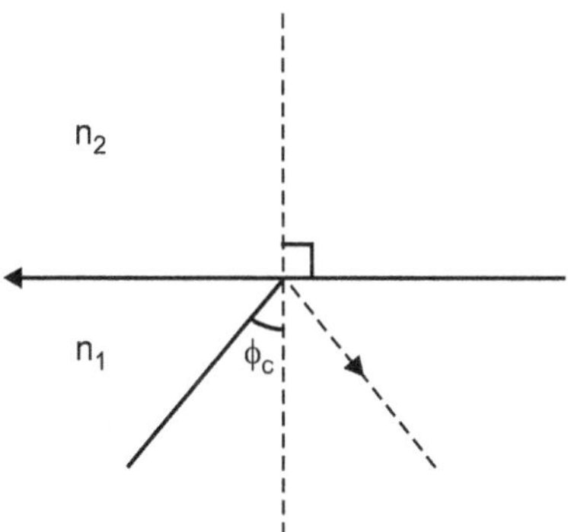

Fig. 1.18 (c) : The limiting case of refraction showing the critical ray at an angle ϕ_c

- Hence it may be observed from Fig. 1.18 (b) that total internal reflection occurs at the interface between two dielectrics of differing refractive indices when light is incident on the dielectric of lower index from the dielectric of higher index and the angle of incidence of the ray exceeds the critical value.

- This is the mechanism by which light at a sufficiently shallow angle (less than $90° - \phi_c$) may be considered to propagate down an optical fiber with low loss.

- Fig. 1.19 shows the transmission of a light ray in an optical fiber via a series of total internal reflections at the interface of the silica core and the slightly lower refractive index silica cladding.

- The ray has an angle of incidence at the interface which is greater than the critical angle and is reflected at the same angle to the normal.

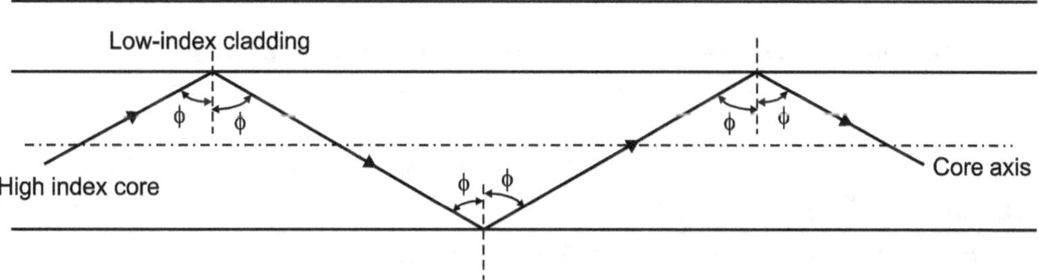

Fig. 1.19 : The transmission of a light ray in a perfect optical fiber

B) Acceptance Angle (θ_a)   (Dec. 2014)

- After studying the propagation of light in an optical fiber through total internal reflection at the core-cladding surface, now we need to study how the light enters into the fiber.

- Since only rays with sufficiently shallow grazing angle (i.e. with an angle to the normal greater than ϕ_c) at the core-cladding interface are transmitted by total internal reflection, it is clear that not all rays entering the fiber core will continue to be propagated down its length.

- The geometry concerned with launching a light ray into an optical fiber is shown in Fig. 1.20.
- In the Fig. 1.20 a meridional ray A is at the critical angle ϕ_c within the fiber at the core-cladding interface. It may be observed that this ray enters the fiber core at an angle θ_a to the fiber axis and is refracted at the air-core interface before transmission to the core-cladding interface at the critical angle.
- Hence, any ray which is incident into the fiber core at an angle greater than θ_a will be transmitted to the core-cladding interface at an angle less than θ_c and will not be totally internally reflected.
- This situation is also shown in the Fig. 1.20, where the incident ray B at an angle greater than θ_a is refracted into the cladding and eventually lost by radiation.
- Thus, for rays to be transmitted by total internal reflection within the fiber core they must be incident on the fiber core within an acceptance cone defined by the conical half angle θ_a.
- Hence, θ_a is the maximum angle to the axis at which light may enter the fiber in order to be propagated, and is often referred to as the acceptance angle for the fiber.

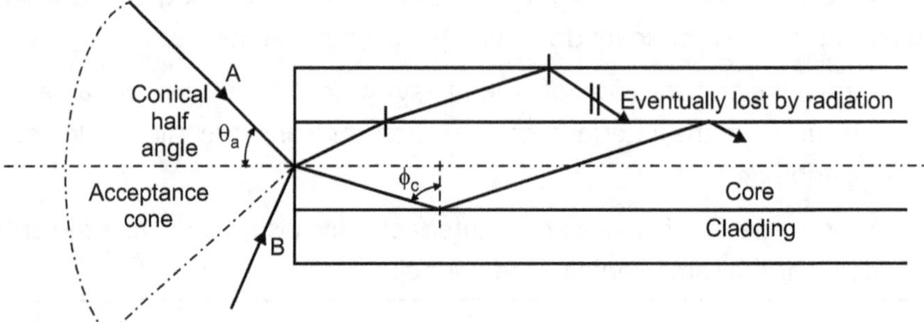

Fig 1.20 : The acceptance angle θ_a when launching light into an optical fiber

- If the fiber has a regular cross-section (i.e. the core-cladding interfaces are parallel and there are no discontinuities) a meridional ray incident at an angle greater than the critical angle will continue to be reflected and will be transmitted through the fiber.

C) Numerical Aperture (NA)   (Dec. 2014)

- To obtain the relationship between the acceptance angle and the refractive indices of the three media involves namely the core, cladding and air, the numerical aperture must be known.

Calculation of Numerical Aperture:

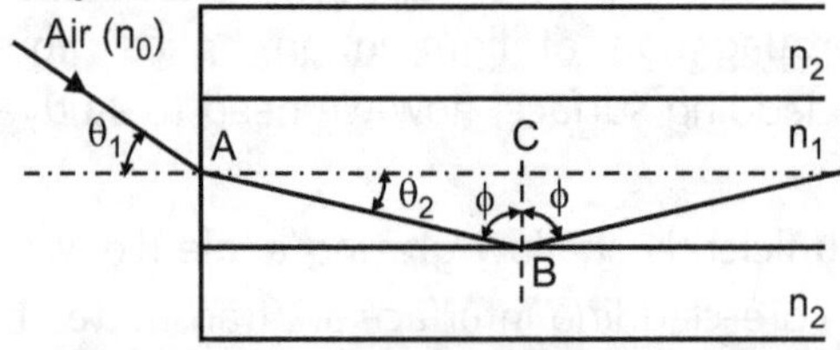

Fig. 1.21 : The ray path for a meridional ray launched into an optical fiber in air at an input angle less than the acceptance angle for the fiber

- The Fig. 1.21 shows a light ray incident on the fiber core at an angle θ_1 to the fiber axis which is less than the acceptance angle for the fiber θ_a.

- The ray enters the fiber from a medium (air) of refractive index n_0, and the fiber core has a refractive index n_1, which is slightly greater than the cladding refractive index n_2.

$$n_0 \sin \theta_1 = n_1 \sin \theta_2 \qquad \text{[– Snell's law]} \quad \ldots (1.43)$$

- Consider the right angled triangle ABC

$$\phi = \frac{\pi}{2} - \theta_2 \qquad \ldots (1.44)$$

where ϕ is greater than the critical angle at the core-cladding interface.

- Hence equation (1.42) becomes

$$n_0 \sin \theta_1 = n_1 \cos \phi \qquad \ldots (1.45)$$

Using the trigonometrical relationship $\sin^2 \phi + \cos^2 \phi = 1$.

- Equation (1.44) can be written as

$$n_0 \sin \theta_1 = n_1 (1 - \sin^2 \phi)^{1/2} \qquad \ldots (1.46)$$

- When the limiting case for total internal reflection is considered, ϕ becomes equal to the critical angle for the core-cladding and is given by

$$\sin \phi_c = \frac{n_2}{n_1}$$

- Also in this limiting case, θ_1 becomes the acceptance angle for the fiber θ_a. Combining these limiting cases into equation (1.45) gives,

$$n_1 \sin \phi_c = n_2 \qquad \ldots (1.47)$$

$$\text{and} \qquad n_0 \sin \theta_1 = n_1 (1 - \sin^2 \phi)^{1/2} \qquad \ldots (1.48)$$

$$\therefore \qquad n_0 \sin \theta_1 = (n \qquad \ldots (1.49)$$

$$\therefore \qquad n_0 \sin \theta_1 = (n \qquad \ldots (1.50)$$

$$NA = n_0 \sin \theta_a = \left(n_1^2 - n_2^2\right)^{1/2} \qquad \ldots (1.51)$$

- Since the NA is often used with the fiber in air where n_0 is unity, it is simply equal to $\sin \theta_a$.

- The NA may also be given in terms of the relation refractive index difference, Δ, between the core and the cladding which is defined as:

$$\Delta = \frac{n_1^2 - n_2^2}{2n_1^2} \qquad \ldots (1.52)$$

$$\simeq \frac{n_1 - n_2}{n_1} \qquad \text{[for } \Delta << 1] \ldots (1.53)$$

Hence, $\qquad n = 2\Delta n$ $\qquad\qquad$ ... (1.54)

Substitute this value in equation (1.51),

$$NA = n_0 \sin \theta_a = n_1^2 \left(2\Delta n_1^2\right)^{1/2} \qquad\qquad ... (1.55)$$

$$NA = n_1 (2\Delta)^{1/2} \qquad\qquad ... (1.56)$$

- The relation given in equation (1.51) and (1.56) for the numerical aperture is a very useful measure of the light-collecting ability of a fiber. They are independent of the fiber core diameter and will hold for diameters as small as 8 μm.

Example 1.1 : *A silica optical fiber with a core diameter large enough to be considered by ray theory analysis has a core refractive index of 1.50 and a cladding refractive index of 1.47. Determine: (a) the critical angle at the core-cladding interface, (b) the NA for the fiber, (c) the acceptance angle in air for the fiber.* **(May 2013, 6 Marks)**

Solution :

(a) The critical angle ϕ_c at the core-cladding interface is given by

$$\phi_c = \sin^{-1}\left(\frac{n_2}{n_1}\right) = \sin^{-1}\left(\frac{1.47}{1.50}\right) = 78.5°$$

(b) $\qquad\qquad NA = \left(n_1^2 - n_2^2\right)^{1/2} = (1.50^2 - 1.47^2)^{1/2}$

$$= (2.25 - 2.16)^{1/2} = 0.30$$

(c) The acceptance angle in air θ_a is given by

$$\theta_a = \sin^{-1} NA = \sin^{-1} 0.30 = 17.4°$$

Example 1.2 : *A typical relative refractive index difference for an optical fiber designed for long-distance transmission is 1%. Estimate the NA and the solid acceptance angle in air for the fiber when the core index is 1.46. Calculate the critical angle at the core-cladding interface within the fiber.* **(May 2015, 6 Marks)**

Solution :

$$\Delta = 0.01 = 1\%$$

$$NA = n_1 (2\Delta)^{1/2}$$

$$= 1.46 (0.02)^{1/2}$$

$$= 0.21$$

For a small angle, the solid acceptance angle in air ζ is given by,

$$\zeta \simeq \pi (NA)^2 = \pi \times 0.04$$

$$= 0.13 \text{ rad}$$

The relative refractive index difference Δ is given as :

$$\Delta \simeq \frac{n_1 - n_2}{n_1} = 1 - \frac{n_2}{n_1}$$

Hence,

$$= 1 - \Delta$$
$$= 1 - 0.01$$
$$= 0.99$$

The critical angle at the core-cladding interface is given as :

$$\phi_c = \sin^{-1}\left(\frac{n_2}{n_1}\right)$$

$$\therefore \qquad \phi_c = \sin^{-1} 0.99$$
$$\therefore \qquad \phi_c = 81.9°$$

D) Skew Rays

- In the previous sections we have considered the propagation of merdional rays in the optical waveguide.

- Another category of ray exists which is transmitted without passing through the fiber axis.

- These rays which greatly outnumber the meridonal rays, follows a helical path through the fiber and are called skew rays.

- It is not easy to visualize the skew ray paths in two dimensional but it may be observed from Fig. 1.22 (b) that the helical path traced through the fiber gives a change in direction of 2γ at each reflection where γ is the angle between the projection of the ray in two dimension and the radius of the fiber core at the point of reflection.

- Hence unlike meridonal rays, the point of emergence of skew rays from the fiber in air will depend upon the number of reflections they undergo rather than the input conditions to the fiber.

- When the light input to the fiber is non-uniform, skew rays will therefore tend to have a smoothing effect on the distribution of the light as it is transmitted, giving a more uniform output.

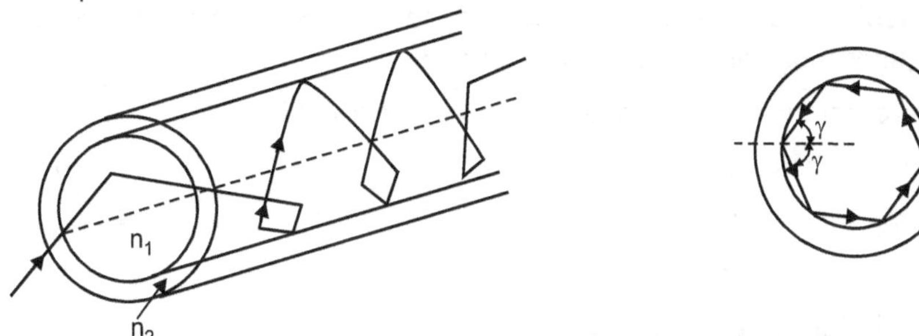

(a) Skew ray path down the fiber   (b) Cross-sectional view of the fiber

Fig. 1.22 : The helical path taken by a skew ray in an optical fiber

Acceptance Angle and NA for Skew Rays

In order to calculate the acceptance angle for a skew ray it is necessary to define the direction of the ray in two perpendicular planes.

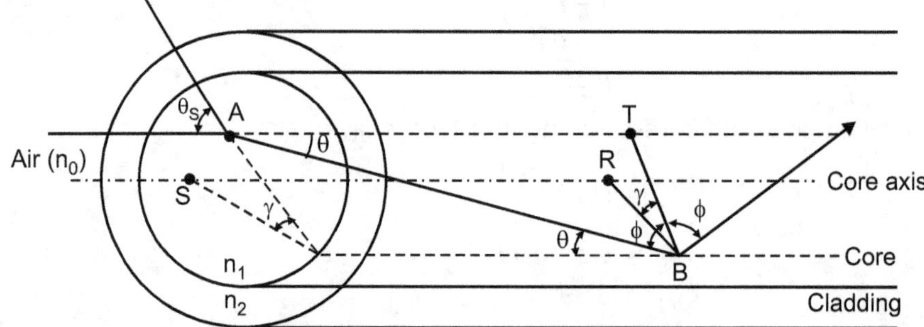

Fig. 1.23 : The ray path within the fiber core for a skew ray incident at an angle θ_s to the normal at the air-core interface

- A skew ray is shown incident on the fiber core at the point A, at an angle θ_s to the normal at the fiber end face.

- The ray is refracted at the core-air interface before travelling to the point B in the same plane.

- The angles of incidence and reflection at the point B are ϕ which is greater than the critical angle for the core-cladding interface.

- When considering the ray between A and B it is necessary to resolve the direction of the ray path AB to the core radius at the point B.

- As the incidence and reflected rays at the point B are in the same plane, this is simply $\cos \phi$.

- However, if the two perpendicular planes through which the ray path AB traverses are considered then γ is the angle between the core radius and the projection of the ray on a plane BRS normal to the core axis.

- Thus, to resolve the ray path AB relative to the radius BR in these two perpendicular planes requires multiplication by $\cos \gamma$ and $\sin \theta$.

  Hence the reflection at point B at an angle may be given by

$$\cos \gamma \sin \theta \; = \; \cos \phi \qquad\qquad \dots (1.57)$$

  Using the trigonometric relationship

$$\sin^2 \phi + \cos^2 \phi \; = \; 1$$

  Equation (1.21) becomes

$$\cos \gamma \sin \theta \; = \; \cos \phi \, (1 - \sin^2 \phi)^{1/2} \qquad\qquad \dots (1.58)$$

- If the limiting case for total internal reflection is now considered, then ϕ becomes equal to the critical angle ϕ_c for the core-cladding interface. Hence, equation (1.57) becomes or may be written as

$$\cos \gamma \sin \theta \ \leq \ \cos \phi_c = \left(1 - \frac{n_2^2}{n_1^2} \right)^{1/2} \qquad \qquad \dots (1.59)$$

- Using Snell's law at the point A we can write,

$$n_0 \sin \theta_a \ = \ n_1 \sin \theta \qquad \qquad \dots (1.60)$$

where θ_a represents the maximum input axial angle for meridional rays and θ is the internal axial angle. Hence, substituting for $\sin \theta$.

$$\sin \theta_{as} \ = \ \frac{n_1}{n_0} \frac{\cos \phi_c}{\cos \gamma} \ = \ \frac{n_1}{n_0 \cos \gamma} \left(1 - \frac{n_2^2}{n_1^2} \right)^{1/2} \qquad \qquad \dots (1.61)$$

where θ_{as} now represents the maximum input angle or acceptance angle for skew rays. Thus, the acceptance conditions for skew rays are

$$n_0 \sin \theta_{as} \cos \gamma \ = \ \left(n_1^2 - n_2^2 \right)^{1/2} = NA \qquad \qquad \dots (1.62)$$

and in the case of the fiber in air ($n_0 = 1$)

$$\sin \theta_{as} \cos \gamma \ = \ NA \qquad \qquad \dots (1.63)$$

- It may be noted that skew rays are accepted at larger axial angles in a given fiber than meridional rays, depending upon the value of $\cos \gamma$.

- It may be observed from Fig. 1.23 that skew rays tend to propagate only in the annular region near the outer surface of the core and do not fully utilize the core as a transmission medium. However, they are complementary to meridional rays and increase the light gathering capacity of the fiber.

Example 1.3 : *An optical fiber in air has an NA of 0.4. Compare the acceptance angle for meridional rays with that for skew rays which change direction by 100° at each reflection.*

Solution :

The acceptance angle for meridional rays is given as

$$n_0 \ = \ 1$$

and

$$\theta_a \ = \ \sin^{-1} NA$$

$$= \ \sin^{-1} 0.4$$

$$= \ 23.6°$$

The skew rays change direction by 100° at each reflection, therefore $\gamma = 50°$. Hence using equation $\sin \theta_{as} \cos \gamma = NA$ the acceptance angle for skew rays is:

$$\theta_{as} \ = \ \sin^{-1} \left(\frac{NA}{\cos \gamma} \right) = \sin^{-1} \left(\frac{0.4}{\cos 50°} \right) = 38.5°$$

- In this example, the acceptance angle for the skew rays is about 15° greater than the corresponding angle for meridional rays. It must be noted that we have only compared the acceptance angle of one particular skew ray path. When the light input to the fiber is at an angle to the fiber axis, it is possible that γ will vary from zero for meridional rays to 90° for rays which enter the fiber at the core-cladding interface giving acceptance of skew rays over a conical half angle of $\pi/2$ radians.

1.8.4 Wave Representation in a Dielectric slab Waveguide

- The ray theory appears to allow rays at an angle ϕ greater than the critical angle ϕ_c to propagate along the fiber. However, when the interference effect due to the phase of the plane wave associated with the ray is taken into account, it is seen that only waves at certain discrete angles greater than or equal to ϕ_c are capable of propagating along the fiber.

- To see this, let us consider wave propagation in an infinite dielectric slab waveguide of thickness d. its refractive index n_1 is greater than the index n_2 of the material above and below the slab. A wave will thus propagate in this guide through multiple reflections, provided that an angle of incidence with respect to the upper and lower surfaces satisfies the condition given in Equation (1.62)

- Fig. 1.24 shows the geometry of the waves reflecting at the material interfaces. Here, we consider two rays, designated ray 1 and ray 2, associated with the same wave. The rays are incident on the material interface at an angle $\theta < \theta_c = \pi/2 - \phi_c$. The ray paths in Fig. 1.24 are denoted by solid lines and their associated constant-phase fronts by dashed lines.

- The condition required for wave propagation in the dielectric slab is that all points on the same phase front of a plane wave must be in phase. This means that the phase change occurring in ray 1 when traveling from point A to point B minus the phase change in ray 2 between points C and D must differ by an integer multiple of 2π. As the wave travels through the material, it undergoes a phase shift Δ given by

$$\Delta = k_2\, s = n_1\, ks = n_1\, 2\pi s/\lambda$$

Where k_1 = the propagation constant in the medium of refractive index n_1

   $K = k_1\, n_1$ is the free-space propagation constant

   S = the distance the wave has traveled in the material

- The phase of the wave changes not only as the wave travels but also upon reflection from a dielectric interface.

- In going from point A to point B, ray 1 travels a distance $s_1 = d/\sin\theta$ in the material, and undergoes two phase changes δ at the reflection points. Ray 2 does not incur any reflections in going from point C to point D. to determine its phase change, first note that the distance from point A to point D is $AD = \left(\dfrac{d}{\tan\theta}\right) - d\tan\theta$. Thus, the distance between points C and D is

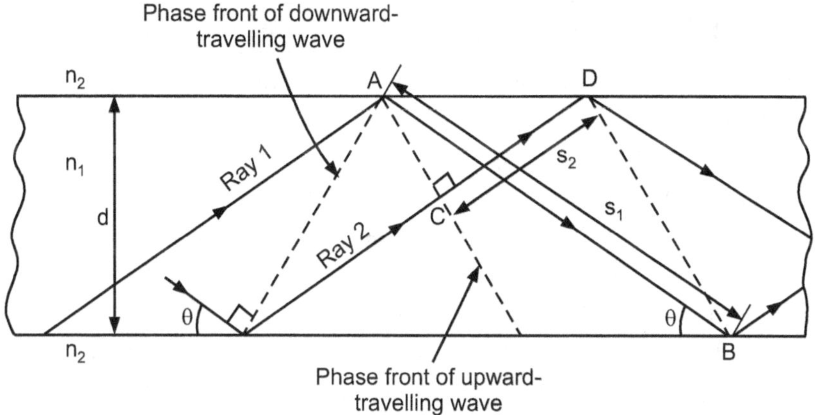

Fig 1.24: Light wave propagating along a fiber waveguide

The requirement for wave propagation can then be written as

$$\frac{2\pi n_1}{\lambda}(s_1 - s_2) + 2\delta = 2\pi m \qquad \text{... (1.64 a)}$$

Where m = 0, 1, 2, 3 ..... Substituting the expressions for s_1 ^ s_2 into Equation (1.64 a) then yields

$$\frac{2\pi n_1}{\lambda}\left\{\frac{d}{\sin\theta} - \left[\frac{(\cos^2\theta - \sin^2\theta)\,d}{\sin\theta}\right]\right\} + 2\delta = 2\pi m \qquad \text{... (1.64 b)}$$

Which can be reduced to

$$\frac{2\pi n_1\, d\,\sin\theta}{\lambda} + \delta = \pi m \qquad \text{... (1.64 c)}$$

Considering only electric waves with components normal to the plane of incidence, we have seen that the phase shift upon reflection is

$$\delta = -2\arctan\left[\frac{\sqrt{\cos^2\theta - (n_2^2/n_1^2)}}{\sin\theta}\right] \qquad \text{... (1.65)}$$

The negative sign is needed here since the wave in the medium must be a decaying and not a growing wave. Substituting this expression into Equation (1.64 c) yields

$$\frac{2\pi n_1\, d\,\sin\theta}{\lambda} - \pi m = 2\arctan\left[\frac{\sqrt{\cos^2\theta - (n_2^2/n_1^2)}}{\sin\theta}\right] \qquad \text{... (1.66 a)}$$

$$\text{Or} \quad \tan\left(\frac{\pi n_1\, d\,\sin\theta}{\lambda} - \frac{\pi m}{2}\right) = \left[\frac{\sqrt{n_1^2\cos^2\theta - n_2^2}}{n_1\sin\theta}\right] \qquad \text{... (1.66 b)}$$

Thus, only waves that have those angles θ which satisfy the condition in Equation (1.66) will propagate in the dielectric slab waveguide.

1.9   MODE THEORY FOR CIRCULAR WAVEGUIDES

- To understand the optical power propagation mechanism in a fiber, it is necessary to solve Maxwell's equations subject to the cylindrical boundary conditions at the interface between the core and the cladding of the fiber.

- Before presenting the basic mode theory in circular optical fibers, we first give a qualitative overview of the concepts of modes in a waveguide.

- When solving Maxwell's equations for hollow metallic waveguides, only Transverse Electric (TE) modes and transverse magnetic.

- TM modes are found. However, in optical fibers the core-cladding boundary conditions lead to a coupling between the electric and magnetic field components.

- This gives rise to hybrid modes, which makes optical waveguide analysis more complex than metallic waveguide analysis. The hybrid modes are designated as HE or EH modes, depending on whether the transverse electric field (the E field) or the transverse magnetic field (the H field) is larger for that mode.

- The two lowest-order modes are designated by HE_{11} and TE_{01}, where the subscripts refer to possible modes of propagation of the optical field.

- Although the theory of light propagation in optical fibers is well understood, a complete description of the guided and radiation modes is rather complex since it involves six-component hybrid electromagnetic fields that have very involved mathematical expressions.

- A simplification of these expressions can be carried out, in practice, since fibers usually are constructed so that the difference in the core and cladding indices of refraction is very small; that is, $n_1 - n_2 << 1$. With this assumption, only four field components need to be considered and their expressions become significantly simpler. The field components are called Linearly Polarized (LP) modes and are labeled LP_{jm} where j and m are integers designating mode solutions.

- In this scheme for the lowest-order modes, each LP_{0m} mode is derived from an HE_{1m} mode and each LP_{1m} mode comes from TE_{0m}, TM_{0m}, and HE_{0m} modes. Thus, the fundamental LP_{01} mode corresponds to an HE_{11} mode.

- Although the analysis required for even these simplifications is still fairly involved, this material is key to understanding the principles of optical fiber operation.

1.9.1 Overview of Modes

- Before we progress with a discussion of mode theory in circular optical fibers, let us qualitatively examine the appearance of modal fields in a planner dielectric slab waveguide shown in Fig. 1.25.

- The core of this waveguide is a dielectric slab of index n_1 that is sandwiched between two dielectric layers which have refractive indices $n_2 < n_1$. These surrounding layers are called the cladding.

- This represents the simple form of an optical waveguide and can serve as a model to gain an understanding of wave propagation in optical fibers. In fact, a cross-sectional view of the slab waveguide looks the same as the cross sectional view of an optical fiber cut along its axis. Fig. 1.25 shows the field patterns of several of the lower-order Transverse Electric (TE) modes (which are solutions of Maxwell's equations for the order of the mode is also related to the angle that the ray congruence corresponding to this mode makes with the plane of the waveguide (or the axis of a fiber); that is, the steeper the angle, the higher the order of the mode.

- The plot show that the electric fields of the guided modes are not completely confined to the central dielectric slab (i.e., they do not go to zero at the guide-cladding interface), but instead, they extend partially into the cladding.

- The fields vary harmonically in the guiding region of refractive index n_1 and decay exponentially outside of this region.

- For low-order modes the fields are tightly concentrated near the center of the slab (or the axis of an optical fiber), with little penetration into the cladding region and penetrate farther into the cladding region.

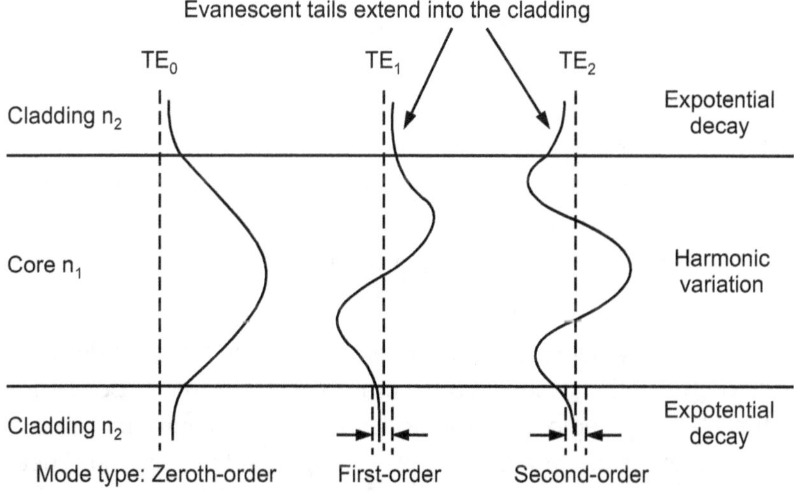

Fig. 1.25 : Electric field distributions for several of the lower-order guided modes in a symmetrical-slab waveguide

- Solving Maxwell's equations shows that, in addition to supporting a finite number of guided modes, the optical fiber waveguide has an infinite continuum of radiation modes that are not trapped in the core and guided by the fiber but are still solutions of the same boundary-value problem.

- The radiation field basically results from the optical power that is outside the fiber acceptance angle being refracted out of the core.

- Because of the finite radius of the cladding, some of this radiation gets trapped in the cladding, thereby causing cladding modes to appear.

- As the core and cladding modes propagate along the fiber, mode coupling occurs between the cladding modes and the higher-order core modes.

- This coupling occurs because the electric fields of the guided core modes are not completely confined to the core but extend partially into the cladding and likewise for the cladding modes.

- A diffusion of power back and forth between the core and cladding modes thus occurs; this generally results in a loss of power from the core modes.

- In practice, the cladding modes will be suppressed by a lossy coating which covers the fiber or they will scatter out of the fiber after traveling a certain distance because of roughness on the cladding surface.

- In addition to bound and refracted modes, a third category of modes called leaky modes is present in optical fibers.

- These leaky modes are only partially confined to the core region, and attenuate by continuously radiating their power out of the core as they propagate along the fiber.

- This power radiation out of the waveguide results from a quantum mechanical phenomenon known as the tunnel effect.

- Its analysis is fairly lengthy and beyond the scope of this book. However, it is essentially based on the upper and lower bounds that the boundary conditions for the solutions of Maxwell's equations impose on the propagation factor β. A mode remains guided as long as β satisfies the condition

$$n_2 k < \beta < n_1 k$$

- Where n_1 and n_2 are the refractive indices of the core and cladding, respectively, and $k = 2\pi/\lambda$. The boundary between truly guided modes and leaky modes is defined by the cutoff condition $\beta = n_2 k$. As soon as β becomes smaller than $n_2 k$, power leaks out of the core into the cladding region. Leaky modes can carry significant amounts of optical power in short fibers. Most of these modes disappear after a few centimeters, but a few have sufficiently low losses to persist in fiber lengths of a kilometer.

1.9.2 Summary of Key Modal Concepts

An important parameter connected with the cutoff condition is the V number defined by

$$V = \frac{2\pi a}{\lambda} (n_1^2 - n_2^2)^{1/2} = \frac{2\pi a}{\lambda} NA \qquad \qquad \text{... (1.67)}$$

- This is the dimensionless number that determines how many modes a fiber can support. Except for the lowest-order HE_{11} mode, each mode can exist only for values of V that exceed a certain limiting value (with each mode having a different V limit). The modes are cut off when $\beta = n_2k$.

- This occurs when $v \leq 2.405$. The HE_{11} mode has no cutoff and ceases to exist only when the core diameter is zero. This is the principle on which single-mode fibers are based.

- The V number also can be used to express the number of modes M in a multimode fiber when V is large. For this case, an estimate of the total number of modes supported in a fiber is

$$M \approx \frac{1}{2}\left(\frac{2\pi a}{\lambda}\right)^2 (n_1^2 - n_2^2) = \frac{V^2}{2} \qquad \text{... (1.68)}$$

- Since the field of a guided mode extends partly into the cladding, as shown in Fig. 1.25, a final quantity of interest for a step-index fiber is the fractional power flow in the core and cladding for a given mode.

- As the V number approaches cutoff for any particular mode, more of the power of that mode is in the cladding.

- At the cutoff point, the mode becomes radiative with all the optical ower of the mode residing in the cladding. Far from cutoff that is, for large values of V the fraction of the average optical power residing in the cladding can be estimated by

$$\frac{P_{clad}}{P} \approx \frac{4}{3\sqrt{M}} \qquad \text{... (1.69)}$$

- Where P is the total optical power in the fiber. Note that since M is proportional to V^2, the power flow in the cladding decreases as V increases. However, this increases the number of modes in the fiber, which is not desirable for a high-bandwidth capability.

1.9.3 Maxwell's Equations

Electromagnetic Waves :

- In order to obtain an improved model for the propagation of light in an optical fiber, electromagnetic wave theory must be considered. The basis for the study of electromagnetic wave propagation is provided by Maxwell's equations

$$\nabla \times E = -\frac{\partial B}{\partial t} \qquad \text{... (1.70)}$$

and

$$\nabla \times H = \frac{\partial D}{\partial t} \qquad \text{... (1.71)}$$

where,

$$E = \text{Electric field}$$

$$D = \text{Electric flux}$$

$$H = \text{Magnetic field}$$

$$B = \text{Magnetic flux density}$$

and the divergence conditions:

$$\nabla \cdot D = 0 \text{ (no free charges)} \qquad \text{... (1.72)}$$

$$\nabla \cdot B = 0 \text{ (no free poles)} \qquad \text{... (1.73)}$$

where ∇ is a vector operator.

The four field vectors are related by the relations

$$D = \varepsilon E \qquad \text{... (1.74)}$$

$$B = \mu H \qquad \text{... (1.75)}$$

where, ε is the dielectric permittivity.

μ is the magnetic permeability of the medium.

Substituting for D and B and taking curl of equations (1.74) and (1.75)

$$\nabla \times (\nabla \times E) = -\mu\varepsilon \frac{\partial^2 E}{\partial t^2} \qquad \text{... (1.76)}$$

$$\nabla \times (\nabla \times H) = -\mu\varepsilon \frac{\partial^2 H}{\partial t^2} \qquad \text{... (1.77)}$$

Then using divergence conditions with the vector identity.

$$\nabla \times (\nabla \times Y) = \nabla (\nabla \cdot Y) - \nabla^2 (Y) \qquad \text{... (1.78)}$$

We obtain the nondispersive wave equations:

$$\nabla^2 E = \mu\varepsilon \frac{\partial^2 E}{\partial t^2} \qquad \text{... (1.79)}$$

and

$$\nabla^2 H = \mu\varepsilon \frac{\partial^2 H}{\partial t^2} \qquad \text{... (1.80)}$$

where ∇^2 is the Laplacian operator.

The equation can be written in the scalar form as:

$$\nabla^2 \psi = \frac{1}{\upsilon_p^2} = \frac{\partial^2 \psi}{\partial t^2} \qquad \text{... (1.81)}$$

where ψ may represent a component of the E or H field and υ_p is the phase velocity in the dielectric medium.

$$\upsilon_p = \frac{1}{(\mu\varepsilon)^{1/2}} = \frac{1}{(\mu_r \mu_o \varepsilon_r \varepsilon_o)^{1/2}} \qquad \text{... (1.82)}$$

where μ_r and ε_r are the relative permeability and permitivity for the dielectric medium and μ_o and ε_o are the permeability and permitivity of free space. The velocity of light in free space is given by,

$$c = \frac{1}{(\mu_o \varepsilon_o)^{1/2}} \qquad \text{... (1.83)}$$

The basic solution of the wave equation is a sinusoidal wave, the most important form of which is a uniform plane wave given by:

$$\psi = \psi_o \exp [j(\omega t - k \cdot \gamma)] \qquad \text{... (1.84)}$$

where ω is the angular frequency of the field, t is the time, k is the propagation vector, which gives the direction of propagation and the rate of change of phase with distance while the components of γ specify the co-ordinate point at which the field is observed when λ is the optical wavelength in a vacuum. The magnitude of the propagation vector or the vacuum phase propagation constant K is given by

$$k = \frac{2\pi}{\lambda} \qquad \text{... (1.85)}$$

1.9.4 Waveguide Equations

- Consider electromagnetic wave propagating along the cylindrical fiber shown in Fig. 1.26. For this fiber, a cylindrical coordinate system {r, ϕ, z} is defined with the z axis lying along the axis of the waveguide. If the electromagnetic waves are to propagate along the z axis, they will have a functional dependence of the form

$$E = E_0(r, \phi)\, e^{j(\omega t - \beta z)} \qquad \text{... (1.86 a)}$$

$$H = H_0(r, \phi)\, e^{j(\omega t - \beta z)} \qquad \text{... (1.86 b)}$$

- Which are harmonic in time t and coordinate z. the parameter β is the z component of the propagation vector and will be determined by the boundary conditions on the electromagnetic fields at the core-cladding interface. When equation (1.86 a) and (1.86 b) are substituted into Maxwell's curl equations, we have, from equation (1.70)

$$\frac{1}{r}\left(\frac{\partial E_z}{\partial \phi} + jr\beta E_\phi\right) = -j\omega\mu H_r \qquad \text{... (1.87 a)}$$

$$j\beta E_r + \frac{\partial E_z}{\partial z} = -j\omega\mu H_0 \qquad \text{... (1.87 b)}$$

$$\frac{1}{r}\left(\frac{\partial r}{\partial}(rE_\phi) - \frac{\partial E_r}{\partial \phi}\right) = -j\mu\omega H_z \qquad \text{... (1.87 c)}$$

And, from equation (1.86 b),

$$\frac{1}{r}\left(\frac{\partial H_z}{\partial \phi} + jr\beta J H_\phi\right) = j\in \omega E_r \qquad \text{... (1.88 a)}$$

$$j\beta H_r + \frac{\partial H_z}{\partial r} = -j\in \omega E_\phi \qquad \text{... (1.88 b)}$$

$$\frac{1}{r}\left(\frac{\partial}{\partial r}(rH_\phi) - \frac{\partial H_r}{\partial \phi}\right) = j\in \omega E_z \qquad \text{... (1.88 c)}$$

- By eliminating variables these equations can be rewritten such that, when E_z and H_z are known, the remaining transverse components E_r, E_ϕ, H_r and H_ϕ can be determined. For example, E_ϕ or H_r, respectively, can be found in terms of E_z or H_z. Doing so yields

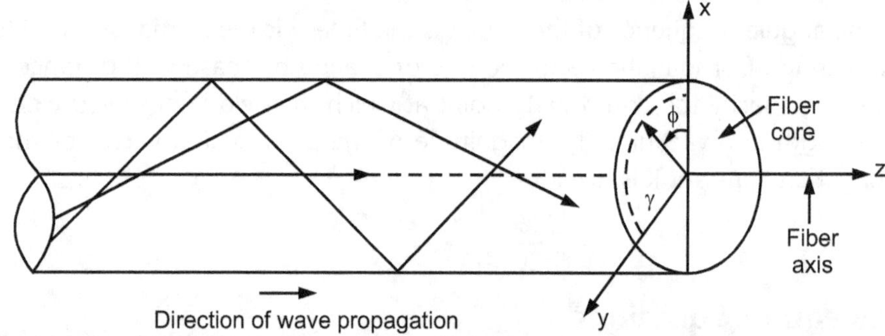

Fig. 1.26 : cylindrical coordinate system used for analyzing electromagnetic wave propagation in an optical fiber

$$E_r = \frac{j}{q^2}\left(\beta\,\frac{\partial E_z}{\partial r} + \frac{\mu\omega}{r}\,\frac{\partial H_z}{\partial \phi}\right) \qquad \text{... (1.89 a)}$$

$$E_\phi = \frac{-j}{q^2}\left(\frac{\beta}{r}\,\frac{\partial E_z}{\partial \phi} - \mu\omega\,\frac{\partial H_z}{\partial r}\right) \qquad \text{... (1.89 b)}$$

$$H_r = \frac{-j}{q^2}\left(\beta\,\frac{\partial H_z}{\partial r} - \frac{\omega\in}{r}\,\frac{\partial E_z}{\partial \phi}\right) \qquad \text{... (1.89 c)}$$

$$H_\phi = \frac{-j}{q^2}\left(\frac{\beta}{r}\,\frac{\partial H_z}{\partial \phi} + \omega\in\,\frac{\partial E_z}{\partial r}\right) \qquad \text{... (1.89 d)}$$

where $q^2 = \omega^2\in\mu - \beta^2 = k^2 - \beta^2$.

- Substitution of equation (1.89 c) and (1.89 d) into equation (1.89 c) results in the wave equation in cylindrical coordinates,

$$\frac{\partial^2 E_z}{\partial r^2} + \frac{1}{r}\,\frac{\partial E_z}{\partial r} + \frac{1}{r^2}\,\frac{\partial^2 E_z}{\partial \phi^2} + q^2 E_z = 0 \qquad \text{... (1.90)}$$

And substitution of equation (1.88 a) and (1.88 b) into equation (1.88 c) leads to

$$\frac{\partial^2 H_z}{\partial r^2} + \frac{1}{r}\,\frac{\partial H_z}{\partial r} + \frac{1}{r^2}\,\frac{\partial^2 H_z}{\partial \phi^2} + q^2 H_z = 0 \qquad \text{... (1.91)}$$

- It is interesting to note that equations (1.90) and (1.91) each contain either only E_z or only H_z. This appears to imply that the longitudinal components of E and H are uncoupled and can be chosen arbitrarily provided that they satisfy equations (1.90) and (1.91). However, in general, coupling of E_z and H_z is required by the boundary conditions of the electromagnetic field components. If the boundary conditions do not lead to coupling between the field components, mode solutions can be obtained in which either $E_z = 0$ or $H_z = 0$. When $E_z = 0$ the modes are called transverse electric or TE modes, and when $H_z = 0$ they are called tranverse magnetic or TM modes. Hybrid modes exist if both E_z and H_z are nonzero. These are designated as HE or EH modes, depending on whether H_z or E_z, respectively, makes a larger contribution to the transverse field. The fact that the hybrid modes are present in optical waveguides makes their analysis more complex than in the simpler case of hollow metallic waveguides where only TE and TM modes are found.

1.9.5 Wave Equations for Step-Index Fibers

- We now use the above results to find the guided modes in a step-index fiber. A standard mathematical procedure for solving equations such as equation (1.86) is to use the separation-of-variables method, which assumes a solution of the form

$$E_z = AF_1(r)\, F_2(\phi)\, F_3(z)\, F_4(t) \qquad \ldots (1.92)$$

- As we already assumed, the time- and z-dependent factors are given by

$$F_3(z)\, F_4(t) = e^{j(\omega t - \beta z)} \qquad \ldots (1.93)$$

- Since the wave is sinusoidal in time and propagates in the z direction. In addition, because of the circular symmetry of the waveguide, each field component must not change when the coordinate ϕ is increases by 2π. We thus assume a periodic function of the form

$$F_2(\phi) = e^{jv\phi} \qquad \ldots (1.94)$$

- The constant v can be positive or negative, but it must be an integer since the fields must be periodic in ϕ with a period of 2π.

- Substituting equation (1.94) into equation (1.92), the wave equation for E_z [equation (1.90)] becomes

$$\frac{\partial^2 F_1}{\partial r2} + \frac{1}{r}\frac{\partial F_1}{\partial r} + \left(q^2 - \frac{v^2}{r^2} \right) F_1 = 0 \qquad \ldots (1.95)$$

which is a well-known differential equation for Bessel functions. An exactly identical equation can be derived for H_z.

- For the configuration of the step-index fiber we consider a homogeneous core of refractive index n_1 and radii a, which is surrounded by an infinite cladding of index n_2.

- The reason for assuming an infinitely thick cladding is that the guided modes in the core have exponentially decaying fields outside the core and these must have insignificant values at the outer boundary of the cladding.

- In practice, optical fibers are designed with claddings that are sufficiently thick so that the guided-mode field does not reach the outer boundary of the cladding. To get an idea of the field patterns, the electric field distributions for several of the lower-order guided modes in a symmetrical-slab waveguide were shown in Fig. 1.26. The fields vary harmonically in the guiding region of refractive index n_1 and decay exponentially outside of this region.

- Equation (1.97) must now be solved for the regions inside and outside the core. For the inside region the solutions for the guided modes must remain finite as $r \to 0$, whereas on the outside the solutions must decay to zero as $r \to \infty$. Thus, for $r < a$ the solutions are Bessel functions of the first kind of order v. for these functions we use the common designations $J_v(ur)$. Here, $u^2 = k$ with $k_1 = 2\pi n_1/\lambda$. The expressions for E_z and H_z inside the core are thus

$$E_z(r < a) = AJ_v(ur)\, e^{jv\phi}\, e^{j(\omega t - \beta z)} \qquad \ldots (1.96)$$

$$H_z(r < a) = BJ_v(ur)\, e^{jv\phi}\, e^{j(\omega t - \beta z)} \qquad \ldots (1.97)$$

where A and B are arbitrary constants.

- Outside of the core the solutions to equation (1.93) are given by modified Bessel functions of the second kind, $K_v(wr)$, where $w^2 = \beta^2 - k$ with $k_2 = 2\pi n_2/\lambda$. The expressions for E_z and H_z outside the core are therefore

$$E_z(r > a) = CK_v(wr)\, e^{jv\phi}\, e^{j(\omega t - \beta z)} \qquad \ldots (1.98)$$

$$H_z(r > a) = DK_v(wr)\, e^{jv\phi}\, e^{j(\omega t - \beta z)} \qquad \ldots (1.99)$$

- With C and D being arbitrary constants.

- The definitions of $J_v(ur)$ and $K_v(wr)$ and various recursion relations are given in App.C From the definition of the modified Besel function, it is seen that $K_v(wr) \to e^{-wr}$ as $wr \to \infty$. Since $K_v(wr)$ must go to zero as $r \to \infty$, it follows that $w > 0$. This, in turn, implies that $\beta \geq K_2$, which represents a cutoff condition. The cutoff condition is the point at which a mode is no longer bound to the core region. A second condition on β can be deduced from the behavior of $J_v(ur)$. Inside the core the parameter u must be real for F_1 to be real, from which it follows that $K_1 \geq \beta$. The permissible range of β for bound solutions is therefore

$$n_2 k = k_2 \leq \beta \leq k_1 = n_1 k \qquad \ldots (1.100)$$

where $k = 2\pi/\lambda$ is the free-space propagation constant.

1.9.6 Modal Equation

- The solutions for β must be determined from the boundary conditions. The boundary conditions require that the tangential components E_ϕ and E_z of e inside and outside of the dielectric interface at $r = a$ must be the same, and similarly for the tangential components H_ϕ and H_z. Consider first the tangential components of E. For the z component we have, from equation (1.94) at the inner core-cladding boundary ($E_z = E_{z1}$ and from equation (1.96) at the outside of the boundary ($E_z = E_{z2}$), that

$$E_{z1} - E_{z2} = AJ_v(ua) - CK_v(wa) = 0 \qquad \ldots (1.101)$$

- The ϕ component is found from equation (1.86 b). Inside the core the factor q^2 is given by

$$q^2 = u^2 = k_1^2 - \beta^2 \qquad \ldots (1.102)$$

where $k_1 = \dfrac{2\pi n_1}{\lambda} = \omega\sqrt{\epsilon_1 \mu}$, while outside the core

$$w^2 = \beta^2 - k_2^2 \qquad \ldots (1.103)$$

where $k_2 = 2\pi n_2/\lambda = \omega\backslash r(\epsilon_2\mu)$. substituting Equations (1.94) and (1.95) into Equation (1.88 b) to find $E_{\phi 1}$ and similarly, using Equations (1.95) and (1.96) to determine $E_{\phi 2}$, yields, at $r = a$,

$$E_{\phi 1} - E_{\phi 2} = \frac{-j}{u^2}\left[A\,\frac{jv\beta}{a}\,J_v(ua) - B\omega\mu u J_v'(ua)\right] - \frac{j}{w^2}\left[C\,\frac{jv\beta}{a}\,K_v(wa) - D\omega\mu w K_v'(wa)\right] = 0 \quad \ldots (1.104)$$

where the prime indicates differentiation with respect to the argument.

- Similarly, for the tangential components of H it is readily shown that, at $r = a$,

$$H_{z1} - H_{z2} = BJ_v(ua) - DK_v(wa) = 0 \qquad \ldots (1.105)$$

and $H_{\phi 1} - H_{\phi 2} = \dfrac{-j}{u^2}\left[B\,\dfrac{jv\beta}{a}\,J_v(ua) + A\omega\epsilon_1 u J_v'(ua)\right] - \dfrac{j}{w^2}\left[D\,\dfrac{J_v\beta}{a}\,K_v(wa) + C\omega\epsilon_2 w K_v'(wa)\right] = 0$

$$\ldots (1.106)$$

- Equations (1.99) to (1.104) are a set of four equations with four unknown coefficients, A, B, C, and D. A solution to these equations exists only if the determinant of these coefficients is zero:

$$\begin{vmatrix} J_v(ua) & 0 & -K_v(wa) & 0 \\[2mm] \dfrac{\beta v}{au^2}J_v(ua) & \dfrac{j\omega\mu}{u}J_v'(ua) & \dfrac{\beta v}{aw^2}K_v(wa) & \dfrac{j\omega\mu}{w}K_v'(wa) \\[2mm] \dfrac{-j\omega\epsilon_1}{u}J_v'(ua) & \dfrac{\beta v}{au^2}J_v(ua) & \dfrac{-j\omega\epsilon_2}{w}K_v'(wa) & \dfrac{\beta v}{aw^2}K_v(wa) \end{vmatrix} = 0 \qquad \ldots (1.107)$$

- Evaluation of this determinant yields the following eigen value equation for β :

$$(j_v + K_v)(k_1^2 j_v + k_2^2 K_v) = \left(\frac{\beta v}{a}\right)^2\left(\frac{1}{u^2} + \frac{1}{w^2}\right)^2 \qquad \ldots (1.108)$$

where $\qquad j_v = \dfrac{J_v'(ua)}{uJ_v(ua)}$ and $K_v = \dfrac{K_v'(wa)}{wK_v(wa)}$

- Upon solving Equation (1.108) for β, it will be found that only discrete values restricted to the range given by Equation (1.100) will be allowed. Although Equation (1.108) is a complicated transcendental equation which is generally solved by numerical techniques, its solution for any particular mode will provide all the characteristics of that mode. We shall now consider this equation for some of the lowest-order modes of a step-index waveguide.

1.9.7 Modes in Step-Index Fibers

- To help describe the modes, we shall first examine the behavior of the J-type Bessel functions. These are plotted in Fig. 1.27 for the first three orders. The J-type Bessel functions are similar to harmonic functions since they exhibit oscillatory behavior for real k, as is the case for sinusoidal functions. Because of the oscillatory behavior of J_v, there will be m roots of Equation (1.108) for a given v value. These roots will be designated by β_{vm} and the corresponding modes are either TE_{vm}, TM_{vm}, EH_{vm}, EH_{vm} or HE_{vm}. Schematics of the transverse electric field patterns for the four lowest-order modes over the cross section of a step-index fiber are shown in Fig. 1.27.

- For the dielectric fiber wavelength, all modes are hybrid modes except those for which v = 0. When v = 0 the right-hand side of Equation (1.108) vanishes and two different eigen value equations result. These are

$$j_0 + K_0 = 0 \qquad \text{... (1.109 a)}$$

- Or, using the relations for J in App. C.

$$\frac{J_2(ua)}{uJ_0(ua)} + \frac{K_1(wa)}{wK_0(wa)} = 0 \qquad \text{... (1.109 b)}$$

which corresponds to TE_{0m} modes ($E_z = 0$),

$$k_1^2 j_\theta + k_2^2 K_0) = 0 \qquad \text{... (1.110 a)}$$

Or $\qquad \dfrac{k_1^2 J_1(ua)}{uJ_0(ua)} + \dfrac{k_2^2 K_1(wa)}{wK_0(wa)} = 0 \qquad \text{... (1.110 b)}$

which corresponds to TM_{0m} modes ($H_z = 0$).

- When v $\neq$ 0 the situation is more complex and numerical methods are needed to solve Equation (1.108) exactly. However, simplified and highly accurate approximations based on the principle that the core and cladding refractive indices are nearly the same have been derived. The condition that $n_1 - n_2 \ll 1$ was referred to by Gloge as giving rise to weakly guided modes.

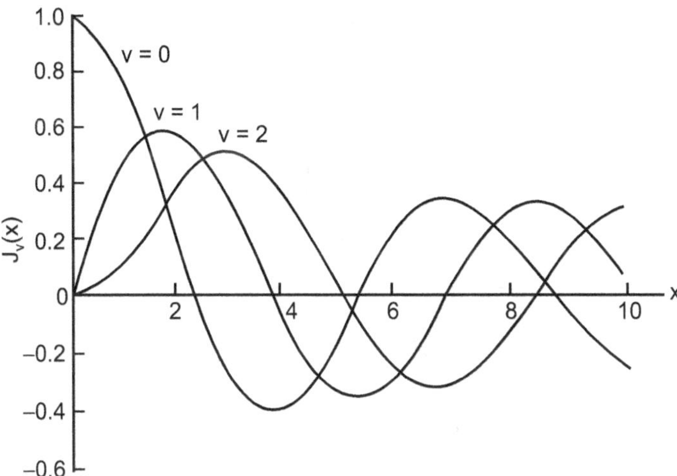

Fig. 1.27 : Variation of the Bessel function $J_v(x)$ for the first three orders (v = 0,1,2) plotted as a function of x.

- Let us examine the cutoff conditions for fiber modes. As was mentioned in relation to Equation (1.100), a mode is referred to as being cut off when it is no longer bound to the core of the fiber, so that its field no longer decays on the outside of the core. The cutoffs for the various modes are found by solving Equation (1.108) in the limit $w^2 \to 0$. This is, in general, fairly complex, so that only the results, which are listed in Table 1.3, will be given here.

- An important parameter connected with the cutoff condition is the normalized frequency V (also called the V number or V parameter) defined by

$$V^2 = (u^2 + w^2)\, a^2 = \left(\frac{2\pi a}{\lambda}\right)^2 (n_1^2 - n_2^2) = \left(\frac{2\pi a}{\lambda}\right)^2 NA^2 \qquad \text{... (1.111)}$$

which is dimensionless number that determines how many modes a fiber can support. The number of modes that can exist in a waveguide as a function of V may be conveniently represented in terms of a normalized propagation constant b defined by

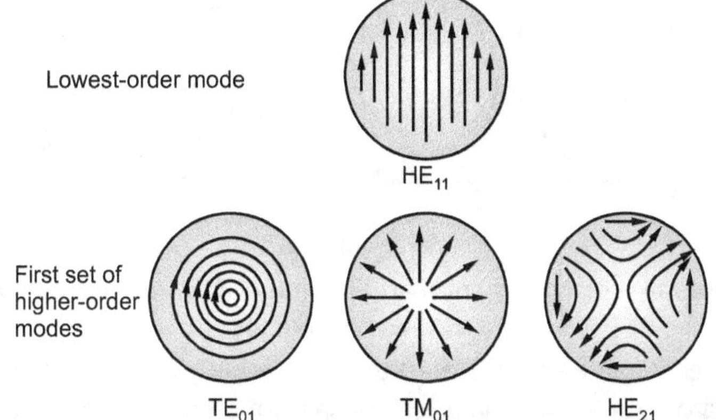

Fig. 1.28 : Fiber end views of the transverse electric field vectors for the four lowest-order modes in a step-index fiber

Table 1.3 : Cutoff Conditions for Some lower-Order Modes

v	Mod	Cutoff condition
0	TE_{0m}, TM_{01}	$J_0(ua) = 0$
1	HE_{1m}, EH_{1m}	$J_1(ua) = 0$
≥ 2	EH_{vm}	$J_v(ua) = 0$
	HE_{vm}	

$$b = \frac{a^2 w^2}{V^2} = \frac{(\beta/k)^2 - n_2^2}{n_1^2 - n_2^2}$$

- A plot of b (in terms of β/k) as a function of V is shown in Fig. 1.28 for a few of the low-order modes. This Fig. 1.28 shows that each mode can exist only for values of V that exceed a certain limiting value. The modes are cut off when $\frac{\beta}{k} = n_2$. The HE_{11} mode has no cutoff and ceases to exist only when the core diameter is zero. This is the principle on which the single mode fiber is based. By appropriately choosing a, n_1 and n_2 so that

$$V = \frac{2\pi a}{\lambda} (n_1^2 - n_2^2)^{1/2} \leq 2.405 \qquad \qquad \dots (1.112)$$

which is the value at which the lowest-order Bessel function $J_0 = 0$, all modes except the HE_{11} modes are cut off.

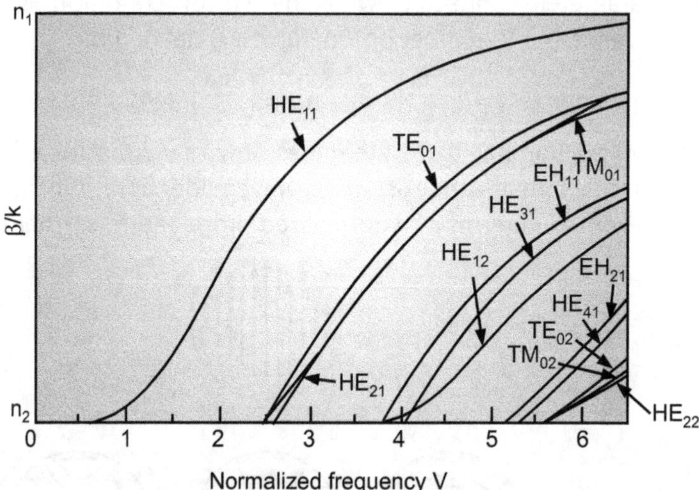

Fig. 1.29 : Plots of the propagation constant (in terms of β/k) as a function of V for a few of the lowest –order modes .

- The parameter V can also be related to the number of modes M in a multi-mode fiber when M is large. An approximate relationship for step-index fibers can be derived from ray theory. A ray congruence will be accepted by the fiber if it lies within an angle θ defined by the numerical aperture as given in Equation (1.112).

$$NA \ = \ \sin \theta = (n_1^2 - n_2^2)^{1/2} \qquad \ldots (1.113)$$

- For practical numerical apertures, $\sin \theta$ is small so that $\sin \theta \cong \theta$. The solid acceptance angle for the fiber is therefore

$$\Omega \ = \ \pi\theta^2 = \pi \, (n_1^2 - n_2^2) \qquad \ldots (1.113)$$

- For electromagnetic radiation of wavelength λ emanating from a laser or a waveguide, the number of modes per unit solid angle is given by $2A/\lambda^2$, where A is the area the mode is leaving or entering. The area A in this case is the core cross section πa^2. The factor 2 comes from the fact that the plane wave can have two polarization orientations. The total number of modes M entering the fiber is thus given by

$$M \ \cong \ \frac{2A}{\lambda^2} \, \Omega \ = \ \frac{2\pi^2 \, a^2}{\lambda^2} \, (n_1^2 - n_2^2) = \frac{V^2}{2} \qquad \ldots (1.115)$$

1.9.8 Linearly Polarized Modes

- The exact analysis for the modes of a fiber is mathematically complex. However, a simpler but highly accurate approximation can be used, based on the principle that in a typical step-index fiber the difference between the indices of refraction of the core and cladding is very small; that is, $\Delta << 1$.

- This is the basis of the weakly guiding fiber approximation.

- In this approximation the electromagnetic field patterns and the propagation constants of the mode pairs $HE_{v+1,m}$ and $EH_{v-1,m}$ are very similar.

- This holds likewise for the three modes TE_{0m}, TM_{0m} and HE_{2m}. This can be seen from Fig. 1.30 with $(v, m) = (0, 1)$ and $(2,1)$ for the mode groupings HE_{11}, TE_{01}, TM_{01}, HE_{21}, HE_{31}, EH_{11}, HE_{12}, HE_{41}, EH_{21} and TE_{02}, TM_{02}, HE_{22}.

- The result is that only four field components need to be considered instead of six, and the field description is further simplified by the use of Cartesian instead of cylindrical coordinates.

- When $\Delta << 1$ we have that k Using these approximations, Equation (1.108) becomes

$$j_v + K_v \ = \ \pm\frac{v}{a}\left(\frac{1}{u^2} + \frac{1}{w^2}\right) \qquad \ldots (1.116)$$

- Thus, Equation (1.109 b) for TE_{0m} modes is the same as Equation (1.110 b) for TM_{0m} modes. Using the recurrence relations for J given in App. C., we get two sets of equations for Equation (1.116) for the positive and negative signs. The positive sign yields

$$\frac{J_{v+1}(ua)}{uJ_v(ua)} + \frac{K_{v+1}(wa)}{wK_v(wa)} \ = \ 0 \qquad \ldots (1.117)$$

- The solution of this equation gives a set of modes called the EH modes. For the negative sign in Equation (1.116) we get

$$\frac{J_{v-1}(ua)}{uJ_v(ua)} + \frac{K_{v-1}(wa)}{wK_v(wa)} = 0 \qquad \ldots (1.118\ a)$$

Or, alternatively, taking the inverse of Equation (1.118 a) and using the first expressions for $J_v(ua)$ and $K_v(wa)$

$$\frac{-uJ_{v-2}(ua)}{J_{v-1}(ua)} = \frac{wK_{v-2}(wa)}{K_{v-1}(wa)} \qquad \ldots (1.118\ b)$$

- This results in a set of modes called the HE modes.

- If we define a new parameter

$$J = \begin{cases} 1 & \text{For TE } \wedge \text{ TM modes} \\ v+1 & \text{for EH modes} \\ v-1 & \text{for HE modes} \end{cases} \qquad \ldots (1.119)$$

Then Equations (1106 b), (1.115 b) can be written in the unified form

$$\frac{uJ_{j-1}(ua)}{J_j(ua)} = \frac{-wK_{j-1}(wa)}{K_j(wa)} \qquad \ldots (1.120)$$

- Equations (1.119) and (1.120) show that within the weakly guiding approximation all modes characterized by a common set of j and m satisfy the same characteristic equation.

- This means that these modes are degenerate. Thus, if an $HE_{v+1,m}$ mode is degenerate with an $EH_{v-1,m}$ mode (i.e., if HE and EH modes of corresponding radial order m and equal circumferential order v form degenerate pairs), then any combination of an $HE_{v+1,m}$ mode with an $EH_{v-1,m}$ mode will likewise constitute a guided mode of the fiber.

- Such degenerate modes are called Linearly Polarized (LP) modes, and designed LP_{jm} modes regardless of their TM, TE, EH, or HE field configuration. The normalized propagation constant b as a function of V is given for various LP_{jm} modes in Fig. 1.30 general, we have the following:

  (1)   Each LP_{0m} mode is derived from an HE_{1m} mode.

  (2)   Each LP_{1m} mode comes from TE_{0m}, TM_{0m}, $\wedge$ HE_{2m} modes.

  (3)   Each LP_{vm} mode ($v \geq 2$ is from an $HE_{v+1,m}$ and an $EH_{v-1,m}$ mode.

- The correspondence between the ten lowest LP modes (i.e., those having cutoff frequencies) and the traditional TM, TE, EH, and HE modes is given in Table 1.4. This table also shows the number of degenerate modes.

- A very useful feature of the LP mode designation is the ability to readily visualize a mode. In a complete set of modes only one electric and one magnetic field component are significant.

- The electric field vector E can be chosen to lie along an arbitrary axis, with the magnetic field vector H being perpendicular to it. In addition, there are equivalent solutions with the field polarities reversed. Since each of the two possible polarization directions can be coupled with either a $\cos j\phi$ or a $\sin j\phi$ azimuthal dependence, four discrete mode patterns can be obtained from a single LP_{jm} label. As an example, the four possible electric and magnetic field directions and the corresponding intensity distributions for the LP_{11} mode are shown in Fig. 1.30. Fig. 1.31 (a) and 1.31 (b) illustrate how two LP_{11} modes are composed from the exact HE_{21} plus TE_{01} and the exact HE_{21} plus TM_{01} modes respectively.

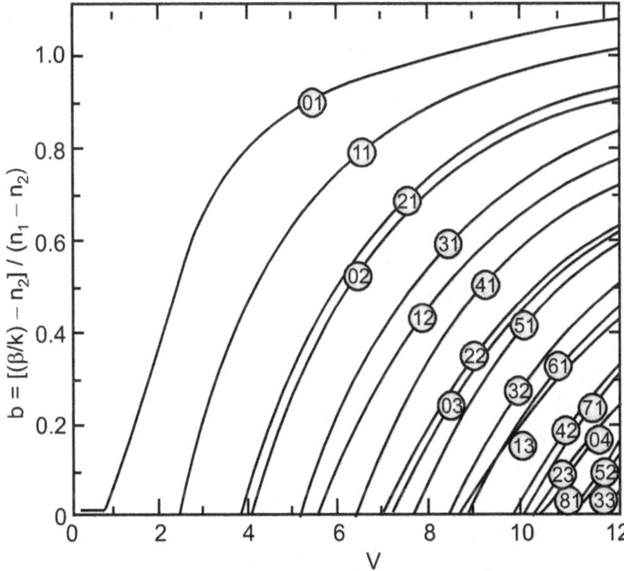

Fig. 1.30 : Plots of the Propagation Constant b as a
Function of V for various LP_{jm} modes.

Table 1.4 : Composition of the Lower-Order Linearly Polarized Modes

LP-Mode Designation	Traditional-Mode Designation and Number of Modes	Number of Degenerate Modes
LP_{01}	$HE_{11} \times 2$	2
LP_{11}	$TE_{01}, TM_{01}, HE_{21} \times 2$	4
LP_{21}	$EH_{11} \times 2, HE_{31} \times 2$	4
LP_{02}	$HE_{12} \times 2$	2
LP_{31}	$EH_{21} \times 2, HE_{41} \times 2$	4
LP_{12}	$TE_{02}, TM_{02}, HE_{22} \times 2$	4

LP$_{41}$	EH$_{31}$ × 2HE$_{51}$ × 2	4
LP$_{22}$	EH$_{12}$ × 2, HE$_{32}$ × 2	4
LP$_{03}$	HE$_{13}$ × 2	2
LP$_{51}$	EH$_{41}$ × 2, HE$_{61}$ × 2	4

1.9.9 Power Flow in Step-Index Fibers

- A final quantity of interest for step-index fibers is the fractional power flow in the core and cladding for a given mode. As illustrated in Fig. 1.30, the electromagnetic field for a given mode does not go to zero at the core-cladding interface, but changes from an oscillating form in the core to an exponential decay in the cladding.

- Thus, the electromagnetic energy of a guided mode is carried partly in the core and partly in the cladding. The further away a mode is from its cutoff frequency, the more concentrated its energy is in the core.

- As cutoff is approached, the field penetrates farther into the cladding region and a greater percentage of the energy travels in the cladding. At cutoff the field no longer decays outside the core and the mode now becomes a fully radiating mode.

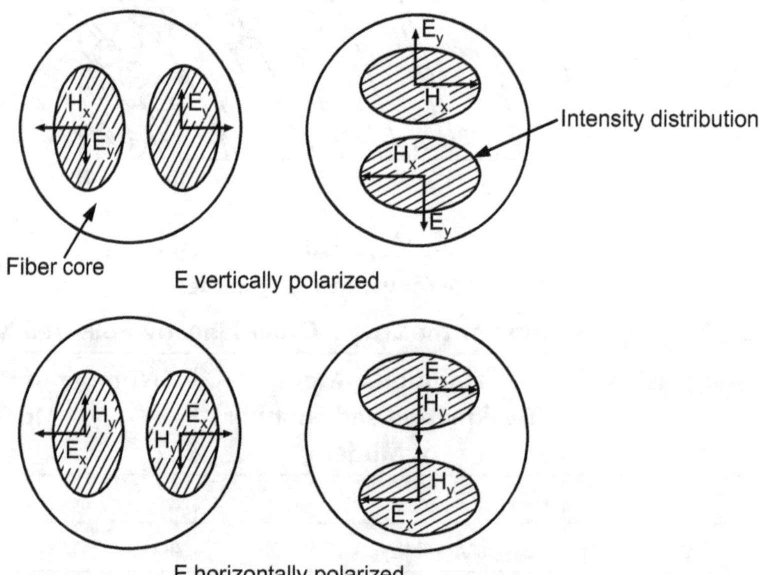

Fig. 1.31 : the four possible transverse electric field and magnetic field directions and the corresponding intensity distributions for the LP$_{11}$ mode

- The relative amounts of power flowing in the core and the cladding can be obtained by integrating the Poynting vector in the axial direction,

$$S_z = \frac{1}{R} \Re (E \times H^*) \cdot e_z \qquad \ldots (1.121)$$

- Over the fiber cross section. Thus, the powers in the core and cladding, respectively, are given by

$$P_{core} = \frac{1}{2} \int_0^a \int_0^{2\pi} r(E_x H_y^* - E_y H_x^*) \, d_\phi d_r \qquad \ldots (1.112)$$

$$P_{clad} = \frac{1}{2} \int_0^a \int_0^{2\pi} r(E_x H_y^* - E_y H_x^*) \, d_\phi d_r \qquad \ldots (1.123)$$

where the asterisk denotes the complex conjugate. Based on the weakly guided mode approximation, which has an accuracy on the order of the index difference Δ between the core and cladding, the relative core and cladding powers for a particular mode v are given by

$$\frac{P_{core}}{P} = \left(1 - \frac{u^2}{V^2}\right)\left[1 - \frac{J_v^2(ua)}{J_{v+1}(ua) \, J_{v-1}(ua)}\right] \qquad \ldots (1.124)$$

and $$\frac{P_{clad}}{P} = 1 - \frac{P_{core}}{P} \qquad (1.125)$$

Where P is the total power in the mode v. the relationships between P_{core} and P_{clad} are plotted in Fig. 1.33 in terms of the fractional powers P_{core}/P and P_{clad}/P for various LP_{jm} modes. In addition, far from cutoff the average total power in the cladding has been derived for fibers in which many modes can propagate. Because of this large number of modes, those few modes that are appreciably close to cutoff can be ignored to a reasonable approximation. The derivation assumes an incoherent source, such as a tungsten filament lamp or a light-emitting diode, which, in general, excites every fiber mode with the same amount of power. The total average cladding power is thus approximated by

$$\left(\frac{P_{clad}}{P}\right)_{total} = \frac{4}{3} M^{-1/2} \qquad \ldots (1.126)$$

Where, from Equation (1.125), M is the total number of modes entering the fiber. From Fig. 1.32 and Equation (1.126) it can be seen that, since M is proportional to V^2, the power flow in the cladding decreases as V increases.

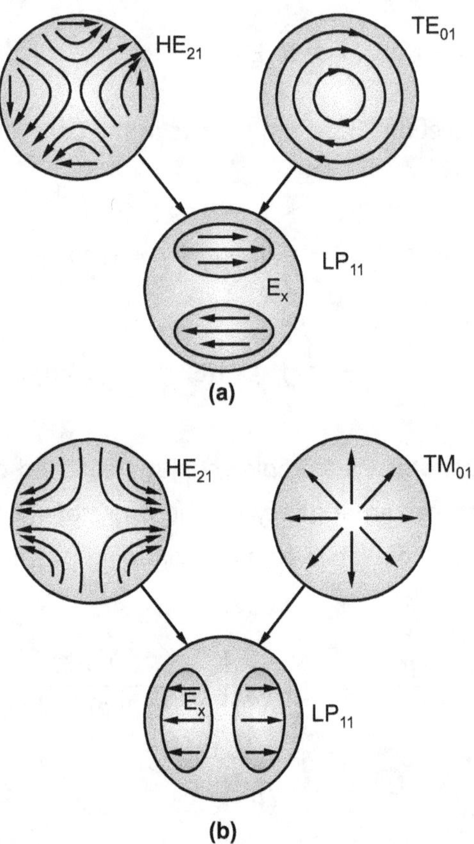

Fig. 1.32 : Composition of two LP$_{11}$ modes from exact field and intensity distributions

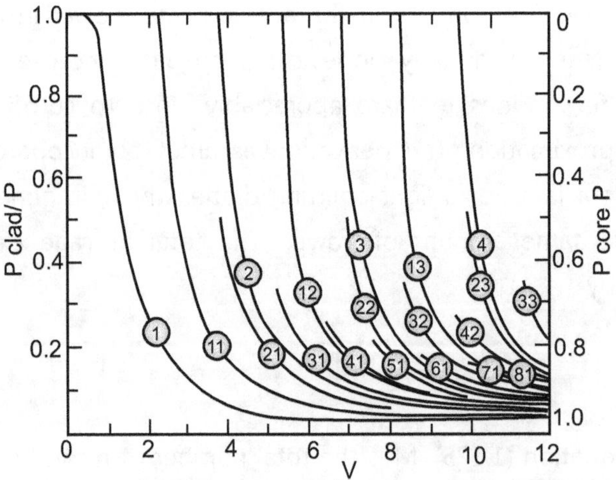

**Fig. 1.33 : Fractional power flow in the cladding of
a step-index optical fiber as a function of V.**

1.10 Single Mode Fibers

- Single mode fibers are constructed by letting the dimensions of the core diameter be a few wavelengths (usually 8-12) and by having small index differences between the core and the cladding. From Eq. (1.67) or (1.112) with V=2.4, it can be seen that single-mode propagation is possible for fairly large variations in values of the physical core size a and the core-cladding index difference Δ. However, in practical design of single-mode fibers, the core-cladding index difference varies between 0.2 and 1.0 percent, and the core diameter should be chosen to be just below the cutoff of the first higher-order mode; that is, for V slightly less than 2.4. for example, atypical single-mode fiber may have a core radius of 3 μm and a numerical aperture of 0.1 at a wavelength of 0.8 μm. From Eqs (1.56) and (1.111) , this yields V=2.356.

1.10.1 Mode Field Diameter

- For multimode fibers the core diameter and numerical aperture are key parameters for describing the signal transmission properties. In single mode fibers the geometric distribution of light in the propagating mode is what is needed when predicting the performance characteristics of these fibers. Thus a fundamental parameter of a single-mode fiber is the mode-field diameter (MFD). This parameter can be determined from the mode field distribution of the fundamental fiber mode, and is a function of the optical source wavelength, the core radius, and the refractive index profile of the fiber. The mode-field diameter is analogous to the core diameter in multimode fibers, except that in single-mode fibers not all the light that propagates through the fiber is carried in the core. Figure 1.34 illustrates this effect.

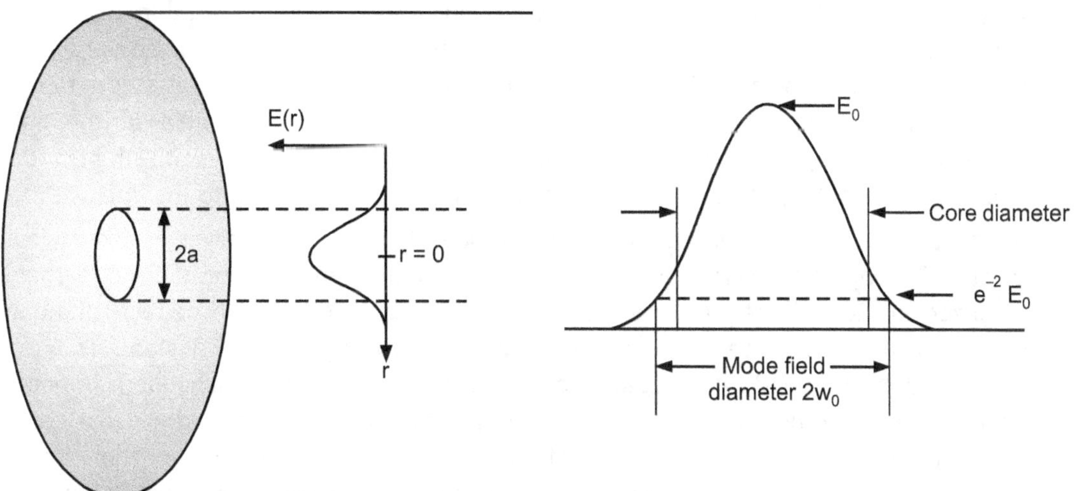

Fig. 1.34: Distribution of light in a single-mode fiber above its cutoff wavelength

- For example, at V=2 only 75 percent of the optical power is confined to the core. This percentage increases for larger values of V and is less for smaller V values.

- The MFD is an important parameter for single-mode fiber, since it is used to predict fiber properties such as splice loss, bending loss, cut-off wavelength, and waveguide dispersion. A variety of models have been proposed for characterizing and measuring the MFD. These include far field scanning, near-field scanning, transverse offset, variable aperture in the far field, knife-edge, and mask methods. The main consideration of all these methods is how to approximate the optical power distribution.

A standard technique to find the MFD is to measure the far-field intensity distribution $E^2(r)$ and then calculate the MFD using the Petermann II equation

$$\text{MFD} = 2w_0 = 2 \left[\frac{2 \int_0^\infty E^2(r)\, r^3\, dr}{\int_0^\infty E^2(r)\, r\, dr} \right]^{1/2} \qquad \text{... (1.127)}$$

Where $2w_0$ (called the spot size) is the full width of the far-field distribution. For calculation simplicity the exact field distribution can be fitted to a Gaussian function.

$$E(r) = E_0 \exp\left(-\frac{r^2}{w_0^2}\right) \qquad \text{... (1.128)}$$

Where r is the radius and E_0 is the field at zero radius, as shown in Fig. 1.34. Then the MFD is given by the $1/e^2$ width of the optical power.

1.10.2 Propagation Modes in Single-Mode Fibers

- In any ordinary single-mode fiber there are actually two independent degenerate propagation modes. These modes are very similar but their polarization planes are orthogonal. These may be chosen arbitrarily as the horizontal (H) and the vertical (v) polarizations as shown in figure. 1.34. Either one of these two polarization modes constitutes the fundamental HE_{11} mode. In general, the electric field of the light propagating along the fiber is a linear superposition of these two polarization modes and depends on the polarization of the light at the launching point into the fiber.

- Suppose we arbitrarily choose one of the modes to have its transverse electric field polarized along the x direction and the other independent orthogonal, mode to be polarized in the y direction as shown in Fig. 1.34. in ideal fibers with perfect rotational symmetry, the two modes are degenerate with equal propagation constants ($k_x = k_y$) and any polarization state injected into the fiber will propagate unchanged. In actual fibers there are imperfections, such as asymmetrical lateral stresses, noncircular cores, and variations in refractive-index profiles. These imperfections break the circular symmetry of the ideal fiber and lift the degeneracy of the two modes. The modes propagate with different phase velocities, and the difference between their effective refractive indices is called the fiber birefringence.

$$B_f = n_y - n_x \qquad \text{... (1.129)}$$

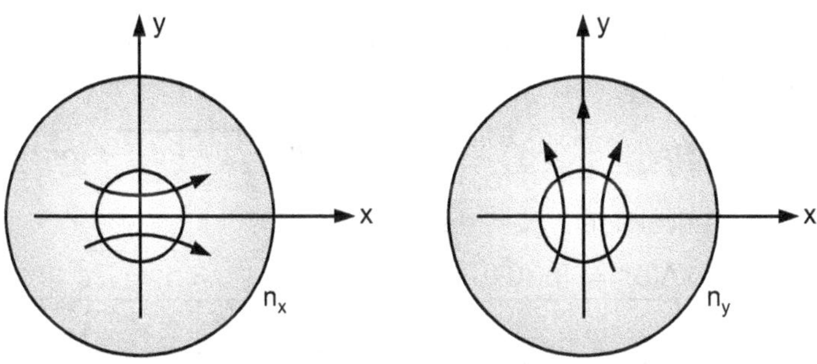

Fig. 1.35: Two polarizations of the fundamental HE_{11} mode in a single-mode fiber

Equivalently, we may define the birefringence as

$$\beta = k_0 (n_y - n_x) \qquad \text{... (1.130)}$$

Where $k_0 = 2\pi/\lambda$ is the free-space propagation constant.

If light is injected into the fiber so that both modes are excited, then one will be delayed in phase relative to the other as they propagate. When this phase difference is an integral multiple of 2π, the two modes will beat at this point and the input polarization state will be reproduced. The length over which this beating occurs is the fiber beat length,

$$L_p = 2\pi/\beta \qquad \text{... (1.131)}$$

1.11 Graded-index fiber Structure

- In the graded index fiber design the core refractive index decreases continuously with increasing radial distance r from the center of the fiber, but is generally constant in the cladding. The most commonly used construction for the refractive-index variation in the core is the power law relationship

$$n(r) = n_1 \left[1 - 2\Delta \left(\frac{r}{a} \right)^a \right]^{1/2} \qquad \text{for } 0 \leq r \leq 0$$

$$n_1 (1 - 2\Delta)^{1/2} \cong n_1 (1 - \Delta) = n_2 \qquad \text{for } r \geq 0 \qquad \text{... (1.132)}$$

Here r is the radial distance from the fiber axis, a is the core radius, n_1 is the refractive index at the core axis, n_2 is the refractive index of the cladding, and the dimensionless parameter α defines the shape of the index profile. The index difference Δ for the graded-index fiber is given by

$$\Delta = \frac{n_1^2 - n_2^2}{2n_1^2} \cong \frac{n_1 - n_2}{n_1} \qquad \text{... (1.333)}$$

The approximation on the right-hand side of this equation reduces the expression for Δ to that of the step-index fiber given by Eq. (1.132). thus, the same symbol is used in both cases. For $\alpha = \infty$, Eq. (1.129) reduces to the step-index profile $n(r) = n_1$.

- Determining the NA for graded-index fibers is more complex than for step-index fibers, since it is a function of position across the core end face. This is in contrast to the step-index fiber, where the NA is constant across the core. Geometrical optics considerations show that light incident on the fiber core at position r will propagate as a guided mode only if it is within the local numerical aperture NA at that point. The local numerical aperture is defined as

$$NA(r) = \left\{ \begin{array}{l} [n^2(r) - n_2^2]^{1/2} \\ 0 \text{ for } r > 0 \end{array} \right\} \approx NA(0)\sqrt{1 - (r/a)^{\alpha}} \text{ for } r \leq a \qquad \dots (1.34 \text{ a})$$

Where the axial numerical aperture is defined as

$$NA(0) = [n^2(0) - n_2^2]^{1/2} = (n_1^2 - n_2^2)^{1/2} \approx n_1\sqrt{2\Delta} \qquad \dots (1.34 \text{ b})$$

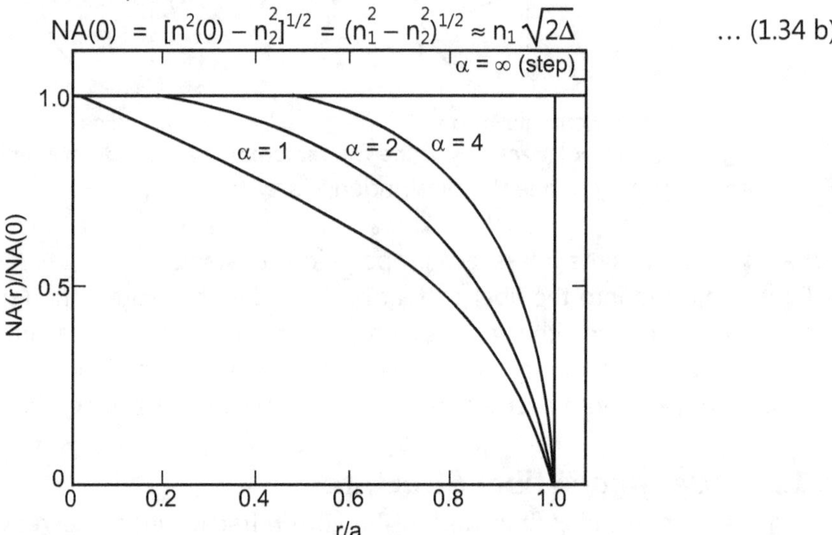

Fig. 1.36: A comparison of the numerical apertures for fibers having various core index profiles

- Thus, the NA of a graded-index fiber decreases from NA(0) to zero as r moves from the fiber axis to the core-cladding boundary. A comparison of the numerical apertures for fibers having various α profiles is shown in fig. 1.36. The number of bound modes in a graded-index fiber is

$$M_g = \frac{\alpha}{\alpha + 2} a^2 k^2 n_1^2 \Delta \approx \frac{\alpha}{\alpha + 2} \frac{V^2}{2} \qquad \dots (1.235)$$

- Where $k = 2\pi/\lambda$ and the right-hand approximation is derived using Eqs. (1.52) and (1.63). Manufacturers typically choose a parabolic refractive index profile given by $\alpha = 2.0$. In this case, $M_g = V^2/4$, which is half the number of modes supported by a step-index fiber (for which $\alpha = \infty$) that has the same V value, as Eq. (1.111) shows.

1.12 SIGNAL DEGRADATION IN OPTICAL FIBERS

- The transmission characteristics are of much importance when the suitability of optical fibers for communication purposes is investigated.
- The two transmission characteristics which are of most important are attenuation (or/loss) and bandwidth.
- Attenuation occurs due to absorption in glass, caused by impurities such as iron, copper, manganese and other transition metals which occur in the third row of the periodic table.

- Since 1970, tremendous improvements have been made leading to silica-based glass fibers with losses of less than 0.2 dB km^{-1} in the laboratory by the late 1980's.
- The other characteristic of primary importance is the bandwidth of the fiber. This is limited by the signal distribution or dispersion within the fiber, which determines the number of bits of information transmitted in a given time period. Therefore, once the attenuation was reduced to acceptable levels, attention was directed towards the dispersive properties of fibers.

1.12.1 ATTENUATION

- Channel attenuation largely determines the maximum transmission distance prior to signal restoration.
- Signal attenuation in optical fibers is determined in decibels. The decibel is used for comparing two power levels and is defined as 'the ratio of the input optical power P_i into the fiber to the output optical power P_o from the fiber'.

$$\text{Number of decibels (dB)} = 10 \log_{10} \qquad \text{.... (1.136)}$$

- In optical fiber communications the attenuation is usually expressed in decibels per unit length (i.e. dB km^{-1})

$$\alpha_{dB}L = 10 \log_{10} \frac{P_i}{P_o} \qquad \text{.... (1.137)}$$

where α_{dB} is the signal attenuation per unit length in decibels and L is the fiber length.

1.2.2.1 Attenuation Units

- When light travels along a fiber, its power reduces exponentially with distance. If P(0) is the optical power in a fiber at the origin (at x=0), then the power P(x) at a distance x further down the fiber is

$$P(x) = P(0) \, e^{-\alpha_v x} \qquad \text{... (1.38 a)}$$

Where

$$\alpha_p = \frac{1}{z} \ln \left[\frac{P(0)}{P(x)} \right] \qquad \text{... (1.38 b)}$$

- α_p is the fiber attenuation coefficient given in units of, for example, km-1. Note that the units for $2 \times \alpha_p$ can also be designed by nepers.
- To determining optical signal attenuation in a fiber, the common procedure is to express the attenuation coefficient in units of decibels per kilometer, denoted by dB/km. designing this parameter by α, we have

$$\alpha \left(\frac{dB}{km} \right) = \frac{10}{x} \log \left[\frac{P(0)}{P(x)} \right] = 4.343 \, \alpha_p \, (km^{-1}) \qquad \text{... (1.38 c)}$$

- This parameter is known as the fiber loss or the fiber attenuation. It depends on different variables, as is shown in the following sections, and it is a function of the wavelength.

Example 1.10 : *When the mean optical power Launched into an 8 km. length of fiber is 120 μw, the mean optical power at the fiber output is 3 μw.*
Determine:
(a) The overall signal attenuation or loss is decibels through the fiber assuming there are no connectors or splices.

(b) The signal attenuation per kilometre for the fiber.

(c) The overall signal attenuation for a 10 km optical link using the same fiber with splices at 1 km intervals, each giving an attenuation of 1 dB;

(d) The numerical input/output power ratio in (c).

Solution :

(a) The overall signal attenuation is decibels through the fiber is:

$$\text{Signal attenuation} = 10 \log_{10} \frac{P_i}{P_o} = 10 \log_{10} \frac{120 \times 10^{-6}}{3 \times 10^{-6}}$$

$$= 10 \log_{10} 40 = 16.0 \text{ dB}$$

(b) The signal attenuation per kilometer for the fiber may be simply obtained by dividing the result in (a) by the fiber length using equation (1.125).

$$\therefore \qquad \alpha_{dB} L = 16.0 \text{ dB}$$

hence,

$$\alpha_{dB} = \frac{16.0}{8}$$

$$= 2.0 \text{ dB km}^{-1}$$

(c) As $\alpha_{dB} = 2$ dB km^{-1}, the loss incurred along 10 km of the fiber is given by:

$$\alpha_{dB} L = 2 \times 10 = 20 \text{ dB}$$

However, the link has nine splices (at 1 km intervals) each with an attenuation of 1 dB. Therefore, the loss due to the splices is 9 dB.

Hence, the overall signal attenuation for the link is

$$\text{Signal attenuation} = 20 + 9$$

$$= 29 \text{ dB}$$

(d) To obtain a numerical value for the input/output power ratio.

$$\frac{P_i}{P_o} = 10^{29/10} = 794.3$$

Number of mechanisms are responsible for the signal attenuation within optical fibers. These mechanisms are influenced by the material composition, the preparation and purification technique and the waveguide structure. They may be categorized within several major areas which include material absorption, material scattering (linear and nonlinear scattering) curve and microbending losses, mode coupling radiation losses and losses due to leaky modes. There are also losses at connectors and splices.

1.12.2 ABSORPTION

1.12.2.1 Absorption

Absorption occurs due to three different mechanisms:

1. Absorption due to atomic defects in the glass compositions.

2. Extrinsic absorption due to impurity atoms in the glass material

3. Intrinsic absorption due to the basic constituent atoms of the fiber material

Table :1.5 Examples of Absorption Loss in Silica glass at Different Wavelengths due to 1 ppm of Water-Ions and Various Transition-Metal Impurities

Impurity	Loss due to 1 ppm of Impurity(dB/km)	Absorption Peak (nm)
Iron: Fe^{2+}	0.68	1100
Iron: Fe^{3+}	0.15	400
Copper: Cu^{2+}	1.1	850
Chromium: Cr^{2+}	1.6	625
Vanadium: V^{4+}	2.7	725
Water: OH^-	1.0	950
Water: OH^-	2.0	1240
Water: OH^-	4.0	1380

- Material absorption is a loss mechanism related to the material composition and fabrication process for the fiber, which results in the dissipation of some of the transmitted optical power as heat in the waveguide.

- The absorption of light may be intrinsic or extrinsic. Intrinsic absorption is caused due to the interaction with one or more of the major components of the glass. Extrinsic absorption is caused due to impurities within the glass.

1.12.2.2 Intrinsic Absorption

- A pure silicate glass has little intrinsic absorption due to it's basic material structure in the near-infrared region. It does have two major intrinsic absorption mechanisms at optical wavelengths, which leave a low intrinsic absorption window over the 0.8 to 1.7 μm wavelength range.

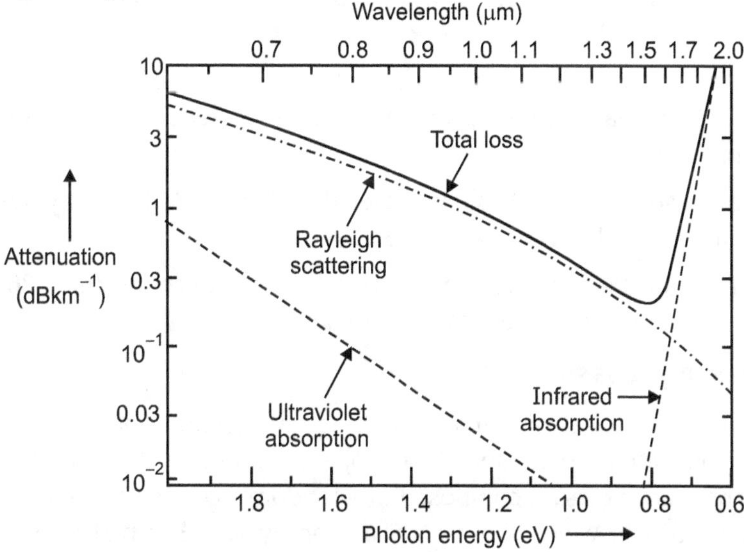

Fig. 1.37 : The attenuation spectra for the intrinsic loss mechanisms in pure G_eO_2 - S_iO_2 glass

- It may be observed that there is a fundamental absorption edge, the peaks of which are centred in the ultraviolet wavelength region.

- This is due to the stimulation of electron transitions within the glass by higher energy excitations.

- The tail of this peak may extend into the window region at the shorter wavelengths as shown in Fig. 1.37.

- Also in the infrared and far infrared, normally at wavelengths above 7 μm, fundamentals of absorption bands due the interaction of photons with molecular vibrations within the glass occur. These give absorption peaks which again extend into the window region.

- The strong absorption bands occur due to oscillations of structural units such as Si - O (9.2 μm), P - O (8.1 μm) B - O (7.2 μm) and Ge - O (11.0 μm) within the glass.

- Hence, above 1.5 μm the tails of these largely far-infrared absorption peaks tend to cause most of the pure glass losses.

- The effects of both processes may be minimized by suitable choice of both core and cladding compositions.

1.12.2.3 Extrinsic Absorption

- Optical fibers which are prepared by conventional melting techniques are the major source of signal attenuation due to extrinsic absorption from transition metal element impurities. Another major extrinsic loss mechanism is caused by absorption due to water (as the hydroxyl or OH ion) dissolved in the glass.

- These Hydroxyl groups are bounded into the glass structure and have fundamental stretching vibrations which occur at wavelengths between 2.7 and 4.2 μm depending on the group position in the glass network.

- A more recent major advance, has enabled the production of a revolutionary fiber type in which 1.383 μm water peak has been permanently reduced to such levels, that it is virtually eliminated.

- The attenuation spectrum for this low Water-Peak Fiber (LWPF), or dry fiber is compared with the Standard Single - Mode Fiber (SSMF).

- The LWPF permits the transmission of optical signals over the full 1.260 to 1.675 μm wavelength range with losses less than 0.4 dB km^{-1}.

1.12.3 Scattering losses

- Scattering losses in glass are mainly due to microscopic variations in the material density, compositional fluctuations, and non-homogenous structure or manufacturing defects in fiber. Since glass is composed of a randomly connected network of molecules, it contains regions in which the molecular density is either higher or lower than the average density in the glass. As glass is made up of several oxides, such as SiO_2, GeO_2, and P_2O_5, compositional fluctuations occurs. Due to these effects refractive-index varies within the glass over distances that are small compared with the wavelength. Due to these index variations a Rayleigh-type scattering of the light occurs. Rayleigh scattering in glass is similar to the phenomenon which scatters light from the sun in the atmosphere, causes to a blue sky.

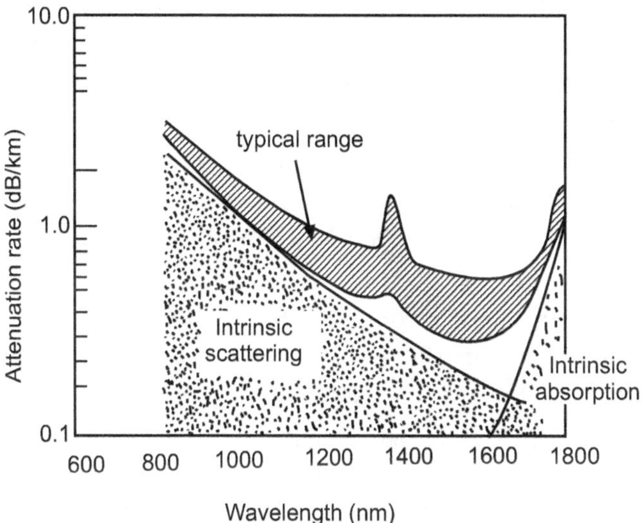

Fig. 1.38: A comparison of the infrared absorption induced by various doping materials in low-loss silica fibers.

Since glass is composed of a randomly connected network of molecules and the various oxide constituents of glass, the expressions for scattering-induced attenuation are fairly complex. For single-component glass the scattering loss at a wavelength λ resulting due to density fluctuations can be expressed as:

$$\alpha_{scat} = \frac{8\pi^2}{3\lambda^4}(n^2-1)^2\,KT_f\,\beta_{iT} \qquad\qquad \dots (1.39\ a)$$

Here, n is the refractive index, K is Boltzmann's constant, β_{iT} is the isothermal compressibility of the material, and the fictive temperature T_f is the temperature at which the density fluctuations are frozen into the glass as it solidifies (after having been drawn into a fiber). Alternatively, the relation becomes

$$\alpha_{scat} = \frac{8\pi^3}{3\lambda^4}n^8\,p^2\,KT_f\,B_{iT} \qquad\qquad \dots (1.39\ b)$$

p is the photo elastic coefficient. Note that Eqs. (1.139 a) and (1.139 b) are given in units of nepers (that is, base e units). As shown in Eq. (1.138), to change this to decibels for optical power attenuation calculations, multiply these equations by 10 log e=4.343

In multi component glasses the scattering is given by

$$\alpha_s = \frac{8\pi^2}{3\lambda^4}(\delta n^2)^2\,\delta V \qquad\qquad \dots (1.140)$$

In which the square of the mean-square refractive-index fluctuation $(\delta n^2)^2$ over a volume of δV is

$$(\delta n^2)^2 = \left(\frac{\partial \pi^2}{\partial p}\right)^2 (\delta p)^2 + \sum_{i=1}^{m} \left(\frac{\partial n^2}{\partial C_i}\right) (\partial C_i)^2 \qquad \ldots (1.141)$$

- Here, δp is the density fluctuation and δC_i, is the concentration fluctuation of the ith glass component. The magnitudes of the composition and density fluctuations are determined from experimental scattering data. Once they are determined, the scattering loss can be calculated.

- Non-homogenous structure and defects created during fiber fabrication causes scattering of materials, and crystallized regions in the glass. These extrinsic effects can be minimized to the point where scattering which results from them is negligible compared with the intrinsic Rayleigh scattering

- In general, the pre-form manufacturing methods which have evolved, minimizes these extrinsic effects to the point where scattering which results from them is negligible compared with the intrinsic Rayleigh scattering.

- As Rayleigh scattering follows a characteristic λ^{-4} dependency, it reduces dramatically with increasing wavelength, as shown in Fig. 1.39. It is the dominant loss mechanisms in a fiber below about 1 μm wavelength and gives the attenuation-versus-wavelength plots their characteristic downward trend with increasing wavelength. At wavelengths longer than 1 μm, infrared absorption effects dominates optical signal attenuation.

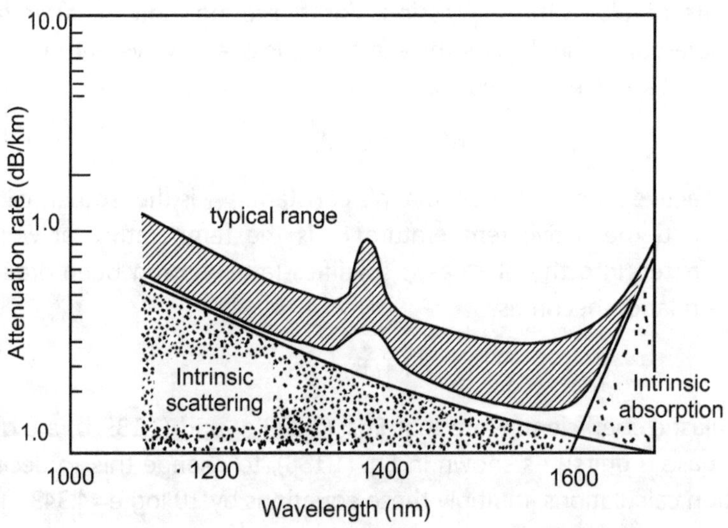

Fig. 1.39: Typical spectral attenuation range for production-run graded-index multimode fibers.

- We get the results shown in fig. 1.37 for multimode fibers and fig. 1.38 for single-mode fibers by combining the infrared, ultraviolet, and scattering losses,. Both of these figures are for typical commercial-grade silica fibers. The losses for multi-mode fibers are generally higher than those for single-mode fibers. This is a result of higher dopant concentrations and the accompanying larger scattering loss due to greater compositional fluctuation in multimode fibers. In addition, multimode fibers are subject to higher-order-mode losses due to perturbations at the core-cladding interface.

1.12.4 Bending losses

- Whenever an optical fiber undergoes a bend of finite radius of curvature radiative losses occurs. Fibers can be subjected to two types of bends: (a) macroscopic bends having radii that are large compared with the fiber diameter, for example, such as those that occur when a fiber cable turns a corner, and (b) random microscopic bends of the fiber axis that can arise when the fibers are incorporated into cables.

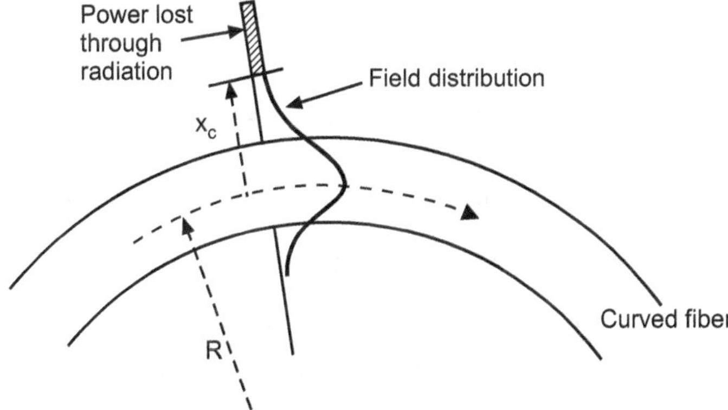

Fig. 1.40: Typical spectral attenuation range for production-run single-mode fibers

- Let us study first large-curvature radiation losses, which are also called as macrobending losses or simply bending losses. For slight bends the excess loss is extremely small and is essentially unobservable. As the radius of curvature decreases, the loss increases exponentially until at a certain critical radius the curvature loss becomes observable. If the bend radius is reduced until this threshold point has been reached, the losses suddenly become extremely large.

Any bound core mode has an evanescent field tail in the cladding which decays exponentially as a function of distance from the core. As this field tail moves along with the field in the core, part of the energy of a propagating mode travels in the fiber cladding. When a fiber is bent, the field tail on the far side of the center of curvature must move faster to keep up with the field in the core, as is shown in fig. 1.41 for the lowest-order fiber mode. At a certain critical distance x_c from the center of the fiber, the field tail would have to move faster than the speed of light to keep up with the core field. Since this is not possible the optical energy in the field tail beyond x_c radiates away.

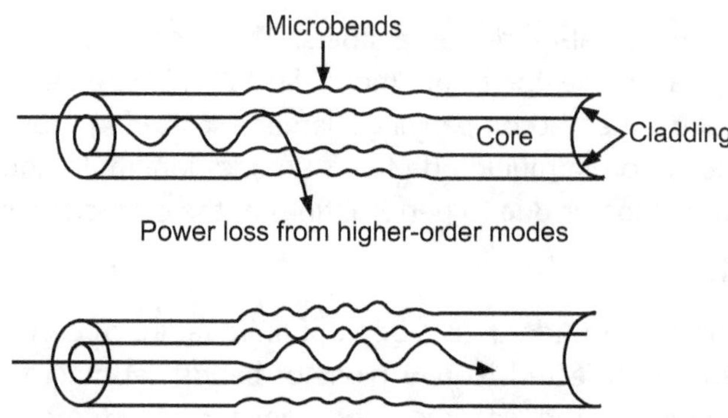

Fig. 1.41: Sketch of the fundamental mode field in a curved optical waveguide

- The amount of optical radiation from a bent fiber depends on the field strength at x_c and on the radius of curvature R. since higher-order modes are bound less tightly to the fiber core than lower-order modes, the higher-order modes will radiate out of the fiber first. Thus, the total number of modes that can be supported by a curved fiber is less than in a straight fiber. Gloge has derived the following expression for the effective number of modes N_{eff} that are guided by a curved multimode fiber of radius a :

$$N_{eff} = N_{\infty}\left\{1 - \frac{\alpha + 2}{2\alpha\Delta}\left[\frac{2a}{R} + \left(\frac{3}{2n_1kR}\right)^{2.3}\right]\right\} \qquad \ldots (1.142)$$

- Where α defines the graded-index profile, Δ is the core-cladding index difference, n_2 is the cladding refractive index, $k = 2\pi/\lambda$ is the wave propagation constant, and

$$N_{\infty} = \frac{\alpha}{\alpha + 2}(n_1ka)^2 \Delta \qquad \ldots (1.143)$$

is the total number of modes in a straight fiber.

- Another form of radiation loss in optical waveguide results from mode coupling caused by random microbends of the optical fiber. Microbends are repetitive small-scale fluctuations in the radius of curvature of the fiber axis, as is illustrated in Fig. 1.42. They are caused either by non-uniformities in the manufacturing of the fiber or by non-uniform lateral pressures created during the cabling of the fiber. The latter effect is often referred to as cabling or packaging losses. An increase in attenuation results from microbending because the fiber curvature causes repetitive coupling of energy between the guided modes and the leaky or non-guided modes in the fiber.

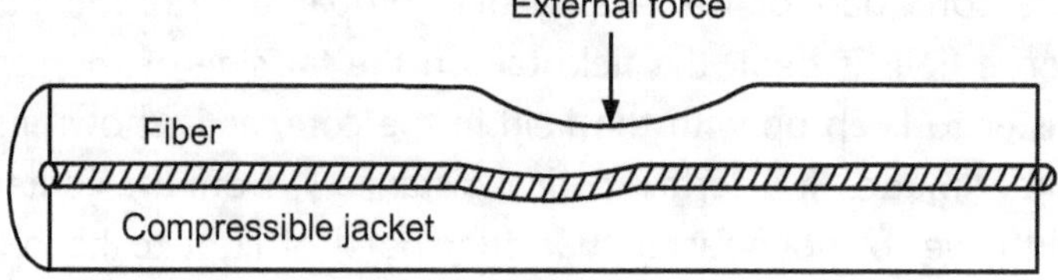

Fig. 1.42: Small scale fluctuations in the radius of curvature of the fiber axis lead to microbending losses

One method of minimizing microbending losses is by extruding a compressible jacket over the fiber. When external forces are applied to this configuration, the jacket will be deformed but the fiber will tend to stay relatively straight, as shown in fig. 1.41. For a multimode graded-index fiber having a core radiusa, outer radius b (excluding the jacket), and index difference Δ, the microbending loss α_M of a jacketed fiber is reduced from that of an unjacketed fiber by a factor.

$$F(\alpha_M) = \left[1 + \pi\Delta^2 \left(\frac{b}{a}\right)^4 \frac{E_f}{E_j} \right]^{-2} \qquad \ldots (1.144)$$

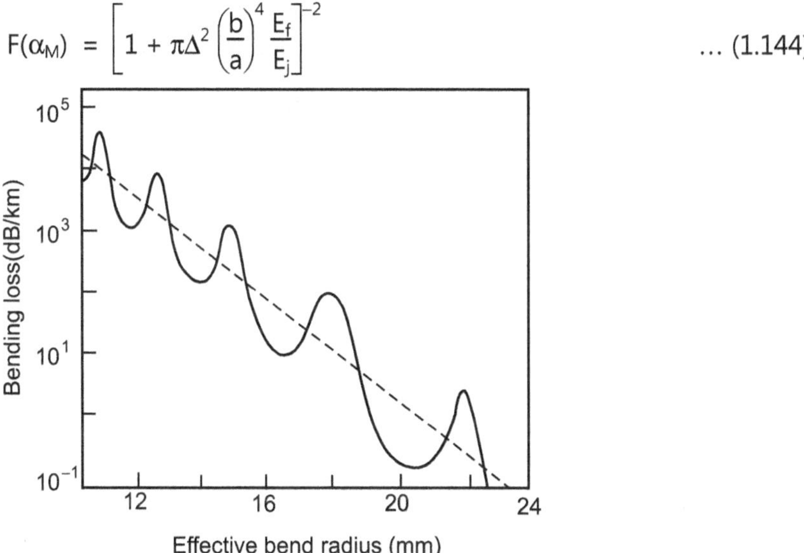

Fig. 1.43: A compressible jacket extruded over a fiber reduces microbending resulting from external forces

Here E_j and E_f are the Young's moduli of the jacket and fiber, respectively. The Young's modulus of common jacket materials ranges from 20 to 500 MPa. The Young's modulus of fused silica glass is about 65 GPa.

Example 1.2.3:

Two step index fibers exhibit the following parameters:

    (a)   a multimode fiber with a core refractive index of 1.500, a relative refractive index difference of 3 % and an operating wavelength of 0.82 µm;

    (b)   an 8 µm core diameter single-mode fiber with a core refractive index the same as (a), a relative refractive index difference of 0.3 % and an operating wavelength of 1.55 µm.

Estimate the critical radius of curvature at which large beding losses occur in both cases.

Solution:

    (a)   The relative refractive index difference is given by equation as:

$$\Delta = \frac{n_1^2 - n_2^2}{2n_1^2}$$

Hence,
$$n = n_1^2 - 2\Delta n_1^2$$

$$= 2.250 - 0.06 \times 2.250$$

$$= 2.115$$

Critical radius of curvature for the multimode fiber is given as:

$$R_c = \frac{3n_1^2 \lambda}{4\pi \, (n_1^2 - n_2^2)^{1/2}}$$

$$= \frac{3 \times 2.250 \times 0.82 \times 10^{-6}}{4\pi \times (0.135)^{1/2}}$$

$$= 9 \ \mu m$$

$$= n_1^2 - 2\Delta n_1^2$$

$$= 2.250 - (0.006 \times 2.250)$$

$$= 2.237$$

The cut-off wavelength for the single mode fiber is given by

$$\lambda_c = \frac{2\pi a n_1 \, (2\Delta)^{1/2}}{2.405}$$

$$= \frac{2\pi \times 4 \times 10^{-6} \times 1.500 (0.06)^{1/2}}{2.405}$$

$$= 1.214 \ \mu m$$

Substitute this value in equation for R_{cs}.

$$R_{cs} \simeq \frac{20 \times 1.55 \times 10^{-6}}{(0.043)^{3/2}} \left(2.748 - \frac{0.996 \times 1.55 \times 10^{-6}}{1.214 \times 10^{-6}} \right)^{-3}$$

$$= 34 \ mm$$

1.12.5 Core and Cladding Losses

- Upon measuring the propagation losses in an actual fiber, all the dissipative and scattering losses will be manifested simultaneously.

- Since the core and cladding have different indices of refraction and therefore differ in composition, the core and cladding generally have different attenuation coefficients, denoted α_1 and α_2, respectively.

- If the influence of modal coupling is ignored, the loss for a mode of order (v, m) for a step-index waveguide is

$$\alpha_{v,\,m} \;=\; \alpha_1 \frac{P_{core}}{P} + \alpha_2 \frac{P_{clad}}{P} \qquad\qquad \dots (1.145\ a)$$

- Where the fractional powers P_{core}/P and P_{clad}/P for several low-order modes. Using Equation (1.145 a), this can be written as

$$\alpha_{v,\,m} \;=\; \alpha_1 + (\alpha_2 - \alpha_1)\frac{P_{clad}}{P} \qquad\qquad \dots (1.145\ b)$$

- The total loss of the waveguide can be found by summing over all modes weighted by the fractional power in that mode.

- For the case of a graded-index fiber the situation is much more complicated. In this case, both the attenuation coefficients and the modal power tend to be functions of the radial coordinate. At a distance r from the core axis the loss is

$$\alpha((r) \;=\; \alpha_1 + (\alpha_2 - \alpha_1)\frac{n^2(0) - n^2(r)}{n^2(0) - n_2^2} \qquad\qquad \dots (1.146)$$

- Where α_1 and α_2 are the axial and cladding attenuation coefficients, respectively, and the n terms are defined. the loss encountered by a given mode is then

$$\alpha_{gi} \;=\; \frac{\displaystyle\int_0^\infty \alpha(r)\,p(r)r\,dr}{\displaystyle\int_0^\infty p(r)r\,dr} \qquad\qquad \dots (1.147)$$

- Where P(r) is the power density of that mode at r. the complexity of the multimode waveguide has prevented an experimental correlation with a model. However, it has generally been observed that the loss increases with increasing mode number.

1.13 SIGNAL DISTORTION IN OPTICAL FIBERS

- Dispersion of the transmitted optical signal causes distortion for both digital and analog transmission along optical fibers.

- Dispersion mechanisms within the fiber causes broadening of the transmitted light pulses as they travel along the channel.

- It may be observed that each pulse broadens and overlaps with it's neighbours and becomes indistinguishable at the receiver input. The effect will be known as Inter Symbol Interference (ISI).

- A number of errors will occur on the digital optical channel as more ISIs are pronounced. The error rate is also a function of the signal attenuation on the link and the Signal-to-Noise Ratio (SNR) at the receiver.

- The signal dispersion alone limits the maximum possible bandwidth attainable with a particular optical fiber to the point where individual symbols can no longer be distinguished.

- To avoid dispersion, the light pulses should not overlap and the overlapping of pulse can be reduced if the digital bit rate B_T must be less than the reciprocal of the broadened pulse duration (2τ).

$$B_T \leq \frac{1}{2\tau} \qquad\qquad\qquad \ldots (1.148)$$

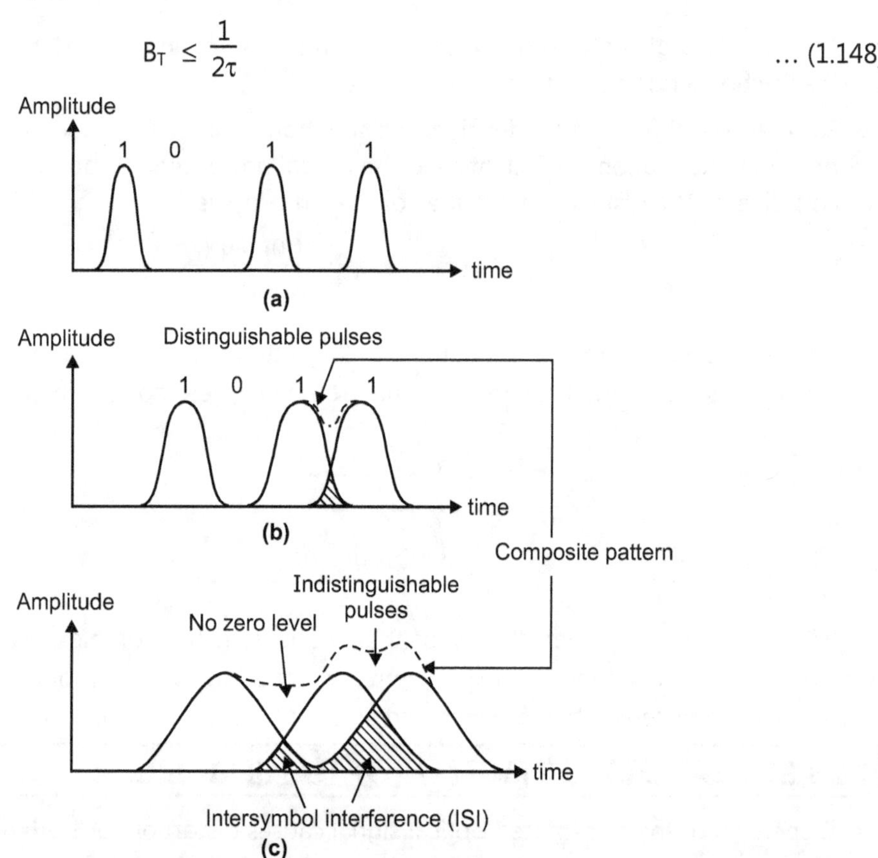

Fig. 1.44 : (a) Fiber input (b) Fiber output at a distance L_1

(c) Fiber output at a distance $L_2 > L_1$

- Another more accurate estimate of the maximum bit rate for an optical channel with dispersion may be obtained by considering the light pulses at the output to have a Gaussian shape with a rms width of σ.

- This analysis allows for the existence of a certain amount of signal overlap on the channel, while avoiding any SNR penalty which occurs when ISI becomes pronounced.

- The maximum bit rate is given approximately by:

$$B_T \text{ (max)} \simeq \frac{0.2}{\sigma} \text{ bit s}^{-1} \qquad \text{... (1.149)}$$

- The conversion of bit rate of bandwidth in hertz depends on the digital coding format used. For metallic conductors when a nonreturn-to-zero code is employed the binary 1 level is held for the whole bit period τ.

- In this case, there are two bit periods in one wavelength (i.e. 2 bits per second per hertz).

- Hence, the maximum bandwidth B is one-half the maximum data rate or:

$$B_T \text{ (max)} = 2B \qquad \text{... (1.150)}$$

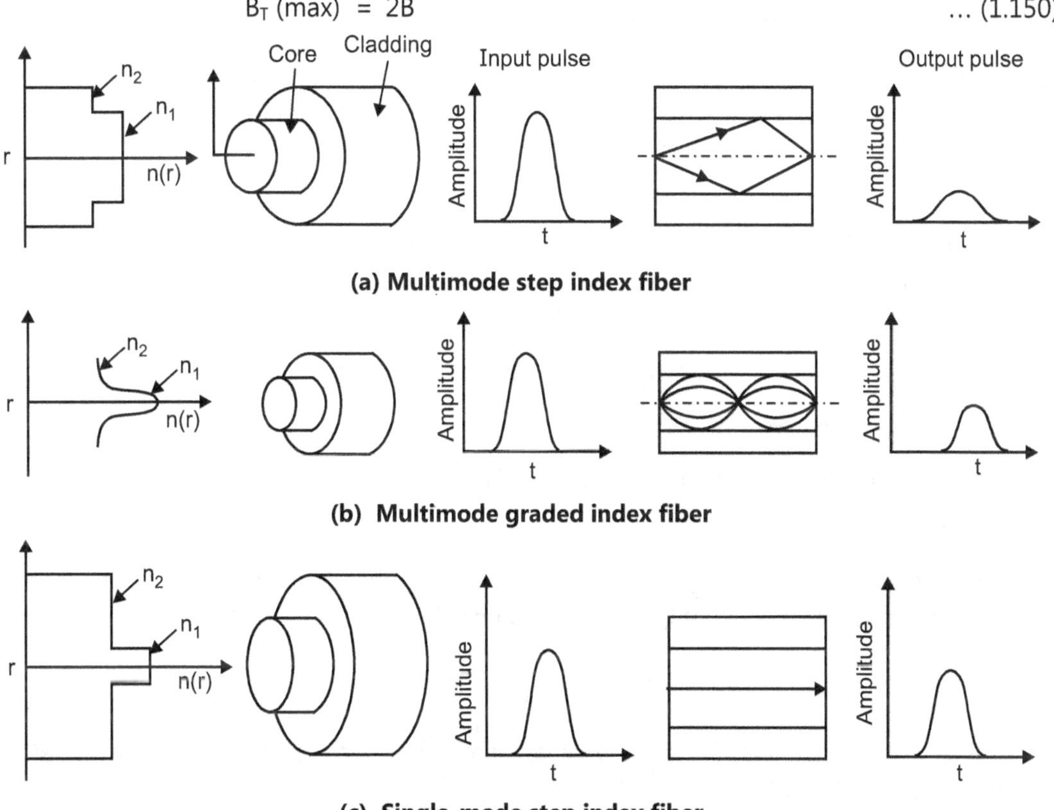

Fig. 1.45 : Schematic diagram showing a multimode step index fiber, multimode graded index fiber and single mode step index fiber and illustration of the pulse broadening due to intermodel dispersion in each fiber.

- The above Fig. 1.45 shows the three common optical fiber structures, namely multimode step index, multimode graded index and single-mode step index and their respective pulse broadening associated with each fiber type.

- It is to be noted that the multimode step index fiber exhibits the greatest dispersion of a transmitted light pulse and multimode graded index fiber gives a considerably improved performance.

- The single mode fiber gives the minimum pulse broadening and thus is capable of the greatest transmission bandwidths which are currently in the gigahertz range, whereas transmission via multimode step index fiber is usually limited to bandwidths of a few tons of megahertz.

- The amount of pulse broadening depends upon the distance travelled by the pulse in the fiber.

- Hence, the number of optical signal pulses which may be transmitted in a given period and therefore the information-carrying capacity of the fiber, is restricted by the amount of pulse dispersion per unit length.

- In absence of mode coupling or filtering, the pulse broadening increases linearly with fiber length and thus the bandwidth is inversely proportional to the distance. This leads to the adoption of a more useful parameter known as Bandwidth - length product i.e. $(B_{opt} \times L)$.

Example 1.12 : *A multimode graded index fiber exhibits a total pulse broadening of 0.1 μs over a distance of 15 km.*

Estimate:

(a) The maximum possible bandwidth on the link assuming no intersymbol interference.

(b) The pulse dispersion per unit length.

(c) The bandwidth - length product for the fiber.

Solution :

(a) The maximum possible optical bandwidth which is equivalent to the maximum possible bit rate (for return to zero pulses) assuming no ISI may be obtained.

Where,
$$B_{opt} = BT = \frac{1}{2\tau} = \frac{1}{0.2 \times 10^{-6}} = 5 \text{ MHz}$$

(b) The dispersion per unit length may be acquired simply by dividing the total dispersion by the total length of the fiber:

$$\text{Dispersion} = \frac{0.1 \times 10^{-6}}{15} = 6.67 \text{ ns km}^{-1}$$

(c) The bandwidth-length product may be obtained in two ways, first by simply multiplying the maximum band width for the fiber link by its length.

Hence,
$$B_{opt} L = 5 \text{ MHz} \times 15 \text{ km} = 75 \text{ MHz km}$$

Alternatively, it may be obtained from the dispersion per unit length.

where,
$$B_{opt} L = \frac{1}{2 \times 6.67 \times 10^{-6}} = 75 \text{ MHz km}$$

1.14 INTRAMODAL DISPERSION

- Chromatic or intramodel dispersion occurs in all types of optical fibers and results from the finite spectral linewidth of the optical source.

- Since optical sources emits a band of frequencies and not a single frequency there may be propagation delay differences between the different spectral components of the transmitted signal.

- This causes broadening of each transmitted mode and is called as Intramodal dispersion.

- The delay differences may be caused by the dispersive properties of the waveguide material (material dispersion) and also guidance effects within the fiber structure (waveguide dispersion).

1.14.1 Material Dispersion

- Pulse broadening due to material dispersion results from the different group velocities of the various spectral components launched into the fiber from the optical source.

- It occurs when the phase velocity of a plane wave propagating in the dielectric medium varies nonlinearly with wavelength and the material is said to exhibit material dispersion when the second differential of the refractive index w.r.t. wavelength is not zero (i.e. $d^2n/d\lambda^2 \neq 0$).

- The pulse spread due to material dispersion may be obtained by considering the group delay τ_g in the optical fiber which is the reciprocal of the group velocity υ_g equations.

- Hence, the group velocity is given by:

$$\tau_g = \frac{d\beta}{dw} = \frac{1}{c}\left(n_1 - \lambda\frac{dn_1}{d\lambda}\right) \qquad \text{... (1.151)}$$

where n_1 is the refractive index of the core material. The pulse delay τ_m due to material dispersion in a fiber of length L is therefore:

$$\tau_m = \frac{L}{c}\left(n_1 - \lambda\frac{dn_1}{d\lambda}\right) \qquad \text{... (1.152)}$$

For a source with rms spectral width σ_λ and a mean wavelength λ the rms pulse broadening due to material dispersion σ_m may be obtained from the above expression in a Taylor series about λ where:

$$\sigma_m = \sigma_\lambda\frac{d\tau_m}{d\lambda} + \sigma_\lambda\frac{2d^2\tau_m}{d\lambda^2} + \text{...} \qquad \text{... (1.163)}$$

As the first term usually dominates, especially for sources operating over the 0.8 to 0.9 μm wavelength range therefore:

$$\sigma_m \approx \sigma_\lambda\frac{d\tau_m}{d\lambda} \qquad \text{... (1.154)}$$

Hence, the pulse spread may be evaluated by considering the dependence of τ_m on λ,

where,
$$\frac{d\tau_m}{d\lambda} = \frac{L\lambda}{c}\left[\frac{dn_1}{d\lambda} - \frac{d^2n_1}{d\lambda^2} - \frac{dn_1}{d\lambda}\right] \qquad \ldots (1.155)$$

$$= \frac{-L\lambda}{c}\frac{d^2n_1}{d\lambda^2} \qquad \ldots (1.156)$$

Substituting this equation into equation (1.143), the rms pulse broadening due to material dispersion is given by:

$$\sigma_m \simeq \frac{\sigma_\lambda L}{c}\left|\lambda\frac{d^2n_1}{d\lambda^2}\right| \qquad \ldots (1.157)$$

The material dispersion for optical fibers is sometimes quoted as a value for $|\lambda^2(d^2n_1|d\lambda^2)|$ or simply $|d^2n_1|d\lambda^2|$.

It may be given in terms of the material dispersion parameter M which is defined as:

$$M = \frac{1}{L}\frac{d\tau_m}{d\lambda} = \frac{\lambda}{c}\left|\frac{d^2n_1}{d\lambda^2}\right| \qquad \ldots (1.158)$$

and which is often expressed in units of ps $\text{nm}^{-1}\text{km}^{-1}$.

Example 1.13 : *A glass fiber exhibits material dispersion given by $|\lambda^2(d^2n_1|d\lambda^2)$ of 0.025. Determine the material dispersion parameter at a wavelength of 0.85 μm and estimate the rms pulse broadening per kilometer for a good LED source with an rms spectral width of 20 nm at this wavelength.*

Solution :

The material dispersion parameter may be obtained as:

$$M = \frac{1}{c\lambda}\left|\frac{d^2n_1}{d\lambda^2}\right|$$

$$= \frac{\lambda}{c\lambda}\left|\lambda^2\frac{d^2n_1}{d\lambda^2}\right| = \frac{0.025}{2.998\times10^5\times850}\ \text{snm}^{-1}\text{km}^{-1}$$

$$= 98.1\ \text{ps nm}^{-1}\ \text{km}^{-1}$$

The rms pulse broadening is given by the equation as

$$\sigma_m = \frac{\sigma_\lambda L}{c}\left|\lambda\frac{d^2n_1}{d\lambda^2}\right|$$

Therefore in terms of the material dispersion, parameter M is defined by the equation as

$$\sigma_m \simeq \sigma_\lambda\, LM$$

Hence, the rms pulse broadening per kilometer due to material dispersion:

$$\sigma_m \,(1 \text{ km}) \;=\; 20 \times 1 \times 98.1 \times 10^{-12} = 1.96 \text{ ns km}^{-1}$$

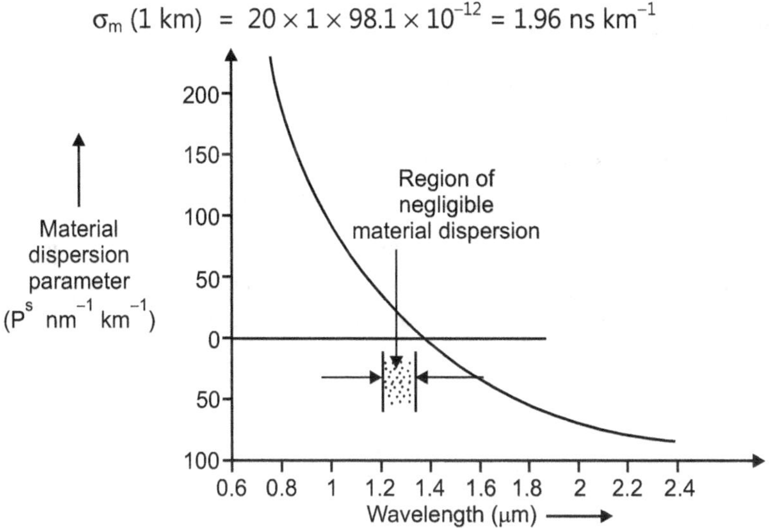

Fig. 1.46 : The material dispersion parameter for silica as a function of wavelength

The Fig. 1.46 shows the variation of the material dispersion parameter M with wavelength for pure silica. It may be observed that the material dispersion tends to zero in the longer wavelength region around 1.3 µm (for pure silica). This provides an additional incentive (other than low attenuation) for operation at longer wavelengths where the material dispersion may be minimized. Also, the use of an injection laser with a narrow spectral width rather than an LED as the optical source leads to a substantial reduction in the pulse broadening due to material dispersion, even in the shorter wavelength region.

Example 1.14 : *Estimate the rms pulse broadening per kilometer for the fiber in above example 2.4 when the optical source used is an injection laser with a relative spectral width $\sigma_\lambda|\lambda$ of 0.0012 at a wavelength of 0.85 µm.*

Solution :

The rms spectral width may be obtained from the relative spectral width by:

$$\sigma_\lambda = 0.0012\, \lambda \;=\; 0.0012 \times 0.85 \times 10^{-6}$$

$$= 1.02 \text{ nm}$$

The rms pulse broadening in terms of the material dispersion parameter is given by

$$\sigma_m \;\simeq\; \sigma_\lambda\, LM$$

Therefore, the rms pulse broadening per kilometer due to material dispersion is:

$$\sigma_m \;\simeq\; 1.02 \times 1 \times 98.1 \times 10^{-12}$$

$$= 0.10 \text{ ns km}^{-1}$$

Hence, in this example the r.m.s. pulse broadening is reduced by a factor of around 20.

1.14.2 Waveguide Dispersion

The waveguiding of the fiber also creates intramodal dispersion. This intramodal dispersion results from the variation in group velocity with wavelength for a particular mode.

The effect of waveguide dispersion on pulse spreading can be approximated by assuming that the refractive index of the material is independent of the wavelength.

First consider the group delay, that is the time required for a mode to travel along a fiber of length L. To make the results independent of fiber configuration the group delay can be expressed in terms of the normalized propagation constant b defined as

$$b = 1 - \left(\frac{ua}{v}\right)^2 = \frac{\beta^2 \mid k^2 - n_2^2}{n_1^2 - n_2^2} \qquad \text{... (1.159)}$$

For small values of the index difference $\Delta = (n_1 - n_2)/n_1$

$$b \simeq \frac{\beta \mid k - n_2}{n_1 - n_2} \qquad \text{... (1.160)}$$

Solving equation for β, we have

$$\beta \simeq n_2 k \, (b\Delta + 1) \qquad \text{... (1.161)}$$

with this expression for β and using the assumption that n_2 is not a function of wavelength we find that the group delay τ_{wg} arising from waveguide dispersion is

$$\tau_{wg} = \frac{L}{c} \frac{d\beta}{dk} = \frac{L}{c}\left[n_2 + n_2\Delta \frac{d(kb)}{dk}\right] \qquad \text{... (1.162)}$$

The modal propagation constant β is obtained from the eigenvalue equation expressed and is generally given in terms of the normalized frequency v defined as :

$$v = ka(n_1^2 - n_2^2)^{1/2} \simeq k \, an_1 \sqrt{2\Delta} \qquad \text{... (1.163)}$$

which is valid for small values of Δ writing the group delay in terms of v instead of k yields.

$$\tau_{wg} = \frac{L}{c}\left[n_2 + n_2 \Delta \frac{d(vb)}{dv}\right] \qquad \text{... (1.164)}$$

The first term in above equation is a constant and the second term represents the group delay arising from waveguide dispersion. The factor d(vb)/dv can be expressed as :

$$\frac{d(vb)}{dv} = b\left[1 - \frac{2 \, J_v^2 \, (ua)}{J_{v+1} \, (ua) \, J_{v-1} \, (ua)}\right] \qquad \text{... (1.165)}$$

where u is defined by equation $u^2 = k_1^2 - \beta^2$ and a is the fiber radius.

For single mode fibers, waveguide dispersion is important and can be of the same order of magnitude as material dispersion.

The pulse spreading σ_{wg} occuring over a distribution of wavelengths σ_λ is obtained from the derivative of the group delay w.r.t. wavelength.

$$\sigma_{wg} = \left|\frac{d\tau_{wg}}{d\lambda}\right| \sigma_\lambda = L\,|D_{wg}(\lambda)|\,\sigma_\lambda \qquad \qquad \text{... (1.166)}$$

$$= \frac{v}{\lambda}\left|\frac{d\tau_{wg}}{d\lambda}\right| \sigma_\lambda \qquad \qquad \text{... (1.167)}$$

$$= \frac{n_2\,L\,\Delta\,\sigma_\lambda}{c\lambda} \cdot \frac{v\,d^2(vb)}{dv} \qquad \qquad \text{... (1.168)}$$

where $D_{wg}(\lambda)$ is the waveguide dispersion.

1.14.3 Polarization Mode Dispersion

- The effect of fiber birefringence on the polarization states of an optical signal are another source of pulse broadening.
- This is critical particularly for high rate long haul transmission links that are designed to operate near the zero dispersion wavelength of the fiber.
- Birefringence can result from intrinsic factors such as geometric irregularities of the fiber core or internal stresses on it.
- Deviations of less than 1 % in the circularities of the core can have a noticeable effect in a high speed lightwave system.
- In addition, external factors, such as bending, twisting or pinching of the fiber, can also lead to birefringence. Since all these mechanisms exist to some extents in any field installed fiber, there will be a varying birefringence along it's length.
- A fundamental property of an optical signal is it's polarization state.
- Polarization refers to the electric field orientation of a light signal, which can vary significantly along the length of a fiber.

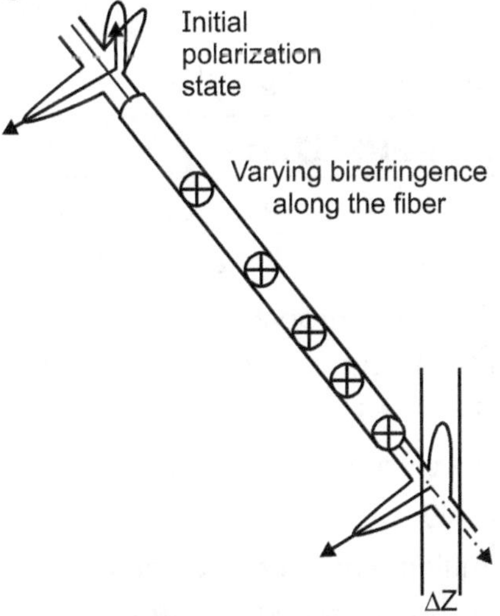

Fig. 1.47 : Polarization mode dispersion

- As shown in Fig. 1.47 the signal energy at a given wavelength occupies two orthogonal polarization modes. A varying birefringence along it's length will cause each polarization mode to travel at a slightly different velocity and the polarization orientation will rotate with distance. The resulting difference in propagation times ΔZ, between the two orthogonal polarization modes will result in pulse spreading. This is the Polarization Mode Dispersion (PMD).

- If the group velocities of the two orthogonal polarization modes are v_{gx} and v_{gy} then the differential time delay $\Delta\tau_{pol}$ between the two polarization components during propagation of the pulse over a distance L is

$$\Delta\tau_{pol} = \left| \frac{L}{v_{gx}} - \frac{L}{v_{gy}} \right| \qquad \ldots (1.169)$$

- In contrast to chromatic dispersion which is a relatively stable phenomenon along a fiber, PMD varies randomly along the fiber.

- The principal reason for this is that the perturbations causing the birefringence effects, vary with temperature.

- In practice, this shows up as a random, time varying fluctuations in the value of the PMD at the fiber output.

- Thus, $\Delta\tau_{pol}$ given in the above equation cannot be used directly to estimate PMD. A useful means of characterizing PMD for long fiber lengths is in terms of the mean value of the differential group delay.

- This can be calculated according to the relationship.

$$\Delta\tau_{pol} \approx D_{PMD}\sqrt{L} \qquad \ldots (1.170)$$

Where D_{PMD} which is measured in $ps/\sqrt{km}$ is the average PMD parameter.

Typical values of D_{PMD} range from 0.1 to 1.0 $ps/\sqrt{km}$.

1.15 INTERMODAL DISPERSION

- Pulse broadening due to intermodal dispersion results from the propagation delay differences between modes within a multimode fiber.

- As there are number of modes propagating along the channel at different group velocities the pulse width at the output is dependent upon the transmission times of the slowest and fastest modes.

- Multimode step index fibers exhibit a large amount of intermodal dispersion which gives the greatest pulse broadening.

- Intermodal dispersion in multimode fibers may be reduced by adoption of an optimum refractive index profile which is provided by the near-parabolic profile of most graded index fibers.

- The overall pulse broadening in multimode graded index fibers is far less than that obtained in multimode step index fibers (typically by a factor of 100). Thus, graded index fibers used with a multimode source give a tremendous bandwidth advantage over multimode step index fibers.

- For a single-mode operation, there is no inter-modal dispersion and therefore pulse broadening is solely due to the intramodal dispersion mechanisms.

1.15.1 Multimode Step Index Fiber

- Using Ray theory model, the fastest and slowest modes propagating in the step index fiber may be represented by the axial ray and the extreme meridional ray respectively. The paths taken by these two rays in a perfectly structured step index fiber are shown in Fig. 1.48.

- The dealy difference between these two rays while travelling in the fiber core allows estimation of the pulse broadening, resulting from intermodal dispersion within the fiber.

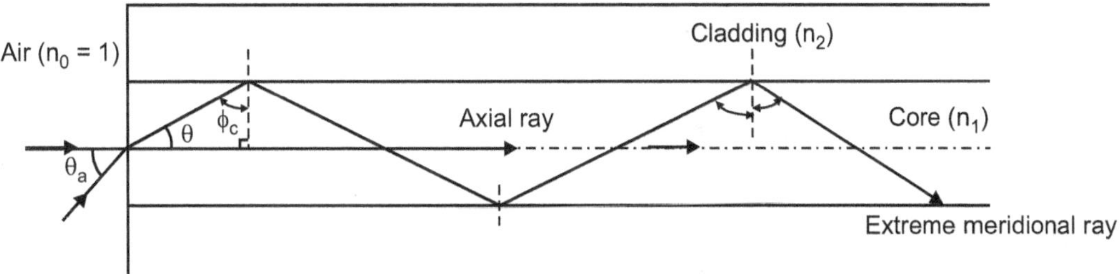

Fig. 1.48 : The paths taken by the axial and an extreme meridional ray in a perfect multimode step index fiber

- As both rays are travelling at the same velocity within the constant refractive index fiber core, the delay difference is directly related to their respective path lengths within the fiber. Hence, the time taken for the axial ray to travel along a fiber of length L gives the minimum delay time T_{min} and

$$T_{min} = \frac{distance}{velocity} = \frac{L}{(c/n_1)} = \frac{L\,n_1}{c} \qquad \ldots (1.171)$$

Where n_1 is the refractive index of the core and c is the velocity of light in a vacuum. The extreme meridional ray exhibits the maximum delay time, T_{max}

where, $\qquad T_{max} = \dfrac{L/\cos\theta}{c/n_1} = \dfrac{L\,n_1}{c\,\cos\theta} \qquad \ldots (1.172)$

using Snell's law of refraction at the core-cladding interface.

$$\sin\phi_c = \frac{n_2}{n_1} = \cos\theta \qquad \ldots (1.173)$$

where n_2 is the refractive index of the cladding substituting the value of $\cos \theta$ in

$$T_{max} \;=\; \frac{L n_1^2}{c n_2} \qquad \text{... (1.174)}$$

The delay difference δT_s between the extreme meridional ray and the axial ray may be obtained as

Hence,
$$\delta T_s \;=\; T_{max} - T_{min}$$

$$=\; \frac{L\, n_1^2}{c n_2} - \frac{L\, n_1}{c}$$

$$=\; \frac{L\, n_1^2}{c n_2} \left(\frac{n_1 - n_2}{n_1} \right) \qquad \text{... (1.175)}$$

$$\approx\; \frac{L\, n_1^2\, \Delta}{c n_2} \qquad \text{[where } \Delta << 1] \text{ ... (1.176)}$$

where Δ is the refractive index difference.

When $\Delta << 1$,

$$\Delta \;\simeq\; \frac{n_1 - n_2}{n_2} \qquad \text{... (1.177)}$$

Hence rearranging equation

$$\delta T_s \;=\; \frac{L n_1}{c} \left(\frac{n_1 - n_2}{n_2} \right) \qquad \text{... (1.178)}$$

$$\simeq\; \frac{L n_1 \Delta}{c} \qquad \text{... (1.179)}$$

Also substituting for Δ,

$$\delta T_s \;\simeq\; \frac{L\,(NA)^2}{2 n_1 c} \qquad \text{... (1.180)}$$

where, NA = Numberical aperture of the fiber.

The approximate equations for delay difference are usually employed to estimate the maximum pulse broadening in time due to intermodal dispersion in multimode step index fibers.

When the optical input to the fiber is a pulse $P_i(t)$ of unit area.

$$\int_{-\infty}^{\infty} P_i(t)\, dt \;=\; 1 \qquad \text{... (1.181)}$$

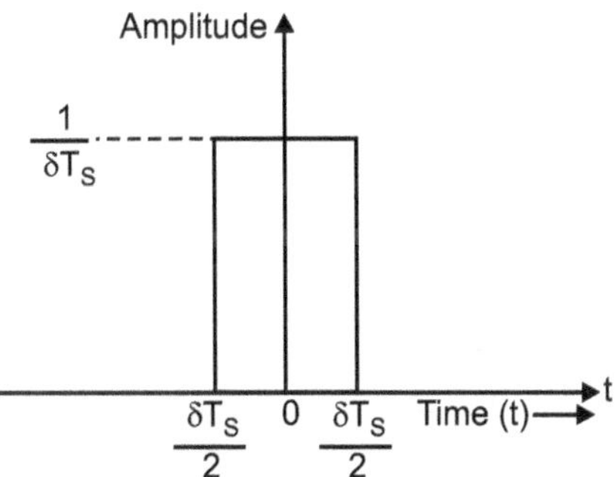

Fig. 1.49 : Light input to the multimode step index fiber consisting of an ideal pulse or rectangular function with unit area

$P_i(t)$ has a constant amplitude of $1/\delta T_s$ over the range.

$$\frac{-\delta T_s}{2} \leq P(t) \leq \frac{\delta T_s}{2} \qquad \text{.. (1.182)}$$

The rms pulse broadening at the fiber output due to intermodal dispersion for the multimode step index fiber σ_s(i.e. the standard deviation) may be given in terms of the variance as

$$\sigma_s^2 = M_2 - M_1^2 \qquad \text{... (1.183)}$$

where M_1 is the temporal moment which is equivalent to the mean value of the pulse and M_2, the second temporal moment, is equivalent to the mean square value of the pulse.

Hence:

$$M_1 = \int_{-\infty}^{\infty} t\, P_i(t)\, dt \qquad \text{... (1.184)}$$

and

$$M_2 = \int_{-\infty}^{\infty} t^2 P_i(t)\, dt \qquad \text{... (1.185)}$$

The mean value M_1 for the unit input pulse is zero and assuming this is maintained for the output pulse.

$$\sigma_s^2 = M_2 = \int_{-\infty}^{\infty} t^2 P_i(t)\, dt \qquad \text{... (1.186)}$$

integrating over the limits of the input pulse and substituting for $P_i(t)$ in equation above over this range gives:

$$\sigma_s^2 = \int_{-\delta T_s/2}^{\delta T_s/2} \frac{1}{\delta T_s} t^2\, dt \qquad \text{... (1.187)}$$

$$= \frac{1}{\delta T_s} \left[\frac{t^3}{3} \right]_{-\delta T_s/2}^{\delta T_s/2} \qquad \dots (1.188)$$

$$= \frac{1}{3} \left[\frac{\delta T_s}{2} \right]^2 \qquad \dots (1.189)$$

Hence, substitution value for δT_s gives:

$$\sigma_s \simeq \frac{L n_1 \Delta}{2\sqrt{3}\, c} \simeq \frac{L\,(NA)^2}{4\sqrt{3}\, n_1 c} \qquad \dots (1.190)$$

This equation allows estimation of the rms impulse response of a multimode step index fiber, if it is assumed that intermodal dispersion dominates and there is a uniform distribution of light rays over the range $0 \le \theta \le \theta_a$. The pulse broadening is directly proportional to the relative refractive index difference Δ and the length of the fiber L.

Example 1.15 : *A 6 km optical link consists of multimode step index fiber with a core refractive index of 1.5 and a relative refractive difference of 1 %.*

Estimate:

(a) the delay difference between the slowest and fastest modes at the fiber output;

(b) the rms pulse broadening due to intermodal dispersion on the link;

(c) the maximum bit rate that may be obtained without substantial errors on the link assuming only intermodal dispersion;

(d) the bandwidth - length product corresponding to (c).

Solution :

(a) The delay difference is given by equation as

$$\delta T_s \simeq \frac{L n_1 \Delta}{c} = \frac{6 \times 10^3 \times 1.5 \times 0.01}{2.998 \times 10^8} = 300 \text{ ns}$$

(b) The rms pulse broadening due to intermodal dispersion may be obtained from equation as

$$\sigma_s = \frac{L n_1 \Delta}{2\sqrt{3}\, c} = \frac{1}{2\sqrt{3}} = \frac{6 \times 10^3 \times 1.5 \times 0.01}{2.998 \times 10^8} = 88.7 \text{ ns}$$

(c) The maximum bit rate may be estimated in two ways. Firstly, to get an idea of the maximum bit rate when assuming no pulse overlap.

$$B_{T\,(max)} = \frac{1}{2\tau} = \frac{1}{2\delta\, \tau_s}$$

$$= \frac{1}{600 \times 10^{-9}} = 1.7 \text{ M bit s}^{-1}$$

Alternatively an improved estimate may be obtained using the calculated rms pulse broadening where:

$$B_{T\,(max)} = \frac{0.2}{\sigma_s} = \frac{0.2}{86.7 \times 10^{-9}} = 2.3 \text{ M bit s}^{-1}$$

(d) Using the most accurate estimate of the maximum bit rate from (c) and assuming return to zero pulses, the bandwidth - length product is:

$$B_{opt} \times L = 2.3 \text{ MHz} \times 6 \text{ km} = 13.8 \text{ MHz km}$$

Intermodal dispersion can be reduced by propagation mechanisms within particular fibers. Another mechanism which reduces intermodal pulse broadening in nonperfect multimode fibers is the mode coupling or mixing. The coupling between guided modes transfers optical power from the slower to the faster modes and vice versa. Hence, with strong coupling the optical power tends to be transmitted at an average speed, which is the mean of the various propagating modes. This reduces the intermodal dispersion on the link and makes it advantageous to encourage mode coupling within multimode fibers.

$$\delta T_{SC} \simeq \frac{n_1 \Delta}{c} (L\, L_C)^{1/2} \qquad\qquad \text{... (1.191)}$$

This is the modified expression for the delay difference for a particular step index fiber for the fiber with mode coupling among all guided modes.

Where L_C is the characteristic length for the fiber which is inversely proportional to the coupling strength. Hence, the delay difference increases at a slower rate proportional to $(LL_C)^{1/2}$ instead of the direct proportionality to L. However, the most successful technique for reducing intermodal dispersion in multimode fibers is by grading the core refractive index to follow a near-parabolic profile.

1.15.2 Multimode Graded Index Fiber

Intermodal dispersion in multimode fibers in minimized with the use of graded index fibers. Hence, multimode graded index fibers show substantial bandwidth improvement over multimode step index fibers. The fiber has a parabolic index profile with a maximum at the core axis.

The index profile with $\alpha = 2$ is given as:

$$n(r) = n_1\left[1 - 2\Delta(r/a)^2\right]^{1/2} \qquad r < a \text{ (core)}$$

$$= n_1\left[1 - 2\Delta\right]^{1/2} = n_2 \qquad r \geq a \text{ (cladding)} \qquad \text{... (1.192)}$$

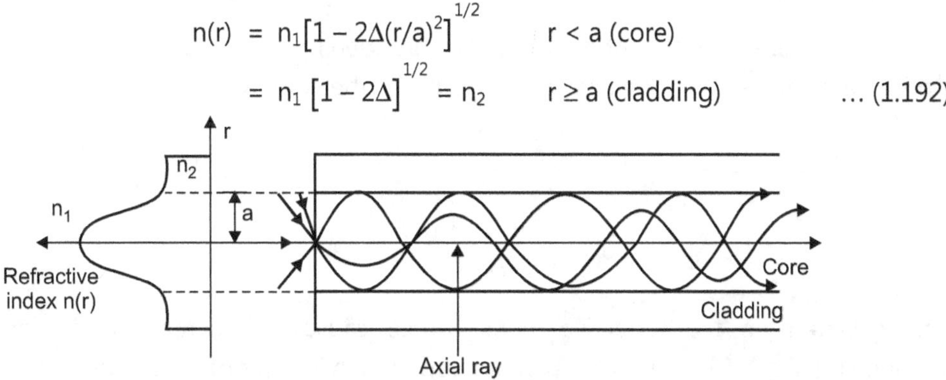

Fig. 1.50 : A multimode graded index fiber

It may be observed that apart from the axial ray, the meridional rays follow sinusoidal trajectories of different path lengths which result from the index grading. The local group velocity is inversely proportional to the local refractive index and therefore the longer sinusoidal paths are compensated for by higher speeds in the lower index medium away from the axis. Hence, there is an equalization of the transmission times of the various trajectories towards the transmission time of the axial ray which travels exclusively in the higher-index region at the core axis, and at the slowest speed.

Improvement in multimode fiber bandwidth achieved with a parabolic or near-parabolic refractive index profile is highlighted by consideration of the reduced delay difference between the fastest and slowest modes for this graded index fiber δT_g.

$$\delta T_g \simeq \frac{Ln_1\Delta^2}{2c} \simeq \frac{(NA)^4}{8\,n_1^3 c} \qquad \ldots (1.193)$$

Hence, a more rigorous analysis using electromagnetic mode theory gives an absolute temporal width at the fiber output of

$$\delta T_g \simeq \frac{Ln_1\Delta^2}{8c} \qquad \ldots (1.194)$$

which corresponds to an increase in transmission time for the slowest mode at $\Delta^2/8$ over the fastest mode. Hence, the rms pulse broadening is a useful parameter for assessment of intermodal dispersion in multimode graded index fibers. σ_g the rms pulse broadening of a near-parabolic index profile graded index fiber is reduced compared with similar broadening for the corresponding step index fiber σ_s.

$$\sigma_g = \frac{\Delta}{D}\,\sigma_s \qquad \ldots (1.195)$$

where D is a constant between 4 and 10 depending on the precise evaluation and the exact optimum profile chosen.

The best minimum intermodal rms pulse broadening for a graded index fiber with an optimum characteristic refractive index profile for the core, $\propto_{op}$ is

$$\alpha_{op} = 2 - \frac{12\Delta}{5} \qquad \ldots (1.196)$$

$$\sigma_g = \frac{Ln_1\Delta^2}{20\sqrt{3}c} \qquad \ldots (1.197)$$

Any deviation in the refractive index profile causes an increase in intermodal pulse broadening. Fig. 1.51 shows the curve for variation in intermodal pulse broadening (δT_g) as a function of the characteristic refractive index profile α for typical graded index fibers.

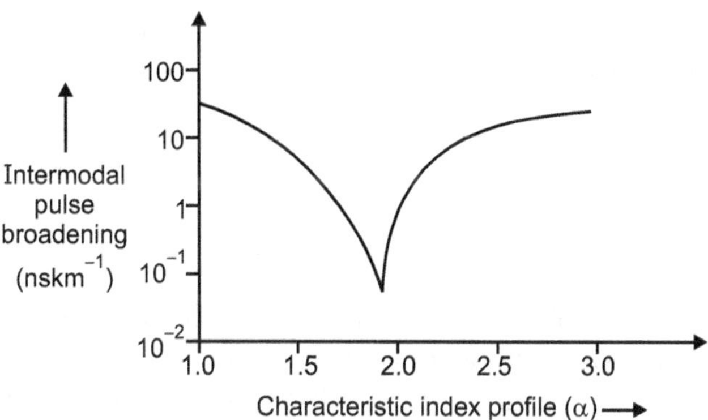

Fig. 1.51 : The intermodal pulse broadening δT_g for graded index fibers having Δ = 1 % verses the characteristic index profile α

Another important factor in the determination of the optimum refractive index profile is the dispersion occurring due to the difference in the refractive index between fiber core and cladding.

1.15.3 Modal Delay

- Intermodal distortion or modal delay appears only in multimode fibers. This signal distorting mechanism is a result of each mode having a different value of the group velocity at a single frequency.

- To see why the delay arises, consider the meridional ray picture for a multimode step-index fiber.

- The steeper the angle of propagation of the ray congruence, the higher is the mode number and, consequently, the slower the axial group velocity.

- This variation in the group velocities of the different modes results in a group delay spread, which is the intermodal distortion. This distortion mechanism is eliminated by single-mode operation, but is important in multimode fibers.

- The maximum pulse broadening arising from the modal delay is the difference between the travel time T_{max} of the longest ray congruence paths (the highest-order mode) and the travel time T_{min} of the shortest ray congruence paths (the fundamental mode). This broadening is simply obtained from ray tracing and for a fiber of length L is given by

$$\Delta T = T_{max} - T_{min} = \frac{n_1}{c}\left(\frac{L}{\sin \phi_c} - L\right) = \frac{Ln_1^2}{cn_2} \qquad \ldots (1.198)$$

where from Equation (1.173) $\sin \phi_c = n_2/n_1$ and Δ is the index difference.

- The question now arises as to what maximum bit rate B can be sent over a multimode step-index fiber.

- Typically the fiber capacity is specified in terms of the bit rate-distance product BL, that is, the bit rate times the possible transmission distance L. in order for neighbouring signal pulses to remain distinguishable at the receiver, the pulse spread should be less than 1/B, which is the width of a bit period.

- For example, a stringent requirement for a high-performance link might be $\Delta T \leq 0.1/B$. In general, we need to have $\Delta T < 1/B$. This inequality gives the bit rate-distance product

$$BL \; < \; \frac{n_2}{n_1}\frac{c}{\Delta} \qquad\qquad \ldots (1.199)$$

- Taking values of $n_1 = 1.480$, $n_2 = 1.465$ and $\Delta = 0.01$, the capacity of multimode step-index fiber is BL=20 Mb/s-km. in graded-index fibers, careful selection of the radial refractive-index profile can lead to bit rate-distances products of up to 1 Gb/s-km.

1.15.4 Modal Noise

- Intermodal dispersion properties of multimode optical fibers creates another phenomenon which affects the transmission of optical signals on the channel.

- It is exhibited within the speckle patterns observed in the multimode fiber, as fluctuations which have characteristic times longer than the resolution time of the detector and is known as modal or speckle noise.

- The speckle patterns are formed by the interference of the modes from a coherent source when the coherence time of the source is greater than the intermodal dispersion time δT within the fiber.

- The coherence time for a source with uncorrelated source frequency width δF is simply $1/\delta f$. The modal noise occurs when

$$\delta f >> \frac{1}{\delta T} \qquad\qquad \ldots (1.200)$$

- Disturbances along the fiber, such as vibrations, discontinuities, connectors, splices and source/detector coupling may cause fluctuations in the speckle patterns and hence modal noise. It is generated when the correlation between two or more modes which gives the original interference is differentially delayed by these disturbances.

- The conditions which give rise to modal noise are therefore specified as,

(a) a coherent source with a narrow spectral width and long coherence length (propagation velocity multiplied by the coherence time);

(b) disturbances along the fiber which give differential mode delay or modal and spatial filtering.

(c) phase correlation between the modes.

- Modal noise may be avoided by removing one of the conditions which give rise to this degradation.

(1) The use of broad spectrum source in order to eliminate the modal interference effects: This may be achieved by either (a) increasing the width of the single longitudinal mode

and hence decreasing it's coherence time or (b) by increasing the number of longitudinal modes and averaging out of the interference patterns.

(2) In conjunction with 1(b) it is found that fibers with large numerical apertures support the transmission of a large number of modes giving a greater number of speckles, and hence reduce the modal noise generating effect of individual speckles.

(3) The use of single-mode fiber which does not support the transmission of different modes and thus there is no intermodal interference.

(4) The removal of disturbances along the fiber has been investigated with regard to connector design in order to reduce the shift in speckles pattern induced by mechanical vibration and fiber misalignment.

- Hence, modal noise may be prevented by suitable choice of the system components.

- Modal noise can be present in single mode fiber links when propagation of the two fundamental modes with orthogonal polarization is allowed or when second-order modes are not sufficiently attenuated.

1.15.5 Factors Contributing to Dispersion

- The wave propagation constant β is a function of the wavelength, or, equivalently, of the angular frequency ω. Since β is a slow varying function of this angular frequency, one can see where various dispersion effects arise by expanding β in a Taylor series about a central frequency ω_0. Inserting such an expression into the waveform equation.

- Expanding β to third order in a Taylor series yields

$$\beta(\omega) \approx \beta_0(\omega_0) + \beta_1(\omega_0)\,(\omega - \omega_0) + \frac{1}{2}\beta_2(\omega_0)\,(\omega - \omega_0)^2 + \frac{1}{6}\beta_3(\omega_0)\,(\omega - \omega_0)^3 \qquad \dots (1.201)$$

where, $\beta_m(\omega_0)$ denotes the mth derivative of β with respect to ω evaluated at $\omega = \omega_0$; that is,

$$\beta_m = \left(\frac{\partial^m \beta}{\partial \omega^m}\right)_{\omega\,=\,\omega_0} \qquad \dots (1.202)$$

- Now let us examine the different components of the product β_z, where z is the distance traveled along the fiber.

- The resulting first term $\beta_0 z$ describes a phase shift of the propagating optical wave. From the second term of Equation (1.188), the factor $\beta_1(\omega_0)z$ produces a group delay $\tau_g = z/V_g$, where z is the distance traveled by the pulse and $V_g = 1/\beta_1$ is the group velocity. Hence, the expression

$$\Delta\tau_{PMD} = z\,|\beta_{1x} - \beta_{1y}| \qquad \dots (1.203)$$

is called the polarization mode dispersion (PMD) of the ideal uniform fiber. Note that in a real fiber the PMD varies stastically.

- In the third term of Equation (1.195), the factor β_2 shows that the group velocity of a monochromatic wave depends on the wave frequency. This means that the different group velocities of the frequency components of a pulse cause it to broaden as it travels along a fiber. This spreading of the group velocities is known as chromatic dispersion or Group Velocity Dispersion (GVD). The factor β_2 thus is known as the GVD parameter. As Equation (1.203) notes, the dispersion D is related to β_2 through the expression

$$D = \frac{2\pi c}{\lambda^2}\,\beta^2 \qquad\qquad \ldots(1.204)$$

- In the fourth term of Equation (1.201), the factor β_3 is known as the third-order dispersion. This term is important around the wavelength at which β_2 equals zero. The third order dispersion can be related to the dispersion D and the dispersion slope $S_0 = \partial D/\partial\lambda$ (the variation in the dispersion D with wavelength) by transforming the derivative with respect to ω into a derivative with respect to λ. Thus we have

$$\beta_3 = \frac{\partial\beta_2}{\partial\omega} = -\frac{\lambda^2}{2\pi c}\frac{\partial\beta_2}{\partial\lambda} = -\frac{\lambda^2}{2\pi c}\frac{\partial}{\partial\lambda}\left[-\frac{\lambda^2}{2\pi c}D\right]$$

$$= \frac{\lambda^2}{(2\pi c)^2}(\lambda^2 S_0 + 2\lambda D) \qquad\qquad \ldots (1.205)$$

1.15.6 Group Delay

- The information-carrying capacity of a fiber link can be determined by examining the deformation of short light pulses propagating along the fiber.

- The following discussion on signal distortion thus is carried out primarily from the viewpoint of pulse broadening, which is representative of digital transmission.

- First consider an electrical signal that modulates an optical source.

- For this case, assume that the modulated optical signal excites all modes equally at the input of the fiber.

- Each waveguide mode thus carries an equal amount of energy through the fiber.

- Furthermore, each mode contains all the spectral components in the wavelength band over which the source emits. In addition, assume that each of these spectral components is modulated in the same way.

- As the signal propagates along the fiber, each spectral component can be assumed to travel independently and to undergo a time delay or group delay per unit length τ_g/L in the direction of the propagation given by

$$\frac{\tau_g}{L} = \frac{1}{V_g} = \frac{1}{c}\frac{d\beta}{dk} = -\frac{\lambda^2}{2\pi c}\frac{d\beta}{d\lambda} \qquad\qquad \ldots (1.206)$$

- Here, L is the distance traveled by the pulse, β is the propagation constant along the fiber axis, $k = \dfrac{2\pi}{\lambda}$, and the group velocity

$$V_g = c\left(\frac{d\beta}{dk}\right)^{-1} = \left(\frac{\partial\beta}{\partial\omega}\right)^{-1} \qquad \ldots (1.207)$$

The velocity at which the energy in a pulse travels along a fiber.

- Since the group delay depends on the wavelength, each spectral component of any particular mode takes a different amount of time to travel a certain distance.

- As a result of this difference in time delays, the optical signal pulse spreads out with time as it is transmitted over the fiber. Thus, the quantity we are interested in is the amount of pulse spreading that arises from the group delay variation.

- If the spectral width of the optical source is not too wide, the delay difference per unit wavelength along the propagation path is approximately $d\tau_g/d\lambda$. For spectral components which are $\delta\lambda$ apart and which lie $\delta\lambda/2$ above and below a central wavelength λ_0, the total delay difference $\delta\tau$ over a distance L is

$$\delta\tau = \frac{d\tau_g}{d\lambda}\,\delta\lambda = -\frac{L}{2\pi c}\left(2\lambda\,\frac{d\beta}{d\lambda} + \lambda^2\,\frac{d^2\beta}{d\lambda^2}\right)\delta\lambda \qquad \ldots (1.208)$$

In terms of the angular frequency ω, this is written as

$$\delta\tau = \frac{d\tau_g}{dw}\,\delta\omega = \frac{d}{d\omega}\left(\frac{L}{V_g}\right)\delta\omega = L\left(\frac{d^2\beta}{d\omega^2}\right)\delta\omega \qquad \ldots (1.209)$$

- The factor $\beta_2 \equiv d^2\beta/d\omega^2$ is the GVD parameter, which determines how much a light pulse broadens as it travels along an optical fiber.

- If the spectral width $\delta\lambda$ of an optical source is characterized by its rms value σ_λ, then the pulse spreading can be approximated by the rms pulse width,

$$\sigma_g \approx \left|\frac{d\tau_g}{d\lambda}\right|\sigma_\lambda = \frac{L\sigma_\lambda}{2\pi c}\left|2\lambda\,\frac{d\beta}{d\lambda} + \lambda^2\,\frac{d^2\beta}{d\lambda^2}\right| \qquad \ldots (1.210)$$

The factor

$$D = \frac{1}{L}\frac{d\tau_g}{d\lambda} = \frac{d}{d\lambda}\left(\frac{1}{V_g}\right) = -\frac{2\pi c}{\lambda^2}\beta_2 \qquad \ldots (1.211)$$

- It is designated as the dispersion. It defines the pulse spread as a function of wavelength and is measured in picoseconds per kilometer per nanometer [ps/(nm.km)].

- It is a result of material and waveguide dispersion.

- In many theoretical treatments of intramodal dispersion it is assumed, for simplicity, that material dispersion and waveguide dispersion can be calculated separately and then added to give the total dispersion of the mode.

- In reality, these two mechanisms are intricately related, since the dispersive properties of the refractive index (which gives rise to material dispersion) also affects the waveguide dispersion.
- However, an examination of the interdependence of material and waveguide dispersion has shown that, unless a very precise value to a fraction of a percent is desired, a good estimate of the total intramodal dispersion can be obtained by calculating the effect of signal distortion arising from one type of dispersion in the absence of the other.
- Thus, to a very good approximation, D can be written as the sum of the material dispersion D_{mat} and the waveguide dispersion D_{wg}.

1.16 SIGNAL DISTORTION IN SINGLE-MODE FIBERS

- For single-mode fibers, waveguide dispersion is of importance and can be of the same order of magnitude as material dispersion.
- To see this, let us compare the two dispersion factors. The pulse spread σ_{wg} occurring over a distribution of wavelengths σ_λ is obtained from the derivative of the group delay with respect to wavelength :

$$\sigma_{wg} \approx \left| \frac{d\tau_{wg}}{d\lambda} \right| \sigma_\lambda = L \, |D_{wg}(\lambda)| \, \sigma_\lambda$$

$$= \frac{v}{\lambda} \left| \frac{d\tau_{wg}}{dV} \right| \sigma_\lambda = \frac{n_2 L \Delta \sigma_\lambda}{c\lambda} \, V \, \frac{d^2(vb)}{dV^2} \qquad \ldots (1.212)$$

where $D_{wg}(\lambda)$ is the waveguide dispersion.

- To see the behavior of the waveguide dispersion, consider the expression of the factor ua for the lowest-order mode (i.e., the HE_{11} mode or, equivalently, the LP_{01} mode) in the normalized propagation constant. This can be approximated by

$$ua = \frac{(1 + \sqrt{2})V}{1 + (4 + V^4)^{1/4}} \qquad \ldots (1.213)$$

For the HE_{11} mode, $$b(V) = 1 - \frac{(1 + \sqrt{2})^2}{[1 + (4 + V^4)^{1/4}]^2} \qquad \ldots (1.214)$$

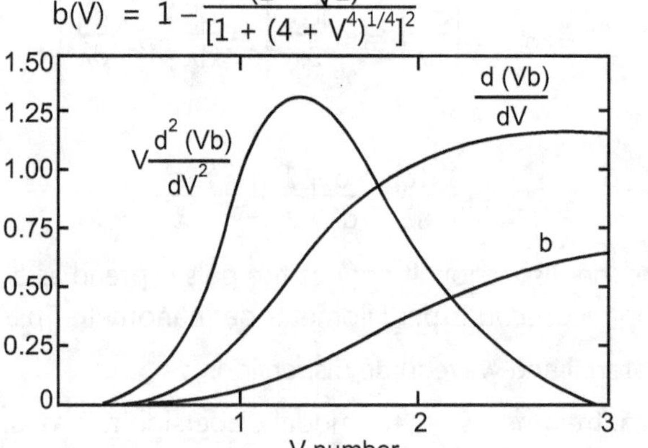

Fig. 1.52 : The waveguide parameter b and its derivatives d(Vb)/dV and Vd^2(Vb)/dV^2 plotted as a function of the V number for the HE_{11} mode

- Fig. 1.52 shows plots of this expression for b and its derivatives d(Vb)/dV and $Vd^2(Vb)/dV^2$ as functions of V.

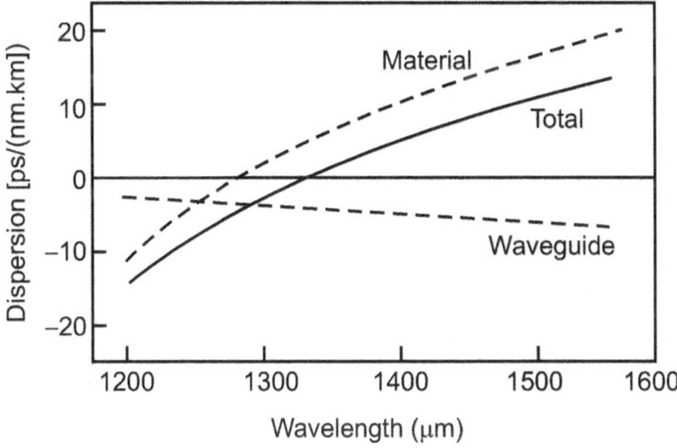

Fig. 1.53 : Examples of the magnitudes of material and waveguide dispersion as a function of optical wavelength for a single-mode fused-silica-core fiber. of optical wavelength for a single-mode fused-silica-core fiber.

- Fig. 1.53 gives examples of the magnitudes of material and waveguide dispersion for a fused-silica-core single-mode fiber having V = 2.4. Comparing the waveguide dispersion with the material dispersion, we see that for a standard non-dispersion-shifted fiber, waveguide dispersion is important around 1320 nm.

- At this point, the two dispersion factors cancel to give a zero total dispersion. However, material dispersion dominates waveguide dispersion at shorter and longer wavelengths; for example, at 900 nm and 1550 nm.

- This Fig. 1.53 used the approximation that material and waveguide dispersions are additive.

1.16.1 POLARIZATION-MODE DISPERSION

- The effect of fiber birefringence on the polarization states of an optical signal are another source of pulse broadening.

- This is particularly critical for high-rate long-haul transmission links (e.g., 10 and 40 Gb/s over tens of kilometers).

- Birefringence can result from intrinsic factors such as geometric irregularities of the fiber core or internal stresses on it. Deviations of less than 1 percent in the circularity of the core can already have a noticeable effect in a high-speed lightwave system. In addition, external factors, such as bending, twisting, or pinching of the fiber, can also lead to birefringence.

- Since all these mechanisms exist to some extent in any field-installed fiber, there will be a varying birefringence along its length.

- A fundamental property of an optical signal is its polarization state. Polarization refers to the electric-field orientation of a light signal, which can vary significantly along the length of a fiber.

- As shown in Fig. 1.54, signal energy at a given wavelength occupies two orthogonal polarization modes. A varying birefringence along its length will cause each polarization mode to travel at a slightly different velocity.

- The resulting difference in propagation times $\Delta\tau_{PMD}$ between the two orthogonal polarization modes will result in pulse spreading.

- This is the polarization-mode dispersion (PMD). If the group velocities of the two orthogonal polarization modes are v_{gx} and v_{gy}, then the differential time delay $\Delta\tau_{PMD}$ between the two polarization components during propagation of the pulse over a distance L is

$$\Delta\tau_{PMD} = \left| \frac{L}{v_{gx}} - \frac{L}{v_{gy}} \right| \qquad \text{... (1.215)}$$

- An important point to note is that, in contrast to chromatic dispersion, which is a relatively stable phenomenon along a fiber, PMD varies randomly along a fiber.

- A principal reason for this is that the perturbations causing the birefringence effects vary with temperature and stress dynamics. In practice, the effect of these perturbations shows up a random, time varying fluctuation in the value of the PMD at the fiber output. Thus, $\Delta\tau_{PMD}$ given in Equation (1.202) cannot be used directly to estimate PMD. Instead, statistical estimations are needed to account for its effects.

- A useful means of characterizing PMD for long fiber lengths in its terms of the mean value of the differential group delay. This can be calculated according to the relationship

$$\Delta\tau_{PMD} \approx D_{PMD} \sqrt{L} \qquad \text{... (1.216)}$$

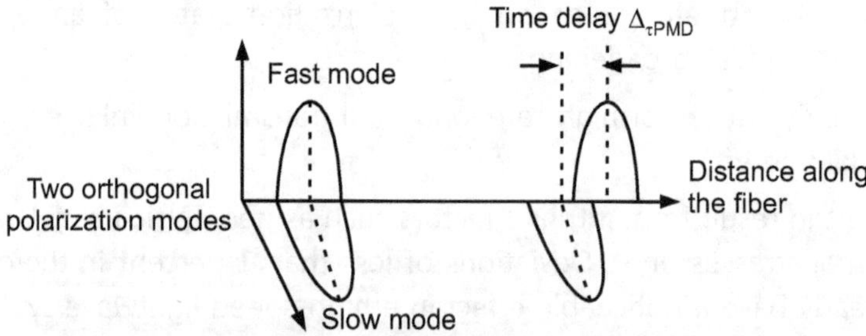

Fig. 1.54 : Differences in the polarization-mode propagation times as an optical pulse passes through a fiber with varying birefringence along its length

- Where D_{PMD}, which is measured in $ps/\sqrt{km}$, is the average PMD parameter. Typical values of D_{PMD} range from 0.05 to 1.0 $ps/\sqrt{km}$.

- As an example, one experiment measured values of PMD for three types of cable installations that were subjected to different environments.

- The setups were a 36-km aerial cable. Over a 12- to 15-h period, the average PMD parameters were measured to be 0.028, 0.29, and 1.28 ps/$\sqrt{km}$, respectively.

- The larger value of PMD for the aerial cable is caused by both gradual and rapid stress variations in the fiber due to temperature fluctuations or from sudden movements of the fiber due to wind.

- To keep the probability of errors due to PMD low, a standard limit on the maximum tolerable value of $\Delta\tau_{PMD}$ ranges between 10 to 20 percent of a bit duration. Thus $\Delta\tau_{PMD}$ should be no more than 10 to 20 ps for 10-Gb/s data rates and 3 ps at 40 Gb/s. for example, taking the lower tolerance limit, this means that for a 10-Gb/s link which has 20 spans of 80 km each, the PMD of the transmission fiber must be less than 0.2 ps/$\sqrt{km}$.

- Various optical and electronic means to monitor and mitigate PMD in a fiber have been investigated. In addition, fibers with low polarization-mode dispersion are being developed and characterized.

1.17 CHARACTERISTICS OF SINGLE MODE FIBERS

- This section addresses the basic design and operational characteristics of single mode fibers.

- These characteristics include index-profile configurations used to produce different fiber types, the concept of cutoff wavelength, signal dispersion designations and calculations, the definition of mode field diameter, and signal loss due to fiber bending.

1.17.1 Refractive-Index Profiles

- When creating single mode fibers, manufacturers pay special attention to how the fiber design affects both chromatic and polarization-mode dispersions.

- Such considerations are important since these dispersions set the limits on long-distance and high-speed data transmission.

- As Fig. 1.55 illustrates, the chromatic dispersion of a step-index silica fiber is lowest at 1310 nm. However, if the goal is to transmit a signal as far as possible, it is better to operate the link at 1550 nm (in the C-band) where the fiber attenuation is lower.

- For high speed links the C-band presents a problem, since chromatic dispersion is much larger at 1550 nm than at 1310 nm.

- Consequently, fiber designers devised methods for adjusting the fiber parameters to shift the zero-dispersion point to longer wavelengths.

- The basic material dispersion is hard to alter significantly. However, it is possible to modify the waveguide dispersion by changing from a simple step-index design to more complex index profiles for the cladding, thereby creating different chromatic-dispersion characteristics in single mode fibers. Fig. 1.55 shows representative refractive-index profiles of four fiber-design categories.

- These are 1310 nm optimized fibers, dispersion-shifted fibers, dispersion-flattened fibers, and large-effective-core-area fibers. To get a better feeling of what this geometry looks like.

- Popular single mode fibers that are used widely in telecommunication networks are near step-index fibers, which are optimized for use in the O-band around 1310 nm.

- These 1310 nm optimized single mode fibers are of either the matched-cladding or the depressed-cladding design, as shown in Fig 1.55 (a). Matched-cladding fibers have a uniform refractive index throughout the cladding.

- Typical mode field diameters are 9.5 μm and the core-to-cladding index differences are around 0.37 percent.

- In depressed-cladding fibers the cladding material next to the core has a lower index than the outer cladding region. Mode field diameters are around 9.0 μm, and typical positive and negative index differences are 0.25 and 0.12 percent, respectively.

- As material dispersion depends only on the composition of the material, waveguide dispersion is a function of the core radius, the refractive index difference, and the shape of the refractive index profile.

- Thus the waveguide dispersion can vary dramatically with the fiber design parameters. By creating a fiber with large negative waveguide dispersion and assuming the same values for material dispersion as in a standard single-mode fiber, the addition of waveguide and material dispersion can then shift the zero dispersion point to longer wavelengths.

- The resulting optical fiber is known as a Dispersion Shifted Fiber (DSF).

- Examples of refractive-index profiles for dispersion-shifted fibers are shown in Fig. 1.55 (b) a typical waveguide dispersion curve for this type of fiber is depicted in Fig. 1.55 (a) the resultant total dispersion curve is shown in Fig. 1.55 (b) for fibers with a zero-dispersion wavelength at 1550 nm.

- Since the zero dispersion value of a DSF falls at 1550 nm, the chromatic dispersion is negative for wavelengths less than 1550 nm and positive for longer wavelengths.

- These positive and negative dispersions will seriously affect closely spaced WDM signals within the C-band because of nonlinear effects in the fiber.

- To reduce the effects of fiber nonlinearities, fiber designers developed the Nonzero Dispersion Shifted Fiber (NZDSF).

- These fibers have a small amount of either all positive or all negative dispersion throughout the C-band. A typical positive chromatic dispersion value for a NZDSF is 4.5 ps/(nm-km) at 1550 nm.

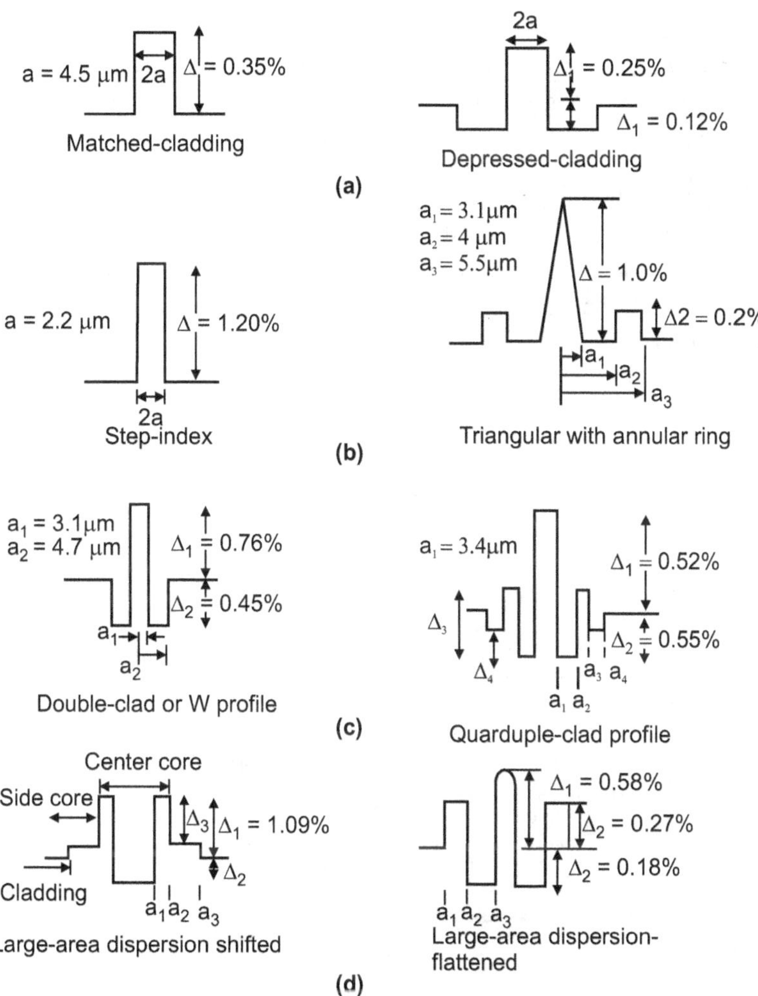

Fig. 1.55 : Representative cross-sections of index profiles for (a) 1310-nm optimized (b) dispersion-shifted, (c) dispersion-flattened, and (d) large-effective-core-area fibers

- Among the NZDSF types is a single-mode optical fiber with a larger effective core area. The larger core areas reduce the effects of fiber nonlinearities, which limit system capacities of transmission systems that have densely spaced WDM channels.

- Fig. 1.55 (d) gives two examples of the index profile for these Large-Effective Area (LEA) fibers. Whereas standard single-mode fibers have effective core areas of about 55 μm^2, these profiles yield values greater than 100 μm^2.

- An alternative fiber design concept is to distribute the dispersion minimum over a wider spectral range. This approach is known as dispersion flattening.

- Dispersion-flattened fibers are more complex to design than dispersion-shifted fibers, because over a much broader range of wavelengths.

- However, they offer desirable characteristics over a wide span of wavelengths. Fig. 1.55 (c) show typical cross-sectional and three-dimensional refractive-index profiles, respectively. A typical waveguide dispersion curve for this type of fiber is depicted in Fig. 1.55 (a). Fig. 1.55 gives the resultant total flattened dispersion characteristic.

1.17.2 Cutoff Wavelength

- The cutoff wavelength of the first-order mode (LP_{11}) is an important transmission parameter for single-mode fibers, since it separates the single-mode from the multimode regions. That single-mode operation occurs above the theoretical cutoff wavelength given by

$$\lambda_{cith} = \frac{2\pi a}{V} (n_1^2 - n_2^2)^{1/2} \qquad \ldots (1.217)$$

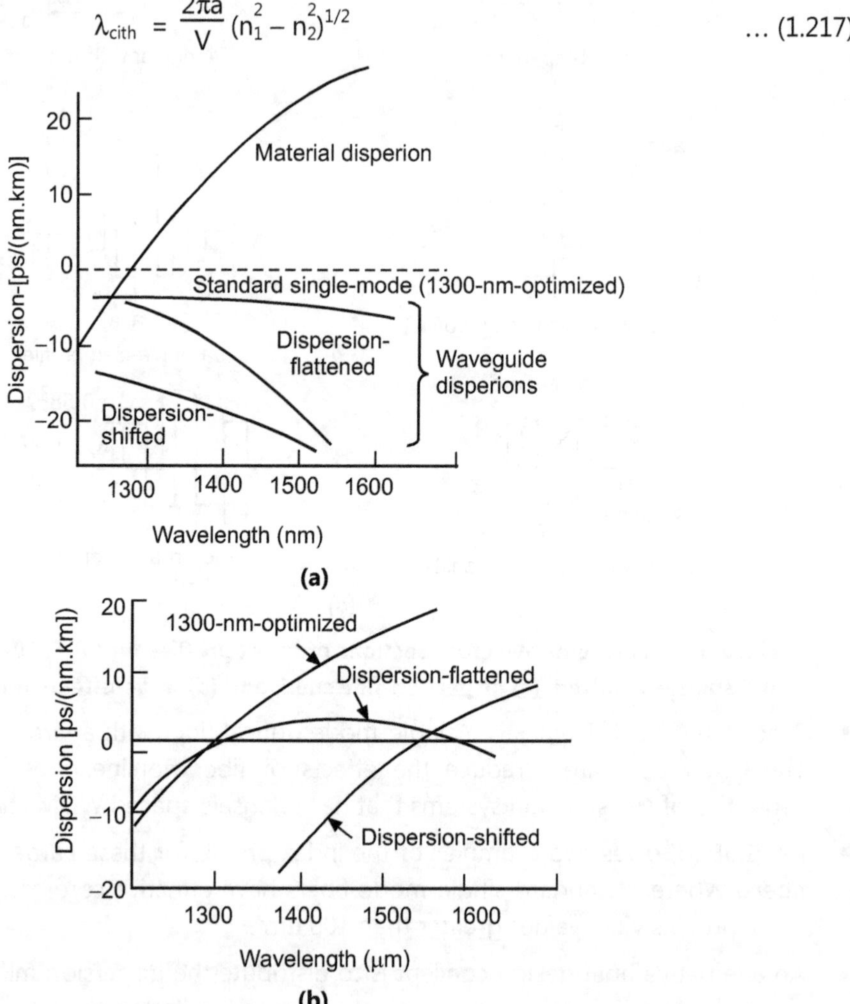

Fig. 1.56 : (a) Typical waveguide dispersions and the common material dispersion for three different single-mode fiber designs. (b) Resultant total dispersions

- With V = 2.405 for step-index fibers. At this wavelength, only the LP_{01} mode (i.e., the HE_{11} mode) should propagate in the fiber.

- Since in the cutoff region the field of the LP_{11} mode is widely spread across the fiber cross section (i.e., it is not tightly bound to the core), its attenuation is strongly affected by fiber bends, length, and cabling. Recommendation G.650.1 of the ITU-T and the EIA-455-80C. standard specify methods for determining an effective cutoff wavelength λ_c.

- The setup consists of a 2-m length of fiber that contains a single 14-cm radius loop or several 14-cm radius curvatures that add up to one complete loop.

- Using a tunable light source that a full-width half-maximum linewidth not exceeding 10 nm, light is launched into the fiber so that both the LP_{01} and the LP_{11} modes are uniformly excited.

- First, the output power $P_1(\lambda)$ is measured as a function of wavelength in a sufficiently wide range around the expected cutoff wavelength.

- Next, the output power $P_2(\lambda)$ is measured over the same wavelength range when a loop of sufficiently small radius is included in the test fiber to filter the LP_{11} mode. A typical radius for this loop is 30 mm.

- With this method, the logarithmic ratio $R(\lambda)$ between the two transmitted powers $P_1(\lambda)$ and $P_2(\lambda)$ is calculated as

$$R(\lambda) \; = \; 10 \log \left[\frac{P_1(\lambda)}{P_2(\lambda)} \right] \qquad \qquad \ldots (1.218)$$

- Fig. 1.56 gives a typical curve of the result. The effective cutoff wavelength λ_c is defined as the largest wavelength at which the higher-order LP_{11} mode power relative to the fundamental LP_{01} mode power is reduced to 0.1 dB; that is, when, $R(\lambda)$ = 0.1 dB, as is shown in Fig. 1.56 recommended values of λ_c range from 1100 o 1280 nm, to avoid modal noise and dispersion problems.

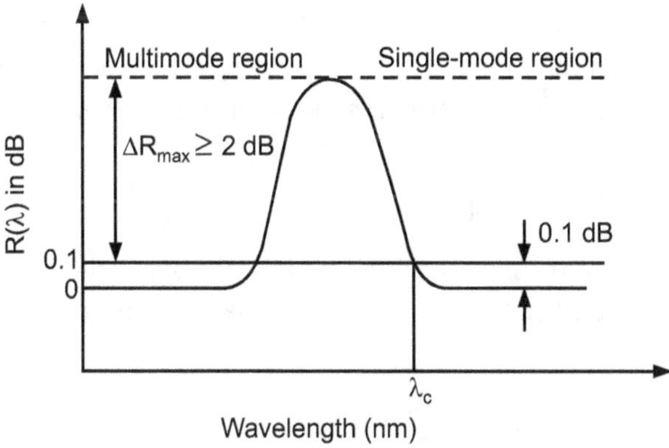

Fig. 1.57 : Typical attenuation-ratio versus wavelength using the bend-reference (or single-mode reference) transmission method.
The peak ration should be at least 2 dB above the cutoff level.

1.17.3 Dispersion Calculations

- The total chromatic dispersion in single mode fibers consists mainly of material and waveguide dispersions. The resultant intramodal or chromatic dispersion is represented by

$$D(\lambda) = \frac{1}{L}\frac{d\tau}{d\lambda} \qquad \ldots (1.219)$$

Where τ is the group delay. The dispersion is commonly expressed in ps/(nm-km). The broadening σ of an optical pulse over a fiber of length L is given by

$$\sigma = D(\lambda)L\sigma_\lambda \qquad \ldots (1.220)$$

- Where σ_λ is the half-power spectral width of the optical source. To measure the dispersion, one examines the pulse delay over a desired wavelength range.

- The dispersion behavior varies with wavelength and also with fiber type.

- Thus, the EIA and the ITU-T have recommended different formulas to calculate the chromatic dispersion for specific fiber types operating in a given wavelength region.

- To calculate the dispersion for a non-dispersion-shifted fiber (called a Class Iva fiber by the EIA) in the 1270-to-1340-nm region, the standards recommend fitting the measured group delay per unit length to a three-term Sellmeier equation of the form

$$\tau = A + B\lambda^2 + C\lambda^{-2} \qquad \ldots (1.221)$$

- To the measured pulse date. Here A, B and C are the curve-fitting parameters. An equivalent expression is

$$\tau = \tau_0 + \frac{S_0}{8}\left(\lambda - \frac{\lambda_0^2}{\lambda}\right)^2 \qquad \ldots (1.222)$$

- Where τ_0 is the relative delay minimum at the zero-dispersion wavelength λ_0 and S_0 is the value of the dispersion slope $S(\lambda) = dD/d\lambda$ at λ_0, which is given in ps/(nm^2.km). Using Eq. (1.2.81), the dispersion for a non-dispersion-shifted fiber is

$$D(\lambda) = \frac{\lambda S_0}{4}\left[1 - \left(\frac{\lambda_0}{\lambda}\right)^4\right] \qquad \ldots (1.223)$$

- To calculate the dispersion for a dispersion-shifted fiber (called a Class IVb fiber by the EIA) in the 1500-to-1600-nm region, the standard recommend using the quadratic expression

$$\tau = \tau_0 + \frac{S_0}{2}(\lambda - \lambda_0)^2 \qquad \ldots (1.224)$$

Which results in the dispersion expression

$$D(\lambda) = (\lambda - \lambda_0)S_0 \qquad \ldots (1.225)$$

- Finally, recall from that third-order dispersion β_3 can be given as

$$\beta_3 \;=\; \frac{\lambda^2}{(2\pi c)^2}\,[\lambda^2 S_0 + 2\lambda D] \qquad\qquad \ldots (1.226\ b)$$

- When measuring a set of fibers, one will get values of λ_0 ranging from $\lambda_{0,min}$ to $\lambda_{0,max}$. Fig. 1.58 shows the range of expected dispersion values for a set of non-dispersion-shifted fibers in the 1270-to-1340-nm region.

- Typical values of S_0 are 0.092 ps/(nm^2.km) for standard non-dispersion-shifted fibers, and are between 0.06 and 0.08 ps/(nm^2.km) for dispersion-shifted fibers.

- Alternatively, the ITU-T Rec.G.652 has specified this as a maximum dispersion of 3.5 ps/(nm.km) in the 1285-to-1330-nm region, as denoted by the dashed lines in Fig. 1.58.

- Fig. 1.58 illustrates the importance of controlling dispersion in single-mode fibers.

- As optical pulses travel down a fiber, temporal broadening occurs because material and waveguide dispersion cause different wavelengths in the optical pulse to propagate with different velocities.

- Thus, as Equation (1.205)) implies, the broader the spectral width σ_λ of the source, the greater the pulse dispersion will be.

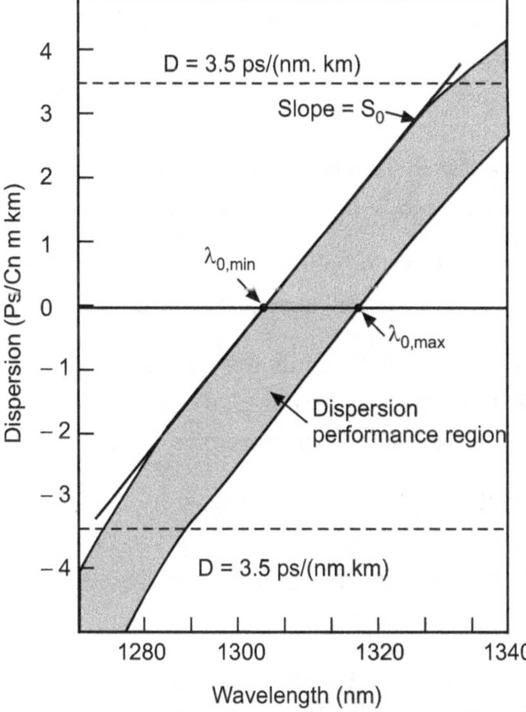

Fig. 1.58 : Examples of a dispersion performance curve for a set of single-mode fibers

1.17.4 Mode Field Diameter

- Properties of the fundamental modes are determined by the radial extent of its electromagnetic field including losses at launching and jointing, microbend losses, waveguide dispersion and the width of the radiation pattern.

- Therefore, the mode field diameter is an important parameter for characterizing single-mode fiber properties which takes into account the wavelength dependent field penetration into the fiber cladding.

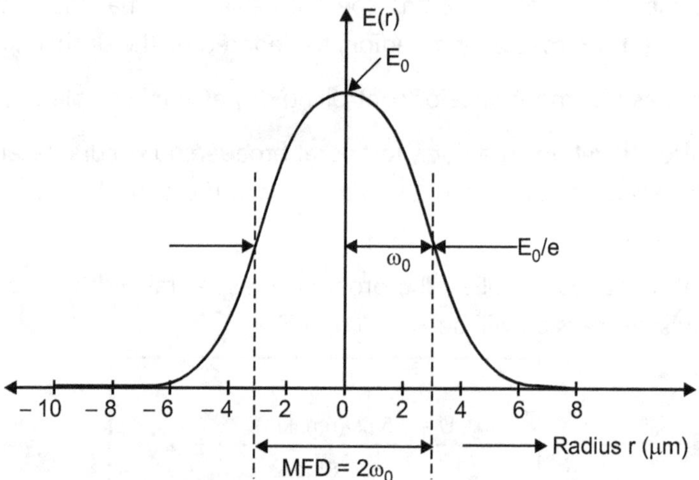

Fig. 1.59 : Field amplitude distribution E(r) of the fundamental mode in a single mode fiber illustrating the mode-field diameter (MFD) and spot size (ω_0)

- For step index and graded (near parabolic profile) single mode fibers operating near the cut-off wavelength λ_c, the field is well approximated by a Gaussian distribution.

- In this case, the MFD is generally taken as the distance between the opposite $1/e = 0.37$ field amplitude points and the power $1/e^2 = 0.135$ points in relation to the corresponding values on the fiber axis as shown in Fig. 1.60.

- Another parameter related to the MFD of a single-mode fiber is the spot size (or mode-field radius) ω_0. Hence MFD = $2\omega_0$, where ω_0 is the nominal half width of the input excitation. The MFD can therefore be regarded as the single-mode analog of the fiber core diameter in multimode fibers.

- For many refractive index profiles and at typical operating wavelengths the MFD is slightly larger than the single-mode fiber core diameter.

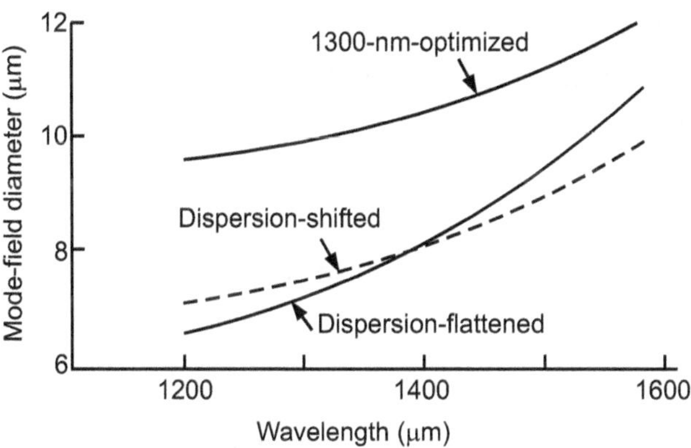

Fig. 1.60 : Typical mode field diameter variations with wavelength for (a) 1300 nm optimized, (b) dispersion-shifted, and (c) dispersion-flattened single-mode fibers

1.17.5 Bending Loss

- Macrobending and microbending losses are important in the design of single-mode fibers.

- These losses are principally evident in the 1550-nm region, and show up as a rapid increase in attenuation when the fiber is bent smaller than a certain bend radius.

- The lower the cutoff wavelength relative to the operating wavelength, the most susceptible single-mode fibers are to bending.

- For example, in a fiber which is optimized for operation at 1300 nm, both the microbending and macrobending losses are greater at 1550 nm that at 1300 nm by a factor of 3 to 5, as Fig. 1.61 illustrates. A fiber thus might be transmitting well at 1300 nm but have a significant loss at 1550 nm.

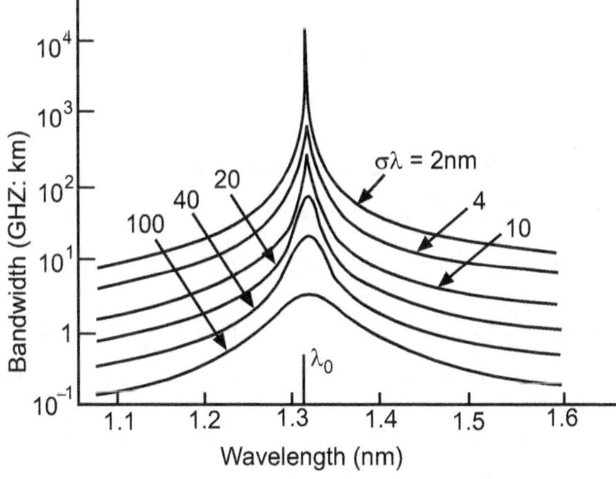

Fig. 1.61 : Examples of bandwidth versus wavelength for different source spectral widths

- The bending losses are primarily a function of the mode-field diameter. Generally, the smaller the mode-field diameter (i.e., the tighter the confinement of the mode to the core), the smaller the bending loss. This is true for both match-clad and depresse-clad fibers, as shown in Fig. 1.62.

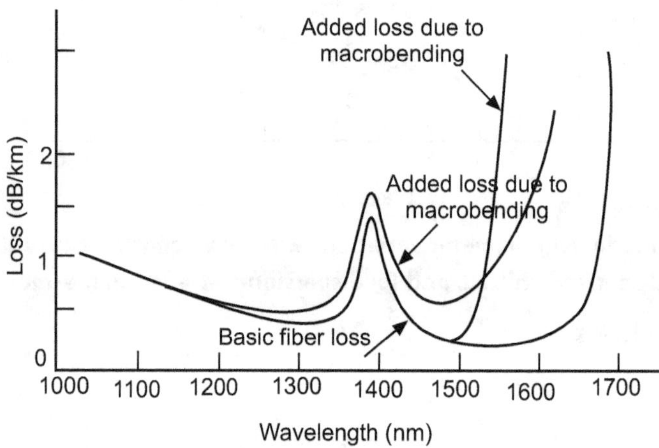

Fig. 1.62 : Representative increases in single-mode fiber attenuation owing to microbending and macrobending effects

- In examining the bending loss, early theories assume a simple model of a fiber with an infinitely extending cladding.

- This results in the prediction of a smooth exponential increase of bending loss with increasing wavelength or radius of curvature.

- In an actual fiber, oscillations in the bend loss versus both the wavelength and bending radius are observed.

- These oscillations can be attributed to coherent coupling between the field propagating in the core and the fraction of the radiated field that is reflected at the boundary between the cladding and the fiber-coating material.

- Fig. 1.63 gives an example of calculated bend loss as a function of bend radius at a 1300-nm wavelength. The fiber parameters were core radius a = 3.6 μm, cladding radius b = 60 μm, $\dfrac{n_1 - n_2}{n_2} = 3.56 \times 10^{-3}$ and $\dfrac{n_3 - n_2}{n_2} = 0.07$, where n_1, n_2 and n_3 are the core, cladding, and coating indices of refraction, respectively.

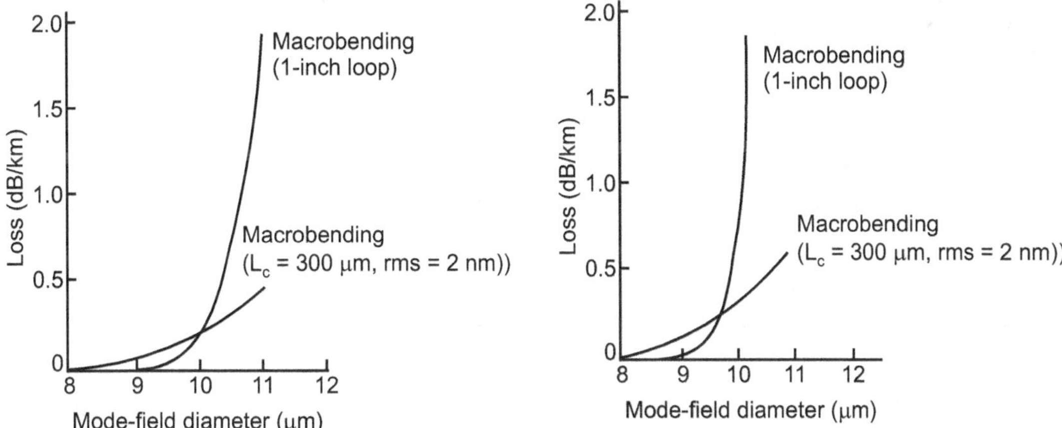

Fig. 1.63 : Calculated increase in attenuation at 1310 nm from microbending and macrobending effects as a function of mode-field diameter for (a) depressed-cladding single-mode fiber and (b) matched-cladding single-mode fiber.

- By specifying bend-radius limitations when installing standard single-mode fibers, one can largely avoid high microbending losses.

- Manufacturers usually recommend a fiber or cable bend diameter no smaller than 40-50 mm (1.6-2.0 in.).

- This is consistent with bend diameters limitations of 50-75 mm specified by installation guides for cable placement in ducts, fiber-splice enclosures, and equipment racks.

- Furthermore, describes, the development of bend-intensive fibers allows much tighter coiling of these fibers in optoelectronic packages.

- In addition, use of these bend-intensive fibers in jumper cables greatly reduces bending loss effects when they are installed in highly confined equipment racks.

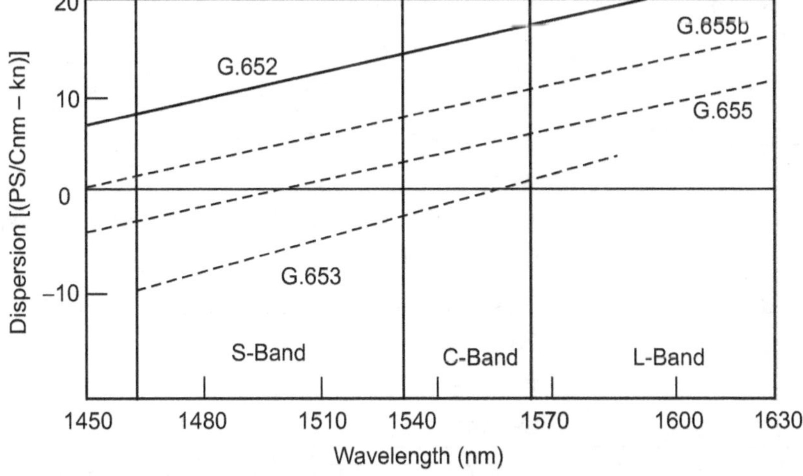

Fig. 1.64 : Calculated bend loss as a function of bend radius at 1300 nm

1.18 INTERNATIONAL STANDARDS

- The ITU-T, the TIA, and the EIA are leading organizations that develop and publish a wide range of internationally recognized recommendations and standards.

- In particular, the ITU-T has created a series of recommendations for manufacturing and testing various classes of multimode and single-mode optical fibers used in telecommunications.

- These documents give guidelines for bounds on fiber parameters, such as core and cladding sizes and circularity, attenuation, cutoff wavelength, and chromatic dispersion.

- The recommendations allow a reasonable degree of design flexibility, so that fiber manufacturers can improve products and develop new ones within the guidelines given in the performance specifications.

- Table 1.2.2 summarizes the ITU-T recommendations for multimode and single-mode optical telecommunication fibers. The following subsections describe the basic characteristics of these fibers.

1.18.1 Recommendation G.651

- The economic demand for low-cost installations of high-speed short-distance optical fiber links created an extensive market for multimode fibers.

- These fiber links use moderately priced light sources that operate in either the short-wavelength region (770 to 860 nm) or in the O-band (around 1310 nm).

- Applications include links in an office or government building, a medical facility, a university campus, or a manufacturing plant, where the desired transmission distance is typically 2 km or less.

Table 1.6: Recommendations for Multimode and Single-Mode Telecommunication Fibers

ITU-T Rec. No.	Title and Description
G.651 (Revised Feb. 1998)	Title: Characteristics of multimode graded index optical fibre cable Description: Multimode fiber for short-wavelength and O-band use in a LAN
G.652 (Revised June 2005)	Title: Characteristics of Single-mode Optical Fiber and Cable Description: Standard single-mode fiber optimized for O-band use
G.653 (Version 5, Dec. 2003)	Title: Characteristics of a dispersion-shifted Single-mode Optical Fiber and Cable

	Description: Original dispersion-shifted fiber for use at 1550 nm
G.654 (Revised June 2004)	Title: Characteristics of a cut-off Shifted Single-Mode Optical Fiber and cable Description: Undersea applications (1500 nm cutoff wavelength)
G.655 (Revised March 2006)	Title: Characteristics of a Non-zero Dispersion-Shifted Single-Mode Optical Fiber and Cable Description: For applications in long-haul links
G.656 (Issued June 2004)	Title: Characteristics of a Fiber and Cable with Non-Zero Dispersion for Wideband Optical Transport Description: Low chromatic dispersion fiber for expanded WDM applications

- Recommendation G.651 addresses the two principal multimode fiber types for these applications. The fibers have either 50- or 62.5 µm core diameters and both have 125-µm cladding diameters. The attenuation values range from 2.5 dB/km at 850 nm to less than 0.6 dB/km at 1310 nm.

- Table 1.7 lists the possible transmission distances when using fibres with different core sizes and bandwidths for Ethernet, Fiber Channel, and SONET/SDH applications.

- The light source used for these examples is a Vertical-Cavity Surface-Emitting Laser (VCSEL) operating at 850 nm. In particular, Ethernet links running at data rates up to 10 Gb/s over distances up to 550 m can use multimode fibers.

Table 1.7: Transmission Distances in Meters in Multimode Fibers using an 850-nm VCSEL

Application	Data rate (Gb/s)	50 - µm core		62.5 - µm core	
		500 MHz.km	2000 MHz.km	160 MHz.km	200 MHz.km
Ethernet	1	550	860	220	275
	10	82	300	26	33
Fiber Channel	1	500	860	250	300
	2	300	500	120	150
	10	82	300	26	33
SONET/SDH	10	85	300	25	33

1.18.2 Recommendation G.652

- Recommendation G.652 deals with the geometrical, mechanical, and transmission characteristics of a single-mode fiber that has a zero-dispersion value at 1310 nm.

- Fig. 1.65 compares the dispersion of the G.652 fiber with other single-mode fiber types.

- This fiber consists of a germanium-doped silica core that has a diameter between 5 and 8 μm and a 125 μm silica cladding diameter.

- The nominal attenuation is 0.4 dB/km at 1310 nm and 0.35 dB/km at 1550 nm. The maximum polarization mode dispersion is 0.2 ps/

- Four subsets ranging from G.652a to G.652d describe different variations of this type of fiber.

- Since G.652a/b fibers were installed widely in telecommunication networks in the 1990s, they are commonly known as standard single-mode fibers or 1310-nm optimized fibers.

- The G.652c/d fibers allow operation in the E-band and are used widely for fiber-to-the-premises (FTTP) installations.

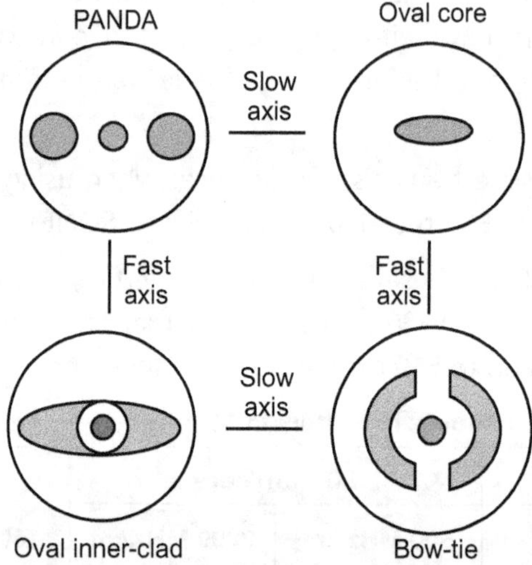

Fig. 1.65 : Chromatic dispersion as a function of wavelength in various spectral bands for several different optical fiber types.

- Although many long-distance cable plant installations now are using nonzero dispersion shifted fiber, the huge base of G.652 fiber that is installed worldwide will be in service for many years.

- If the G.652 fiber is used at 1550 nm, the chromatic dispersion value of about 17 ps/(nm-km) must be taken into account.

- This requires implementation of chromatic dispersion-compensation techniques or special data formats at high data rates.

- As an example, a number of field experiments have demonstrated the ability to transmit 160-Gb/s data rates over long distances of installed G.652a/b fiber.

- The G.652c/d fibers are created by reducing the water ion concentration in order to eliminate the attenuation spike in the 1360-to-1460-nm E-band.

- They are called low-water-peak fiber and allow operation over the entire wavelength range from 1260 to 1625 nm.

- One use of this fiber is for low-cost short-reach CWDM (coarse wavelength division multiplexing) applications in the E-band.

- In CWDM the wavelength channels are spaced by 20 nm, so that minimum wavelength stability control is needed for the optical sources. Another important application is in a passive Optical Network (PON) for Fiber-To-The-Premises (FTTP) access networks.

- Typically a FTTP link transmits three independent bidirectional channels at 1310, 1490, and 1550 nm over the same fiber.

1.18.3 Recommendation G.653

- Dispersion-Shifted Fiber (DSF) was developed for use with 1550-nm lasers. As Fig. 1.65 illustrates, in this fiber type the zero-dispersion point is shifted to 1550 nm where the fiber attenuation is about half that at 1310 nm.

- Therefore this fiber allows a high-speed data stream of a single-wavelength channel at or near 1550 nm to maintain its fidelity over long distances.

- However, it presents dispersion-related problems in Dense Wavelength Division Multiplexing (DWDM) applications in the center of the C-band where many wavelengths are packed tightly into one or more of the operational bands.

- To prevent undesirable nonlinear effects in DWDM systems, the chromatic dispersion values should be positive (or negative) over the entire operational band.

- Fig. 1.66 shows that for G.653 fibers the chromatic dispersion has a different sign above and below 1550 nm.

- Therefore the use of G.653 fibers for DWDM should be restricted to either the S-band (wavelengths lower than 1550 nm) or the L-band (wavelengths higher than 1550 nm).

- These fibers are seldom deployed anymore, since G.655 fibers offer a better solution.

1.18.4 Recommendation ITU-T G.654

- This recommendation deals with cutoff wavelength shifted fiber that is designed for long-distance high-power signal transmission.

- It describes the geometrical, mechanical and transmission characteristics of a single-mode optical fiber, which has the zero-dispersion wavelength around 1300 nm wavelength.

- The fiber has a very low loss in the 1550-nm band, which is achieved by using a pure silica core. Since it has a high cutoff wavelength of 1500 nm, this fiber is restricted to operation in the 1500 to 1600-nm region. It typically is used only in long-distance undersea applications.

1.18.5 Recommendation ITU-T G.655

- Nonzero Dispersion-Shifted Fiber (NZDSF) was introduced in the mid-1990s for WDM applications. Its principal characteristic is that it has a positive nonzero dispersion value over the entire C-band, which is the spectral operating region for erbium-doped optical fiber amplifiers.

- This is in contrast to G.653 fibers in which the dispersion varies from negative through zero to positive values in the C-band.

- Version G.655b was introduced to extend WDM applications into the S-band.

- As shown in Fig. 1.67, the principle characteristic of a G.655b fiber is that it has a nonzero dispersion value over the entire S-band and the C-band.

- This is in contrast to standard G.655 fibers in which the dispersion varies from negative through zero to positive values in the S-band. Version G.655c specifies a lower PMD value of 0.2 ps/than the 0.5 ps/ value of G.655a/b.

1.18.6 RECOMMENDATION G.656

- This recommendation describes the characteristics of a single-mode optical fiber which has a positive chromatic dispersion value ranging from 2 to 14 ps/(nm-km) in the 1460-to-1625-nm wavelength band.

- This means that the dispersion slope is significantly lower than in G.655 fibers for which the chromatic dispersion ranges from 1 to 10 ps/(nm-km) in the 1530-to-1565 band.

- The consequence of a lower dispersion slope means that the chromatic dispersion changes slower with wavelength so that dispersion compensation is simpler or not needed.

- This allows the use of CWDM without chromatic dispersion compensation and also means that 40 additional DWDM channels can be implemented in this wavelength band.

- Other G.656 attributes are similar to those of G.655 fibers. For example, the mode-field diameter ranges from 7 to 11 μm (compared to 8 to 11 μm for G.655 fibers), the maximum PMD value of cabled fiber is 0.2 ps/ and the cutoff wavelength is 1310 nm (the same as for G.655).

1.19 SPECIALITY FIBERS

- Telecommunication fibers are designed to transmit light with minimal change in the signal fidelity.

- In contrast, speciality fibers are designed to interact with light and thereby manipulate or control some characteristic of an optical signal.

- The light manipulation applications include optical signal amplification, optical power coupling, dispersion compensation, wavelength conversion, and sensing of physical parameters such as temperature, stress, pressure, vibration, and fluid levels.

- For light-control applications a speciality fiber can be insensitive to bends, maintain polarization states, redirect specific wavelengths, or provide a very high attenuation for fiber terminations.

- Speciality fibers can be of either a multimode or a single-mode design. Among the optical devices that may use a speciality fiber are light transmitters, light signal modulators, optical receivers, wavelength multiplexers, light couplers and splitters, optical amplifiers, optical switches, wavelength add/drop modules, and optical power attenuators. Table 1.8 gives a summary of some speciality fibers and their applications.

Table 1.8: Examples of Speciality Fibers and their Applications

Speciality Fiber Type	Application
Erbium-doped fiber	Gain medium for optical fiber amplifiers
Photosensitive fibers	Fabrication of fiber Bragg gratings
Bend-insensitive fibers	Tightly looped connections in device packages
Termination fiber	Termination of open optical fiber ends
Polarization-preserving fibers	Pump lasers, polarization-sensitive devices, sensors
High-index fibers	Fused couplers, short-λ sources, DWDM devices
Photonic crystal fibers	Switches; dispersion compensation

1.19.1 Erbium-Doped Fiber

- These fibers have small amounts of erbium ions (for example, 1000 parts per million weight) added to the silica material to form a basic building block for optical fiber amplifiers.

- A length of Er-doped fiber ranging from 10 to 30 m serves as a gain medium for amplifying optical signals in either the C-band (1530 to 1560 nm) or the L-band (1560 to 1625 nm).

- There are many variations on the doping level, cutoff wavelength, mode-field diameter, numerical aperture and cladding diameter for these fibers.

- Specific erbium-doped fiber configurations will yield a variety of optical amplifier designs that can be selected according to pump laser power requirement, noise figure, signal gain, and flatness of the output spectrum.

- Higher erbium concentrations allow the use of shorter fiber lengths, smaller claddings are useful for compact packages and a higher numerical aperture allows the fiber to be coiled tightly in small packages.

- Table lists some generic parameter values of an erbium-doped fiber for use in the C-band.

1.19.2 Photosensitive Sensitive Fiber

- The refractive index of a photosensitive sensitive fiber changes when it is exposed to ultraviolet light. This sensitivity may be provided by doping the fiber material with germanium and boron ions.

- The main application is to create a fiber Bragg grating, which is a periodic variation of the refractive index along the fiber axis.

- Applications of fiber Bragg gratings include light-coupling mechanisms for pump lasers used in optical amplifiers, wavelength add/drop modules, optical filters, and chromatic dispersion compensation modules.

1.19.3 Bend-Insensitive Fiber

- Increasing the Numerical Aperture (NA) reduces the sensitivity of a single-mode fiber to bending loss.

- The higher NA decreases the Mode-Field Diameter (MFD), thereby confining optical power more tightly within the core than in conventional single-mode fibers.

- For example, at 1310 nm a fiber designed with an NA of 0.16 can have a MFD of 6.7 μm.

- An increase of the NA to 0.21 decreases the MFD to 5.1 μm.

- Bend insensitive fibers are available commercially in a range of core diameters to provide optimum performance at specific operating wavelengths, such as 820, 1310 nm, or 1550 nm.

- These fibers are offered with either an 80 μm or a 125 μm cladding diameter as standard products. The 80 μm reduced cladding fiber results in a much smaller volume compared with a 125 μm cladding diameter when a fiber length is coiled up within a device package.

- Whereas there is a high bending loss for tightly wound conventional single-mode fibers, the induced attenuation when bend-insensitive fiber is wound into five coils with a 10-mm radius is less than 0.01 dB at 1310 nm and less than 0.5 dB at 1550 nm.

1.19.4 Termination Fiber

- Often an optical device with multiple ports will have one or more unused or open branches. Back reflections from these ports can cause instabilities and need to be suppressed.

- This can be achieved by using a termination fiber.

- An example of such a fiber is a coreless silica construction. A termination that has a return loss of better than 65 dB can be achieved by splicing about 25 cm of a termination fiber onto the end of unused fiber branches.

1.19.5 Polarization-Preserving Fiber

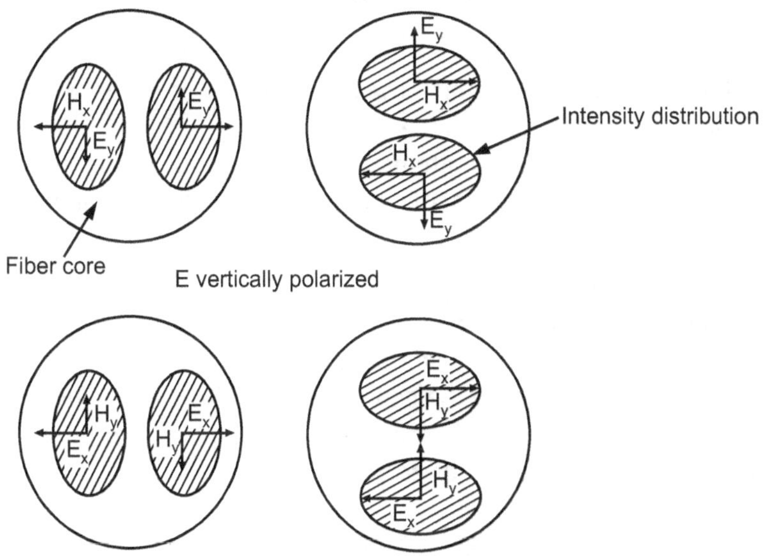

Fig. 1.66 : Cross-sectional geometry of four different polarization-maintaining fibers

- In contrast to standard single-mode optical fibers in which that state of polarization fluctuates as a light signal propagates through the fiber, polarization-preserving fibers have a special core design that maintains the state of polarization.

- Applications of these fibers include light signal modulators fabricated from lithium niobate, optical amplifiers for polarization multiplexing, light-coupling fibers for pump lasers, and polarization-mode dispersion compensators.

- Fig. 1.66 illustrates the cross-sectional geometry of four different polarization-maintaining fibers.

- The light circles represent the cladding and the dark areas are the core configurations.

- The goal in each design is to use stress-applying parts to create slow and fast axes in the core.

- Each of these axes will guide light at a different velocity.

- Crosstalk between the two axes is suppressed so that polarized light launched into either of the axes will maintain its state of polarization as it travels along the fiber.

1.20 OVERALL FIBER DISPERSION

1.20.1 Multimode Fibers

- The overall dispersion in multimode fibers consists of both chromatic and intermodal terms.
- The total rms pulse broadening σ_T is given by

$$\sigma_T = \left(\sigma_c^2 + \sigma_n^2\right)^{1/2} \qquad \ldots (1.227)$$

where σ_c is the intramodal chromatic broadening and σ_n is the intermodal broadening caused by delay differences between the modes.

- The chromatic term σ_c consists of both material and waveguide dispersion.
- Since waveguide dispersion is negligible compared with material dispersion in multimode fibers hence $\sigma_c \simeq \sigma_m$.

1.20.2 Single-Mode Fibers

- The pulse broadening in single mode fibers results almost entirely from chromatic or intramodal dispersion as only a single mode is allowed to propagate.
- Hence, the bandwidth is limited by the finite spectral width of the source.
- The transit time or specific group delay τ_g for a light pulse propagating along a unit length of single mode fiber may be given as:

$$\tau_g = \frac{1}{c}\frac{d\beta}{dk} \qquad \ldots (1.228)$$

where c is the velocity of light in a vacuum, β is the propagation constant for a mode within the fiber core of refractive index n_1 and k is the propagation constant for the mode in a vacuum.

- The total first-order dispersion parameter or the chromatic dispersion of a single-mode fiber D_T is given by the derivative of the specific group delay wrt the vacuum wavelength λ as:

$$D_T = \frac{d\tau_g}{d\lambda} \qquad \ldots (1.229)$$

- When the variable λ is replaced to ω, then the total dispersion parameter becomes:

$$D_T = -\frac{\omega}{\lambda}\frac{d\tau_g}{d\omega} = -\frac{\omega}{\lambda}\frac{d^2\beta}{d\omega^2} \qquad \ldots (1.230)$$

- The fiber exhibits intramodal dispersion when β varies nonlinearly with wavelength. β may be expressed in terms of the relative refractive index difference Δ and the normalized propagation constant b as:

$$\beta = kn_1\left[1 - 2\Delta\left(1 - b\right)\right]^{1/2} \qquad \ldots (1.231)$$

$$\text{Total rms pulse broadening} = \sigma_\lambda L \left|\frac{d\tau_g}{d\lambda}\right| \qquad \ldots (1.232)$$

$$= \frac{\sigma_\lambda L 2\pi}{c\lambda^2} \frac{d^2\beta}{dk^2} \qquad \qquad \text{... (1.223)}$$

where σ_λ is the source rms spectral linewidth centered at a wavelength λ.

- The waveguide dispersion parameter D_W may be obtained as

$$D_W = -\left(\frac{n_1 - n_2}{\lambda c}\right) v \frac{d^2(vb)}{dv^2} \qquad \qquad \text{... (1.234)}$$

- Where v is the normalized frequency for the fiber. Since the normalized propagation constant b for the specific fiber is only dependent on v, the normalized waveguide dispersion coefficient $vd^2(vb)/dv^2$ also depends on v.

- A profile dispersion parameter D_P which is proportional to $d\Delta/d\lambda$.

- Total first order dispersion D_T in a practical single-mode fiber is given by:

$$D_T = D_M + D_W + D_P \qquad \qquad \text{... (1.235)}$$

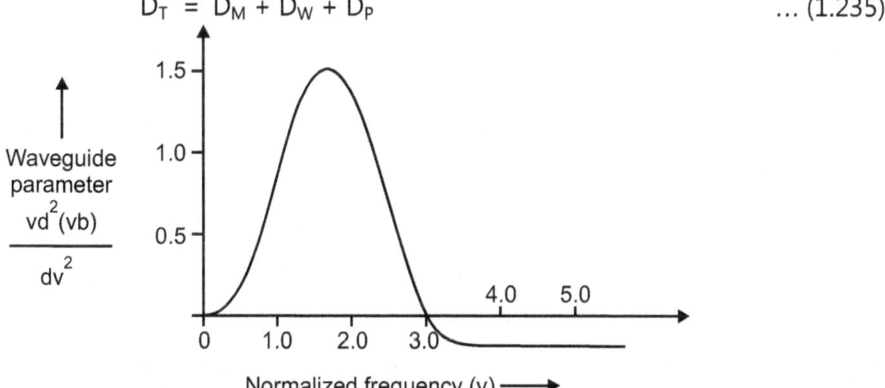

Fig. 1.67 : The waveguide parameter $vd^2(vb)/dv^2$ as a function of the normalized frequency v for the LP_{01} mode

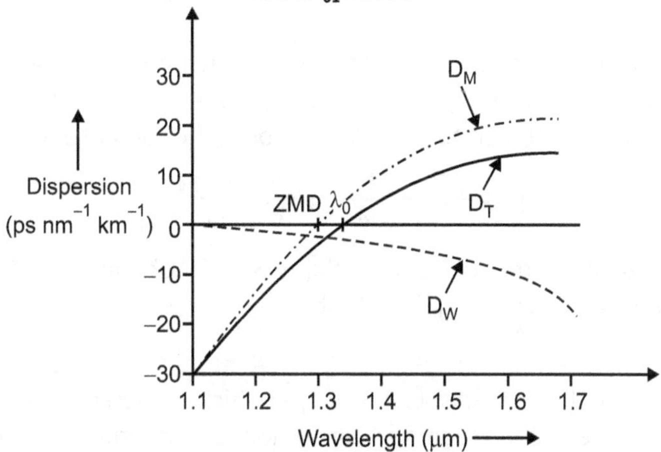

Fig. 1.68 : The material dispersion parameter (D_M), the waveguide dispersion parameter (D_W), and the total dispersion parameter (D_T) as a function for a single mode fiber

- From Fig. 1.68 it may be observed that the characteristic curve goes through zero at a wavelength of 1.27 μm.

- This Zero Material Dispersion (ZMD) point can be shifted anywhere in the wavelength range 1.2 to 1.4 µm by the addition of suitable dopants.

- The total fiber dispersion, which depends on both the fiber material composition and dimensions, may be minimized by trading off material and waveguide dispersion while limiting the profile dispersion.

- For wavelengths longer than the ZMD point, the material dispersion parameter is positive whereas the waveguide dispersion parameter is negative.

- For a particular wavelength for designed λ_O, which is slightly larger than the ZMD point wavelength, the waveguide dispersion compensates for the material dispersion and the total first-order dispersion parameter D_T becomes zero.

- The wavelength at which the first order dispersion is zero, λ_o may be selected in the range 1.3 to 2 µm by careful control of the fiber core diameter and profile.

- The wavelength at which first order dispersion is zero, λ_o may be extended to wavelengths of 1.55 µm and beyond, by a combination of three techniques.

- These are:

  (a) Lowering the normalized frequency (v value) for the fiber.

  (b) Increasing the relative refractive index difference Δ for the fiber.

  (c) Suitable doping of the silica with germanium.

- The variation of the chromatic dispersion with wavelength is usually characterized by the second order dispersion parameter or dispersion slopes which may be written as

$$S = \frac{dD_T}{d\lambda} = \frac{d^2\tau_g}{d\lambda^2} \qquad \ldots (1.236)$$

- Whereas the first order dispersion parameter D_T may be seen to be related only to the second derivative of the propagation constant β with respect to angular frequency. The dispersion slope can be shown to be related to both the second and third derivatives.

$$S = \frac{(2\pi c)^3}{\lambda^4} \frac{d^3\beta}{d\omega^3} + \frac{4\pi c}{\lambda^3} \frac{d^2\beta}{d\omega^2} \qquad \ldots (1.237)$$

- An important value of the dispersion slope $S(\lambda)$ is obtained at the wavelength of minimum chromatic dispersion λ_o such that:

$$S_o = S(\lambda_o)$$

- Where S_o is called the zero-dispersion slope which is determined only by the third derivative of β. The total chromatic dispersion at an arbitrary wavelength can be estimated when the two parameters λ_o and S_o are specified according to:

$$D_T(\lambda) = \frac{\lambda S_o}{4} \left[1 - \left(\frac{\lambda_o}{\lambda}\right)^4 \right] \qquad (1.238)$$

Example 1.16 : *A multimode step index fiber has a numerical aperture of 0.3 and a core refractive index of 1.45. The material dispersion parameter for the fiber is 250 Ps $nm^{-1}km^{-1}$ which makes material dispersion the totally dominating chromatic dispersion mechanism. Estimate (a) the total rms pulse broadening per kilometer when the fiber is used with an LED source of rms spectral width 50 nm and (b) the corresponding bandwidth length product for the fiber.*

Solution :

(a) The rms pulse broadening per kilometer due to material dispersion may be obtained as:

$$\sigma_m \ (1 \ km) \ \simeq \ \frac{\sigma_\lambda \ L\lambda}{c} \left| \frac{d^2 n_1}{d\lambda^2} \right|$$

$$= \ \sigma_\lambda LM$$

$$= \ 50 \times 1 \times 250 \ ps \ km^{-1}$$

$$= \ 12.5 \ ns \ km^{-1}$$

The rms pulse broadening per kilometer due to intermodal dispersion for the step index fiber is given by

$$\sigma_s \ (1 \ km) \ \simeq \ \frac{L \ (NA)^2}{4 \sqrt{3} \ n_1 c}$$

$$= \ \frac{10^3 \times 0.09}{4\sqrt{3} \times 1.45 \times 2.998 \times 10^8}$$

$$= \ 29.9 \ ns \ km^{-1}$$

The total rms pulse broadening per kilometer may be obtained where $\sigma_c \simeq \sigma_m$ as the waveguide dispersion is negligible and $\sigma_n = \sigma_s$ for the multimode step index fiber.

Hence,
$$\sigma_T \ = \ \left(\sigma_m^2 + \sigma_s^2 \right)^{1/2}$$

$$= \ \left(12.5^2 + 29.9^2 \right)^{1/2}$$

$$= \ 32.4 \ ns \ km^{-1}$$

(b) The bandwidth-length product may be estimated from the relationship given below :

where,
$$B_{opt} \times L \ = \ \frac{0.2}{\sigma_T}$$

$$= \ \frac{0.2}{32.4 \times 10^{-9}}$$

$$= \ 6.2 \ MHz \ km$$

Example 1.17 : *A typical single-mode fiber has a zero-dispersion wavelength of 1.31 μm with a dispersion slope of 0.09 ps nm^{-2} km^{-1}. Compare the total first order dispersion for the fiber at the wavelengths of 1.28 μm and 1.55 μm when the material dispersion and profile dispersion at the latter wavelength are 13.5 ps nm^{-1} and 0.4 ps nm^{-1} km^{-1} respectively, determine the waveguide dispersion at this wavelength.*

Solution :

The total first-order dispersion for the fiber at the two wavelengths may be obtained as:

$$D_T(1280 \text{ nm}) = \frac{\lambda S_o}{4}\left[1 - \left(\frac{\lambda_o}{\lambda}\right)^4\right]$$

$$= \frac{1280 \times 0.09 \times 10^{-12}}{4}\left[1 - \left(\frac{1310}{1280}\right)^4\right]$$

$$= -2.8 \text{ ps nm}^{-1} \text{ km}^{-1}$$

and

$$D_T(1550 \text{ nm}) = \frac{1550 \times 0.09 \times 10^{-12}}{4}\left[1 - \left(\frac{1310}{1550}\right)^4\right]$$

$$= 17.1 \text{ ps nm}^{-1}\text{km}^{-1}$$

The total dispersion at the 1.28 μm wavelength exhibits a –ve sign due to the influence of the waveguide dispersion. Furthermore, as anticipated the total dispersion at the longer wavelength (1.55 μm) is considerably greater than that obtained near the zero-dispersion wavelength.

The waveguide dispersion for the fiber at a wavelength of 1.55 μm is given by equation

$$D_W = D_T - (D_M + D_P)$$

$$= 17.1 - (13.5 + 0.4)$$

$$= 3.2 \text{ ps nm}^{-1} \text{ km}^{-1}$$

1.21 OPTICAL SOURCES

The optical source is the major active component in an optical fiber communication system. The main function of the optical source is to convert electrical energy into optical or light energy, such that it must be launched or coupled into the optical fiber.

There are three main sources of optical light available:

- Wideband 'continuous spectra' sources (incandescent lamps);
- Monolithic incoherent sources (light emitting diodes, LEDs);
- Monochromatic coherent sources (lasers).

Among these three sources, semiconductor injection laser and the LED fulfill the following major requirements for an optical fiber.

- A size and configuration compatibility with launching light into an optical fiber. Ideally, the light output should be highly directional.

- Must accurately track the electrical input signal to minimize the distortion and noise. Ideally, the source should be linear.

- Should emit light at wavelengths where the fiber has low losses and low dispersion and where the detectors are efficient.

- Capable of signal modulation over a wide bandwidth extending from audio frequencies to beyond the gigahertz range.

- Must couple sufficient optical power to overcome attenuation in the fiber plus additional connector losses and leave adequate power to drive the detector.

- Should have a very narrow spectral bandwidth (linewidth) in order to minimize dispersion in the fiber.

- Must be capable of maintaining a stable optical output which is largely unaffected by changes in the ambient conditions (e.g. temperature).

- Source should be comparatively cheap and highly reliable in order to compete with convention transmission techniques.

1.21.1 MATERIAL CONSIDERATIONS

The semiconductor materials used for the optical sources must broadly fulfill several conditions. Thee conditions are as follows:

1. **p-n Junction Formation:** The materials must lend themselves to the formation of p-n junctions with suitable characteristics for carrier injection.

2. **Efficient Electroluminescence:** The devices fabricated must have a high probability of radiative transitions and therefore a high internal quantum efficiency. Hence, the materials utilized must be either direct bandgap semiconductors or indirect bandgap semiconductors with appropriate impurity centers.

3. **Useful emission wavelength:** The materials must emit light at a suitable wavelength to be utilized with current optical fibers and detectors (0.8 to 1.7 µm). Ideally, they should allow bandgap variation with appropriate doping and fabrication so that emission at a desired specific wavelength may be achieved.

- Initially to obtain electroluminescence the direct bangap III-V alloy semiconductors including the binary components gallium arsenide (GaAs) and gallium phosphide (GaP) and the ternary gallium arsenide phosphide ($GaAsP_{1-x}$) are used.

- Gallium arsenide gives efficient electroluminescence over an appropriate wavelength band (0.88 to 0.91 µm). It was the first material to be fabricated into homojunction semiconductor lasers operating at low temperature for the first generation optical fiber communication systems.

- Then comes hetrojunction semiconductor devices. These hetrostructure devices were first fabricated using Liquid-Phase Epitaxy (LPE) to produce GaAs/Al$_x$Ga$_{1-x}$As as single hetrojunction lasers.

- The same technique was used to produce double hetrojunctions consisting of Al$_x$Ga$_{1-x}$As/ GaAs/Al$_x$Ga$_{1-x}$As epitaxial layers, which give continuous operation at room temperature.

- The GaAs/AlGaAs DH system is best developed and is used for fabricating both lasers and LEDs for the shorter wavelength region.

- The bandgap in this material is used to span the entire 0.8 to 0.9 μm wavelength band by changing the AlGa composition.

- In the longer wavelength region (1.1 to 1.6 μm) a number of III-V alloys have been utilized which are compatible with GaAs, InP and GaSb substrates. These include ternary alloys such as GaAs$_{1-x}$Sb$_x$ and In$_x$Ga$_{1-x}$As grown on GaAs.

- The most advanced are In$_{1-x}$Ga$_x$As$_y$P$_{1-y}$ lattice matched to InP and Ga$_{1-y}$Al$_y$As$_{1-x}$Sb$_x$ lattice matched to GaSb. Both these material systems allow emission over the entire 1.0 to 1.7 μm wavelength band.

- The InGaAsP/InP material system remains the most favourable for both long wavelength light sources and detectors.

- This is due to ease of fabrication with lattice matching on InP which is also a suitable material for the active region with a bandgap energy of 1.35 eV at 300 K. Hence, InP/InGaAsP devices may be fabricated.

- Furthermore, ternary - nitride based alloys also have an advantage over GaAs or InP based alloys because of their better index match with silica optical fibers.

- Some common material systems used in the fabrication of electroluminescent source for optical fiber communications are summarized in Table 1.2 shown below.

Table 1.8 : Some Common Material Systems used in the Fabrication of Electroluminescent Sources for Optical Fiber Communications

Material systems Active Layer/Confining Layers	Useful Wavelength Range (μm)	Substrate
GaAs/Al$_x$Ga$_{1-x}$As	0.8 – 0.9	GaAs
GaAs/In$_x$Ga$_{1-x}$P	0.9	GaAs
Al$_y$Ga$_{1-y}$As/Al$_x$Ga$_{1-x}$As	0.65 – 0.9	GaAs
In$_y$Ga$_{1-y}$As/In$_x$Ga$_{1-x}$P	0.85 – 1.1	GaAs
GaAs$_{1-x}$Sb$_x$/Ga$_{1-y}$Al$_y$As$_{1-x}$Sb$_x$	0.9 – 1.1	GaAs
Ga$_{1-y}$Al$_y$As$_{1-x}$Sb$_x$/GaSb	1.0 – 1.7	GaSb

$In_{1-x}Ga_xAs_yP_{1-y}/InP$	0.92 – 1.7	InP
$In_xGa_{1-x}As/InGaA/As$	1.3	InGaAs
$In_{1-x}GaN_yAs_{1-y}/GaNAs$	1.3 – 1.55	GaAs
$In_{1-x}Ga_xN_{1-y}As_ySb/Ga_{1-x}Al_xAs$	1.31	GaAs

1.22 OPTICAL SOURCE : LIGHT-EMITTING DIODE

- The normally empty conduction band of the semiconductor is populated by electrons injected into it by the forward current through the junction and light is generated when these electrons recombine with holes in the valence band to emit a photon. This is the mechanism by which light is emitted from an LED, but stimulated emission is not encouraged.

- The LED can therefore operate at low current densities than the injection lasers but the emitted photons have random phases and the device is an incoherent optical source.

- Also, the energy of the emitted photons is only roughly equal to the bandgap energy of the semiconductor material which gives a much wider spectral linewidth than the injection laser.

- The linewidth for an LED corresponds to a range of photon energy between 1 and 3.5 KT, where K is Boltzmann's constant and T is the absolute temperature.

- This gives a linewidth of 30 to 40 nm for GaAs based devices operating at room temperature. Thus, the LED supports many optical modes within its structure and therefore is used as a multimode source.

1.22.1 Disadvantages of LEDs Compared to Injection Lasers

- Generally lower optical power coupled into a fiber (microwatts);
- Usually lower modulation bandwidth;
- Harmonic distortion.

1.22.2 Advantages of LED

- Simple fabrication.
- Simple construction leads to low cost.
- Reliability is more. The LED does not exhibit catastrophic degradation and has proved far less sensitive to gradual degradation than the injection laser. It is also immune to self-pulsation and modal-noise problems.
- Less dependent on temperature. The light output against current characteristics is less affected by temperature than the corresponding characteristics of the laser. LED is not a threshold device.

- Simple drive circuits. This is due to the lower drive currents and reduced temperature dependence which reduces the necessity of temperature compensation circuits.

- Linearity is more. The LED has a linear light output against current characteristics, unlike the injection laser. This proves advantageous where analog modulation is needed.

Thus, LED has high-radiance and relatively high-bandwidth, which makes the device an extensively used source for optical fiber communications.

GaAs/AlGaAs LED structures are suitable for shorter wavelength region.

In GaAsP/InP material structure is used for the longer wavelength especially around 1.3 μm.

1.22.3 LED STRUCTURES

- There are six major types of LED structures but only two have found extensive use in optical fiber communications.

- These are surface emitter, the edge emitter, the superluminescent and the resonant cavity LED respectively. The other two structures, the planar and dome LEDs, find more application as cheap plastic encapsulated visible devices for use in such areas as intruder alarms TV channel changers and industrial counting.

- However, infrared versions of these devices have been used in optical communications mainly with fiber bundles.

1.22.3.1 Planar LED

- The planar LED is the simplest of the structures that is available and is fabricated by either the liquid or vapour phase epitaxial processes over the whole surface of a GaAs substrate.

- This involves a p-type diffusion into the n-type substrate in order to create the junction as shown in Fig. 1.69.

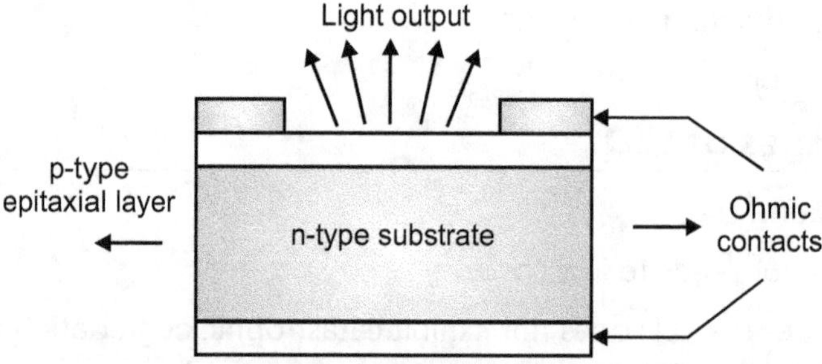

Fig. 1.69 : Structure of the planar LED

- Forward current flow through the junction gives Lambertian spontaneous emission and the device emits light from all surfaces.

- However, only a limited amount of light escapes the structure due to total internal reflection and therefore the radiance is low.

1.22.3.2 Dome LED

- The structure of a typical dome LED is shown in Fig. 1.70. A hemisphere of n-type GaAs is formed around a diffused p-type region.

- The diameter of the dome is chosen to maximize the amount of internal emission reaching the surface within the critical angle of the GaAs - air interface. Hence, this device has a higher external power efficiency than the planar LED.

- The geometry of the structure is such that the dome must be far larger than the active recombination area, which gives a greater effective emission area and thus reduces the radiance.

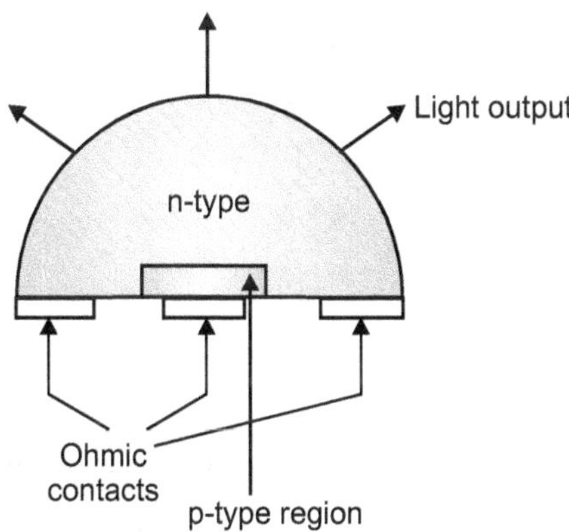

Fig. 1.70 : The structure of a dome LED

1.22.3.3 Surface Emitting LED

- A method to obtain a high radiance is to restrict the emission to a small active region within the device.

- The technique pioneered by Burrus and Dawson with homostructure devices was to use an etched well in a GaAs substrate in order to prevent heavy absorption of the emitted radiation and physically to accommodate the fiber.

- These structures have a low thermal impedance in the active region allowing high current densities and giving high radiance emission into the optical fiber.

- The advantage of employing DH structures is its increased efficiency from electrical and optical confinement as well as less absorption of the emitted radiation.

- This type of surface emitted LED (SLED) has been widely employed with optical communications.

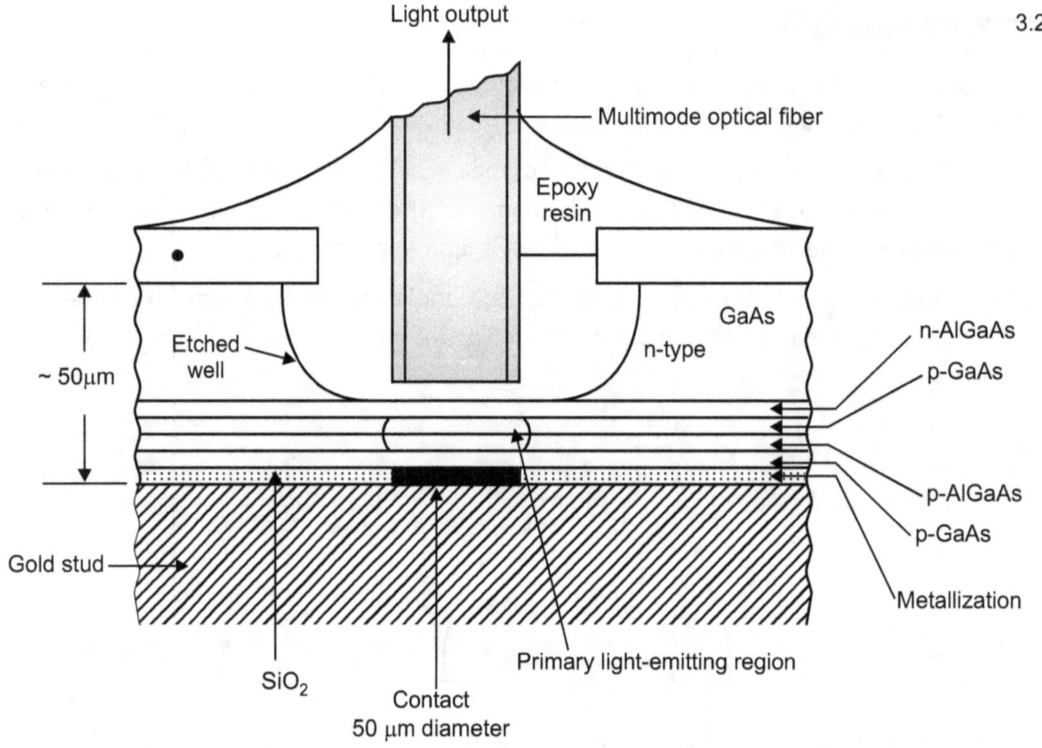

Fig. 1.71 : The structure of an AlGaAs DH surface emitting LED (Burrus type)

- The structure of a high radiance etched well DH structure for the 0.8 to 0.9 µm wavelength bond is shown in Fig. 1.71.

- The internal absorption in this device is very low due to the larger bandgap confining layers and the reflection coefficient at the back crystal face is high giving good forward radiance. The emission from the active layer is essentially isotropic.

- The external emission distribution may be considered as Lambertian with a beam width of 120° due to refraction from a high to a low refractive index at the GaAs fiber interface.

- The power coupled P_C into a multimode step index fiber may be obtained from the relationship.

$$P_C = \pi(1 - r)\, AR_D(NA)^2 \qquad\qquad \dots (1.239)$$

where, r = Fresnel reflection coefficient at the fiber surface

A = Smaller of the fiber core cross-section or the emission area of the source

R_D = Radiance of the source

- Power coupled into the fiber also depends on any other factors including the distance and alignment between the emission area and the fiber. DH surface emitters often give more coupled optical power than predicted by the above equation.

1.22.3.4 Edge Emitter LEDs

- Another basic high radiance structure currently used in optical communications is the stripe Geometry DH edge emitter LED (ELED).

- The edge emitter consists of an active junction region, which is the source of the incoherent light and two guiding layers.

- The guiding layers both have a refractive index which is lower than that of the active region but higher than the index of the surrounding material. This structure forms a waveguide channel that directs the optical radiation towards the fiber core.

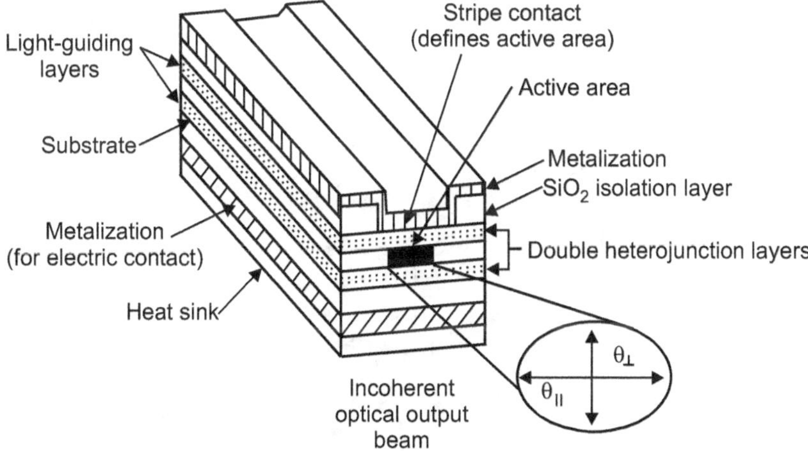

Fig. 1.72 : Schematic of edge-emitting double hetrojunction LED

- The output beam is Lambertian in a plane of the p-n junction ($\theta_{||}$ = 120°) and highly directional perpendicular to the p-n junction ($\theta_{\perp} \approx 30°$).

- To match the typical fiber core diameter, the contact stripes for the edge emitter are 50 - 70 µm wide. Lengths of the active regions usually range from 100 to 150 µm.

- The emission pattern of the edge emitter is more directional than that of the surface emitter.

- In the plane parallel to the junction, where there is no waveguide effect, the emitted beam is Lambertian with a half power width of $\theta_{||}$ = 120°. In the plane perpendicular to the junction, the half power beamwidth $\theta_{\perp}$ has been made as small as 25 – 35° by a proper choice of the waveguide thickness.

1.22.3.5 Superluminescent LEDs

- Another device geometry which provides significant benefits over both SLEDs and ELEDs for communication applications is the superluminescent diode or SLD.

Advantages over SLED and ELED :

- A high output power.

- A directional output beam.

- A narrow spectral linewidth.

- Furthermore the superradiant emission process within the SLD tends to increase the device modulation bandwidth over that of the more conventional LEDs.

- Fig. 1.73 shows two forms of construction for the SLD. It is observed that the structures are very similar to those of ELEDs. The SLD has optical properties that are bounded by the ELED and the injection laser.

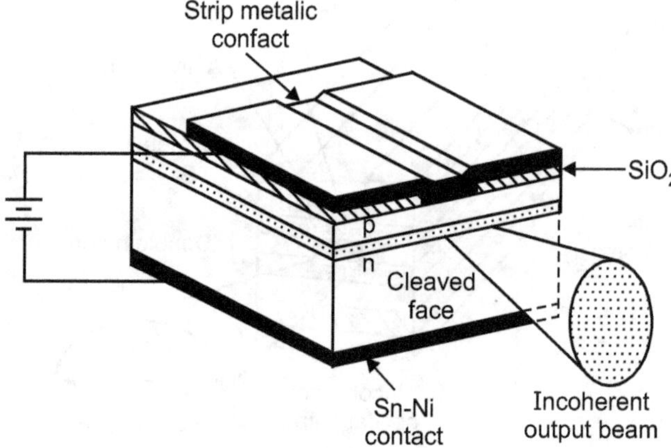

Fig. 1.73 : Superluminescent LED structure: AlGaAs contact stripe SLD

- SLD structure requires a p-n junction in the form of a long rectangular stripe, a ridge waveguide. One end of the device is made optically lossy to prevent reflections and thus suppress lasing, the output being from the opposite end.

- For operation, the injected current is increased until stimulated emission and hence amplification occurs. But because there is high loss at one end of the device, no optical feedback takes place.

- High optical power can therefore be obtained, together with the narrowing of the spectral width which also results from the stimulated emission.

- An early SLD is shown in Fig. 1.74 which employs a contact stripe together with an absorbing region at one end to suppress the laser action.

- Such devices have provided peak output power of 60 mw at a wavelength of 0.87 μm in a pulsed mode.

- Antireflection (AR) coatings can be applied to the cleaved facets of the SLD in order to suppress fabry-perot resonance.

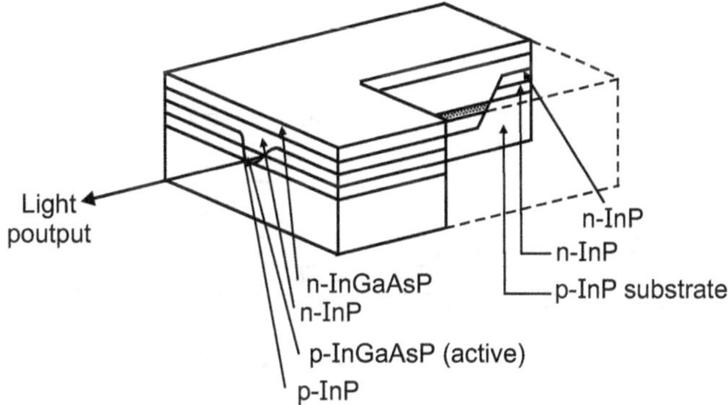

Fig. 1.74: High output power InGaAsP SLD

- The structure of an InGaAsP/InP SLD is shown in Fig. 1.75. The device which emits at 1.3 µm comprises a buried active layer within a V-shaped groove on the p-type InP substrate.

- This technique provides an appropriate structure for high-power operation because of its low leakage current. SLD structures incorporate AR coatings on both end facets. To prevent feedback, a light diffusion surface is placed within this device.

- The surface, which is applied diagonally on the active layer of length 350 µm, serves to scatter the backward light emitted from the active layer and thus decreases feedback into this layer.

- AR coating is provided on the output facet. As it is not possible to achieve a perfect AR coating, the above structure is therefore not left totally dependent on this feedback suppression mechanism.

- The coupling of 1 mw of optical power into the spherically lensed end of a single mode fiber (10 µm diameter) has been demonstrated with this device operating at a drive current of 150 mA.

- The spectral distribution from the SLD was observed to be a smooth envelope with an FWHP of 30 nm, while the device modulation bandwidth reached 350 MHz at the −1.5 dB point.

1.22.3.6 Resonant Cavity and Quantum-Dot LEDs

- The Resonant Cavity Light Emitting Diode (RC−LED) is based on planar technology containing a fabry-perot active resonant cavity between Distributed Bragg Reflector (DBR) mirrors.

- A quantum well is then embedded in this active cavity.

- Since the cavity is confined to a micrometer size, the RC-LED is therefore also referred to as a microcavity light-emitting diode.

- The basic structure of an RC-LED is shown in Fig. 1.75 where an active region consisting of InGaAsP multiquantum wells is positioned in the optical resonant cavity which is located between two DBR mirrors, one each at the bottom and the top of the activity cavity.

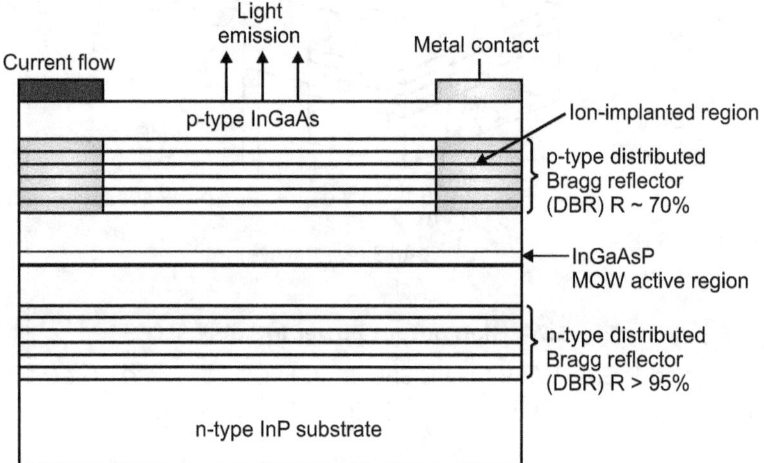

Fig. 1.75: Structures of resonant - cavity light emitting diodes : surface emitting using DBR mirrors

- Current confinement is obtained through the ion implantation technique in the top mirror while the RC-LED structure constitutes a Fabry-Perot resonator where the optical cavity mode is in resonance, amplifying the spontaneous emission from the active layer.
- The reflectivity of the Bottom DBR mirror is kept to a maximum (i.e. higher than 90%) by incorporating a large number of gratings (i.e. more than 40) whereas the surface DBR mirror is made semitransparent by introducing fewer gratings (i.e. about 15) creating low facet reflectivity (i.e. 40 to 60%) to allow the optical signal to exit through this mirror.
- Since these devices incorporate DBR mirrors they may also be referred to as grating assisted RC-LEDs.

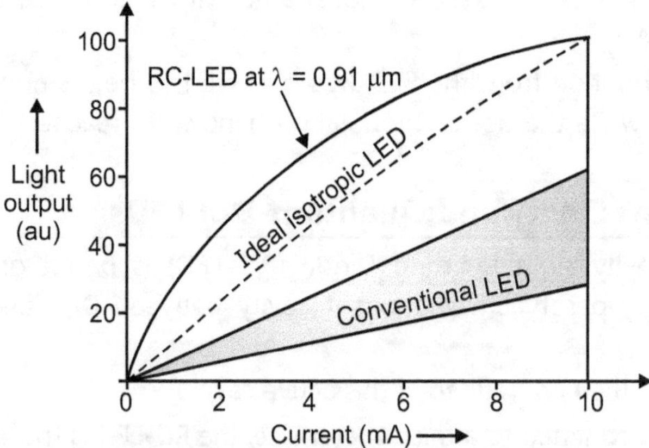

Fig. 1.76 : Optical intensity against drive current for a conventional LED and an RC-LED for an output signal wavelength of 0.91 μm

- Fig. 1.76 shows the comparison of the output optical powers for a conventional LED and that of an RC-LED with increasing operating current at an output signal wavelength of 0.91 μm.
- The dashed line represents the characteristics of an ideal isotropic emitting device possessing zero facet reflectivity which is assumed to emit light isotropically with 100% quantum efficiency for all wavelengths emitted from the active cavity.
- It can be seen that the RC-LED provides a higher optical intensity than a conventional LED and it also surpasses the theoretical limit of an isotropic optical emitter.
- This higher optical intensity is due to the resonant amplified spontaneous emission output from the surface of the device.
- Hence the combination of both high efficiency and high radiance makes the RC-LED an ideal optical source for multimode fiber coupling in a range of applications.

1.23 LED CHARACTERISTICS

1.23.1 Optical Output Power

- The ideal output power against current characteristic for an LED is shown in Fig. 1.77.

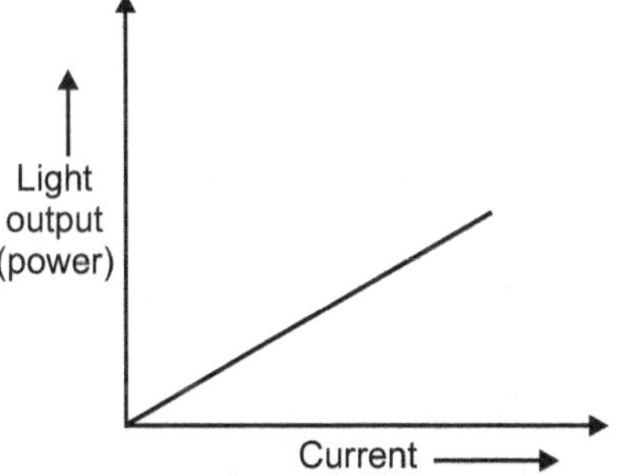

Fig. 1.77 : Ideal light output against current characteristics for an LED

- It is linear device in comparison with the majority of injection laser and hence it is more suitable for analog transmission where severe constraints are put on the linearity of the optical source.

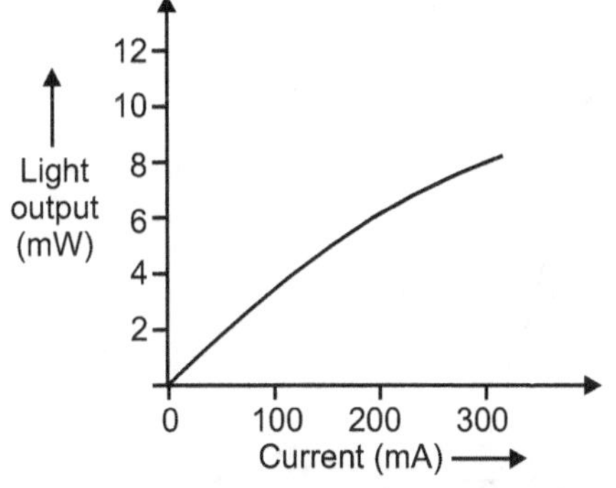

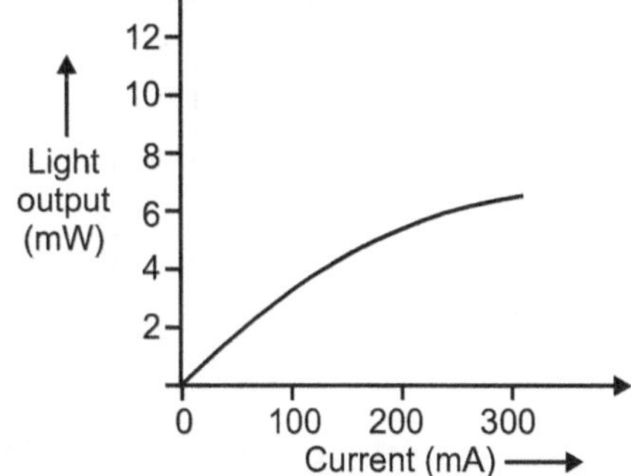

Fig. 1.78: An AlGaAs surface emitter with a 50μm diameter dot contact

Fig. 1.79: An AlGaAs edge emitter with a 65 μm wide stripe and 100 μm length

- Fig. 1.78 and 1.79 show the light output against current characteristics for a typically good surface and edge emitters respectively. It may be noted that the surface emitter radiates significantly more optical power into the air than the edge emitters, and that both devices are reasonably linear at moderate drive currents.

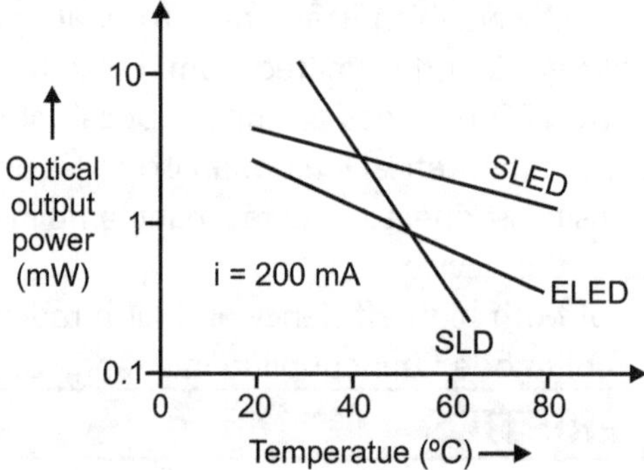

Fig. 1.80 : Light output temperature dependence for three important LED structures emitting at a wavelength of 1.3 μm

- The light output power against temperature characteristics for three important LED structures operating at a wavelength of 1.3 μm are shown in Fig. 1.80.

- It may be observed that the edge emitting device exhibits a greater temperature dependence than the surface emitter and that the output of the SLD with its stimulated emission is strongly dependent on the junction temperature.

1.23.2 Output Spectrum

- The spectral linewidth of an LED operating at room temperature in the 0.8 to 0.9 μm wavelength band is usually between 25 and 40 nm at the half maximum intensity points.

- For materials with smaller bandgap energies operating in the 1.1 to 1.7 μm wavelength region the linewidth tends to increase to around 50 to 160 nm.

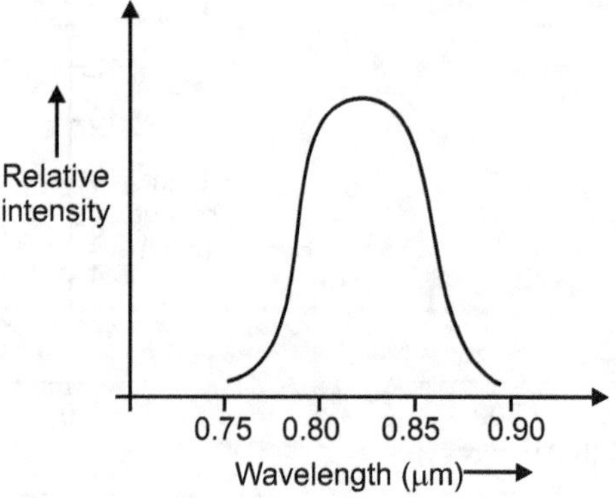

(a) Output spectrum for an AlGaAs surface emitter with doped active region

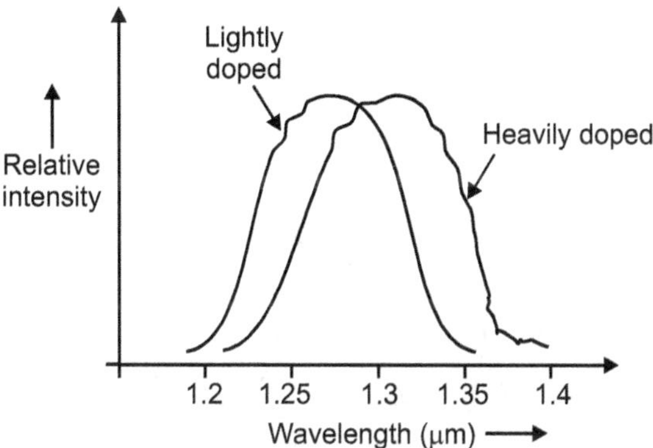

(b) Output spectra for an InGaAsP surface emitter showing both the lightly doped and heavily doped cases

Fig. 1.81 : LED output spectra

- Fig. 1.81 (b) shows the increase in linewidth due to increased doping levels and the formation of bandtail states. This becomes apparent in the differences in the output spectra between the surface and edge-emitting LEDs where the devices have generally heavily doped and lightly doped active layers respectively.

- It may also be noted that there is a shift to the lower peak emission wavelength (i.e. higher energy) through reduction in doping and hence the active layer composition must be adjusted if the same center wavelength is to be maintained.

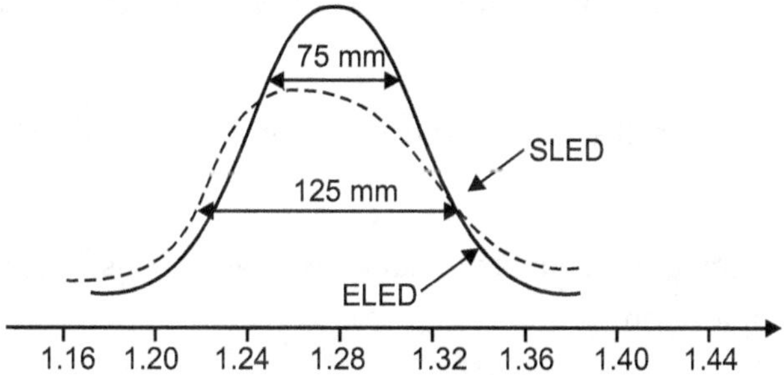

Fig. 1.82 : Typical spectral output characteristics for InGaAsP surface and edge-emitting LEDs operating in the 1.3 µm wavelength region

- The difference in the output spectra between InGaAsP SLEDs and ELEDs caused by self-absorption along the active layer of the devices are displayed in Fig. 1.82.

- It may be observed that the FWHP points are around 1.6 times smaller for the ELED than the superluminescent operation due to the onset of stimulated gain and in this case the linewidth can be far smaller than that obtained with the SLED.

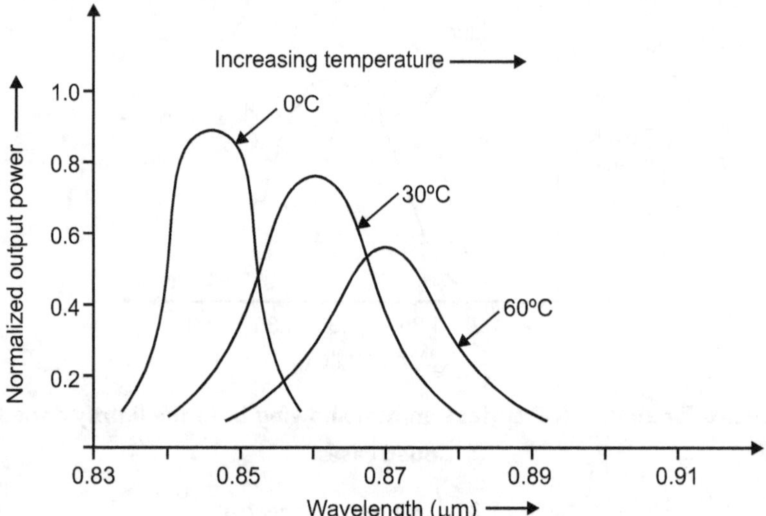

Fig. 1.83 : Typical spectral variation of the output characteristic with temperature for an AlGaAs surface emitting LED

- The output spectra also tends to broaden at a rate of 0.1 to 0.3 nm° C^{-1} with increase in temperature due to the greater energy spread in the carrier distributions at higher temperatures.

- Increase in temperature of the junction affect the peak emission wavelength as well and it is shifted by +0.3 to 0.4 nm° C^{-1} for AlGaAs devices and by +0.6 nm° C^{-1} for InGaAsP devices.

- The combined effects on the output spectrum for a typical AlGaAs surface emitter are illustrated in Fig. 1.83.

- It is therefore necessary to utilize heat sinks with LEDs for certain optical fiber communication applications.

1.23.3 Modulation Bandwidth

- The modulation bandwidth may be defined in either electrical or optical terms in optical communications. this corresponds to the electrical 3 dB point of the frequency at which the output electrical power is reduced by 3 dB w.r.t. the input electric power.

- As optical sources operate down to d.c. level, we only consider the high frequency 3 dB point, the modulation bandwidth being the frequency range between zero and this high frequency 3 dB point.

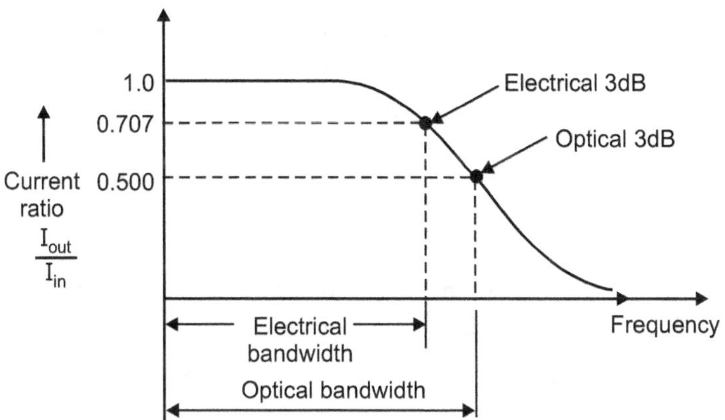

Fig. 1.84 : The frequency response for an optical fiber system shows the electrical and optical bandwidths

- Alternatively, if the 3 dB bandwidth of the modulated optical carrier (optical bandwidth) is considered, we obtain an increased value for the modulation bandwidth.

Relation between Optical and Electrical Bandwidth :

- In order to compare the two bandwidths it is necessary to compare the electric current through the system.

- Current rather than voltage is compared as both the optical source and optical detector may be considered to have a linear relationship between light and current.

Electrical Bandwidth : The ratio of electrical output power to the electrical input power in decibels RE_{dB} is given by

$$RE_{dB} \; = \; 10 \, \log_{10} \frac{\text{Electrical power out}}{\text{Electrical power in}} \qquad \ldots (1.240)$$

$$= \; 10 \, \log_{10} \frac{I_{out}^2/R_{out}}{I_{in}^2/R_{in}} \qquad \ldots (1.241)$$

$$\propto \; 10 \, \log_{10} \left[\frac{I_{out}}{I_{in}}\right]^2 \qquad \ldots (1.242)$$

The electrical 3 dB points occur when the ratio of the electrical powers shown above is 1/2. Hence it follows that this must occur when :

$$\left[\frac{I_{out}}{I_{in}}\right]^2 \; = \; \frac{1}{2} \qquad \ldots (1.243)$$

OR
$$\frac{I_{out}}{I_{in}} \; = \; \frac{1}{\sqrt{2}} \qquad \ldots (1.244)$$

Thus in electrical terms, the bandwidth may be defined by the frequency when the output current has dropped to $\frac{1}{\sqrt{2}}$ or 0.707 of the input current to the system.

Optical Bandwidth : The ratio of the optical output power to the optical input power in decibels RO_{dB} is given by:

$$RO_{dB} = 10 \log_{10} \frac{\text{optical power out}}{\text{optical power in}} \qquad \text{... (1.245)}$$

$$\propto 10 \log_{10} \frac{I_{out}}{I_{in}} \qquad \text{... (1.246)}$$

(due to the linear light/current relationships of the source and detector). Hence the optical 3 dB points occur when the ratio of the currents is equal to 1/2 and

$$\frac{I_{out}}{I_{in}} = \frac{1}{2} \qquad \text{... (1.247)}$$

Therefore in optical terms, the bandwidth is defined by the frequencies at which the output current has dropped to $\frac{1}{2}$ or 0.5 of the input current to the system. This corresponds to an electric power attenuation of 6 dB.

The modulation bandwidth of LEDs is generally determined by three mechanisms. These are:

(a) The doping level in the active layer;

(b) The reduction in radiative lifetime due to the injected carriers;

(c) The parasitic capacitance of the device.

Assuming negligible parasitic capacitance, the speed at which an LED can be directly current modulated is fundamentally limited by the recombination lifetime of the carriers, where the optical output power $P_e(\omega)$ of the device and angular modulation frequency ω is given by:

$$\frac{P_e(\omega)}{P_{dc}} = \frac{1}{[1 + (\omega \tau_i)^2]^{1/2}} \qquad \text{... (1.248)}$$

where τ_i is the injected (minority) carrier lifetime in the recombination region and Pdc is the d.c. optical output power for the same drive circuit.

1.23.4 LED Power and Efficiency

- The power generated internally by an LED may be determined by consideration of the excess electrons and holes in the P and n type material respectively. (i.e. the minority carriers) when it is forward biased and carrier injection takes place at the device contacts.

- Generally, the excess minority carrier density decays exponentially with time t according to the relation:

$$\Delta n = \Delta n(0) \exp(-t/\tau) \qquad \text{... (1.249)}$$

where $\Delta n(0)$ is the initial injected excess electron density and τ represents the total carrier recombination lifetime.

- In most cases Δn is only a small fraction of the majority carriers and comprises all the minority carriers. Therefore, the carrier recombination lifetime becomes the minority or injected carrier lifetime τ_i.

- The total rate at which the carriers are generated will be the sum of the externally supplied and the thermal generation rates.

- The current density J in amperes per square meter may be written as J/ed in electronics per cubic meter per second, where e is the charge on the electron and d is the thickness of the recombination region.

- Hence a rate equation for carrier recombination in the LED can be expressed in the form:

$$\frac{d(\Delta n)}{dt} = \frac{J}{ed} - \frac{\Delta n}{\tau} \; (m^{-3}\, s^{-1}) \qquad \text{... (1.250)}$$

The condition for equilibrium is obtained by setting the derivative to zero. Hence,

$$\Delta n = \frac{J\tau}{ed} \; (m^{-3}) \qquad \text{... (1.251)}$$

Therefore equation (1.243) gives the steady-state electron density when a constant current is flowing in the steady-state the total number of carrier recombinations per second or the recombination rate r_t will be:

$$r_t = \frac{J}{ed} \; (m^{-3}) \qquad \text{... (1.252)}$$

$$= r_r + r_{nr} \; (m^{-3}) \qquad \text{... (1.253)}$$

where r_r is the radiative recombination rate per unit volume and r_{nr} is the non-radiative recombination rate per unit volume, when the forward-biased current into the device is i, then from equation (1.244) the total number of recombinations per second R_t becomes:

$$R_t = \frac{i}{e} \qquad \text{... (1.254)}$$

The excess carriers can recombine either radiatively or non-radiatively.

The LED internal quantum efficiency η_{int} can be defined as 'the ratio of the radiatively recombination rate to the total recombination rate'.

$$\therefore \quad \eta_{int} = \frac{r_r}{r_t} = \frac{r_r}{r_r + r_{nr}} = \frac{R_r}{R_t} \qquad \text{... (1.255)}$$

where, R_r is the total number of radiative recombinations per second. Rearranging equation (1.240) and substituting from equation (1.248) gives:

$$R_r = \eta_{int} \frac{1}{e} \qquad \text{... (1.256)}$$

Since R_r is also equivalent to the total number of photons generated per second and each photon has an energy equal to hf joules, the optical power generated internally by the LED, P_{int}, is

$$P_{int} = \eta_{int} \frac{i}{e} hf \quad (\omega)$$ ... (1.257)

The internally generated power in terms of wavelength gives:

$$P_{int} = \eta_{int} \frac{h\,c\,i}{e\lambda} \quad (\omega)$$ ... (1.258)

'i' is the drive current.

To obtain a linear relationship between the optical power generated in the LED and the drive current in the device, the constant of proportionality η_{int} must be multiplied by a factor representing the external quantum efficiency η_{ext} to provide an overall quantum efficiency for the device.

The radiative minority carrier lifetime is $\tau_r = \dfrac{\Delta n}{r_r}$ and the non-radiative minority carrier lifetime is $\tau_{nr} = \dfrac{\Delta n}{r_{nr}}$. Therefore, the internal quantum efficiency is:

$$\eta_{int} = \frac{1}{1 + \left(\dfrac{r_{nr}}{r_t}\right)}$$ ... (1.259)

$$= \frac{1}{1 + \left(\dfrac{\tau_r}{\tau_{nr}}\right)}$$ ... (1.260)

The total recombination lifetime τ can be written as $\tau = \dfrac{\Delta n}{r_t}$

$$\frac{1}{\tau} = \frac{1}{\tau_r} + \frac{1}{\tau_{nr}}$$ ... (1.261)

The external quantum efficiency may be defined as 'the ratio of photons emitted from the device to the photons internally generated'. However, it is sometimes defined as 'the ratio of the number of photons emitted to the total number of carrier recombinations (raditive and non-raditive)'.

Hence,　　　　　　$$\eta_{int} = \frac{\tau}{\tau_r}$$ ... (1.262)

Example 1.18 : *The radiative and non-radiative recombination lifetimes of the minority carriers in the active region of a double hetrojunction LED are 60 and 100 ns respectively. Determine the total carrier recombination lifetime and the power internally generated within the device.*

When the peak emission wavelength is 0.87 μm at a drive current of 40 mA.

Solution :

Total carrier recombination lifetime is given by as

$$\tau = \frac{\tau_r \, \tau_{nr}}{\tau_r + \tau_{nr}}$$

$$= \frac{60 \times 100 \text{ ns}}{60 + 100} = 37.5 \text{ ns}$$

To calculate the power internally generated, it is necessary to obtain the internal quantum efficiency of the device.

$$\eta_{int} = \frac{\tau}{\tau_r} = \frac{37.5}{60} = 0.625$$

Thus,

$$P_{int} = \eta_{int} \frac{h \, c \, i}{e \, \lambda}$$

$$= \frac{0.625 \times 6.626 \times 10^{-34} \times 2.998 \times 10^{8} \times 40 \times 10^{-3}}{1.602 \times 10^{-19} \times 0.87 \times 10^{-6}}$$

$$= 35.6 \text{ mW}$$

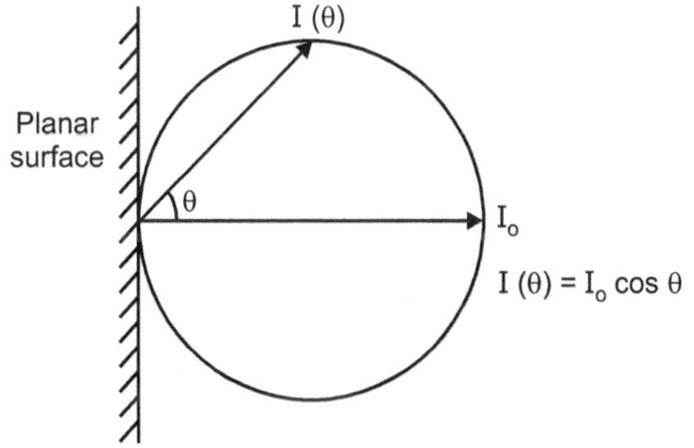

Fig. 1.85 : The Lambertian intensity distribution typical of a planar LED

- Although, the possible internal quantum efficiency can be high, the radiation geometry for an LED which emits through a planar surface is essentially Lambertian. In that, the surface radiance is constant in all directions.

- The Lambertian intensity distribution is illustrated in Fig. 1.85 where the maximum intensity I_o is perpendicular to the plane surface but is reduced on the sides in proportion to the cosine of the viewing angle θ as the apparent area varies with this angle.

- This reduces the external power efficiency to a few per cent as most of the light generated within the device is trapped by total internal reflection. When it is radiated at an angle greater than the critical angle for the crystal air interface.

- The external power efficiency η_{ep} is defined as 'the ratio of the optical power emitted externally, P_e, to the electric power provided to the device, P, or

$$\eta_{ep} = \frac{P_e}{P} \times 100\% \qquad \qquad \ldots (1.263)$$

- Also, the optical power emitted, P_e, into a medium of low refractive index n from the face of a planar LED fabricated from a material of refractive index η_x is given approximately by

$$P_e = \frac{P_{int}\, Fn^2}{4n_x^2} \qquad \qquad \ldots (1.264)$$

where P_{int} is the power generated internally and F is the transmission factor of the semiconductor external interface. Hence, it is possible to estimate the percentage of optical power emitted.

1.24 THE SEMICONDUCTOR INJECTION LASER

Stimulated emission by the recombination of the injected carriers is encouraged in the semiconductor injection laser by the provision of an optical cavity in the crystal structure in order to provide the feedback of photons. This gives the injections laser several major advantages over other semiconductor sources that may be used for optical communications.

The advantages are given below:

- High radiance due to the amplifying effect of stimulated emission. Injection lasers will generally supply milliwatts of optical output power.

- Narrow linewidth of the order of 1 nm (10 A°) or less which is useful in minimizing the effects of material dispersion.

- Modulation capabilities which at present extend up into the gigahertz range.

- Relative temporal coherence which is considered essential to allow heterodyne (coherent) detection in high capacity systems.

- Good spatial coherence which allows the output to be focused by a lens into a spot which has a greater intensity than the dispersed unfocused emission.

- These advantages, together with the compatibility of the injection laser with optical fibers led to the early developments of the device in the 1960s. Early injection lasers had the form of a Fabry-Perot cavity often fabricated in gallium arsenide which was the major III - V compound semiconductor with electroluminescent properties at the appropriate wavelength for the first generation systems. The basic structure of this homomjunction device is shown in Fig. 1.86.

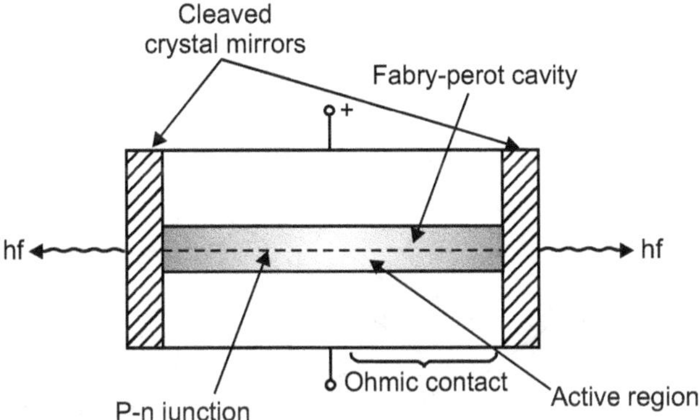

Fig. 1.86 : Schematic of a GaAs homojunction injection laser with a Fabry-Perot cavity

- Where the cleaved ends of the crystal acts as partial mirrors in order to encourage stimulated emission in the cavity when electrons are injected into the p-type region.

- These devices had a high threshold current density (greater than 10^4 A cm^{-2}) due to lack of carrier containment and proved inefficient light sources.

- Improved carrier containment and lower threshold current densities were achieved using heterojunction structures.

- The DH injection laser fabricated from the lattice - matched III - V alloys, provided both carrier and optical confinement on both sides of the p-n junction, giving the injection laser a greatly enhanced performance.

- In order to provide reliable Continuous Wave (CW) operation of the DH injection laser, it was necessary to provide further carrier and optical confinement which led to the introduction of stripe geometry DH laser configurations.

1.24.1 STRIPE GEOMETRY

- The DH laser structure provides optical confinement in the vertical direction through the refractive index step at the heterojunction interfaces but lasing takes place across the whole width of the device.

- This situation is illustrated in Fig. 1.87 which shows the broad-area DH laser where the sides of the cavity are simply formed by roughening the edges of the device in order to reduce unwanted emission in these directions and limit the number of horizontal transverse modes.

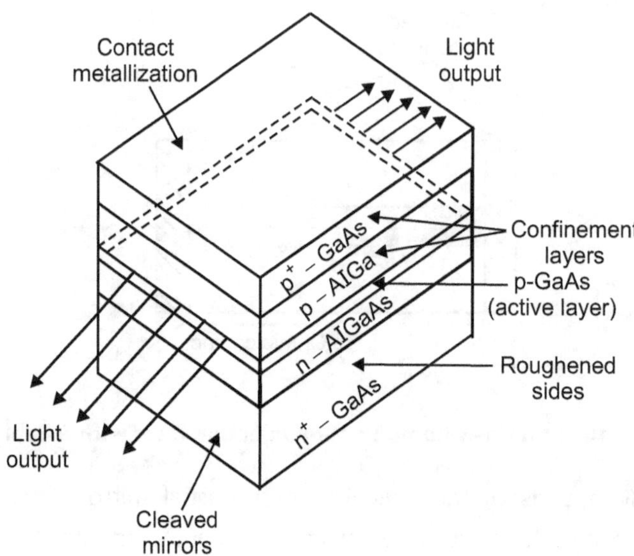

Fig. 1.87 : A broad-area GaAs/AlGaAs DH injection laser

- However, the broad emission area creates several problems including difficult heat sinking, lasing from multiple filaments in the relatively wide active area and unsuitable light output geometry for efficient coupling to the cylindrical fibers.

- To overcome these problems while also reducing the required threshold current, laser structures in which the active region does not extend to the edges of the device region were developed.

- A common technique to provide optical containment in the horizontal plane and the structure of a DH stripe contact laser is shown in Fig. 1.88. The major current flow through the device and hence the active region is within the stripe.

- Generally, the stripe is formed by the creation of high-resistance areas on either side by techniques such as photon bombardment or oxide isolation. The stripe therefore acts as a guiding mechanism which overcomes the major problems of the broad-area device.

- Although, the active area width is reduced, the light output is still not particularly well collimated due to isotropic emission from a small active region and diffraction within the structure.

- The optical output and far field emission patterns are illustrated in the Fig. 1.88. The output beam divergence is typically 45° perpendicular to the plane of the junction and 9° parallel to it.

- It also gives the correct balance of guiding and single transverse mode operation. Various stripe geometry laser structures have been investigated with stripe width ranging from 2 to 65 µm.

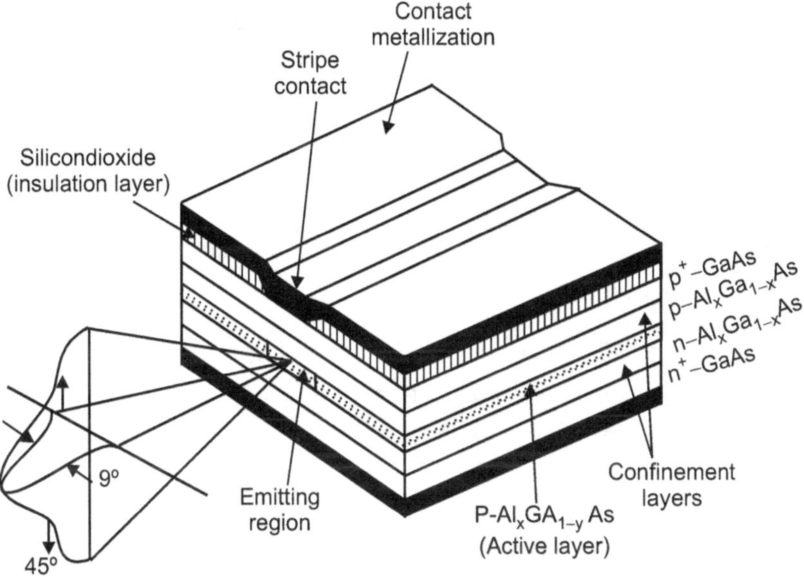

Fig. 1.88 : Schematic representation of an oxide stripe AlGaAs DH injection laser

1.24.2 INJECTION LASER STRUCTURES

1.24.2.1 Gain Guided Lasers

- Multimode injection lasers can be achieved by the use of stripe geometry and are often called gain guided lasers.

- Two basic techniques for the fabrication of gain guided laser structures are shown in Fig. 1.89 (a) and (b). The Fig. 1.89 shows the photon isolated stripe and the p-n junction isolated stripe structures respectively.

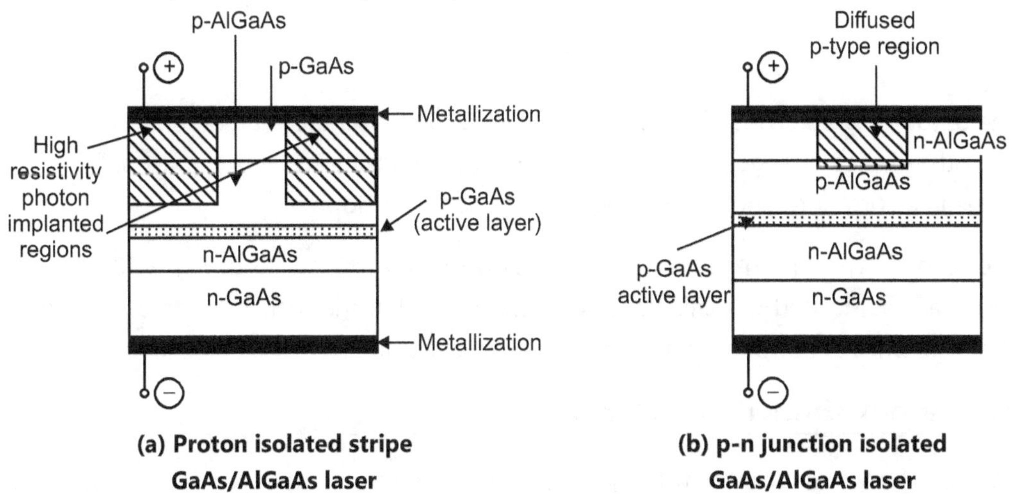

(a) Proton isolated stripe　　　　　**(b) p-n junction isolated**
GaAs/AlGaAs laser　　　　　　　　**GaAs/AlGaAs laser**

Fig. 1.89 : Schematic representation of structures for stripe geometry injection lasers

- In Fig. 1.90 (a) the resistive region formed by the photon bombardment gives better current confinement than the simple oxide stripe and has superior thermal properties due to the absence of silicon dioxide layer; p-n junction isolation involves a selective diffusion through the n-type surface region in order to reach the p-type layers as shown in Fig. 1.90 (b).

- None of these structures confines all the radiation and current to the stripe region and spreading occurs on both sides of the stripe.

- With stripe widths of 10 μm or less, such planar stripe lasers provide highly efficient coupling into multimode fibers, but significantly lower coupling efficiency is achieved into small core-diameter single mode fibers.

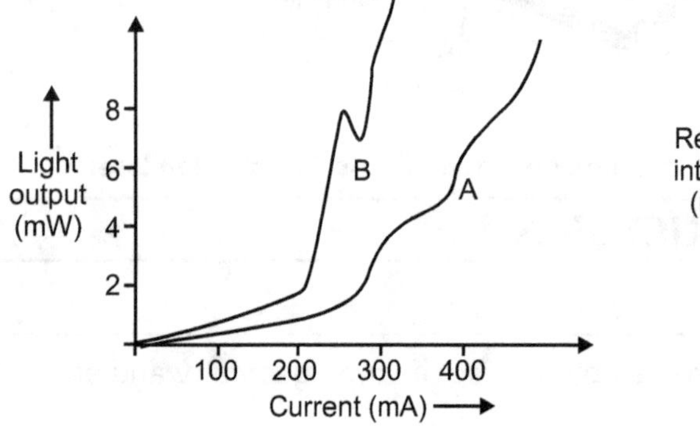

(a) The light output against current characteristics of an injection laser

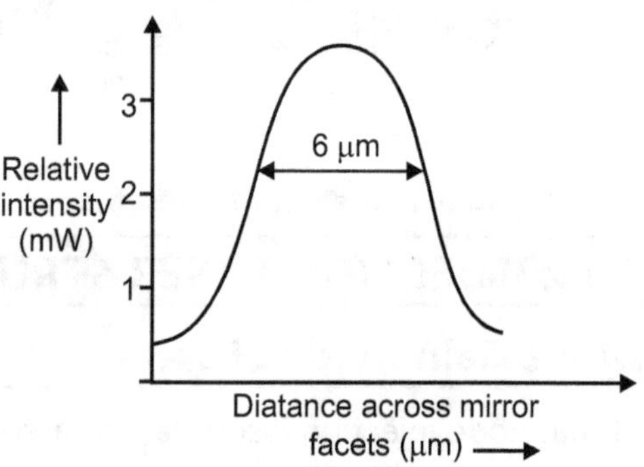

(b) A typical near field intensity distribution in the plane of the junction for an injection laser

Fig. 1.90

- The output characteristics for laser A in Fig. 1.90 (a) shows this type of Kink where lasing from the device changes from the fundamental lateral mode to a higher order lateral mode in a current region corresponding to a change in slope.

- The second type of Kink involves a spike as observed for laser B of Fig. 1.90 (a). These spikes are associated with filamentary behaviour within the active region of the device. The filaments result from defects within the crystal structure.

1.24.2.2 Index Guided Structures

- The drawbacks associated with gain guided laser structures were largely overcome through the development of index guided injection lasers.

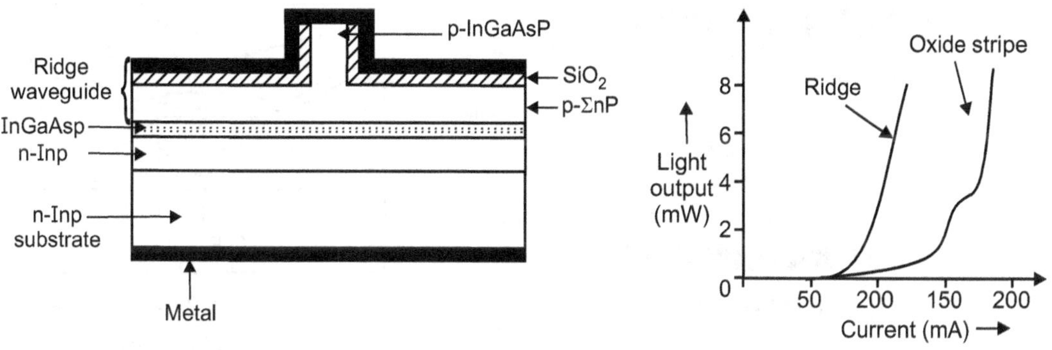

(a) Ridge wave guide injection laser structures　　　**(b) Light output versus current characteristics**

Fig. 1.91

- In such structures with weak index guiding, the active region waveguide thickness is varied by growing it over a channel or ridge in the substrate.

- A ridge is produced above the active region and surrounding areas are etched close to it.

- Insulating coatings on these surrounding areas confine the current flow through the ridge and active stripe, while the edges of the ridge reflect light, guiding it within the active layer and thus forming a waveguide.

- The ridge not only provides the location for the weak index guiding but also acts as the narrow current confining stripe.

- These devices are fabricated to operate at various wavelengths with a single lateral mode.

- More typically, the threshold currents for such weakly index-guided structures are in the range 40 to 60 mA as shown in Fig. 1.91 (b) which compares a light output versus current characteristics for a ridge waveguide laser with that of an oxide stripe gain guided device.

- Strong index guiding along the junction plane can provide improved transverse mode control in injection lasers.

- This can be achieved using a Buried Heterostructure (BH) device in which the active volume is completely buried in a material of wider bandgap and lower refractive index.

- The structure of a BH laser is shown in the Fig. 1.92.

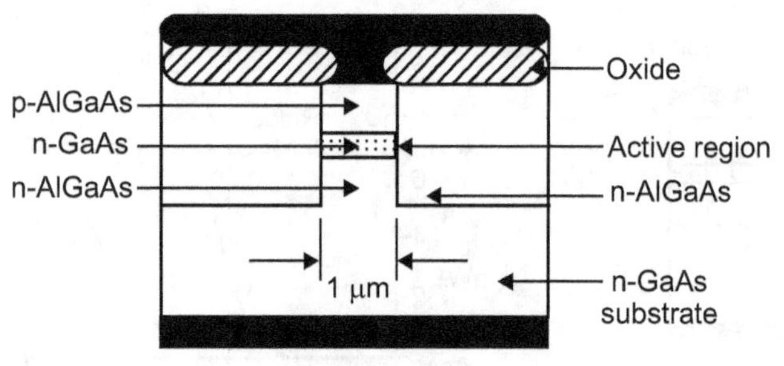

(a) GaAs/AlGaAs BH device

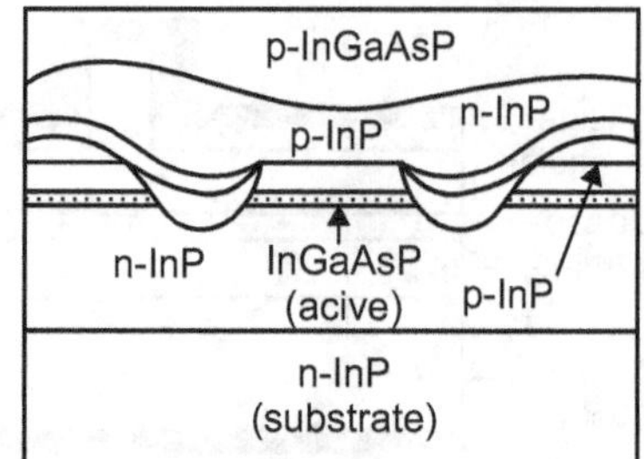

(b) InGaAsP/InP double channel planar BH device

Fig. 1.92 : Buried heterostructure laser structures

- The optical field is well confined in both the transverse and lateral directions within these lasers, providing strong index guiding of the optical mode together with good carrier confinement.

- Confinement of the injected current to the active region is obtained through the reverse biased junctions of the higher bandgap material.

- In Fig. 1.92, the higher bandgap, low refractive index, confinement material is AlGaAs for GaAs lasers operating in the 0.8 to 0.9 μm wavelength range, whereas it is InP in InGaAsP devices operating in the 1.1 to 1.6 μm wavelength range.

1.24.2.3 Quantum Well Lasers

- DH lasers are fabricated with very thin active layer thickness of around 10 nm instead of the typical range for conventional DH structures of 0.1 to 0.3 μm.

- The carrier motion normal to the active layer in these devices is restricted, resulting in a quantization of the kinetic energy into discrete energy levels for the carriers moving in that direction.

- This effect is similar to the well-known quantum mechanical problem of a one dimensional potential well, and therefore these devices are known as quantum well lasers.

- In this structure, the thin active layer causes drastic changes to the electronic and optical properties in comparison with a conventional DH laser.

- Quantum well lasers exhibit inherent advantages over conventional DH devices. In that, they allow high gain at low carrier density, thus providing the possibility of significantly lower threshold currents.

- Both Single Quantum Well (SQW) and Multi-Quantum Well (MQW) lasers are utilized, better confinement of the optical mode is obtained in MQW lasers in comparison with SQW lasers which result in lower threshold current density for these devices.

1.24.2.4 Quantum Dot Lasers

- Quantum well lasers that have been developed in the device, contain a single discrete atomic structure or so-called Quantum Dot (QD).

- Quantum dots are small elements that contain a tiny droplet of free electrons forming quantum well structures.

- Hence, a QD laser is also referred to as a dot-in-a well device.

- QD does not suffer from thermal broadening and their threshold current is also temperature insensitive.

- When the conventional injection lasers diode is considered as three dimensional and a quantum well is confined to two dimensions, then the QD structure can be considered to be zero dimensional.

- The size and shape of the structure for a QD laser can be altered as required during the fabrication process. Shapes such as cube, circular, disk, cylinder, pyramid or truncated pyramid can be created from self-organized crystalline growth of InGaAs material on the GaAs substrate.

- One of the important features of the QD laser is its very low-threshold current density. These low values of threshold current density makes it possible to create stacked or cascaded QD structures which provide high optical gain suitable for the short cavity transmitters and vertical cavity surface emitting lasers.

1.25 INJECTION LASER CHARACTERISTICS

1.25.1 Efficiency

- The operational efficiency of the semiconductor laser may be defined in a number of ways.

- A useful definition is that of the differential external quantum efficiency, η_D, which is the ratio of the increase in photon output rate for a given increase in the number of injected electrons. If P_e is the optical power emitted from the device, I is the current, e is the charge on an electron and hf is the photon energy, then

$$\eta_D = \frac{dP_e/hf}{dI/e} \simeq \frac{dP_e}{dI(Eg)} \qquad \dots (1.266)$$

- where Eg is the bandgap energy expressed in eV. η_D gives a measure of the rate of change of the optical output power with current and hence defines the slope of the output characteristics in the lasing region for a particular device.

- Hence, η_D is sometimes referred to as the slope quantum efficiency. For a CW semiconductor laser it usually has values in the range 40 to 60%.

- The internal quantum efficiency of the semiconductor laser η_i defined as:

$$\eta_i = \frac{\text{Number of photons produced in the laser cavity}}{\text{Number of injected electrons}} \quad \text{... (1.267)}$$

- May be quite high with values usually in the range 50 to 100%.
- It is related to the differential quantum efficiency by the expression:

$$\eta_D = \eta_i \left[\frac{1}{1 + 2\bar{\alpha} \, L/\ln(1/r_1 r_2)} \right] \quad \text{... (1.268)}$$

where is the loss coefficient of the laser cavity, L is the length of the laser cavity and r_1, r_2 are the cleaved mirror reflectivities.

- Total efficiency η_T which is defined as:

$$\eta_T = \frac{\text{Total number of output photons}}{\text{Total number of injected photons}} \quad \text{... (1.269)}$$

$$= \frac{P_e/hf}{I/e} \simeq \frac{P_e}{IEg} \quad \text{... (1.270)}$$

As power emitted P_e, changes linearly when the injection current I is greater than the threshold current I^{th} then:

$$\eta_T \simeq \eta_D \left(1 - \frac{I^{th}}{I} \right) \quad \text{... (1.271)}$$

For high injection current (e.g. I = 5 I^{th}) then $\eta_T \simeq \eta_D$, whereas for lower currents (I $\simeq$ 2 I^{th}) the total efficiency is lower and around 15 to 25%.

The external power efficiency of the device η_{ep} in converting electrical input to optical output is given by:

$$\eta_{ep} = \frac{P_e}{P} \times 100 \quad \text{... (1.272)}$$

$$= \frac{P_e}{IV} \times 100\% \quad \text{... (1.273)}$$

where,   P = IV is the d.c. electrical input power.

$$\eta_{ep} = \eta_T \left(\frac{Eg}{V} \right) \times 100\% \quad \text{... (1.274)}$$

Example 1.19 : *The total efficiency of an injection laser with a GaAs active region is 18%. The voltage applied to the device is 2.5 V and the bandgap energy for GaAs is 1.43 eV. Calculate, the external power efficiency of the device.*

Solution :

The external power efficiency is given by :

$$\eta_{ep} = 0.18 \left(\frac{1.43}{2.5} \right) \times 100$$

$$\simeq 10\%$$

This indicates the possibility of achieving high overall power efficiencies from semiconductor lasers which are much larger than the other laser types.

1.25.2 Threshold Current Temperature Dependence

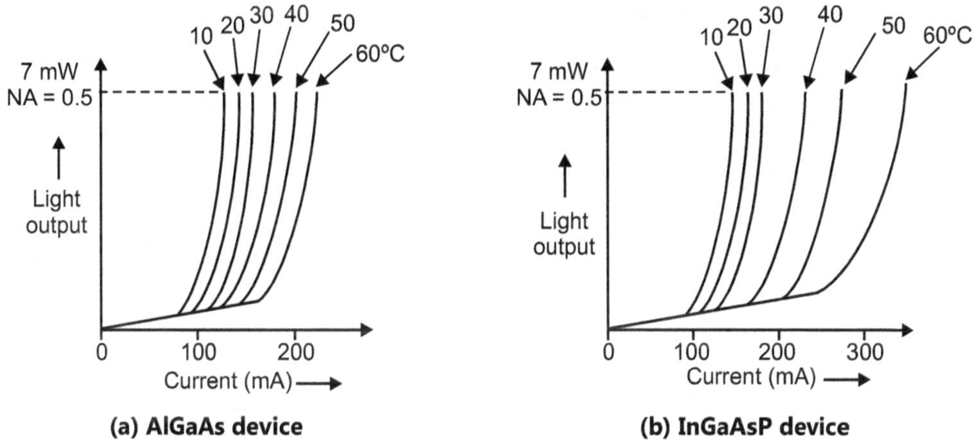

Fig. 1.93 : Variation in threshold current with temperature for gain guided injection lasers

- Fig. 1.93 shows the variation in threshold current with temperature for two gain guided injection lasers.

- In general, the threshold current tends to increase with temperature, the temperature dependence of the threshold current density J^{th} being approximately exponential for most of the common structures.

$$J^{th} \propto \exp \frac{T}{T_o} \qquad \qquad \text{... (1.275)}$$

where T is the device absolute temperature and T_o is the threshold temperature coefficient which is a characteristic temperature describing the quality of the material.

- For AlGaAs devices, T_o is usually in the range of 120 to 190 K, whereas for InGaAsP devices it is between 40 and 75 K.

- Intrinsic physical properties of the InGaAsP material system may cause it to have higher temperature sensitivity, these include Auger recombination, intervalance band absorption and carrier leakage effects over the heterojunctions.

- Auger recombination is a process where the energy released during the recombination of an electron-hole event is transferred to another carrier.

- During this process, when a carrier is excited to a higher energy level, it loses its surplus energy by emitting a photon in order to maintain thermal equilibrium.

- Auger recombination is not a single process but consists of many different processes, each of which may involve at least three particles. Auger recombination is not the main loss mechanism at room temperature. It dominates at elevated threshold current densities.

- These adverse effects may be reduced by using strained MQW structure for the laser.

1.25.3 Dynamic Response

- The dynamic behaviour of an injection laser is critical, especially when it is used in high bit rate optical communication systems. The application of a current step to the device results in a switch-on delay followed by high-frequency damped oscillations known as Relaxation Oscillations (ROs).

- Fig. 1.94 shows the dynamic behaviour of an injection laser and the corresponding injection current of the device showing relaxation oscillations and the switch-on delay.

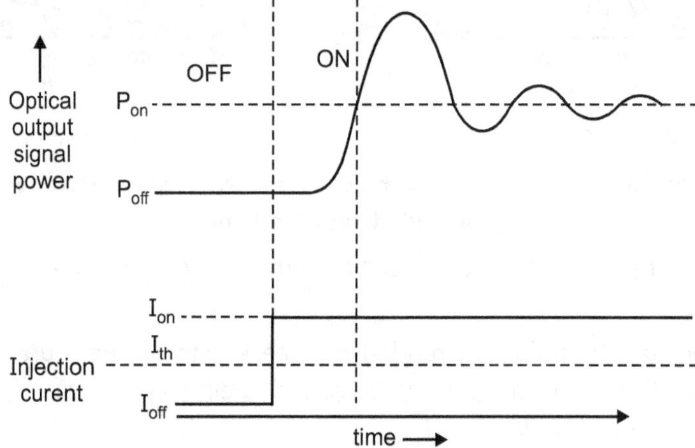

Fig. 1.94 : The dynamic behaviour of an injection laser

- The switch on or turn on delay is caused by the initial build-up of photon density resulting from stimulated emission. It is related to the minority carrier lifetime and the current through the device.

- The switch-on delay, may be reduced by biasing the laser near the threshold.

1.25.4 Frequency Chirp

- The d.c. modulation of a single longitudinal mode semiconductor laser can cause a dynamic shift of the peak wavelength emitted from the device.

- This phenomenon, which results in dynamic linewidth broadening under the direct modulation of the injection current, is referred to as **frequency chirping.**

- It arises from gain-induced variations in the laser refractive index due to the strong coupling between the free carrier density and the index of refraction which is present in any semiconductor structure.

- Hence, even small changes in carrier density will result in a phase shift of the optical field, giving an associated change in the resonance frequency within both Fabry-Perot and DFB laser structures.

- A number of techniques can be employed to reduce frequency chirp. One approach is to bias the laser sufficiently above threshold so that the modulation current does not drive the device below the threshold where the rate of change of optical output power varies rapidly with time.

1.25.5 Noise

- Another important characteristic of injection laser operation involves the noise behaviour of the device especially when considering analog transmission.

- The sources of noise are:

(a) Phase or frequency noise.

(b) Instabilities in operation such as Kinks in the light output against current characteristics and self pulsation.

(c) Reflection of light back into the device.

(d) Mode partition noise.

- Phase noise is an intrinsic property of all laser types. It results from the discrete and random spontaneous or stimulated transitions which cause intensity fluctuations in the optical emission.

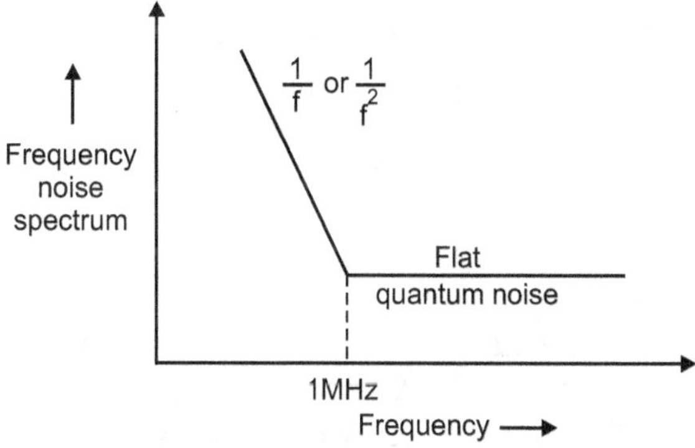

Fig. 1.95 : Spectral characteristic showing injection laser phase noise

- It has been observed that the spectral density of this phase of frequency noise has a characteristic represented by $1/f$ or $1/f^2$ upto a frequency of around 1 MHz as shown in Fig. 1.95.

- At frequencies above 1 MHz the noise spectrum is flat or white and is associated with quantum fluctuations which are a principal cause of linewidth broadening within semiconductor lasers.

- Optical feedback from unwanted external reflections can also affect the intensity and frequency stability of semiconductor lasers.

- Mode partition noise is a phenomenon which occurs in multimode semiconductor lasers where the modes are not well stabilized.

- The spectral fluctuations combined with the fiber dispersion produce random distortion of received pulses on a digital channel, causing an increase in bit-error rate.

- As mode partition noise is a function of laser spectral fluctuations, a reduced number of modes results in less pulse-width spreading.

- Thus, it provides low values of intermodal dispersion in the fiber. Reducing the number of modes in a multimode fiber decreases the mode partition noise.

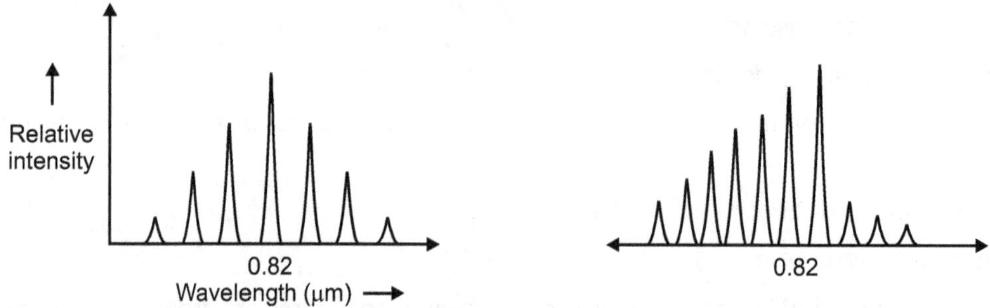

Fig. 1.96 : The effect of partition noise in a multimode injection laser

1.25.6 Mode Hopping

- Mode hopping to a longer wavelength as the current is increased above threshold is shown by comparison with the output spectrum in Fig. 1.97 (b).

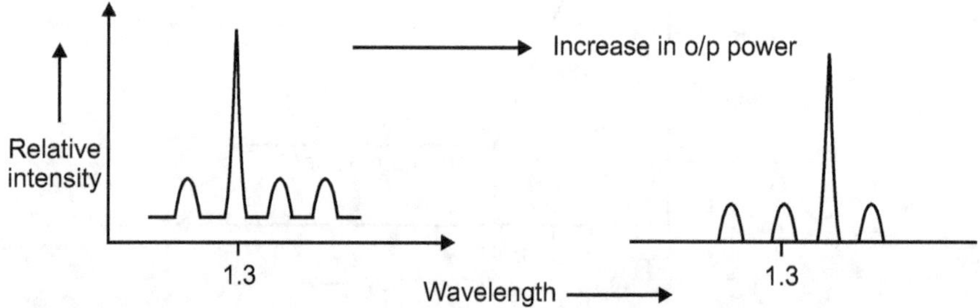

(a) Single longitudinal mode optical output   **(b) Mode hop to a longer peak emission wavelength at an increased optical power**

Fig. 1.97 : Mode hopping in a single mode injection laser

- The transition (hopping) from one mode to another is not a continuous function of the drive current but occurs suddenly over only 1 to 2 mA.

- Mode hopping alters the light output against current characteristic of the laser and is responsible for the Kinks observed in the characteristics of many single-mode devices.

1.25.7 Reliability

- Device reliability has been a major problem with injection lasers.

- Much progress has been made since the early days when device lifetimes were very short.

- The degradation behaviour may be separated into two major processes known as catastrophic and gradual degradation.

- Catastrophic degradation results from mechanical damage of the mirror facets and leads to a partial or complete laser failure.

- It happens due to the average optical flux density within the structure at the facet. Due to its occurrence the device is restricted for the operation and lifetime of CW devices.

- Gradual degradation mechanisms can be separated into two categories which are:

(a) Defect formation in the active region.

(b) Degradation of the current confining junctions.

These degradations are normally characterized by an increase in the threshold current for the laser which decreases its external quantum efficiency.

1.28 COMPARISON BETWEEN LED AND LASER SOURCE

LED Source	Laser Source
1. Output is coherent.	1. Highly coherent.
2. Optical cavity is not present for wavelength selectivity.	2. Optical cavity is present for wavelength selectivity.
3. Large beam divergence.	3. Highly directional monochromatic beam.
4. Can be easily coupled to multimode fibers.	4. Can be easily coupled to single mode fibers.
5. LEDs are used for high speed short haul local area applications.	5. Lasers can be used for high speed long haul wide area connection.
6. Less reactant towards the temperature changes.	6. More reactant towards the temperature changes.

1.29 OPTICAL DETECTOR

- The detector is an essential component of an optical fiber communication system. Its function is to convert the received optical signal into an electrical signal, which is then amplified before processing it further.

- Therefore the performance of the system is determined at the detector.

- The detector plays an important role and hence it must satisfy very stringent requirements for performance and compatibility.

The following criteria define the important performance and compatibility requirements for detectors:

- High sensitivity is required at the operating wavelength.

- To reproduce the received signal with fidelity, high fidelity is required. For analog communication linearity must be provided for a wide range of input signals.

- Large electrical response is required to the received optical signal. The quantum efficiency should be high.

- Short response time to obtain a suitable bandwidth.

- A minimum noise must be introduced by the detector.

- Stability of performance characteristics.

- The physical size of the detector must be small for efficient coupling to the fiber.

- Ideally, the detector should not require excessive bias voltages or currents.

- The detector must be capable of continuous stable operation at room temperature for many years. Therefore, high reliability is required.

- Low cost.

1.29.1 MATERIAL CONSIDERATION

- To detect an optical signal both external and internal photoemission of electrons may be utilized.

- Semiconductor photodiodes with or without internal gain, provide good performance and compatibility with relatively low cost.

- The semiconductor materials which are used for manufacturing photodiodes are Silicon, Germanium and increasing number of III - V alloys.

- Silicon photodiodes have high sensitivity over the 0.8 - 0.9 μm wavelength band and adequate speed, negligible shunt conductance, low dark current and long-term stability. Therefore, they are used in first generation systems.

- Their usefulness is limited to the first generation wavelength region because silicon has an indirect bandgap energy of 1.14 eV giving a loss in response above 1.09 μm.

- For second generation system in the wavelength range 1.1 to 1.6 μm which requires narrower bandgaps in the semiconductor, interest has focused on germanium and III - V alloys which gives a good response at longer wavelengths.

- Ideally, a photodiode material should be chosen with a bandgap energy slightly less than the photon energy corresponding to the longest operating wavelength of the system.

- This gives a high absorption coefficient to ensure a good response and yet limits the number of thermally generated carriers in order to achieve a low dark current.

- Germanium photodiodes have relatively large dark currents due to their narrow bandgap in comparision with other semiconductor materials.

- This is the major disadvantage with the use of germanium photodiodes, especially at shorter wavelengths.

- Due to the drawbacks with germanium direct bandgap III - V alloys are employed for the longer wavelength region.

- These materials are superior to germanium because their bandgaps can be changed to the desired wavelength by changing the relative concentrations of their constituents which results in lower dark currents.

- They may also be fabricated in heterojunction structures which increases their high-speed operation.

- Ternary alloys such as InGaAs and GaAlSb deposited on InP and GaSb substrates respectively has been used to fabricate photodiodes for the longer wavelength band.

- The alloy $In_{0.53}$ $Ga_{0.47}$ As lattice matched to InP which responds to the wavelength upto 1.7 μm has been used for the fabrication of photodiodes for operation at both 1.3 and 1.55 μm. Quaternary alloys can also be used for detection of these wavelengths.

- Both InGaAsP grown on InP and GaAlAsSb grown on GaSb have been studied, with the former material system finding significant application within advanced photodiode structures.

REVIEW QUESTIONS

1. Explain following types of fibers with their characteristics :

   (i) Single-mode step-index fibers.

   (ii) Multimode step-index fibers.

   (III) Multimode graded index fibers.

2. An optical fiber has core refractive index of 1.5 and cladding refractive index 1.45. Calculate the following :

   (i) Critical angle.

   (ii) Numerical aperture.

   (iii) Acceptance angle.

3. What is LASER? Explain the working of LASER. Compare LASER with LED.

4. Explain how light is propagated within a fiber. Determine the following terms with respect to an optical fiber

    (i)   Acceptance cone.

    (ii) Numerical aperture.

5. What is dispersion? Explain intermodal dispersion and intramodal dispersion

6. Describe the system design considerations involved in establishing point-to-point optical fiber link.   **(May-Jun 2014) [8]**

7. An engineer selects a fiber with a 25 µm core radius, a core index n_1 = 1.48 and Δ = 0.01

    (i)   If λ = 1310 nm, what is the value of normalized frequency V and how many modes propagate in the fiber?

    (ii) What percent of optical power flows in the cladding?

    (iii) If the core-cladding difference is reduced to Δ = 0.003, how many modes does the fiber support and what fraction of the optical power flows in the cladding?

8. An installed fiber has following specifications :

    Core diameter = 62.5 µm; NA= 0.275 and its operating wavelength is 1310 nm. Calculate the V number, the number of modes if the fiber is graded index and has a parabolic refractive index profile. What number of modes would be supported if instead, the fiber is of step index type. (May-Jun 2012)

9. Draw neat characteristics and show the operating ranges of the four key optical fiber link components on it . Comment precisely on these characteristics.

10. The International Telecommunication Union (ITU) has designated six spectral bands for use in optical fiber communication. State the name, designation and spectrum of each band.

11. State the key system requirements needed in analyzing a link. To fulfill these requirements explain the choice of components and their associated characteristics in a point-to-point optical link.

12. With a neat block diagram, explain the features of the key elements of an optical fiber transmission link.

13. The velocity of light in the core of a step index fiber is 2.01×10^8 m/s , and the critical angle at the core-clad interface is 80°. Determine the numerical aperture and the acceptance angle for the fiber in air, assuming it has a core diameter suitable for

consideration by ray analysis.

14. With reference to mode theory for optical propagation explain the terms: phase velocity, group velocity and group delay.

15. A graded index fiber with a parabolic index profile supports the propagation of 742 guided modes. The fiber has a numerical aperture in air of 0.3 and a core diameter of 70 µm. Determine the wavelength of the light propagating in the fiber. Further estimate the new maximum core diameter for single-mode operation at the same wavelength. Is the dispersion value positive or negative in this example? State the interpretation of negative sign.

16. Explain the terms: mode field diameter, spot size and cut off wavelength for single mode fibers.

17. A graded index fiber has a core with a parabolic refractive index profile which has a diameter of 50 µm. The fiber has numerical aperture of 0.2 Estimate the total number of guided modes propagating in the fiber when it is operating at a wavelength of 1.3 µm.

18. State and explain the advantages of optical fiber communication system.

19. A silica optical fiber with core diameter large enough to be considered by ray theory analysis has core refractive index of 1.5 and cladding refractive index of 1.47. Determine

   (i)   The critical angle at core cladding interface.

   (ii) The NA of the fiber.

   (iii) The acceptance angle in air for the fiber.

20. Compare (i) Multimode and Single mode fibers. (ii) Step index and Graded index fibers.

21. A graded index fiber with a parabolic refractive index profile core has a refractive index at the core axis of 1.5 and refractive index difference of 1% Estimate the maximum possible core diameter which allows single mode operation at wavelength of 1.55 µm.

22. Draw a neat block diagram of an optical fiber communication link and explain the function of each block.

23. A graded index fiber with a core axis refractive index of 1.5 has a refractive index profile 1.90, a relative refractive index difference of 1.3% and a core diameter of 40 µm. Estimate the number of guided modes propagating in the fiber when the transmitted light has a wavelength of 1.55 µm.

24. Compare in detail multimode and single mode step index fiber.

25. A step index fiber has core refractive index 1.5 and $\Delta = 1.3\%$ with core diameter of 100 μm. The operating wavelength is 850 nm. Calculate assuming that the fiber is kept in air, the :

    (i) Numerical aperture of fiber and acceptance angle.

    (ii) V parameter and number of modes.

    (iii) Does the number of modes in the fiber increase or decrease if :

        (A) n_1 increases and

        (B) if wave length increases.

26. A laboratory setup is tuned at 1310 nm, and a 62.5/125 multimode step index fiber with core refractive index 1.48 and clad index of 1.46 is used.

    Calculate :

    (i) Critical angle.

    (ii) Numerical aperture.

    (iii) Acceptance angle in air.

    (iv) Normalized frequency.

    (v) Total number of modes supported by this fiber.

    (vi) Fraction of power residing in the cladding if the total optical power in the fiber is 1 mW.

27. Describe with the aid of a neat diagram the basic principle of total internal reflection that enables the fiber to work as a light conduit.

28. Explain what is meant by a graded index optical fiber by giving an expression for refractive index profile n(r). State the major advantage of this type of fiber with regard to multimode propagation.

29. Using ray theory, derive an expression for the Numerical Aperture and the solid acceptance angle in terms of the physical parameters of a step index fiber and explain their importance in the propagation of optical signal through the fiber. Why do we need cladding?

30. Calculate the number of modes propagating at 820 nm wavelength in graded index fiber having parabolic refractive index profile. The core radius is 25 μm. The refractive index at the center of the core is 1.48 and cladding refractive index is 1.46.

31. Under what conditions of the propagation constant β mode remains guided in the core? Write an expression for the V number which is connected with the cutoff condition and determines the number of modes a fiber can support?

32. A step index fiber has core refractive index 1.5 and Δ = 1.3% with core diameter of 100 µm. The operating wavelength is 850 nm. Calculate assuming that the fiber is kept in air the

    (i)   Numerical Aperture of fiber.

    (ii) Acceptance angle.

    (iii) Critical angle.

    (iv) Angle of incidence.

33. What does the term the state of polarization mean? Does it describes the fiber properties? Explain.

34. A typical relative refractive index difference for an optical fiber designed for long distance transmission is 1.3%. Estimate the NA and the solid acceptance angle in air for the fiber when the core index is 1.48. Further, calculate the critical angle at the core-clading interface within the fiber. It may be assumed that the concepts of geometric optics for the fiber.

35. Explain the characteristics and operating ranges of the four key optical fiber link components.

36. Derive an expression for the acceptance angel for a skew ray which   changes direction by an angle 2γ at each reflection in a step index fiber   in terms of the fiber NA and γ. It may be assume that ray theory holds   for the fiber.

37. A single mode step index fiber has core and cladding refractive indices of 1.498 and 1.495 respectively. Determine the core diameter required for the fiber to permit its operation over the wavelength range 1.48 to 1.60 µm. Calculate the new fiber core diameter to enable single -mode transmission at a wavelength of 1.30 µm.

38. A step index fiber in air has a numerical aperture of 0.16, a core refractive index of 1.45 and a core diameter of 60 µm. Determine the normalized frequency for the fiber when light at a wavelength of 0.9 µm. is transmitted. Further, estimate the number of guided modes propagating in the fiber

---

39. An analog optical fiber communication system requires an SNR of 40 dB at the detector with a post-detection bandwidth of 30 MHz. Calculate the minimum optical power required at the detector if it is operating at a wavelength of 0.9 μm with a quantum efficiency of 70%. State any assumption made.

40. With reference to mode theory for optical propagation explain the following terms:

    (i)   Group velocity.

    (ii) Phase velocity.

    (iii) Group delay.

41. Compare :

    (i)   Multimode and single mode fibers.

    (ii) Step Index and graded Index fibers.

42. An optical fiber with 25μm core radius has core refractive index 1.48 and relative refractive index difference of 0.01.

    (i)   Calculate the value of normalized frequency and the number of   modes that can propagate through this fiber, if the wavelength of operation is 1310 nm.

    (ii) Calculate the percentage of optical power flow in the cladding.

    (iii) If the relative refractive difference is reduced to 0.001, how many modes are supported by the fiber and what fraction of the optical power flows in the cladding?

43. A graded index fiber with parabolic index profile supports the propagation of 742 guided modes. The fiber has numerical aperture in air of 0.3 and core diameter of 70 μm. Determine the wavelength of light propagating in the fiber. Also estimate the new maximum core diameter for single mode operation at same wavelength.

44. Velocity of light in the core of step index fiber is 2×10^8 m/sec and critical angle at core-cladding interface is 80o. Determine numerical aperture and acceptance angle for the fiber in the air, assuming it has core diameter suitable for consideration by ray analysis.

Unit II

LIGHT WAVE SYSTEMS

2.1 INTRODUCTION

- The preceding chapter focused on the three main components of a Fiber-optic communication system optical fibers, optical transmitters, and optical receivers.

- In this chapter we consider the issues related to system design and performance when the three components are put together to form a practical lightwave system.

2.2 SYSTEM ARCHITECTURES

- From an architectural standpoint, fiber-optic communication systems can be classified into three broad categories point-to-point links, distribution networks, and local-area networks. This section focuses on the main characteristics of these three system architectures.

2.2.1 Point-to-Point Links

- Point-to-Point links constitute the simplest kind of lightwave systems. Their role is to transport information, available in the form of a digital bit stream, from one place to another as accurately as possible.

- The link length can vary from less than a kilometer (short haul) to thousands of kilometers (long haul), depending on the specific application.

- For example, optical data links are used to connect computers and terminals within the same building or between two buildings with a relatively short transmission distance (< 10 km).

- The low loss and the wide bandwidth of optical fibers are not of primary importance for such data links; fibers are used mainly because of their other advantages, such as immunity to electromagnetic interference. In contrast, undersea lightwave systems are used for high-speed transmission across continents with a link length of several thousands of kilometers.

- Low losses and a large bandwidth of optical fibers are important factors in the design of transoceanic systems from the standpoint of reducing the overall operating cost.

- When the link length exceeds a certain value, in the range 20-100 km depending on the operating wavelength, it becomes necessary to compensate for fiber losses, as the signal would otherwise become too weak to be detected reliably.

- Fig. 2.1 shows two schemes used commonly for loss compensation.

- Until 1990 optoelectronic repeaters, called regenerators because they regenerate the optical signal, were used exclusively.

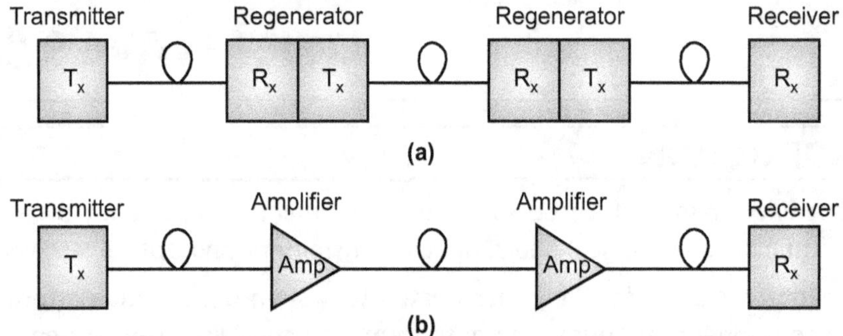

Fig. 2.1 : Point-to-point fiber links with periodic loss compensation through

(a) regeneration and (b) optical amplifiers.

- As seen in Fig. 2.1(a), a regenerator is nothing but a receiver-transmitter pair that detects the incoming optical signal, recovers the electrical bit stream, and then converts it back into optical form by modulating an optical source.

- Fiber losses can also be compensated by using optical amplifiers, which amplify the optical bit stream directly without requiring conversion of the signal to the electric domain. The advent of optical amplifiers around 1990 revolutionized the development of fiber-optic communication systems.

- Amplifiers are especially valuable for wavelength division multiplexed (WDM) lightwave systems as they can amplify many channels simultaneously.

- Optical amplifiers solve the loss problem but they add noise and worsen the impact of fiber dispersion and nonlinearity since signal degradation keep on accumulating over multiple amplification stages.

- Indeed, periodically amplifier lightwave systems are often limited by fiber dispersion unless dispersion-compensation techniques are used.

- Optoelectronic repeaters do not suffer from this problem as they regenerate the original bit stream and thus effective compensate for all sources of signal degradation automatically.

- An optical regenerator should perform the same three functions reamplification, reshaping, and retiming (the 3Rs) to replace an optoelectronic repeater. Although considerable research effort is being directed toward developing such all-optical regenerators, most terrestrial systems use a combination of the two techniques shown in Fig. 2.1 and place an optoelectronic regenerator after a certain number of optical amplifiers.

- Until 2000, the regenerator spacing was in the range of 600-800 km. since then, ultralong-haul systems have been developed that are capable of transmitting optical signals over 3000 km or more without using a regenerator.

- The spacing L between regenerators or optical amplifiers, often called the repeater spacing, is a major design parameter simply because the system cost reduces as L increases.

- The distance L depends on the bit rate B because of fiber dispersion.

- The bit rate-distance product, BL, is generally used as a major of the system performance for point-to-point links. The BL product depends on the operating wavelength, since both fiber losses and fiber dispersion are wavelength dependent.

- The first three generations of lightwave systems correspond to three different operating wavelengths near 0.85, 1.3 and 1.66 μm. Whereas the BL product was ~ 1(Gb/s) - km for the first generation systems operating near 0.85 μm, it becomes ~1(Tb/s) – km for the third generation systems operating near 1.55 μm and can exceed 100 (Tb/s) – km for the fourth generation systems.

2.2.2 Distributed Networks

- Many applications of optical communication systems require that information is not only transmitted but is also distributed to a group of subscribers.

- Examples include local-loop distribution of telephone services and broadcast of multiple video channels over cable television (CATV, short for common antenna television).

- Considerable effort is directed toward the integration of audio and video services through a broadband integrated-services digital network (ISDN).

- Such a network has the ability to distribute a wide range of services, including telephone, facsimile, computer data, and video broadcasts.

- Transmission distances are relatively short (L < 50 km), but the bit rate can be as high as 10 Gb/s for a broadband ISDN.

- Fig. 2.2 shows two topologies for distribution networks. In the case of hub topology, channel distribution takes place at central locations (or hubs), where an automated cross-connect facility switches channels in the electrical domain.

- Such networks are called metropolitan-area networks (MANs) as hubs are typically located in major cities.

- The role of fiber is similar to the case of point-to-point links.

- Since the fiber bandwidth is generally much larger than that required by a single hub office, several offices can share a single fiber headed for the main hub.

- Telephone networks employ hub topology is related to its reliability outage of a single fiber cable can affect the service to a large portion of the network.

- Additional point-to-point links can be used to guard against such a possibility by connecting important hub locations directly.

- In the case of bus topology, a single fiber cable carries the multichannel optical signal throughout the area of service.

- Distribution is done by using optical taps, which divert a small fraction of the optical power to each subscriber.

- A simple CATV application of bus topology consists of distributing multiple video channels within a city.

- The use of optical fiber permits distribution of a large number of channels (100 or more) because of its large bandwidth compared with coaxial cables.

- The advent of high definition television (HDTV) also requires lightwave transmission because of a large bandwidth (about 100 Mb/s) of each video channel unless a compression technique (such as MPEG-2 or 2nd recommendation of the motion picture entertainment group) is used.

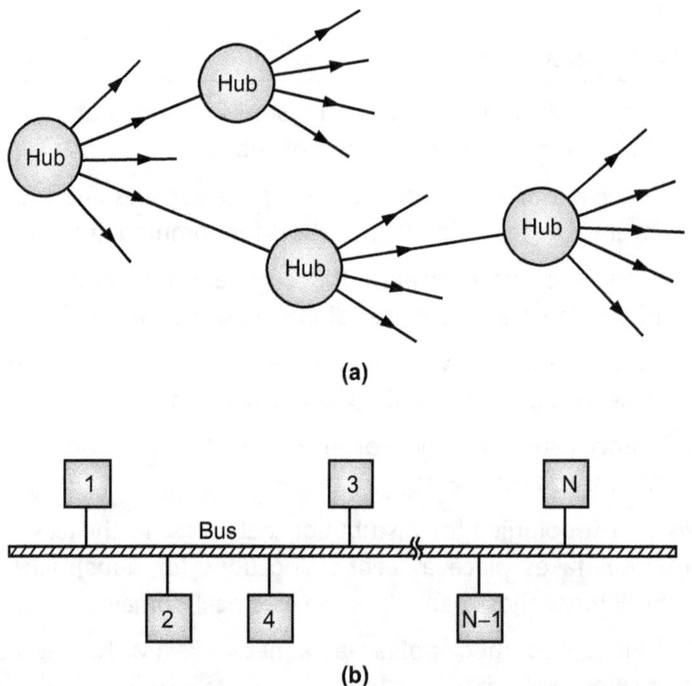

Fig. 2.2 : (a) Hub topology and (b) bus topology for distribution networks.

- A problem with the bus topology is that the signal loss increases exponentially with the number of taps and limits the number of subscribers served by a single optical bus. Even when fiber losses are neglected, the power available at the Nth tap is given by

$$P_N = P_T C[(1 - \delta)(1 - C)]^{N-1} \qquad \ldots (2.1)$$

- Where P_T is the transmitted power, C is the fraction of power coupled out at each tap, and δ accounts for insertion losses, assumed to be the same at each tap.

- If we use $\delta = 0.05$, $C = 0.05$, $P_T = 1$ mW and $P_N = 0.1$ μW as illustrative values, N should not exceed 60.

- A solution to this problem is offered by optical amplifiers which can boost the optical power of the bus periodically and thus permit distribution to a large number of subscribers as long as the effects of fiber dispersion remain negligible.

2.2.3 Local Area Networks

- Many applications of fiber optic communication technology require networks in which a large number of users within a local area (e.g., a university campus) are interconnected in such a way that any user can access the network randomly to transmit data to any other user.

- Such networks are called local-area networks (LANs). Optical access networks used in a local subscriber loop also fall in this category.

- Since the transmission distances are relatively short (< 10 km), fiber losses are not of much concern for LAN applications.

- The major motivation behind the use of optical fibers is the large bandwidth offered by fiber optic communication systems.

- The main difference between MANs and LANs is related to the random access offered to multiple users of a LAN.

- The system architecture plays an important role for LANs. Since the establishment of predefined protocol rules is a necessity in such an environment.

- Three commonly used topologies are known as bus, ring, and star configurations. The bus topology is similar to that shown in Fig. 2.2 (b).

- A well known example of bus topology is provided by the Ethernet, a network protocol used to connect multiple computers and used by the Internet.

- The Ethernet operates at speeds up to 1 Gb/s by using a protocol based on carrier-sense multiple access (CSMA) with collision detection.

- Although the Ethernet LAN architecture has proven to be quite successful when coaxial cables are used for the bus, a number of difficulties arise when optical fibers are used.

- A major limitation is related to the losses occurring at each tap, which limits the number of users.

- Fig. 2.3 shows the ring and star topologies for LAN applications. In the ring topology, consecutive nodes are connected by point-to-point links to form a closed ring.

- Each node can transmit and receive the data by using a transmitter-receiver pair which also acts as a repeater.

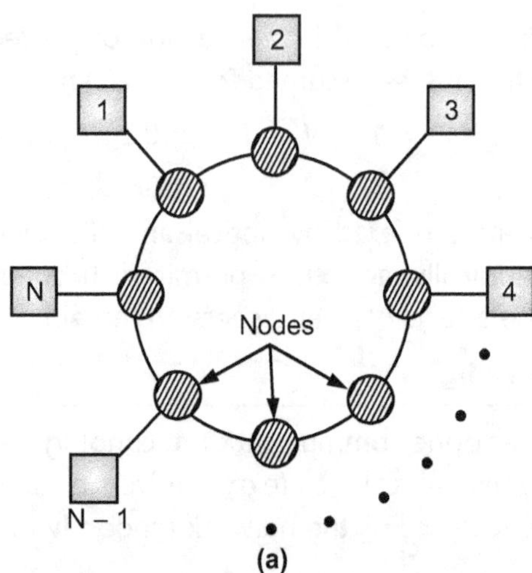

Fig. 2.3 : (a) Ring topology and (b) star topology for local area networks

- A token (a predefined bit sequence) is passed around the ring.
- Each node monitors the bit stream to listen for its own address and to receive the data.
- It can also transmit by appending the data to an empty token.
- The use of ring topology for fiber-optic LANs has been commercialized with the standardized interface known as the fiber distributed data interface, FDDI for short.
- The FDDI operates at 100 Mb/s by using multimode fibers and 1.3 µm transmitters based on light emitting diodes (LEDs). It is designed to provide backbone services such as the interconnection of lower speed LANs or mainframe computers.
- In the star topology, all nodes are connected through point-to-point links to a central node called a hub, or simply a star.
- Such LANs are further subclassified as active-star or passive-star networks, depending on whether the central node is an active or passive device.
- In the active star configuration, all incoming optical signals are converted to the electrical domain through optical receivers.
- The electrical signal is then distributed to drive individual node transmitters. Switching operations can also be performed at the central node since distribution takes place in the electrical domain.
- In the passive star configuration, distribution takes place in the optical domain through devices such as directional couplers.
- Since the input from one node is distributed to many output nodes, the power transmitted to each node depends on the number of users.
- Similar to the case of bus topology, the number of users supported by passive-star LANs is limited by the distribution losses. For an ideal $N \times N$ star coupler, the power reaching each node is simply P_T/N (if we neglect transmission losses) since the transmitted power P_T is divided equally among N users.

- For a passive star composed of directional couplers, the power is further reduced because of insertion losses and can be written as

$$P_N = (P_T/N)(1 - \delta) \log_2 N \qquad \text{... (2.2)}$$

- Where δ is the insertion loss of each directional coupler. If we use $\delta = 0.05$, $P_T = 1$ mW and $P_N = 0.1$ µW as illustrative values, N can be as large as 500. This value of N should be compared with N = 60 obtained for the case of bus topology by using Equation (2.1). A relatively large value of N makes star topology attractive for LAN applications.

2.3 DESIGN GUIDELINES

- The design of fiber-optic communication systems requires a clear understanding of the limitations imposed by the loss, dispersion and nonlinearity of the fiber. Since fiber properties are wavelength dependent, the choice of operating wavelength is a major design issue. In this section we will discuss how the bit rate and the transmission distance of a single channel system are limited by fiber loss and dispersion.

2.3.1 Loss-limited Lightwave Systems

- Except for some short-haul fiber links, fiber losses play an important role in the system design. Consider an optical transmitter that is capable of launching an average power $\overline{P}_{tr}$. If the signal is detected by a receiver that requires a minimum average power $\overline{P}_{rec}$ at the bit rate B, the maximum transmission distance is limited by

$$L = \frac{10}{a_f} \log_{10} \left(\frac{\overline{P}_{tr}}{\overline{P}_{rec}} \right) \qquad \text{... (2.3)}$$

In this equation it is α_f, make the changes

- Where α_f is the net loss (in dB/km) of the fiber cable, including splice and connector losses. The bit-rate dependence of L arises from the linear dependence of $\overline{P}_{rec}$ on the bit rate B.

- Noting that $P_{rec} = N_p hvB$, where hv is the photon energy and $\overline{N}_p$ is the average number of photons/bit required by the receiver, the distance L decreases logarithmically as B increases at a given operating wavelength.

- The solid lines in Fig. 2.4 show the dependence of L on B for three common operating wavelengths of 0.85, 1.3 and 1.55 µm by using $\alpha_f = 2.5$, 0.4 and 0.25 dB/km, respectively.

- The transmitted power is taken to be $\overline{P}_{tr} = 1$ mW at the three wavelengths, whereas $\overline{N}_p = 500$ at 1.3 and 1.55 µm.

- The smallest value of L occurs for first-generation systems operating at 0.85 µm because of relatively large fiber losses near that wavelength.

- The repeater spacing of such systems is limited to 10-25 km, depending on the bit rate and the exact value of the loss parameter. In contrast, a repeater spacing of more than 100 km is possible for lightwave systems operating near 1.55 µm.

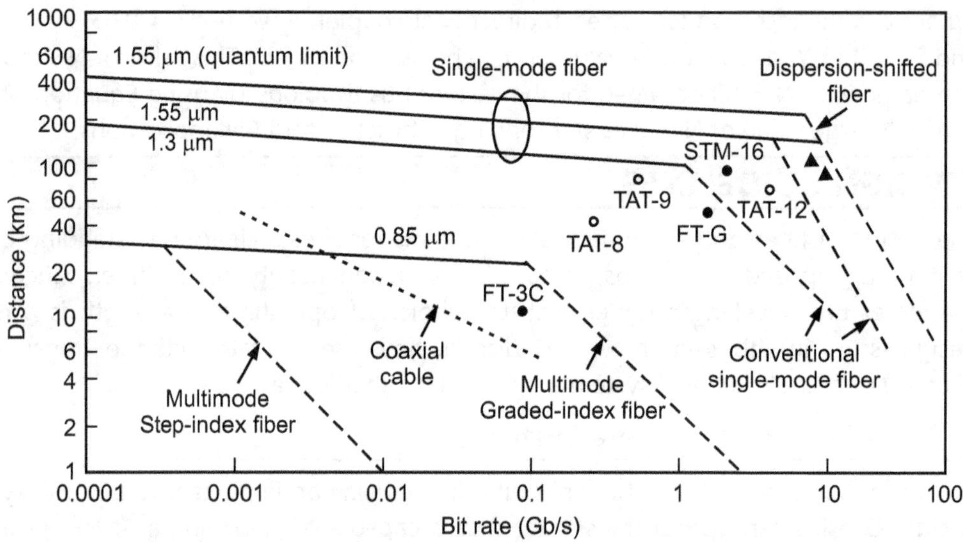

Fig. 2.4 : Loss (solid lines) and dispersion (dashed lines) limits on transmission distance L as a function of bit rate B for the three wavelength windows.

- It is interesting to compare the loss limit of 0.85 µm lightwave systems with that of electrical communication systems based on coaxial cables.

- The dotted line in Fig. 2.4 shows the bit-rate dependence of L for coaxial cables by assuming that the loss increases as $\sqrt{B}$.

- The transmission distance is larger for coaxial cables at smaller bit rates (B < Mb/s), but fiber-optic systems take over at bit rates in excess of 5 Mb/s. Since a longer transmission distance translates into a smaller number of repeaters in a long-haul point-to-point link, fiber-optic communication systems offer an economic advantage when the operating bit rate exceeds 10 Mb/s.

- The system requirements typically specified in advance are the bit rate B and the transmission distance L. the performance criterion is specified through the Bit-Error Rate (BER), a typical requirement being BER < 10^{-9}. The first decision of the system designer concerns the choice of the operating wavelength.

- As a practical matter, the cost of components is lowest near 0.85 µm and increases as wavelength shifts toward 1.3 and 1.55 µm.

- Fig. 2.4 can be quite helpful in determining the appropriate operating wavelength. Generally speaking, a fiber-optic link can operate near 0.85 µm is B < 200 Mb/s and L < 20 km. This is the case for many LAN applications.

- On the other hand, the operating wavelength is by necessity in the 1.55 μm region for long haul lightwave systems operating at bit rates in excess of 2 Gb/s. The curves shown in Fig. 2.4 provide only a guide to the system design.

- Many other issues need to be addressed while designing a realistic fiber-optic communication system.

- Among them are the choice of the operating wavelength, selection of appropriate transmitters, receivers, and fibers, compatibility of various components, issue of cost versus performance, and system reliability and upgradability concerns.

2.3.2 Dispersion-Limited Lightwave Systems

- When the dispersion limited transmission distance is shorter than the loss-limited distance of Equation (2.3), the system is said to be dispersion limited.

- The dashed lines in Fig. 2.4 show the dispersion–limited transmission distance as a function of the bit rate. Since physical mechanisms leading to dispersion limitation can be different for different operating wavelengths.

- Consider first the case of 0.85 μm lightwave systems, which often use multimode fibers to minimize the system cost. The most limiting factor for multimode fibers is intermodal dispersion. In the case of step-index multimode fibers, provides an approximate upper bound on the BL product.

- A slightly more restrictive condition BL = $c/(2n_1\Delta)$ is plotted in Fig. 2.4 by using typical values n_1 = 1.46 and Δ = 0.01. Even at a low bit rate of 1 Mb/s, such multimode systems are dispersion-limited, and their transmission distance is limited to below 10 km. For this reason, multimode step-index fibers are rarely used in the design of fiber-optic communication systems.

- Considerable improvement can be realized by using graded index fibers for which intermodal dispersion limits the BL product to values given the condition BL = $2c/(n_1\Delta^2)$ is plotted in Fig. 2.4 and shows that 0.85 μm lightwave systems are loss-limited, rather than dispersion-limited, for bit rates up to 100 Mb/s when graded-index fibers are used.

- The first generation of terrestrial telecommunication systems took advantage of such an improvement and used graded-index fibers. The first commercial system became available in 1980 and operated at a bit rate of 45 Mb/s with a repeater spacing of less than 10 km.

- The second generation of lightwave systems used primarily single-mode fibers near the minimum-dispersion wavelength occurring at about 1.31 μm.

- The most limiting factor for such systems is dispersion-induced pulse broadening dominated by a relatively large source spectral width. The BL product is then limited by

$$BL \leq (4\,|\,D\,|\,\sigma_\lambda)^{-1} \qquad\qquad ... (2.4)$$

- Where σ_λ is the root-mean-square (RMS) width of the source spectrum. The actual value of $|D|$ depends on how close the operating wavelength is to the zero-dispersion wavelength of the fiber and is typically ~ 1 ps/(km-nm).

- Fig. 2.4 shows the dispersion limit for 1.3 µm lightwave systems by choosing $|D|\ \sigma_\lambda = 2$ ps/km so that $BL \leq 125$ (Gb/s)-km as seen there, such systems are generally loss-limited for bit rates up to 1 Gb/s but become dispersion-limited at higher bit rates.

- Third and fourth generation lightwave systems operate near 1.55 µm to take advantage of the smallest fiber losses occurring in this wavelength region.

- However, fiber dispersion becomes a major problem for such systems since $D \approx 16$ ps/(km-nm) near 1.55 µm for standard silica fibers. Semiconductor lasers operating in a single longitudinal mode provide a solution to this problem. The ultimate limit is then given by

$$B^2 L \ < \ (16\,|\beta_2|) - 1 \qquad\qquad \dots (2.5)$$

- Where β_2 is related to D as in Equation (2.5). Fig 2.4 shows this limit by choosing $B^2 L = 4000$ (Gb/s)^2-km. as seen there, such 1.55 µm systems becomes dispersion-limited only for $B > 5$ Gb/s.

- In practice, the frequency chirp imposed on the optical pulse during direct modulation provides a much more severe limitation.

- The effect of frequency chirp on system performance is qualitatively speaking, the frequency chirp manifests through a broadening of the pulse spectrum. If we use Equation (2.4) with $D = 16$ ps/(km-nm) and $\sigma_\lambda = 0.1$ nm, the BL product is limited to 150 (Gb/s)-m as a result, the frequency chirp limits the transmission distance to 75 km at $B = 2$ Gb/s, even though loss-limited distance exceeds 150 km the frequency chirp problem is often solved by using an external modulator for systems operating at bit rates > 5 Gb/s.

- A solution to the dispersion problem is offered by dispersion-shifted fibers for which dispersion and loss both are minimum near 15.55 µm. Fig. 2.4 shows the improvement by using Equation (2.5) with $|\beta_2| = 2$ ps^2/km.

- Such systems can be operated at 20 Gb/s with a repeater spacing of about 80 km, further improvement is possible by operating the lightwave system very close to the zero-dispersion wavelength, a task that requires careful matching of the laser wavelength to the zero-dispersion wavelength and is not always feasible because of variations in the dispersive properties of the fiber along the transmission link.

- In practice, the frequency chirp makes it difficult to achieve even the limit indicated in Fig. 2.4. By 1989, two laboratory experiments had demonstrated transmission over 81 km at 11 Gb/s and over 100 km at 10 Gb/s by using low-chirp semiconductor lasers together with dispersion-shifted fibers.

- The triangles in Fig. 2.4 shows that such systems operate quite close to the fundamental limits set by fiber dispersion. Transmission over longer distances requires the use of dispersion-management techniques.

2.4 OPTICAL POWER BUDGET

- The purpose of the power budget is to ensure that enough power will reach the receiver to maintain reliable performance during the entire system lifetime.

- The minimum average power required by the receiver is the receiver sensitivity $\bar{P}_{rec}$ the average launch power $\bar{P}_{tr}$ is generally known for any transmitter.

- The power budget takes an especially simple form in decibel units with optical powers expressed in dBm units. More specifically,

$$\bar{P}_{tr} = \bar{P}_{rec} + C_L + M_S \qquad \ldots (2.6)$$

- Where C_L is the total channel loss and M_s is the system margin.

- The purpose of system margin is to allocate a certain amount of power to additional sources of power penalty that may develop during system lifetime because of component degradation or other unforeseen events. A system margin of 4-6 dB is typically allocated during the design process.

- The channel loss C_L should take into account all possible sources of power loss, including connector and splice losses. If α_f is the fiber loss in decibels per kilometer, C_L can be calculated as

$$C_L = \alpha_f L + \alpha_{con} + \alpha_{splice} \qquad \ldots (2.7)$$

- Where α_{con} and α_{splice} account for the connector and splice losses throughout the fiber link.

- Sometimes splice loss is included within the specified loss of the fiber cable. The connector loss α_{con} includes connectors at the transmitter and receiver ends but must include other connectors if used within the fiber link.

- Equations (2.6) and (2.7) can be used to estimate the maximum transmission distance for a given choice of the components.

- As a illustration, consider the design of a fiber link operating at 100 Mb/s and requiring a maximum transmission distance of 8 km. as seen in Fig. 2.4, such a system can be designed to operate near 0.85 µm provided that a graded-index multimode fiber is used for the optical cable.

- The operation near 0.85 µm is desirable from the economic standpoint. Once the operating wavelength is selected, a decision must be made about the appropriate transmitters and receivers.

- The GaAs transmitter can use a semiconductor laser or an LED as an optical source. Similarly, the receiver can be designed to use either a p-i-n or an avalanche photodiode.

- Keeping the low cost in mind, let us choose a p-i-n receiver and assume that it requires 2500 photons/bit on average to operate reliably with a BER below 10^{-9}.

- Using the relation $P_{rec} = N_p\, h\nu B$ with $N_p = 2500$ and $B = 100$ Mb/s, the receiver sensitivity is given by $P_{rec} = -42$ dBm. The average launch power for LED and laser-based transmitters is typically 40 μW and 1 mW, respectively.

- Table 2.1 shows the power budget for the two transmitters by assuming that the splice loss is included within the cable loss.

- The transmission distance L is limited to 6 km in the case of LED-based transmitters. If the system specification is 8 km, a more expensive laser-based transmitter must be used. The alternative is to use an Avalanche Photodiode (APD) receiver.

- If the receiver sensitivity improves by more than 7 dB when an APD is used in place of a p-i-n photodiode, the transmission distance can be increased to 8 km even for an LED-based transmitter. Economic considerations would then dictate the choice between the laser-based transmitters and APD receivers.

Table 2.1 : Power Budget of a 0.85 μm Lightwave System

Quantity	Symbol	Laser	LED
Transmitter power	$\bar{P}_{tr}$	0 dBm	– 13 dBm
Receiver sensitivity	$\bar{P}_{rec}$	– 42 dBm	– 42 dBm
System margin	M_s	6 dB	6 dB
Available channel loss	C_L	36 dB	23 dB
Connector loss	α_{con}	2 dB	2 dB
Fiber cable loss	α_f	3.5 dB/km	3.5 dB/km
Maximum fiber length	L	9.7 km	6 km

Fig. 2.5 shows the link power budget which can be represented graphically as below.

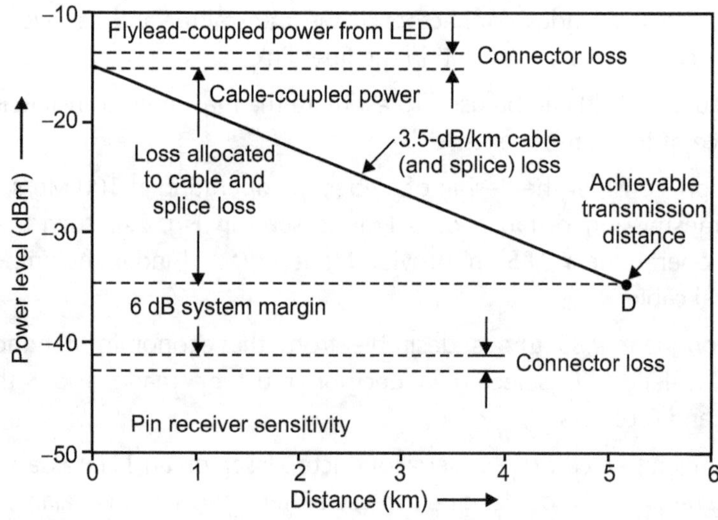

Fig. 2.5 : Graphical representation of a link loss budget for an 850 nm LED/pin system operating at 20 Mb/s

The vertical axis represents the optical power loss allowed between the transmitter and the receiver. The horizontal axis give the transmission distance. Here, we show a silicon pin receiver with a sensitivity of – 42 dBm (at 20 Mb/s) and a LED with an output power of –13 dBm coupled into a fiber flylead. We subtract a 1-dB connector loss at each end, which leaves a total margin of 27 dB. Subtracting a 6-dB system safety margin leaves us with a tolerable loss of 21-dB that can be allocated to the cable and splice loss. The slope of the line shown in Fig. 2.5 is the 3.5 dB/km cable loss. This line starts at the – 14-dBm point and ends at the 35-dBm level. The intersection point D then defines the maximum possible transmission path length.

Another example is for a 2.5 Gb/s link that may be used for SONET OC-48 or SDH STM-16.

Consider a 1550 nm laser diode that launches a +3-dBm (2 mw) optical power level into a fiber flylead, an INGaAs APD with a –32 dBm sensitivity at 2.5 Gb/s and a 60 km long optical cable with a 0.3 dB/km attenuation. Assume that here, because of the way the equipment is arranged, a 5 m optical jumper cable is needed at each end between the end of the transmission cable and the SONET equipment rack as shown in Fig. 2.6. Assume that each jumper cable introduces a loss of 3-dB. In addition, assume that a 1-dB connector loss occurs at each fiber joint.

Table 2.2 lists the components in column 1 and the associated optical output, sensitivity or loss in column 2. Column 3 gives the power margin available after subtracting the component loss from the total optical power loss that is allowed between the light source and the photodetector, which, in this case, is 35-dB, adding all the losses results in a final power margin of 7-dB.

Table 2.2: Example of a Spreadsheet for Calculating an Optical-Link Power Budget

Component/Loss parameters	Output/Sensitivity/Loss	Power Margin
Laser output	3 dBm	–
APD sensitivity at 2.5 Gb/s Allowed loss [3 – (–32)]	–32 dBm	35
Source connector loss	1 dB	34
Jumper + Connector loss	3 + 1 dB	30
Cable attenuation (60 km)	18 dB	12
Jumper + Connector loss	3 + 1 dB	8
Receiver connector loss	1 dB	7 (final margin)

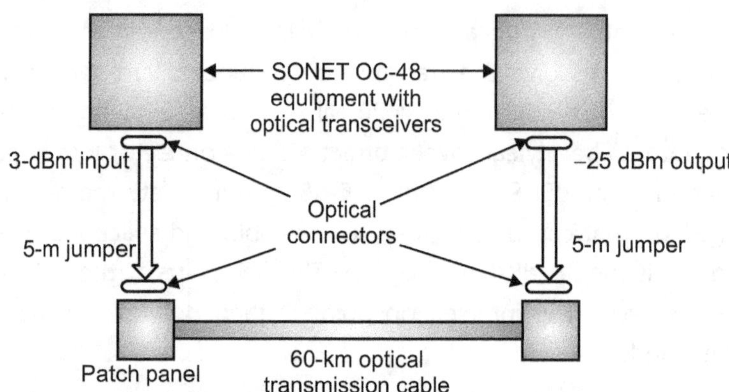

Fig. 2.6 : A 2.5 Gb/s 60 km optical fiber link with 5 m optical jumper cables at each end

2.5 Rise-Time Budget

A rise-time budget is a convenient method for determining the dispersion limitation of an optical fiber link. This is helpful for digital system. In this approach, the total rise-time t_{sys} of the link is the root sum square of the rise times from each contributor t_i to the pulse rise-time degradation:

$$t_{sys} = \left(\sum_{i=1}^{N} t_i^2 \right)^{1/2} \qquad \ldots (2.8)$$

The elements which limit the system speed are the transmitter rise-time t_{tx} , the group Velocity Dispersion (GVD), rise-time t_{GVD} of the fiber, the modal dispersion rise-time t_{mod} of the fiber and the receiver rise-time t_{rx}.

Single mode fibers do not exhibit modal dispersion, so rise-time in these fibers is related only to GVD.

The rise time of the transmitters and receiver are generally known to the designer. The transmitter rise time is attributable primarily to the light source and its drive circuitry. The receiver rise time results from the photodetector response and the 3-dB electrical bandwidth of the receiver front end.

The rise time t_{rx} of the receiver is usually defined as 'the time interval between g(t) = 0.1 and g(t) = 0.9'. This is known as the 10 to 90% rise time.

If B_{rx}, 3-dB electrical bandwidth of the receiver, is given in megahertz, then the receiver front end rise time in nanoseconds is

$$t_{rx} = \frac{350}{B_{rx}} \qquad \ldots (2.9)$$

Determining the fiber rise times resulting from GVD and modal dispersion is more complex than that for the case of a single uniform fiber.

The fiber rise time, t_{GVD}, resulting from GVD over a length L can be approximated as

$$t_{GVD} \approx |D|\,L\sigma_\lambda \qquad \qquad \text{... (2.10)}$$

where σ_λ is the half power spectral width of the source and the dispersion (D) value changes from fiber section to section in a long link, an average value should be used for D.

The bandwidth B_M in a link of length L can be expressed to a reasonable approximation as

$$B_M(L) = \frac{B_O}{L^q} \qquad \qquad \text{... (2.11)}$$

where the parameter q ranges between 0.5 and 1 and B_O is the bandwidth of a 1 km length of cable. A value of q = 0.5 indicates that a steady state model equilibrium has been reached, whereas q = 1 indicates little mode mixing. Based on field experience, a reasonable estimate is q = 0.7.

Another expression for B_M based on curve fitting of experimental data, is

$$\frac{1}{B_M} = \left[\sum_{n=1}^{N} \left(\frac{1}{B_n}\right)^{1/q}\right]^q \qquad \qquad \text{... (2.12)}$$

where the parameter q ranges between 0.5 and 1.0 and B_n is the bandwidth of the nth fiber section.

$$t_M(N) = \left[\sum_{n=1}^{N} (t_n)^{1/q}\right]^q \qquad \qquad \text{... (2.13)}$$

where $t_M(N)$ is the pulse broadening occurring over N cable sections in which the individual pulse broadenings are given by t_n.

Now find out the relation between the fiber rise time and the 3-dB bandwidth. Assume that the optical power emerging from the fiber has a Gaussian temporal response.

$$G(t) = \frac{1}{\sqrt{2\pi\sigma}}\, e^{-t^2/2\sigma^2} \qquad \qquad \text{... (2.14)}$$

where σ is the rms pulse width.

The Fourier transform of this function is

$$G(\omega) = \frac{1}{\sqrt{2\pi}}\, e^{-\omega^2\sigma^2/2} \qquad \qquad \text{... (2.15)}$$

The time required for the pulse to reach its half maximum value i.e. the time required to have

$$g(t_{1/2}) = 0.5\, g(0) \qquad \qquad \text{... (2.16)}$$

is given by

$$t_{1/2} = (2ln2)^{1/2}\, \sigma \qquad \qquad \text{... (2.17)}$$

The relation between full width half maximum rise time t_{FWHM} and the 3-dB optical bandwidth is

$$f_{3dB} \;=\; B_{3dB} = \frac{0.44}{t_{FWHM}} \qquad \qquad \dots (2.18)$$

t_{FWHM} is given as

$$t_{FWHM} \;=\; 2\, t_{1/2} = 2\sigma\,(2\ln2)^{1/2} \qquad \qquad \dots (2.19)$$

Let t_{FWHM} be the rise time resulting from modal dispersion then

$$t_{mod} \;=\; \frac{0.44}{B_M} = \frac{0.44\,L^q}{B_O} \qquad \qquad \dots (2.20)$$

If t_{mod} is expressed in nanoseconds and B_M is given in megahertz, then

$$t_{mod} \;=\; \frac{440}{B_M} = \frac{440\,L^q}{B_O} \qquad \qquad \dots (2.21)$$

A total system rise time

$$t_{sys} \;=\; [t_{tx}^2 + t_{mod}^2 + t_{GVD}^2 + t_{rx}^2]^{1/2} \qquad \qquad \dots (2.22)$$

$$=\; \left[t_{tx}^2 + \left(\frac{440\,L^q}{B_o}\right)^2 + D^2\,\sigma_\lambda^2\,L^2 + \left(\frac{350}{B_{rx}}\right)^2 \right]^{1/2} \qquad \dots (2.23)$$

where all times are given in nanoseconds. σ_λ is the half power spectral width of the source and the dispersion D.

2.6 LONG-HAUL SYSTEMS

- With the advent of optical amplifiers, fiber losses can be compensated by inserting amplifiers periodically along a long-haul fiber link.

- At the same time, the effects of Fiber Dispersion (GVD) can be reduced by using dispersion management. Since neither the fiber loss nor the GVD is then a limiting factor, one may ask how many in-line amplifiers can be cascaded in series, and what limits the total link length.

- Here we focus on the factors that limit the performance of amplified fiber links and provide a few design guidelines. The section also outlines the progress realized in the development of terrestrial and undersea lightwave systems since 1977 when the first field trial was completed.

2.6.1 Performance-Limiting Factors

- The most important consideration in designing a periodically amplified fiber link is related to the nonlinear effects occurring inside all optical fibers.

- For single channel lightwave systems, the dominant nonlinear phenomenon that limits the system performance is self-phase modulation (SPM).

- When optoelectronic regenerators are used, the SPM effects accumulate only over one repeater spacing (typically < 100 km) and are of little concern if the launch power satisfies or the condition $P_{in} << 22$ mW when $N_A = 1$.

- In contrast, the SPM effects accumulate over long lengths (~ 1000 km) when in-line amplifiers are used periodically for loss compensation.

- A rough estimate of the limitation imposed by the SPM is again obtained from Equation (2.15). This equation predicts that the peak power should be below 2.2 mW for 10 cascaded amplifiers when the nonlinear parameter $\gamma = 2$ W^{-1}/km the condition on the average power depends on the modulation format and the shape of optical pulses.

- It is nonetheless clear that the average power should be reduced to below 1 mW for SPM effects to remain negligible for a lightwave system designed to operate over a distance of more than 1000 km the limiting value of the average power also depends on the type of fiber in which light is propagating through the effective core area A_{eff}.

- The SPM effects are most dominant inside dispersion-compensating fibers for which A_{eff} is typically close to 20 μm^2.

- The forgoing discussion of the SPM-induced limitations is too simplistic to be accurate since it completely ignores the role of fiber dispersion.

- In fact, as the dispersive and nonlinear effects act on the optical signal simultaneously, their mutual interplay becomes quite important. The effect of SPM on pulses propagating inside an optical fiber can be included by using the nonlinear Schrodinger (NLS) equation. This equation is of the form

$$\frac{\partial A}{\partial z} + \frac{i\beta_z}{2}\frac{\partial^2 A}{\partial t^2} = -\frac{\alpha}{2}A + i\gamma\,|A|^2\,A \qquad \qquad \ldots (2.24)$$

- Where, fiber losses are included through the α term. This term can also include periodic amplification of the signal by treating α as a function of z. The NLS equation is used routinely for designing modern lightwave systems.

- Because of the nonlinear nature of Equation (2.24), it should be solved numerically in general. A numerical approach has indeed been adopted since the early 1990s for quantifying the impact of SPM on the performance of long-haul lightwave systems.

- The use of a large-effective area fiber (LEAF) helps by reducing the nonlinear parameter γ defined as $\gamma = 2\pi n_2/(\lambda A_{eff})$.

- Appropriate chirping of input pulses can also be beneficial for reducing the SPM effects. This feature has led to the adoption of a new modulation format known as the chirped RZ or CRZ format.

- Numerical simulations how that, in general, the launch power must be optimized to a value that depends on many design parameters such as the bit rate, total link length, and amplifier spacing. In one study, the optimum launch power was found to be about 1 mW for a 5 Gb/s signal transmitted over 9000 km with 40 km amplifier spacing.

- The combined effects of GVD and SPM also depend on the sign of the dispersion parameter β_2. In the case of anomalous dispersion ($\beta_2 < 0$), the nonlinear phenomenon of modulation instability can affect the system performance drastically.

- This problem can be overcome by using a combination of fibers with normal and anomalous GVD such that the average dispersion over the entire fiber link is normal.

- However, a new kind of modulation instability, referred to as sideband instability, can occur in both the normal and anomalous GVD regions.

- It has its origin in the periodic variation of the signal power along the fiber link when equally spaced optical amplifiers are used to compensate for fiber losses.

- Since the quantity $\gamma\,|A|^2$ in Equation (2.24) is then a periodic function of z, the resulting nonlinear-index grating can initiate a four-wave-mixing process that generates sidebands in the signal spectrum.

- It can be avoided by making the amplifier spacing nonuniform.

- Another factor that plays a crucial role is the noise added by optical amplifiers. Similar to the case of electronic amplifiers, the noise of optical amplifiers is quantified through an amplifier noise figure F_n.

- The nonlinear interaction between the amplified spontaneous emission and the signal can lead to a large spectral broadening through the non-linear phenomenon such as cross-phase modulation and four-wave mixing.

- Because the noise has a much larger bandwidth than the signal, its impact can be reduced by using optical filters.

- Numerical simulations indeed show a considerable improvement when optical filters are used after every in-line amplifier.

- The polarization effects that are totally negligible in the traditional nonamplified lightwave systems become of concern for long-haul systems with in-line amplifiers.

- In addition to PMD, optical amplifiers can also induce polarization-dependent gain and loss.

- Although the PMD effects must be considered during system design, their impact depends on the design parameters such as the bit rate and the transmission distance.

- For bit rates as high as 10 Gb/s, the PMD effects can be reduced to an acceptable level with a proper design.

- However, PMD becomes of major concern for 40 Gb/s systems for which the bit slot is only 25 ps wide. The use of a PMD-compensation technique appears to be necessary at such high bit rates.

- The fourth generation of lightwave systems began in 1995 when lightwave systems employing amplifiers first became available commercially.

- Of course, the laboratory demonstrations began as early as 1989.

- Many experiments used a recirculating fiber loop to demonstrate system feasibility as it was not practical to use long lengths of fiber in a laboratory setting. Alredy in 1991, an experiment showed the possibility of data transmission over 21,000 km at 2.5 Gb/s and over 14,300 km at 5 Gb/s, by using the recirculating loop configuration.

- In a system trial carried out in 1995 by using actual submarine cables and repeaters, a 5.3 Gb/s signal was transmitted over 11,300 km with 60 km of amplifier spacing.

- This system trial led to the deployment of a commercial transpacific cable (TPC-5) that began operating in 1996.

- The bit rate of fourth generation systems was extended to 10 Gb/s beginning in 1992. As early as 1995, a 10 Gb/s signal was transmitted over 6480 km with 90 km amplifier spacing. With a further increase in the distance, the SNR decreased below the value needed to maintain the BER below 10^{-9}.

- One may think that the performance should improve by operating close to the zero-dispersion wavelength of the fiber.

- However, an experiment, performed under such conditions, achieved a distance of only 6000 km at 10 Gb/s even with 40 km amplifier spacing, and the situation became worse when the RZ modulation format was used. Starting in 1999, the single channel bit rate was pushed toward 40 Gb/s in several experiments.

- The design of 40 Gb/s lightwave systems requires the use of several new ideas including the CRZ format, dispersion management with GVD-slope compensation, and distributed Raman amplification.

- Even then, the combined effects of the higher order dispersion, PMD and SPM degrade the system performance considerably at a bit rate of 40 Gb/s.

2.6.2 Terrestrial Lightwave Systems

- An important application of fiber-optic communication links is for enhancing the capacity of telecommunication networks worldwide.

- Indeed, it is this application that started the field of optical fiber communications in 1977 and has propelled it since then by demanding systems with higher and higher capacities. Here we focus on the status of commercial systems by considering the terrestrial and undersea systems separately.

Table 2.3 : Terrestrial Lightwave Systems

system	Year	λ (μm)	B (Mb/s)	L (km)	Voice Channels
FT-3	1980	0.85	45	< 10	672
FT-3C	1983	0.85	90	< 15	1,344
FT-3X	1984	1.30	180	< 25	2,688
FT-G	1985	1.30	417	< 40	6,048
FT-G-1.7	1987	1.30	1,668	< 46	24,192
STM-16	1991	1.55	2,488	< 85	32,256
STM-64	1996	1.55	9,953	< 90	129,024
STM-256	2002	1.55	39,813	< 90	516,096

- After a successful Chicago field trial in 1977, terrestrial lightwave systems became available commercially beginning in 1980. Table 2.3 lists the operating characteristics of several terrestrial systems developed since then.

- The first generation systems operated near 0.85 μm and used multimode graded-index fibers as the transmission medium.

- As seen in Fig. 2.4, the BL product of such systems is limited to 2(Gb/s)-km a commercial lightwave system (FT-3C) operating at 90 Mb/s with a repeater spacing of about 12 km realized a BL product of nearly 1 (Gb/s)-km; it is shown by a filled circle in Fig. 2.4.

- The operating wavelength moved to 1.3 μm in second-generation lightwave systems to take advantage of low fiber losses and low dispersion near this wavelength.

- The BL product of 1.3 μm lightwave systems is limited to about 100 (Gb/s)-km when a multimode semiconductor laser is used inside the transmitter.

- In 1987, a commercial 1.3 μm lightwave system provided data transmission at 1.7 Gb/s with a repeater spacing of about 45 km a filled circle in figure 2.4 shows that this system operates quite close to the dispersion limit.

- The third generation of lightwave systems became available commercially in 1991.

- They operate near 1.55 μm at bit rates in excess of 2 Gb/s, typically at 2.488 Gb/s, corresponding to the OC-48 level of the synchronized optical network (SONET) [or the STS-16 level of the synchronous digital hierarchy (SDH) specifications.

- The switch to the 1.55 μm wavelength helps to increase the loss-limited transmission distance to more than 100 km because of fiber losses of less than 0.25 dB/km in this wavelength region.

- However, the repeater spacing was limited to below 100 km because of the high GVD of standard telecommunication fibers.

- In fact, the deployment of third-generation lightwave systems was possible only after the development of distributed feedback (DFB) semiconductor lasers, which reduce the impact of fiber dispersion by reducing the source spectral width to below 100 MHz.

- The fourth generation of lightwave systems appeared around 1996. Such systems operate in the 1.55 µm region at a bit rate as high as 40 Gb/s by using dispersion-shifted fibers in combination with optical amplifiers.

- However, more than 50 million kilometers of the standard telecommunication fiber is already installed in the world-wide telephone network.

- Economic reasons dictate that the fourth generation of lightwave systems make use of this existing base. Two approaches are being used to solve the dispersion problem.

- First, several dispersion-management schemes make it possible to extend the bit rate to 10 Gb/s while maintaining an amplifier spacing of up to 100 km. Second, several 10 Gb/s signals can be transmitted simultaneously by using the WDM technique.

- Moreover, if the WDM technique is combined with dispersion management, the total transmission distance can approach several thousand kilometers provided that fiber losses are compensated periodically by using optical amplifiers.

- Such WDM lightwave systems were deployed commercially worldwide beginning in 1996 and allowed a system capacity of 1.6 Tb/s by 2000 for the 160-channel commercial WDM systems.

- The fifth generation of lightwave systems was just beginning to emerge in 2001. The bit rate of each channel in this generation of WDM systems is 40 Gb/s (corresponding to the STM-256 or OC-768 level).

- Several new techniques developed in recent years make it possible to transmit a 40 Gb/s optical signal over long distances.

- New fibers known as reverse-dispersion fibers have been developed with a negative GVD slope.

- Their use in combination with tunable dispersion-compensating techniques can compensate the GVD for all channels simultaneously.

- The PMD compensators help to reduce the PMD-induced degradation of the signal. The use of Raman amplification helps to reduce the noise and improves the signal-to-noise artio (SNR) at the receiver.

- The use of a forward-error correction technique helps to increase to increase the transmission distance by reducing the required SNR.

- The number of WDM channels can be increased by using the L and S bands located on the long- and short wavelength sides of the conventional C band occupying the 1530-1570 nm spectral region.

- In one 3 Tb/s experiment, 77 channels, each operating at 42.7 Gb/s, were transmitted over 1200 km by using the C and L bands simultaneously. In another experiment, the system capacity was extended to 10.2 Tb/s by transmitting 256 channels over 100 km at 42.7 Gb/s per channel using only the C and L bands, resulting in a spectral efficiency of 1.28 (b/s)/Hz.

- The bit rate was 42.7 Gb/s in both of these experiments because of the overhead associated with the forward-error-correction technique. The highest capacity achieved in 2001 was 11 Tb/s and was realized by transmitting 273 channels over 117 km at 40 Gb/s per channel while using all three bands simultaneously.

Table 2.4 : Commercial Transatlantic Lightwave Systems

System	Year	Capacity (Gb/s)	L (km)	Comments
TAT-8	1988	0.28	70	1.3 μm, multimode lasers
TAT-9	1991	0.56	80	1.55 μm, DFB lasers
TAT-10/11	1993	0.56	80	1.55 μm, DFB lasers
TAT-12/13	1996	5.00	50	1.55 μm, optical amplifiers
AC-1	1998	80.0	50	1.55 μm, WDM with amplifiers
TAT-14	2001	1280	50	1.55 μm, dense WDM
AC-2	2001	1280	50	1.55 μm, dense WDM
360 Atlantic-1	2001	1920	50	1.55 μm, denser WDM
Tycom	2001	2560	50	1.55 μm, dense WDM
FLAG Atlantic-1	2001	4800	50	1.55 μm, dense WDM

2.6.3 Undersea Lightwave Systems

- Undersea or submarine transmission systems are used for intercontinental communications and are capable of providing a network spanning the whole earth.

- Reliability is of major concern for such systems as repairs are expensive. Generally, undersea systems are designed for a 25-year service life, with at most three failures during operation.

- Table 2.4 lists the main characteristics of several transatlantic fiber-optic cable systems. The first undersea fiber-optic cable (TAT-8) was a second generation system. It was installed in 1988 in the Atlantic Ocean for operation at a bit rate of 280 Mb/s with a repeater spacing of up to 70 km.

- The system design was on the conservative side, mainly to ensure reliability. The same technology was used for the first transpacific lightwave system (TPC-3), which became operational in 1989.

- By 1990 the third generation lightwave systems had been developed. The TAT-9 submarine system used this technology in 1991; it was designed to operate near 1.55 μm at a bit rate of 560 Mb/s with a repeater spacing of about 80 km.

- The increasing traffic across the Atlantic Ocean led to the deployment of the TAT-10 and TAT-11 lightwave systems by 1993 with the same technology.

- The advent of optical amplifiers prompted their use in the next generation of undersea systems, and the TAT-12 submarine fiber-optic cable became operational by 1996.

- This fourth-generation system employed optical amplifiers in place of optoelectronic regenerators and operated at a bit rate of 5.3 Gb/s with an amplifier spacing of about 50 km.

- The bit rate is slightly larger than the STM-32 level bit rate of 5 Gb/s because of the overload associated with the forward-error correction technique.

- As discussed earlier, the design of such lightwave systems is much more complex than that of previous undersea system because of the cumulative effects of fiber dispersion and nonlinearity, which must be controlled over long distances.

- The transmitter power and the dispersion profile along the link must be optimized to combat such effects.

- Even then, amplifier spacing is typically limited to 50 km and the use of an error-correction scheme is essential to ensure a bit-error rate of $< 2 \times 10^{-11}$.

- A second category of undersea lightwave systems requires repeaterless transmission over several hundred kilometers.

- Such systems are used for interisland communication or for looping a shoreline such that the signal is regenerated on the shore periodically after a few hundred kilometers of undersea transmission.

- The dispersive and nonlinear effects are of less concern for such systems than for transoceanic lightwave systems, but fiber losses become a major issue.

- The reason is easily appreciated by noting that the cable loss exceeds 100 dB over a distance of 500 km even under the best operating conditions.

- In the 1990s several laboratory experiments demonstrated repeaterless transmission at 2.5 Gb/s over more than 500 km by using two in-line amplifiers that were pumped remotely from the transmitter and receiver ends with high-power pump lasers. Another amplifier at the transmitter boosted the launched power to close to 100 mW.

- Such high input powers exceed the threshold level for stimulated Brillouin scattering (SBS), a nonlinear phenomenon.

- The suppression of SBS is often realized by modulating the phase of the optical carrier such that the carrier linewidth is broadened to 200 MHz or more from its initial value of < 10 MHz.

- Directly modulated DFB lasers can also be used for this purpose.

- In a 1996 experiment a 2.5 Gb/s signal was transmitted over 465 km by direct modulation of a DFB laser.

- Chirping of the modulated signal broadened the spectrum enough that an external phase modulator was not required provided that the launched power was kept below 100 mW.

- The bit rate of repeaterless undersea systems can be increased to 10 Gb/s by employing the same techniques used at 2.5 Gb/s. In a 1996 experiment the 10 Gb/s signal was transmitted over 442 km by using two remotely pumped in-line amplifiers.

- Two external modulators were used, one for SBS suppression and another for signal generation.

- In a 1988 experiment, a 40 Gb/s signal was transmitted over 240 km using the RZ format and an alternating polarization format.

- These results indicate that undersea lightwave systems looping a shoreline can operate at 10 Gb/s or more with only shore-based electronics.

- The use of the WDM technique in combination with optical amplifiers, dispersion management, and error-correction has revolutionized the design of submarine fiber-optic systems.

- In 1998, a submarine cable known as Atlantic-crossing 1 (AC-1) with a capacity of 80 Gb/s was deployed using the WDM technology. An identically designed system (Pacific-Crossing 1 or PC-1 crossed the Pacific Ocean.

- The use of dense WDM, in combination with multiple fiber pairs per cable, resulted in systems with much larger capacities. By 2001, several systems with a capacity of > 1 Tb/s became operational across the Atlantic Ocean.

- These systems employ a ring configuration and cross the Atlantic Ocean twice to ensure fault tolerance. The 360 Atlantic submarine system can operate at speed up to 1.92 Tb/s and spans a total distance of 11,700 km.

- Another system, known as FLAG Atlantic-1, is capable of carrying traffic at speeds up to 4.8 Tb/s as it employs six fiber pairs.

- A global network, spanning 250,000 km and capable of operating at 3.2 Tb/s using 80 channels (at 10 Gb/s) over 4 fibers, was under development in 2001 such a submarine network can transmit nearly 40 million voice channels simultaneously, a capacity that should be contrasted with the TAT-8 capacity of 8000 channels in 1988, which in turn should be compared to the 48-channel capacity of TAT-1 in 1959.

REVIEW QUESTIONS

1. Prove that the rise time T_r and the 3-dB bandwidth Δf of a RC circuit are related by $T_r \Delta f = 0.35$.

2. Make a rise time budget for a 0.85μm, 10-km fiber link designed to operate at 50 Mb/s. The LED transmitter and the Si p-i-n receiver have rise times of 10 and 15 ns, respectively. The graded-index fiber has a core index of 1.46, $\Delta = 0.01$, and $D = 80$ ps/(km-nm). The LED spectral width is 50 nm. Can the system be designed to operate with the NRZ format?

3. A 1.3 μm long-haul lightwave system is designed to operate at 1.5 Gb/s. it is capable of coupling 1 mW of average power into the fiber. The 0.5-dB/km fiber cable loss includes splice losses. The connectors at each end have 1-dB losses. The InGaAs p-i-n receiver has a sensitivity of 250 nW. Make the power budget and estimate the repeater spacing.

4. Explain the various topologies for the distribution networks.

5. Write short notes on:

    (i)   Loss-limited lightwave systems

    (ii) Dispersion-limited lightwave systems

6. Write short notes on:

    (i)   Power budget

    (ii) Rise time budget

7. What are the two analysis usually carried out to ensure the desired performance of optical fiber transmission link? Explain any one of them in detail.

8. An optical fiber system is to be designed to operate on 8 km length without repeaters. The rise times of chosen components are source (LED) : 8 ns.

    Fiber cable: Intermodal   :   5 ns/km

    Intramodal   :   1 ns/km

    Detector (PIN)   =   6 ns

    Estimate maximum bit rate that may be achieved on the link when using NRZ and RZ formats.

9. Determine the maximum bit rate for RZ and NRZ encoding for the following pulse spreading constants and cable lengths.

    (i) $\Delta t = 10$ ns/m,   L = 100 m

    (ii) $\Delta t = 20$ ns/m,   L = 1000 m

    (iii) $\Delta t = 2000$ ns/m,   L = 2 km

10. A D-Im analog optical fiber link of length 2 km employs on LED which launchs mean optical power of −10 dBm into a multimode optical fiber. The fiber cable exhibits a loss of 3.5 dB km^{-1} with splice losses calculated at 0.7 dB km^{-1}. In addition there is a connector loss at the receiver of 1.6 dB. The Pin photodiode receiver has a sensitivity of −25 dBm for an SNR of 50 dB and with a modulation index of 0.5. It is estimated that a safety margin of 4 dB is required. Assuming there is no dispersion equalization penalty.

(i) Perform an optical power budget for the system operating under the above conditions and ascertain its viability.

(ii) Estimate any possible increase in link length which may be achieved using an injection laser source which launches mean optical power of 0 dBm into the fiber cable. In this case, the safety margin must be increased to 7 dB.

Questions from university question papers

May-Jun 2012

1. An engineer has the following components available: [8]
   (i) GaAs laser diode operating at 850 nm and capable of coupling 1 mW into a fiber.
   (ii) 10 sections of cable each of which is 500m long, has a 4 dB/km attenuation and has connectors on both ends
   (iii) Connector loss of 2dB/connector
   (iv) A p-i-n photodiode receiver (− 45 dBm sensitivity)
   (v) An avalanche photodiode receiver (− 56 dBm sensitivity)

   Using these components, the engineer wishes to construct a 5-km link operating at 20 Mb/s. Perform optical budget and state which receiver should be used if a 6-dB system operating margin is required?

2. State the key system requirements needed in analyzing a link. To fulfill these requirements explain the choice of components and their associated characteristics in a point-to-point optical link. [8]

Nov-Dec 2012

1. Following are the parameters of a point-to-point optical link:

Optical power launched	:	+3 dBm
Sensitivity of detector	:	− 32 dBm
Source/Detector connector loss	:	1 dB each
Length of optical cable	:	60 km
Cable attenuation	:	0.3 dB/km
Jumper cable loss	:	3 dB
Connector loss at each fiber joint	:	1 dB

Assume two jumper cables and two cable joints at the two ends of transmission fiber. Compute the power margin of the link using spreadsheet method.

2. A lab setup of optical fiber demo-system is to be tested over an 8 km length. The rise times of the chosen components are:

LED	:	10 ns
p-i-n photodiode	:	6 ns
Intermodal pulse broadening	:	10 ns/km
Intramodal pulse broadening	:	5 ns/km

From system rise time considerations, estimate the maximum bit rate achievable on the link when using an NRZ format.

3. Write a short note on performance analysis of analog optical fiber system.

May-Jun 2013

1. Components chosen for a digital optical fiber link of overall length 10 km and operating at a 20M bit/s using an RZ code are given below :
   (i) LED capable of launching an average power of 0.1 mW at 0.85 µm [including connector loss into a 50µm core diameter graded index fiber]
   (ii) Fiber attenuation 2.5 dB/km and
   (iii) Requires splicing every 2 km with a loss of 0.3 dB per splice. There is also a connector loss at the receiver of 1.5 dB.
   (iv) The receiver requires mean incident optical power of -46 dBm in order to give the necessary BER of 10-10
   (v) Predicted safety margin of 6 dB.
   Write down the optical power budget for the system and hence determine its viability.

2. Write short notes no :   [08]

   (i) Rise Time Budgeting.

3. An analog optical fiber system operating at a wavelength of 1.3 µm has a post detection bandwidth of 5 MHz. Assuming an ideal detector and considering only quantum noise on the signal, calculate the incident the incident optical power necessary to achieve an SNR of 50 dB at the receiver.   [8]

Nov-Dec 2013

1. Explain in detail the importance of budgets. What are different system considerations for rise time budget?

---

2. The 10 - 90% rise times for possible components to be used in a D-IM analog optical fiber link are specified below : [8]

Source (LED) 10 ns

Fiber cable : intermodal 9 ns/km

Intramodal : 2 ns/km

Detector (APD) : 3ns

The desired link length without repeaters is 6 km and the required optical bandwidh is 6 MHz. Determine whether the above combination of components give an adequate temporal response.

May-Jun 2014

1. Describe the system design considerations involved in establishing point-to-point optical fiber link. [8]

2. Following components are available for 5 Km link operating at 20 Mb/sec: [8]

   (i) GaAs LED operating at 850 nm and capable of coupling 1 mW into fiber.

   (ii) 10 sections of cable each of which is 500 m long, has 4 dB/km attenuation and has connectors on both ends.

   (iii) Connector loss of 2 dB/connector.

   (iv) PIN photo diode receiver (- 45 dBm sensitivity).

   (v) Avalanche photo diode receiver (- 56 dBm sensitivity).

   Perform Optical power budget and state which receiver should be used if 6-dB system operating margin is required.

3. Explain the concept of link power budget and rise time budget in optical fiber communication system. [8]

Nov-Dec 2014

1. Explain the design procedure with graphical representation for link loss budget analysis.

   [8]

2. Components are chosen for a digital optical link of overall length of 6 km. LED chosen is capable of launching - 10 dBm into a graded index fiber, which has an attenuation of 3 dbkm^{-1}. It requires splicing every kilometer with a loss of 0.5 dB. per splice. The connector loss at the receiver is 1.5 dB. The receiver requires mean optical power of - 41 dBm in order to give necessary BER of 10^{-10}. It is also predicted that a safety margin of 6 dB will be required. Write down the optical power budget for the system and hence determine its viability. [8]

3. An optical fiber system is to be designed to operate over an 8km length without repeaters. The rise times of the chosen components are

Source LED = 8ns

Fiber: Intermodal = 5 ns/km

  Intramodal = 1 ns/km

Pin Detector = 6 ns

Estimate the maximum bit rate that may be achieved on the link using NRZ format.   [8]

May-Jun 2015

1. A 1550-nm single mode digital fiber optic link needs to operate at 622 Mbps over 80 km without amplifiers. A single-mode InGaAsP laser launches an average optical power of 13 dBm into the fiber. The fiber has a loss of 0.35 dB/km and there is a splice with a loss of 0.1 dB every kilometer. The coupling loss at the receiver is 0.5 dB, and the receiver uses InGaAs APD with a sensitivity of −39 dBm. Excess-noise penalties are predicted to be 1.5 dB. Setup an optical power budget for this link and find the system margin. Represent link loss budget graphically.   [10]

2. An optical fiber system is to be designed to operate over an 8 km length without repeaters. The rise times of the chosen components are: [8]

Source LED 8 ns

Fiber: Intermodal 6 ns/km

(Pulse broadening) intramodal 1 ns/km

Detector (p-i-n photodiode) 5ns

From system rise time considerations, estimate the maximum bit rate that may be achieved on the link when using an NRZ format.

Nov-Dec 2015

1. Draw the block diagram of optical fiber communication link. Explain the system design considerations in a point-to-point optical fiber communication link.   [8]

2. Using graphical method calculate the maximum attenuation-limited transmission distance of the following two systems operating at 100 Mb/s: [8]

System I operating at 850 nm

(i) GaAlAs laser diode: 0 dBm fiber-coupled power.

(ii) Silico APD with -50 dBm sensitivity.

(iii) Graded-index fiber: 3.5 dB/ km attenuation at 850 nm.

(iv) Connector loss: 1dB/connector.

System II operating at 1300 nm

(i)   InGaAsP LED diode: 13 dBm fiber-coupled power.

(ii) InGaAs pin photodiode with -38 dBm sensitivity.

(iii) Graded-index fiber: 1.5 dB/km attenuation at 1300 nm.

(iv) Connector loss: 1 dB/connector.

Allow a 6 dB system operating margin in each case. Comment on the result.

3. Explain in detail: Rise time Budget   [8]

4. Draw the block diagram of optical fiber communication link. Explain the system design considerations in a point-to-point optical fiber communication link.   [8]

MULTICHANNEL SYSTEMS

3.1 INTRODUCTION

- A distinctive operational feature of an optical fiber is that there is a wide spectral region in which optical signals can be transmitted efficiently.

- For full-spectrum fibers this region includes the O-band through the L-band, which ranges from about 1260 to 1675.

- Since the light sources used in high-capacity optical fiber communication systems emit in a narrow wavelength band of less than 1 nm, then many different independent optical channels can be used simultaneously in different segments of this wavelength range.

- The technology of combining a number of such independent information-carrying wavelengths onto the same fiber is known as wavelength division multiplexing or WDM.

- This chapter addresses the operating principles of WDM, examines the functions of a generic WDM link, and discusses the internationally standardized spectral grids for two different wavelength multiplexing schemes.

- Various categories of passive optical components that are needed to combine wavelengths at the transmitting end and separate them back into individual channels at the destination.

- An important factor in deploying these components in a WDM system is to ensure that optical signal power from one channel does not drift into the spectral territory occupied by adjacent channels.

- The design of complex wavelength division multiplexed links requires choosing many optical sources with narrow spectral emission bands.

- The most straight forward method is to select a series of individual; lasers, each of which emits at a specific wavelength.

- This selection process is adequate for a small number of wavelength channels, but can be cumbersome for links carrying many wavelengths.

- To simplify this process, a variety of wavelength-tunable components and schemes have been investigated concerning the administration of channels in a WDM transmission system. Among these are tunable light sources and tunable optical signal-conditioning and receiving devices.

- Applications of WDM techniques are found in all levels of communication links including long-distance terrestrial and undersea transmission systems, metro networks, and fiber-to-the premises (FTTP) networks.

3.2 OVERVIEW OF WDM

- A distinct operational feature of an optical fibers is that there is a wider spectral region in which the optical signals can be transmitted efficiently. This region includes the O-band through the L-band, which ranges from about 1260 to 1675 nm. Hence, if the light sources used in high capacity fibers emit in a narrow wavelength band of less than 1 nm, then many different optical channels can be used simultaneously in this range.

- 'The technology of combining a number of such independent information carrying wavelengths onto the same fiber' is known as wavelength division multiplexing or WDM.

- The design of complex wavelength division multiplexed links requires choosing many optical sources with narrow spectral emission bands.

- The first use of WDM was to upgrade the capacity of installed point-to-point transmission links. This was achieved with wavelengths that were separated from several tens upto 200 nanometers in order not to impose strict wavelength tolerance requirements on the different laser sources and the receiving wavelength separating components at the receiving end.

- WDM is a technology which can be used in all levels of communication links including long distance terrestrial and undersea transmission systems, metro networks and fiber to the premises (FTTP) networks.

- With the invention of high quality light sources with extremely narrow spectral emission widths, many independent wavelength channels which are spaced less than a nanometer apart could be placed on the same fiber. These light sources allow the WDM technology to increase its capacity of an optical link compared to simple point-to-point link that is carried by only a single wavelength.

- The second advantage of WDM is that the various optical channels can support different transmission formats. Thus by using separate wavelengths, differently formatted signals at any data rate can be sent simultaneously and independently over the same fiber without the need for a common signal structure.

3.2.1 Operating Principle of WDM

- WDM has the characteristics that the discrete wavelengths form an orthogonal set of carriers which can be separated, routed and switched without interfering with each other. The implementation of WDM requires active and passive devices to combine distribute, isolate and amplify optical power at different wavelengths. Passive devices do not require external control for their operation. The functions of these passive devices are to split and combine or tap off the optical signal. The performance of active devices can be controlled electronically, which provides a large degree of network flexibility. Active components are turnable optical filters, tunable sources and optical amplifiers.

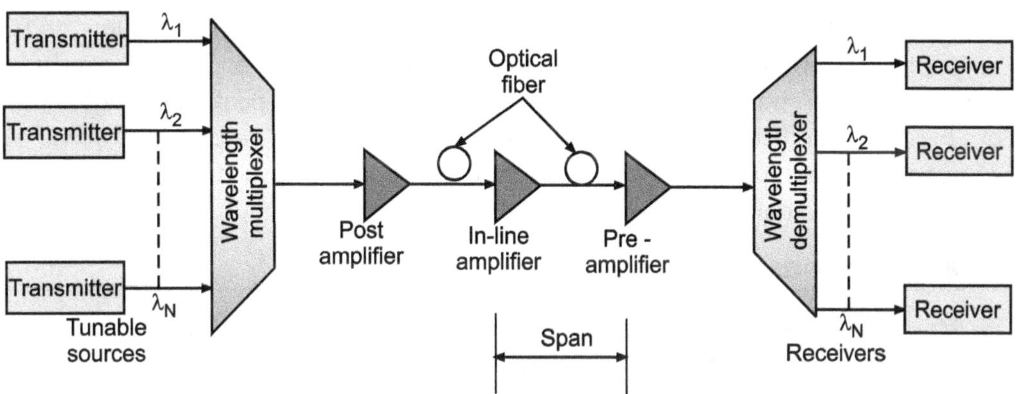

Fig. 3.1 : Implementation of WDM network with various types of optical amplifiers

- Fig. 3.1 shows the implementation of active and passive components in a typical WDM network which contains various types of optical amplifiers.

- At the end of the transmitter, there are several independently modulated light sources, each emitting signals at a unique wavelength. Here a multiplexer is used to combine these optical outputs into a continuous spectrum of signals and couple them onto a single fiber. At the end of the receiver the demultiplexer is used to separate the optical signals into appropriate detection channels for signal processing.

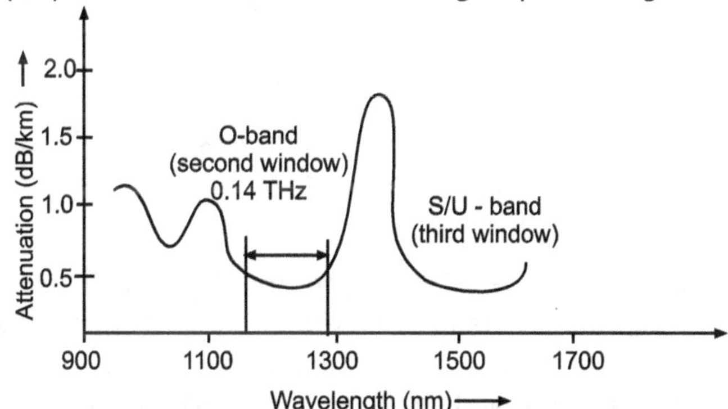

Fig. 3.2 : The transmission bandwidths in the O and C-bands which allow the use of many simultaneous channels for sources with narrow spectral widths

- Fig. 3.2 shows the operating regions across the spectrum ranging from the O-band through the L-band in which narrow line width optical sources can be used simultaneously. These regions can be viewed in terms of spectral width or optical bandwidth. To find the optical bandwidth corresponding to a particular spectral width in these regions, the fundamental relationship $c = \lambda v$, which relates the wavelength λ to the carrier frequency v, where c is the speed of the light. Differentiating this, we have for $\Delta\lambda << \lambda^2$.

$$|\Delta v| = \frac{c}{\lambda^2} |\Delta\lambda| \qquad \qquad \dots (3.1)$$

where the frequency deviation Δv corresponds to the wavelength deviation $\Delta\lambda$ around λ.

- The operational frequency band which is allocated to a particular light source normally ranges from 25 to 100 GHz. The exact width of the frequency or spectral band that is selected needs to be taken into account, possible drifts in the peak wavelength emitted by the laser and temporal variations in the wavelength response of other link components. These parameter changes can result from effects such as component aging or temperature variations.

3.2.2 WDM Standards

- WDM standards are developed by the International Telecommunication Union (ITU) specify channel spacing in terms of frequency.

- Recommendation G.692 was the first ITU-T specification for WDM. This document specifies selecting the channels from a grid of frequencies referenced to 193.100 THz and spacing them by 100 GHz which corresponds to spectral widths of 0.4 and 1.6 nm, respectively at 1550 nm.

- In 2002, the ITU-T released recommendation G.694.1, which is aimed specifically at DWDM (dense WDM). This document specifies WDM operation in the S, C and L-bands for high quality, high-rate Metro Area Network (MAN) and Wide Area Network (WAN) services. It calls for a narrow frequency spacing of 100 to 12.5 GHz. This implementation requires the use of stable, high quality temperature controlled and wavelength controlled laser diode light sources.

- To designate which C-band channel is under consideration in 100 GHz applications, the ITU-T uses a channel numbering convention. For this, the frequency 19 N·M THz is designated as ITU channel number NM.

- The concept of coarse WDM (CWDM) emerged from the combination of the production of full spectrum (low water content) G.652C and 9.652 D fibers, the development of relatively inexpensive optical sources and the desire to have low-cost optical links operating in access networks and local area network. In 2002, the ITU-T released recommendations 6.694.2 which defines the spectral grid for CWDM.

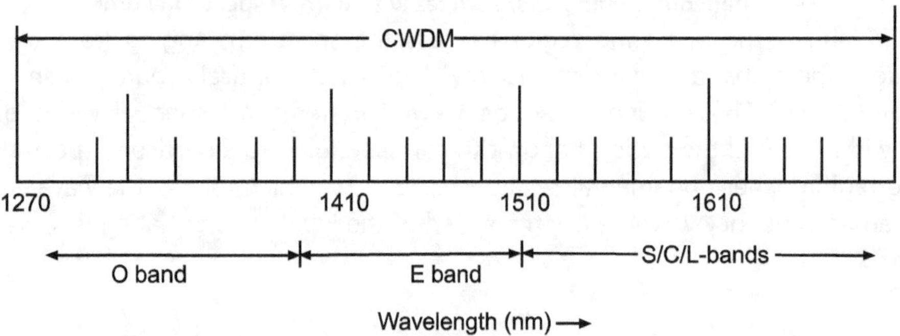

Fig. 3.3 : Spectral grid from coarse wavelength division multiplexing (CWDM)

- Fig. 3.3 shows the CWDM grid which is made up of 18 wavelengths defined within the range 1270 nm to 1610 nm (O-through L-bands) spaced by 20 nm with wavelength - drift tolerances of ±2 nm. This can be achieved with inexpensive light sources that are not temperature - controlled.

- ITU-T Recommendation G.965 released in 2004 outlines the specifications for multiple-channel CWDM over distances of 40 to 80 km. The Recommendation includes both unidirectional and bidirectional systems.

- Table 3.1 lists part of the ITU-T G.694.1 dense WDM frequency grid for 100 and 50 GHz spacings in the L- and C-bands. The column labeled "50 GHz offset" means that for the 50 GHz grid one uses the 100 GHz spacings with these 50 GHz values interleaved.

- For example, the 50 GHz channels in the L-band would be at 186.00 THz, 186.05 THz, 186.10 THz and so on. Note that when the frequency spacing is uniform, the wavelengths are not spaced uniformly because of the relationship given in Equation (3.1)

Table 3.1 : Portion of the ITU-T G.694.1 Dense WDM Grid for 100- and 50-GHz Spacings in the L- and C-bands

L-band		C-band					
100 GHz	50 GHz offset	100 GHz	50 GHz offset				
THz	nm	THz	nm	THz	nm	THz	nm
186.00	1611.79	186.05	1611.35	191.00	1569.59	191.05	1569.18
186.10	1610.92	186.15	1610.49	191.10	1568.77	191.15	1568.36
186.20	1610.06	186.25	1609.62	191.20	1576.95	191.25	1567.54
186.30	1609.19	186.35	1608.76	191.30	1567.13	191.35	1566.72
186.40	1608.33	186.45	1607.90	191.40	1566.31	191.45	1565.09
186.60	1606.60	196.65	1606.17	191.60	1564.68	191.65	1564.27
186.60	1606.60	186.65	1606.17	191.60	1564.68	191.65	1564.27
186.70	1605.74	186.75	1605.31	191.70	1563.86	191.75	1563.45
186.80	1604.88	186.85	1604.46	191.80	1563.05	191.85	1562.64
186.90	1604.03	186.95	1603.60	191.90	1562.23	191.95	1561.83

- To designate which C-band channel is under consideration in 100 GHz applications, the ITU-T uses a channel numbering convention.

- For this, the frequency 19 N.M THz is designated as ITU channel number NM. For example, the frequency 194.3 THz is ITU channel 43.

- The concept of coarse WDM (CWDM) emerged from the combination of the production of full spectrum (low-water-content) G. 652D and G. 652D fibers, the development of relatively inexpensive optical sources, and the desire to have low-cost optical links operating in access networks and local area networks.

- In 2002 the ITU-T released Recommendation G. 694.2 which defines the spectral grid for CWDM. As shown in Fig. 3.3, the DWDM grid is made up of 18 wavelengths defined within the range 1270 nm to 16010 nm (0-through L-bands) spaced by 20 nm with wavelength-drift tolerances of ± 2 nm. This can be achieved with inexpensive light sources that are not temperature-controlled.

- The ITU-T Recommendation G. 695 released in 2004 outlines optical interface specifications for multiple-channel CWDM over distances of 40 and 80 km.

- Both unidirectional and bidirectional systems (such as used in passive optical network applications) are included in the recommendation.

- The applications for G. 695 cover all or part of the 1270-to-1610 range.

- The main deployments are for single-mode fibers, such as those specified in ITU-T Recommendations G. 652 and G. 655.

3.3 PASSIVE OPTICAL COUPLERS

- WDM devices operate completely in the optical domain to split and combine light signals. The devices are called passive devices. These devices include N × N couplers (with N ≥ 2), power splitters, power taps and star couplers. These components are fabricated from planar optical waveguides using materials such as lithium niobate ($LiNbO_3$), Inp, silica, silicon oxynitride or various polymers.

- Most passive WDM components are variations of a star-coupler for combining and splitting optical power. In the broadest application, star couplers combine light streams from two or more input fibers and split them among several output fibers. Splitting is done with uniformity for all wavelengths. NXN splitter is used to fuse together the cores of N single mode fibers over a length of a few millimeters.

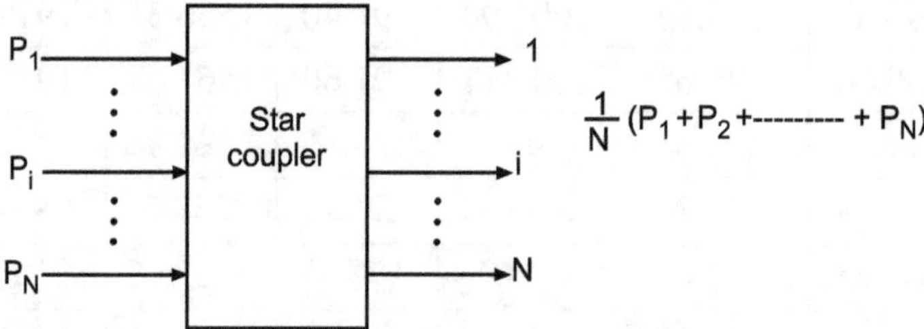

Fig. 3.4 : Basic star coupler

- A star coupler can be made of any size, provided that all fibers must be heated uniformly during the coupler-fabrication process. The maximum inputs and outputs are 64. One simple device is a power tap. Taps are non-uniform 2 × 2 couplers which are used to extract a small portion of optical power from a fiber line for monitoring the signal quality.

- Three fundamental technologies are used for fabrication of passive components. These are based on optical fibers, integrated optical waveguides and bulk micro-optics. Couplers using micro-optic designs are not widely used because the strict tolerances required in the fabrication and alignment processes affect their cost, performance and robustness.

3.3.1 2 × 2 Fiber Coupler

- A coupler with two inputs and two outputs can be called as 2 × 2 coupler.

- The 2 × 2 fiber coupler is a fused-fiber coupler. It is fabricated by twisting together, melting and pulling two single mode fibers so that they get fused together over a uniform section of length w. Each input and output has a long tapered section of length L. Transverse dimensions are gradually reduced down to that of the coupling region when the fibers are pulled during the fusion process. The total draw length $= \mathscr{L} = 2L + w$. It is called a fused biconical tapered coupler.

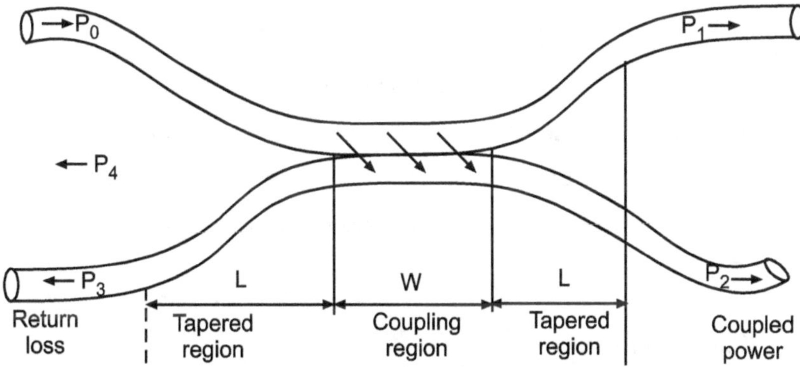

Fig. 3.5 : Cross-sectional view of fused fiber coupler

- When the light P_o, propagates long the fiber there is a reduction in the V number. Depending upon the dimension of the coupling region, any desired fraction of this decoupled field can be recoupled into the other fiber. A small amount of incoming optical power is reflected back into either of the input ports and hence these are called directional couplers.

- The optical power coupled from one fiber to another can be varied by three parameters:

1. By the axial length of the coupling region.

2. By the size of the reduced radius r in the coupling region.

3. By Δr, the difference in the radii of the two fibers in the coupling region.

- Assuming that the coupler is lossless, power P_2 coupled from one fiber to another fiber over an axial distance z can be expressed as:

$$P_2 = P_o \sin^2 (kz) \qquad \qquad \text{... (3.2)}$$

where k = Coupling coefficient

$$P_1 = P_0 - P_2 \qquad \qquad \ldots(3.3)$$

$$= P_0 [1 - \sin^2 (kz)] \qquad \ldots(3.4)$$

$$= P_0 \cos^2 (kz) \qquad \ldots(3.5)$$

- This shows that the phase of the driven fiber always lags 90° behind the phase of the driving fiber.

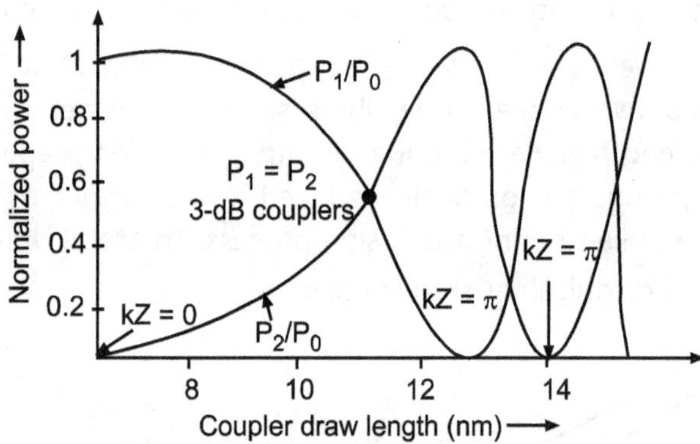

Fig. 3.6 : Normalized coupler power P_2/P_0 and P_1/P_0 as a function of the coupler draw length

- To specify the performance of an optical coupler, splitting ratio or coupling ratio is used.

  If P_0 is the input power and P_1 and P_2 are the output powers then,

$$\begin{matrix} \text{Splitting ratio} \\ \text{OR} \\ \text{Coupling ratio} \end{matrix} = \left(\frac{P_2}{P_1 + P_2} \right) \times 100\% \qquad \ldots(3.6)$$

- By adjusting the parameters, power gets divided evenly with half of the input power going to each output and the coupler acts as 3-dB coupler.

- Here we assume that the device is loss less. But practically there always will be a loss when the signal passes through a coupler.

- The two basic losses are excess loss and insertion loss.

Excess Loss: It is defined as 'the ratio of the input power to the total output power'.

It is expressed in decibels.

$$\boxed{\text{Excess loss } = 10 \log \left(\frac{P_0}{P_1 + P_2} \right)} \qquad \ldots(3.7)$$

Insertion Loss: The insertion loss occurs for a particular port to port path. For example, for the path from input port i to output port j, we have,

$$\boxed{\text{Insertion loss} = 10 \log \left(\frac{P_i}{P_j} \right)} \qquad \ldots(3.8)$$

Another parameter is return loss which measures the degree of isolation between the input at one port and the optical power scattered or reflected back into the other input port.

$$\text{Return loss} = 10 \log \left(\frac{P_3}{P_0} \right) \qquad \ldots (3.9)$$

3.3.2 Tap Coupler

- To monitor the light signal level or quantity in a link, one can use a 2×2 device that has a coupling fraction of around 1 to 5%, which is selected and fixed during fabrication. This is known as the **tap coupler.**

- Nominally the tap coupler is packaged as a three port device with one arm of the 2×2 coupler being terminated inside the package.

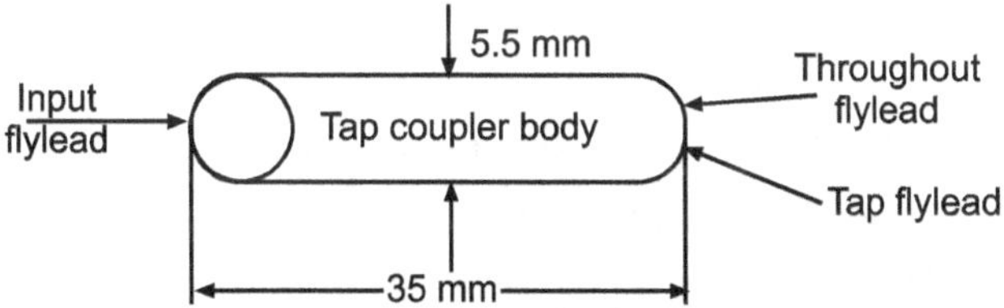

Fig. 3.7: Configuration and package dimensions for a tap coupler

- Fig. 3.7 shows a typical package for such a tap coupler and table 3.2 lists some representative specifications.

Table 3.2 Representative Specifications for a 2 × 2 Tap Coupler

Parameter	Unit	Specification
Tap ratio	percent	1 to 5
Insertion loss	dB	0.5
Return loss	dB	55
Power handling	mW	1000
Flylead length	m	1
Size (diameter × length)	mm	5.5 × 35

Example 3.1 : A 2×2 biconical tapered fiber coupler has an input optical power level of $P_0 = 200\ \mu W$. The output powers at the other three ports are $P_1 = 90\ \mu W$, $P_2 = 85\ \mu W$ and $P_3 = 6.3\ nW$. Find all the losses which occur in the fiber.

Solution : The coupling ratio is

$$\text{Coupling ratio} = \left(\frac{85}{90 + 85} \right) \times 100\% = 48.6\%$$

$$\text{Excess loss} = 10 \log \left(\frac{200}{90 + 85} \right) = 0.58\ dB$$

$$\text{Insertion loss (part 0 to part 1)} = 10 \log \left(\frac{200}{90} \right) = 3.47\ dB$$

$$\text{Insertion loss (part 0 to part 2)} = 10 \log\left(\frac{200}{85}\right) = 3.72 \text{ dB}$$

$$\text{Return loss} = 10 \log\left(\frac{6.3 \times 10^{-3}}{200}\right) = -45 \text{ db}$$

3.3.3 Scattering matrix Representation

- One can also analyze a 2×2 guided wave coupler as a four terminal device that has two inputs and two outputs, as shown in Fig. 3.8. Either all-fiber or integrated-optics devices can be analyzed in terms of the scattering matrix (also called the propagation matrix) S, which defines the relationship between the two input field strengths a_1 and a_2 and the two output field strengths b_1 and b_2 By definition,

$$B = Sa, \quad \text{where} \quad b = \begin{bmatrix} b_1 \\ b_2 \end{bmatrix}, \quad a = \begin{bmatrix} a_1 \\ a_2 \end{bmatrix} \quad \text{and} \quad S = \begin{bmatrix} S_{11} & S_{21} \\ S_{12} & S_{22} \end{bmatrix} \qquad \dots (3.10)$$

- Here $S_{ij} = |S_{ij}| \exp(j\phi_{ij})$ represents the coupling coefficient of optical power transfer from input port i to output port j, with $|s_{ij}|$ being the magnitude of S_{ij} and ϕ_{ij} being its phase at port j relative to port i.

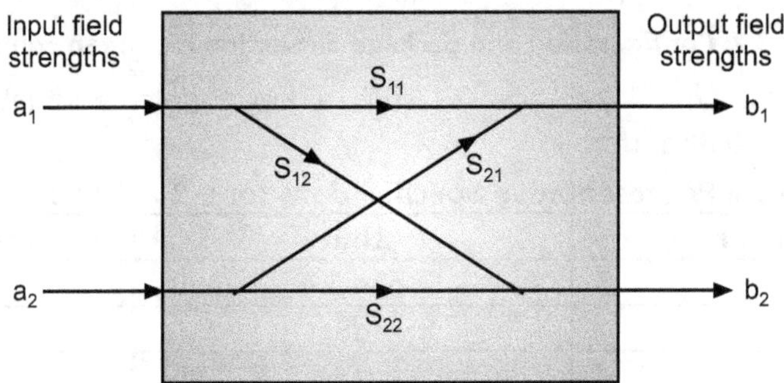

Fig. 3.8 : Generic 2×2 guided wave coupler

- For an actual physical device, two restrictions apply to the scattering matrix S. One is a result of the reciprocity condition arising from the fact that Maxwell's equations are invariant for time inversion; that is, they have two solutions in opposite propagating directions through the device, assuming single-mode operation.

- The other restriction arises from energy-conservation principles under the assumption that the device is lossless. From the first condition, it follows that

$$S_{12} = S_{21} \qquad \dots (3.11)$$

- From the second restriction, if the device is lossless, the sum of the output intensities I_0 must equal the sum of the input intensities I_i :

$$I_0 = b_1^* b_1 + b_2^* b_2 = I_i = a_1^* a_1 + a_2^* a_2 \quad \text{or} \quad b + b = a + a \qquad \dots (3.12)$$

- Where the superscript $*$ means the complex conjugate and the superscript + indicates the transpose conjugate. Substituting Equation (3.10) and (3.11) into Equation (3.12) yields the following set of three equations :

$$S^*_{11} S_{11} + S^*_{12} S_{12} = 1 \qquad \qquad \text{... (3.13)}$$

$$S^*_{11} S_{12} + S^*_{12} S_{22} = 0 \qquad \qquad \text{... (3.14)}$$

$$S^*_{22} S_{22} + S^*_{12} S_{12} = 1 \qquad \qquad \text{... (3.15)}$$

- If we now assume that the coupler has been constructed so that the fraction $(1 - \epsilon)$ of the optical power from input 1 appears at output port 1, with the remainder ϵ going to port 2, then we have $s_{11} = \sqrt{1 - \epsilon}$, which is a real number between 0 and 1.

- Here, we have assumed, without loss of generality, that the electric field at output 1 has a zero phase shift relative to the input at port 1; that is $\phi_{11} = 0$.

- Since we are interested in the phase change that occurs when the coupled optical power from input 1 emerges from port 2, we make the simplifying assumption that the coupler is symmetric. Then, analogous to the effect at port 1, we have $s_{22} = \sqrt{1 - \epsilon}$, with $\phi_{22} = 0$.

- Using these expressions, we can determine the phases ϕ_{12} of the coupled outputs relative to the input signals and find the constraints on the composite outputs when both input ports are receiving signals.

- Inserting the expressions for s_{11} and s_{22} into Equation (3.14) and letting $s_{12} = |s_{12}|$ exp $(j\phi_{12})$, where $|s_{12}|$ is the magnitude of s_{12} and ϕ_{12} is its phase, we have

$$\exp(j2\phi_{12}) = 1 \qquad \qquad \text{... (3.16)}$$

which holds when

$$\phi_{12} = (2n + 1)\frac{\pi}{2} \quad \text{where } n = 0, 1, 2, \ldots\ldots \qquad \text{... (3.17)}$$

- So that the scattering matrix from Equation (3.10) becomes

$$S = \begin{bmatrix} \sqrt{1 - \epsilon} & j\sqrt{\epsilon} \\ j\sqrt{\epsilon} & \sqrt{1 - \epsilon} \end{bmatrix} \qquad \qquad \text{... (3.18)}$$

- Assume we have a 3 db coupler, so that half of the input power gets coupled to the second fiber. Then, $\epsilon = 0.5$ and the output field intensities $E_{out,1}$ and $E_{out,2}$ can be found from the input intensities $E_{in,1}$ and $E_{in,2}$ and the scattering matrix in Equation (3.8) :

$$\begin{bmatrix} E_{out,1} \\ E_{out,2} \end{bmatrix} = \frac{1}{\sqrt{2}} \begin{bmatrix} 1 & j \\ j & 1 \end{bmatrix} \begin{bmatrix} E_{in,1} \\ E_{in,2} \end{bmatrix}$$

Letting $E_{in,2} = 0$, we have $E_{out,1} = \left(1/\sqrt{2}\right) E_{in,1}$ and $E_{out,2} = \left(j/\sqrt{2}\right) E_{in,1}$

The output powers are then given by

$$P_{out,\,1} = E_{out,\,1}\, E^{*}_{out,\,1} = \frac{1}{2} E^{2}_{in,\,1} = \frac{1}{2} P_0$$

Similarly, $$P_{out,\,2} = E_{out,\,2}\, E^{*}_{out,\,2} = \frac{1}{2} E^{2}_{in,\,1} = \frac{1}{2} P_0$$

So that half the input power appears at each output of the coupler.

- It is also important to note that when we want a large portion of the input power from, say, port 1 to emerge from output 1, we need $\in$ be small.

- However, this, in turn, means that the amount of power at the same wavelength coupled to output 1 from input 2 is small.

- Consequently, if one is using the same wavelength, it is not possible, in a passive 2×2 coupler, to have all the power from both inputs coupled simultaneously to the same output.

- The best that can be done is to have half of the power from each input appear at the same output.

- However, if the wavelengths are different at each input, it is possible to couple a large portion of both power levels onto the same fiber.

3.4 OPTICAL ISOLATORS AND CIRCULATORS

In a number of applications it is desirable to have a passive optical device that is nonreciprocal, that is, it works differently when its inputs and outputs are reversed. Two examples of such a device are isolators and circulators. To understand the operation of these devices, we need to recall some facts about polarization and polarization-sensitive components.

1) Light can be represented as a combination of a parallel vibration and a perpendicular vibration, which are called the two orthogonal plane polarization states of a lightwave.

2) A polarizer is a material or device that transmits only one polarization component and blocks the other.

3) A Faraday rotator is a device that rotates the state of polarization (SOP) of light passing through it by a specific angular amount.

4) A device made from birefringent materials (called a walk-off polarizer)splits the light signal entering it into two orthogonally (perpendicularly) polarized beams, which then follow different paths through the material.

5) A half-wave plate rotates the SOP clockwise by 45^0 for signals going from left to right, and counterclockwise by 45^0 for signals propagating in the other direction.

3.4.1 Optical Isolators

- In some applications it is desirable to have a passive optical device that is non-reciprocal, that is it works differently when its inputs and outputs are reversed.

- Optical isolators are devices that allow light to pass through them only in one direction. One common application of an optical isolator is to keep such backward travelling light from entering a laser diode and possibly causing instabilities in the output.

- Various design configurations are available for optical isolators. One of the designs is a polarization independent isolator which is made of three miniature optical components. The core of the device consist of 45° Faraday rotator that is placed between two wedge-shaped birefringent plates or walk-off polarizers. These plates consists of a material YVO_4 or TiO_2. Light travelling in the forward direction is separated into ordinary and extraordinary rays by the first birefringent plate.

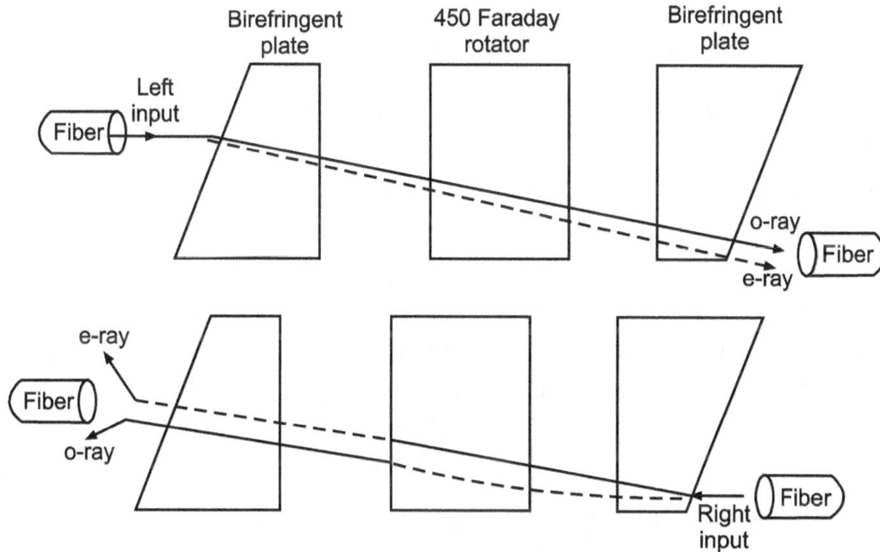

Fig. 3.9 : Polarization independent isolator

- The Faraday rotator then rotates the polarization plane of each ray by 45°. After passing the Faraday rotator the two rays pass through the second birefringent plate. The axis of this polarizer plate is oriented in such a way that the relationship between the two types of rays is maintained. Thus, when they exit the polarizer they both are refracted in an identical parallel direction.

- Going in the reverse direction (right to left) the relationship of the ordinary and extraordinary ray is reversed when exiting the Faraday rotator due to the non-reciprocity of the Faraday rotation. The rays diverge when they exit the left hand birefringent plate and are not coupled to the fiber anymore.

Table 3.3 : The Typical Parameter Values of Commercially Available Optical Isolators

Parameter	Unit	Value
Central wavelength λ_C	nm	1310, 1550
Peak isolation	dB	40
Isolation at $\lambda_C \pm 20$ nm	dB	30
Insertion loss	dB	< 0.5
Polarization - dependent loss	dB	< 0.1
Polarization - mode dispersion	ps	< 0.25
Size (diameter $\times$ length)	mm	6×35

3.4.2 Optical Circulators

- An optical circulator is a non-reciprocal multi-port passive device that directs light sequentially from port to port in only one direction.

- This device is used in optical amplifiers, add/drop multiplexers, and dispersion compensation modules.

- The operation of a circulator is similar to that of an isolator except that its construction is more complex.

- Typically it consists of a number of walk-off polarizers, half-wave plates, and Faraday rotators and has three or four ports, as shown in Fig. 3.10. To see how it works, Consider the three-port circulator. Here an input on port 1 is sent out on port 2, an input on port 2 is sent out on port 3, and an input on port 3 is sent out on port 1.

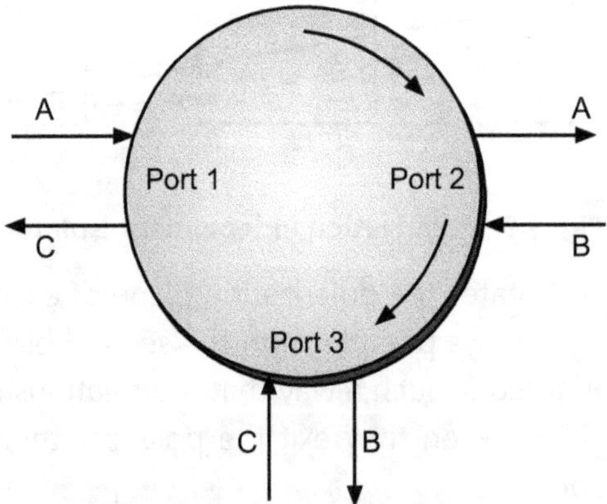

Fig. 3.10 : Operational concept of a three port circulator

- Similarly, in a four port device ideally one could have four inputs and four outputs if the circulator is perfectly symmetrical. However, in actual applications usually it is not necessary to have four inputs and four outputs.

- Furthermore, such a perfectly symmetrical circulator is rather complex to fabricate. Therefore in a four-port circulator it is common to have three input ports and three output ports, making port 1 be an input-only port, 2 and 3 being input and output ports, and port 4 be an output-only port.

- A variety of circulators are available commercially. These devices have low insertion loss, high isolation over a wide wavelength range, minimal polarization-dependent loss (PDL) and low polarization-mode dispersion (PMD). Table 3.4 lists some operational characteristics of commercially available circulators.

Table 3.4 : Typical Parameter Values of Commercially Available Optical Circulators

Parameter	Unit	Value
wavelength band	nm	C-band : 1525-1565 L-band : 1570-1610
Insertion loss	dB	< 0.6
Channel Isolation	dB	> 40
Optical return loss	dB	> 50
Operating power	mW	< 500
Polarization-dependent loss	dB	< 0.1
Polarization-mode dispersion	ps	< 0.1
Size (diameter × length)	mm	5.5×50

3.5 FIBER GRATING

- A grating is an important element in WDM systems for combining and separating individual wavelengths. Basically, a grating is a periodic structure or perturbation in a material.

- This variation in the material has the property of reflecting or transmitting light in a certain direction depending on the wavelength. Thus, gratings can be categorized as either transmitting or reflecting gratings.

3.5.1 Grating Basics

- Fig. 3.11 defines various parameters for a reflecting grating. Here, θ_i is the incident angle of the light, θ_d is the diffracted angle, and Λ is the period of the grating (the periodicity of the structural variation in the material).

- In a transmission grating consisting of a series of equally spaced slits, the spacing between two adjacent slits is called the pitch of the grating. Constructive interference at a wavelength λ occurs in the imaging plane when the rays diffracted at the angle θ_d satisfy the grating equation given by

$$\Lambda (\sin \theta_i - \sin \theta_d) = m\lambda \qquad \qquad \dots (3.19)$$

- Here, m is called the order of the grating. In general, only the first-order diffraction condition m = 1 is considered.

- (Note that in some texts the incidence and refraction angles are defined as being measured from the same side of the normal to the grating.

- In this case, the sign in front of the term sin θ_d changes) a grating can separate individual wavelengths since the grating equation is satisfied at different points in the imaging plane for different wavelengths.

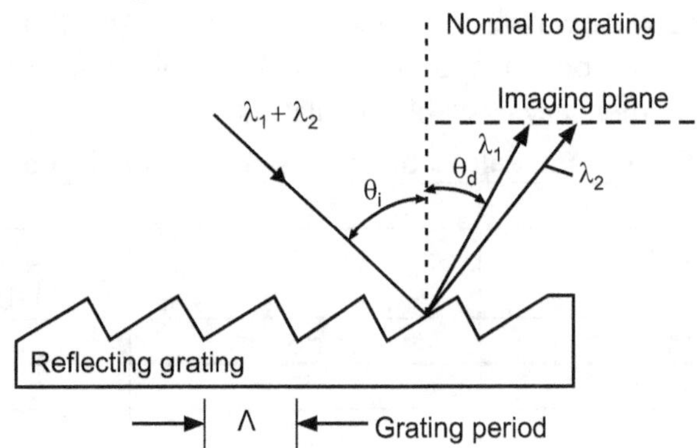

Fig. 3.11: Basic parameters in a reflection grating

3.5.2 Fiber Bragg Grating

- A Bragg grating constructed within an optical fiber constitutes a high performance device for accessing individual wavelengths in the closely spaced spectrum of dense WDM systems.

- Since this is an all fiber device, its main advantages are low cost, low loss (around 0.3 dB), ease of coupling with other fibers, polarization insensitivity, low temperature coefficient (< 0.7 pm/°C) and simple packaging.

- A fiber grating is a narrowband reflection filter that is fabricated through a photo imprinting process.

- The technique is based on the observation that germanium-doped silica fiber exhibits high photosensitivity to ultraviolet light.

- This means that one can induce a change in the refractive index of the core by exposing it to ultraviolet radiation such as 244 nm.

- Several methods can be used to create a fiber phase-grating. Fig. 3.12 demonstrates the so-called external-writing technique.

- The grating fabrication is accomplished by means of two ultraviolet beams transversely irradiating the fiber to produce an interference pattern in the core.

- Here, the regions of high intensity (denoted by the shaded ovals) cause an increase in the local refractive index of the photosensitive core, whereas it remains unaffected in the zero-intensity regions.

- A permanent reflective Bragg grating is thus written into the core.

- When a multi-wavelength signal encounters the grating, those wavelengths that are phase-matched to the Bragg reflection condition are not transmitted.

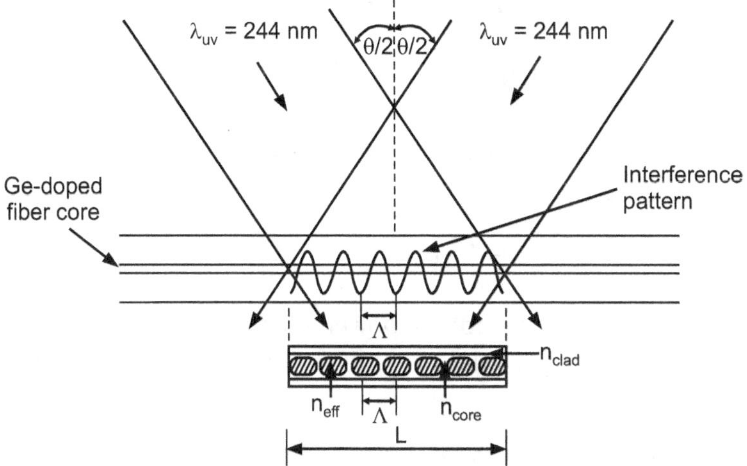

Fig. 3.12: Formation of a Bragg grating in a fiber core

by means of two intersecting ultraviolet light beams

- Using the standard grating equation given by Equation (3.19), with λ being the wavelength of the ultraviolet light λ_{uv}, the period Λ of the interference pattern (and hence the period of the grating) can be calculated from the angle θ between the two interfering beams of free-space wavelength λ_{uv}. Note from Fig. 3.12 that θ is measured outside of the fiber.

- The imprinted grating can be represented as a uniform sinusoidal modulation of the refractive index along the core:

$$n(z) \;=\; n_{core} + \delta_n\left[1 + \cos\left(\frac{2\pi z}{\Lambda}\right)\right] \qquad \text{... (3.20)}$$

where n_{core} is the unexposed core refractive index and δ_n is the photoinduced change in the index. The maximum reflectivity R of the grating occurs when the Bragg condition holds; that is, at a reflection wavelength λ_{Bragg} where

$$\lambda_{Bragg} \;=\; 2\Lambda n_{eff} \qquad \text{... (3.21)}$$

and n_{eff} is the mode effective index of the core. At this wavelength, the peak reflectivity R_{max} for the grating of length l and coupling coefficient K is given by

$$R_{max} \;=\; \tanh^2 (KL) \qquad \text{... (3.22)}$$

- The full bandwidth $\Delta\lambda$ over which the maximum reflectivity holds is

$$\Delta\lambda \;=\; \frac{\lambda_{Bragg}^2}{\pi n_{eff} L}\,[(KL)^2 + \pi^2]^{1/2} \qquad \text{... (3.23)}$$

- An approximation for the full width half-maximum (FWHM) bandwidth is

$$\Delta\lambda_{\text{FWHM}} \approx \lambda_{\text{Bragg}}\, S\left[\left(\frac{\delta n}{2n_{\text{core}}}\right)^2 + \left(\frac{\wedge}{L}\right)^2\right]^{1/2} \qquad \ldots (3.24)$$

where s = 1 for strong gratings with near 100 percent reflectivity, and s $\approx$ 0.5 for weak gratings.

- For a uniform sinusoidal modulation of the index throughout the core, the coupling coefficient K is given by

$$K = \frac{\pi\delta_n\eta}{\lambda_{\text{Bragg}}} \qquad \ldots (3.25)$$

- With η being the fraction of optical power contained in the fiber core. Under the assumption that the grating is uniform in the core, η can be approximated by

$$\eta \approx 1 - v^{-2} \qquad \ldots (3.26)$$

where V is the V number of the fiber. A more precise evaluation is needed for nonuniform or nonsinusoidal index variations.

- Fiber Bragg gratings are available in a wide range of reflection bandwidths varying from 25 GHz and higher. Table 3.5 lists some operational characteristics of commercially available 25 –, 50 – and 100 GHz fiber Bragg gratings for use in optical communication systems.

Table 3.5 : Typical Parameter Values of Commercially Available Fiber Bragg Gratings

Parameter	Typical value		
Channel spacing	**25 GHz**	**50 GHz**	**100 GHz**
Reflection bandwidth	> 0.08 nm @ - 0.5 dB	0.15 nm @ – 0.5 dB	> 0.3 nm @ – 0.5 dB
	< 0.2 nm @ – 3 dB	< 0.4 nm @ – 3 dB	< 0.75 mm @ – 3 dB
	< 0.25 nm @ – 25 dB	< 0.5 nm @ – 25 dB	< 1 nm @ – 25 dB
Transmission bandwidth	> 0.05 nm @ – 25 dB	> 0.1 nm @ – 25 dB	> 0.2 nm @ – 25 dB
Adjacent channel isolation		> 30 dB	
Insertion loss		< 0.25 dB	
Central λ tolerance		< ± 0.05 nm @ 25°C	
Thermal λ drift		< 1 pm/°C (for an a thermal design)	
Package size		5 mm (diameter) × 80 mm length)	

- In the fiber Bragg grating (FBG) illustrated in Fig. 3.13, the grating spacing is uniform along its length. It is also possible to have the spacing vary along the length of the fiber, which means that a range of different wavelengths will be reflected by the FBG. This is the basis of what is known as a chirped grating.

3.5.3 FBG Applications

- Fig. 3.13 shows a simple concept of a demultiplexing function using a fiber Bragg grating. To extract the desired wavelength, a circulator is used in conjunction with the grating.

- Here the four wavelengths enter through port 1 of the circulator and leave from port 2.

- All wavelengths except λ_2 pass through the grating. Since λ_2 satisfies the Bragg condition of the grating, it gets reflected, enters port 2 of the circulator, and exits at port 3.

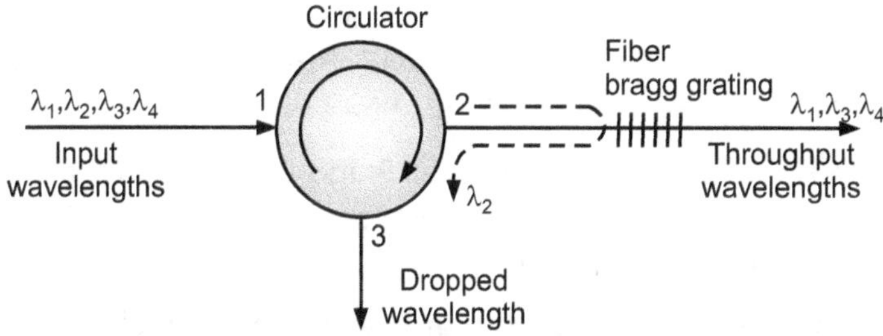

Fig.. 3.13 : Simple concept of a demultiplexing function

using a fiber grating and an optical circulator

- To create a device for combining or separating N wavelengths, one needs to cascade N − 1 FBGs and N − 1 circulators. Fig. 3.14 illustrates a multiplexing function for the four wavelengths λ_1, λ_2, λ_3 and λ_4 using three FBGs and three circulators (labeled C_2, C_3 and C_4).

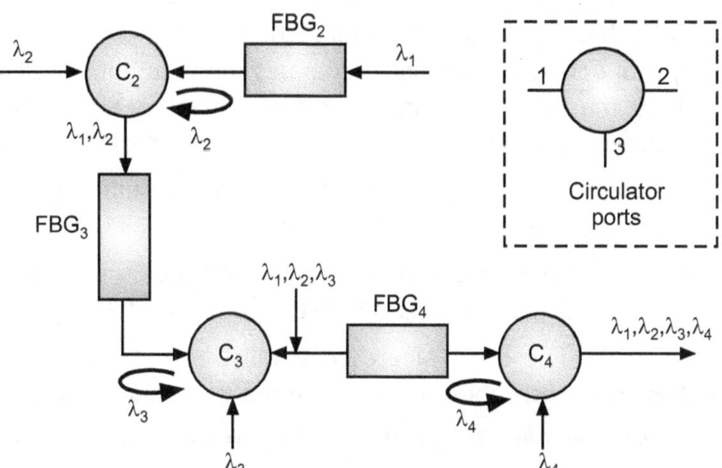

Fig. 3.14: Multiplexing of four wavelengths using three FBG devices and three circulators

- The fiber grating filters labeled FBG_2, FBG_3 and FBG_4 are constructed to reflect wavelengths λ_2, λ_3 and λ_4, respectively, and to pass all others.

- To see how the multiplexer functions, first consider the combination of circulator C_2 and fiber filter FBG_2.

- Here filter FBG_2 reflects wavelength λ_2 and allows wavelength λ_1 to pass through. After wavelength λ_1 passes through FBG_2, it enters port 2 of circulator C_2 and exits from port 3. Wavelength λ_2 enters port 1 of circulator C_2 and exits from port 2.

- After being reflected from FBG_2 it enters port 2 of circulator C_2 and exits from port 3 together with wavelength λ_1.

- Next at circulator C_3 wavelength λ_3 enters port 3 of circulator C_3 and exits from port 1 and travels toward FBG_3.

- After being reflected from FBG_3 it enters port 1 of circulator C_3 and exits from port 2 together with wavelengths λ_1 and λ_2. After a similar process at circulator C_4 and filter FBG_4 to insert wavelength λ_4, the four wavelengths all exit together from port 2 of circulator C_4 and can be coupled easily into a fiber.

- The coupler size limitation when using fiber Bragg gratings is that one filter is needed for each wavelength and normally the operation is sequential with wavelengths being transmitted by one filter after another.

- Therefore the losses are not uniform from channel to channel, since each wavelength goes through a different number of circulators and fiber gratings, each of which adds loss to that channel.

- This may be acceptable for a small number of channels, but the loss differential between the first and last inserted wavelengths is a restriction for large channel counts.

3.6 DIFFRACTION GRATINGS

- Another DWDM technology is based on diffraction gratings. A diffraction grating is a conventional optical device that spatially separates the different wavelengths contained in a beam of light. The device consists of a set of diffracting elements, such as narrow parallel slits or grooves, separated by a distance comparable to the wavelength of light.

- These diffracting elements can be either reflective or transmitting, thereby forming a reflection grating or a transmission grating, respectively.

- Separating and combining wavelengths with diffraction gratings is a parallel process, as opposed to the serial process that is used with the fiber-based Bragg gratings.

- Reflection gratings are fine ruled or etched parallel lines on some type of reflective surface. With these gratings, light will bounce off the grating at an angle.

- The angle at which the light leaves the grating depends on its wavelength, so the reflected light fans out in a spectrum.

- For DWDM applications, the lines are spaced equally and each individual wavelength will be reflected at a slightly different angle, as shown in Fig. 3.15.

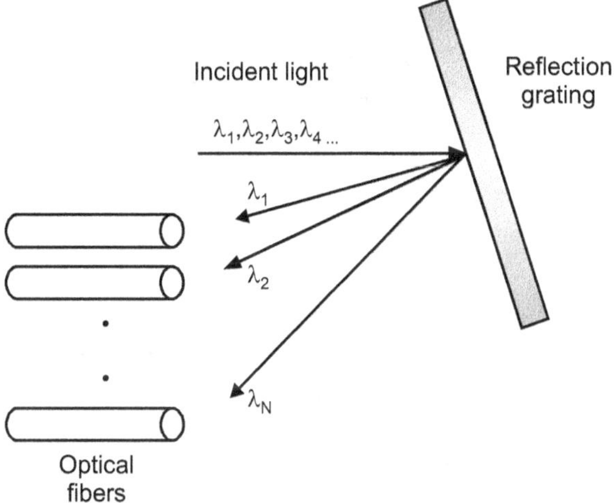

Fig. 3.15: The angle at which reflected light leaves

a reflection grating depends on its wavelength

- There can be reception fiber at each of the positions where the reflected light gets focused. Thus, individual wavelengths will be directed to separate fibers.

- The reflective diffraction grating works reciprocally, that is, if different wavelengths come into the device on the individual input fibers, all of the wavelengths will be focused back into one fiber after traveling through the device.

- One also could have a photodiode array in place of the receiving fibers for functions such power-per-wavelength monitoring.

- One type of transmission grating, which is known as a phase grating, consists of a periodic variation of the refractive index of the grating.

- These may be characterized by a Q-parameter which is defined as

$$Q = \frac{2\pi\lambda d}{n_g{}^{\wedge 2} \cos \alpha} \qquad \ldots (3.27)$$

- Where λ is the wavelength, d is the thickness of the grating, n_g is the refractive index of the material, $^\wedge$ is the grating period, and α is the incident angle, as shown in Fig. 3.16.

- The phase grating is called thin for Q < 1 and thick for Q > 10. After a spectrum of wavelength channels passes through the grating, each wavelength emerges at a slightly different angle and can be focused into a receiving fiber.

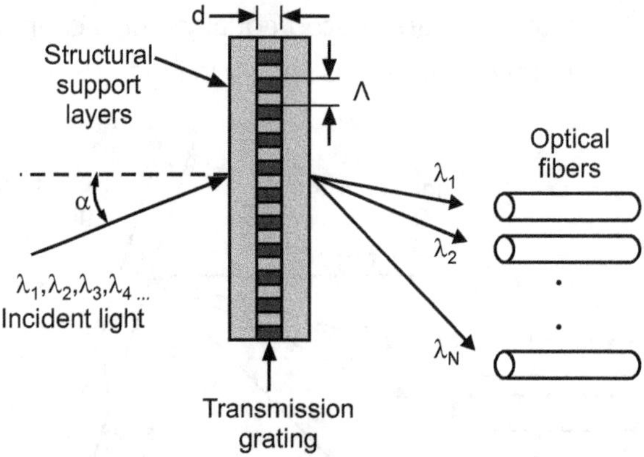

Fig. 3.16: Each wavelength emerges at a slightly different angle after passing through a transmission grating

3.7 OPTICAL AMPLIFIERS

- Optical amplifiers have widespread applications ranging from ultra-long undersea links to short links in access networks. In long distance undersea and terrestrial point-to-point links, the traffic patterns are relatively stable, so that the input power levels to an optical amplifier do not vary significantly. The amplifier must have a wide spectral response range and should be highly reliable.

- The optical amplifiers are classified into three categories :

1. In-line Optical Amplifiers :

In a single-mode link, the dispersion may be small so the main limitation to repeater spacing is fiber attenuation. Such a link does not require a complete regeneration of the signal. A simple amplification of optical signal is sufficient. Thus, an in-line optical amplifier can be used to compensate for the transmission loss and increase the distance between regeneration repeaters as shown in Fig. 3.17 (a).

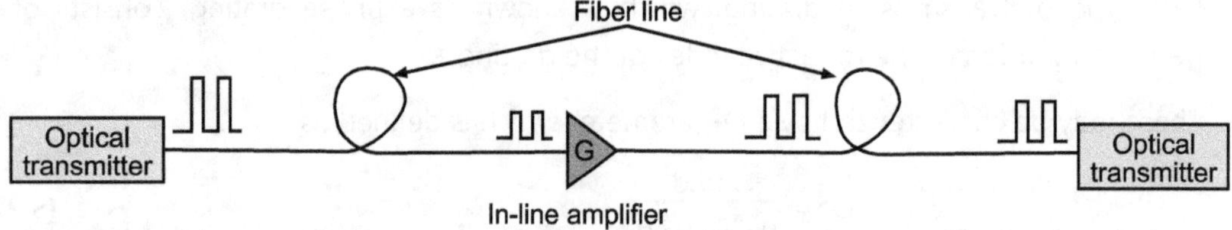

Fig. 3.17 (a) : In-line amplifier to increase transmission distance

2. Pre-amplifier :

- Fig. 3.17 (b) shows the front-end preamplifier for an optical receiver. A weak optical signal is amplified before photodetection so that the signal-to-noise ratio degradation caused by thermal noise in the receiver can be suppressed. Compared with other front-end devices, an optical amplifier provides a larger gain factor and a broader bandwidth.

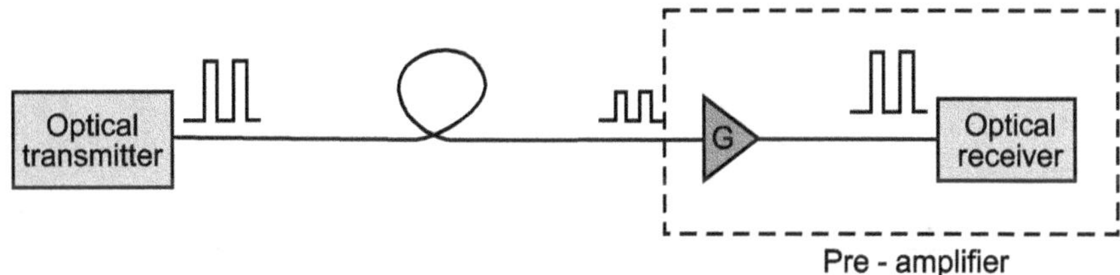

Fig. 3.17 (b) : Pre-amplifier to improve receiver sensitivity

3. Power Amplifier :

- Power amplification includes the applications in which the device is placed immediately after the optical transmitter to boost the transmitted power. This increases the transmission distance by 10 – 100 km depending upon the amplifier gain and fiber loss. One can also apply an optical amplifier in a local area network as a booster amplifier to compensate for the coupler-insertion loss and power-splitting loss.

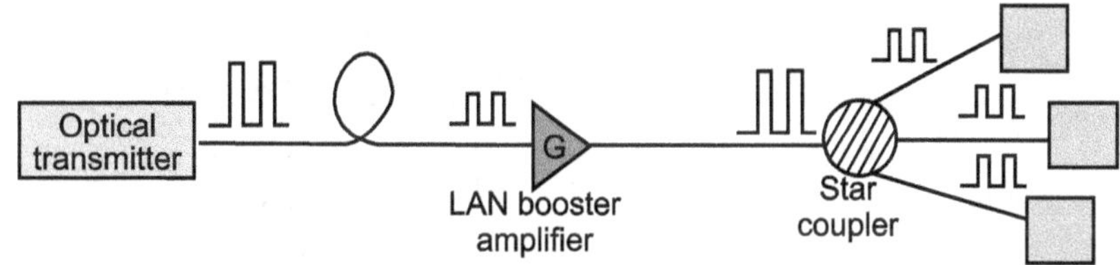

Fig. 3.17 (c) : Power amplifier or booster of signal level in a local area network

3.8 AMPLIFIER TYPES

- The optical amplifiers can be classified as :

(1) Semiconductor Optical Amplifiers (SOA).

(2) Active-fiber or doped-fiber amplifiers (DFAs).

(3) Raman amplifiers.

- All optical amplifiers increase the power level of incident light through a stimulated emission process or an optical power transfer process. An optical amplifier can boost the incoming signal levels, but it cannot generate a coherent optical output by itself.

- The basic operation of the amplifier consists of a pump which provides energy to the device. The pump supplies energy to electrons in an active medium which raises them to higher energy levels to produce a population inversion. An incoming signal photon will trigger these excited electrons to drop to lower levels through a stimulated emission process. Since one incoming trigger photon simulates many excited electrons to emit photons of equal energy as they drop to the ground state, the result is the amplification of the optical signal.

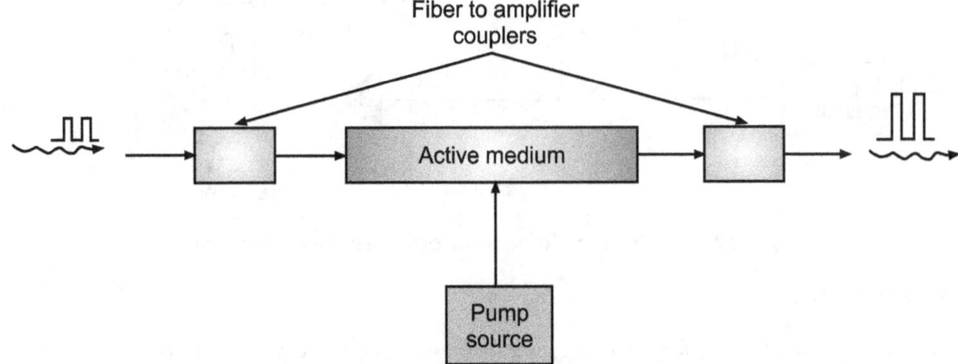

Fig. 3.18 : Basic operation of an optical amplifier

- The typical gain profiles for various optical amplifiers based around the 1.3 and 1.5 μm wavelength regions are shown in Fig. 3.19.

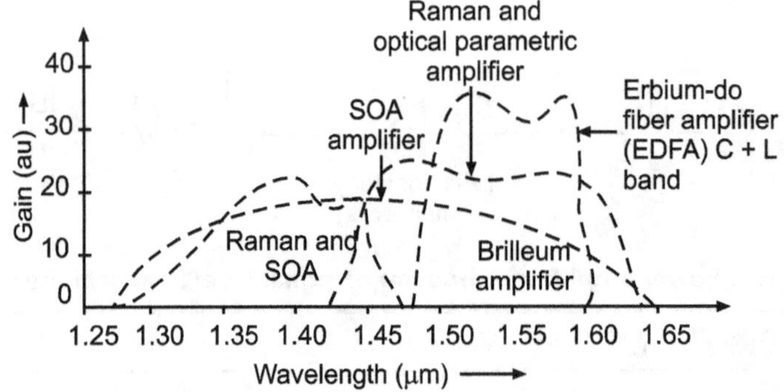

Fig. 3.19: Gain bandwidth characteristics of different optical amplifiers

- It may be observed that the Semiconductor optical amplifier (SOA), the Erbium-Doped Fiber Amplifier (EDFA) and the Raman amplifier all provide wide spectral bandwidths. In comparison, Brillouin fiber amplifiers have a very narrow spectral bandwidth, possibly around 50 MHz and therefore cannot be employed for wideband amplification. However, SOA's exhibit low power consumption and their single mode waveguide structures make them suitable for use with a single-mode fiber.

3.9 SEMICONDUCTOR OPTICAL AMPLIFIERS (SOA)

- The SOA is based on the conventional laser structure. Semiconductor optical amplifiers can be used in both linear and non-linear modes of operation.

- Semiconductor optical amplifiers can be classified into two main groups :

1. Fabry-Perot Amplifiers (FPAs).

2. Travelling-wave amplifiers (TWAs).

3.9.1 Fabry-Perot Amplifiers (FPAs)

Fig. 3.20 shows the schematic structure of the semiconductor optical amplifier.

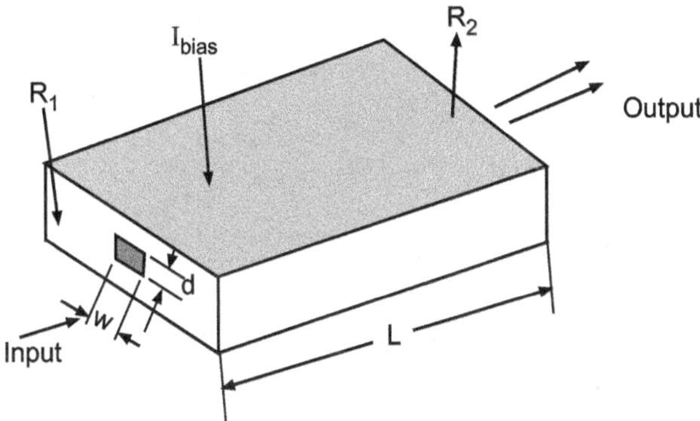

Fig. 3.20 : Schematic structure of the semiconductor optical amplifier

- It is based on the conventional semiconductor optical structure (gain or index guided) with an active region width w, thickness d and length L. When the input and output laser facet reflectivities denoted by R_1 and R_2 are each around 0.3, which depicts a normal semiconductor laser, then an FPA is obtained.

- For operation, the FPA is biased below the normal lasing threshold current and light entering one facet appears amplified at the other facet together with inherent noise. The amplifier chip is bonded into a package with single-mode fiber pigtails which are used to guide light into and out of the amplifier. The inherent filtering of the FPA means the devices are very sensitive to fluctuations in bias current, temperature and signal polarization. Because of the resonant nature of FPAs, combined with their high internal fields, they are used within non-linear applications.

3.9.2 Travelling Wave Amplifiers

- To form a travelling wave semiconductor optical amplifier, anti-reflection coatings may be applied to end reflectivities. This can be achieved by depositing a thin layer of silicon oxide, silicon nitride or titanium oxide on the end facets such that the reflectivities are reduced to 1×10^{-4} or less. Such a device becomes a TWA operating in the single-pass amplification mode in which the Fabry-Perot resonance is suppressed by the reduction in facet reflectivity. This has the effect of increased amplifier spectral bandwidth and it makes the transmission characteristics less dependent upon fluctuations in bias current, temperature and input signal polarization. Hence, the TWA proves superior to the FPA. Anti-reflection facet coatings have the effect of increasing the lasing current threshold, so such SOAs are operated at currents far beyond the normal lasing threshold current.

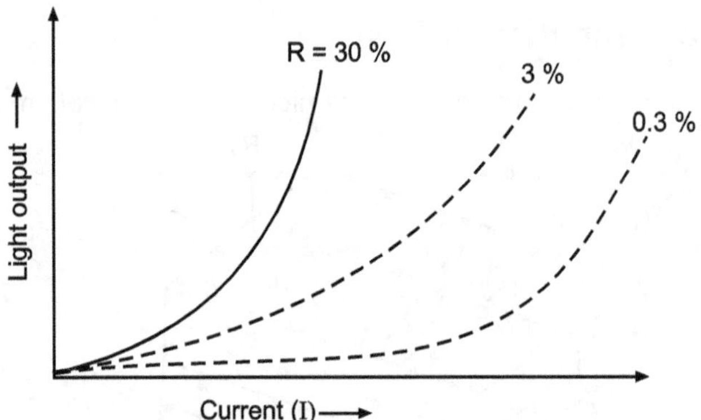

Fig. 3.21 : Light output against current characteristics for the semiconductor optical amplifier with different values of facet relectivity R

- The general equation for the cavity gain G of an SOA as a function of signal frequency f is

$$G(f) \; = \; \frac{(1 - R_1)(1 - R_2)\, G_s}{\left(1 - \sqrt{R_1\, R_2}\, G_s\right)^2 + 4\sqrt{R_1\, R_2}\, G_s \sin^2 \phi} \qquad \ldots (3.28)$$

where R_1 and R_2 are the input and output facet reflectivities respectively.

G_s is the single pass gain.

ϕ is the single pass phase shift through the amplifier.

- The above equation does not include coupling losses to and from the amplifier and the phase shift is given by

$$\phi \; = \; \frac{\pi (f - f_0)}{\delta f} \qquad \ldots (3.29)$$

where f_0 is the Fabry-Perot resonant frequency and δf is the free spectral range of the SOA.

- The 3 dB spectral bandwidth of an FPA or essentially the ± 3 dB single longitudinal mode bandwidth defined by the FWHP points B_{FPA} is expressed as

$$B_{FPA} \; = \; 2\,(f - f_0) = \frac{2\delta f}{\pi} \sin^{-1} \left[\frac{1 - \sqrt{R_1 R_2\, G_s}}{2 \left(\sqrt{R_1 R_2\, G_s}\right)^{1/2}} \right] \qquad \ldots (3.30)$$

$$= \; \frac{c}{\pi n L} \sin^{-1} \left[\frac{1 - \sqrt{R_1 R_2\, G_s}}{2 \left(\sqrt{R_1 R_2\, G_s}\right)^{1/2}} \right] \qquad \ldots (3.31)$$

where the mode separation frequency interval δf combines the velocity of light c and the refractive index of the amplifier medium n with its length L. The 3-dB spectral or optical bandwidth may be expressed as a function of the FPA cavity gain G:

$$B_{FPA} \; = \; \frac{c}{\pi n L} \sin^{-1} \left[\frac{1}{2} \left(\frac{(1 - R_1)(1 - R_2)}{\sqrt{R_1 R_2}\, G} \right) \right] \qquad \ldots (3.32)$$

- The single-pass gain (G_s), defined in terms of the device parameters and the applied bias current for the semiconductor laser is written as:

$$G_s = \exp(\bar{g}L) \qquad \qquad \text{... (3.33)}$$

where $\bar{g}$ is the net gain coefficient per unit length and L = amplifier active length.

- The net gain per unit length $\bar{g}$ may be defined in terms of the material gain coefficient g_m, the optical confinement factor Γ and the effective loss coefficient per unit length $\bar{\alpha}$ as

$$\bar{g} = \Gamma g_m - \bar{\alpha} \qquad \qquad \text{... (3.34)}$$

- The material gain coefficient g_m is further related to the signal intensity I, as

$$g_m = \frac{g_o}{1 + I/I_s} \qquad \qquad \text{... (3.35)}$$

where, g_o = Unsaturated material gain coefficient in the absence of the input signal

I_s = Saturation intensity

- Substituting equation (3.34) and (3.35) in equation (3.33)

$$G_s = \exp\left[(\Gamma g_m - \bar{\alpha})L\right] \qquad \qquad \text{... (3.36)}$$

$$= \exp\left[\left(\frac{\sqrt{\Gamma}g_o}{1 + I/I_s} - \bar{\alpha}\right)L\right] \qquad \qquad \text{... (3.37)}$$

- The Phase shift ϕ_s associated with the single-pass amplifier includes the nominal phase shift ϕ_o and an additional component resulting from the change in carrier density from the nominal density in the absence of a signal. Hence, the total phase shift is given by

$$\phi_s = \phi_o + \frac{g_o bL}{2}\left(\frac{I}{1 + I_s}\right) \qquad \qquad \text{... (3.38)}$$

where b is the linewidth broadening factor and the nominal phase shift is

$$\phi_o = \frac{2\pi nL}{\lambda} \qquad \qquad \text{... (3.39)}$$

where, n = material refractive index

- Equations (3.37) and (3.38) indicate that both single pass gain and phase are functions of optical intensity. For a constant signal intensity there is no inherent signal distortion. But with a time varying intensity the gain and phase may also change with time which causes the signal distortion.

- As G_s and ϕ_s are the functions of the input signal intensity, the SOA will exhibit non-linear and bistable characteristics at high input powers.

- The 3dB spectral bandwidth of a TWA is determined by the full gain width of the amplifier medium itself rather than the Fabry-Perot gain profile. Hence, the 3dB bandwidth of TWA is three times larger than that of FPA.

- The passband comprises peaks and troughs whose relative amplitudes are determined by the facet reflectivities, the single pass gain and the input intensity. This gain undulation or peak-trough ratio of the passband ripple, ΔG, is defined as 'the difference between the resonant and non-resonant signal gain'.

$$\Delta G = \left(\frac{1 + \sqrt{R_1 R_2}\ G_s}{1 - \sqrt{R_1 R_2}\ G_s} \right)^2 \qquad \qquad \text{... (3.40)}$$

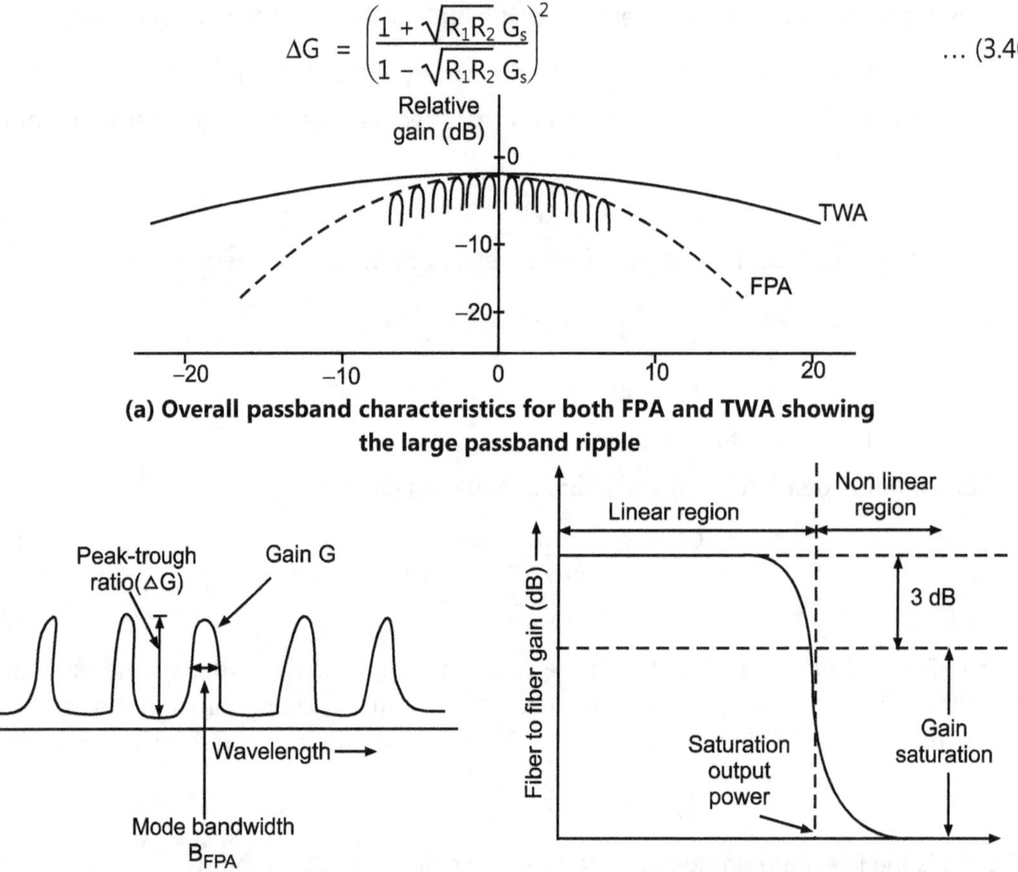

(a) Overall passband characteristics for both FPA and TWA showing the large passband ripple

(b) Illustration of the peak-trough ratio of the passband ripple

(c) Typical fiber to fiber gain against output signal power characteristics

Fig. 3.22 : Characteristics of a semiconductor amplifier

Example 3.2 : *An uncoated FPA has facet reflectivities of 30% and a single pass gain of 4.8 dB. The amplifier has a 300 μm long active region, a mode spacing of 1 nm and a peak gain wavelength of 1.5 μm. Determine the refractive index of the active medium and the 3dB spectral bandwidth of the device.*

Solution :

The refractive index of the active medium at the peak gain wavelength is given as

$$n = \frac{\lambda^2}{2\delta\lambda L} = \frac{(1.5 \times 10^{-6})^2}{2 \times 1 \times 10^{-9} \times 300 \times 10^{-6}} = 3.75$$

The 3 dB spectral bandwidth is given by

$$B_{FPA} = \frac{c}{\pi nL} \sin^{-1}\left[\frac{1 - \sqrt{R_1 R_2}\, G_s}{2\left(\sqrt{R_1 R_2}\, G_s\right)^{1/2}}\right]$$

$$= \frac{2.998 \times 10^8}{\pi \times 3.75 \times 300 \times 10^{-6}} \sin^{-1}\left[\frac{1 - \sqrt{0.09 \times 3.020}}{2\left(\sqrt{0.09} \times 3.020\right)^{1/2}}\right]$$

$$= 8.482 \times 10^{10} \sin^{-1}\left[\frac{0.040}{1.904}\right]$$

$$= 8.482 \times 10^{10} \times 0.494 = 4.2 \text{ GHz}$$

Example 3.3 : *Derive an approximate expression for the cavity gain of an SOA in the limiting case of a 3dB peak-trough ratio.*

Solution :

For a 3 dB peak-trough ratio

$$\left(\frac{1 + \sqrt{R_1 R_2}\, G_s}{1 - \sqrt{R_1 R_2}\, G_s}\right)^2 = 0.5$$

Therefore, $1 + \sqrt{R_1 R_2}\, G_s = 0.707 \left(1 - \sqrt{R_1 R_2}\, G_s\right)$

$$\sqrt{R_1 R_2}\, G_s = \frac{0.293}{1.707} = 0.172$$

For a TWA, R_1, $R_2 << 1$ and assuming a zero single pass phase shift

$$G \equiv \frac{G_s}{\left(1 - \sqrt{R_1 R_2}\, G_s\right)^2}$$

Substituting for $\sqrt{R_1 R_2}\, G_s$ gives:

$$G \equiv \frac{G_s}{(1 - 0.172)^2} = \frac{0.172}{(1 - 0.172)^2 \sqrt{R_1 R_2}} = \frac{0.25}{\sqrt{R_1 R_2}}$$

The approximate equation for the cavity gain for an SOA in the limiting case is $\dfrac{0.25}{\sqrt{R_1 R_2}}$. Thus, for wide spectral bandwidth operation the available cavity gain is determined by the quality of the anti-reflection coatings on the device.

The gain of the backward travelling signal G_b is defined as 'the ratio of the power in the backward travelling signal, P_b, to the input signal power, P_{in}, into the amplifier'. Hence, the gain of the backward travelling signal is given by:

$$G_b = \frac{P_b}{P_{in}} \frac{\left(\sqrt{R_1} - \sqrt{R_2}\, G_s\right)^2 + 4\sqrt{R_1 R_2}\, G_s \sin^2 \phi}{\left(1 - \sqrt{R_1 R_2}\, G_s\right)^2 + 4\sqrt{R_1 R_2}\, G_s \sin^2 \phi} \qquad \ldots (3.41)$$

Another important characteristic of the SOA is the noise generated. It also determines the number of devices which can be cascaded as linear repeaters within an optical fiber communication system.

During the amplification process the spontaneously emitted photons are amplified together with the signal photons and they are also accumulated as the output of the amplifier to cause the phenomenon known as Amplified Spontaneous Emission (ASE). It is the main source of noise in SOAs and as it occurs randomly it may cause fluctuations in the optical output signal.

The ASE is considered as an additive noise with constant amplitude, hence it is referred to as white noise. Since the ASE noise power depends upon the amplifier gain, the noise power spectral density P_{ASE}, is given as:

$$P_{ASE} = mn_{sp} (G_s - 1) h_f B \qquad \qquad \text{... (3.42)}$$

$$\text{where,} \qquad m = \text{mode number}$$
$$B = \text{optical bandwidth}$$
$$h_f = \text{energy of photon}$$

The parameter, n_{sp}, represents the spontaneous emission factor which is the spontaneous emission being emitted into the cavity mode.

n_{sp} lies in the range of $1 \le n_{sp} \le 4.0$.

Another parameter to quantify optical amplifier noise is the noise figure, F_n, that is defined as 'the ratio of the input and output signal to noise ratios' and is related to ASE noise as:

$$F_n = \frac{P_{ASE}}{G_s h_f B} \qquad \qquad \text{... (3.43)}$$

The ASE noise is present in both polarization states of the amplified signal and it beats with the signal within each polarization state generating a signal spontaneous noise for each of them.

Example 6.4 : *An SOA operating at a signal wavelength of 1.55 μm produces a gain of 30dB with an optical bandwidth of 1 THz. The device has a spontaneous emission factor of 4 and the mode number is equal to 2.2 when the net gain coefficient over the length of the amplifier is 200. Determine: (a) the length of the device, (b) the ASE noise signal power at the output of the amplifier.*

Solution :

(a)
$$G = \exp(\bar{g}L)$$

$$L = \frac{G_s \text{ (dB)}}{10 \times \bar{g} \times \log_e} = \frac{30}{10 \times 200 \times 0.434} = 34.56 \times 10^{-3} \text{ m.}$$

The length of the SOA is therefore 34.6 mm.

(b) The noise power spectral density P_{ASE} is given by

$$P_{ASE} = mn_{sp} (\sigma_s - 1) h_f B$$
$$= 2.2 \times 4 \times (1000 - 1) \times 6.63 \times 10^{-34} \times 1.94 \times 10^{14} \times 1.0 \times 10^{12}$$
$$= 1.13 \text{ mw}$$

The ASE noise power generated within the SOA is a high level of 1.13 mw which is mainly caused by the large value of the spontaneous emission factor for the device.

3.9.3 Gain Clamping

- Gain clamping is used to maintain or clamp the carrier concentrations to a fixed level in the SOA active cavity medium. This technique is used to avoid the situation where the gain of the SOA can change due to variation of the input signal power.

- Gain clamping is achieved by incorporating lasing action into the amplifier, since the steady-state conditions for the laser can be obtained when the round trip gain is kept constant and equal to the round trip loss. To provide the facility of a gain-clamped SOA, mirrors are placed at either end of the device. This arrangement creates a resonant cavity, similar to Fabry-Perot laser, which is used to stabilize the gain of the optical amplifier.

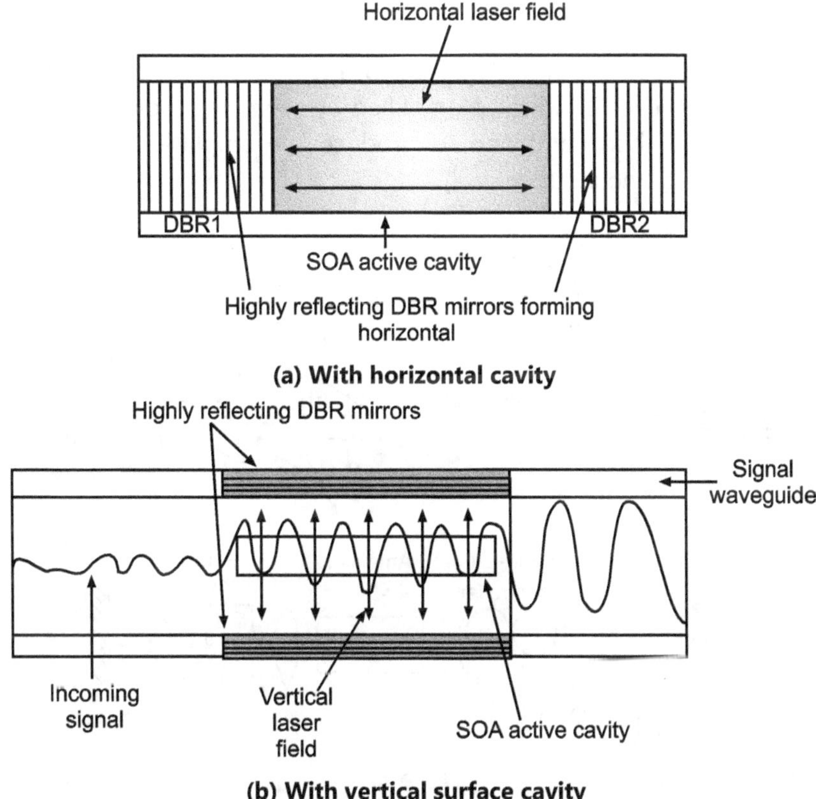

(a) With horizontal cavity

(b) With vertical surface cavity

Fig. 3.23 : Gain clamped SOA with high reflective distributed Bragg reflectors

- Fig. 3.23 shows the two Distributed Bragg Reflectors (DBR1 and DBR2) which are used as mirrors. The lasing field is longitudinal and parallel to the direction of the optical signal. Hence highly reflective DBR mirrors are required to stabilize the gain of the device. Either one or both of the DBR sections can be selected as the active region.

3.9.4 Polarization Sensitivity

- An undesirable characteristic of SOAs is their polarization sensitivity. The amplifier gain 'G', differs for the TM and TE modes by as much as 5-8 dB, simply because both G and σ_g are different for the two orthogonally polarized modes. This feature makes the amplifier gain sensitive to the polarization state of the input beam.

- Several schemes are used to reduce the polarization sensitivity by using two amplifiers or two passes through the same amplifier. Fig. 3.24 shows such three configurations.

- In Fig. 3.24 (a), the TE-polarized signal in one amplifier becomes TM polarized in the second amplifier and vice versa. If both amplifiers have identical gain characteristics, the twin-amplifier configuration provides signal gain that is independent of the signal polarization. A drawback of the series configuration is that the residual facet reflectivities lead to mutual coupling between the two amplifiers.

- In parallel configuration shown in Fig. 3.24 (b) the incident signal is split into a TE and TM polarized signal, each of which is amplified by separate amplifiers. The amplified TE and TM signals are then combined to produce the amplified signal with the same polarization as that of the input beam.

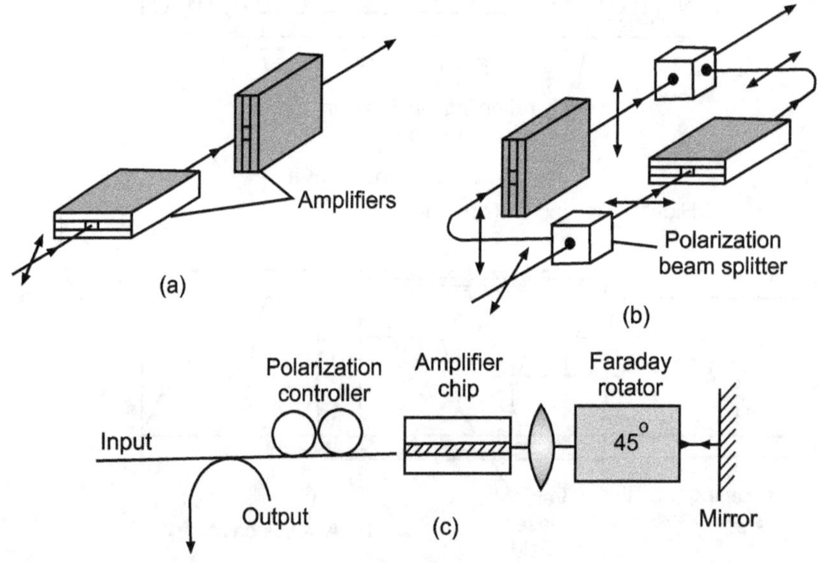

Fig. 3.24

- The double pass configuration as shown in Fig. 3.24 (c) passes the signal through the same amplifier twice, but the polarization is rotated by 90° between the two passes. Since the amplified signal propagates in the backward direction, a 3-dB fiber coupler is needed to separate it from the incident signal. Despite a 6-dB loss occurring the fiber coupler, this configuration provides high gain from a single amplifier, as the same amplifier supplies gain on the two passes.

3.10 SOA APPLICATIONS

- SOA's can be used as a preamplifier to the receiver because it permits monolithic integration of the SOA with the receiver.
- SOAs were used as in-line amplifiers in several system experiments.
- SOAs have also been employed to overcome distribution losses in local area network (LAN) applications.
- SOAs can be used as a dual function device for e.g. It can be used as an amplifier as well as to monitor the network performance through a baseband control channel.
- SOAs can be used to amplify several channels simultaneously.

Drawbacks of SOAs :

- Polarization sensitivity.
- Interchannel crosstalk.
- Large coupling losses.

3.11 ERBIUM - DOPED FIBER AMPLIFIERS (EDFA)

- An important class of fiber amplifiers make use of rare-earth elements as a gain medium by doping the fiber core during the manufacturing process. Amplifier properties such as the operating wavelength and the gain bandwidth are determined by the dopants rather than by the silica fiber, which plays the role of a host medium. Many different rare-earth elements, such as erbium, holmium, neodymium, samarium, thulium and ytterbium, can be used to realize fiber amplifiers operating at different wavelengths in the range 0.5 - 3.5 μm. Erbium doped fiber amplifiers (EDFAs) have attracted the most attention because they operate in the wavelength region near 1.55 μm.

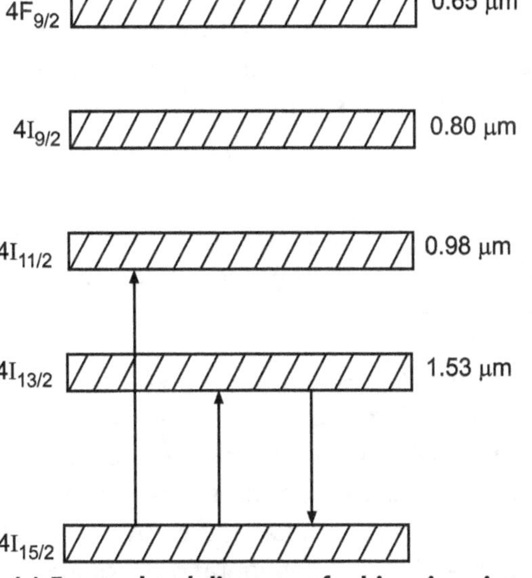

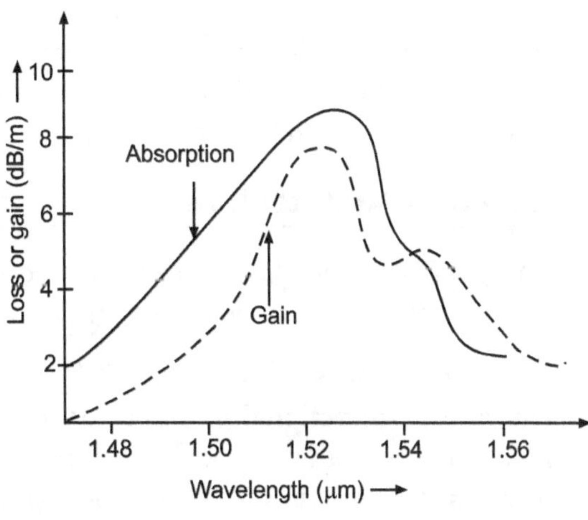

(a) Energy level diagram of erbium ions in silica fiber

(b) Absorption and gain spectra of an EDFA whose core was codoped with germania

Fig. 3.25

- To understand the principle working of EDFA we need to look at the energy-level structure of erbium. The erbium atoms in silica are Er^{3+} ions which are erbium atoms that have lost three of their outer electrons.

- Fig. 3.25 (a) shows the energy-level diagram. Here the two principal levels for telecommunication applications are the **metastable level** (4 $I_{13/2}$ level) and the 4 $I_{11/2}$ **pump level.**

- The term metastable means that the lifetimes for transitions from this state to the ground state are very long compared with the lifetimes of the states that led to this level. The metastable, the pump, and the ground state levels are actually bands of closely spaced energy levels that form a manifold due to the effect known as **stark splitting**. Each stark level is broadened by thermal effects into an almost continuous band.

- Pumping at a suitable wavelength provides gain through population inversion. The gain spectrum depends on the pumping scheme as well as on the presence of other dopants, such as germania and alumina, within the fiber core.

- Many transitions can be used to pump on EDFA.

- Efficient EDFA pumping is possible using semiconductor lasers operating near 0.98 and 1.48 μm wavelengths. Most EDFAs use 980-nm pump lasers. As such lasers are commercially available and can provide more than 100 mw of pump power. Pumping at 1480 nm requires longer fibers and higher powers because it uses the tail of the absorption band.

- Absorption and emission response of an EDFA depend on the composition of the host glass and on the types of dopants such as Ge and Al, in the glass. Fig. 3.30 (b) gives an example for a Ge-doped silicon glass that has Al codopants added. The Al atoms help to absorb the Er ions in the glass and they broaden the amplifier gain spectrum.

3.11.1 EDFA Architecture

- An optical fiber amplifier consist of a doped fiber, one or more pump lasers, a passive wavelength coupler, optical isolators and tap couplers.

- The pump light is usually injected from the same direction as the signal flow. This is known as **codirectional pumping** or **forward pumping**. It is also possible to inject the pump power in the opposite direction to the signal flow which is known as **counter-directional pumping** or **backward pumping**. In **bidirectional pumping** or **dual pumping**, the amplifier is pumped in both directions simultaneously by using two semiconductor lasers located at the two fiber ends. This configuration requires two pump lasers but has the advantage that the population inversion and hence the small signal gain, is relatively uniform along the entire amplifier length.

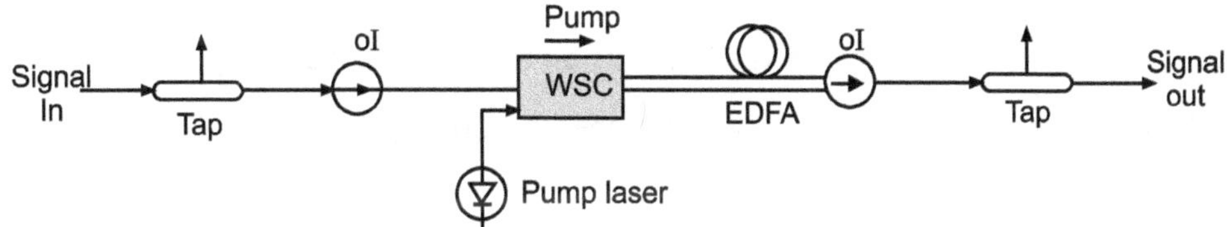

(a) Codirectional or forward pumping

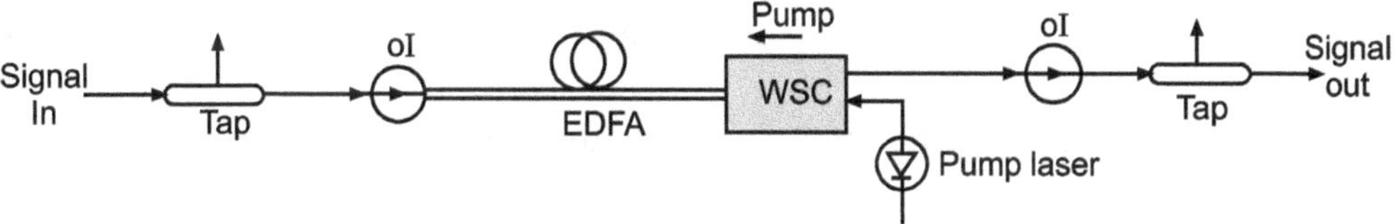

(b) Counter directional or backward pumping

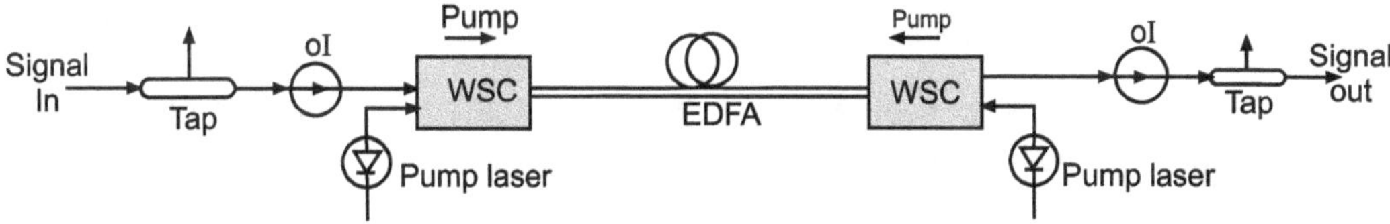

(c) Dual or bidirectional pumping

Fig. 3.26

Wavelength Selective Coupler (WSC) :

- The dichroic (two wavelength) coupler handles either 980/1550 nm or 1480/1550 nm wavelength combinations to couple both the pump and signal optical powers efficiently into the fiber amplifier. The tap couplers are wavelength insensitive with typical splitting ratios ranging from 99 : 1 to 95 : 5. They are generally used on both sides of the amplifier to compare the incoming signal with the amplified output.

- The optical isolator prevents the amplified signal from reflecting back into the device, where it could increase the amplifier noise and decrease the amplifier efficiency.

3.11.2 EDFA Gain and Power Conversion Efficiency

- The input and output powers of an EDFA can be expressed in terms of the principle of energy conservation:

$$P_{s,\,out} \leq P_{s,\,in} + \frac{\lambda_p}{\lambda_s}\, P_{p,\,in} \qquad\qquad \dots (3.44)$$

where $\qquad\qquad P_{p,\,in}$ – input pump power

$\qquad\qquad \lambda_p$ and λ_s – pump and signal wavelengths

- The fundamental physical principle here is that the amount of signal energy that can be extracted from an EDFA cannot exceed the pump energy that is stored in the device. The inequality in the above equation shows the possibility of effects such as pump photons being lost due to various causes or pump energy lost due to spontaneous emission.

- The maximum output signal power depends on the ratio $\frac{\lambda_p}{\lambda_s}$. For the pumping scheme to work, it is required that $\lambda_p < \lambda_s$ and to have an appropriate gain, it is necessary that $P_{s,\,in} << P_{p,\,in}$.

- Thus, power conversion efficiency is defined as:

$$PCE = \frac{P_{s,\,out} - P_{s,\,in}}{P_{p,\,in}} \le \frac{P_{s,\,out}}{P_{p,\,in}} \le \frac{\lambda_p}{\lambda_s} \le 1 \qquad \dots (3.45)$$

is less than unity. Maximum theoretical value of the PCE is $\frac{\lambda_p}{\lambda_s}$.

$$\text{Quantum conversion efficiency (QCE)} = \frac{\lambda_s}{\lambda_p} \, PCE \qquad \dots (3.46)$$

The maximum value of QCE is unity.

- Assuming that there is no spontaneous emission, the above equation can be written in terms of the amplifier gain G.

$$G = \frac{P_{s,\,out}}{P_{s,\,in}} \le 1 + \frac{\lambda_p \, P_{p,\,in}}{\lambda_s \, P_{s,\,in}} \qquad \dots (3.47)$$

- When the input signal power is very large so that $P_{s,\,in} >> \left(\frac{\lambda_p}{\lambda_s}\right) P_{p,\,in}$ the maximum amplifier gain is unity. This means that the device is transparent to the signal.

- In order to achieve a specific maximum gain G, the input signal power cannot exceed a value given by,

$$P_{s,\,in} \le \frac{\left(\frac{\lambda_p}{\lambda_s}\right) P_{p,\,in}}{G - 1} \qquad \dots (3.48)$$

- The gain depends on the pump power as well as on the fiber length. The maximum gain in a three level laser medium of length L, such as EDFA is given by

$$G_{max} = \exp\,(p\sigma_e L) \qquad \dots (3.49)$$

where σ_e is the signal-emission cross-section and P is the rare-earth element concentration.

- The maximum possible EDFA gain is given by the lowest of the two gain expressions :

$$G \le min \left\{ \exp\,(p\sigma_e L),\, 1 + \frac{\lambda_p \, P_{p,\,in}}{\lambda_s \, P_{s,\,in}} \right\} \qquad \dots (3.50)$$

Since, $$G = \frac{P_{s,\,out}}{P_{p,\,in}} = \exp\,(p\sigma_e L) \qquad \dots (3.51)$$

- It follows similarly that the maximum possible EDFA output power is given by the minimum of the two expressions:

$$P_{s,\,out} \leq \min \left\{ P_{s,\,in} \exp (p\sigma_e L),\ P_{s,\,in} + \frac{\lambda_p}{\lambda_s} P_{p,\,in} \right\} \qquad \dots (3.52)$$

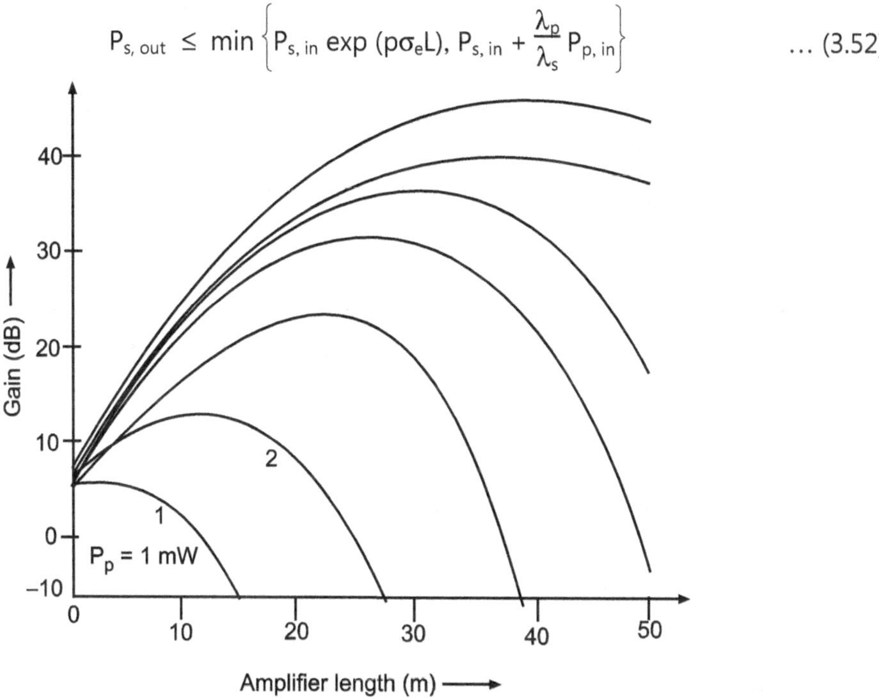

Fig. 3.27 : Calculation of the dependence of EDFA gain on fiber length and pump power for a 1480-nm pump and a 1550-nm signal

- Fig. 3.27 shows the onset of gain saturation for various doped-fiber lengths as the pumping power increases. The gain was measured for a 100-nw input signal at 1550 nm. As the fiber length increases for low pumping powers, the gain starts to decrease after a certain length because the pump does not have enough energy to create a complete population inversion in the downstream of the amplifier.

3.11.3 Amplifier Noise

- Amplified Spontaneous Emission (ASE) is the dominant noise generated in an optical amplifier. This noise is generated due to spontaneous recombination of electrons and holes in the amplifier medium. This recombination gives rise to a broad spectral background of photons that get amplified along with the optical signal. The spontaneous noise can be modeled as a stream of random infinitely short pulses that are distributed all along the amplifying medium. Such a random process is characterized by a noise power spectrum that is flat with frequency. The power spectral density of the ASE noise is

$$S_{ASE} (f) = h\nu\, n_{sp} [G(F) - 1] = \frac{P_{ASE}}{\Delta V_{opt}} \qquad \dots (3.53)$$

- P_{ASE} is the ASE noise power in one polarization state in an optical bandwidth ΔV_{opt} and n_{sp}, the spontaneous emission or population inversion factor is defined as

$$n_{sp} = \frac{n_2}{n_2 - n_1} \qquad \ldots (3.54)$$

where n_1 and n_2 are the fractional densities or populations of electrons in a lower state 1 and an upper state 2, respectively.

- The ASE noise level depends on whether codirectional or counterdirectional pumping is used.

- ASE gives rise to three different noise components in an optical receiver in addition to the normal thermal noise of the photodetector. This occurs because the photocurrent consists of a number of beat signals between the signal and the optical noise fields.

- The total photocurrent is given by

$$i_{tot} \propto (E_s + E_n)^2 = E_s^2 + E_n^2 + 2E_s \cdot E_n \qquad \ldots (3.55)$$

- The first two terms arise due to signal and noise respectively. The third term is a mixed component (a beat signal) between the signal and noise.

- The optical power incident on the photodetector is

$$P_{in} = GP_{s,\,in} + P_{ASE} = GP_{s,\,in} + S_{ASE}\,\Delta V_{opt} \qquad \ldots (3.56)$$

- The total mean-square shot-noise current

$$(i_{shot}^2) = \sigma_{shot}^2 = \sigma_{shot\text{-}S}^2 + \sigma_{shot-ASE}^2$$

$$= 2q\,\Re G\,P_{s,\,in}\,B_e + 2q\,\Re S_{ASE}\,\Delta V_{opt}\,B_e \qquad \ldots (3.57)$$

where, B_e is the front-end receiver electrical bandwidth.

- The other noises arises from the mixing of the different optical frequencies contained in the light signal and the ASE, which generates two sets of beat frequencies. Since, the signal and the ASE have different optical frequencies, the beat noise of the signal with the ASE noise that is in the same polarization state as the signal is

$$\sigma_{s\text{-}ASE}^2 = 4\,(\Re GP_{s,\,in})\,(\Re S_{ASE}\,B_e) \qquad \ldots (3.58)$$

- Since the ASE spans a wide optical frequency range it can beat against itself giving rise to the noise current.

$$\sigma_{ASE-ASE}^2 = \Re^2\,S_{ASE}^2\,(2\Delta V_{opt} - B_e)\,B_e \qquad \ldots (3.59)$$

- The total mean-square receiver noise current then becomes

$$(i_{total}^2) = \sigma_{total}^2 = \sigma_T^2 + \sigma_{shot-s}^2 + \sigma_{shot-ASE}^2 + \sigma_{S-ASE}^2 + \sigma_{ASE-ASE}^2$$

$$\ldots (3.60)$$

- Signal-to-noise ratio (S/N) at the photodetector output:

$$\left(\frac{S}{N}\right)_{out} = \frac{\sigma^2_{ph}}{\sigma^2_{total}} = \frac{\Re_2\, G^2\, P^2_{s,\,in}}{\sigma^2_{total}} \approx \frac{\Re\, P_{s,\,in}}{2q\, B_e}\;\frac{G}{1 + 2\eta\, n_{sp}\,(G-1)} \qquad \ldots (3.61)$$

where η is the quantum efficiency of the photodetector.

- The mean square input photocurrent is

$$(i^2_{ph}) = \sigma^2_{ph} = \Re^2\, G^2\, P^2_{s,\,in} \qquad \ldots (3.62)$$

and

$$\left(\frac{S}{N}\right)_{in} = \frac{\Re\, P_{s,\,in}}{2q\, B_e} \qquad \ldots (3.63)$$

Using the standard definition of noise figure as the ratio between the S/N at the input and S/N at the amplifier output.

$$\text{Noise figure} = F_{EDFA} = \frac{(S/N)_{in}}{(S/N)_{out}} = \frac{1 + 2\, n_{sp}\,(G-1)}{G} \qquad \ldots (3.64)$$

When G is large, this becomes $2\, n_{sp}$. A perfect amplifier would have $n_{sp} = 1$, yielding a noise figure of 2, assuming n = 1. That is, using an ideal receiver with a perfect amplifier would degrade the S/N ratio by a factor of 2.

Example 3.5 : *Consider an EDFA being pumped at 980 nm with a 30-mw pump power. If the gain at 1550 nm is 20dB then calculate the maximum input power and the maximum output power.*

Solution :

$$P_{s,\,in} \leq \frac{(980/1550)\,(30\text{ mw})}{100-1} \approx 190\ \mu w$$

$$P_{s,\,out}\,(max) \leq P_{s,\,in}\,(max) + \frac{\lambda_p}{\lambda_s}\, P_{p,\,in}$$

$$= 190\ \mu w + 0.63\,(30\text{ mw})$$

$$= 19.1\text{ mw}$$

$$= 12.8\text{ dB m}$$

3.12 RAMAN AMPLIFIERS (RFA)

- A Raman optical amplifier is based on a nonlinear effect called Stimulated Raman Scattering (SRS), which occurs in fibers at high optical powers.

- The SRS effect is due to an interaction between an optical energy field and the vibrational modes of the lattice structure in a material.

- Basically what happens is that an atom first absorbs a photon at a particular energy and then releases another photon at a lower energy, that is, at a longer wavelength than that of the absorbed photon.

- The energy difference between the absorbed and the released photon is transformed into a phonon, which is a vibrational mode of the material.

- The power transfer to higher wavelengths occurs over a broad spectral range of 80 to 100 nm. The shift to a particular longer wavelength is reffered to as the Stokes shift for that wavelength.

- Fig. 3.28 shows the Raman gain spectrum for a pump laser operating at 1445 nm and illustrates the SRS-induced power transfer to a signal at 1535 nm, which is 90 nm away from the pump wavelength.

- The gain curve is given in terms of the Raman gain coefficient gR units of 10^{-14} m/W.

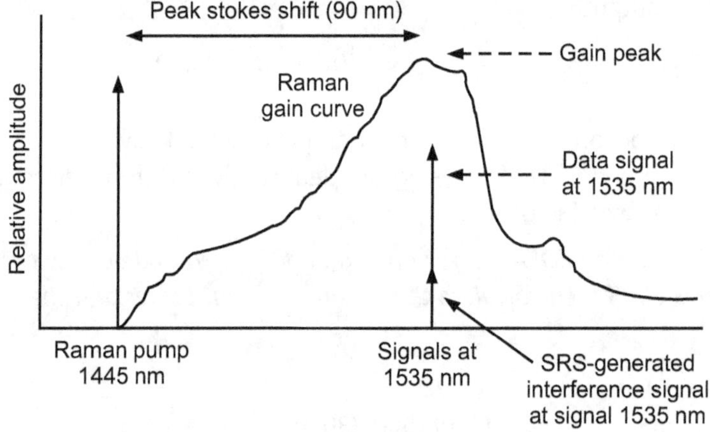

Fig. 3.28: Stokes shift and the resulting Raman gain spectrum from a pump laser operating at 1445 nm.

- Whereas an EDFA requires a specially constructed optical fiber for its operation, a Raman amplifier makes use of the standard transmission fiber itself as the amplification medium.

- The Raman gain mechanism can be achieved through either a lumped (or discrete) amplifier or a distributed amplifier.

- In the lumped Raman amplifier configuration, a spool of about 80 m of small-core fiber along with appropriate pump lasers is inserted into the transmission path as a distinct packaged unit.

- For the distributed Raman amplifier application, optical power from one or more Raman pump lasers is inserted into the end of the transmission fiber toward the transmitting end.

- This process converts the final 20 to 40 km of the transmission fiber into a pre-amplifier.

- Hence the word distributed is used, since the gain is spread out over a wide distance.

- Fig. 3.29 shows this effect on a single wavelength for several different pump levels.

- In this Fig. 3.29 the term on-off Raman gain is defined as the increase in signal power at the receiver amplifier output when the Raman pump lasers are turned on.

- As the optical power from the pumps travels upstream (from the receiver toward the sender), the SRS effect progressively transfers power from shorter pump wavelengths to longer signal wavelengths.

- This occurs over the characteristic Raman-gain length $L_G = g_R P / A_{eff}$, where P is the pump laser power and A_{eff} is the effective area of the transmission fiber, which is approximately equal to the actual fiber cross-sectional area. In general, noise factors limit the practical gain of a distributed Raman amplifier to less than 20 dB.

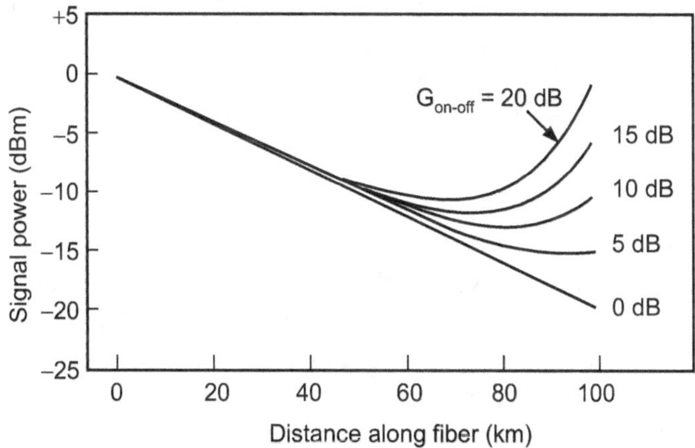

Fig. 3.29 : Simulated signal power evolution along a 100-km fiber link for different values of on-off Raman gain, which is the increase in signal power at the amplifier output when the pump lasers are turned on

- In practice, link design engineers use several pump lasers to generate a flat wideband gain spectrum. Fig. 3.30 shows a typical Raman gain spectrum for six pump lasers at different wavelengths.

- As indicated in the figure, when using several pump lasers it is important to remember that there is a strong Raman interaction between the pumps themselves.

- Since pumps at short wavelengths amplify the power of longer-wavelength pumps, the shorter-wavelength pumps typically need to have higher power levels. In addition, note that as a result of the asymmetry of the Raman gain efficiency spectrum, the power level and wavelength of the longest-wavelength pump needs to be calculated carefully.

- For example, in this case shown in Fig. 3.30, although only ten percent of the total pump power comes from the laser operating at 1495 nm, since it is amplified by the other pumps it contributes 80 percent of the gain for the longest signal wavelengths.

- The top right curve of figure 3.31 illustrates that by using an appropriate combination of pump wavelengths and pump powers, it is possible to achieve a fairly flat gain over a wide spectral range.

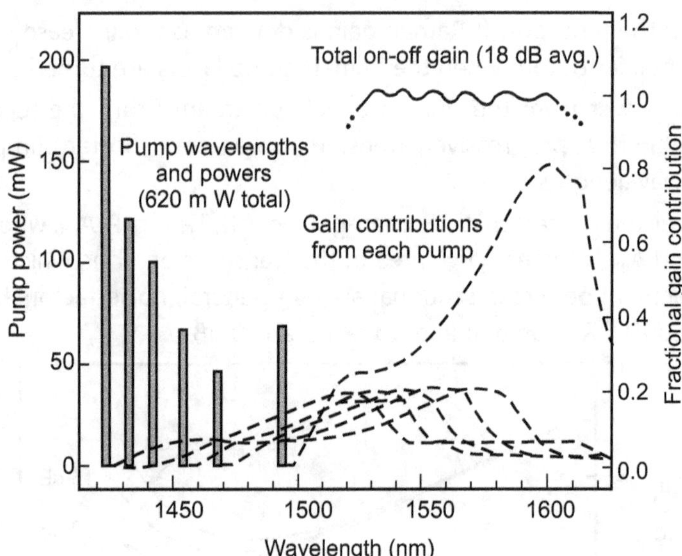

Fig. 3.30 : Numerical example of broadband Raman gain in a nonzero-dispersion shifted fiber when using six pump lasers. The bars show the pump wavelengths and their input powers. The solid line shows the total small-signal on-off gain and the dashed lines show the fractional gain contribution from each pump wavelength

- Pump lasers with high output powers in the 1400 to 1500 nm region are required for Raman amplification of C and I band signals. Lasers that provide fiber-launch powers of up to 300 mW are available in standard 14-pin butterfly packages.

- Fig. 3.31 shows the setup for a typical Raman amplification system. Here a pump combiner multiplexes the outputs from four pump lasers operating at different wavelengths onto a single fiber.

- These pump-power couplers are referred to popularly as 14XX-nm pump-pump combiners. Table 3.6 lists the performance parameters of a pump combiner based on fused-fiber coupler technology.

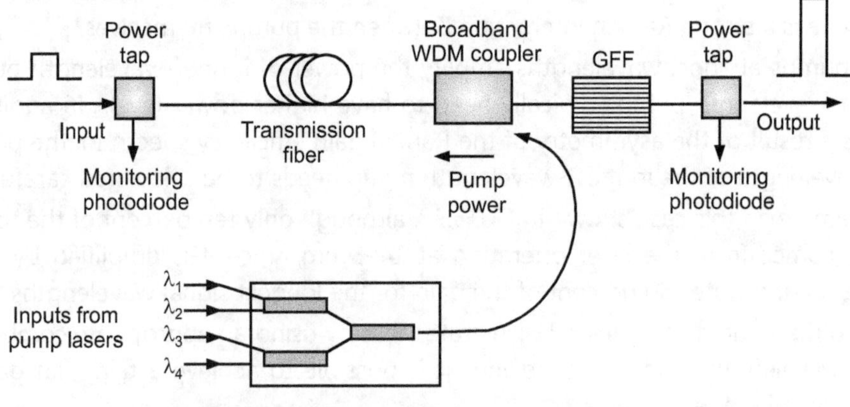

Fig. 3.31 : Setup for a typical Raman amplification system

- This combined pump power then is coupled into the transmission fiber in a counter-propagating direction through a broadband WDM coupler, such as those listed in Table 3.7. the differences in the power levels measured between the two monitoring photodiodes gives the amplification gain. The Gain-Flattering Filter (GFF) is used to equalize the gains at different wavelengths.

Table 3.6 : Performance Parameters of a 14XX-nm Pump-Pump Combiner Based on Fused-Fiber Coupler Technology

Parameter	Performance Value
Device technology	Fused-fiber coupler
Wavelength range	1420 to 1500 nm
Channel spacing	Customized : 10 to 40 nm Standard : 10, 15, 20 nm
Insertion loss	< 0.8 dB
Polarization dependent loss	< 0.2 dB
Directivity	> 55 dB
Optical power capability	3000 mW

Table 3.7 : Performance Parameters of Broadband WDM Couplers for Combining 14XX-nm Pumps and C-band or L-band Signals

Parameter	Performance Value	Performance Value
Device technology	Micro-optics	Thin-film-filter
Reflection channel λ range	1420 to 1490 nm	1440 to 1490 nm
Pass channel λ range	1505 to 1630 nm	1528 to 1610 nm
Reflection channel insertion loss	0.30 dB	0.6 dB
Pass channel insertion loss	0.45 dB	0.8 dB
Polarization dependent loss	0.05 dB	0.10 dB
Polarization mode dispersion	0.05 ps	0.05 ps
Optical power capability	2000 mW	500 mW

REVIEW QUESTIONS

May-Jun 2012

1. An optical transmitter uses a DH structure InGaAsP LED operating at a wavelength of 1550 nm and τr = 25 nsec; τnr = 90 nsec.

2. If a LED is driven with a current of 35 mA, I) find internal quantum efficiency and the power generated internally. ii) if n= 3.5 of the light source material, find the power emitted from the device. (May-Jun 2012)

3. State and explain the requirements of a good optical source from link design point of view. (May-Jun 2012)

4. Consider a 870 nm receiver with a silicon p-i-n photodiode. Assume 20 MHz bandwidth, 65% quantum efficiency, 1 nA dark current, 8 pF junction capacitance, and 3 dB amplifier noise figure. The receiver is illuminated with a 5 µW of optical power. Determine the RMS noise currents due to shot noise, thermal noise and amplifier noise. Also calculate the SNR. (May-Jun 2012)

5. A laboratory set up uses an InGaAsP hetrojunction phototransistor which has a common emitter current gain of 170, when operating at a λ = 1300 nm with an incident optical power of 80 µW. The base-collector quantum efficiency at this wavelength is 65%. Estimate the collector current in the device. (May-Jun 2012)

6. Answer the following:

    (i)   The responsivity of a PD is 0.9 A/w and its saturation power is 2 mW. What is the photocurrent if the received power is 1 mW?

    (ii) What is the responsivity of an InGaAs photodiode if its quantum efficiency is 95%?

    (iii) Draw a neat responsivity curve of a PD and explain precisely the reasons that explains the curve.

    (iv) What factors restrict the bandwidth of a p-n photodiode?

    (v)   List four advantages of using reverse bias in a PD.   (May-Jun 2012)

7. What is multichannel transmission in optical links? Explain any one method to achieve multi channel transmission.   (May-Jun 2012)

Nov-Dec 2012

1. Explain the conditions necessary to attain lasing action in LASERs. Also state the advantages of Laser diodes over LEDs, for use in context of fiber-optic communication.

(Nov-Dec 2012)

2. The radiative and nonradiative recombination lifetime of majority carriers in active region of double heterojunction InGaAsP LED are 30 ns and 100 ns respectively. Determine bulk recombination life time and power internally generated within the device when peak emission wavelength is 1310 nm at a LED drive current of 40 mA.

(Nov-Dec 2012)

3. Explain and compare PIN photodiode with APD with suitable field diagram.

(Nov-Dec 2012)

4. An InGaAs avalanche photodetector has a quantum efficiency of 90% at a wavelength of 1310 nm. If an incident optical power of 0.5 µW produces a multiplied photocurrent of 15µA, calculate the responsivity and multiplication factor.   (Nov-Dec 2012)

5. Explain the terms quantum efficiency and responsivity of a photodetector. How are these terms related to each other.   (Nov-Dec 2012)

May-Jun 2013

1. Radiative and non – radiative recombination lifetimes of the minority carriers in the active region of a DH InGaAsP-LED are 60 ns and 100 ns respectively. Determine the total carrier recombination lifetime and the power internally generated within the device when the peak emission wavelength is 1.55 μm at a drive current of 40 mA.   [8]

(May-Jun 2013)

2. A GaAlAs laser diode has 500 μm cavity-length which has an effective absorption coefficient of 10 cm-1. Calculate the optical gain at the lasing threshold for the following cases :

   (i)   For uncoated facets the reflectivities are 32% at each end.

   (ii) If one end of the laser is coated with dielectric reflector with 90% reflectivity. Comment on the results.   (May-Jun 2013) [8]

3. A Silicon photodiode has quantum efficiency of 70% when photons of energy $1.5 \times 10\text{-}19$ J are incident upon it.

   (i)   At what wavelength is the photodiode operating?

   (ii) Calculate the incident optical power required to obtain a photocurrent of 2.5 μA when the photodiode is operating as describe above.

   (iii) A silicon photodiode can be used for detection in the first transmission window only. Justify.   (May-Jun 2013)[10]

4. Explain the following with respect to optical receivers:

   (i)   Shot Noise

   (ii) Thermal Noise

   (iii) Signal to Noise ratio in p-n or p-i-n receivers   (May-Jun 2013) [8]

4. Explain the following factors limiting the speed of response of a photo diode:

   (i)   Drift time of carriers

   (ii) Diffusion time

   (iii) Time constant

5. A silicon p-i-n photodiode has 25 μm depletion layer width and carrier velocity 3x104 m/s. Determine the maximum bandwidth and the corresponding response time for the device.   (May-Jun 2013) [10]

6. An analog optical fiber system operating at a wavelength of 1.3 μm has a post detection bandwidth of 5 MHz. Assuming an ideal detector and considering only quantum noise on the signal, calculate the incident the incident optical power necessary to achieve an SNR of 50 dB at the receiver.   (May-Jun 2013) [8]

Nov-Dec 2013

1. The power generated internally within a double heterojunction LED is 28.4 mW at a drive current of 600 mA. Determine the peak emission wavelength from the device when the radiative and non – radiative recombination lifetimes of the minority carriers in the active region are equal.   (Nov-Dec 2013)

2. Draw the schematic and energy band diagram of double hetero – junction LED and explain the operation? State why it is more efficient in its action than homo – junction?
                                                                (Nov-Dec 2013) (Nov-Dec 2014)

3. A p-i-n photodiode on average generates one electron - hole pair per three incident photons at a wavelength of 0.8 μm. Assuming all the electrons are collected calculate :
                                                                                                    [6]

   (i) The quantum efficiency of the device.

   (ii) Its maximum possible bandgap energy.

   (iii) The mean output photocurrent when the received optical power is 10^{-7} W.

                                                                                (Nov-Dec 2013)

4. A p-n photodiode has a quantum efficiency of 50% at a wavelength of 0.9 μm.
   Calculate :   [6]
   (i) Its responsivity at 0.9 μm.
   (ii) The received optical power if the mean photocurrent is 10^6 A;
   (iii) The corresponding number of received photons at this wavelength.   (Nov-Dec 2013)

5. Explain the working of PIN photo detector with relevant diagrams.   [6] (Nov-Dec 2013)

6. An analog optical fiber system operating at a wavelength of 1 μm has a post detection bandwidth of 5 MHz. Assuming an ideal detector and considering only quantum noise on the signal, calculate the incident optical power necessary to achieve an SNR of 50 dB at the receiver.   [6] (Nov-Dec 2013)

May-Jun 2014

1. Explain the concept of intensity modulation of LEDs and Laser diodes using their I-P characteristics.   (May-Jun 2014) [8]

2. Radiative and non radiative recombination lifetimes of the minority carriers in the active region of a double-heterojunction LED are 60 ns and 100 ns respectively. Determine the total carrier recombination lifetime and the power internally generated within the device when the peak emission wavelength is 1.31 m at a drive current of 40 mA.
                                                                                (May-Jun 2014) [8]

3. Explain the wavelength and material considerations with reference to optical sources used for communication. Also compare the performance of laser diode versus light emitting diode.   (May-Jun 2014) [8]

4. Explain the working of PIN photo-detector with relevant diagrams.   (May-Jun 2014) [6]

5. State the various merits and demerits of p-n, p-i-n and avalanche photo detectors.

(May-Jun 2014) [6]

6. An InGaAs Avalanche photo detector has quantum efficiency 90% at a wavelength of 1310nm. If an incident optical powered of 0.5 W produces a multiplied photo current of 15 A. Calculate responsivity and the multiplication factor.   (May-Jun 2014) [6]

7. When photons of energy 1.5×10^{19} J are incident on a photo diode, its quantum efficiency is found to be 70%. Find out the wavelength of operation, incident optical power and responsivity when the photo current in the diode is 4 A.   (May-Jun 2014) [6]

8. Draw and explain the nature of responsivity curves of optical detectors.

(May-Jun 2014) [6]

Nov-Dec 2014

1. Distinguish between spontaneous and stimulated emission. How is stimulated emission assured in laser diode? Give comparison between LED and Laser?   (Nov-Dec 2014)

2. Explain what is $P+\Pi Pn+$ structure of an avalanche photodiode? How the term reach through is concerned with its operation? Which type of carriers are responsible for the avalanche action? How this avalanche effect causes a gain in the responsivity of the diode?   (Nov-Dec 2014)

3. The quantum efficiency of RAPD is 80% for the direction of radiation at wavelength of 0.9 µm, when the incident optical power is 0.5 µw, the output current from the device is 11 µA. Determine the multiplication factor or gain of the photodiode under this condition.   (Nov-Dec 2014)

May-Jun 2015

1. The radiative and nonradiative recombination lifetimes of the minority carriers in the active region of a double-heterojunction LED are 30 ns and 80 ns respectively. Determine the total carrier recombination life time and the power internally generated within the device when the peak emission wavelength is 0.87 µ m at a drive current of 40 mA.   (May-Jun 2015) [8]

2. State and explain the various advantages of LED in comparison with injection lasers.

(May-Jun 2015) [8]

3. Explain the conditions necessary to attain lasing action in LASERs.   (May-Jun 2015) [8]

4. When 2.5×10^{11} photons each with a wavelength of 0.85 µm are incident on a photodiode, on average 1×10^{11} electrons are collected at the terminals of the device. Determine the following of the photodiode at 0.85 µm.   (May-Jun 2015) [6]

    (i)   The quantum efficiency

    (ii) Responsivity

5. Given that the following measurements were taken for an APD, calculate the multiplication factor for the device. *(May-Jun 2015)* [6]

   (i)   Received optical power at 1.35 μm = 0.2 μW

   (ii) Corresponding output photocurrent = 4.9 μA

         (After avalanche gain)

   (iii) Quantum efficiency at 1.35 μm = 40%

6. Explain the requirements that must be satisfied by detectors forperformance and compatibility. *(May-Jun 2015)* [6]

Nov-Dec 2015

1. Explain the mechanism of optical feedback to provide oscillation and hence amplification within the laser. [8]

2. The longitudinal modes of GaAs injection laser emitting at a wavelength of 0.87 μm are separated in frequency by 278 GHz. Determine the length of the optical cavity and the number of longitudinal modes emitted. Consider the refractive index of GaAs as 3.6.

3. Explain the various modulation schemes applicable to optical sources. [8]

4. Draw and explain the principle of working and characteristics of LASER. [8]

5. For the wavelength range 1300 nm < λ < 1600 nm, the quantum efficiency for InGaAs is around 90%. [6]

   (i)   Calculate the responsivity at 1300 nm;

   (ii) Calculate the cutoff wavelength of this detector considering the energy gap of InGaAs as E_g = 0.73 eV.

   (iii) State the reason for the rapid decrease in responsivity for smaller wavelengths.

6. Explain the principle of working and characteristics of photo transistor. [6]

7. A silicon based avalanche photo diode has a quantum efficiency of 65% at a wavelength of 900nm. Optical power of 0.5 μW produces a multiplied photocurrent of 10 μA. Calculate : [6]

   (i) Primary photo current and (ii) Multiplication factor M.

8. Explain the principle of working and characteristics of avalanche photodiode. [6]

9. Write short note on: Noise considerations in p-n, p-i-n and APDs. [6]

●●●

ORBITAL MECHANICS AND LAUNCHERS

4.1 INTRODUCTION

- Space segment is a very strong and effective communication media. Telecommunication systems have now made it possible to communicate with virtually anyone at any time. Early telegraph and telephone systems used copper wire to carry signals over the earth's surface and across oceans, and High Frequency (HF) radio, also commonly called short wave radio made it possible intercontinental telephone links.

- Artificial earth satellites have been used in communication systems for more than 35 years and have become an essential part of the world's telecommunication's infrastructure.

- Satellite allows people to talk by telephone and exchange electronic mail from anywhere in the world and to receive hundreds of TV channels in their homes.

- The origins of satellite communications can be traced to an article written by Arthur C. Clarke in the British radio magazine Wireless World in 1945. At that time, the Clarke was serving in the British Royal Air Force and was interested in long distance radio communication. In 1945, HF radio was the only available method for radio communication over transcontinental distances, and it was not reliable at all sunspots and ionospheric disturbances could disrupt HF radio links for days at a time.

- Telegraph cables had been laid across the oceans as early as the mid-1800s, but cables capable of carrying voice signals across the Atlantic did not begin service until 1953.

- Clarke suggested that a radio relay satellite in an equatorial orbit with a period of 24h would remain stationary with respect to the earth's surface and make possible long distance radio links. At the time Clarke wrote, there were no satellites in orbit or rockets powerful enough to launch them.

- Satellite communication systems were originally developed to provide long distance telephone service. In the late 1960's launch vehicles had been developed that could place a 500 kg satellite in Geostationary Earth Orbit (GEO , with a capacity of 5000 telephone circuits marking the start of an era of expansion for telecommunication satellites.

4.2 SOME BASIC DEFINITIONS

Space :

- It is defined as a place free from obstacles. The Outer Space Act 1986 was introduced to ensure that the governments of various countries have no claim of sovereignty over the space or the moon. In the UN treaty on 'Exploration and use of Outer Space' including the moon and other celestial bodies in space may not be subject to any claim of national sovereignty. Most of the members of UN involved in space activities and ITU have signed this treaty.

Space is classified into :

(a) Air space

(b) Outer space

(c) Deep space

Air Space: Region below 100 km above the earth's surface.

Outer Space: This is also called cosmic space and falls between 100 km and 42,000 km in this region, aerodynamic lift is ineffective and is taken over by the centrifugal force.

Deep Space: Regions beyond 42,000 km fall in this category which is not in use for the communication satellites.

Satellite:

- Satellite can be defined as a heavy object which goes around another object in space due to the effect of mutual gravitational forces. The path followed by the orbiting body may be as per the, Kepler's laws of orbiting bodies.

- During the 17th century, Kepler had predicted that the path followed by the satellite of mass m around a primary body of mass M in space will be an ellipse.

- The body centre mass M of the primary body should coincide with one of the foci of the ellipse. In such a case, eccentricity would exist and the angular velocity of the revolving body will change.

Types of Satellites :

The satellites can be classified as :

1. Active satellites

2. Passive satellites

Active Satellites:

- Active satellites are used for both linking and also for processing and transmitting signals are active satellites. This type of linkage is called Bend Pipe Technology where frequency translation and power amplification take place.

- Some active satellites also use Regenerative technology in which demodulation, processing, frequency translation, switching and power amplification are carried out. The block used for this purpose is called transponder. All communication satellites are active satellites of one or the other kind.

Passive Satellites:

- These satellites do not have on-board processing and are just used to link two stations through space. In the process, there is loss of power. These are not very useful for regular communication or sensing applications.

Satellite Systems:

- Broadly, there are three types of satellite systems:

  1. **Ground to Ground:** In this an earth station A sends signals to the satellite, which after processing retransmits to another earth station B as shown in Fig. 4.1 (a).

  2. **Ground Cross Link Ground:** If the earth stations are situated such that they are not in the line of sight of a common satellite, it becomes essential that the help of another satellite is taken. The link between the two satellites in space is such that the signal from the earth station A goes to satellite S_1 and the satellite S_1 sends the processed signal to another satellite S_2 which in turn retransmits the processed signal to the earth station B, as shown in Fig. 4.1 (b).

  3. **Ground to relay platform:** The earth station can send signals to the satellite, which can be further retransmitted from the satellite to several other relay platforms, and the data can be utilized. Even the direct reception could be considered under this category, as shown in Fig. 4.1 (c).

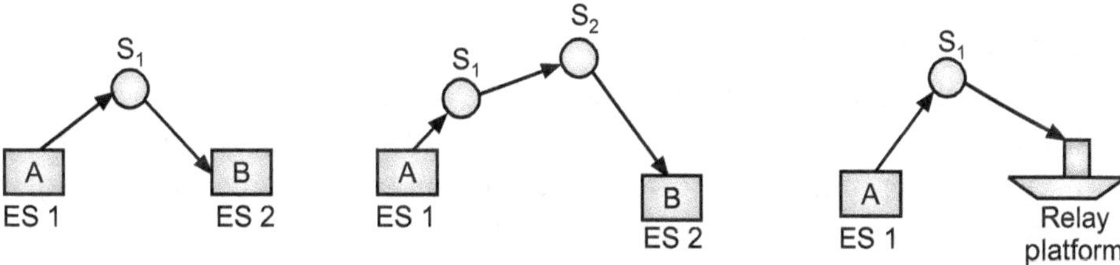

Fig. 4.1 : Satellite Systems

4.3 SATELLITE ORBIT

- Whether the satellite is natural like the moon or artificial like the one launched by man, they revolve round the planet as per the Kepler's laws in space.

- The path in which satellite goes round the primary body or the mother body is called orbit path and the distance from the center of the primary body to the satellite is called orbit radius.

- The height of the satellite from the surface of the earth is called altitude.

- In case of eccentric orbits, the radius varies while in circular orbits, it is constant. If we consider the earth as a primary body then the satellite can be classified in terms of altitude as follows :

Low Earth Orbit (LEO):

- Satellites that orbit below an altitude of around 1000 km are called low earth orbit satellites. Satellites at such low heights are useful for mobile communication but a number of such satellites are required for the continuous communication between a user and satellite.

- The height being low, the transmitter power required is small and hand held transreceivers can be used. However, the main disadvantage in such orbits is that the life of the satellite is limited because of the fuel requirement.

- The rotation period of such satellite is about 1 hour 30 min while they remain insight for a quarter hour from a particular earth station.

Intermediate Circular Orbit (ICO):

- In the altitudes lying between 2000 km to 10000 km, there is excessive radiation and the satellite cannot be kept in these altitudes.
- This is called Van Allen belt and the satellites have to be below this belt or above this belt. Satellites above this belt are said to be in the intermediate circular orbit (ICO).
- Satellites in this orbit are better than in LEO as far as the life and coverage area are concerned. Hence, the number of satellites required is less than that in LEO.
- This orbit is being visualized as the ultimate for global communication such as telephone, e-mail, fax etc.
- For the continuous communication, earth stations have to be used for switching. In this orbit, the rotation period of satellites is 5 to 12 hours and the line of sight visibility period is 3 hours.

Highly Eccentric Orbit (HEO):

- These orbits are also called as Molniya orbits and are used for communication by countries, which are in the Polar Regions such as Russia, Uzbekistan, etc. The inclination of such orbits is around 63°. However, for continuous coverage over long hours, a number of satellites in the same orbit path are to be used.
- At the inclination of about 63°, continuous communication is possible for about eight hours for orbit heights above 20,000 km. Therefore, theoretically three satellites are required for the continuous communication throughout the 24 hours.

Geosynchronous Earth Orbit (GEO):

- Any satellite above 36,000 km orbiting at an angular velocity equal to the angular velocity of revolution of earth around its polar axis is called geosynchronous. Though the orbit height for these satellites is very high still these are very useful for communication.
- A special case of geosynchronous is the geostationary orbit.
- When the satellite is in equatorial plane and is geosynchronous, the satellite is said to be in the geostationary orbit, i.e. the satellite will look to be stationary when seen from any point on the earth.
- These orbits are not useful for places in the Polar Regions because there is a visibility limitation. At this height, the coverage area is limited to less than 80 of the earth's surface excluding countries lying in the Polar Regions.

4.4 FEATURES OF GEOSTATIONARY SATELLITES

Advantages

- Tracking equipment is avoided.
- Earth stations remain at constant distance and line of sight from the satellite.
- Because of larger coverage area, a number of earth stations can access the satellite.

- Small number of satellites can provide global coverage.
- Quality of service is same for the rural and urban areas.
- Almost no Doppler shift.
- Cost effective services.

Disadvantages

- Earth stations in latitudes greater than 81.5° in northern and southern Hemisphere cannot access the satellite.
- Received signal strength is weak because of large distance.
- Time delays of send-receive more than 270 milliseconds.
- More powerful launching vehicles required.
- High free space loss.
- Finite number of satellites can be parked as parking longitudes are fixed.

4.5 HISTORY OF SATELLITE COMMUNICATION

- In view of the enormous advantages of satellites, many countries tried to launch their own satellites initially on experimental basis, but now it is a profitable proposition and is widely used for commercial communications and military applications.
- Looking back over the years, one finds the development in this field has been quite significant and speedy.

Table 4.1 : Basic Information about Satellites Communication

1945	• Theoretical studies carried out by Clarke proving that a satellite orbiting in an equatorial orbit at a radius of 42,242 km would look as if the satellite is stationary. • He also proved that three such satellites spaced at 120° apart in space could cover the whole world.
1957	• Sputnik-I was launched by USSR.
1958	• SCORE (Signal communication by orbiting relay equipment) was launched by USA. • This satellite was used to record messages sent uplink on a carrier of 150 MHz and on request was received back at 60 wpm on a carrier of 132 MHz. The lifetime of this satellite was about 35 days.
1960	• First communication satellite ECHO-I and II were launched as floating balloons. These were passive satellites.
1962	• Bell laboratories launched TELSTAR-I. It was a real time broadband active satellite with on-board transponders. • It was a LEO satellite with 50 MHz bandwidth and a uplink frequency of 6.389 GHz and downlink frequency of 4.169 GHz.

1963	• First geostationary satellite as visualized by Clarke in 1945 called SYNCOM (Synchronous Communication Satellite) was launched jointly by NASA and defence department of US. • It had uplink of 7 GHz and downlink of 1 GHz. This used FM/PSK transponders and for two years.
1965	• First communication satellite INTELSAT-I, also called early bird, developed by International Telecommunication Satellite Organization was launched. • This was a joint venture of Europe and USA. It had two 25 MHz bandwidth transponders. • The 6.031 GHz center frequency transponder was used by Europe and the 6.390 GHz center frequency transponder was used by USA. • The corresponding downlink being 4.081 GHz and 4.161 GHz, respectively. This satellite was active till 1969.
1970's	• About fourteen INTELSAT series 3 and 4 satellites were launched for weather forecasting and communication.
1980's	• About fifteen INTELSAT series 5 and 6 were launched for T.V. transmission, satellite switched multiple access, weather forecasting, etc. First generation Arabsat activities also started.
1990's	• INTELSAT series 7 and 8 in Ku band were launched. Arabsat-2 and 3 series as well as Asia-sat first commercial Chinese launch took place.
2000's	• Third generation Arabsat and INTELSAT9 series have started.

- Subsequently a number of INTELSAT satellites have been parked in space during the years 1968, 1971, 1981, 1983, 1986 and onwards.

- From 1976 onwards, many countries have launched their own satellites for communication applications. It was in 1980's that most of the countries realized the potential of the satellite communication and spent huge sums from their annual budget on space and satellite research.

4.5.1 Indian Scenario

- The space program in India has come a long way from early 60's when experiments were conducted with the help of American satellite ATS-6 to indigenously designed INSAT series of satellites by the Indian Space Research Organization (ISRO) under government of India.

- Indian space research organization (ISRO), initiated a number of programs and initiated studies in this direction as early as 1962. Aryabhatta was the first step towards indiginization. This satellite was launched on April 19, 1975.

- The space application studies were started side by side with the help of NASA'sATS-6 (application technology satellite) during 1975-76. This program is popularly known as SITE program.

- This covered limited areas, covering 2400 villages in the states of Andhra Pradesh, Karnataka, Madhya Pradesh, Orissa, Bihar and Rajasthan. Later on in 1977-79, with the help of Franco German, SYMPHONIE, STEP program was launched. The then post and telegraph department gained useful experience from this program.

- In 1979 remote sensing experiments were conducted using Bhaskara-I. Meanwhile Arian series of launch vehicles were developed by European space agency and they offered to send an Indian satellite free of cost.

- On 18th June, 1981 APPLE (Arian Passenger Payload Experiment) satellite was launched. This was the first geosynchronous satellite. This helped ISRO, Department of telecommunication, Indian space application centre, Vikram Sarabhai space centre, etc., to carry out the space application experiments that they had taken during the STEP program.

- With all these experiences and studies carried out on the different socio-economic application aspects, ISRO decided to have a multipurpose satellite instead of dedicated satellite.

- This was the first of its kind in the world and was called INSAT (Indian National Satellite). INSAT-I was the first generation satellite with a weight of 1200 kg in the transfer orbit and 650 kg in the geostationary orbit.

- The average electrical power required was about 1000 W, mainly provided by a solar panel of about 11 sq.m.

- Since a number of such INSAT satellites have been launched.

- The INSAT series is multipurpose satellite catering to the needs of Department of space, Department of telecommunications, Indian meterological department, All India Radio, Doordarshan (T.V. Broadcasting agency under ministry of information) and now is also shared by private operators.

- INSAT system has virtually revolutionized the long distance voice communication and television broadcasting in India. With INSAT-2 having five T.V. Channels, it is a boon for long distance coverage from South-east Asia to Middle East in the areas of education, entertainment, sports, etc. Other than communication INSAT is serving many applications, some of which are highlighted below:

  - National Informatics Centre Network (CNET) is an interactive data communication network. It has helped in socio-economic growth. Customized master earth stations support thousands of remote duplex small earth stations. The master station is located in the country's capital (New Delhi) with a host computer and connected to all district head quarters through INSAT.

- Satellite based Rural Telegraph Network (SBRTN) is a low cost digital messaging network operating in TDM/TDMA mode. It uses C-band. All rural telegraph terminals (RTT) are connected through a master HUB.

- Radio broadcast of message and DATA for the benefit of subscribers to this service. All the PTI (Press Trust of India) bureaus are connected through the INSAT network.

- Meteorological data transmission, standard time and frequency is another service provided by INSAT.

- In some INSATs there is an automatic remote DATA collection service called Data Collection Platform (DCP). It supports 406 MHz, search and rescue beacons. It also has the disaster warning system, which has been highly useful in coastal and north-eastern areas.

4.5.2 Milestones of Indian Space Programs

1962	Indian National Committee for Space Research (INCOSPAR) formed by the department of atomic energy and work on establishing Thumba equatorial rocket launching station (TERLS) started.
1963	First sounding rocket launched from TERLS on Nov. 21st.
1965	Space science and technology centre (SSTC) established in Thumba.
1967	Satellite telecommunication earth station set up at Ahmedabad.
1968	TERLS dedicated to United Nations on Feb. 2nd.
1969	ISRO formed under Department of atomic energy on Aug. 15th.
1972	Space commission and department of space set up. ISRO brought under DOS on June 1st.
1972-76	Air-Bourne remote sensing experiments.
1975	ISRO became government organization on April 1st. First Indian Satellite, Aryabhatta launched on April 19th.
1975-76	Satellite instructional television experiment conducted.
1977	Satellite telecommunication experiments project carried out.
1979	Bhaskara-I, an experimental satellite for earth observation launched on 7th of June. First experimental launch of Sunsynchronous Launch Vehicle-3 (SLV-3) for Rohini technology payload.
1980	Second experimental launch of SLV-3. Rohini satellite successfully placed in orbit on July 18th.
1981	With the help of first developmental SLV3. RS – D1 placed in orbit May 31st. Apple, an experimental geostationary communication satellite successfully launched on June 19th. Bhaskara-II launched.

1982	INSAT – 1A launched on April 10th. Deactivated on Sept. 6th.
1983	Second developmental SLV3 launched. RS-D2 placed in orbit on April 17th. INSAT-1B, launched on AUG. 30th.
1987	First developmental ASLV launched on March 24th with SROSS-1 satellite on-board. Satellite could not be placed in orbit.
1988	Launch of first operational Indian remote sensing satellite, IRS-1A on March 17th. Second developmental launch of ASLV with SROSS-2 on-board on July 13th.
1990	INSAT-1D launched on June 12th.
1991	Launch of second operational remote sensing satellite, IRS-1B on August 29th.
1992	Third developmental launch of ASLV with SROSS-C on-board on May 20th.. Satellite placed in orbit 2A, the first satellite of the indigenously built second generation INSAT series launched on July 10th.
1993	INSAT-2B, second satellite in INSAT-2 series launched on July 23rd. First developmental launch of PSLV with IRS-1E on-board on Sept. 20th. Satellite could not be placed in orbit.
1994	Fourth developmental launch of ASLV with SROSS-C2 on-board on May 4th. Satellite placed in orbit. Second developmental launch of PSLV with IRS-P2 on-board on Oct. 15th. Satellite successfully placed in polar sunsynchronous orbit.
1995	INSAT-2C, the third satellite in INSAT-2 series, launched on Dec. 7th. Launch of third operational IRS, IRS-1C on December 28th.
1996	Third developmental launch of PSLV with IRS-P3 on-board on Mar 21st. Satellite placed in polar sunsynchronous orbit.
1997	INSAT-2D, the fourth satellite in INSAT series, launched on June 4th. Becomes inoperable on October 4th, ARABSAT-1C, since renamed INSAT-2DT, was acquired in November 1997 to partly augment the INSAT system. First operational launch of PSLV with IRS-1D on-board on Sept. 29th. IRS-1D satellite was placed in orbit.
1998	INSAT system capacity augmented with the readiness of INSAT-2DT acquired from ARABSAT.
1999	The latest in multipurpose INSAT-2 series, launched by Ariane form Kourou French Guyana on April 3rd. IRS-P4 (OCEANSAT) launched by polar satellite launch vehicle (PSLV-C2) along with Korean KITSAT-3 and German DLR-TUBSAT from Sriharikota on May 26th.

2000	Geosynchronous launch vehicle launched from SHAR center. INSAT-3B weighting 2070 kg and GSAT-1 launched.
2001	Technology experiment satellite designed and developed to evaluate advanced designed procedures.
2002	INSAT-3C with 24C-band transponders and Z, S-band transponder. Also a meterological satellite METSAT was designed to be launched as a payload of PSLV-C4 from India. Efforts to Implement MEMS (Micro Electro Mechanical systems) for ST $^\wedge$ C.
2003	Department of space has several patents and qualified as one of the export earning agencies. An international standard compact Antenna Test Facility set-up at Bangalore, Karnataka.

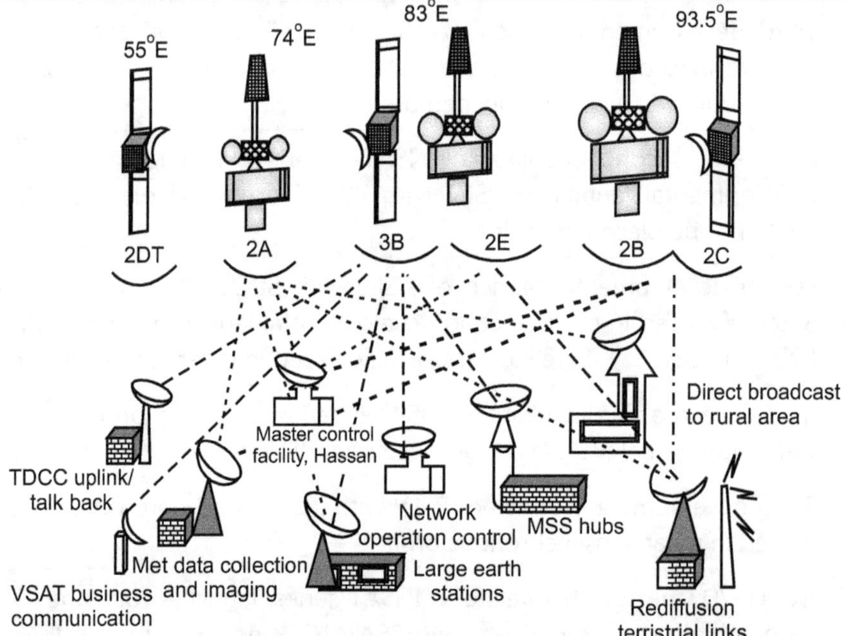

Fig. 4.2 Indian space programmes

- Satellites have always been the backbone of the commercial satellite communications industry. Large GEO satellites can serve one-third of the earth's surface, and can carry up to 4 Gbps of data, or transmit up to 16 high power direct broadcast satellite television (DBS-TV) signals, each of which can deliver several video channels.

- The weight and power of GEO satellites have also increased. In 2000 a large GEO satellite could weigh 10,000 kg (10 ton), might generate 12 kW of power, and carry 60 transponders, with a trend toward even higher powers but lower weight. Satellites generating 25 kW and carrying antennas with hundreds of beams are planned for the time frame 2005-2010.

- Television program distribution and DBS-TV have become the major source of revenue for commercial satellite system operators, earning more than half of the industry's $30 B revenues for 1998.

- By the end of 2000 there were over 14 million DBS-TV customers in the United States.

- The high capacity of GEO satellites results from the use of high-power terrestrial transmitters and relatively high gain earth station antennas.

- Earth station antenna gain translates directly into communication capacity, and therefore into revenue. Increased capacity lowers the delivery cost per bit for a customer.

- Systems with fixed directional antennas can deliver bits at a significantly lower cost than systems using low gain antennas, such as those designed for use by mobile users. Consequently, GEO satellites look set to be the largest revenue earners in space for the foreseeable future.

- All radio systems require frequency spectrum, and the delivery of high-speed data requires a wide bandwidth.

- Satellite communication systems started in C band, with an allocation of 500 MHz, shared with terrestrial microwave links.

- As the GEO orbit filled up with satellites operating at C band, satellites were built for the next available frequency band, Ku band.

- There is a continuing demand for ever more spectrum to allow satellites to provide new services, with high speed access to the Internet forcing a move to Ka band and even higher frequencies. Access to the Internet from small transmitting Ka-band earth stations located at the home offers a way to bypass the terrestrial telephone network and achieve much higher bit rates.

- SES began two-way Ka-band Internet access in Europe in 1998 with the Astra-K satellite, and the next generation of Ka-band satellites in the United States will offer similar services.

- Successive World Radio Conferences have allocated new frequency bands for commercial satellite services that now include L, S, C, Ku, K, Ka, V and Q bands.

- Mobile satellite systems use VHF, UHF, L and S bands with carrier frequencies from 137 to 2500 MHz and GEO satellites use frequency bands extending from 3.1 to 50 GHz. Despite the growth of fiber optic links with very high capacity, the demand for satellite systems continues to increase.

- Satellites have also become integrated into complex communications architectures that use each element of the network to its best advantage.

- Examples are VSAT/WLL (Very Small Aperture Terminals/Wireless Local Loop) in countries where the communications infrastructure is not yet mature and GEO/LMDS (Local Multipoint Distribution Systems) for the urban fringes of developed nations where the build-out of fiber has yet to be an economic proposition.

4.5.3 Overview of Satellite Communications

- Satellite communication exists because the earth is sphere. Radio waves travel in straight lines at the microwave frequencies, used for wideband communications, so a repeater is needed to convey signals over long distances.

- Satellites can link places on the earth that are thousands of miles apart, and are a good place to locate a repeater, and a GEO satellite is the best place of all.

- A repeater is simply a receiver linked to a transmitter, always using different radio frequencies that can receive a signal from one earth station, amplify it, and retransmit it to another earth station.

- The repeater derives its name from nineteenth century telegraph links, which had a maximum length of about 50 miles.

- Telegraph repeater stations were required every 50 miles in a long distance link so that the Morse code signals could be re-sent before they become too weak to read.

- The majority of communication satellites are in geostationary earth orbit, at an altitude of 35,786 km.

- Typical path length from an earth station to a GEO satellite is 38,500 km. Radio signals get weaker in proportion to the square of the distance traveled, so signals reaching a satellite are always very weak.

- Similarly, signals received on earth from a satellite 38,500 km away are also very weak, because of limits on the weight of GEO satellites and the electrical power they can generate using solar cells. It costs roughly $25,000 per kilogram to get a geostationary satellite in orbit.

- Obviously, there are severe restrictions on the size and weight of GEO satellites, since the high cost of building and launching a satellite must be recovered over a 10 to 15 year lifetime by selling communications capacity.

- Satellite communication systems are dominated by the need to receive very weak signals.

- In the early days, very large receiving antennas, with diameters up to 30 m, were needed to collect sufficient signal power to drive video signals or multiplexed telephone channels.

- As satellites have become larger, heavier, and more powerful, smaller earth station antennas have become feasible, and Direct Broadcast Satellite TV (DBS-TV) receiving systems can use dish antennas as small as 0.5 m in diameter.

- Satellite systems operate in the microwave and millimeter wave frequency bands, using frequencies between 1 and 50 GHZ. Above 10 GHz, rain causes significant attenuation of the signal and the probability that rain will occur in the path between the satellite and an earth station must be factored into the system design.

- Above 20 GHz, attenuation in heavy rain (usually associated with thunder storms) can cause sufficient attenuation that the link will fail.

- Initially analog signals were used for almost the first 20 years of satellite communications, with most links using frequency modulation (FM).

- Wideband FM can operate at low carrier-to-noise ratios (C/N), in the 5 to 15 dB range, but adds a signal-to-noise improvement so that video and telephone signals can be delivered with signal-to-noise ratios (S/N) of 50 dB.

- The penalty for the improvement is that the radio frequency (RF) signal occupies a much larger bandwidth than the baseband signal. In satellite links, that penalty results because signals are always weak and the improvement in signal-to-noise ratio is essential.

- The move toward digital communications in terrestrial telephone and data transmission has been mirrored by a similar move toward digital transmission over satellite links.

- In the United States, only TV distribution at C band remains as the major analog satellite transmission system.

- Even this last bastion of analog signaling seems destined to disappear as cable TV stations switch over to digital receivers that allow six TV signal to be sent through a single Ku-band transponder.

- More, importantly, dual standards permitting the transmission of not only digital TV but also High Definition TV (HDTV), will eventually remove analog TV from consideration.

- Almost all other signals are digital- telephony, data, DBS-TV, radio broadcasting, and navigation with GPS all use digital signaling technique.

- All of the LEO and MEO mobile communication systems are digital, taking advantage of voice compression techniques that allow a digital voice signal to be compressed into a bit stream at 4.8 kbps.

- Similarly, MPEG2 and other video compression techniques allow video signal to be transmitted in full fidelity at rates less than 6.2 Mbps.

4.6 ORBITAL MECHANICS

- In the beginning of the 17th century, it was Kepler who predicted the motion of bodies in space by the observations he made.

- Later on these laws were proved by Newton. Since it was Kepler's work that assisted the modern day scientists to predict and design the orbiting satellites, the laws are still known as Kepler's laws or Kepler's principles of orbiting bodies. He predicted that when the two bodies are in space uninfluenced by aerodynamic lift and other disturbances they are acted upon by mutual gravitation.

Some important definitions:

- Let us study some important definitions and understand important terms that would be used in subsequent discussions.

- **Orbit :** When a body are volves around another body B, body A is said to be orbiting around body B. Body A is called the satellite of body B. B can be termed as primary body or mother body.

- **Orbit Path :** The path followed by an orbiting body is called path of orbit. Depending on the shape of the path the satellite follows, orbit path is further categorized as elliptical or circular orbit.

- **Elliptical Orbit :** Every satellite revolves with a certain angular velocity ω around the primary body. If ω varies the path tends to become elliptical. There are certain disadvantages of elliptical orbit which are discussed hereafter:

  (1) Velocity of satellite changes depending on the orbit path parameters.

  (2) As the distance varies power received also varies.

- **Circular Orbit :** When angular velocity ω remains constant the orbital path is circular. For communication/broadcast satellites, circular orbit is preferred, as power requirement remains constant.

- **Radius of Orbit :** In a circular orbit the primary body lies at the centre of the circular path and the satellite on the circumference of the circle. Hence the radius of this circle is called radius of orbit. See Fig. 4.3 (b). Evidently elliptical orbit has variable radius.

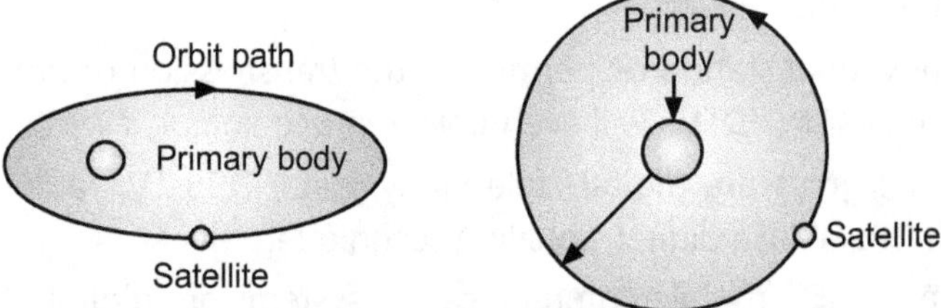

Fig. 4.3 : Radius of Orbit

- **Orbit Plane :** The plane in which the satellite orbits is called the plane of orbit. A man made satellite can lie in any of the following planes depending on the application :

  Polar Plane : It is the plane assumed to be cut along the poles of the earth. If one sees this plane as a section from east or west it looks to be a circle of radius r_e (radius of the earth).

  Equatorial Plane : It is the plane assumed to be cut along the equator. If one sees this section from poles it looks to be a circle of radius r_e. A satellite revolving in this plane is called equatorial satellite. A special case of a satellite orbiting in this plane is the geostationary satellite. (see Fig. 4.3 b)

  Inclined Plane : The plane of the orbit, which is at an angle to both polar plane and equatorial plane, is called inclined plane. (see Fig. 4.4 c)

  Prograde : When a man made satellite orbits in the same direction as the direction of revolution of earth, the orbit is called prograde orbit. Launching of the satellite is necessarily in prograde orbit. (see Fig. 4.4 d)

  Retrograde : When a man made satellite orbits in the opposite direction than that of the direction of revolution of earth, the orbit is called retrograde orbit. (see Fig. 4.4 d)

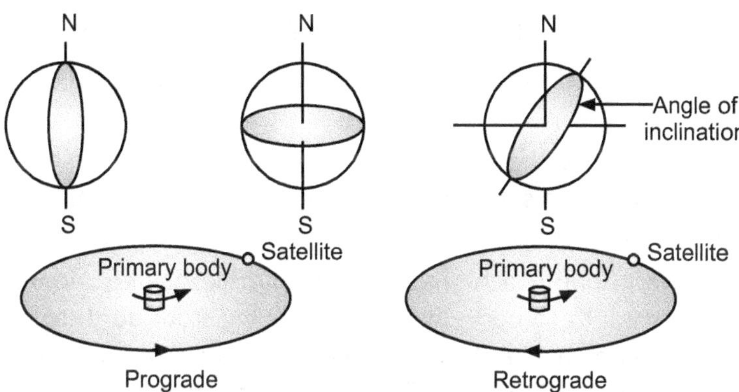

Fig. 4.4 : (a) Polar Plane (b) Equatorial Plane (c) Inclined Plane (d) Orbits

- **Geosynchronous :** A satellite which moves with the same angular velocity (in the orbit path) as that of revolution of earth around its axis of rotation (pitch axis), is called geosynchronous. A geosynchronous satellite has an orbit period of 24 hours.

- **Geostationary Orbit :** A satellite which is geosynchronous in the equatorial plane and additionally has prograde circular orbit, is said to be geostationary. The minimum radius of orbit to achieve this condition is 42000 km.

- **Sub-Satellite Point :** The imaginary point S' on the earth's surface created by a normal drawn from the centre of the satellite to the centre of the earth is called sub-satellite point.(see Fig. 4.6)

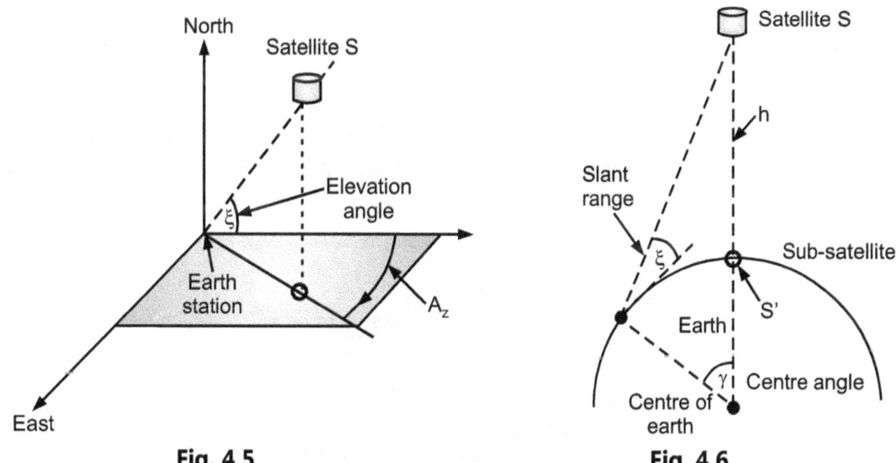

Fig. 4.5   **Fig. 4.6**

- **Azimuth :** The angle made eastward from a geographic north by an earth station to satellite along the horizontal plane is called azimuth angle. As the sub-satellite point is directly below the satellite on the horizontal plane, azimuth is also the angle from earth station eastward to sub-satellite point. (see Fig. 4.5)

- **Elevation Angle :** The angle subtended by an antenna looking at the satellite from the horizontal plane in the vertical direction is called the elevation angle. It is also called earth-satellite angle. (see Fig. 4.5)

- **Look Angle :** The angle subtended and determined by azimuth and elevation angle.

- **Slant Range :** The line of sight distance from a particular point on the earth to satellite is called slant range.

- **Height of Satellite :** It is the height h or altitude of satellite from the sub-satellite point on the surface of earth to satellite. In an elliptical orbit this varies. Radius of orbit is the sum of height and the radius of earth, $(r_e + h)$.

- **Ascending Node :** During each orbit a satellite crosses the equatorial plane twice, once while going from south to north and once traveling from north to south. The point of intersection of orbit path with the equatorial plane while traveling from south to north is called ascending node. The ascending node is specified by the right ascension Ω. (see Fig. 4.7)

- **Descending Node :** The point of intersection of orbit path with the equatorial plane while traveling from north to south is called descending node.

- **Perigee :** In an elliptical orbit the distance of satellite from primary body varies, hence a point in orbit when satellite is nearest the earth or primary body is called perigee. The perigee depends on the eccentricity and is equal to a $(1 - e)$, where a is the major axis of the ellipsoid and e is the eccentricity.

- **Apogee :** It is a point in orbit when the satellite is farthest from the earth. The apogee height is given by $a(1 + e)$. Note, in case of circular orbit apogee and perigee coincide as e is zero.

- **Inclination :** The angle between orbital plane and earth's equatorial plane is called angle of inclination. (see Fig. 4.7)

- **Satellite Axes :** The satellite being in space, to keep the spacecraft in proper position it is necessary to define the axes that control the spacecraft. The three axes of control are roll, pitch and yaw.

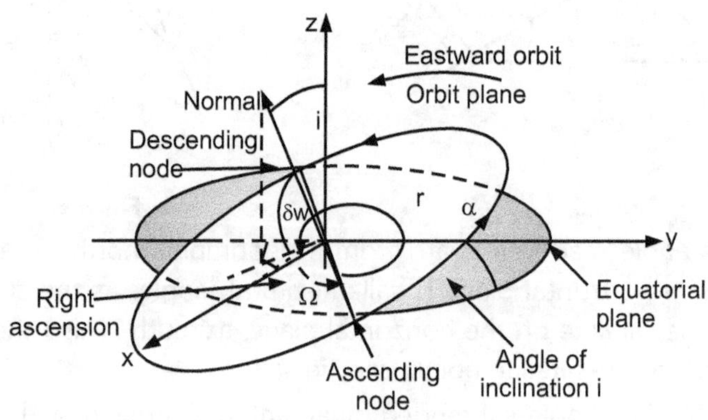

Fig. 4.7

- **Roll :** The tangent along the orbit path is called the roll axis which is shown in Fig. 4.6. Around the roll axis the satellite can either tilt towards north or south. A tilt towards north is said to be positive roll while a tilt towards south is called negative roll.

- **Pitch :** The axis of satellite perpendicular to the orbit path is called pitch axis as exhibited in Fig. 4.6. A satellite rotates around the pitch axis. The pitch rotation can be either eastwards called positive pitch or westwards called negative pitch. Earth's pitch axis polar axis.

- **Yaw :** The third axis of satellite is the axis, which is directed towards the centre of the earth along this axis the satellite can either rotate clockwise or anticlockwise hence it is called yawing (see Fig. 4.8). A clockwise rotation is positive yaw and anticlockwise rotation is negative yaw.

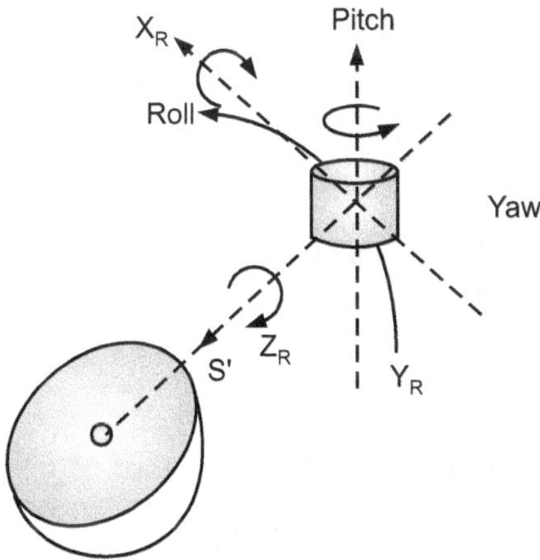

Fig. 4.8

4.6.1 Kepler's Laws

Law 1 :

- Whenever two bodies of mass m_1 and m_2 are in free space, such that $m_1 >> m_2$, the body with mass m_2 goes around the body of mass m_1 in an elliptical orbit. This happens when the centre of mass m_1 of the body lies at one of the foci of the ellipse. The body of mass m_2 can be called as the satellite of body having mass m_1. The motion in an orbit is governed by the eccentricity e such that

$$e = \frac{\sqrt{a^2 - b^2}}{a} \qquad \qquad \dots (4.1)$$

where a is the major axis and b is the minor axis of elliptical path.

- The velocity of the satellite is variable from point to point in the orbit path and this creates eccentricity. Theoretically, e can take any value between 0 and 1. When a= b, the orbit is circular and there is no eccentricity (change of angular velocity is zero)

Law 2 :

- If a satellite travels from x to y in an arc distance S_1 in one second during its orbit and during the same period travels arc of distance S_2 $\left(\begin{matrix} x' \\ y' \end{matrix}\right)$ then the area covered under OXY is equal to area covered under OX'Y', as shown in Fig. 4.9

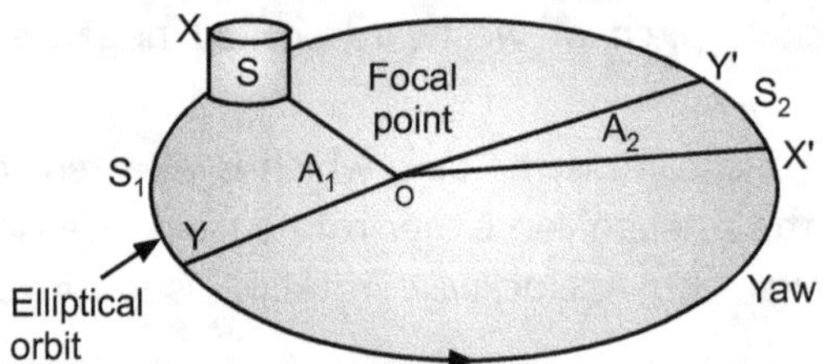

Fig. 4.9 : Kepler's law

- That means as the satellite moves away from the earth or primary body its velocity decreases, while it moves faster when it is nearer to the primary body.

Law 3 :

- If the period of orbit of satellite is t_0 and the mean distance between the primary body and satellite is d_0, then square of the periodic time of orbit is proportional to the cubic distance. Such that

$$t_0^2 = a d_0^3 \qquad \qquad \dots (4.2)$$

where a is called orbital constant or Kepler's constant.

4.7 SATELLITES IN CIRCULAR ORBIT

- Communication satellites are preferably launched in geostationary orbit and they move in circular orbit. If the satellite is in any other orbit the relative velocity between earth station and the satellites will not be zero and more than one satellite will be required for uninterrupted communication. Therefore our main interest would be to study satellites in circular orbit in the equatorial plane, moving in space, free from aerodynamic lift or any influence of external torques.

- Let M be the mass of earth and m be the mass of satellite. If the satellite is moving with an angular velocity ω under the influence of earth's gravitation G and its own gravitation, the satellite would go into circular orbit provided it satisfies the conditions derived hereunder.

  For an orbit height of h or orbit radius $(r_e + h)$, the velocity of satellite would be

$$v_s = \omega(r_e + h) \qquad \qquad \dots (4.3)$$

where r_e is is the radius of the earth.

- If the satellite has to orbit stably, then the centrifugal force that tries to take away the satellite should be equal to the centrifugal force with which the satellite is attracted towards the earth.

- If F_1 is the force acting upon by satellite due to its own mass m and velocity v, the satellite tends to pull away from earth, such that

$$F_1 = \frac{mv^2}{d} = \frac{mv_s^2}{r_e + h} = \frac{m\omega^2 (r_e + h)^2}{r_e + h} \qquad \text{... (4.4)}$$

$$F_1 = m (2\pi T)^2 (r_e + h) \qquad \text{... (4.5)}$$

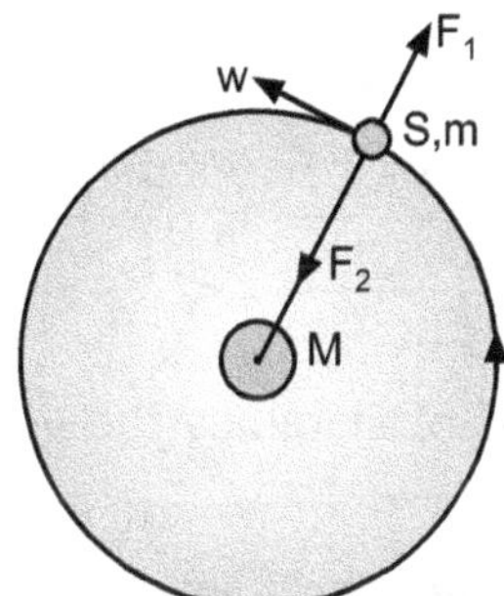

Fig. 4.10 : Orbit parameters calculation

- On the other hand, F_2, the force that attracts the satellite towards earth is given by

$$F_2 = \frac{GMm}{d^2} = \frac{GMm}{(r_e + h)^2} \qquad \text{... (4.6)}$$

- In equilibrium the centrifugal force should be equal to the centripetal force. For example, if a stone tied to a string is made to orbit by rotating the hand holding it, the stone will go round and round till the force acting on it due to motion of hand is equal to the inertial force that is trying to take the stone.

$$F_1 = F_2$$

$$\therefore \quad \frac{m(2\pi)^2 (r_e + h)}{T^2} = \frac{GMm}{(r_e + h)^2} \qquad \text{... (4.7)}$$

- If any one of the forces increases or decreases, the stone no longer remains in orbit. For example, if the motion of hand disturbs or reduces, the stone will fall on the head or on the other hand if the string breaks F_1 becomes very large and F_2 tends to zero making the stone fly away.

- Rearranging Equation (4.7), the time of orbit would be

$$T_s^2 = \frac{4\pi^2 (r_e + h)^3}{g_0}$$

$$T_s = \frac{2\pi}{\sqrt{g_0}} (r_e + h)^{3/2} \qquad \text{... (4.8)}$$

Where g_0 = GM called the gravitational coefficient or Kepler's coefficient.

For earth, $G = 6.672 \times 10^{-11}$ newton metre/ kg^2 and $M = 5.97 \times 10^{24}$ kg.

Therefore, $\qquad g_0 = 3.9861 \times 10^5 \ km^3/s^2$

Is it not the same as predicted by Kepler in his third law?

i.e. $$t_0^2 = a d_0^3$$

where $a = 2\pi/\sqrt{g_0}$.

- Equation (2.4) indicates that, as the radius of orbit increases, the time of the orbit also increases.

- Now, let us find the velocity of satellite.

  Substituting $v_s = \omega(r_e + h) = (2\pi/T)(r_e + h)$, we get

$$v_s = \sqrt{\frac{GM}{(r_e + h)}} = \sqrt{\frac{g_0}{(r_e + h)}} \qquad \ldots (4.9)$$

- This shows with the increase in orbit radius the velocity of the satellite decreases as predicted by Kepler in his second law.

- For such a satellite to look stationary in geostationary orbit, it is necessary that the relative velocity between the orbiting satellite and orbiting earth (earth orbits round the sun) should be zero. That means, at sub-satellite point S' the velocity of the satellite and earth should be same, i.e. 7.905364 km/s and as the satellite goes farther away from the earth the velocity should correspondingly decrease. Also if the satellite has to be geosynchronous, the time taken for one full orbit should be24 hrs. The solar day of 24 hrs does not give exact calculations as both sun and earth are moving objects, therefore sidereal day referred to fixed stars is used used for better accuracy in orbiting satellites. A sidereal day is of 23 hrs 56 mins and 4 seconds which is 0.9972 times the solar day.

- Additionally for the satellite to orbit in space, it should also revolve round its pitch axis like a top to create necessary gyroscopic stiffness. Imagine a revolving top, when this top attains a certain angular velocity, it revolves around its pitch axis stably without falling and at higher speeds even leaves the surface. This is possible because of stiffness it attains due to high angular velocity. But as the velocity decreases the top tends to wobble. This is analogous to a revolving satellite.

Example 4.1: A satellite is orbitting in a geosynchronous orbit of radius 41500 km. Find the velocity and time of orbit. What will be the change in velocity if the radius reduces to 36000 km. If $g_0 = 398600.5$ km^3/s^2.

Solution: Given: The gravitational coefficient 398600.5 km^3/s^2.

Radius of orbit = 41500 km.

Since, $$v_s = \sqrt{\frac{GM}{(r_e + h)}} = \sqrt{\frac{398600.5}{41500}} = 3.099 \text{ km/s}$$

and   Period of orbit, $$T_s = \frac{2\pi d^{3/2}}{\sqrt{g_0}} = \frac{2\pi (41500)^{3/2}}{\sqrt{398600.5}} = 84136.26 \text{ s}$$

For　　　　　　　　　$(r_e + h) = 36000$ km

$$g_s = \sqrt{\frac{GM}{(r_e + h)}} = \sqrt{\frac{398600.5}{36000}} = 3.3274 \text{ km/s}$$

Thus, increase in velocity,

$$3.3274 - 3.099 = 0.2284 \text{ km/s}$$

4.7.1 Developing the Equations of the Orbit of a Satellite

- The initial coordinate system can be used to describe the relationship between the earth and a satellite. A Cartesian coordinate system with the geographical axes of the earth as the principle axes is the simplest coordinate system to set up. The rotational axis of the earth is about the axis cz, where c is the center of the earth and cz passes through the geographic north pole. Axes cx, cy, $\wedge$ cz are mutually orthogonal axes, with cx and cy passing through the earth's geographic equator. The vector r locates the moving satellite with respect to the center of the earth.

- Fig. 4.11 illustrates one of these using a Cartesian coordinate system with the earth at the center and the reference planes coinciding with the equator and the polar axis. This is referred to as a geocentric coordinate system.

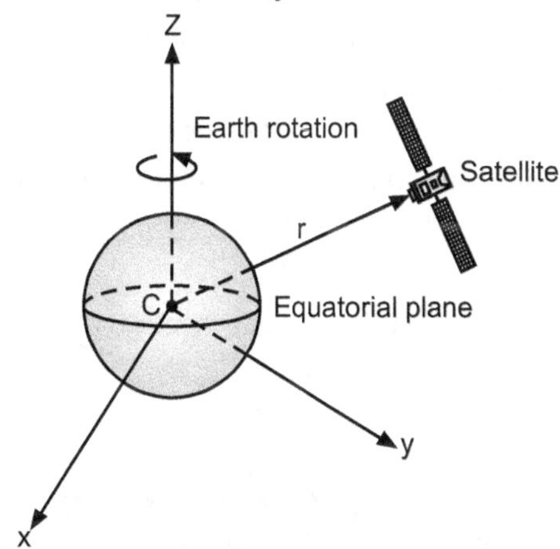

Fig. 4.11: The initial coordinate system

- With the coordinate system set up as in Fig. 4.11 and with the satellite mass m located at a vector distance r from the center of the earth, the gravitational force F on the satellite is given by

$$F' = \frac{-GM_{Emr'}}{r^3} \qquad \qquad \dots (4.10)$$

where M_E is the mass of the earth and $G = 6.672 \times 10^{-11}$ newton metre/ kg^2. But force = mass $\times$ acceleration and Equation (4.9) can be written as

$$F' = m\frac{d^2r'}{dt^2} \qquad \qquad \dots (4.11)$$

From equations (4.10) and (4.11), we have

$$\frac{-r'}{r^3}\mu = \frac{d^2r'}{dt^2} \qquad \ldots (4.12)$$

which yields $\qquad \dfrac{d^2r'}{dt^2} + \dfrac{r'}{r^3}\mu = 0 \qquad \ldots (4.13)$

- This is the second order linear differential equation and its solution will involve six undetermined constants called the orbital elements. The orbit described by these orbital elements can be shown to lie in a plane and to have a constant angular momentum. The solution to Equation (4.13) is difficult since the second derivative of r involves the second derivative of the unit vector r to remove this dependency, a different set of coordinates can be chosen to describe the location of the satellite such that the unit vectors in the three axes are constant. This coordinate system uses the plane of the satellite's orbit as the reference plane. This is shown in Fig. 4.11.

The orbital plane coordinate system:

- In this coordinate system, the orbital plane of the satellite is used as the reference plane. The orthogonal axes x_0 and y_0 lie in the orbital plane. The third axis, z_0, is perpendicular to the orbital plane. The geographical z-axis of the earth (which passes through the true North Pole and the center of the earth, c) does not lie in the same direction as the z_0 axis except for satellite orbits that are exactly in the plane of the geographical equator.

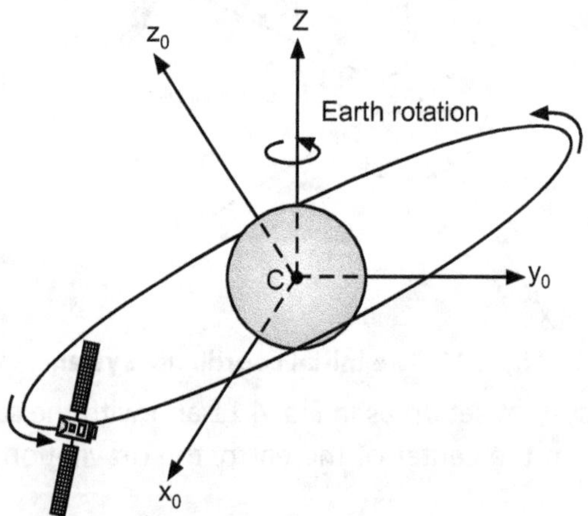

Fig. 4.12: Orbital plane coordinate system

- Expressing Equation (4.13) in terms of the new coordinate axes x_0, y_0 and z_0 gives

$$\hat{x}_0\left(\frac{d^2x_0}{dt^2}\right) + \hat{y}_0\left(\frac{d^2y_0}{dt^2}\right) + \frac{\mu(x_0\hat{x}_0 + y_0\hat{y}_0)}{(x_0^2 + y_0^2)^{3/2}} = 0 \qquad \ldots (4.14)$$

- Equation (4.14) is easier to solve if it is expressed in a polar coordinate system rather than a Cartesian coordinate system. The polar coordinate system is shown in Fig. 4.12 and using the transformations

$$x_0 = r_0 \cos \phi_0 \qquad \text{... (4.15 a)}$$

$$y_0 = r_0 \sin \phi_0 \qquad \text{... (4.15 b)}$$

$$\hat{x}_0 = \hat{r}_0 \cos \phi_0 - \hat{\phi}_0 \sin \phi_0 \qquad \text{... (4.15 c)}$$

$$\hat{y}_0 = \hat{\phi}_0 \cos \phi_0 - \hat{r}_0 \sin \phi_0 \qquad \text{... (4.15 d)}$$

and equating the vector components of r_0 and ϕ_0 in turn in Equation (4.14) yields

$$\frac{d^2 r_0}{dt^2} - r_0 \left(\frac{d\phi_0}{dt}\right) = \frac{-\mu}{r_0^2} \qquad \text{... (4.16)}$$

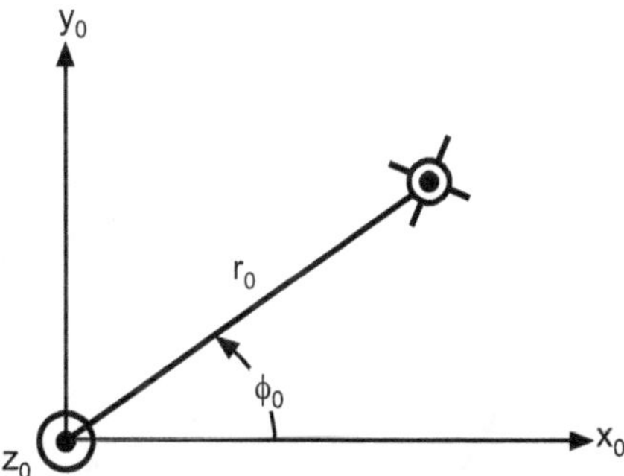

Fig. 4.13: Polar coordinate system in the plane of the satellite's orbit

- The plane of the orbit coincides with the plane of the paper. The axis z_0 is straight out of the paper from the center of the earth, and is normal to the plane of the satellite's orbit.

The satellite's position is described in terms of the radius from the center of the earth r_0 and the angle this radius makes with the x_0 axis, ϕ_0,

$$r_0 \left(\frac{d^2 \phi_0}{dt^2}\right) + 2 \left(\frac{dr_0}{dt}\right)\left(\frac{d\phi_0}{dt}\right) = 0 \qquad \text{... (4.17)}$$

- Using standard mathematical procedures, we can develop an equation for the radius of the satellite's orbit, r_0 namely

$$r_0 = \frac{p}{1 + e \cos (\phi_0 - \theta_0)} \qquad \text{... (4.18)}$$

Where θ_0 is a constant and e is the eccentricity of an ellipse whose semilatus rectum p is given by

$$p = (h^2)/\mu \qquad \text{... (4.19)}$$

and h is magnitude of the orbital angular momentum of the satellite. That the equation of the orbit is an ellipse is Kepler's first law of planetary motion.

4.7.2 Describing the Orbit of a Satellite

- The quantity θ_0 in Equation (4.16) serves to orient the ellipse with respect to the orbital plane axes x0 and y0. Now that we know that the orbit is an ellipse, we can always choose x_0 and y_0 so that θ_0 is zero. This now gives the equation of the orbit as

$$r_0 = \frac{p}{1 + e \cos \phi_0} \qquad \qquad \text{... (4.20)}$$

- The path of the satellite in the orbital plane is shown in figure 4.14. The lengths a and b of the semimajor and semiminor axes are given by

$$a = p/(1 - e^2) \qquad \qquad \text{... (4.21)}$$
$$b = a(1 - e^2)^{1/2} \qquad \qquad \text{... (4.22)}$$

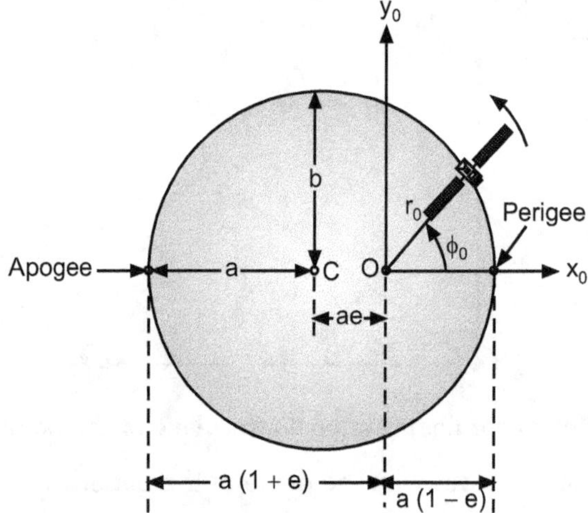

Fig. 4.14: Orbital Plane

- The point in the orbit where the satellite is closest to the earth is called the perigee and the point where the satellite is farthest from the earth is called the apogee. The perigee and apogee are always exactly opposite each other. To make θ_0 equal to zero, we have chosen the x_0 axis so that both the apogee and the perigee lie along it and the x_0 axis is therefore the major axis of the ellipse.

- The differential area swept out by the vector r0 from the origin to the satellite in time dt is given by

$$dA = 0.5r_0^2 \left(\frac{d\phi_0}{dt}\right) dt = 0.5 \, hdt \qquad \qquad \text{... (4.23)}$$

- Remembering that h is the magnitude of the orbital angular momentum of the satellite, the radius vector of the satellite can be seen to sweep out equal areas in equal times. This is Kepler's second law of planetary motion. By equating the area of the ellipse (πab) to the area swept out in one orbital revolution, we can derive an expression for the orbital period T as

$$T^2 = (4\pi^2 a^3)/\mu \qquad \qquad \text{... (4.24)}$$

- This equation is the mathematical expression of Kepler's third law of planetary motion: the square of the period of revolution is proportional to the cube of the semi-major axis. Equation (4.24) is extremely important in satellite communication systems. This equation determines the period of the orbit of any satellite, and it is used in every GPS receiver in the calculation of the positions of GPS satellites. Equation (4.24) is also used to find the orbital radius of a GEO satellite, for which the period T must be made exactly equal to the period of one revolution of the earth for the satellite to remain stationary over a point on the equator.

- An important point to remember is that the period of revolution T, is referenced to inertial space, namely to the galactic background.

- The orbital period is the time the orbiting body takes to return to the same reference point in space with respect to the galactic background.

- Nearly always, the primary body will also be rotating and so the period of revolution of the satellite may be different from the perceived by an observer who is standing still on the surface of the primary body. This is the most obvious with a geostationary earth orbit (GEO) satellite.

- The orbital period of a GEO satellite is exactly equal to the period of rotation of the earth, 23 h 46 min 4.1 s, but, to an observer on the ground, the satellite appears to have an infinite orbital period: it always stays in the same place in the sky.

To be perfectly geostationary, the orbit of a satellite needs to have three features:

- It must be exactly circular (i.e. have an eccentricity of zero);

- It must be at the correct altitude(i.e. have the correct period); and

- It must be in the plane of the equator (i.e. have a zero inclination with respect to the equator).

- If the inclination of the satellite is not zero and/or if the eccentricity is not zero, but the orbital period is correct, then the satellite will be in a geosynchronous orbit.

- The position of a geosynchronous satellite will appear to oscillate about a mean look angle in the sky with respect to a stationary observer on the earth's surface. The orbital period of a GEO satellite, 23 h 56 min 4.1 s is one sidereal day.

- A sidereal day is the time between consecutive crossings of any particular longitude on the earth by any star, other than the sun.

- The mean solar day of 24 h is the time between any consecutive crossings of any particular longitude by the sun, and is the time between successive sunrises (or sunsets) observed at one location on earth, averaged over an entire year.

- Because the earth moves round the sun once per $365\frac{1}{4}$ days, the solar day is 1440/365.25 = 3.94 min longer than a sidereal day.

4.7.3 Locating the Satellite in the Orbit

- Consider now the problem of locating the satellite in its orbit. The equation of the orbit may be rewritten by combining Equations (4.18) and (4.21) to obtain

$$r_0 = \frac{a(1 - e^2)}{1 + e \cos \phi_0} \qquad \qquad \ldots (4.25)$$

- The angle ϕ_0 is measured from the x_0 axis and is called the true anomaly. [Anomaly was a measure used by astronomers to mean a planet's angular distance from its perihelion (closest approach to the sun), measured as if viewed from the sun. the term was adopted in celestial mechanics for all orbiting bodies.] Since we defined the positive x_0 axis so that it passes through the perigee, ϕ_0 measures the angle from the perigee to the instantaneous position of the satellite. The rectangular coordinates of the satellite are given by

$$x_0 = r_0 \cos \phi_0 \qquad \qquad \ldots (4.26)$$

$$y_0 = r_0 \sin \phi_0 \qquad \qquad \ldots (4.27)$$

- As noted earlier, the orbital period T is the time for the satellite to complete a revolution in inertial space, traveling a total of 2π radians. The average angular velocity η is thus

$$\eta = \frac{(2\pi)}{T} = (\mu^{1/2})/(a^{3/2}) \qquad \qquad \ldots (4.28)$$

- If the orbit is an ellipse, the instantaneous angular velocity will vary with the position of the satellite around the orbit. If we enclose the elliptical orbit with a circumscribed circle of radius a then an object going around the circumscribed circle with a constant angular velocity η would complete one revolution in exactly the same period T as the satellite requires completing one (elliptical) orbital revolution.

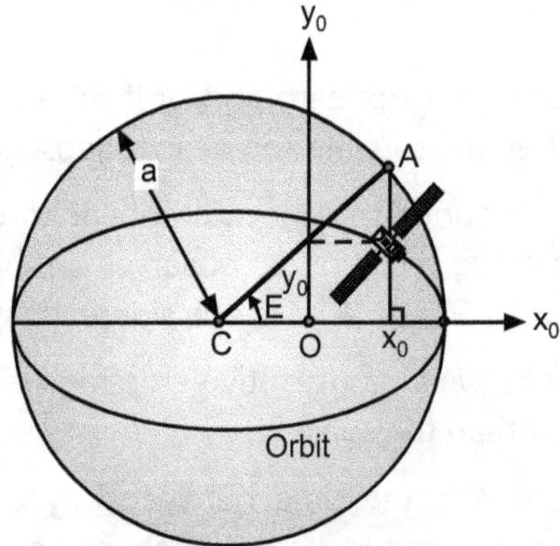

Fig. 4.15: The circumscribed circle and the eccentric anomaly E

- Consider the geometry of the circumscribed circle as shown in Fig. 4.15 . Locate the point (indicated as A) where a vertical line drawn through the position of the satellite intersects the circumscribed circle. A line from the center of the ellipse (C) to this point (A) makes an angle E with the x_0 axis; E is called the eccentric anomaly of the satellite.

It is related to the radius r_0 by

$$r_0 = a(1 - e \cos E) \qquad \qquad \text{... (4.29)}$$

Thus $\qquad \qquad a - r_0 = ae \cos E \qquad \qquad \text{... (4.30)}$

- We can also develop an expression that relates eccentric anomaly E to the average angular velocity η, which yields

$$\eta dt = (1 - e \cos E) dE \qquad \qquad \text{... (4.31)}$$

- Let t_p be the time of perigee. This is simultaneously the time of closest approach to the earth; the time when the satellite is crossing the x_0 axis; and the time when E is zero. If we integrate both sides of Equation (4.31), we obtain

$$\eta(t - t_p) = E - e \sin E \qquad \qquad \text{... (4.32)}$$

The left side of Equation (4.33) is called the mean anomaly, M. Thus

$$M = \eta(t - t_p) = E - e \sin E \qquad \qquad \text{... (4.33)}$$

- The mean anomaly M is the arc length (in radians) that the satellite would have traversed since the perigee passage if it were moving on the circumscribed circle at the mean angular velocity η.

- If we know the time of perigee, t_p, the eccentricity, e and the length of the semi major axis, a, we now have the necessary equations to determine the coordinates (r_0, ϕ_0) and (x_0, y_0) of the satellite in the orbital plane. The process is as follows :

1. Calculate η
2. Calculate M
3. Solve Equation (4.33) for E
4. Find r_0 from E
5. Solve Equation (4.25) for ϕ_0
6. Use Equations (4.26) and (4.27) to calculate with respect to calculate x_0 and y_0

Now we must locate the orbital plane with respect to the earth.

4.7.4 Locating the Satellite with Respect to the Earth

- At the end of the last section, we summarized the process for locating the satellite at the point (x_0, y_0, z_0) in the rectangular coordinate system of the orbital plane.

- The location was with respect to the center of the earth.

- In most cases, we need to know where the satellite is from an observation point and not at the center of the earth. Let us therefore develop the transformations that permit the satellite to be located from any given point on the rotating surface of the earth.

- We will begin with a geocentric equatorial coordinate system as shown in Fig. 4.16. The rotational axis of the earth is the z_i axis, which is through the geographic North Pole.

- The x_i axis is from the center of the earth toward a fixed location in space called the first point of Aries (see Fig. 4.16). This coordinate system moves through space; it translates as the earth moves in its orbit around the sun, but it does not rotate as the earth rotates.

- The x_i direction is always the same, whatever the earth's position around the sun and is in the direction of the first point of Aries. The (x_i, y_i) plane contains the earth's equator and is called the equatorial plane.

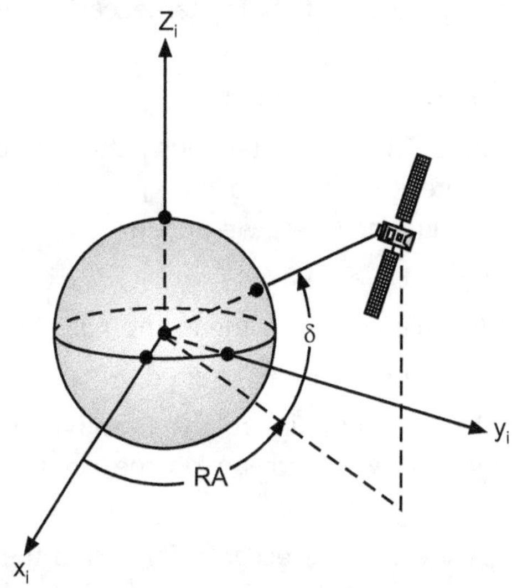

Fig. 4.16 : The geocentric equatorial system

- Angular distance measured eastward in the equatorial plane from the x_i axis is called right ascension and given the symbol RA.

- The two points at which the orbit penetrates the equatorial plane are called nodes; the satellite moves upward through the equatorial plane at the ascending node and downward through the equatorial plane at the descending node, given the conventional picture of the earth, with north at the top, which is in the direction of the positive z axis for the earth centered coordinate set.

- Remember that in space there is no up or down; that is a concept we are familiar with because of gravity at the earth's surface.

- For a weightless body in space, such as an orbiting spacecraft, up and down have no meaning unless they are defined with respect to a reference point. The right ascension of the ascending node is called Ω.

- The angle that the orbital plane makes with the equatorial plane (the planes intersect at the line joining the nodes) is called the inclination, Fig. 4.17 illustrates these quantities.

- The variables Ω and i together locate the orbital plane with respect to the equatorial plane. To locate the orbital coordinate system with respect to the equatorial coordinate system we need ω, the argument of perigee west.

- This is the angle measured along the orbit from the ascending node to the perigee.

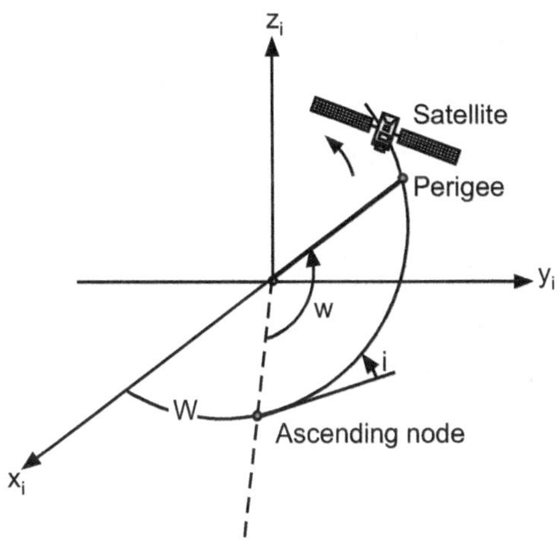

Fig. 4.17 : Locating the orbit in the geocentric equatorial system

- Standard time for space operations and most other scientific and engineering purposes is universal time (UT), also known as Zulu time (z).

- This is essentially the mean solar time at the Greenwich Observatory near London, England. Universal time is measured in hours, minutes and seconds or in fractions of a day. It is 5 h later than Eastern Standard Time, so that 0.7:00 EST is 12:00 hUT.

- The civil or calendar day begins at 00:00:00 hours UT, frequently written as 0 h.

- This is, of course, midnight (24:00:00) on the previous day.

- Astronomers employ a second dating system involving Julian days and Julian dates. Julian days start at noon UT in a counting system whereby noon on December 31, 1899, was the beginning of Julian day 2415020, usually written 2415020.

4.7.5 Orbital Elements

- To specify the absolute (i.e., the inertial) coordinates of a satellite at time t, we need to know six quantities.

- These quantities are called the orbital elements. More than six quantities can be used to describe a unique orbital path and there is some arbitrariness in exactly which six quantities are used.

- We have chosen to adopt a set that is commonly used in satellite communications: eccentricity (e), semimajor axis (a), time of perigee (t_p), right ascension of ascending node (Ω), inclination (i) and argument of perigee (ω). Frequently, the mean anomaly (M) at a given time is substituted for t_p.

Example 4.2 : A satellite is in an elliptical orbit with a perigee of 1000 km and an apogee of 4000 km. Using a mean earth radius of 6378.14 km, find the period of the orbit in hours, minutes, and seconds, and the eccentricity of the orbit.

Solution: The major axis of the elliptical orbit is a straight line between the apogee and perigee. Hence, for a semimajor axis length a, earth radius r_e, perigee height h_p and apogee height h_a.

$$2a = 2r_e + h_p + h_a = 2 \times 6378.14 + 1000.0 + 4000.0 = 17{,}756.28 \text{ km}$$

Thus the semimajor axis of the orbit has a length a = 8878.14 km. Using this value of a in Equation (4.24) gives an orbital period T seconds where

$$T^2 = \frac{(4\pi^2 a^3)}{\mu} = 4\pi^2 \times (8878.07)_3 / 3.986004418 \times 10^5 \ s^2$$

$$6.930872802 \times 10^7 \ s^2$$

T = 8325.1864 s = 138 min 45.19 s= 2 h 18 min 45.19 s

The eccentricity of the orbit is given by e, which can be found from Equation (2.28) by considering the instant at which the satellite is at perigee. Rearranging to Figure 2.7, when the satellite is at perigee, the eccentric anomaly E = 0 and $r_0 = r_e + h_p$. From Equation (2.28), at perigee

$$r_e + h_p = a(1 - e)$$

$$e = 1 - \frac{(r_e + h_p)}{a} = 1 - \frac{7378.14}{8878.14} = 0.169$$

4.8 LOOK ANGLE DETERMINATION

- Navigation around the earth's oceans became more precise when the surface of the globe was divided up into a grid like structure of orthogonal lines: latitude and longitude.

- Latitude is the angular distance, measured in degrees, north or south of the equator and longitude is the angular distance, measured in degrees, from a given reference longitudinal line.

- By the time this grid reference became popular, there were two major seafaring nations vying for dominance: England and France. England drew its reference zero longitude through Greenwich, a town close to London, England, and France, drew its reference longitude through Paris, France.

- Since the British Admiralty chose to give away their maps and the French decided to charge a fee for theirs, it was not surprising that the use of Greenwich as the zero reference longitude became dominant within a few years.

- Thus, there are 360° of longitude and ± 90° of latitude, plus being measured north of the equator and minus south of the equator. Latitude 90° N (or + 90°) is the North Pole and latitude 90° S (or – 90°) is the South Pole.

- When GEO satellite systems are registered in Geneva, their (sub-satellite) location over the equator is given in degrees east to avoid confusion. Thus, the INTELSAT primary location in the Indian Ocean is registered at 60°E and the primary location in the Atlantic Ocean is at 355.5°E (not 24.5°W).

- Earth stations that communicate with satellites are described in terms of their geographic latitude and longitude when developing the pointing coordinates that the earth station must use to track the apparent motion of the satellite.

- The coordinates to which an earth station antenna must be pointed to communicate with a satellite are called the look angles.

- These are most commonly expressed as azimuth (A_z) and elevation (E_l), although other pairs exist. For example, right ascension and declination are standard for radio astronomy antennas.

- Azimuth is measured eastward (clockwise) from geographic north to the projection of the satellite path on a (locally) horizontal plane at the earth station to the satellite path. Fig. 4.18 illustrates these look angles.

- In all look angle determinations, the precise location of the satellite is critical. A key location in many instances is the subsatellite point.

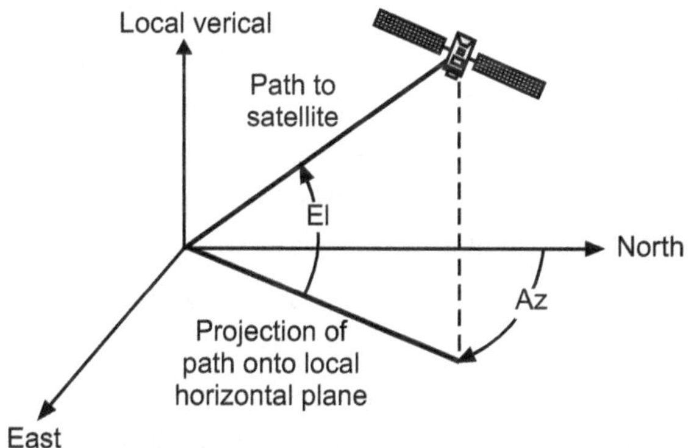

Fig. 4.18: The definition of elevation (E_l) and azimuth (A_z)

4.8.1 The Subsatellite Point

- The subsatellite point is the location on the surface of the earth that lies directly between the satellite and the center of the earth.

- It is the nadir pointing direction from the satellite and, for a satellite in an equatorial orbit, it will always be located on the equator.

- Since geostationary satellites are in equatorial orbits and are designed to stay stationary over the earth., it is usual to give their orbital location in terms of their subsatellite point.

- As noted in the example given earlier, the INTELSAT primary satellite in the Atlantic Ocean Region (AOR) is at 335.5°E longitude.

- Operators of international geostationary satellite systems that have satellites in all three ocean regions(Atlantic, Indian and pacific) tend to use longitude east to describe the subsatellite points to avoid confusion between using both east and west longitude descriptors. For U.S.

- Geostationary satellite operators, all of the satellites are located west of the Greenwich meridian and so it has become accepted practice for regional systems over the United States to describe their geostationary satellite locations in terms of Degrees W.

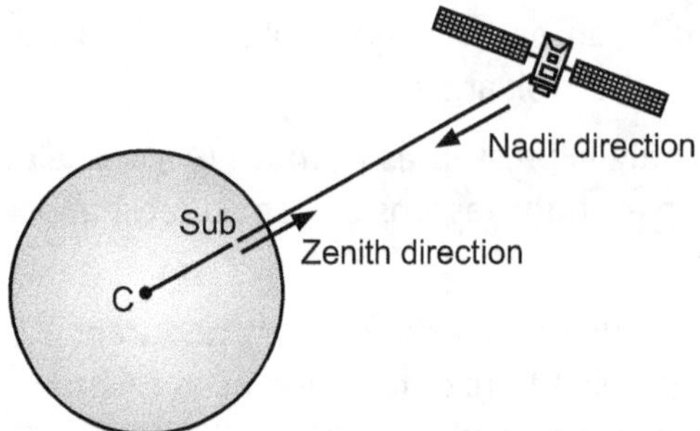

Fig. 4.19: Zenith and nadir pointing directions

- To an observer of a satellite standing at the subsatellite point, the satellite will appear to be directly above his head, in the zenith direction from the observing location.

- The zenith and nadir paths are therefore in opposite directions along the same path (see Fig. 4.18). Designers of satellite antennas reference the pointing direction of the satellite's antenna beams to the nadir direction.

- The communications coverage region on the earth from a satellite is defined by angles measured from nadir at the satellite to the edges of the coverage.

- Earth station antenna designers, however, do not reference their pointing direction to zenith.

- As noted earlier, they use the local horizontal plane at the earth station to define elevation angle and geographical compass points to define azimuth angle. Thus giving the two look angles for the earth station antenna toward the satellite (A_z, E_l).

4.8.2 Elevation Angle Calculation

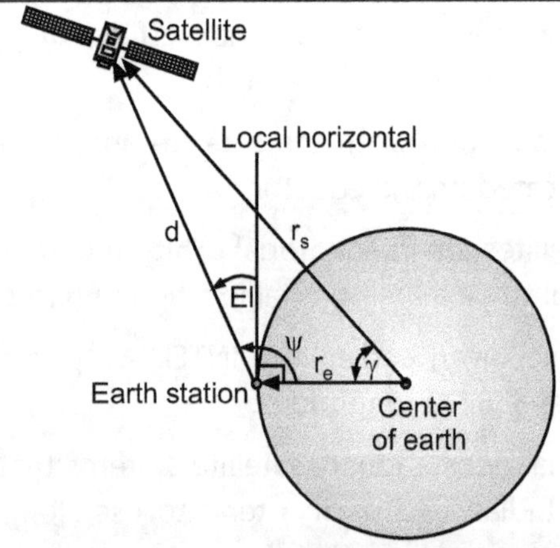

Fig. 4.20 : The geometry of elevation angle calculation

- Fig. 4.20 shows the geometry of the elevation angle calculation. In figure 4.20 r_s is the vector from the center of the earth to the satellite; r_e is the vector from the center of the earth to the earth station; and d is the vector from the earth station to the satellite.

- These three vectors lie in the same plane and form a triangle.

- The central angle γ measured between r_e and r_s is the angle between the earth station and the satellite, and ψ is the angle (within the triangle) measured from r_e to d defined so that it is non-negative, γ related to the earth station north latitude L_e (L_e is the number of degrees in latitude that the earth station is north from the equator) and west longitude l_e (l_e is the number of degrees in longitude that the earth station is west from the Greenwich meridian) and the subsatellite point at north latitude L_s and west longitude l_s by

$$\cos(\gamma) = \cos(L_e)\cos(L_s)\cos(l_s - l_e) + \sin(L_e)\sin(L_s) \qquad \ldots (4.34)$$

- The law of cosines allows us to relate the magnitudes of the vectors joining the center of the earth, the satellite, and the earth station. Thus

$$d = r_s\left[1 + \left(\frac{r_e}{r_s}\right)^2 - 2\left(\frac{r_e}{r_s}\right)\cos(\gamma)\right]^{1/2} \qquad \ldots (4.35)$$

- Since the local horizontal plane at the earth station is perpendicular to r_e, the elevation angle ξ is related to the central angle ψ by

$$\xi = \psi - 90^0 \qquad \ldots (4.36)$$

By the law of sines we have

$$\frac{r_s}{\sin(\psi)} = \frac{d}{\sin(\gamma)} \qquad \ldots (4.37)$$

Combining the last three equations yields

$$\cos(\xi) = \frac{r_s\sin(\gamma)}{d}$$

$$= \frac{\sin(\gamma)}{\left[1 + \left(\frac{r_e}{r_s}\right)^2 - 2\left(\frac{r_e}{r_s}\right)\cos(\gamma)\right]^{1/2}} \qquad \ldots (4.38)$$

- Equations (4.38) and (4.34) permit the elevation angle ξ to be calculated from knowledge of the subsatellite point and the earth station coordinates, the orbital radius r_s and the earth's radius r_e. An accurate value for the average earth radius is 6378.137 km but a common value used in appproximate determinations is 6370 km.

4.8.3 Azimuth Angle Calculation

- As the earth station, the center of the earth, the satellite, and the subsatellite point all lie in the same plane, the azimuth angle A_z from the earth station to the subsatellite point.

- Azimuth angle is difficult to compute than the elevation angle because the exact geometry involved depends on whether the subsatellite point is east or west of the earth station, and in which of the hemispheres the earth station and the subsatellite point are located.

- The problem simplifies somewhat for geosynchronous satellites, which will be treated in the next section. For the general case, in particular for constellations of LEO satellites, the tedium of calculating the individual look angles on a second-by-second basis has been considerably eased by a range of commercial software packages that exist for predicting a variety of orbital dynamics and intercept solutions.

Specialization to Geostationary Satellites:

- For most geostationary satellites, the subsatellite point is on the equator at longitude l_s and the lattitude L_s is 0. The geosynchronous radius r_s is 42,164.17 km. Since L_s is zero, Equation (4.34) simplifies to

$$\cos(\gamma) \;=\; \cos(L_e)\cos(l_s - l_e) \qquad\qquad \dots (4.39)$$

- Substituting r_s = 42,164.17 km and r_e = 6,3780137 km in Equations (4.35) and (4.38) gives the following expressions for the distance d from the earth station to the satellite and the elevation angle ξ at the earth stationary

$$d \;=\; 42{,}164.17\,[1.02288235 - 0.30253825\cos(\gamma)]^{1/2} \qquad \dots (4.40)$$

$$\cos(\xi) \;=\; \frac{\sin(\gamma)}{[1.02288235 - 0.30253825\cos(\gamma)]^{1/2}} \qquad \dots (4.41)$$

- For a geostationary satellite with an orbital radius of 42,164.17 km and a mean earth radius of 6378.137 km, the ratio r_s/r_e = 6.6107345 giving

$$\xi \;=\; \tan^{-1}/\sin\gamma - \gamma \qquad\qquad \dots (4.42)$$

- To find the azimuth angle, an intermediate angle α must first be found. The intermediate angle α permits the correct 90° quadrant to be found for the azimuth since the azimuth angle can lie anywhere between 0° (true north) and clockwise through 360° (back to true north again). The intermediate angle is found from

$$\alpha \;=\; \tan^{-1}\left[\frac{\tan|(l_s - l_e)|}{\sin(L_e)}\right] \qquad\qquad \dots (4.43)$$

- Having found the intermediate angle α, the azimuth look angle A_z can be found from:

Case 1: Earth station in the Northern Hemisphere with

- Satellite to the SE of the earth station: $A_z = 180° - \alpha$
- Satellite to the SW of the earth station: $A_z = 180° + \alpha$

Case 2: Earth station in the Southern Hemisphere with

- Satellite to the NE of the earth station: $A_z\ \alpha$
- Satellite to the NW of the earth station: $A_z = 360° - \alpha$

4.8.4 Visibility Test

- For a satellite to be visible from an earth station, its elevation angle E_l must be above some minimum value, which is at least 0°. A positive or zero elevation angle requires that (see Fig. 4.20)

$$r_s \;\geq\; \frac{r_e}{\cos(\gamma)} \qquad\qquad \dots (4.44)$$

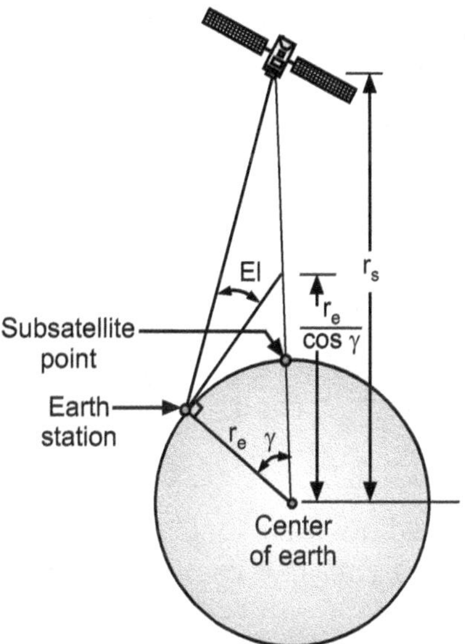

Fig. 4.21: The geometry of the visibility calculations

- This means that the maximum central angular separation between the earth station and the subsatellite point is limited by

$$\gamma \le \cos^{-1}\left(\frac{r_e}{r_s}\right) \qquad\qquad \dots (4.45)$$

- For a nominal geostationary orbit, the last equation reduces to $\gamma \le 81.3°$. For the satellite to be visible.

Example 4.3 : A Hypothetical satellite is orbiting at a distance of 68400 km. the earth station antenna makes a vertical angle of 30° for a LOS communication with this satellite. Calculate slant range for this case using first approximation?

Solution: From first approximation,

$$\varepsilon_\infty = \varepsilon = 30°$$

$$\therefore \qquad \gamma = 90 - 30 = 60°$$

Then,

Slant range, $d_s = 68400\ [1 + (6378/68400)^2 - 2(6378/68400) \times \cos 60°]^{1/2}$

$$65444.51 \text{ km}$$

Always, $\qquad\qquad d_s < d$

Example 4.4 : Calculate the slant range of a geostationary satellite orbiting at 42200 km from an earth station making an elevation angle of 25°. Also find the viewing angle of the satellite.

Solution: $\qquad\qquad d = 42200$ km

Let us assume the radius of earth to be 6378 km.

Now, $\lambda = \cos^{-1}\left[\dfrac{r_e \cos \xi}{d}\right] - \xi = \cos^{-1}\left(\dfrac{6378 \cos 25}{42200}\right) - 25 = 57.12°$

The slant range therefore will be

$$d_s = d\left[1 + \left(\dfrac{r_e}{d}\right)^2 - \dfrac{2r_e}{d}\cos\gamma\right]^{1/2} = 42200\left[1 + \left(\dfrac{6378}{42200}\right)^2 - \dfrac{2 \times 6378}{42200}\cos 57.12\right]^{1/2}$$

$$39135.637 \text{ km}$$

Viewing angle δ is given by

$$\sin\delta = \dfrac{r_e}{r_e + h}\cos\xi = \dfrac{6378}{42200}\cos 25 = 0.1369$$

$\therefore$ $\qquad\qquad\qquad\qquad \delta = 7.872°$

Calculation of ξ can be carried out if the longitude and latitude of the earth station and the longitude of the geostationary satellite is known using the equation:

$$\xi = \tan^{-1}\left[\dfrac{\cos\lambda_{AE}\cos\lambda - 0.151}{\sqrt{(1 - \cos^2\lambda_{AE}\cos^2\lambda)}}\right]$$

where λ_{AE} is the earth station's latitude.

and $\qquad\qquad\qquad\qquad \lambda = \lambda_E - \lambda_s$

The difference between the longitudes of the earth station and satellite.

Thus substituting different values of λ_{AE} and λ, it is found that if the latitude of earth station is greater than $\pm\,81.3°$ the satellite will go below horizon, indicating that the satellite is out of sight.

$$A_{z(cal)} = \tan^{-1}\left[\dfrac{\tan\lambda}{\sin\lambda_{AE}}\right]$$

The value of azimuth angle depends upon the relative positions of satellite (sub-satellite point on the earth) and earth station.

Example 4.5 : An earth station is located at a longitude of 76° east and latitude of 13° north while the satellite is at 83° east. Calculate the elevation and azimuth requirement of a transmitting antenna.

Solution: From the data given

$\lambda = \lambda_E - \lambda_s = 76 - 83 = -7$ or satellite is 7° west of earth station.

$$\xi = \tan^{-1}\left[\dfrac{\cos\lambda_{AE}\cos\lambda - 0.151}{\sqrt{\sqrt{1 - \cos^2\lambda_{AE}\cos^2\lambda}}}\right] = \tan^{-1}\left[\dfrac{\cos 13 \cos 7 - 0.151}{\sqrt{(1 - \cos^2 13 \cos^2 7)}}\right] = 72.86°$$

$$A_{z(cal)} = \tan^{-1}\left[\dfrac{\tan\lambda}{\sin\lambda_{AE}}\right] = \tan^{-1}\left[\dfrac{\tan 7}{\sin 13}\right] = 28.62°$$

Since the sub-satellite point (sat. itself) is SW of earth station

$$A_z = A_{z(cal)} + 180° = 208.62°$$

Example 4.6 : A LEO satellite is at 1000 km from the sub-satellite point on the earth. Determine the angular velocity and time of orbit, assuming ideal orbiting conditions. If this satellite has to scan from 20° south-east to 40° north-east. Estimate the number of satellites required for communication throughout 24 hours.

Solution: Given: $\qquad h = 1000$ km

Then $\qquad\qquad\qquad d = r_e + h$

$$6378 + 1000 = 7378 \text{ km}$$

$$3.98 \times 10^6$$

$$(7378) = 7.344 \text{ km/s}$$

$$v = \sqrt{g_0/d)}$$

$$\omega = \frac{v}{d} = \frac{7.344}{7378} = 9.95 \times 10^{-4} \text{ rad/s}$$

Time of orbit to cover 360° is:

$$T_0 = \frac{2\pi}{\omega} = \frac{2\pi}{1.2 \times 10^{-4}} = 6311.67 \text{ s}$$

$$\therefore \qquad \text{Time to cover } 60° = \left(\frac{6311.67}{360}\right) \times 60 = 1051.95 \text{ s} = 17.53 \text{ min}$$

No. of satellites required for 24 hrs or 1440 min = 1440/17.53 = 82 to 83 satellites.

4.9 ORBITAL PERTURBATIONS

- The orbital equations developed in section 4.7 modeled the earth and the satellite as point masses influenced only by gravitational attraction.

- Under these ideal conditions, a "Keplerian" orbit results, which is an ellipse whose properties are constant with time.

- In practice, the satellite and the earth respond to many other influences including asymmetry of the earth's gravitational field, the gravitational field of the sun and the moon, and solar radiation pressure.

- For low earth orbit satellites, atmospleric drag can also be important.

- All of these interfering forces cause the true orbit to be different from a simple Keplerian ellipse; if unchecked, they would cause the subsatellite point of a nominally geosynchronous satellite to move with time.

- Historically, much attention has been given to techniques for incorporating additional perturbing forces into orbit descriptions. The approach normally adopted for communications satellites is first to derive an osculating orbit for some instant in time (the Keplerian orbit the spacecraft would follow if all perturbing forces were removed at that time) with orbital elements $(a, e, t_p, \Omega, i, \omega)$.

- The perturbations are assumed to cause the orbital elements to vary with time and the orbit and satellite location at any instant are taken from the osculating orbit calculated with orbital elements corresponding to that time. To visualize the process, assume that the osculating orbital elements at time t_0 are (a_0, e_0, t_p, Ω_0, i_0, ω_0).

- Then assume that the orbital elements vary linearly with time at constant rates given by (da/dt, de/dt) etc. the satellite's position at any time t_1 is then calculated from a Keplerian orbit with elements

$$a_0 + \frac{da}{dt}(t_1 - t_0),\ e_0 + \frac{de}{dt}(t_1 - t_0)\ \text{etc.}$$

- This approach is particularly useful in practice because it permits the use of either theoretically calculated derivatives or empirical values based on satellite observations.

- As the perturbed orbit is not an ellipse, some care must be taken in defining the orbital period.

- Since the satellite does not return to the same point in space once per revolution, the quantity most frequently specified is the so called anomalistic period: the elapsed time between successive perigee passages.

- In addition to the orbit not being a perfect Keplerian ellipse, there will be other influences that will cause the apparent position of a geostationary satellite to change with time.

- These can be viewed as those causing mainly longitudinal changes and those that principally affect the orbital inclination.

- However, the Keplerian orbit is ideal in the sense that it assumes that the earth is a uniform spherical mass and that the only force acting is the centrifugal force, resulting from satellite motion balancing the gravitational pull of the earth.

- In actual practice it is not true because any satellite in space is also acted upon by torque due to other external as well as internal forces.

External Torques:

1. Gravitational effect of other planetary bodies like sun, moon and other heavenly bodies.
2. Non-spherical earth
3. Atmospheric drag (only in low orbits).
4. Aerodynamic forces (only in low orbits).
5. Solar pressure on the solar cell panel.
6. Magnetic forces acting on the satellite due to earth's magnetic fields.

- The gravitational force on satellite varies due to the earth's oblateness. The earth's polar diameter is about 42 km shorter than the equatorial.

- We also find that the gravitational effect of sun, moon and atmospheric drag are quite significant depending on the position of the satellite.

- The gravitational pulls of sun and moon have negligible effect on LEO satellites but they do affect satellites in the geostationary orbit.

- For satellites in the low earth orbit (below 1000 km), the effect of atmospheric drag is significant and it tries to slow down the satellite. This causes change in eccentricity and position of apogee changes during every successive revolution.

- The solar pressure is another aspect to be considered while designing the shape and architecture of the satellite.

- Since the satellite is in an environment almost free of all forces, the sunrays (which essentially consist of photons) when fall normally on the solar panel, exerts a typical force of 4.63×10^{-6} newton/m^2 or 95.5 *lbs*/ft^2.

- This is quite enormous in space particularly in case of geosynchronous orbits where the sunrays always fall normal to the solar panels.

- Even though this seems to be minute, they are sufficient to tilt the satellite in space.

- To compensate for such forces solar sails or compensating panels are necessary.

Internal Torques:

1. Thruster misalignment.
2. Fuel movement in spacecraft.

- Ideally the thruster is used to control the north-south axis of the satellite and the force that acts due to this should pass through the centre of mass of the satellite but if there is any minute misalignment, it will produce a torque that may change the stability of the satellite.

- Fuel movement is another important factor as the satellite rotates around its own axis, the liquid hydrazine inside churns and produce a rotational torque, which may change the attitude and orbit of satellite.

4.9.1 Longitudinal Changes: Effects of the Earth's Oblateness

- The earth is neither a perfect sphere nor a perfect ellipse; it can be said to be as a triaxial ellipsoid.

- The earth is flat at the poles; the diameter at the equator is about 20 km more than the average diameter at poles.

- The radius at the equator is not constant, though the non-circularity is small, the radius does not vary by more than about 100 m around the equator.

- In addition to these non-regular features of the earth, like there are regions where the average density of the earth appears to be higher.

- These are referred to as regions of mass concentration or Mascons.

- Hence the earth is not an exact spherical and also non-circular at the equatorial radius and the Mascons lead to a non-uniform gravitational field around the earth.

- The force on an orbiting satellite will therefore vary with position.

- For a low earth orbit satellite, the rapid change in position of the satellite with respect to the earth's surface will lead to an averaging out of the perturbing forces in line with the orbital velocity vector.
- The same is not true for a geostationary (or geosynchronous) satellite.
- A geostationary satellite is weightless when in orbit.
- The smallest force on the satellite will cause it to accelerate and then drift away from its nominal location.
- The satellite is required to maintain a constant longitudinal position over the equator, but there will generally be an additional force toward the nearest equatorial bulge in either an eastward or a westward direction along the orbit plane.
- Since this will rarely be in line with the main gravitational force toward the earth's center, there will be a resultant component of force acting in the same direction as the satellite's velocity vector or against it, depending on the exact position of the satellite in the GEO orbit.
- This will lead to a resultant acceleration or deceleration component that varies with longitudinal location of the satellite.
- Due to the position of the Mascons and equatorial bulges, there are four equilibrium points in the geostationary orbit: two of them stable and two unstable.
- The stable points are analogous to the bottom of a valley, and the unstable points to the top of a hill. If a ball is perched on top of a hill, a small push will cause it to roll down the slope onto a valley, where it will roll backwards and forwards until it gradually comes to a final stop at the lowest point. The satellite at an unstable orbital location is at the top of a gravity hill.
- Given a small force, it will drift down the gravity slope into the gravity well (valley) and finally stay there, at the stable position. The stable points are at about 75°E and 252°E and the unstable points are at around 162°E and 348°E. If a satellite is perturbed slightly from one of the stable points, it will tend to drift back to the stable point without any thruster firing required.
- A satellite that is perturbed slightly from one of the unstable points will immediately begin to accelerate its drift toward the nearest stable point and once it reaches this point, it will oscillate in longitudinal position about this point until(centuries later) it stabilizes at that point.
- These stable points are sometimes called the graveyard geosynchronous orbit locations (which is the orbit to which the satellite is raised once the satellite ceases to be useful). Note that, due to the nonsphericity of the earth, etc., the stable points are neither exactly 180°apart, nor are the stable and unstable points precisely 90° apart.

4.9.2 Inclination Changes: Effects of the Sun and the Moon

- The plane of the earth's orbit around the sun the ecliptic is at an inclination of 7.3° to the equatorial plane of the sun. The earth is tilted about 23° away from the normal to the ecliptic. The moon circles the earth with an inclination of around 5° to the equatorial plane of the earth.

- Due to the fact that the various planes the sun's equator, the ecliptic, the earth's equator (a plane normal to the earth's rotational axis), and the moon's orbital plane around the earth are all different, a satellite in orbit around the earth will be subjected to a variety of out of plane forces.

- That is, there will generally be a net acceleration force that is not in the plane of the satellite's orbit, and this will tend to try to change the inclination of the satellite's orbit from its initial inclination.

- Under these conditions, the orbit will process and its inclination will change.

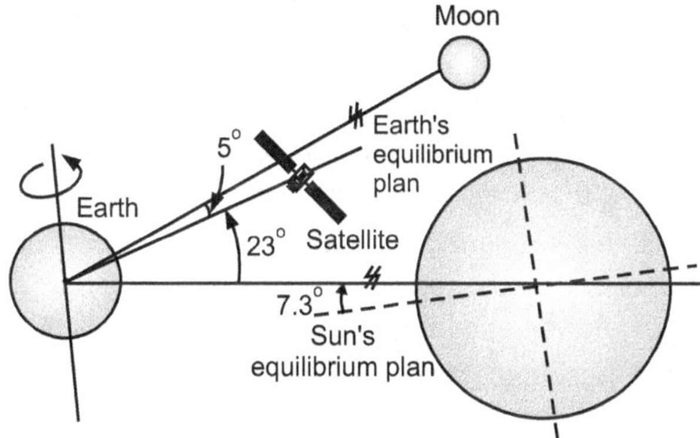

Fig. 4.22: Relationship between the orbital planes of the sun, moon, and earth.

- The mass of the sun is significantly larger than that of the moon but the moon is considerably closer to the earth than the sun.

- For this reason, the acceleration force induced by the moon on a geostationary satellite is about twice as large as that of the sun.

- The net effect of the acceleration forces induced by the moon and the sun on a geostationary satellite is to change the plane of the orbit at an initial average rate of change of 0.85°/year from the equatorial plane.

- When both the sun and moon are acting on the same side of the satellite's orbit, the rate of change of the plane of the geostationary satellite's orbit will be higher than average.

- When they are on opposite sides of the orbit, the rate of change of the plane of the satellite's orbit will be less than average.

- Examples of maximum years are 1988 and 2006 (0.94°/year) and examples of minimum years are 1997 and 2015 (0.75°/year).

- These rates of change are neither constant with time nor with inclination. They are at a maximum when the inclination is zero and they are zero when the inclination is 14.67°. From an initial zero inclination, the plane of the geostationary orbit will change to a maximum inclination of 14.67° over 26.6 years.

- The acceleration forces will then change direction at this maximum inclination and the orbit inclination will move back to zero in another 26.6 years and out to 14.67° over a further 26.6 years, and so on.

- In some cases, to increase the orbital maneuver lifetime of a satellite for a given fuel load, mission planner deliberately place a satellite planned for geostationary orbit into an initial orbit with an inclination that is substantially larger than the nominal 0.05o for a geostationary satellite.

- The launch is specifically timed, however so as to set up the necessary precessional forces that will automatically reduce the inclination "error" to close to zero over the required period without the use of any thruster firings on the spacecraft.

- This will increase the maneuvering lifetime of the satellite at the expense of requiring greater tracking by the larger earth terminals accessing the satellite for the first year or so of the satellite's operational life.

- Under normal operations, ground controllers command spacecraft maneuvers to correct for both the in-plane changes (longitudinal drifts) and out-of-plane changes (inclination changes) of a satellite so that it remains in the correct orbit.

- For a geostationary satellite, this means that the inclination, ellipticity and longitudinal position are controlled so that the satellite appears to stay within a box in the sky that is bounded by $\pm\,0.05°$ in latitude and longitude over the subsatellite point.

- Some maneuvers are designed to correct for both inclination and longitude drifts simultaneously in the one burn of the maneuvering rockets on the satellite.

- In others, the two maneuvers are kept separate: one burn will correct for ellipticity and longitude drift; another will correct for inclination changes.

- The latter situation of separated maneuvers is becoming more common for two reasons. The first is due to the much larger velocity increment needed to change the plane of an orbit (the so-called north-south maneuver) as compared with the longitude/ellipticity of an orbit (the so called east-west maneuver).

- The difference in energy requirement is about 10:1. By alternately correcting for inclination changes and in-phase changes, the altitude of the satellite can be held constant and different sets of thrusters exercised for the required maneuver.

- The second reason is the increasing use of two completely different types of thrusters to control N–S maneuvers on the one hand and E–W maneuvers on the other.

- In the mid-1990 s, one of the heaviest items that carried into orbit on a large satellite was the fuel to raise and control the orbit.

- About 90% of this fuel load was to control the inclination of the satellite, once on orbit.

- Latest rocket motors, particularly arc jets and ion thrusters, offer increased efficiency with lighter mass.

- In general, these low thrust, high efficiency rocket motors are used for N – S maneuvers leaving the liquid propellant thrusters, with their inherently higher thrust (but lower efficiency) for orbit raising and in-plane changes.

- In order to be able to calculate the required orbit maneuver for a given satellite, the controllers must have an accurate knowledge of the satellite's orbit. Orbit determination is a major aspect of satellite control.

Example 4.7: A quasi-GEO satellite is in a circular equatorial orbit close to geosynchronous altitude. The quasi-GEO satellite, however, does not have a period of one sidereal day: its orbital period is exactly 24 h-one solar day. Calculate:

(i) The radius of the orbit.

(ii) The rate of drift around the equator of the subsatellite point in degrees per (solar) day. An observer on the earth sees that the satellite is drifting across the sky.

(iii) Is the satellite moving toward the east or toward the west?

Solution:

(i) The orbital radius is found from Equation (4.24), it gives the square of the orbital period in seconds.

$$T^2 = (4\pi^2 a^3)/\mu$$

Rearranging the equation, the orbital radius a is given by

$$a^3 = T^2\mu/(4\pi^2) = (86,000)^2 \times 3.986004418 \times 10^5/4\pi^2$$

$$7.5371216 \times 10^{13} \text{ km}^3$$

$$a = 42.241.095 \text{ km}$$

(ii) The orbital period of the satellite (one solar day) is longer than a sidereal day by 3 min 55.9 sec = 235.9 s. This will cause the subsatellite point to drift at a rate of 360° × 235.9/86400 per day or 0.983° per day.

(iii) The earth moves toward the east at a faster rate than the satellite, so the drift will appear to an observer on the earth to be toward the west.

4.10 ORBIT DETERMINATION

- Orbit determination requires that sufficient measurements be made to determine uniquely the six orbital elements needed to calculate the future orbit of the satellite, and hence calculate the required changes that need to be made to the orbit to keep it within the nominal orbital location.

- Three angular position measurements are needed because there are six unknowns and each measurement will provide two equations.

- Conceptually, these can be thought of as one equation giving the azimuth and the other the elevation as a function of the six (as yet unknown) orbital elements.

- The control earth stations used to measure the angular position of the satellites also carry out range measurements using unique time stamps in the telemetry stream or communication carrier.

- These earth stations are generally referred to as the TTC&M (Telemetry Tracking Command and Monitoring) stations of the satellite network.

- Major satellite networks maintain their own TTC&M stations around the world. Smaller satellite systems generally contract for such TTC&M functions from the spacecraft manufacturer or from the larger satellite system operators, as it is generally uneconomic to build advanced TTC&M stations with fewer than three satellites to control.

4.11 LAUNCHES AND LAUNCH VEHICLES

- A satellite cannot be placed into a stable orbit unless two parameters that are uniquely coupled together the velocity vector and the orbital height are simultaneously correct.

- There is little point in obtaining the correct height and not having the appropriate velocity component in the correct direction to achieve the desired orbit.

- A geostationary satellite, for example, must be in an orbit at a height of 35,786.03 km above the surface of the earth (42,164.17 km radius from the center of the earth) with an inclination of zero degrees, an ellipticity of zero, and a velocity of 3074.7 m/s tangential to the earth in the plane of the orbit, which is the earth's equatorial plane.

- The further out from the earth the orbit is, the greater the energy required from the launch vehicle to reach that orbit.

- In any earth satellite launch, the largest fraction of the energy expanded by the rocket is used to accelerate the vehicle from rest until it is about 20 miles (32 km) above the earth.

- To make the most efficient use of the fuel, it is common to shed excess mass from the launcher as it moves upward on launch: this is called staging. Figure 4.23 gives a schematic of a proton launch from the Russian Baikonur complex at Kazakhstan, near Tyuratam.

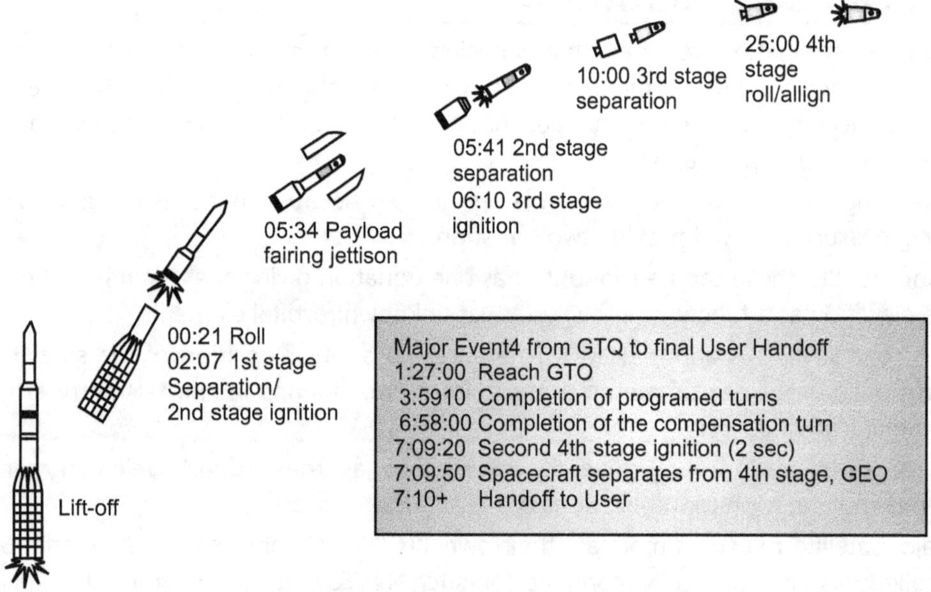

Fig. 4.23 : Schematic of a Proton launch

- Most launch vehicles have multiple stages and, as each stage is completed, that portion of the launcher is expanded until the final stage places the satellite into the desired trajectory. Hence the term: **expandable launch vehicle (ELV)**.

- The space shuttle, called the Space Transportation System (STS) by NASA, is partially reuauable.

- The solid rocket boosters are recovered and refurbished for future missions and the shuttle vehicle itself is flown back to earth for refurbishment and reuse. Hence the term: Reusuable Launch Vehicle(RLV) for such launchers.

- More advanced launch vehicles are being developed that would provide both single stage to orbit (SSTO) and RLV capabilities. The NASA series of X-33 and X-34 test vehicles from the public portion of this quest.

- There are also a number of private ventures that aim to achieve RLV capabilities in the first decade of the twenty first century.

- Equal importance to the orbital height the satellite is intended for is the inclination of the orbit that the spacecraft needs to be launched into.

- The earth spins toward the east. At the equator, the rotational velocity of a sea level site in the plane of the equator is ($2\pi \times$ radius of the earth)/(one sidereal day) = 0.4651 km/s. This velocity increment is approximately 1000 mph (~ 1610 km/h). An easterly launch from the equator has a velocity increment of 0.465 km/s imparted by the rotation of the earth.

- A satellite in a circular, equatorial orbit at an altitude of 900 km requires an orbital velocity of about 7.4 km/s tangential to the surface of the earth. A rocket launched from the equator needs to impart an additional velocity of (7.4 − 0.47) km/s = 6.93 km/s: in other words, the equatorial launch has reduced the energy required by about.

- This equatorial launch "bonus" led to the concept of a sea launch by Hughes and Boeing. If the launch is not to be into an equatorial orbit, the payload capabilities of any given rocket will reduce as the inclination increases.

- A satellite launched into a prograde orbit from latitude of ϕ degrees will enter an orbit with an inclination of ϕ degrees to the equator.

- If the satellite is intended for geostationary orbit, the satellite must be given a significant velocity increment to reorient the orbit into the earth's equatorial plane.

- For example, a satellite launched from Cape Canaveral at 28.5° N latitude requires a velocity increment of 366 m/s to attain an equatorial orbit from a geosynchronous orbit plane of 28.5°.

- Ariane is launched from the Guiana Space Center in French Guiana, located at latitude 5° S in South America, and SeaLaunch can launch from the equator.

- The lower latitude of these launch sites results in significant savings in the fuel used by the Apogee Kick Motor (AKM).

4.11.1 Expandable Launch Vehicle (ELVs)

- 1998 was an important year for ELVs: it was the year when the number of commercial launches in the United States surpassed the number of government launches for the first time.

- The gap between commercial and government launches will continue to grow. The Teal group estimated in mid-1999 that 1447 satellites would be launched worldwide between 2000 and 2009 on 850 to 900 launch vehicles.

- At an average cost of $100 M per launch, this represents a business worth about $90B over 10 years. Of these 1447 satellites, 893 were considered commercial ventures with the remainder split between military and civilian government spacecraft.

- There is therefore a healthy market for ELVs and a number of companies, consortia, and national entities are seeking to enter this expanding field.

- Reference 15 contains a good survey of the ELVs being developed for the 21st century.

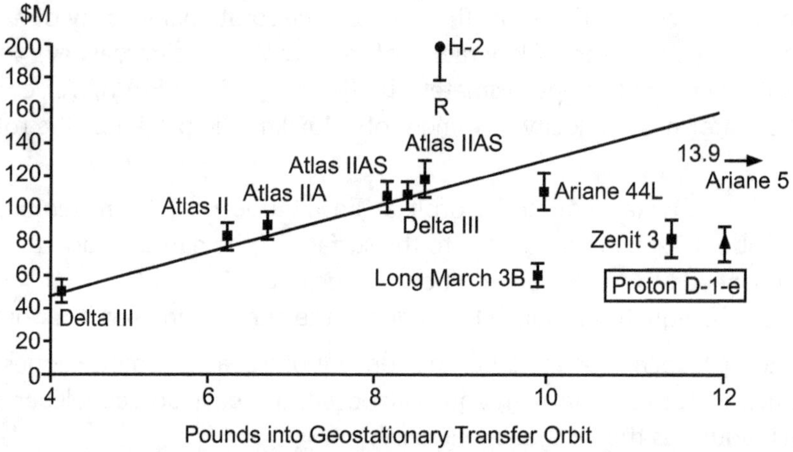

Fig. 4.24 : Launch vehicle market price vs performance

- Fig. 4.24 presents a rough comparison between the main launch vehicles used for Geostationary Transfer Orbit (GTO) injection during the 1990s, plus the Ariane 5 launchers.

- The 1996 pricing of these vehicles is shown in Fig. 4.24. Not included in these data are the advanced Chinese launch vehicles being developed for both unmanned and manned missions in the 21st century.

- The largest of these Chinese launch vehicles rivals the Ariane 5 vehicle with a geostationary transfer orbit capability of 26,000 lb.

Table 4.2 : Some Next Generation Launchers Compared with Ariane 44 and Atlas IIAS Baseline Vehicles(1999 Prices)

Launchers	Weight to orbit(kg)	Total cost($M)	Lead times(months)	Max. payload diameter(m)	Launch latitude($^\circ$)
Ariane 44	4000	130	36	3.65	5.2
Ariane 5	6800	120	36	4.57	5.2
Atlas IIAS	3700	100	36	3.45	28.5
Atlas IIIA	4120	125	36	4.19	28.5
Atlas IIIB	4500	135	48	4.19	28.5
Atlas V	6500	150*	48	5.40	28.5
Delta III	3800	130	36	4.00	28.7
Delta IV(small)	2177	60*	36*	3.00	28.7
Delta IV(med.)	4173	120*	36*	4.00	28.7
Delta IV(heavy)	13200	400*	48*	5.00	28.7
Titan III	4500	260	36	3.65	28.6
Titan IV	5700	435	48	4.57	28.6
Proton M	4800	80	24	3.68	51.6

Table 4.3: Some Launch Vehicle Selection Factors

Price/cost
Reliability
Recent launch success/failure history
Dependable launch schedule
Urgency of your launch requirement
Performance
Spacecraft fit to launcher(size, acoustic, and vibration environment)
Flight proven (see recent launch history)
Safety issues
Launch site location
Availability
What is the launcher backlog of orders?
What is the launch site backlog of launches?
Market issues
What will the market bear at this particular time?

- It can be seen from Fig. 4.22 that there was a well- established trend line of about $25,000 per kg into GTO prior to the introduction of the Chinese Long March and the Russian Zenit and Proton vehicles.

- The pricing of the Chinese and Russian launchers reflected an aggressive marketing strategy to break into the launch services field.

- Ariane 5 was the first of the next generation launchers aimed at both large, simple payloads into GTO and multiple payload injection into LEO and MEO.

- Some more next-generation launchers are shown in Table 4.2. It is anticipated that the bulk of the large satellite launches will be conducted with Atlas V, Delta IV and Ariane vehicles and their Russian and Chinese equivalents over the first 2 decades of the 21st century.

- The decision on which particular rocket to use in a given situation will depend on a variety of factors. Some of these are set out in Table 4.3.

- The decision making routine using the above criteria is shown in Fig. 4.23.

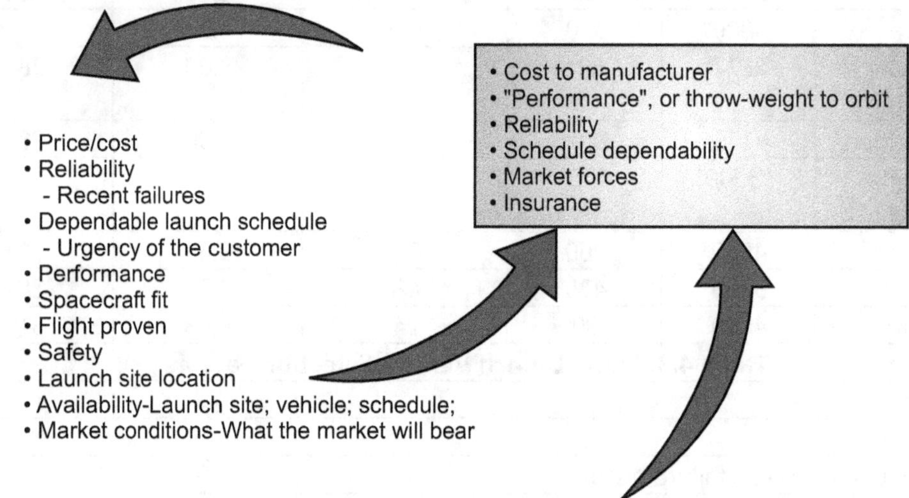

**Fig. 4.25 : Schematic of the decision making process to select
a rocket for a given satellite requirement**

- Some of the launch vehicles deliver the spacecraft directly to geostationary orbit (called a direct-insertion launch) while others inject the spacecraft into a geostationary transfer orbit (GTO).

- Spacecraft launched into GTO must carry additional rocket motors and/or propellent to enable the vehicle to reach the geostationary orbit. There are three basic ways to achieve geostationary orbit.

4.11.2 Placing Satellite into Geostationary Orbit

- **Geostationary Transfer Orbit and AKM** the initial approach to launching geostationary satellites was to place the spacecraft, with the final rocket stage still attached, into low earth orbit.

- After a couple of orbits, during which the orbital elements are measured, the final stage is reignited and the spacecraft is launched into a geostationary transfer orbit.

- The GTO has a perigee that is the original LEO orbit altitude and an apogee that is the GEO altitude. Fig. 4.24 illustrates the process.

- The position of the apogee point is close to the orbital longitude that would be the in-orbit test location of the satellite prior to it being moved to its operational position.

- Again, after a few orbits in the GTO while the orbital elements are measured, a rocket motor (usually contained within the satellite itself) is ignited at apogee and the GTO is raised until it is a circular, geostationary orbit.

- Since the rocket motor fires at apogee, it is commonly referred to as the apogee kick motor (AKM). The AKM is used both to circularize the orbit at GEO and to remove any inclination error so that the final orbit of the satellite is very close to geostationary.

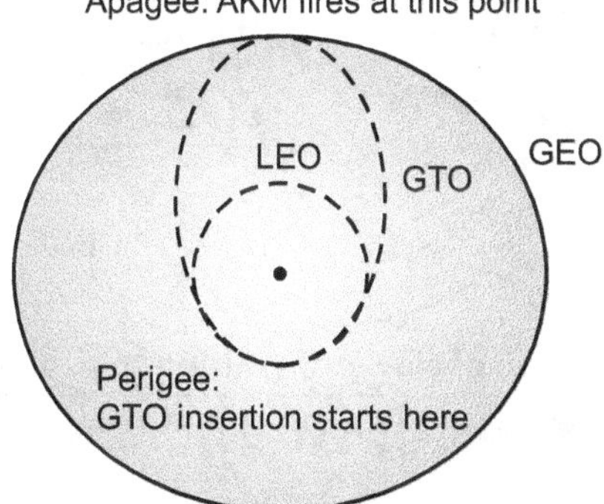

Fig. 4.26 : Illustration of the GTO/AKM approach to geostationary orbit

- **Geostationary Transfer Orbit with Slow Orbit Raising** in this procedure, rather than employ an apogee kick motor that imparts a vigorous acceleration over a few minutes, the spacecraft thrusters are used to raise the orbit from GTO to GEO over a number of burns.

- Since the spacecraft cannot be spin-stabilized during the GTO (so as not to infringe the Hughes patent), many of the satellite elements are deployed while in GTO, including the solar panels.

- The satellite has two power levels of thrusters: one for more powerful orbit raising maneuvers and one for on-orbit (low thrust) maneuvers.

- Since the thrusters take many hours of operation to achieve the geostationary orbit, the perigee of the orbit is gradually raised over successive thruster firings.

- The thruster firings occur symmetrically about the apogee although they could occur at the perigee as well. The burns are typically 60 to 80 min long on successive orbits and up to six orbits can be used. Fig. 4.25 illustrates the process.

- In the first two cases, AKM and slow orbit raising, the GTO may be a modified orbit with the apogee well above the required altitude for GEO.

- The excess energy of the orbit due to the higher-than-necessary altitude at apogee can be traded for energy required to raise the perigee. The net energy to circularize the orbit at GEO is therefore less and the satellite can retain more fuel for on-orbit operations.

- **Direct Insertion to GEO.** This is similar to the GTO technique but, in this case, the launch service provider contracts to place the satellite into GTO.

- The final stages of the rocket are used to place the satellite directly into GEO rather than the satellite using its own propulsion system to go from GTO to GEO.

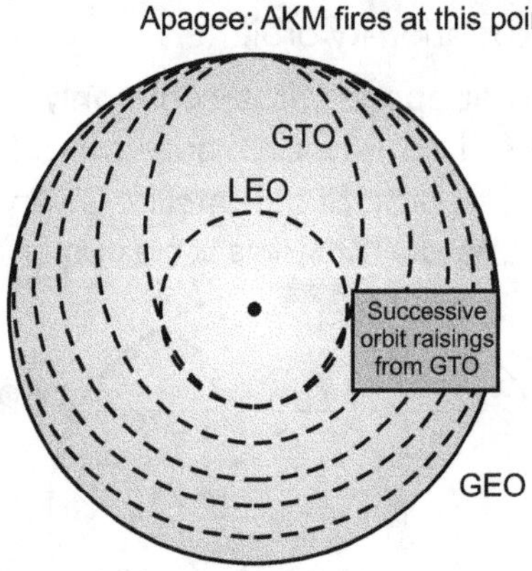

Apagee: AKM fires at this point

GTO
LEO
Successive orbit raisings from GTO
GEO

Fig. 4.27: Illustration of slow orbit raising to geostationary orbit

4.12 ORBITAL EFFECTS IN COMMUNICATIONS SYSTEMS PERFORMANCE

4.12.1 Doppler Shift

- To a stationary observer, the frequency of a moving radio transmitter varies with the transmitter's velocity relative to the observer.

- If the true transmitter frequency (i.e. the frequency that the transmitter would send when at rest) is f_T, the received frequency f_R is higher than f_T when the transmitter is moving towards the receiver and lower than f_T when the transmitter is moving away from the receiver. Mathematically, the relationship [Equation (2.44a) between the transmitted and received frequencies is

$$\frac{f_R - f_T}{f_T} = \frac{QDf}{f_T} = \frac{V_T}{v_p} \qquad \qquad \dots (2.44\ a)$$

Or
$$\Delta f = \frac{V_T f_T}{c} = V_T/\lambda \qquad \qquad \dots (2.44\ b)$$

- Where V_T is the component of the transmitter velocity directed towards the receiver, v_p the phase velocity of light ($2.9979 \times 10^8 = 3 \times 10^8$ m/s in free space), and λ is the wavelength of the transmitted signal. If the transmitter is moving away from the receiver, then V_T is negative.

- This change in frequency is called the Doppler shift, the Doppler effect, or more commonly just Doppler after the German physicist who first studied the phenomenon in sound waves.

- For LEO satellites, Doppler shift can be quite pronounced, requiring the use of frequency-tracking receivers. For geostationary satellites, the effect is negligible.

4.12.2 Range Variations

- The position of a satellite with respect to the earth exhibits a cyclic daily variation even with the best station keeping systems available for geostationary satellites.

- The variation in position will lead to a variation in range between the satellite and user terminals.

- If Time Division Multiple Access (TDMA) is being used, careful attention must be paid to the timing of the frames within the TDMA bursts so that the individual user frames arrive at the satellite in the correct sequence and at the correct time. Range variations on LEO satellites can be significant, as can path loss variations.

- While guard times between bursts can be increased to help in any range and/or timing inaccuracies, this reduces the capacity of the transponder.

- The on-board capabilities of some satellites permit both timing control of the burst sequence and power level control of individual user streams.

4.12.3 Solar Eclipse

- A satellite is said to be in eclipse when the earth prevents sunlight from reaching it, that is, when the satellite is in the shadow of the earth.

- For geostationary satellites, eclipses occur during two periods that begin 23 days before the equinoxes (about March 21 and about September 23) and end 23 days after the equinox periods.

- Fig. 4.28 from reference 11 and Fig. 4.29 from reference 12 illustrate the geometry and duration of the eclipses.

- Eclipses occur close to the equinoxes, as these are the times when the sun, the earth, and the satellite are all nearly in the same plane.

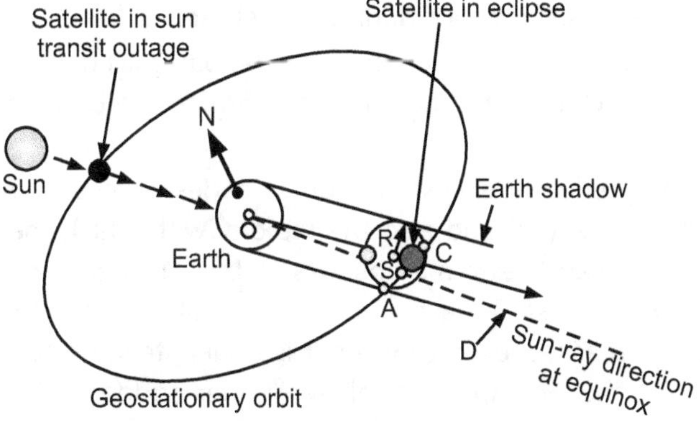

Fig. 4.28: Eclipse geometry

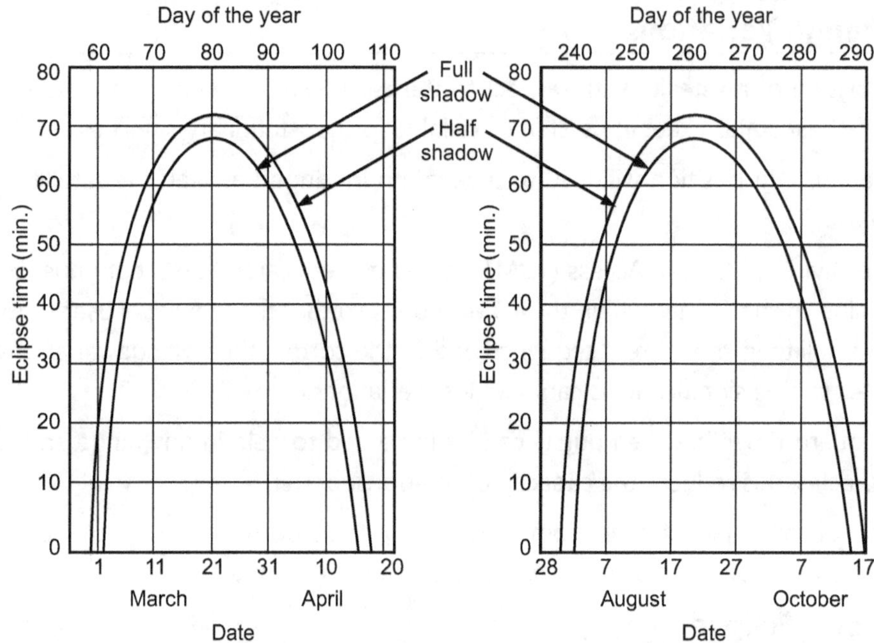

Fig. 4.29: Dates and duration of eclipses

- During full eclipse, a satellite receives no power from its solar array and it must operate entirely from its batteries.

- Batteries are designed to operate with a maximum depth of discharge: the better the battery, the lower the percentage depth of discharge can be. If the battery is discharged below its maximum depth of discharge, the battery may not recover to full operational capacity once recharged.

- The depth of discharge therefore sets the power drain limit during eclipse operations. Nickel-Hydrogen batteries, long the mainstay of communication satellites, can operate at about a 70 depth of discharge and recover fully once recharged.

- Ground controllers perform battery-conditioning routines prior to eclipse operations to ensure the best battery performance during the eclipse.

- The routines consist of deliberately discharging the batteries until they are close to their maximum depth of discharge, and then fully recharging the batteries just before eclipse season begins.

- For spacecraft designers the eclipse season is a design challenge. The main power source is withdrawn (the sun) and also the rapidity with which the satellite enters and exits the shadow can cause extreme changes in both power and heating effects over relatively short periods. Just like a common light bulb is more likely to fail when the current is switched on as opposed to when it is under steady state conditions, satellites can suffer many of their component failures under sudden stress situations. Eclipse periods are therefore monitored carefully by ground controllers, as this is when most of the equipment failures are likely to occur.

Example 4.8 : If a satellite is at a height of 36000 km and orbiting in equatorial plane, comment whether the satellite will be under eclipse on equinox days and find the duration of eclipse.

Solution: Given: h = 36000 km if radius of earth is taken as 6378 km

then

Radius of orbit d = r_e + h = 6378 + 36000 = 42378 km

Since the satellite is in equatorial plane and radius of orbit 42378 km which is nearly geosynchronous radius hence satellite will be under eclipse on equinox days.

The angle of eclipse $\alpha = 2 \sin^{-1} (r_e/d) = 2 \sin^{-1} (6378/42378) = 17.31°$

Taking sidereal day = 23 hrs 56 min 4 s.

Eclipse period $t_e = \dfrac{86164}{360} \times 17.31 = 4143.05$ s

$$1 \text{ hr } 9 \text{ min } 3 \text{ s}$$

Example 4.9 : Calculate the duration of eclipse for a geostationary satellite orbiting at 42378 km and the declination of sunrays is 2.6°. For this declination what should be the radius of orbit so that no eclipse will ever occur?

Solution: Given: d = 42378 km

$$\delta_e = 2.6°$$

Then $\alpha = 2 \cos^{-1}\left(\sqrt{\left(1 - \left(\dfrac{r_e}{d}\right)^2\right)/\cos \delta_e}\right)$

$$= 2 \cos^{-1}\left(\sqrt{\left(1 - \left(\dfrac{6378}{42378}\right)^2\right)/\cos 2.6}\right)$$

$$= 16.51°$$

Now,   Eclipse period, $t_e = \dfrac{\text{Orbital period}}{360} \times \alpha = \dfrac{86164}{360} \times 16.51$

$$= 3953.58 \text{ s} = 1 \text{ hr } 5 \text{ min } 53.58 \text{ s}$$

Comparing this with the earlier result of example without δ the eclipse time is reduced.

For no eclipse to occur, radius of orbit d $> \dfrac{r_e}{\sin \delta_e}$

Substituting   d $> \dfrac{6378}{\sin 2.6} = 140599.203$ km

Which is not practicable for communication satellites using present day technology.

4.12.4 Sun Transit Outage

- During the equinox periods, not only does the satellite pass through the earth's shadow on the dark side of the earth, but the orbit of the satellite will also pass directly in front of the sun on the sunlight side of the earth.

- The sun is a hot microwave source with an equivalent temperature of about 6000 to 10000 K, depending on the time within the 11-year sunspot cycle, at the frequencies used by communication satellites (4 to 50 GHz).

- The earth station antenna will therefore receive not only the signal from the satellite but also the noise temperature transmitted by the sun. The added noise temperature will cause the fade margin of the receiver to be exceeded and an outage will occur. These outages may be precisely predicted.

- For satellite system operators with more than one satellite at their disposal, traffic can be off-loaded to satellites that are just out of, or are yet to enter, a sun outage.

- The outage in this situation can therefore be limited as far as an individual user is concerned. However the outages can be detrimental to operators committed to operations during daylight hours.

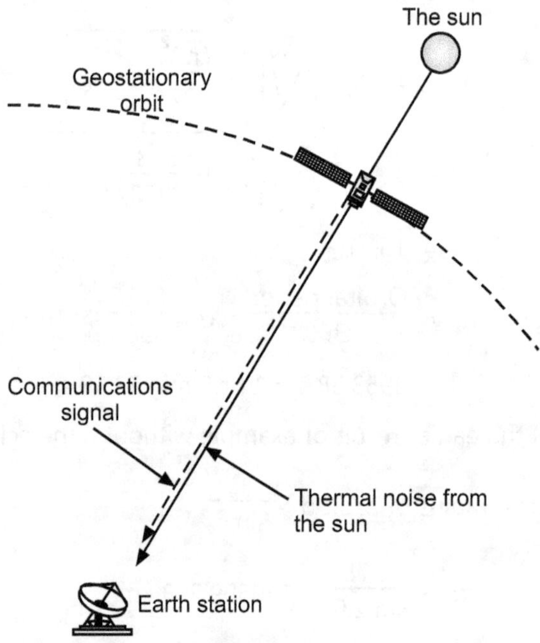

Fig. 4.30 : Schematic of sun outage conditions

REVIEW QUESTIONS

1. Define the following and explain :

   (i)   Satellite orbit.

   (ii) Satellite axes.

   (iii) Gyroscopic stiffness.

   (iv) Earth station look angles.

2. What is the difference between a geosynchronous and geostationary satellite?

3. Define the following with respect to a satellite:

   (i)   Eccentricity.

   (ii) Axes

   (iii) Sub-satellite point

   (iv) Ascending node.

4. Distinguish between synchronous, subsynchronous and non-subsynchronous types of satellites

5. Define Kepler's laws of orbiting bodies and derive an equation to show that the third law is true for any orbiting satellite.

6. What is slant range and what is its importance in satellite communication?

7. What do you mean by eclipse in case of a geostationary satellite and when does it occur?

8. Explain the effect of solar eclipse on the performance of a geostationary satellite. In what way it is related to fixing the parking place of a satellite?

9. (i)   Explain the need for satellite communication.

   (ii) What are the different types of satellite orbits? Discuss their merits and demerits.

   (iii) A low orbiting satellite has an 8-hour prograde orbit. How long during each orbit will an earth station be able to communicate with it above an elevation angle of 15?

10. What are the different methods to achieve stability of satellites in orbit?

11. What are the different torques that affect the position of a geostationary satellite?

12. Describe the steps involved in launching a satellite.

13. If a satellite has an orbiting time of 23 hrs 56 min, calculate the orbiting distance (radius of orbit). Assume suitable data if required.   (Ans: 42160 km)

14. The longitude and latitude of an earth station are 76°E and 13°N. Find the azimuth and elevation from this station to ASIASAT situated at 105°E.

(**Ans. :** A_z = 247.75 °, ξ = 53.12°)

15. A satellite is orbiting round the earth at 42124 km. the earth station is looking at this satellite at an elevation angle of 35°. Calculate the slant range. Make suitable assumptions and give reasons for making such an assumption.   (**Hint:** Take ξ_∞)

(**Ans.** : 35773.56 km)

16. Determine the slant range from an earth station situated at 20°E and 10°N from a geostationary satellite parked at 70°E. The height of satellite from sub-satellite point is 36348 km.   (**Ans. :** ξ = 31.7642°)

•••

SATELLITES

5.1 INTRODUCTION

- Communication satellites are very complex. They are very expensive to develop or purchase and are equally expensive to launch.
- Hence maintaining a microwave communication system in orbit in space is not so simple. A typically large geostationary satellite is estimated to cost anywhere in between $100M to $150M, on station.
- The cost of the satellite and launch are increased further by the need to dedicate an earth station to the monitoring and control, at cost of several million dollars per year.
- These costs is earned from the revenue earned by selling the communication capacity of the satellite to users in many ways like leasing circuits or transponders, or by charging for circuit use, as in the international telephone and data transmission service.
- Communication satellites are usually designed to have a typical operating lifetime of 10 to 15 years.
- The developers or operators of the system expects to recover the initial costs and operating costs well within the expected lifetime of the satellite, and the designer must provide a satellite that can survive the hostile environment of outer space for such a long period. In order to support the communication system, the satellite must provide to mount the antennas, be capable of station keeping, provide the required electrical power for the communication system, and also provide a controlled temperature environment for the communication electronics.
- This unit will cover the topics on subsystems needed on a satellite to support its primary mission of communications and also the communications subsystem itself in brief, and other problems such as reliability.
- The discussion of satellites in this unit is necessarily brief.
- Communications satellites for low earth orbit are in most cases quite similar to small GEO satellites and have similar requirements. Hence the emphasis throughout this unit is on satellites in geostationary orbit.

5.2 SATELLITE SUBSYSTEMS

- Fig. 5.1 shows an exploded view of a typical geostationary (GEO) satellite with several of the subsystems indicated. The major subsystems required on the satellite are explained below.

5.2.1 Attitude and Orbit Control Systems (AOCS)

- This subsystem consists of rocket motors that are used to move the satellite back into the correct orbit whenever external forces cause it to drift off station and also has gas jets or inertial devices that control the attitude of the satellite.

5.2.2 Telemetry, Tracking, Command, and Monitoring (TTC & M)

- These systems are partly mounted on the satellite and partly at the controlling earth station.

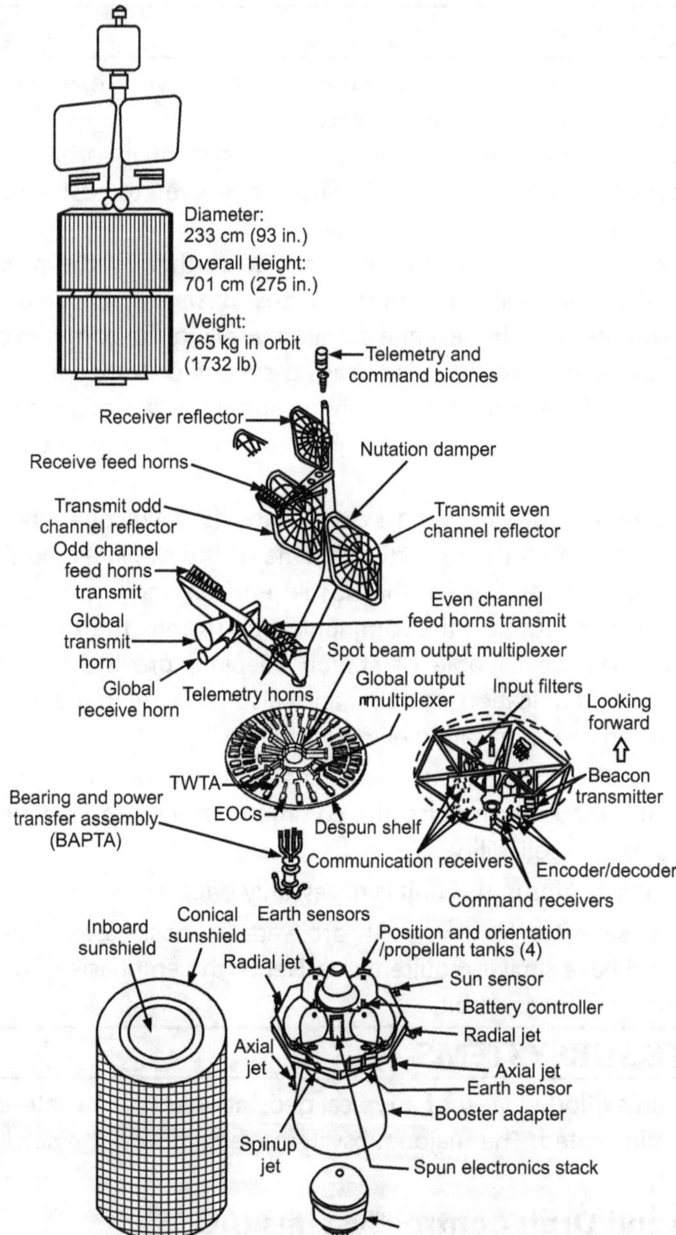

Fig. 5.1 : Exploded view of a spinner satellite based on the Boeing (Hughes) HS376 design

- The telemetry system mounted on satellite sends data derived from many sensors on the satellite, which monitor the satellite's health, via a telemetry link to the controlling earth station.

- The tracking system located at this earth station and provides information on the range and the elevation and azimuth angles of the satellite. Repeated measurements of these three parameters permits computation of orbital elements, from which changes in the orbit of the satellite can be detected.

- The control system is used to correct the position and attitude of the satellite, based on telemetry data received from the satellite and orbital data obtained from the tracking system.

- It's also used to communication system configuration and control antenna pointing to cater to current traffic requirements, and to operate switches on the satellite.

5.2.3 Power System

- Since the whole system works on the electrical power, the communication satellites derive electrical power from solar cells.

- This power is utilized for its transmitters, and also by other electrical system which supports the communication system on satellites.

5.2.4 Communications Subsystems

- The communications subsystem is the major component of a communications satellite, and the remainder of the satellite is there solely to support it.

- Though, the communications equipment is only a small part of the weight and volume of the whole satellite, and is usually composed of one or more antennas and set of receivers and transmitters, which receive and transmit over wide bandwidths at microwave frequencies, and a set of receivers and transmitters that amplify and retransmit the incoming signals.

- The receiver-transmitter units are known as transponders.

- There are two types of transponders in use on satellites: the linear or bent pipe transponder that amplifies the received signals and retransmits it at a different, usually lower frequency and the baseband processing transponder which is used only with digital signals, that converts the received signal to baseband, processes it, and then retransmits a digital signal.

5.2.5 Satellite Antennas

- Though the satellite Antennas are a part of complete communication system, yet they can be considered separately from the transponders.

- On large GEO satellites the antenna systems are very complex and produce beams with shapes carefully tailored to match the areas on the earth's surface served by the satellite.

- The most satellite antennas are designed to operate in a single frequency band, for example, C band or Ku band.

- A satellite which uses multiple frequency bands usually has four or more antennas.

- The other subsystems which are essential to the operation of the satellite are the thermal control system helps regulate the temperature inside a satellite

5.3 Attitude and Orbit Control System (AOCS)

- The attitude and orbit of a satellite need to be controlled, so that the satellites antennas point towards the earth and so the user knows where in the sky to look for the satellite.

- This is particularly important for GEO satellites as the earth stations antennas that are used with GEO satellites are normally fixed and so if the satellite moves away from its appointed position in the sky will cause a loss of signal.

- There are several forces acting on an orbiting satellite that tend to change its attitude and orbit.

- The most important are the gravitational fields of the sun and moon, irregularities in the earth's gravitational field, solar pressure from the sun and variations in the earth's magnetic field.

- Solar pressure acting on a satellite's solar cells and antennas, and the earth's magnetic field generating eddy currents in the satellite's metallic structure as it travels through the magnetic field, tend to cause rotation of the satellite's body.

- Careful design of the structure can minimize these effects, but the orbital period of the satellite makes many of the effects cyclic, which can cause nutation (a wobble) of the satellite.

- The attitude control system must damp out nutation and counter any rotational torque or movement.

- The presence of gravitational fields from the sun and the moon cause the orbit of a GEO satellite to change with time.

- At GEO orbit altitude, the moon's gravitational force is about twice as strong as the sun's.

- The moon's orbit is inclined to the equatorial plane by approximately 5°, which creates a force on the satellite with a component that is normal to the satellite's orbit.

- The plane of the earth's rotation around the sun is inclined by 23° to the earth's equatorial plane.

- There is a net gravitational pull on the satellite that tends to change the inclination of the satellite's orbit, pulling it away from the earth's equatorial plane at an initial rate of approximately 0.86° per year.

- The orbital control system of the satellite must be able to move the satellite back into the equatorial plane before the orbital inclination becomes excessive.

- LEO satellites are less affected by gravitational fields of the sun and moon.
- Since they are much closer to the earth than GEO satellites, the earth's gravity is much stronger, and the pull from the sun and moon are proportionately weaker.
- The earth is not quite a perfect sphere. At the equator, there are bulges of about 65 m at longitudes 162° E and 348° E, with the result that a satellite is accelerated toward one of two stable points in the GEO orbit at longitude 75°E and 252°E, as shown in Fig. 5.2.
- To maintain accurate station keeping, the satellite must be periodically accelerated in the opposite direction to the forces acting on it. This is done as a sequence of station-keeping maneuvers, using small rocket motors (sometimes called gas jets or thrusters) that can be controlled from the earth via the TTC&M system.

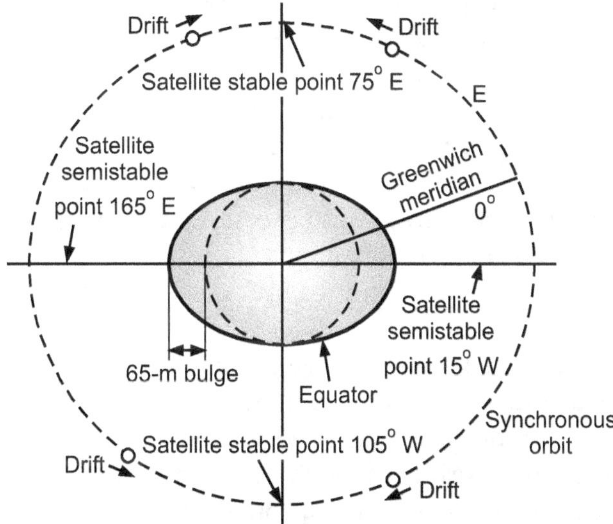

Fig. 5.2: Forces on a synchronous satellite

5.3.1 Attitude Control System

- There are two ways to make a satellite in orbit, when it is weightless. The body of the satellite can be rotated, typically at a rate between 30 and 100 rpm, to create a gyroscopic force that provides stability of the spin axis and keeps it pointing in the same direction.
- Such satellites are known as spinners.
- The popular Hughes 376 (now Boeing 376) satellite is an example of a spinner design.
- Alternatively, the satellite can be stabilized by one or more momentum wheels. This is called a three-axis stabilized satellite, of which the Hughes (Boeing) 701 series is an example.
- The momentum wheel is usually a solid metal disk driven by an electric motor. Either there must be one momentum wheel for each of the three axes of the satellite, or a single momentum wheel can be mounted on gimbals and rotated to provide a rotational force about any of the three axes.

- Increasing the speed of the momentum wheel causes the satellite to precess in the opposite direction, according to the principle of conservation of angular momentum.
- The spinner design of satellite is typified by many satellites built by the Hughes Aircraft Corporation for domestic satellite communication systems.
- As shown in Fig. 5.1, the satellite consists of a cylindrical drum covered in solar cells that contains the power systems and the rocket motors.
- The communications system is mounted at the top of the drum and is driven by an electric motor in the opposite direction to the rotation of the satellite body to keep the antennas pointing toward the earth. Such satellites are called despun.
- The satellite is spun up by operating small radial gas jets mounted on the periphery of the drum. At an appropriate point in the launch phase.
- The despun system is then brought into operation so that the main TTC&M antennas point toward the earth.
- The main TTC&M system operates at 6/4 GHz on the Intelsat satellite, with a 2 GHz backup system for use during the launch phase.
- A variety of liquid propulsion mixes have been used for the gas jets, the most common being a variant of hydrazine (N_2H_4), which is easily liquefied under pressure, but readily decomposes when passed over a catalyst.
- Increased power can be obtained from the hydrazine gas jets by electrically heating the catalyst and the gas.
- Satellites that use liquid fuel thrusters have standardized on bi-propellant fuels, that is fuels that mix together to form the thruster fuel.
- The most common bi-propellant fuels used for thruster operations are mono-methyl hydrazine and nitrogen tetroxide, although standard hydrazine is still used in place of mono-methyl hydrazine by some satellite manufacturers.
- The bi-propellants are hypogolic: that is they ignite spontaneously on contract, and so do not need either a catalyst or a heater.
- By adjusting the flow of the bi-propellants, pulses of thrust can be generated at the correct time and in the correct direction.
- There are two types of rocket motors used on satellites. The traditional bi-propellant thruster described above, and arc jets or ion thrusters.
- The fuel that is stored on a GEO satellite is used for two purposes: to fire the apogee kick motor that injects the satellite into its final orbit, and to maintain the satellite in that orbit over its lifetime.
- If the launch is highly accurate, a minimum amount of fuel is used to attain the final orbit.
- If the launch is less accurate, more fuel must be used up in maneuvering the satellite into position, and that reduces the amount left for station keeping.
- A new development in thrusters uses a high voltage source to accelerate ions to a very high velocity, thus producing thrust.

- The ion engine thrust is not large, but because the engine can be driven by power from the solar cells it saves on expendable fuel. Ion engines can also be used to slowly raise a GEO satellite from a transfer orbit to GEO orbit, although a process takes months rather than hours as with a conventional rocket engine.

- Arc jets or ion thrusters are mainly used for north-south station keeping, which is where the greatest use of fuel is required for station-keeping maneuvers, and became operational on the Hughes (Boeing) 600 series of satellite buses. Arc jets or ion thrusters lack the total thrust required to move satellites quickly (e.g., for major longitudinal changes in position) but a small, continuous thrust is adequate to maintain N – S and E – W position keeping.

- In a three axis stabilized satellite, one pair of gas jets is needed for each axis to provide for rotation in both directions of pitch, roll, and yaw.

- An additional set of controls, allowing only one jet on a given axis to be operated, provides for velocity increments in the X, Y, Z directions.

- When motion is required along a given axis, the appropriate gas jet is operated for a specified period of time to achieve the desired velocity.

- The opposing gas jet must be operated for the same length of time to stop the motion when the satellite reaches its new position.

- Fuel is saved if the velocity of the satellite is kept small, but progress toward the destination is slow.

- Let us define a set of reference Cartesian axes (X_R, Y_R, Z_R) with the satellite at the origin, as shown in Fig. 5.3.

- The Z_R axis is directed towards the center of the earth and is in the plane of the satellite orbit. It is aligned along the local vertical at the satellite's subsatellite point.

- The X_R axis is tangent to the orbital plane and lies in the orbital plane. The Y_R axis is perpendicular to the orbital plane.

- For a satellite serving the Northern Hemisphere, the directions of the X_R and Y_R axes are nominally east and south.

- Rotation about the X_R, Y_R and Z_R axes is defined as roll about the XR axis, pitch about the YR axis, and yaw about the Z_R axis, in exactly the same way as for an aircraft or ship traveling in the X direction.

- The satellite must be stabilized with respect to the reference axes to maintain accurate pointing of its antenna beams.

- The axes X_R, Y_R and Z_R are defined with respect to the location of the satellite; a second set of Cartesian axes, X, Y, Z, as shown in Fig. 5.3, define the orientation of the satellite.

- Changes in a satellite's attitude cause the angles θ, ϕ and ψ in Fig. 5.3 to vary as the X, Y and Z axes move relative to the fixed reference axes X_R, Y_R and Z_R.

- The Z axis is usually directed toward a reference point on the earth, called the Z-axis intercept.

- The location of the Z-axis intercept defines the pointing of the satellite antennas; the Z-axis intercept point may be moved to repoint all the antenna beams by changing the attitude of the satellite with the attitude control system.

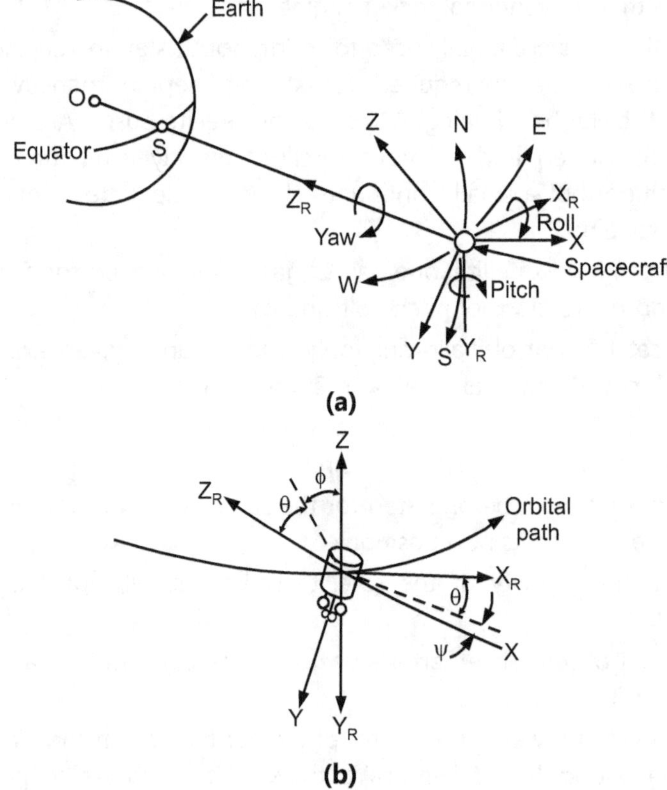

Fig. 5.3 : (a) Forces on a satellite. (b) Relationship between axes of a satellite

- In a spinner-type satellite, the axis of rotation is usually the Y axis, which is maintained close to the Y_R axis, perpendicular to the orbital plane.
- Pitch correction is required only on the despun antenna system and can be obtained by varying the speed of the despin motor.
- Yaw and roll are controlled by pulsing radially mounted jets at the appropriate instant as the body of the satellite rotates.
- Attitude control of a three-axis stabilized satellite requires an increase or a decrease in the speed of the inertia wheel.
- If a constant torque exists about one axis of the satellite, a continual increase or decrease in momentum wheel speed is necessary to maintain the correct attitude.
- When the upper or lower speed limit of the wheel is reached, it must be unloaded by operating a pair of gas jets and simultaneously reducing or increasing the wheel speed.
- Closed-loop control of attitude is employed on the satellite to maintain the correct attitude.

- When large, narrow beam antennas are used, the whole satellite may have to be stabilized within $\pm\,0.1°$ on each axis.

- The references for the attitude control system may be the outer edge of the earth's disk, as observed with infrared sensors, the sun, or one or more stars.

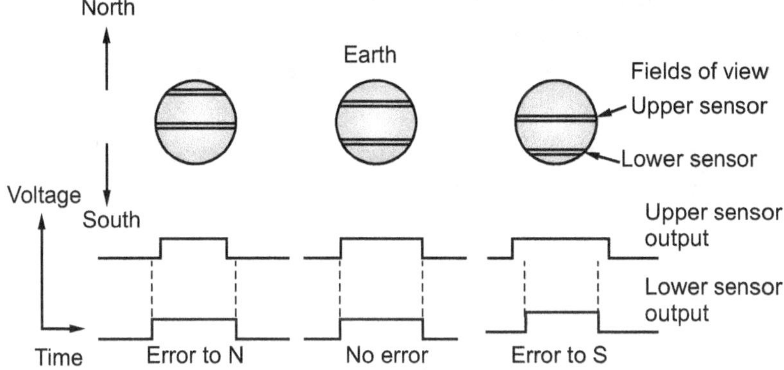

Fig. 5.4 : Principle of N-S control of a spinner satellite using infrared Earth sensors.

- Fig. 5.4 shows how an infrared sensor on the spinning body of a satellite can be used to control pointing towards the earth. Fig. 5.5 shows a typical control system loop using the technique shown in Fig. 5.4.

- The control system will be more complex for a three-axis stabilized satellite and may employ an onboard computer to process the sensor data and command the gas jets and momentum wheels.

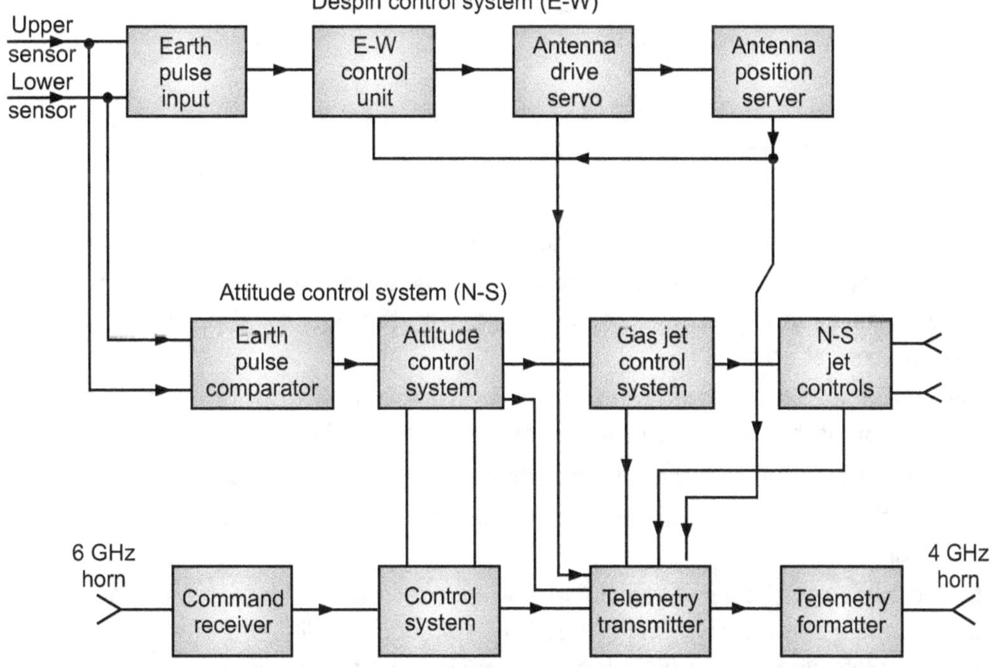

Fig. 5.5 : Typical onboard control system for a spinner satellite.

5.3.2 Orbit Control System

- A geostationary satellite is subjected to several forces that tend to accelerate it away from its required orbit.

- The most important, for the geostationary satellite, are the gravitation forces of the moon and the sun, which cause inclination if the orbital plane, and the nonspherical shape of the earth around the equator, which causes drift of the subsatellite point.

- There are many other smaller forces that act on the satellite causing the orbit to change.

- Accurate prediction of the satellite position a week or 2 weeks ahead requires a computer program with up to 20 force parameters.

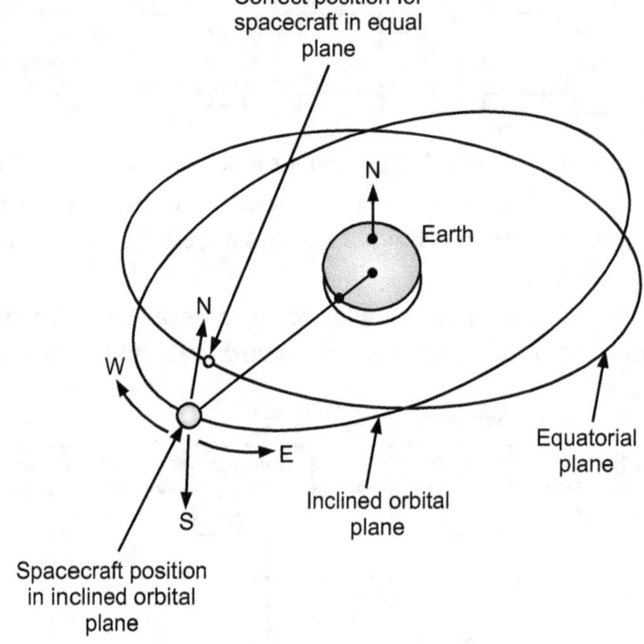

Fig. 5.6: Satellite in inclined orbit

- Fig. 5.6 shows a diagram of an inclined orbital plane close to the geostationary orbit. For the orbit to be truly geostationary, it must lie in the equatorial plane, be circular, and have the correct attitude.

- The various forces acting on the satellite will steadily pull it out of the correct orbit; it is the function of the orbital control system to return it to the correct orbit.

- This cannot be done with momentum wheels since linear accelerations are required.

- Gas jets that can impart velocity changes along the three reference axes of the satellite are required.

- If the orbit is not circular, a velocity increase or decrease will have to be made along the orbit, in the x-axis direction in Fig. 5.3. On a spinning satellite, this is achieved by pulsing the radial jets when they point along the X-axis. On a three-axis stabilized satellite, there will usually be two pairs of X-axis jets acting in opposite directions, one pair of which will be operated for a predetermined length of time to provide the required velocity change.

- The orbit of a geostationary satellite remains approximately circular for long periods of time and does not need frequent velocity corrections to maintain circularity. Altitude corrections are made by operating the Z-axis gas jets.

- The inclination of the orbit of a satellite that starts out in a geostationary orbit increases at an average rate of about 0.85° per year, with an initial rate of change of inclination for a satellite in an equatorial orbit between 0.75° to 0.94° per year.

- The most of GEO satellites are specified to remain within a box of ± 0.05° and so, in practice, corrections, called a north-south station keeping maneuver are made every 2 to 4 weeks to keep the error small.

- It has become normal to split the E – W and N – S maneuvers so that at intervals of 2 weeks the E – W corrections are made first and then after 2 more weeks, the N – S corrections are made.

- If arc jets or ion thrusters are used for N – S station-keeping maneuvers, these tend to operate almost continuously since their thrust levels are low when compared with traditional liquid fueled engines.

- Correcting the inclination of a satellite orbit requires more fuel to be expended than for any other orbital correction.

- This places a weight penalty on those satellites that must maintain very accurate station keeping, and reduces the communications payload they can carry.

- As much as half the total satellite weight at launch may be station keeping fuel when the satellite's expected lifetime on orbit is 15 years.

- East-west station-keeping is effected by use of the X-axis jets of the satellite. For a satellite located away from the stable points at 75°E and 252°E, a slow drift toward these points will occur.

- Typically, the X-axis jets are pulsed every 2 or 3 weeks to counter the drift and add a small velocity increment in the opposite direction.

- The satellite then drifts through its nominal position, stops at a point a fraction of a degree beyond it, and then drifts back again.

- East-west station-keeping requires only a modest amount of fuel and is necessary on all geostationary communications satellites to maintain the spacing between adjacent satellites.

- With orbital locations separated by 2° or 3°, east-west drifts in excess of a fraction of a degree cannot be tolerated, and most GEO satellites are held within ± 0.05° of their alloted longitude.

- Some communications satellites such as the Russian Molniya series are not in geostationary orbit. Early Molniya satellites were launched into a highly elliptical 12-h orbit with a large (65°) inclination angle to provide communication to northerly latitudes like Siberia. The Russian satellite gave its name to any satellite in a highly elliptical inclined orbit.

- Low earth orbit (LETO) and medium earth orbit (MEO) satellites also need AOC systems to maintain the correct orbit and attitude for continuous communication.

- Because of the much stronger gravitational force of the earth in LEO orbit, attitude stabilization is often accomplished with a rigid gravity gradient boom.

- This is a long pole that points toward the center of the earth, providing damping of oscillations about the satellite's z axis by virtue of the difference in gravitational field at the top of the pole and at the bottom.

5.4 TELEMETRY, TRACKING, COMMAND AND MONITORING

- This system is essential for the successful operation of a communications satellite. It is the part of the satellite management task, which also involves an earth station, usually dedicated to that task, and a group of personnel.

- The main functions of satellite management are to control the orbit and attitude of the satellite, monitor the status of all sensors and subsystems on the satellite, and switch on or off sections of the communication system.

- The TTC&M earth station may be owned and operated by the satellite owner, or it may be owned by a third party and provide TTC&M services under contract.

- On large geostationary satellites, some repointing of individual antennas may be possible, under the command of the TTC&M system. Tracking is performed primarily by the earth station. Fig. 5.7 illustrates the functions of a controlling earth station.

5.4.1 Telemetry and Monitoring System

- The monitoring system collects data from many sensors within the satellite and sends these data to the controlling earth station.

- There may be several hundred sensors located on the satellite say to monitor pressure in the fuel tanks, voltage and current in the power conditioning unit, current drawn by each subsystem, and critical voltages and currents in the communications electronics.

- The temperature of many of the subsystems is important and must be kept within predetermined limits, so many temperature sensors are fitted. The sensor data, the status of each subsystem, and the positions of switches in the communication system are reported back to the earth by the telemetry system.

- The sighting devices used to maintain attitude are also monitored via the telemetry link: this is essential in case one should fail and cause the satellite to point in the wrong direction.

- The faulty unit must then be disconnected and a spare brought in, via the command system, or some other means of controlling attitude devised.

- Telemetry data are usually digitized and transmitted as phase shift keying (PSK) of a low-power telemetry carrier using time division techniques.

- A low data rate is normally used to allow the receiver at the earth station to have a narrow bandwidth and thus maintain a high carrier to noise ratio.

- The entire TDM frame may contain thousands of bits of data and take several seconds to transmit.

- At the controlling earth station a computer can be used to monitor, store, and decode the telemetry data so that the status of any system or sensor on the satellite can be determined immediately by the controller on the earth.

- Alarms can also be sounded if any vital parameter goes outside allowable limits.

5.4.2 Tracking

- A number of techniques can be used to determine the current orbit of a satellite. Velocity and acceleration sensors on the satellite can be used to establish the change in orbit from the last known position, by integration of the data.

- The earth station controlling the satellite can observe the Doppler shift of the telemetry carrier or beacon transmitter carrier to determine the rate at which range is changing.

- Together with accurate angular measurements from the earth station antenna, range is used to determine the orbital elements.

- Active determination of range can be achieved by transmitting a pulse, or sequence of pulses, to the satellite and observing the time delay before the pulse is received again.

- The propagation delay in the satellite transponder must be accurately known, and more than one earth station may make range measurements.

- If a sufficient number of earth stations with an adequate separation are observing the satellite, its position can be established by triangulation from the earth station by simultaneous range measurements.

- With precision equipment at the earth stations, the position of the satellite can be determined within 10 m.

- Ranging tones are also used for range measurement. A carrier generated on board the satellite is modulated with a series of sine waves at increasing frequency, usually harmonically related.

- The phase of the sine wave modulation components is compared at an earth station, and the number of wavelengths of each frequency is calculated.

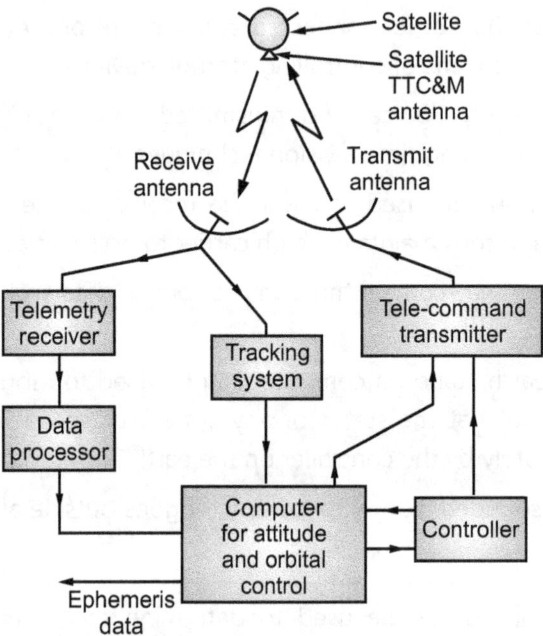

Fig. 5.7: Typical tracking, telemetry, command and monitoring system

- Ambiguities in the numbers are resolved by reference to lower frequencies, and prior knowledge of the approximate range of the satellites.

- If sufficiently high frequencies are used, perhaps even the carrier frequency, range can be measured to millimeter accuracy. The technique is similar to that used in the terrestrial telurometer and in aircraft radar altimeters.

5.4.3 Command

- A secure and effective command structure is vital to the successful launch and operation of any communications satellite.

- The command system is used to make changes in attitude and corrections to the orbit and to control the communication system.

- During launch, it is use to control the firing of the apogee kick motor and to spin up a spinner or extend the solar Cells and antennas of a three-axis stabilized satellite.

- The command structure must possess safeguards against unauthorized attempts to make changes to the satellite's operation, and also against inadvertent operation of a control due to error in a received command.

- Encryption of commands and responses is used to provide security in the command system.

- A typical type of system is shown in Fig. 5.7 will originate commands at the control terminal of the computer.

- After converting the control code into a command word, it is sent in a TDM frame to the satellite. After validity the command word in the satellite, the word is sent back to the control station via the telemetry link where it is checked again in the computer.

- If it is received correctly, an execute instruction will be sent to the satellite and the command is executed.

- The entire process may take 5 or 10 s, but minimizes the risk of erroneous commands causing a satellite malfunction.

- The command and telemetry links are usually separate from the communication system, although they may operate in the same frequency band (6 and 4 GHz).

- Two levels of command system are used in the Intelsat satellite: the main system operates in the 6 GHz band, in a gap between the communication channel frequencies; the main telemetry system uses a similar gap in the 4 GHz band. The TTC&M antennas for the 6/4 GHz system are shown in Fig. 5.1 on the satellite.

- These are earth-coverage horns, so the main system can be used only after correct attitude of the satellite is achieved.

- The main TTC&M system will be in inoperable state during the launch phase and injection into geostationary orbit, because the satellite does not have the correct attitude or has not extended its solar Cells. A backup system is used at this time, which controls only the most important sections of the satellite.

- A great deal of redundancy is built into this system, since its failure will jeopardize the entire mission. Omni directional antennas of either UHF or band (2 − 4 GHz) are used, and sufficient margin is allowed in the signal-to-noise ratio (S/N) at the satellite receiver, this assures control under the most adverse conditions.

- The backup system provides control of the apogee kick motor, the attitude control system and orbit control thrusters, the solar Cells deployment mechanism (if fitted), and the power conditioning unit. With these controls, the satellite can be injected into geostationary orbit, turned to face the earth, and switched to full electrical power so that handover to the main TTC&M system is possible.

- In the event of failure of the main TTC&M system, the backup system can be used to keep the satellite on station. It is also used to eject the satellite from geostationary orbit and to switch off all transmitters when the satellite eventually reaches the end of its useful life.

5.5 POWER SYSTEMS

- Solar cells which convert incident sunlight into electrical energy are the main source of electrical power for all the communication satellites.

- Nuclear Power generators are avoided to avert danger to the people on the earth if the launch should fail and the nuclear fuel spread over an inhabited area. Though some deep space planetary research satellites have used thermonuclear power generators.

- The sun is a powerful source of energy. In the total vacuum of outer space, at geostationary altitude, the radiation falling on a satellite has an intensity of 1.39 kW/m^2. Though Solar Cells do not convert all this incident energy into electrical power, their efficiency is typically 20 to 25 at beginning of life,but falls with time because of aging of the cells and etching of the surface by micrometer impacts.

- To tackle to this problem and to generate sufficient till the end of life (EOL) of the satellite to supply all the systems on-board, about 15% of additional area of solar Cells is usually provided as an allowance for aging.

- A spin-stabilized satellite usually has a cylindrical body covered in solar cells. Because the solar Cells are on a cylindrical surface, at any given time half of the Cells are not illuminated at all, and at the edges of the illuminated half, the low angle of incidence results in little electrical power being generated.

- The output from the solar Cells is slightly higher than would be obtained with normal incidence on a flat panel equal in area to the projected area of the cylinder, i.e. its width times its height. The Cells that are not illuminated by sunlight face cold space, which causes them to cool down.

- The solar Cells on a spinner satellite have a lower temperature than those on other satellites, which increases their efficiency. Early satellites were of small dimensions and had relatively small areas of solar Cells. More recently, large communications satellites for direct broadcast operation generate up to 6 kW from solar power.

- A three-axis stabilized satellite can make better use of its solar cell area, since the cells can be arranged on flat panels that can be rotated to maintain normal incidence of the sunlight. Only one-third of the total area of solar Cells is needed relative to a spinner, with some saving in weight.

- A primary advantage, however, is that by unfurling a folded solar array when the satellite reaches geostationary orbit, power in excess of 10 kW can be generated with large arrays. To obtain 10 kW from a spinner requires a very large body on which to place the solar Cells, which may then exceed the maximum payload dimensions of the launch vehicle.

- Solar Cells must be rotated by an electric motor once per 24h to keep the Cells in full sunlight. This causes the Cells to heat up, typically to 50° to 80°C, which causes a drop in output voltage. In the spinner design, the Cells cool down when in shadow and run at 20° to 30°C, with somewhat higher efficiency.

- The bombardment of the Cells by protons and electrons is also more severe, and a thicker layer of glass may be needed to slow down deterioration of the Cells, which adds consequent weight. A rotary joint must be used with each solar sail to transfer current from the rotating sail to the body of the satellite.

- The satellite also needs to carry batteries to power the subsystems during launch and during eclipses. Eclipses occur twice per year, around the spring and fall equinoxes, when the earth's shadow passes across the satellite, as illustrated in Fig. 4.28 and 4.29.

- The longest duration of eclipse is 70 min, occurring around March 21 and September 21 each year. To avoid the need for large, heavy batteries, part or the entire communications system load may be shut down during eclipse, but this technique is rarely used when telephony or data traffic is carried. TV broadcast satellites may not carry sufficient battery capacity to supply their high-power transmitters during eclipse, and may shut down.

- By locating the satellite 20°W of the longitude of the service area, the eclipse will occur after 1 A.M. Local time for the service area, when shut down is more acceptable. Batteries are usually of the nickel-hydrogen type which do not gas when charging and have good reliability and long life, and can be safely discharged to 70 of their capacity.

- A power conditioning unit controls the charging current and dumps excess current from the solar cells into heaters or load resistors on the cold side of the satellite. Sensors on the batteries, power regulator, and solar cells monitor temperature, voltage, and current and supply these data to both the onboard control system and the controlling earth station via the telemetry downlink. Typical battery voltages are 20 to 50 V with capacities of 20 to 100 ampere-hours.

5.6 COMMUNICATION SUBSYSTEMS

Description of the Communication System:

- A communications satellite exists to provide a platform in geostationary orbit for the relaying of voice, video, and data communications.

- All other subsystems on the satellite exist solely to support the communications system, although this may represent only a small part of the volume, weight, and cost of the satellite in orbit.

- The revenue is earned from the communication system in communication satellite for the system operator, the satellite are designed to provide the largest traffic capacity possible. The growth in capacity is shown in Fig. 5.8 for the Intelsat system.

- Successive satellites have become larger, heavier, and more costly, but the rate at which traffic capacity has increased has been much greater, resulting in a lower cost per telephone circuit or transmitted bit with each succeeding generation of satellite.

- The satellite transponders have limited output power and the earth stations are at least 36,000 km away from a GEO satellite, so the received power level, even with large aperture earth station antennas, is very small and rarely exceeds 10^{-10} W for the system to perform satisfactorily, the signal power must exceed the power of the noise generated in the receiver by between 5 and 25 dB, depending on the bandwidth of the transmitted signal and the modulation scheme used. With low power transmitters, narrow receiver bandwidths have to be used to maintain the required signal-to-noise ratios.

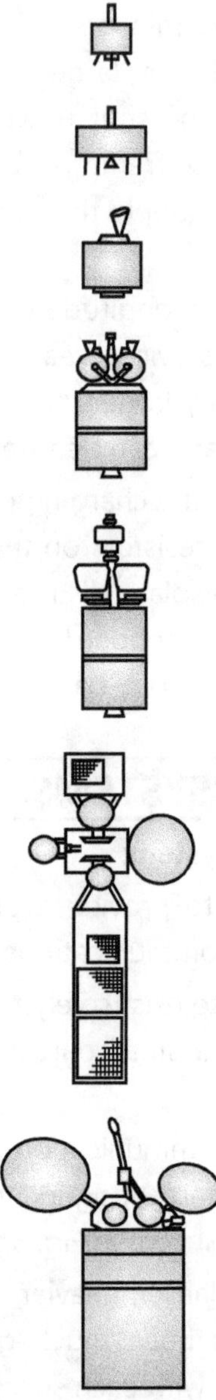

Fig. 5.8

- Early communications satellites were fitted with transponders of 250 or 500 MHz bandwidth, but had low gain antennas and transmitters of 1 or 2 W output power. The earth station receiver could not achieve an adequate signal-to-noise ratio when the full bandwidth was used with the result that the system was power limited.

- Later generations of communications satellites have transponders with greatly increased output power say up to 200 W for DBS-TV satellites and have steadily improved in bandwidth utilization efficiency, as seen in figure 5.8.

- The total channel capacity of a satellite that uses a 500 MHz band at 6/4 GHz can be increased only if the bandwidth can be increased or reused. The trend in high capacity satellites has been to reuse the available bands by employing several directional beams at the same frequency (spatial frequency reuse) and orthogonal polarizations at the same frequency (polarization frequency reuse).

- Large GEO satellites also use both the 6/4 GHz and 14/11 GHz bands to obtain more bandwidth; for example, some GEO satellites have achieved an effective bandwidth of 2250 MHz within a 500 MHz band at 6/4 GHz and a 250 MHz band at 14/11 GHz by a combination of spatial and polarization frequency reuse, and later generations of Intelsat satellites have achieved up to sevenfold reuse of their frequency bands.

- The designer of a satellite communication system is not free to select any frequency and bandwidth he or she chooses.

- International agreements restrict the frequencies that may be used for particular services, and the regulations are administered by the appropriate agency in each country---the Federal Communication Commission (FCC) in the United States.

- The bands currently used for the majority of services are 6/4 GHz and 14/11 GHz, with 30/20 GHz coming into service. The 6/4 GHz band was expanded from 500 MHz bandwidth in each direction to 1000 MHz by a World Administrative Radio Conference in 1979, but other services share the new part of the band and may cause interference to the satellite communication link.

- Similar bandwidth is available at 14/11 GHz and Ka-band satellites will be launched in the first decade of 2000 to exploit the wider bandwidths available in the 30/20 GHz bands.

- A different frequency is required for the transmit path (normally the higher frequency) at the satellite because the high power transmit signal would overload the receiver if they both operated at the same frequency.

- The 500 MHz bands originally allocated for 6/4 and 14/11 GHz satellite communications have become very congested and are now completely filled for some segments of the geostationary orbit, such as that serving North America.

- Extension of the bands to 1000 MHz will eventually provide greater capacity as the new frequencies come into use. Many systems now use 14/11 GHz for TV broadcast and distribution and 30/20 GHz systems are introducing Internet-like services from GEO. The standard spacing between GEO satellites was originally set at 3°, but under regulations covering North America and much of the rest of the world, the spacing has been reduced to 2°.

- The move to 2° spacing opened up extra slots for new satellites in the 6/4 and 14/11 GHz bands.

- Satellite systems designed for Ku band (14/11 GHz) and Ka band (30/20 GHz) have narrower antenna beams, and better control of coverage patterns than satellites using C band (6/4 GHz).

- As the available orbital slots for GEO satellites have filled up with satellites using the 6/4 and 14/11 GHz bands, attention has focused on the use of the 30/20 GHz band.

- Originally, this band has 3 GHz bandwidth allocated to satellite services, but part of the band was reallocated to the Land Multipoint Distribution Services (LMDS). Approximately 2 GHz of bandwidth is still available for satellite systems at Ka band on an exclusive or shared basis, which is equal to the combined allocations of C and Ku bands.

- However, propagation in rain becomes a major factor at frequencies above 10 GHz. Attenuation (in dB) in rain increases at roughly the square of the frequency, so at 20 GHz rain attenuation is four times larger, in dB, than at 10 GHz. It is also impossible to provide rain attenuation margins larger than 20 dB in any system, and many Ka-band systems will have margins of only 4 or 5 dB when operating to small earth station antennas.

Transponders:

- Signals or carriers transmitted by an earth station are received at the satellite by either a spot beam or a zone beam antenna. Spot beams have limited coverage but Zone beams can receive from transmitters anywhere within the coverage zone. Two low noise amplifiers are used to receive signals and is recombined at their output to provide redundancy. If any one amplifier fails, the other one can still carry all the traffic.

- Since all carriers from one antenna must pass through a low noise amplifier, a failure at that point is catastrophic. Redundancy is provided wherever failure of one component will cause the loss of a significant part of the satellite's communication capacity.

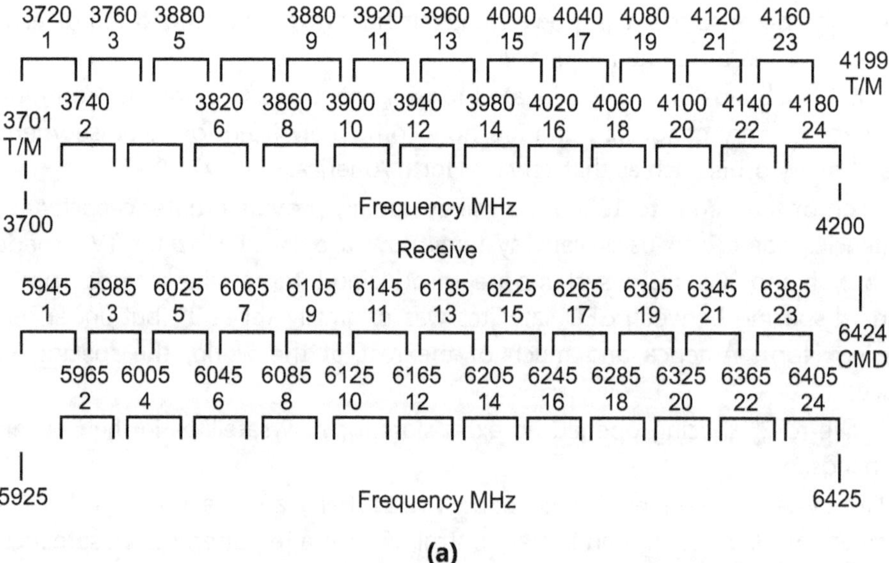

(a)

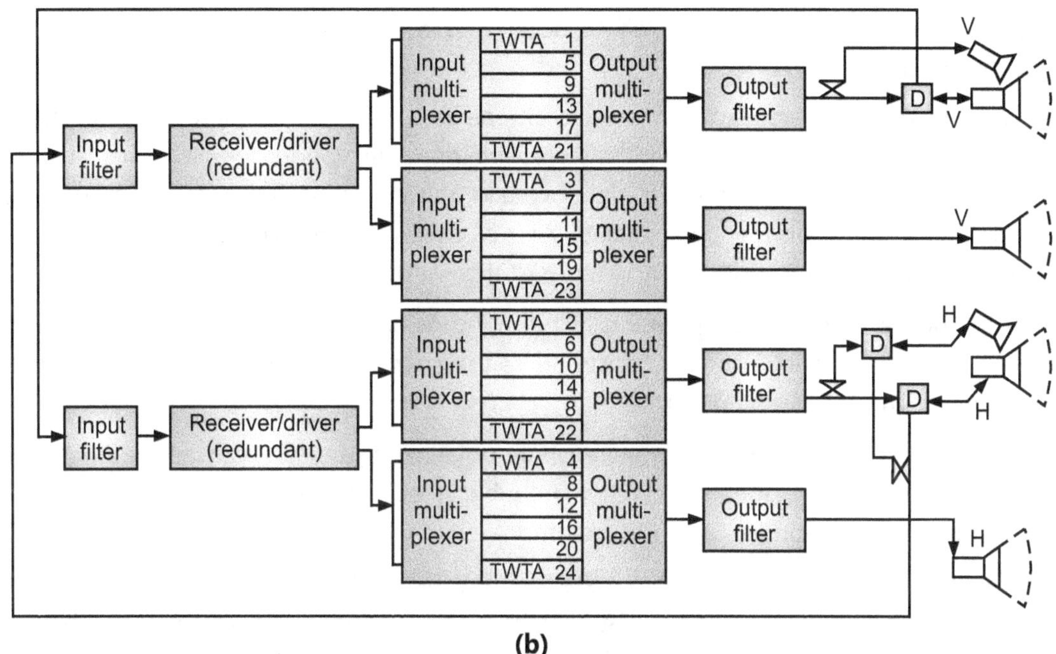

(b)

Fig. 5.9: Transponder arrangement of RCA's SATCOM satellites and frequency plan.

- Fig. 5.9 shows a simplified block diagram of a satellite communication subsystem for the 6/4 GHz band. The 500 MHz bandwidth is divided up into channels, often 36 MHz wide, which are each handled by a separate transponder.

- A transponder consists of a band-pass filter to select the particular channel's band of frequencies, a down converter to change the frequency from 6 GHz at the input to 4 GHz at the output, and an output amplifier.

- The communication system has many transponders, some of which may be spares; typically 12 to 44 active transponders are carried by a high-capacity satellite. The transponders are supplied with signals from one or more receiver antennas and send their outputs are given to a switch matrix that directs each transponder band of frequencies to the appropriate antenna or antenna beam.

- In a large satellite there may be four or five beams to which any transponder can be connected. The switch setting can be controlled from the earth to allow reallocation of the transponders between the downlink beams as traffic patterns change.

- In the early satellites such as INTELSAT I and II, one or two 250 MHz bandwidth transponders were employed.

- This proved unsatisfactory because of the nonlinearity of the traveling wave tube transmitter used at the output of the transponder, and later GEO satellites have used up to 44 transponders each with 36, 54 or 72 MHz bandwidth. The reason for using narrower bandwidth transponders is to avoid excessive intermodulation problems when transmitting several carriers simultaneously with a nonlinear transmitter.

- Intermodulation distortion is likely to occur whenever a high power amplifier is driven close to saturation.

- Since we generally want to have more than one earth station transmitter sending signals via a satellite, one solution would be to provide one transponder for each earth station's signal. In the case of the Intelsat global system, this could result in a requirement for as many as 100 transponders per satellite. As a compromise, 36 MHz has been widely used for transponder bandwidth, with 54 and 72 MHz adopted for some satellites.

- Many domestic satellites operating in the 6.4 GHz band carry 24 active transponders. The center frequencies of the transponders are spaced 40 MHz apart, to allow guard bands for the 36 MHz filter skirts.

- With a total of 500 MHz available, a single polarization satellite can accommodate 12 transponders across the band. When frequency reuse by orthogonal polarizations is adopted, 24 transponders can be accommodated in the same 50 MHz bandwidth.

- Traditional linear transponder-type satellites now have sixfold reuse (INTELSATVI and IX) or even sevenfold reuse (INTELSATVIII) at C band. The reuse is achieved through microwave switch interconnections between subbeams.

- Internet-like satellites need a plethora of beam interconnections-more than 50 in most cases. The only way to achieve this level of beam/path interconnections is via on board processing (OBP).

- Fig. 5.10 shows a simplified diagram of the communication system carried by INTELSATV satellites. The latter series of Intelsat satellites use a similar arrangement. The bulk of the traffic is carried by the 6/4 GHz section, with a total bandwidth of 2000 MHz available by frequency reuse.

- The switch matrix allows a very large number of variations in connecting the 6 GHz receivers to the 4 GHz transmitters, and also interconnects the 6/4 and 14/11 GHz sections.

- This provides Intelsat with a great deal of flexibility in setting up links through the satellite.

- When more than one signal shares a transponder then the power amplifier must be run below its maximum output power to maintain linearity and reduce intermodulation products, this is achieved by using frequency division multiple access (FDMA).

- The degree to which the transmitter output power is reduced below its peak output is known as output backoff: in FDMA systems, 2 to 7 dB of output backoff is typically used, depending on the number of accesses to the transponder and the extent to which the characteristics of the HPA have been linearized.

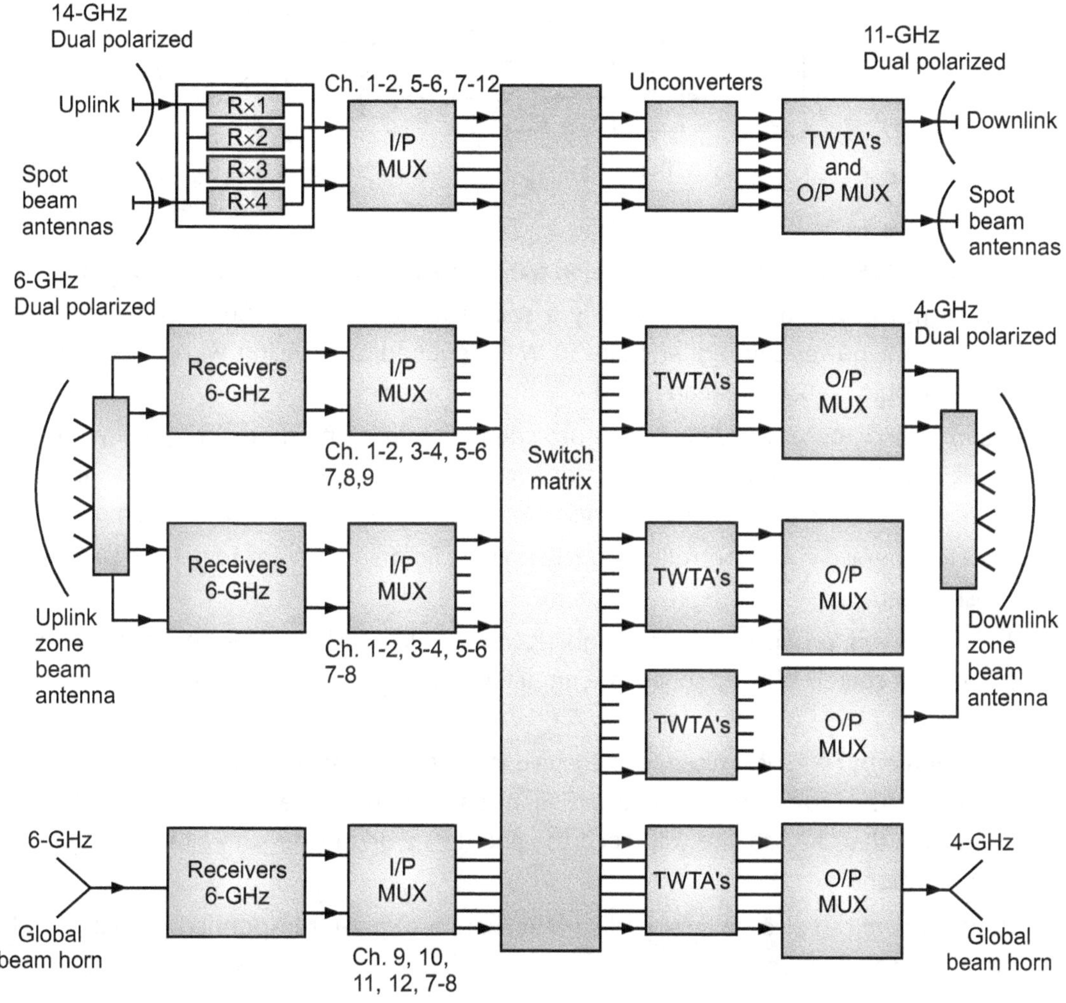

Fig. 5.10: Simplified block diagram of an INTELSAT V communication system.

- Backoff results in a lower downlink carrier-to-noise ratio at the earth station with FDMA when multiple accesses to each transponder are required.

- Time division multiple access (TDMA) can theoretically be used to increase the output power of transponders by limiting the transponder to a single access.

- However, most TDMA systems are hybrid FDMA – TDMA schemes known as multifrequency TDMA (MF – TDMA), in which several TDMA signals share the transponder bandwidth using FDMA. Linearity of the HPA remains an issue for MF – TDMA systems.

- Fig. 5.11 shows a typical single conversion bent pipe transponder used on many satellites for the 6/4 GHz band.

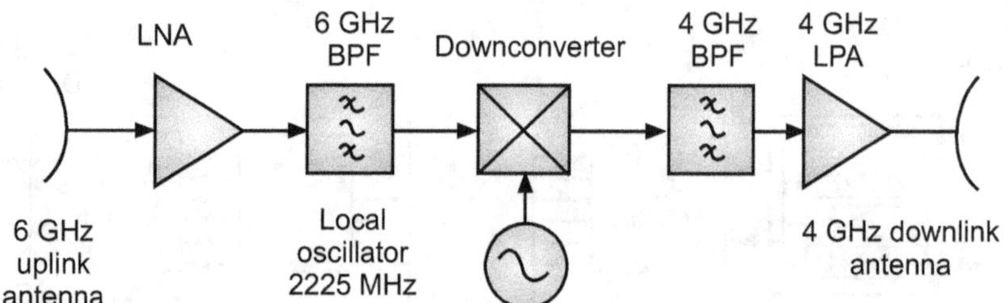

Fig. 5.11: Simplified single conversion transponder (bent pipe) for 6/4 GHz band

- The output power amplifier is usually a solid state power amplifier (SSPA). For a very high output power say higher than 50 W is required, a traveling wave tube amplifier (TWTA) would be used instead of SSPA.

- The local oscillator is at 2225 MHz to provide the appropriate shift in frequency from the 6 GHz uplink frequency to the 4 GHz downlink frequency, and the band pass filter after the mixer removes unwanted frequencies resulting from the down-conversion operation.

- The attenuator can be controlled via the uplink command system to set the gain of the transponder.

- Redundancy is provided for the high power amplifier (HPA) in each transponder by including a spare TWTA or solid state amplifier (SSPA) that can be switched into circuit if the primary power amplifier fails.

- The lifetime of HPAs is limited, and they represent the least reliable component in most transponders. Providing a spare HPA in each transponder greatly increases the probability that the satellite will reach the end if its working life with all its transponders still operational.

- Transponders can also be arranged so that there are spare transponders available in the event of a total failure.

- The arrangement is known as M for N redundancy. For example, it is common to have 16 for 10 redundancy or even 14 for 10.

- That is, 16 (or 14) output amplifiers are connected in a ring such that any of the 10 signals can pass through them. Thus, 6 (or 4) amplifiers are acting as back-up amplifiers while 10 are on line. Most HPAs have bandwidths much larger than the allocated frequency band and so it matters little which signals are passing through them.

- At Ku band, ring redundancy is still used, but it is much more like 2 for 1, that is, one spare for every active unit.

- Transponders for use in the 14/11 GHz bands normally employ a double frequency conversion scheme as illustrated in Fig. 5.12. it is easier to make filters, amplifiers, and equalizers at an intermediate frequency (IF) such as 1100 MHz than at 14 or 11 GHz, so the incoming 14 GHz carrier is translated to an IF of around 1 GHz.

- The amplification and filtering are performed are performed at 1 GHz and a relatively high-level carrier is translated back to 11 GHz for amplification by the HPA.

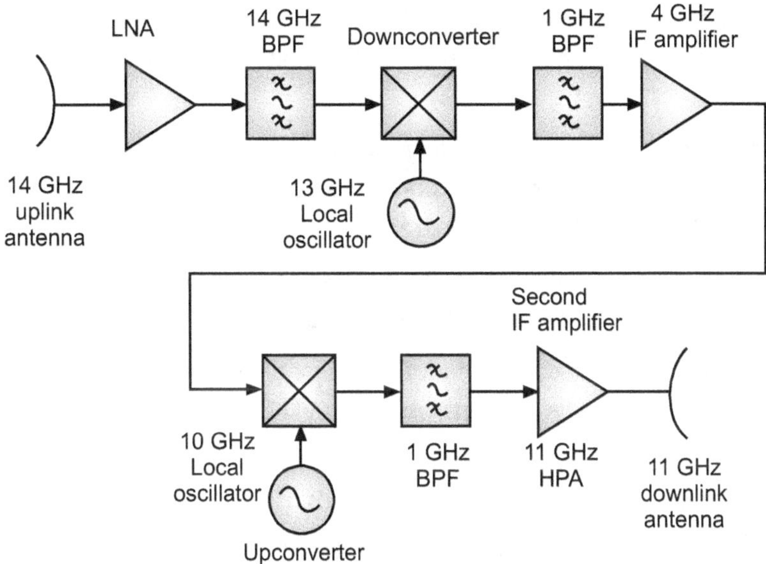

Fig. 5.12: Simplified double conversion transponder (bent pipe) for 14/11 GHz band

- Stringent requirements are placed on the filters used in transponders, since they must provide good rejection of unwanted frequencies, such as intermodulation products, and also have very low amplitude and phase ripple in their pass bands.

- Frequently a filter will be followed by an equalizer that smoothes out amplitude and phase variations in the pass band.

- Phase variation across the pass band produces group delay distortion, which is particularly troublesome with wideband FM signals and high-speed phase shift keyed data transmissions.

- A considerable increase in the communications capacity of a satellite can be achieved by combining onboard processing with switched beam technology.

- A switched beam satellite generates a narrow transmit beam for each earth station with which it communicates, and then transmits sequentially to each one using time division multiplexing of the signals.

- The narrow beam has to cover only one earth station, allowing the satellite transmit antenna to have a very high gain compared to a zone-coverage antenna.

- A narrow scanning beam can also be used, or a combination of fixed and scanning beams.

- Unless the satellite has a zone coverage receiver antenna, data storage is required at the satellite since it communicates with only one earth station at a time.

- The high gain antennas used in switched-beam systems raise the EIRP (effective isotropically radiated power) of the satellite transmitter and thus increase the capacity of the downlink.

- Switched beam systems on GEO satellites work best at Ka band where the wavelength is short enough that the limited dimensions of antennas on the satellite still allow beams of less than 0.4° beamwidth to be generated.

- Multiple beam antennas with baseband processing transponders are used on GEO and LEO satellites providing service to mobile terminals and handheld telephones.

- The low gain of the near omnidirectional antenna of a mobile earth station must be compensated by a high gain antenna on the satellite, necessitating the use of a multiple beam antennas.

- It is possible to conserve uplink bandwidth by using different modulation techniques on the uplink and downlink and by providing a baseband processor on the satellite.

- A high level modulation such as 16 QAM with four bits per symbol can be used on the link between the satellite and a large earth station to improve bandwidth efficiency.

- This approach has been adopted in the Astrolink and Spaceway 30/20 GHz satellites.

- Onboard processing may also be used to advantage to switch between the uplink access technique (e.g., MF – TDMA) and the downlink access technique (e.g., TDM) so that small earth stations may access each other directly via the satellite.

- The processor can provide the data storage needed for a switched-beam system and also can perform error correction independently on the uplink and downlink.

- A typical arrangement of the communication system for a satellite employing onboard processing is shown in Fig. 5.13.

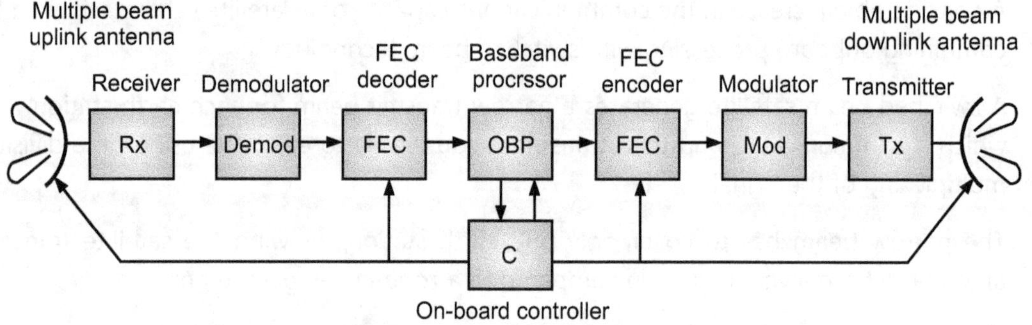

Fig. 5.13: Onboard processing transponder

5.7 SATELLITE ANTENNAS

Basic Antenna Types and RELATIONSHIPS:

- Four main types of antennas are used on satellites, these are :
    1. Wire antennas: monopoles and dipoles.
    2. Horn antennas.
    3. Reflector antennas.
    4. Array antennas.

- Wire antennas are used primarily at VHF and UHF to provide communications for the TTC&M systems.

- They are positioned with great care on the body of the satellite in an attempt to provide omnidirectional coverage.

- Most satellites measure only a few wavelengths at VHF frequencies, which makes it difficult to get the required antenna patterns, and there tend to be some orientations of the satellite in which the sensitivity of the TTC&M system is reduced by nulls in the antenna pattern.

- An antenna pattern is a plot of the field strength in the far field of the antenna when the antenna is driven by a transmitter.

- It is usually measured in decibels (dB) below the maximum field strength. The gain of an antenna is a measure of the antenna's capability to direct energy in one direction, rather than all around.

- At this point, it will be used with the simple definition given above.

- A useful principle in antenna theory is reciprocity.

- Reciprocity means that an antenna has the same gain and pattern at any given frequency whether it transmits or receives. An antenna pattern measured when receiving is identical to the pattern when transmitting.

- Fig. 5.14 shows typical satellite antenna coverage zones. The pattern is frequently specified by its 3 dB beamwidth, the angle between the directions in which the radiated (or received) field falls to half the power in the direction of maximum field strength.

- However, a satellite antenna is used to provide coverage of a certain area, or zone on the earth's surface, and it is more useful to have contours of antenna gain.

- When computing the signal power received by an earth station from the satellite, it is important to know where the station lies relative to the satellite transmit antenna contour pattern, so that the exact EIRP can be calculated.

- If the pattern is not known, it may be possible to estimate the antenna gain in a given direction if the antenna bore-sight or beam axis direction and its beamwidth are known.

- Horn antennas are used at microwave frequencies when relatively wide beams are required, as for global coverage.

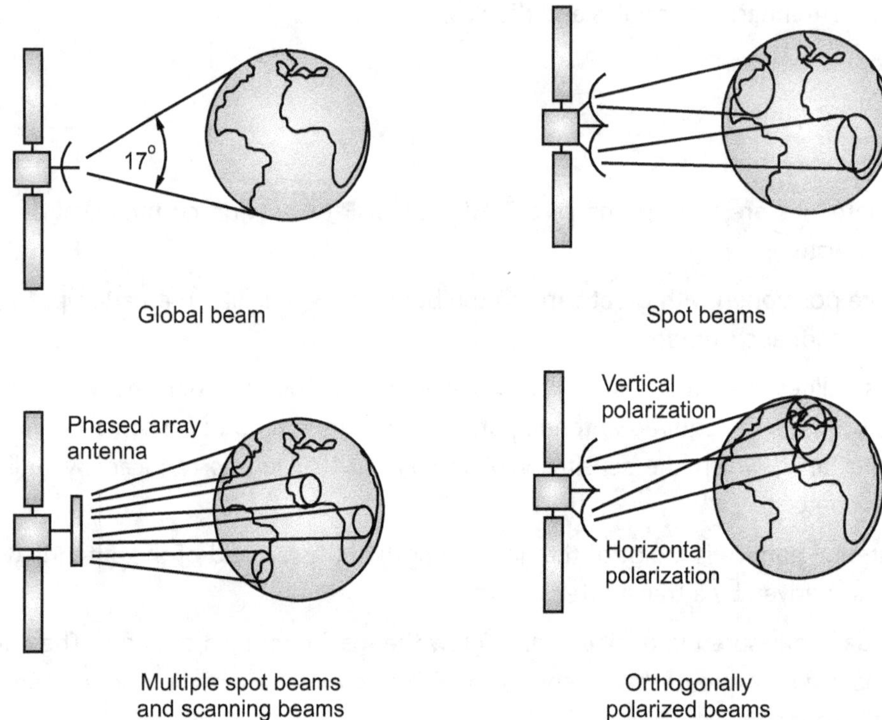

Fig. 5.14: Typical satellite antenna patterns and coverage zones

- A horn is a flared section of waveguide that provides an aperture several wavelengths wide and a good match between the waveguide impedance and free space. Horns are also used as feeds for reflectors, either singly or in clusters.

- Horns and reflectors are examples of aperture antennas that launch a wave into free space from a waveguide. It is difficult to obtain gains much greater than 23 dB or beamwidths narrower than about 10° with horn antennas.

- For higher gains or narrow beamwidths a reflector antenna or array must be used.

- Reflector antennas are usually illuminated by one or more horns and provide a larger aperture that can be achieved with a horn alone. For maximum gain, it is necessary to generate a plane wave in the aperture of the reflector.

- This is achieved by choosing a reflector profile that has equal path lengths from the feed to the aperture, so that all the energy radiated by the feed and reflected by the reflector reaches the aperture with the same phase angle and creates a uniform phase front.

- One reflector shape that achieves this with a point source of radiation is the paraboloid, with a feed placed at its focus.

- The paraboloid is the basic shape for most reflector antennas, and is commonly used for earth station antennas.

- Satellite antennas often use modified paraboloid reflector profiles to tailor the beam pattern to a particular coverage zone.

- Phased array antennas are also used on satellites to create multiple beams from a single aperture, and have been used by Iridium and Globalstar to generate up to 16 beams from a single aperture for their LEO mobile telephone systems.

- Some basic relationships in aperture antennas can be used to determine the approximate size of a satellite antenna for a particular application, as well as the antenna gain.

- More accurate calculations are needed to determine the exact gain, efficiency, and pattern of a satellite antenna, and the interested reader should refer to one of the many excellent texts in this field for details.

- The following approximate relationships will be used here to guide the selection of antennas for a communication satellite.

  An aperture antenna has a gain G given by

  $$G = \eta_A 4\pi A/\lambda^2 \qquad \qquad \text{... (5.1)}$$

- Where A is the area of the antenna aperture in meters, λ the operating wavelength in meters, and η_A is the aperture efficiency of the antenna. The aperture efficiency η_A is not easily determined, but is typically in the range 55 to 68 for reflector antennas with single feeds, lower for antennas with shaped beams.

- Horn antennas tend to have higher efficiencies than reflector antennas, typically in the range 65 to 80. If the aperture is circular, as is often the case, Equation (5.1) can be written as:

  $$G = \eta_A(\pi D/\lambda)^2 \qquad \qquad \text{... (5.2)}$$

  where D is the diameter of the circular aperture in meters.

- The beamwidth of the antenna is related to the aperture dimension in the plane in which the pattern is measured. A useful rule of thumb is that the 3 dB beamwidth in a given plane for an antenna with dimension D in that plane is

  $$\theta_{3dB} \approx 75\ \lambda/D \text{ degrees} \qquad \qquad \text{... (5.3)}$$

- Where θ_{3dB} is the beamwidth between half power points of the antenna pattern and D is the aperture dimension in the same units as the wavelength λ. The beamwidth of a horn antenna may depart from Equation (5.2) quite radically.

- For example, a small rectangular horn will produce a narrower beam than suggested by Equation (5.2) in its E plane and a wider beamwidth in the H plane.

- Since both Equations (5.2) and (5.3) contain antenna dimension parameters, the gain and beamwidth of an aperture antenna are related. For antennas with $\eta_A \approx 60\%$, the gain is approximately

$$G \approx 33,000/(\theta_{3dB})^2 \qquad \ldots (5.4)$$

- Where $\theta_{3\ dB}$ is in degrees and G is not in decibels. If the beam has different beamwidths in orthogonal planes, $\theta_{3\ dB}$ should be replaced by the product of the two 3 dB beamwidths. Values of the constants in Equation (5.3) vary between different sources, with a range 28,000 to 35,000. The value 33,000 is typical for reflector antennas used in satellite communication systems.

Example 5.1 : The earth subtends an angle of 17° when viewed from geostationary orbit. What are the dimensions and gain of a horn antenna that will provide global coverage at 4 GHz ?

Solution: If we design our horn to give a circularly symmetric beam with a 3 dB beamwidth of 17° using Equation (5.2)

$$D/\lambda = 74/(\theta_{3dB}) = 4.4$$

At 4 GHz, $\lambda = 0.075$ m, so D = 0.33 m (just over 1 ft). if we use a circular horn excited in the TE_{11} mode, the beamwidths in the E and H planes will not be equal and we may be forced to make the aperture slightly smaller to guarantee coverage in the H plane. A corrugated horn designed to support the HE hybrid mode has a circularly symmetric beam and could be used in this application. Waveguide horns are generally used for global beam coverage. Reflector antennas are not efficient when the aperture diameter is less than 8λ.

Using Equation (5.4), the gain of the horn is approximately 100 or 20 dB, at the center of the beam. However, in designing our communication system we will have to use the edge of beam gain figure of 17 dB, since those earth stations close to the earth's horizon, as viewed from the satellite, are close to the 3 dB contour of the transmitted beam.

Example 5.2 : The continental United States (48 contiguous states) subtends an angle of approximately 6° × 3° when viewed from geostationary orbit. What dimensions must a reflector antenna have to illuminate half this area with a circular beam 3° in diameter at 11 GHz ?

Can a reflector be used to produce a 6° × 3° beam? What gain would the antenna have?

Solution: Using Equation (5.2), we have for a 3° circular beam

$$D/\lambda = 75/3 = 25$$

And with $\lambda = 0.0272$ m, D = 0.68 m (just over 2 ft). The gain of the antenna, from Equation (5.3) is approximately 35 dB.

To generate a beam with different beamwidths in orthogonal planes we need an aperture with different dimensions in the two planes. In this case, a rectangular aperture $25\lambda \times 12.5\lambda$ would generate a beam $6° \times 3°$ and would have a gain of 32 dB, approximately. In order to illuminate such a reflector, a horn with unequal beamwidths is required, since the reflector must intercept most of the radiation from the feed if it is to have an acceptable efficiency. Rectangular, or more commonly elliptical, outline reflectors are used to generate unequal beamwidths. When orthogonal polarizations are to be transmitted or received, it is better to use a circular reflector with a distorted profile to broaden the beam in one plane, or a feed cluster to provide the appropriate amplitude and phase distribution across the reflector.

Satellite Antennas in Practice :

- The antennas of a communications satellite are often a limiting element in the complete system. In an ideal satellite, there would be one antenna beam for each earth station, completely isolated from all other beams, for transmit and receive.

- However, if two earth stations are 300 km apart on the earth's surface and the satellite is in geostationary orbit, their angular   separation at the satellite is $0.5°$ for $\theta_{3dB \text{ to be } 0.5°}$, D/λ must be 150, which requires an aperture diameter of 11.3 m at 4 GHz.

- Antennas this large have been flown on satellites (ATS-6 deployed a 2.5 GHz, 10 m diameter antenna, for example), and large unfurled antennas are used to create multiple spot beams from GEO satellites serving mobile users.

- However, at 20 GHz, an antenna with $D/\lambda = 150$ is only 1.5 m wide, and such an antenna can readily be flown on a 30/20 GHz satellite. A phased array feed is used to create many $0.5°$ beams which can be clustered to serve the coverage zone of the satellite.

- To provide a separate beam for each earth station would also require one antenna feed per earth station if a multiple-feed antenna with a single reflector were used.

- A compromise between one beam per station and one beam for all stations has been used in many satellites by using zone-coverage beams and orthogonal polarizations within the same beam to provide more channels per satellite.

- Each reflector is illuminated by a complex feed that provides the required beam shape to permit communication between earth stations within a given coverage zone.

- The largest reflector on the satellite transmits at 4 GHz and produces the peanut shaped patterns for the zone beams, which are designed to concentrate the transmitted energy onto densely populated areas such as North America and Western Europe where much telecommunications traffic is generated. The smaller antennas are used to provide hemisphere transmit and receive beams, and the 14/11 GHz spot beams. In addition, there are horn antennas providing global beam coverage.

- Countries such as the United States create an enormous demand for communication services, and a number of domestic satellite communication systems have been established to meet that demand.

- In 2000 the geostationary orbit had domestic satellites spaced every 2°, operating at 6/4 GHz and 14/11 GHz from longitude 60°W to 140°W.

- This encompasses all orbital locations that can be simultaneously viewed by earth stations in the United States and Canada, and each operator has been given a limited number of orbital slots in which to place a satellite.

- As a result, there is a great deal of pressure on the operating companies to obtain the maximum number of channels per satellite in order to give the operator the greatest possible revenue-earning capacity.

- This has encouraged the development of frequency reuse antennas by means of orthogonal polarizations and multiple beams, the combination of 6/4 and 14/11 GHz communication systems on one satellite, and the use of multilevel digital modulation and TDMA to increase capacity.

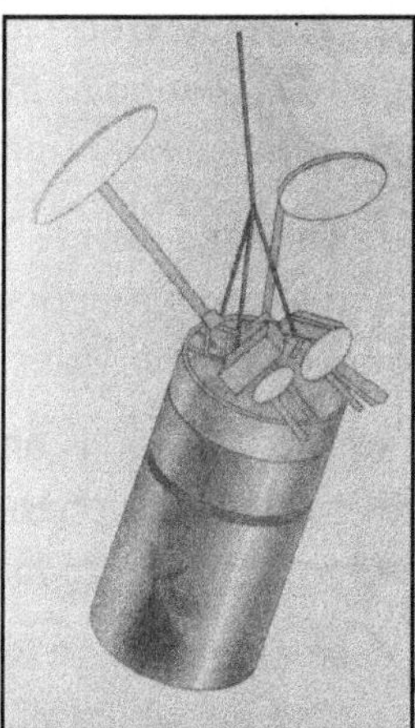

Fig. 5.15: Intelsat VI satellite on station

- The requirements of narrow antenna beams with high gain over a small coverage zone leads to large antenna structures on the satellite. Frequently, the antennas in their operating configuration are too large to fit within the shroud dimensions of the launch vehicle, and must be folded down during the launch phase.

- Once in orbit, the antennas then can be deployed. In many larger satellites, the antennas use offset paraboloidal reflectors with clusters of feeds to provide carefully controlled beam shapes.

- The feed mount on the body of the satellite, close to the communications subsystem, and the reflector is mounted on a hinged arm.

- Fig. 5.15 shows an example of this design of antenna for the INTELSAT VI satellite.

- For launch, the solid reflectors fold down to provide a compact structure; in orbit, the hinged arms are swung out and locked in place to hold the reflectors in the correct position.

- When the satellite is in geostationary orbit it is weightless, so very little energy is required to move the large reflector.

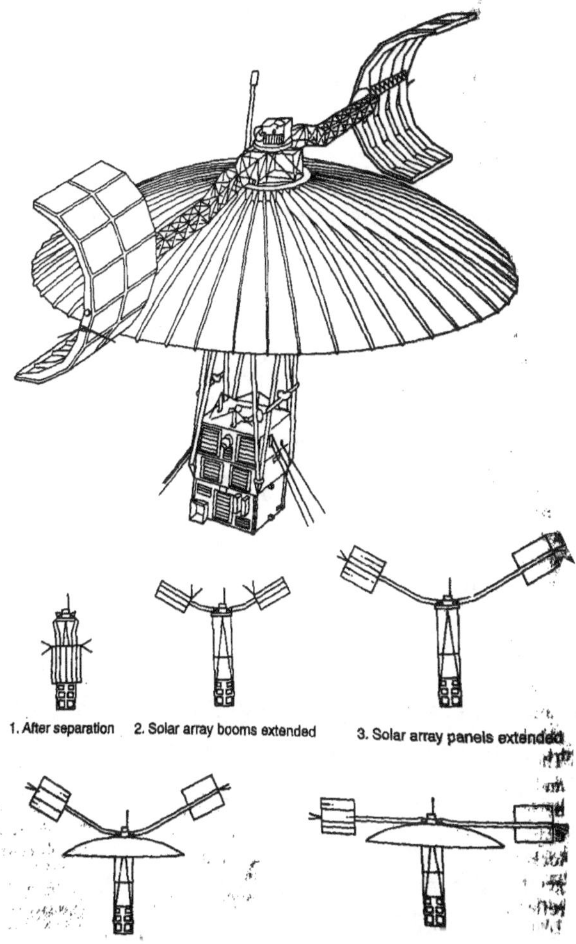

Fig. 5.16: Deployment sequence of ATS-6 10-m antenna

- Fig. 5.16 shows the deployment sequence used for the 30-ft antenna carried by ATS-6: the antenna was built as a series of petals that folded over each other to make a compact unit during launch, which then unfurled in orbit.

- The solar Cells folded down over the antenna, and were deployed first. Springs or pyrotechnic devices can be used to provide the energy for deployment of antennas or solar Cells, with a locking device to ensure correct positioning after deployment.

- Similar unfurlable antennas are used on GEO satellites that provide satellite telephone service at L band using multiple narrow beams.

5.8 EQUIPMENT RELIABILITY AND SPACE QUALIFICATION

- Communications satellites built in the 1980s and 1990s have provided operational lifetimes of up to 15 years. Once a satellite is in geostationary orbit, there is little possibility of repairing components that fail or adding more fuel for station keeping.

- The components that make up the satellite must therefore have very high reliability in the hostile environment of outer space, and a strategy must be devised that allows some components to fail without causing the entire communication capacity of the satellite to be lost.

- Two separate approaches are used: space qualification of every part of the satellite to ensure that it has a long life expectancy in orbit and redundancy of the most critical components to provide continued operation when one component fails.

Space QUALIFICATION:

- Outer space, at geostationary orbit distances, is a harsh environment.

- There is a total vacuum and the sun irradiates the satellite with 1.4 kW of heat and light on each square meter if exposed surface.

- Where surfaces are in shadow, heat is lost to the infinite sink of space, and surface temperature will fall toward absolute zero.

- Electronic equipment cannot operate at such extremes of temperature stays within the range 0° to 75°C.

- This requires a thermal control system that manages heat flow throughout a GEO satellite as the sun moves around once every 24h. Thermal problems are equally severe for a LEO satellite that moves from sunlight to shadow every 100 min.

- The first stage in ensuring high reliability in a satellite is by selection and screening of every component used.

- Past operational and test experience of components indicates which components can be expected to have good reliability.

- Only components that have been shown to have high reliability under outer space conditions will be selected.

- Each component is then tested individually (or as a subsystem) to ensure that it meets its specification.

- This process is known as quality control or quality assurance and is vital in building any equipment that is to be reliable.

- Once individual components and subsystems have been space qualified, the complete satellite must be tested as a system to ensure that its many systems are reliable.

- When a satellite is designed, three prototype models are often built and tested.

- The mechanical model contains all the structural and mechanical parts that will be included in the satellite and is tested to ensure that all moving parts operate correctly in a vacuum, over a wide temperature range.

- It is also subjected to vibration and shock testing to simulate vibration levels and G forces likely to be encountered on launch.

- The thermal model contains all the electronics packages and other components that must be maintained at the correct temperature.

- Often, the thermal, vacuum, and vibration tests of the entire satellite will be combined in a thermal vacuum chamber for what is known in the industry as a shake and bake test.

- The antennas are usually included on the thermal model to check for distortion of reflectors and displacement or bending of support structures. In orbit, an antenna may cycle in temperature from above 100°C to below −100°C as the sun moves around the satellite.

- The electrical model contains all the electronic parts of the satellite and is tested for correct electrical performance under total vacuum and a wide range of temperatures.

- The antennas of the electrical model must provide the correct beamwidth, gain, and polarization properties.

- Testing carried out on the prototype models is designed to overstress the system and induce failure in any weak components: temperature cycling will be carried out to 10% beyond expected extremes; structural loads and G forces 50 above those expected in flight may be applied.

- Electrical equipment will be subjected to excess voltage and current drain to test for good electronic and thermal reliability.

- The prototype models used in these tests will not usually be flown.

- A separate flight model (or several models) will be built and subjected to the same tests as the prototype, but without the extremes of temperature, stress, or voltage.

- Preflight testing of flight models, while exhaustive, is designed more to cause failure of parts, rather than to check that they will operate under worst-case conditions.

- Space qualification is an expensive process, and one of the factors that makes large GEO satellites expensive.

- Some low earth orbit satellites have been built successfully using less expensive techniques and relying on lower performance in orbit.

- LEO satellite systems require large numbers of satellites that are generally less expensive than large GEO satellites.

- The iridium system, for example, was designed with 66 operational satellites in its constellation to provide continuous worldwide coverage, with at least eight spare satellites in orbit at any time. If one operational satellite fails, a spare is moved in to take its place.

- This allowed Iridium satellites to be built with a higher probability of failure than a GEO satellite.

- Experimental satellites have also been built using low cost techniques.

- The University of Surrey, U.K., for example, built a series of digital store and forward satellites that were used by radio amateurs and others which each cost less than $1M. most of the components on the surrey satellites were not space qualified, but were selected carefully to ensure best possible lifetimes at reasonable cost and then the entire satellite was subjected to shake and bake tests.

- Many of the electronic and mechanical components that are used in satellites are known to have limited lifetimes, or a finite probability of failure.

- If failure of one of these components will jeopardize the mission or reduce the communication capacity of the satellite, a backup, or redundant, unit will be provided.

- The design of the system must be such that when one unit fails, the backup can automatically take over or be switched into operation by command from the ground.

- For example, redundancy is always provided for traveling wave tube amplifiers used in the transponders of a communications satellite, as these are known to have a limited lifetime.

- The success of the testing and space qualification procedures use by NASA has been illustrated by the lifetime achieved by many of its scientific satellites.

- Satellites designed for a specific mission lasting 1 or 2 years have frequently operated successfully for up to 25 years.

- Sufficient reliability was designed into the satellite to guarantee the mission lifetime such that the actual lifetime has been much greater.

Reliability :

- We need to calculate the reliability of a satellite subsystem for two reasons: we want to know what the probability is that the subsystem will still be working after a given time period, and we need to provide redundant components or subsystems where the probability of a failure is too great to be accepted.

- The owner of the satellite used for communications expects to be able to use a predetermined percentage of its communications capacity for a given length of time.

- Amortization of purchase and launch costs will be calculated on the basis of an expected lifetime.

- The manufacturers of satellites must provide their customers with predictions (or guarantees) of the reliability of the satellite and subsystems: to do this requires the use of reliability theory.

- Reliability theory is a mathematical attempt to predict the future and is therefore less certain than other mathematical techniques that operate in absolute terms.

- The application of reliability theory has enabled satellites engineers to build satellites that perform as expected, at acceptable construction costs.

- It should be noted, however, that the cost of a satellites is very high compared to other equipment with a comparable number of components: a large GEO satellite costs around $100 M to build, close to the cost of a Boeing 747 jet airliner.

- The cost is acceptable because of the high revenue-earning capability of the satellite.

- The reliability of a component can be expressed in terms of the probability of failure after time t, PF(t). For most electronic equipment, probability of failure is higher at the beginning of life → the burn-in period → than at some later time.

- As the component ages, failure becomes more likely, leading to the bathtub curve shown in figure 5.17

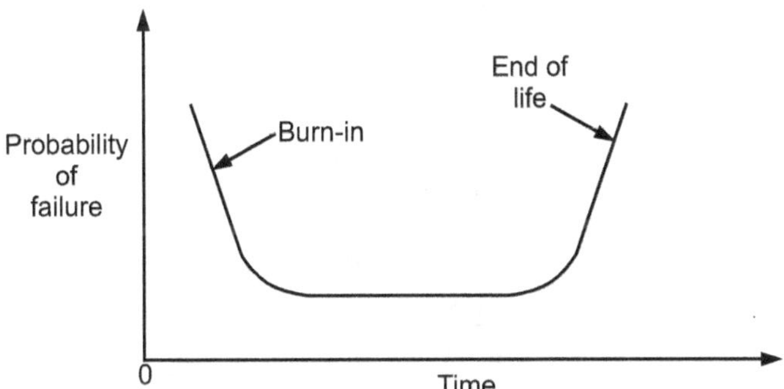

Fig. 5.17: Bathtub curve for probability of failure

- Components for satellites are selected only after extensive testing.

- The aim of the testing is to determine reliability, causes of failure, and expected lifetime. The result is a plot similar to Fig. 5.17.

- Testing is carried out under rigorous conditions, representing the worst operating conditions likely to be encountered in space, and may be designed to accelerate failure in order to shorten the testing duration needed to determine reliability.

- Units that are exposed to the vacuum of space are tested under equivalent radiant heat conditions.

- The initial period of reduced reliability can be eliminated by a integrated circuits that are required to have high reliability are subjected to burn-in periods from 100 to 1000h, often at a high temperature and excess voltage to induce bathtub curve.

The reliability of a device or subsystem is defined as

$$R(t) = \frac{N_s(t)}{N_0} = \frac{\text{Number of surviving components at time}}{\text{Numbers of components at start of test period}} \qquad \ldots (5.5)$$

Correction is number of surviving components at time t

The number of components that failed in time t if $N_f(t)$ where

$$N_f(t) = N_0 - N_s(t) \qquad \ldots (5.6)$$

From the engineering viewpoint, what we need to know is the probability of any one of the N_0 components failing: this is related to the mean time before failure (MTBF). Suppose we continue testing devices until all of them fail. The ith device fails after time t_i where

$$\text{MTBF} = m = \frac{1}{N_0} \sum_{i=1}^{N_0} t_i \qquad \ldots (5.7)$$

The average failure rate λ, is the reciprocal of the MTBF, m. If we assume that λ is a constant, then

$$\lambda = \frac{\text{Number of failures given time}}{\text{Number of surviving components}} \qquad \ldots (5.8)$$

Correction is number of failures in a given time

$$\lambda = \frac{1}{N_s} \frac{\Delta N_f}{\Delta t} = \frac{1}{N_s} \frac{dN_f}{dt} = 1/\text{MTBF} \qquad \ldots (5.9)$$

Failure rate λ is often given as the average failure rate per 10^9 h. The rate of failure, $\dfrac{dN_f}{dt}$, is the negative of the rate of survival dN_s/dt, so we can redefine λ as

$$\lambda = \frac{-1}{N_s} \frac{dN_s}{dt} \qquad \ldots (5.10)$$

By definition from Equation (5.5), the reliability r is N_s/N_0, so

$$\lambda = \frac{-1}{N_0 R} \frac{d}{dt} (N_0 R) = \frac{-1}{R} \frac{dR}{dt} \qquad \ldots (5.11)$$

A solution of Equation (5.11) is

$$R = e^{-\lambda t} \qquad \ldots (5.12)$$

Thus the reliability of a device decreases exponentially with time, with zero reliability after infinite time, that is, certain failure. However, end of useful life is usually taken to be the time t_1, at which R falls to 0.37 $\left(\dfrac{1}{e}\right)$, which is when

$$t_1 = \frac{1}{\lambda} = m \qquad \ldots (5.13)$$

The probability of a device failing, therefore, has an exponential relationship to the MTBF and is represented by the right-hand end of the bathtub curve.

Redundancy :

- The equations in the preceding section allow us to calculate the reliability of a given device when we know its MTBF. In a satellite, many devices are used, each with a different MTBT and failure of one device may cause catastrophic failure of a complete subsystem.

- If we incorporate redundant devices, the subsystem can continue to function correctly.

- We can define three different situations for which we want to compute subsystem reliability.

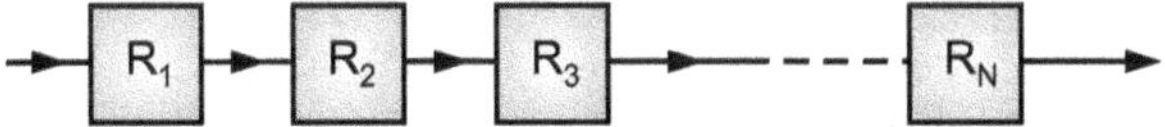

Fig. 5.18: Redundancy connections. (a) Series connection. (b) Parallel connection. (c) Series/Parallel connection. (d) Switched connection.

- Series connection, used in solar cells arrays, parallel connection, used to provide redundancy of the high power amplifiers in satellite transponders, and a switched connection, often used to provide parallel paths with multiple transponders.

- These are illustrated in Fig. 5.18; also shown is a hybrid arrangement, a series/parallel connection, widely used in electronic equipment.

- The switched connection arrangement shown in Fig. 5.18 (d) is also referred to as ring redundancy since any component can be switched in for any other.

- Switches S_1 and S_2 are a little more complicated than as shown, affording the choice of multiple paths in an M and N ring redundancy configuration.

- The important point to note is that the active devices (R_1, R_2, ..., R_n) have sufficient bandwidth, power output range, etc., to be able to handle any of the channels that might be switched through to them.

- Most TWTAs and SSPAs are such wideband, large power range devices.

- An example of parallel redundancy for the HPA of a 6/4 GHz bent pipe transponder is shown in Fig. 5.19 the transponder translates incoming signals in the 6 GHz uplink band by 2225 MHz and retransmits them in the 4 GHz band.

- The high power output stage of the transponder has two parallel TWT amplifiers. One TWTA will be switched off, but must present a matched load when both off and on. If one TWTA fails, the other is switched on either automatically, or by command from earth.

- The TWT is a thermionic device with a heated cathode and a high voltage power supply. In common with other thermoionic devices such as cathode ray tubes and magnetrons, they have a relatively short MTBF.

- Although the MTBF may be 50,000h, this is the period after which 50 of such devices will have failed, on average.

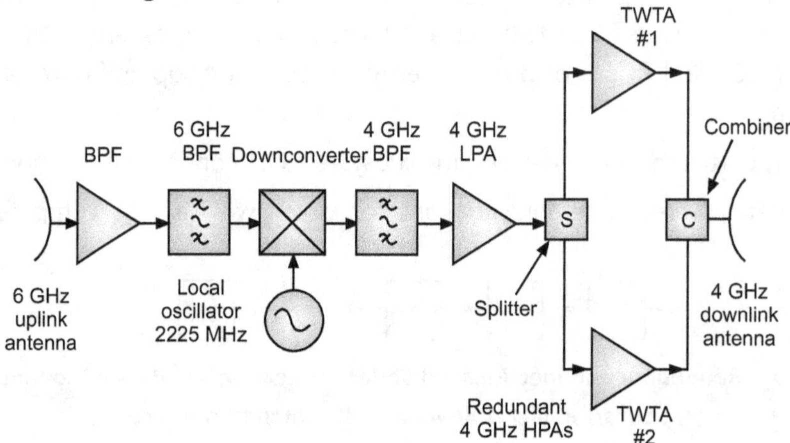

Fig. 5.19: Redundant TWTA configuration in HPA of a 6/4 GHz bent pipe transponder

- The parallel connection of two TWTs, as shown in figure 5.19 raises the reliability of the amplifier stage to 0.60 at the MTBF period, assuming zero probability of a short circuit.

- A lifetime of 50,000h is approximately 6 years of continuous operation, which is close to the typical design lifetime of a satellite.

- To further improve the reliability of the transponders, a second redundant transponder may be provided with switching between the two systems.

- Note that a combination of parallel and switched redundancy is used to combat failures that are catastrophic to one transponder channel and to the complete communication system.

REVIEW QUESTIONS

1. Explain how attitude and orbit control is achieved from an earth station?
2. Why TTC&M are necessary for a satellite system?
3. What is the overall distribution of electrical power requirement in a satellite?
4. Why backup batteries are necessary in spite of solar arrays?
5. What are the different types of batteries used in satellites?
6. What are the characteristics that are most important in satellite antenna?
7. What are global beam and spot beam antennas? Give their applications.
8. Explain briefly antenna tracking systems.
9. What are the different parameters on which the design of a parabolic reflector depends?
10. List the major factors that govern the design of earth station antennas for satellite communication.

●●●

SATELLITESCOMMUNICATION LINK DESIGN

6.1 INTRODUCTION

- The designing of a satellite communication system is a complex process and needs to make compromises between many factors to achieve the best performance at an acceptable and feasible cost.

- Let us first consider geostationary satellite systems, since GEO satellites carry the vast majority of the world's satellite traffic.

- The cost to build and launch a GEO satellite is estimated at $25,000 per kg. Hence weight is the most critical factor in the design of any satellite, since the heavier the satellite the higher the cost, and so may not be possible to recover the capital cost of the satellite which is to be recovered over its lifetime by selling communication services.

- The overall dimensions of the satellite are critical too, since the spacecraft must fit within the confines of the launch vehicle.

- When stowed for launch, typically the diameter of the spacecraft must be less than 3.5 m. most large GEO satellites use deployable solar panels and antennas, but the antenna reflectors require accurate surfaces and are not folded for launch. This limits the maximum aperture dimension to about 3.5 m. as in most radio systems, antennas are a limiting factor in the capacity and performance of the communication system.

- The weight of the satellite is based on two factors: output power and the number of the transponders on the satellite and the weight of station-keeping fuel. As much as half the total weight of satellite which is expected to remain in service for 15 years may be fuel.

- High power transponders require lots of electrical power, which can only be generated by solar cells, increasing the total output power of the transponders raises the demand for electrical power and the dimensions of the solar cells, adding more weight to the satellite.

- Three other factors influence system design: the choice of frequency band, atmospheric propagation effects, and multiple access technique.

- These factors are all related, with the frequency band often being determined by what is available.

- Table 6.1 and 6.2 tabulate the most important frequencies allocated for satellite communications.

Table 6.1 : Major Frequency Allocations for Fixed Satellite Services and Broadcasting Satellites

Frequency	Fixed Satellite Service	Broadcasting Satellites
2320 – 2345 MHz		Radio broadcasting
2500 – 2535		Down region III
2500 – 2655	Down region II	Down region II
2655 – 2690	Down region II	Down region II Up region II, III
3400 – 3700	Down	
3700 – 4200	Down	
4500 – 4800	Down, up	
5725 – 5850	Up region I	
5850 – 5925	Up region I	
5925 – 7075	Up	
7250 – 7450	Down, government	
7450 – 7550	Down, government	
7550 – 7750	Down, government	
8215 – 8400	Up, government	
10.7 – 11.7 GHz	Down	Up region I
11.7 – 12.2	Down region II	Down regions I and III
12.2 – 12.7		Down regions I and II U.S Direct Broadcast Satellite TV
12.50 – 12.75	Up region I and II, down region I	
12.75 – 13.25		Up
14.00 – 14.25	Up	
14.25 – 14.50	Up	
14.5 – 14.8		Up
17.3 – 17.7		Up
17.7 – 18.6	Down	

18.1 – 18.6	Down	
18.6 – 18.8	Down regions I and III	
18.8 – 19.7	Down	
27.0 – 27.5	Up regions II and III	
27.5 – 29.5	Up	
30.0 – 31.0	Up	
37.5 – 39.5	Down	
39.5 – 40.5	Down	
40.5 – 42.5	Down	
42.5 – 43.5	Down	
47.2 – 50.2	Up	
50.4 – 51.4	Up	
71.0 – 75.5	Up	
81 – 84	Down	
84 – 86	Down	
92 – 95	Up	
102 – 105	Down	
149 – 164	Down	
202 – 217	Up	
231 – 241	Down	
265 – 275	Down	

Table 6.2 : Major Frequency Allocations for Mobile Satellite Services

Frequency	Aeronautical Mobile	Maritime Mobile	Land Mobiles and Other Services
137 – 138 MHz			Down, shared
148 – 149.9			Up, shared
149.9 – 150.05			Up, shared
399.9 – 400.05			Up
400.15 – 401			Down, shared

406 – 406.1			Emergency beacons
860 – 896			Region II (limited use) shared with cellular radio
1559 – 1610			Navigation satellite, down
1530 – 1535		Down	Down region I only
1535 – 1544		Down	
1544 – 1545		Down	
1445 – 1555	Down		
1555 – 1559			Down
1559 – 1610			Navigation satellite, down
1610 – 1625.5			Navigation satellite, Up
1625.5 – 1631.5		Up	
1631.5 – 1634.5			Up
1534.5 – 1645.5		Up	shared
1645.5 – 1646.6	Up	UP	Up
1646.5 – 1656.5	Up		
1656.5 – 1660			Up
1660.0 – 1660.5			Up
2483.5 – 2500	Down	Down	Down
5.00 – 5.25 GHz	Up	Up	Up
7.30 – 7.75	Up, government	Up, government	Up, government
15.4 – 15.7	Down	Down	Down
20.2 – 21.2	Down	Down	Down
29.5 – 31.0	Up	Up	Up
39.5 – 40.5	Down	Down	Down
43.5 – 45.5	Up, government	Up, government	Up, government
45.5 – 47.0	Up	Up	Up

66.0 – 71.0	Down	Down	Down
71.0 – 74.0	Up	Up	Down
81.0 – 84.0	Down	Down	Down
95.0 – 100			
134 – 142			
190 – 200			
252 – 265			

*   Region I, II and III are regions of the earth's surface defined by the international Telecommunications Union.

- The major bands are the 6/4 GHz, 14/11 GHz and 30/20 GHz bands. (the uplink frequency is quoted first, by convention.) However, over much of the geostationary orbit there is already a satellite using both 6/4 GHz and 14/11 GHz every 2°.

- This is the minimum spacing used for satellites in GEO to avoid interference from uplink earth stations. Additional satellites can only be accommodated if they use another frequency band, such as 30/20 GHz.

- Rain in the atmosphere attenuates radio signals. The effect is more severe as the frequency increases, with little attenuation at 4 and 6 GHz, , but significant attenuation above 10 GHz.

- Attenuation through rain (in decibels) increases roughly as the square of frequency, so a satellite uplink operating at 30 GHz suffers four times as much attenuation as an uplink at 14 GHz.

- Low Earth Orbit (LEO) and Medium Earth Orbit (MEO) satellite systems have similar constraints to GEO satellite systems, but each serve a smaller area of the earth's surface and thus they need more satellites, serve a smaller area of the earth's surface.

- Although the satellites are much closer to the earth than GEO satellites and therefore produce stronger signals, this advantage is usually lost since the earth terminals need low gain omnidirectional antennas because the position of the satellite is continually changing. LEO and MEO satellites use multiple beam antennas to increase the gain of the satellite antenna beams, and also to provide frequency reuse.

- Mobile satellite terminals must operate with low gain antennas at the mobile unit, and at as low a RF frequency as can be obtained.

- The link between the satellite and the major earth station (often called a hub station) is usually in a different frequency band as it is a fixed link. Fig. 6.1 shows an illustration of a maritime satellite communication system using a GEO satellite and L-band links to mobiles, with C-band links to a fixed hub station.

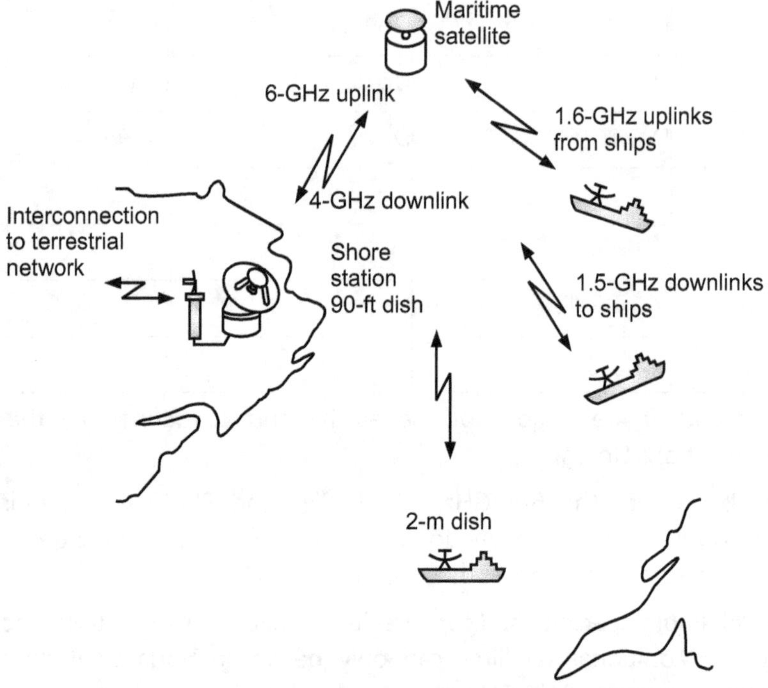

Fig. 6.1 : A maritime satellite communication system

- All communication links are designed to meet certain performance objectives, usually a Bit Error Rate (BER) in a digital link or a signal-to-noise ratio (S/N) in an analog link, measured in the baseband channel.

- The baseband channel is where an information carrying signal is generated or received; for example, a TV camera generates a baseband video signal, and a TV receiver delivers a baseband video signal to the picture tube to form the images that the viewer watches.

- Digital Data are generated by computers at baseband, and BER is measured at baseband.

- The baseband channel BER or S/N ratio is determined by the carrier-to-noise ratio (C/N) at the input to the demodulator in the receiver.

- In most satellite communications applications, the C/N ratio at the demodulator input must be greater than 6 dB for the BER or S/N objective to be achieved.

- Digital links operating at C/N ratios below 10 dB must use error correction techniques to improve the BER delivered to the user.

- Analog links using frequency modulation (FM) require wideband FM to achieve a large improvement in S/N ratio relative to C/N ratio.

- The C/N ratio is calculated at the input of the receiver, at the output terminals (or) port) of the receiving antenna. RF noise received along with the signal and noise generated by the receiver are combined into an equivalent noise power at the input to the receiver, and a noiseless receiver model is used.

- In a noiseless receiver, the C/N ratio is constant at all points in the RF and IF chain, so the C/N ratio at the demodulator is equal to the C/N ratio at the receiver input.

- In a satellite link there are two signal paths: an uplink from the earth station to the satellite, and a downlink from the satellite to the earth station.

- The overall C/N at the earth station receiver depends on both links, therefore both links must achieve the required performance for a specified percentage of time. Path attenuation in the earth's atmosphere may become excessive in heavy rain, causing the C/N ratio to fall below the minimum permitted value, especially when the 30/20 GHz band is used, leading to a link outage.

- Designing a satellite system therefore requires knowledge of the required performance of the uplink and downlink, the propagation characteristics and rain attenuation for the frequency band being used at the earth station locations, and the parameters of the satellite and earth stations.

- Additional constraints may be imposed by the need to conserve RF bandwidth and to avoid interference with other users. Sometimes, all of these information is not available and the designer must estimate values and produce tables of system performance based on assumed scenarios. It is usually impossible to design a complete satellite communication system at the first attempt.

- A trial design must first be tried, and then refined until a workable model is achieved. In this chapter we focus on the basic procedures for the design of satellite communication links, and includes design examples for a digital TV link using a GEO satellite and Quadrature Phase Shift Keying (QPSK) modulation, and a LEO satellite system for personal communication.

6.2 BASIC TRANSMISSION THEORY

- The calculation of the power received by an earth station from a satellite transmitter is fundamental to the understanding of satellite communications. In this section we discuss two approaches to this calculation: the use of flux density and the link equation.

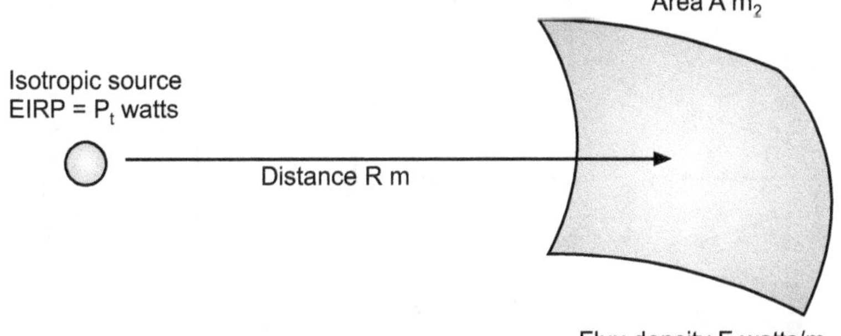

Fig. 6.2 : Flux density produced by an isotropic source

- Consider a transmitting source, in free space, radiating a total power P_t watts uniformly in all directions as shown in Fig. 6.2. Such a source is called isotropic; it is an idealization that cannot be realized physically because it could not create transverse electromagnetic waves.

- At a distance R meters from the hypothetical isotropic source transmitting RF power P_t watts, the flux density crossing the surface of a sphere with radius R is given by

$$F = \frac{P_t}{4\pi R^2} \; W/m^2 \qquad \qquad ... (6.1)$$

- All real antennas are directional and radiate more power in some directions than in others. Any real antenna has a gain $G(\theta)$ defined as the ratio of power per unit solid angle radiated in a direction θ to the average power radiated per unit solid angle.

$$G(\theta) = \frac{P(\theta)}{P_0/4\pi} \qquad \qquad ... (6.2)$$

Where $P(\theta)$ is the power radiated per unit solid angle by the antenna.

P_0 is the total power radiated by the antenna.

$G(\theta)$ is the gain of the antenna at an angle θ.

- The reference for the angle θ is usually taken to be the direction in which maximum power is radiated, often called the boresight direction of the antenna. The gain of the antenna is then the value of $G(\theta)$ at angle $\theta = 0°$ and is a measure of the increase in flux density radiated by the antenna over that from an ideal isotropic antenna radiating the same total power. For a transmitter with output P_t watts driving a lossless antenna with gain G_t, the flux density in the direction of the antenna boresight at distance R meters is

$$F = \frac{P_t G_t}{4\pi R^2} \qquad \qquad ... (6.3)$$

- The product $P_t G_t$ is often called the effective isotropically radiated power or EIRP and it describes the combination of transmitter power and antenna gain in terms of an equivalent isotropic source with power $P_t G_t$ watts, radiating uniformly in all direction.

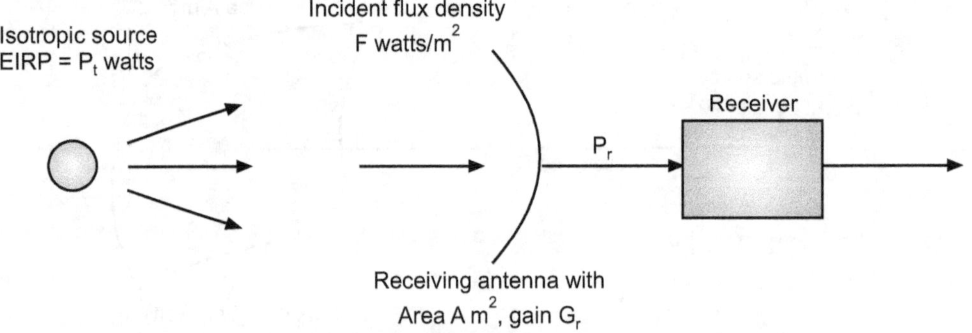

Fig. 6.3 : Power received by an ideal antenna with area Am^2

- If we had an ideal receiving antenna with an aperture area of $A m^2$, as shown in Fig. 6.3, we would collect power P_r watts given by

$$P_r = F \times A \text{ watts} \qquad \text{... (6.4)}$$

- A practical antenna with a physical aperture of $A_r m^2$ will not deliver the power given in Equation (6.4). Some of the energy incident on the aperture is reflected away from the antenna, and some is absorbed by lossy components. This reduction in efficiency is described by using an effective aperture A_e where

$$A_e = \eta_A A_r \qquad \text{... (6.5)}$$

- And η_A is the aperture efficiency of the antenna. The aperture efficiency η_A accounts for all the losses between the incident wavefront and the antenna output port: these include illumination efficiency or aperture taper efficiency of the antenna, which is related to the energy distribution produced by the feed across the aperture, and also other losses due to spillover, blockage, phase errors, diffraction effects, polarization, and mismatch losses.

- For paraboloidal reflector antennas, η_A is typically in the range 50 to 75, lower for small antennas and higher for large Cassegrain antennas.

- Horn antennas can have efficiencies approaching 90 thus the power received by a real antenna with a physical receiving area A_r and effective aperture area $A_e m^2$ is

$$P_r = \frac{P_t G_t A_e}{4\pi R^2} \text{ watts} \qquad \text{... (6.6)}$$

- Note that this equation is essentially independent of frequency if G_t and A_e are constant within a given band, the power received at an earth station depends only on the EIRP of the satellite, the effective area of the earth station antenna, and the distance R.

- A fundamental relationship in antenna theory is that the gain and area of an antenna are related by

$$G = 4\pi A_e/\lambda^2 \qquad \text{... (6.7)}$$

where λ is the wavelength (in meters) at the frequency of operation.

Substituting for A_e in Equation (6.6) gives

$$P_r = \frac{P_t G_t G_r}{(4\pi R/\lambda)^2} \qquad \text{... (6.8)}$$

- This expression is known as the link equation, and it is essential in the calculation of power received in any radio link. The frequency (as wavelength, λ) appears in this equation for received power because we have used the receiving antenna gain, instead of effective area. The term $[4\pi R/\lambda^2]$ is known as the path loss, L_p.

- It is not a loss in the sense of power being absorbed but it accounts for the way energy spreads out as an electromagnetic wave travels away from a transmitting source in three-dimensional space.

Collecting the various factors, we can write

$$\text{Power received} = \frac{\text{EIRP} \times \text{Receiving antenna gain}}{\text{Path loss}} \text{ Watts} \qquad \dots (6.9)$$

- In communication systems, decibel quantities are commonly used to simplify equations like Equation (6.9). In decibel terms, we have

$$P_r = \text{EIRP} + G_r - L_p \text{ dBW} \qquad \dots (6.10)$$

where
$$\text{EIRP} = 10 \log_{10} (P_t G_t) \text{ dBW}$$

$$G_r = 10 \log_{10} (4\pi A_e/\lambda^2) \text{ dB}$$

$$\text{Path loss } L_p = 10 \log_{10} (4\pi R/\lambda^2) = 20 \log_{10} (4\pi R/\lambda) \text{ dB}$$

- Equation (6.10) represents an idealized case, in which there are no additional losses in the link. It describes transmission between two ideal antennas in otherwise empty space.

- In practice, we will need to take account of a more complex situation in which we have losses in the atmosphere due to attenuation by oxygen, water vapor, and rain, losses in the antennas at each end of the link, and possible reduction in antenna gain due to mis-pointing.

- All of these factors are taken into account by the system margin but need to be calculated to ensure that the margin allowed is adequate. More generally, Equation (6.10) can be written

$$P_r = \text{EIRP} + G_r - L_p - L_a - L_{ta} - L_{ra} \text{ dBW} \qquad \dots (6.11)$$

where,
$$L_a = \text{Attenuation in atmosphere}$$

$$L_{ta} = \text{Losses associated with transmitting antenna}$$

$$L_{ra} = \text{Losses associated with receiving antenna}$$

- The conditions in Equation (6.11) are illustrated in Fig. 6.4. The expression dBW means decibels greater or less than 1 W (0 dBW). The units dBW and dBm (dB greater or less than 1 W and 1 mW) are widely used in communication engineering. EIRP, being the product of transmitter power and antenna gain is often quoted in dBW.

- Note that once a value has been calculated in decibels, it can readily be scaled if one parameter is changed. For example, if we calculated G_t for an antenna to be 48 dB, at a frequency of 4 GHz and wanted to know the gain at 6 GHz, we can multiply G_t by $(6/4)^2$.

- Using decibels, we simply add 20 log (6/4) $\vee$ 20 log (3) – 20 log (2) = 9.5 – 6 = 3.5 dB. Thus the gain of our antenna at 6 GHz is 51.3 dB.

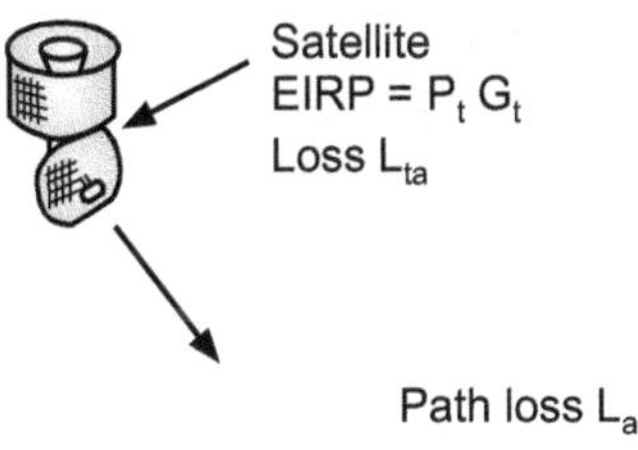

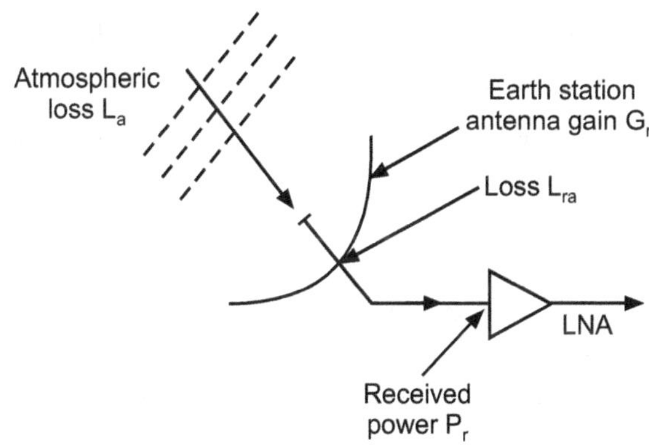

Fig. 6.4 : A satellite link. LNA, low noise amplifier

Example 6.1 : A satellite at a distance of 40,000 km from a point on the earth's surface radiates a power of 10 W from an antenna with a gain of 17 dB in the direction of the observer. Find the flux density at the receiving point, and the power received by an antenna at this point with an effective area of 10 m^2.

Solution:
$$F = \frac{P_t G_t}{4\pi R^2}$$

$$\frac{10 \times 50}{(4\pi \times (4 \times 10^7)^2)} 2.49 \times 10^{-14} \text{ W/m}^2$$

The power received with an effective collecting area of 10 m^2 is therefore

$$P_r = 2.49 \times 10^{-13} \text{ W}$$

The calculation is more easily handled using decibels. Noting that $10 \log_{10} 4\pi = 11.0$ dB

$$F \in \text{dB units} = 10 \log_{10} (P_t G_t) - 20 \log_{10} (R) - 11.0$$

$$= 27.0 - 152.0 - 11.0$$

$$= -136.0 \text{ dB (W/m}^2)$$

Then
$$P_r = -136.0 + 10.0 = -126 \text{ dBW}$$

Here we have put the antenna effective area into decibels greater than 10 m^2 = 10 dB = 1 m^2 greater than 1 m^2).

Example 6.2 : The satellite in Example 6.1 operates at a frequency of 11 GHz. The receiving antenna has a gain of 52.3 dB. Find the receiver power.

Solution: We know that

$$P_t = EIRP + G_t - Pathloss \text{ (dBW)}$$
$$EIRP = 27.0 \text{ dBW}$$
$$G_t = 52.3 \text{ dB}$$
$$Pathloss = (4\pi R/\lambda)^2 = 20 \log_{10}(4\pi R/\lambda) \text{ dB}$$
$$20 \log_{10}[(4\pi \times 4 \times 10^7)/(2.727 \times 10^{-2})] \text{ dB} = -205.3 \text{ dB}$$
$$P_t = 27.0 + 52.3 - 205.3 = -126.0 \text{ dBW}$$

- We have the same answer as in example 6.1 because the figure of 52.3 dB is the gain of a 10 m^2 aperture at a frequency of 11 GHz.

- Equation (6.10), with other parameters for antenna and propagation losses, is commonly used for calculation of received power in a microwave link and is set out as a link power budget in tabular form using decibels.

- This allows the system designer to adjust parameters such as transmitter power or antenna gain and quickly recalculate the received power.

- The received power P_t, calculated by Equations (6.6) and (6.8) is commonly referred to as carrier power, C. this is because most satellite links use either frequency modulation for analog transmission or phase modulation for digital transmission.

- In both of these modulation systems, the amplitude of the carrier is not changed when the data are modulated onto the carrier, so received carrier power C is always equal to received power P_r.

6.3 SYSTEM NOISE TEMPERATURE AND G/T RATIO

6.3.1 Noise Temperature

- Noise temperature provides a way of determining how much thermal noise is generated by active and passive devices in the receiving system, so it is a useful concept in communications receivers. At microwave frequencies, a black body with a physical temperature, T_p degrees Kelvin, generates electrical noise over a wide bandwidth.

  The noise power is given by

$$P_n = kT_pB_n \qquad \qquad \dots (6.12)$$

where, K = Boltzmann's constant = 1.39×10^{-23} J/K = -28.6 dBW/K/Hz

   T_p = Physical temperature of source in Kelvin degrees

   B_n = Noise bandwidth in which the noise power is measured, in hertz

- P_n is the available noise power (in watts) and will be delivered only to a load that is impedance matched to the noise source. The term kT_p is a noise power spectral density, in watts per hertz. The density is constant for all radio frequencies up to 300 GHz.

- The noise produced by the components of a low noise receiver needs to be described and can be conveniently done by equating the component to a black body radiator with an equivalent noise temperature, T_n kelvins.

- A device with a noise temperature of T_n kelvins (symbol k, not oK) produces at its output the same noise power as a black body at a temperature T_n degrees Kelvin followed by a noiseless amplifier with the same gain as the actual device.

- We can add noise temperatures to determine the total noise power in a receiver as shown in the following analysis, so the description of a low noise component by an equivalent noise source at the input of a noiseless amplifier is very useful. Note that the unit of noise temperature is in kelvins, and not degrees Kelvin. This distinction is often lost on the suppliers of consumer satellite broadcast receiving equipment.

- As satellite communication systems involves large distances, we are always working with weak signals and must make the noise level as low as possible to meet the C/N ratio requirements.

- This is done by making the bandwidth in the receiver large enough to allow the signal carrier and sidebands to pass unrestricted, while keeping the noise power to the lowest possible.

- The bandwidth used in Equation (6.12) should be the equivalent noise bandwidth. As we do not know the equivalent noise bandwidth and use the 3 dB bandwidth of our receiving system instead.

- The error introduced by using the 3 dB bandwidth is small when the filter characteristic of the receiver has steep sides.

- Noise temperatures from 30 K to 200 K can be achieved without physical cooling if GaAsFET (gallium arsenide field effect transistor) amplifiers are employed. GaAsFET amplifiers can be built to operate at room temperature with noise temperatures of 30 K at 4 GHz and 100 K at 11 GHz.

- Typically, noise temperatures increases with frequency, and an LNA for a 20 GHz receiver might have a noise temperature of 150 K.

- One might ask how an amplifier can have a noise temperature that is lower than its physical temperature. Noise temperature simply relates the noise produced by an amplifier to the thermal noise from a matched load at the same physical temperature placed at the input to the amplifier.

- If the amplifier produced no noise at all, its noise temperature would be 0 K. if the amplifier produces less noise than a matched load at the same physical temperature, its noise temperature will be lower than its physical temperature.

- To determine the performance of a receiving system we need to be able to find the total thermal noise power against which the signal must be demodulated.

- We do this by determining the system noise temperature, T_s. T_s is the noise temperature of a noise source, located at the input of a noiseless receiver, which gives the same noise power as the original receiver, measured at the output of the receiver and usually includes noise from the antenna.

- If the overall end-to-end gain of the receiver is G_{rx} (G_{rx} is a ratio, not in decibels) and its narrowest bandwidth is B_n Hz, the noise power at the demodulator input is

$$P_{no} = kT_sB_nG_{rx} \text{ watts} \qquad \qquad \text{... (6.13 a)}$$

where G_{rx} is the gain of the receiver from RF input to demodulator input.

The noise power referred to the input of the receiver is P_n where

$$P_n = kT_sB_n \text{ watts} \qquad \qquad \text{... (6.13 b)}$$

- Let the antenna deliver a signal power P_r watts to the receiver RF input. The signal power at the demodulator input is P_rG_{rx} watts, representing the power contained in the carrier and sidebands after amplification and frequency conversion within the receiver. Hence, the carrier-to-noise ratio at the demodulator is given by

$$\frac{C}{N} = \frac{P_rG_{rx}}{kT_sB_nG_{rx}} = \frac{P_r}{kT_sB_n} \qquad \qquad \text{... (6.14)}$$

- The gain of the receiver cancels out in Equation (6.14), so we can calculate C/N ratios for our receiving terminals at the antenna output port. This is convenient, because a link budget will find P_r at this point. Using a single parameter to encompass all of the sources of noise in a receiving terminal is very useful because it replaces several sources of noise in the receiver by a single system noise temperature, T_s.

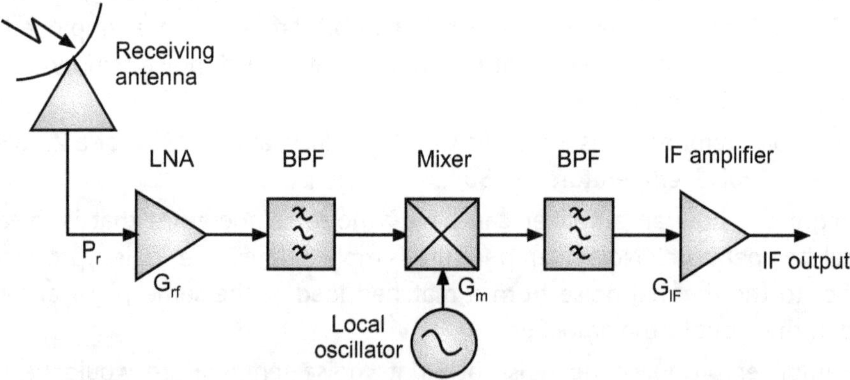

Fig. 6.5 : Simplified earth station receiver, BPF, bandpass filter

6.3.2 Calculation of System Noise Temperature

- Fig. 6.5 shows a simplified communications receiver with an RF amplifier and single frequency conversion, from its RF input to the IF output. This is the form used for all radio receivers, with few exceptions, known as the superhet (short for superheterodyne).

- The superhet receiver has three main subsystems: a front end (RF amplifier, mixer and local oscillator) an IF amplifier (IF amplifiers and filters), and a demodulator and baseband section.

- The RF amplifier in a satellite communications receiver must generate as little noise as possible, so it is called a low noise amplifier or LNA.

- The mixer and local oscillator form a frequency conversion stage that down converts the RF signal to a fixed intermediate frequency (IF), where the signal can be amplified and filtered accurately.

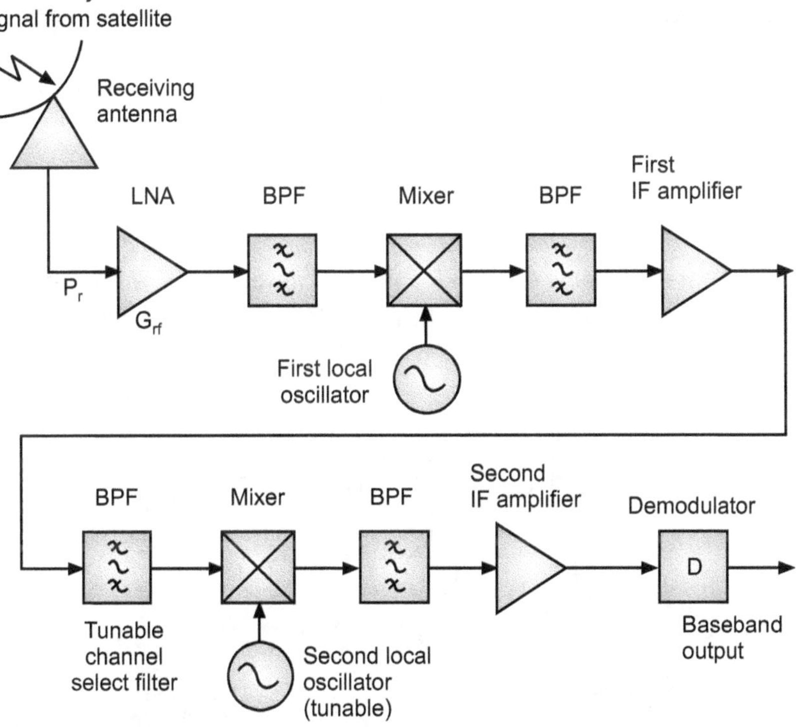

Fig. 6.6 : Double conversion earth station receiver

- Many earth station receivers use the double superhet configuration shown in Fig. 6.6 which has two stages of frequency conversion.

- The front end of the receiver is mounted behind the antenna feed and converts the incoming RF signals to a first IF in the range 900 to 1400 MHz this allows the receiver to accept all the signals transmitted from a satellite in a 500 MHz bandwidth at C band or Ku band, for example.

- The RF amplifier has a high gain and the mixer is followed by a stage of IF amplification. This section of the receiver is called a low noise block converter (LNB).

- The 900 – 1400 MHz signal is sent over a coaxial cable to a set top receiver that contains another down-converter and a tunable local oscillator. The local oscillator is tuned to convert the incoming signal from a selected transponder to a second IF frequency.

- The second IF amplifier has a bandwidth matched to the spectrum of the transponder signal. Direct broadcast satellite TV receivers at Ku band use this approach, with a second IF filter bandwidth of 20 MHz.

- The equivalent circuits in Fig. 6.7 (a) can be used to represent a receiver for the purpose of noise analysis. The noisy devices in the receiver are replaced by equivalent noiseless blocks with the same gain and noise generators at the input to each block such that the block produces the same noise at its output as the device it replaces.

- The entire receiver is then reduced to a single equivalent noiseless block with the same end-to-end gain as the actual receiver and a single noise source at its input with temperature T_n. The total noise power at the output of the IF amplifier of the receiver in Fig. 6.7 (a) is given by

$$P_n = G_{IF}kT_{IF}B_n + G_{IF}G_mkT_mB_n + G_{IF}G_mG_{RF}kB_n (T_{RF} + T_{in}) \qquad \text{... (6.15)}$$

where

G_{RF} G_m and G_{IF} are the gains of the RF amplifier, mixer, and IF amplifier, and T_{RF}, T_m and T_{IF} are their equivalent noise temperatures. T_{in} is the noise temperature of the antenna, measured at its output port.

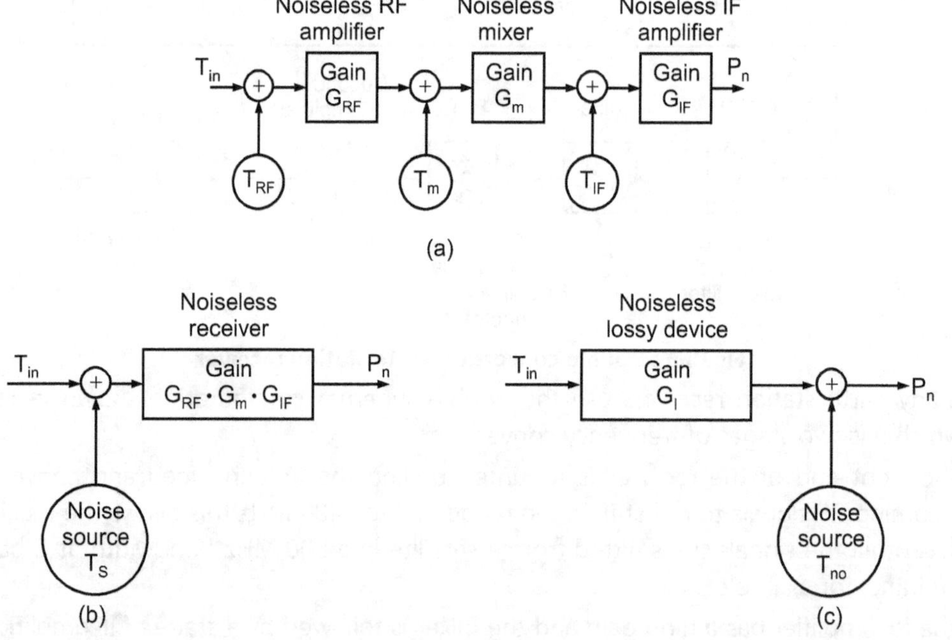

Fig. 6.7 : (a) Noise model of receiver. (b) Noisy model of receiver. All noisy units have been replaced by one noiseless amplifier, with a single noise source T_s at its input. (c) Noise model for a lossy device

Equation (6.15) can be written as

$$P_n = G_{IF} \, G_m \, G_{RF} \, [kT_{IF} \, B_n)/(G_{RF} \, G_m) + (k \, T_{in} \, B_m)/G_{RF} + T_{RF} \, T_{in})]$$

$$G_{IF} \, G_m \, G_{RF} \, k \, B_n \, [T_{RF} + T_{in} + T_{in}/G_{RF} + T_{IF}/G_{RF} \, G_m) \qquad \text{... (6.16)}$$

- The single source of noise shown in figure 6.7b with noise temperature T_s generates the same noise power P_n at its output if

$$P_n = G_{IF} \, G_m \, G_{RF} \, kT_s \, B_n \qquad \text{... (6.17)}$$

- The noise power at the output of the noise model in Figure 6.7b will be the same as the noise power at the output of the noise model in Fig. 6.7 (a) if

$$kT_sB_n = kB_n \, [T_{in} + T_{RF} + T_m/G_{IF} + T_{IF}/(G_mG_{RF})]$$

- Hence the equivalent noise source in Fig. 6.7 (b) has a system noise temperature T_s where

$$T_s = [T_{in} + T_{RF} + T_m/G_{RF} + T_{IF}/(G_mG_{RF})] \qquad \text{... (6.18)}$$

- Succeeding stages of the receiver contribute less and less noise to the total system noise temperature. Frequently, when the RF amplifier in the receiver front end has a high gain, the noise contributed by the IF amplifier and later stages can be ignored and the system noise temperature is simply the sum of the antenna noise temperature and the LNA noise temperature, so $T_s = T_{antenna} + T_{LNA}$. Note that the values for component gains in Equation (6.18) must be linear ratios, not in decibels.

- The noise model shown in Fig. 6.7 (b) replaces all the individual sources of noise in the receiver by a single noise source at the receiver input.

- This assumes that all the noise comes in from the antenna or is internally generated in the receiver.

- In some circumstances, we need to use a different model to deal with noise that reaches the receiver after passing through a lossy medium.

- Waveguide and rain losses are two examples.

- When raindrops cause attenuation, they radiate additional noise whose level depends on the attenuation. We can model the noise emission as a noise source placed at the output of the atmosphere, which is the antenna aperture.

- The noise model for an equivalent output noise source is shown in Fig. 6.7 (c) and produces a noise temperature T_{no} given by

$$T_{no} = T_p \, (1 - G_l) \qquad \text{... (6.19)}$$

Where G_l is the linear gain (less than unity, not in decibels) of the attenuating device or medium, and T_p is the physical temperature in degrees kelvin of the device or medium.

For an attenuation of A dB, the value of G_l is given by

$$G_l = 10^{A/10} \qquad \text{... (6.20)}$$

Example 6.3 : Suppose we have a 4 GHzreceiver with the following gains and noise temperatures : T_{in} = 25 K, G_{RF} = 23 dB, T_{RF} = 50 K, G_{IF} = 30 dB, T_{IF} = 1000 K, T_m = 500 K.

Calculate the system noise temperature assuming that the mixer has a gain G_m = 0 dB. Recalculate the system noise temperature when the mixer has a 10 dB loss. How can the noise temperature of the receiver be minimized when the mixer has a loss of 10 dB ?

Solution: The system noise temperature is given by Equation (6.18)

$$T_s = [25 + 50 + (500/200) + (1000/200)] = 87.5 \text{ K}$$

If the mixer had a loss, as is usually the case, the effect of the IF amplifier would be greater. For G_m = − 10 dB, the linear value is G_m = 0.1 as a ratio. Then

$$T_s = [25 + 50 + (500/200) + (1000/20)] = 137.5 \text{ K}$$

The lowest system noise temperatures are obtained by using a high gain LNA. Suppose we increase the LNA gain in this example to G_{RF} = 50 dB, giving ratio G_{RF} = 10^5

$$T_s = [25 + 50 + (500/105) + (1000/104)] = 75.1 \text{ K}$$

The high gain of the RFLNA amplifier has made the system noise temperature almost as low as it can go : T_s = T_{in} + T_{RF} = 75 K in this example. LNA for use in satellite receivers usually have gains in the range 40 − 55 dB.

Example 6.4 : The system illustrated in example 6.3 has an LNA with a gain of 50 dB. A section of lossy waveguide with an attenuation of 2 dB is inserted between the antenna and the RF amplifier. Find the new system noise temperature for a waveguide temperature of 300°K.

Solution : The waveguide loss of 2 dB (ratio 1.58) can be treated as a gain, G_l, that is less than unity : (G_l = 1/1.58 = 0.631). The lossy waveguide attenuates the incoming noise and adds noise generated by its own ohmic loss. The equivalent noise generator placed at the output of the section of waveguide that represents the noise generated by the waveguide has a noise temperature T_{wg}, where

$$T_{wg} = T_p (1 - G_l) = 300 (1 - 0.631) = 110.7 \text{ K}$$

The waveguide attenuates the noise from the antenna, so

$$T_{in} = 0.63 \times 25 = 15.8 \text{ K}$$

The new system noise temperature, referred to the input of the INA, is

$$T_s = [15.8 + 110.7 + 50 + (500/105) + (1000/104)] = 176.6 \text{ K}$$

We can refer the system noise temperature to the antenna output port by dividing the above result by G_l. this transfers the noise source from the LNA input to the waveguide input.

$$T_s = 176.6/0.631 = 279.9 \text{ K}$$

The new system noise temperature is 5.7 dB higher than the system noise temperature without the lossy waveguide.

Note : When the system noise temperature is low, each 0.1 dB of attenuation ahead of the RF amplifier will add approximately 6.6 K to the system noise temperature. (Using the formula in example 6.4 with T_p = 290° K, G_l = – 0.1 dB = 0.977 and T_{no} = 290 × 0.023 = 6.6 K. This is the reason for placing the front end of the receiver at the output of the antenna feed. Waveguide losses ahead of the LNA can have a disastrous effect on the system noise temperature of low noise receiving systems.

6.3.3 Noise Figure and Noise Temperature

- Noise figure is frequently used to specify the noise generated within a device. The operational noise figure (N/F) is defined by the following formula:

$$(N)F \; = \; \frac{(S/N)_{in}}{(S/N)_{out}} \qquad \qquad \text{... (6.21)}$$

- Because noise temperature is more useful in satellite communication systems, it is best to convert noise figure to noise temperature, T_d. The relationship is

$$T \; = \; T_0 \, (NF - 1) \qquad \qquad \text{... (6.22)}$$

- Where the noise figure is a linear ratio, not in decibels, and where T_0 is the reference temperature used to calculate the standard noise figure-usually 290 K. NF is frequently given in decibels and must be converted to a ratio before being used in Equation (6.18).

- Table 6.3 gives a comparison between noise figure and noise temperature over the range encountered in typical systems.

Table 6.3 : Comparison of Noise Temperature and Noise Figure

Noise temperature (K)	0	20	40	60	80	100	120	150	200	290
Noise Figure (dB)	0	0.29	0.56	0.82	1.06	1.29	1.50	1.81	2.28	3.0
Noise temperature (K)	400	600	800	1,000	1500	2000	3000	5000	10000	
Noise Figure (dB)	3.8	4.9	5.8	6.5	7.9	9.0	10.5	12.6	15.5	

Example 6.5 : An amplifier has a quoted noise figure of 2.5 dB. What is its equivalent noise temperature?

Solution : Using Equation (6.22)

$$T_d \; = \; 290 \, (1.78 - 1) = 226 \text{ K}$$

This value of noise temperature could then be used in Equation (6.17), with other appropriate data, to calculate system noise temperature.

6.3.4 G/T Ration for Earth Stations

- The link equation can be rewritten in terms of (C/N) at the earth station

$$\frac{C}{N} = \left[\frac{P_t G_t G_r}{kT_s B_n}\right]\left[\frac{\lambda}{4\pi R}\right]2 = \left[\frac{P_t G_t}{kB_n}\right]\left[\frac{\lambda}{4\pi R}\right]2\left[\frac{G_r}{T_s}\right]$$

- Thus $C/N \propto G_t/T_s$ and the terms in the square brackets are all constants for a given satellite system. The ratio G_r/T_s, which is usually quoted as simply G/T in decibels, with units dB/K, can be used to specify the quality of a receiving earth station or a satellite receiving system, since increasing G_r/T_s increases the received C/N ratio.

- Satellite terminals may be quoted as having a negative G/T which is below 0 dB/k. This simply means that the numerical value of G_r is smaller than the numerical value of T_s.

Example 6.6 : An earth station antenna has a diameter of 30 m, has an overall efficiency of 68 and is used to receive a signal at 4150 MHz. At this frequency, the system noise temperature is 79 K when the antenna points at the satellite at an elevation angle of 28°. What is the earth station G/T ratio under these conditions? If heavy rain causes the sky temperature to increase so that the system noise temperature rises to 99 K, what is the new G/T value?

Solution: First calculate the antenna gain. For a circular aperture :

$$G_t = \eta_A 4\pi A/\lambda^2 = \eta_A(\pi D/\lambda)^2$$

At 4150 MHz, $\lambda = 0.0723$ m. Then

$$G = 0.68 \times (\pi\, 30/0.0723)^2 = 1.16 \times 10^6 \text{ V } 60.0 \text{ dB}$$

Converging T_s into dBK

$$T_s = 10 \log 79 = 19.0 \text{ dBK}$$

$$G/T = 60.6 - 19.0 = 41.6 \text{ dB/K}$$

If $T_s = 88$ K $\in$ heavy rain, G/T = 60.6 − 19.4 = 41.2 dB/K

6.4 DESIGN OF DOWNLINKS

- The two main objectives in design of any satellite communication are meeting a minimum C/N ratio for a specified percentage of time, and carrying the maximum revenue earning traffic at minimum cost.

- There is an old saying that "an engineer is a person who can do for a dollar what any fool can do for one hundred dollars." This applies to satellite communication systems.

- Any satellite link can be designed with very large antennas to achieve high C/N ratios under all conditions, but the cost will be high.

- The art of good system design is to reach the best compromise of system parameters that meets the specification at the lowest cost.

- For example, if a satellite link is designed with sufficient margin to overcome a 20 dB rain fade rather than a 3 dB fade, earth station antennas with seven times the diameter are required.

- All satellite communication links are affected by rain attenuation. In the 6/4 GHz band the effect of rain on the link is small. In the 14/11 GHz (Ku band) and even more so in the 30/20 GHz (Ka) band, rain attenuation becomes all important.

- Satellite links are designed to achieve reliabilities of 99.5 to 99.99, averaged over a long period of time, typically a year.

- This means the C/N ratio in the receiver will fall below the minimum permissible value for proper operation of the link for between 0.5 and 0.1 of the specified time, the link is then said to suffer an outage.

- The time period over which the percentage of time is measured can be a month, sometimes the worst month in attenuation terms, or a year. Rain attenuation is a very variable phenomenon, both with time and place.

- C-band links can be designed to achieve 99.99 reliability because the rain attenuation rarely exceeds 1 or 2 dB.

- The time corresponding to 0.01 of a year is 52 min; at this level of probability the rain attenuation statistics are usually not stable and wide fluctuations occur from year to year.

- Outages occur in heavy rain, usually in thunderstorms, and thunderstorm occurrence varies widely. A link designed to have outages totaling 52 min each year may well have outages of several hours one year and none the next.

- Most Ka-band links cannot be designed to achieve 99.99 reliability because rain attenuation generally exceeds 10 dB and often 20 dB for 0.01 of the time.

- Outage times of 0.1 to 0.5 of a year (8 to 40 h) are usually tolerated in Ka-band links. The allowable outage time for a link depends partly on the traffic carried.

- Telephone traffic needs real-time channels that are maintained for the duration of a call, so C band or Ku band is used for voice channels with sufficient link margin that outage times are small.

- Internet transmissions are less affected by short outages and generally do not require a real-time channel, making Ka band better suited for Internet access.

6.4.1 Link Budgets

- C/N ratio calculation is simplified by the use of link budgets. A link budget is a tabular method for evaluating the received power and noise power in a radio link.

- Link budgets invariably use decibel units for all quantities so that signal and noise powers can be calculated by addition and subtraction. Since it is usually impossible to design a satellite link at the first attempt, link budgets make the task much easier because, once a link budget has been established, it is easy to change any of the parameters and recalculate the result.

- Tables 6.4 (a) and 6.4 (b) show a typical link budget for a C-band downlink using a global beam on a GEO satellite and a 9 m earth station antenna.

- The link budget must be calculated for an individual transponder, and must be repeated for each of the individual links. In a two-way satellite communication link there will be four separate links, each requiring a calculation of C/N ratio.

- When a bent pipe transponder is used the uplink and downlink C/N ratios must be combined to give an overall C/N . In this section we will calculate the C/N ratio for a single link.

Table 6.4 (a) : C-band GEO Satellite Link Budget in Clear Air

C-band Satellite Parameters	
Transponder saturated output power	20 W
Antenna Gain, on axis	20 dB
Transponder Bandwidth	36 MHz
Downlink frequency band	3.7 – 4.2 GHz
Signal FM-TV analog signal	
FM-TV signal bandwidth	30 MHz
Minimum permitted overall C/N in receiver	9.5 dB
Receiving C-Band Earth Station	
Downlink frequency	4.00 GHz
Antenna gain, on axis, 4 GHz	49.7 dB
Receiver IF bandwidth	27 MHz
Receiving system noise temperature	75 K
Downlink Power Budget	
P_t = satellite transponder output power, 20 W	13.0 dBW
B_0 = Transponder output backoff	– 2.0 dB
G_t = Satellite antenna gain, on axis	20.0 dB

G_r = Earth station antenna gain	49.7 dB
L_p = Free space path loss at 4 GHz	– 196.5 dB
L_{ant} = Edge of beam loss for satellite antenna	– 3.0 dB
L_a = Clear air atmospheric loss	– 0.2 dB
L_m = other losses	– 0.5 dB
P_r = Received power at earth station	– 119.5 dBW
Downlink Noise Power Budget in Clear Air	
K = Boltzmann's constant	– 228.6 dBW/K/hz
T_s = System Noise temperature, 75 K	18.8 dBK
B_n = Noise bandwidth, 27 MHz	74.3 dBHz
N = Receiver noise power	– 135.5 dBW
C/N ratio in receiver in clear air	
C/N = P_r – N = – 119.5 dBW – (– 135.5 dBW) = 16.0 dB	

Table 6.4 (b) : C-band Downlink Budget in Rain

P_{rca} = Received power at earth station in clear air	– 119.5 dBW
A = Rain attenuation	1.0 dB
P_{rain} = Received power at earth station in rain	–120.5 dBW
N_{ca} = Receiver noise power in clear air	– 135.5 dBW
ΔN_{rain} = Increase in noise temperature due to rain	2.3 dB
N_{rain} = Receiver noise power in rain	– 1.33.2 dBW
C/N ratio in receiver in rain	
C/N = P_{rain} – N_{rain} = – 120.5 dBW – (– 133.2 dBW) =	12.7 dB

- Link budgets are usually calculated for a worst case, the one in which the link will have the lowest C/N ratio.

- The factors which contribute to a worst case scenario include, location of an earth station at the edge of the satellite coverage zone where the received signal is typically 3 dB lower than in the center of the zone because of the satellite antenna pattern, maximum path length from the satellite to the earth station, a low elevation angle at the earth station giving the highest atmospheric path attenuation in clear air, and maximum rain attenuation on the link causing loss of received signal power and an increase in receiving system noise temperature.

- The edge of the coverage pattern of the satellite antenna and the longest path usually go together.

- This may not always be the case however, when a satellite has a multiple beam antenna. Earth station antennas are assumed to be pointed directly at the satellite, and therefore operate at their on-axis gain.

- If the antenna is mispointed, a loss factor is included in the link budget to account for the reduction in antenna gain.

- The calculation of carrier to noise ratio in a satellite link is based on the two equations, for received signal power and receiver noise power that were presented in sections 6.1 and 6.2. Equation (6.11) gives the received carrier power in dB watts as

$$P_r = EIRP + G_r - L_p - L_a - L_r - L_t \ dBW \qquad \qquad \text{... (6.24)}$$

- A receiving terminal with a system noise temperature T_s K and a noise bandwidth B_n Hz has a noise power P_n referred to the output terminals of the antenna where

$$P_n = kT_sB_n \ watts \qquad \qquad \text{... (6.25)}$$

- The receiving system noise power is usually written in decibel units as

$$N = K + T_s = B_n \ dBW \qquad \qquad \text{... (6.26)}$$

- Where k is Boltzmann's constant − 228.6 dBW/K/Hz), T_s is the system noise temperature in dBK and B_n is the noise bandwidth of the receiver in dBHz. Note that because we are working in units of power, all decibel conversions are made as $10 \ \log_{10} (T_s)$ or $10 \ \log_{10} (B_n)$. The $20 \ \log_{10}$ factor used in the calculation of path loss results from the $(4\pi R/\lambda)^2$ term in the path loss equation.

6.4.2 Link Budget Example : C-band Downlink for Earth coverage Beam

- The satellite used in this example [see tables 6.4 (a) and 6.4 (b)] is in geostationary earth orbit and carries 24C-band transponders, each with a bandwidth of 36 MHz the downlink band is 3.7 − 4.2 GHz and the satellite uses orthogonal circular polarizations to provide an effective RF bandwidth of 864 MHz.

- The satellite provides coverage of the visible earth, which subtends an angle of approximately 17° from a satellite in a geostationary orbit, by using a global beam antenna.

- Since antenna beamwidth and gain are linked together [3 dB beamwidth $\approx \sqrt{(3300)}/G$ where G is a ratio, not in decibels], the on-axis gain of the global beam antenna is approximately 20 dB.

- However, we must make the link budget calculation for an earth station at the edge of the coverage zone of the satellite where the effective gain of the antenna is 3 dB lower, at 17 dB. The C/N ratio for the downlink is calculated in clear air conditions and also in heavy rain.

- An antenna with a gain of 20 dB has an effective aperture diameter of 5.6 wavelengths $[G = \eta(\pi D/\lambda)^2]$, which gives D = 0.42 m at a frequency of 4 GHz. The calculation of C/N ratio is made at a mid-band frequency of 4 GHz.

- The saturated output power of the transponder is 20 W = 13 dBW. We will assume an output back-off of 2 dB, so that the power transmitted by the transponder is 11 dBW.

- Hence the on-axis EIRP of the transponder and antenna is P_tG_t = 11 + 20 = 31 dBW. The transmitted signal is a single 30 MHz bandwidth analog FMTV channel in this example.

- Following common practice for analog TV transmission, the receiver noise bandwidth is set to 27 MHz, slightly less than the 30 MHz bandwidth of the FMTV signal.

- The receiving earth station has an antenna with an aperture diameter of 9 m and a gain of 49.7 dB at 4 GHz and a receiving system noise temperature of 75 K in clear air conditions.

The G/T ratio for this earth station is G/T = 49.7 − $10 \log_{10} 75$ = 30.9 dBk^{-1}.

- The maximum path length for a GEO satellite link is 40,000 km, which gives a path loss of 195.6 dB at 4 GHz (λ = 0.075 m). We must make an allowance in the link budget for some losses that will inevitably occur on the link.

- At C band, propagation losses are small, but the slant path through the atmosphere will suffer a typical attenuation of 0.2 dB in clear air.

- We will allow an additional 0.5 dB margin in the link design to account for miscellaneous losses, such as antenna mispointing, polarization mismatch, and antenna degradation, to ensure that the link budget is realistic.

- The earth station receiver C/N ratio is first calculated for clear air conditions, with no rain in the slant path. The C/N ratio is then recalculated taking account of the effects of rain.

- The minimum permitted overall C/N ratio for this link is 9.5 dB, corresponding to the FM threshold of the analog satellite TV receiver. Table 6.4 (a) shows that we have a downlink C/N of 16.0 dB in clear air, giving a link margin of 6.5 dB. This link margin is available in clear air conditions, but will be reduced when there is rain in the slant path.

- Heavy rain in the slant path can cause up to 1 dB of attenuation at 4 GHz, which reduces the received power by 1 dB and increases the noise temperature of the receiving system.

- Using the output noise model with a medium temperature of 273 K and a total path loss for clear air plus rain of 1.2 dB (ratio of 1.32), the sky noise temperature in rain is

$$T_{sky} = 273 \times (1 - 1/1.32) = 66 \text{ K}$$

- In clear air the sky noise temperature is about 13 K, the result of 0.2 dB of clear air attenuation. The noise temperature of the receiving system has therefore increased by $(66 - 13)$ K = 53 K to 75 + 53 K = 128 K with 1 dB rain attenuation in the slant path, from a clear air value of 75 K. This is an increase in system noise temperature of 2.3 dB.

- Now the link budget can be very easily adjusted to account for heavy rain in the slant path without having to recalculate the C/N ratio from the beginning. The received carrier power is reduced by 1 dB because of the rain attenuation and the system noise temperature is increased by 2.3 dB. Table 6.4 b shows the new downlink budget in rain.

- The C/N ratio in rain has a margin of 3.2 dB over the minimum permissible C/N ratio of 9.5 dB for an analog FM-TV transmission.

- The C/N margin will translate into a higher than needed S/N ratio in the TV baseband signal, and can be traded off against earth station antenna gain to allow the use of smaller (and therefore lower cost) antenna.

- We should always leave a small margin for unexpected losses if we want to guarantee a particular level of reliability in the link. In this case, we will use a 2 dB margin and examine how the remaining 1/2 dB of link margin can be traded against other parameters in the system.

- A reduction in earth station antenna gain of 1.2 dB is a reduction in the gain value, as a ratio, of 1.32. Antenna gain is proportional to diameter squared, so the diameter of the earth station antenna can be reduced by a factor of $\sqrt{1.32} = 1.15$ from 9 m to 7.8 m.

- We could transmit a QPSK signal from the satellite instead of an analog FM signal.

- Using the 27 MHz noise bandwidth receiver, we could transmit a digital signal at 54 Mbps using QPSK, but would require a minimum C/N ratio in the receiver of 14.6 dB, allowing a 1 dB implementation margin and a minimum BER of 10^{-6}.

- The link margin would be $- 1.9$ dB under heavy rain conditions, so we would need to increase the earth station antenna diameter by a factor of 1.55 to 13.9 m to provide a C/N ratio of 14.6 dB under heavy rain conditions.

- A 54-Mbps digital signal could carry seven digital TV signals using MPEG-2 compression, a much more attractive proposition than carrying a single analog FM-TV signal, although at the cost of a larger earth station antenna.

- Global beam antennas are not widely used, although most Intelsat satellites carry them.

- Regional TV signal distribution is much more common, so the C-band link in table 6.4 a and 6.4 b is more likely to use a regional antenna, serving the United States, for example, with a 6° by 3° beam. The gain of a typical satellite antenna providing coverage of the 48 contiguous states is 32.0 dB on axis ($G = 33,000/\theta_1 \times \theta_2$), which is 12.0 dB higher than the on-axis gain of a global beam.

- Using the link budget in tables 6.4 (a) and 6.4 (b), we can trade the extra 12 dB gain of a regional coverage satellite antenna for a reduction in earth station antenna dimensions. For the example of a 9.0 m antenna receiving analog FM-TV, we could reduce the antenna diameter by a factor of 4 to 2.25 m (approximately 7 ft 6 inch diameter). This is the smallest size of antenna used by home satellite TV systems operating in C band.

- The above examples shows the use of link budget to study different combinations of system parameters.

- Most satellite link analyses do not yield the wanted result at the first try, and the designer or analyst must use the link budget to adjust system parameters until an acceptable result is achieved.

6.5 SATELLITE SYSTEMS USING SMALL EARTH STATIONS

- Many applications are there in which satellites carry only one or two telephone or data channels, or a direct-broadcast TV signal and use small, low-cost earth stations.

- Satellite transmitted power and satellite antenna beamwidth are the two parameters in the equation for received power that can be adjusted at the satellite which makes feasible to use a small receiving antenna.

- In domestic satellite systems, to provide coverage over the region for which the system is designed to serve, narrow beams can be used for transmitting from the spacecraft.

- Since the dimensions of the antennas that can be mounted on most of the spacecraft are limited, the coverage zone cannot be made arbitrarily small.

- The earth's disk subtends an angle of about 17° when viewed from geostationary orbit, and can be illuminated with a microwave horn having an aperture of a few wavelengths in diameter.

- At 4 GHz, to obtain a 4° spot beam, a dish of 1.4 m in diameter is needed. As the frequency is increased, the diameter of the spacecraft antenna in wavelengths is increased for a given dish diameter, making it feasible to use more directive beams.

- However, unless a switched or multiple beam system is used, the single transmit (or receive) beam must cover the whole region that the domestic satellite serves.

- As an example, consider the problem of providing service to the 48 contiguous states of the United States, known as Conus, as illustrated in the constraints then become apparent.

- Viewed from a geostationary orbit, at a longitude of around 100°W, the continental United States subtends an angle of about 3° in the latitude plane (N-S) and 6° in the longitude plane (E – W).

- Regardless of the frequency used, an aperture antenna to produce a single beam with 3 dB beamwidths of 6° by 3° has dimensions approximately 13λ by 26λ and a gain of 32 dB.

- For a receiving earth station at an edge of the coverage zone, the gain of the satellite antenna in that direction is typically 3 dB lower, or 29 dB.

- For the GEO satellite system shown in the received carrier level and C/N ratio can readily be calculated for an earth station with a 3 m antenna at the edge of the coverage zone, using a transponder with an output power of 5 W at 4 GHz, transmitting a single carrier. Ignoring all losses and using a receiving antenna gain of 40.0 dB   (63 efficiency)

$$P_r \ = \ 7.0 + 29.0 - 196.5 + 40.0 = \ - \ 120.5 \ dBW$$

- The noise power at the input to a low noise receiver with noise bandwidth of 30 MHz and system noise temperature of 100 K is

$$N = kT_sB_n \ = \ - \ 228.6 + 20.0 + 74.8 = \ - \ 133.8 \ dBW$$

- Thus for this system the C/N ratio is 13.3 dB. This is some 3.8 dB above an FM threshold of 9.5 dB and provides an adequate margin for an operational system.

- These figures are typical of those used in U.S. domestic satellite systems designed for distribution of television programs to cable TV networks and broadcast TV stations using a single C-band transponder for each video signal and FM with analog video signals.

6.5.1 Direct Broadcast TV

- Direct Broadcast Satellite Television (DBS – TV) originally started in Europe in the 1980s using analog FM transmission in Ku band. It achieved a reasonable measure of success, due in part to the much slower introduction of cable TV systems in Europe than occurred in the United States.

- In the 1990s, digital transmission became possible, and several systems were developed in the United States in the 12.2 to 12.7 GHz band allocated to DBS-TV services.

- In the United States, DIRECTV, a system built by a consortium led by Hughes, has been very successful and had over 10 million customers by year-end 2000, offering two hundred television and audio channels.

- Another DBS-TV provider in the United States, Echostar, offered similar services and had 4 million customers in year 2000. TV and audio channels are available from DBS-TV providers in a mixture of subscription packages, much like cable TV companies offer, and as pay per view for individual movies and special events.

- In rural areas of the United States, DBS-TV offers hundreds of television channels in place of the three or four terrestrial broadcasting stations that are typically available.

- In city areas, DBS-TV offers an alternative to cable television at a similar cost.

- The development of low cost Ku-band antennas and receivers, and high speed digital integrated circuits specifically for DBS television, has made DBS-TV practical.

- The 12.2 to 12.7 GHz band was set aside for exclusive use by DBS-TV satellites in geostationary orbit so that high power transponders could be used on specially designed DBS-TV satellites. Typical transponder output levels are 100 to 200 W with a flux density at the earth's surface of up to $- 100$ dBW/m^2.

- The satellites can carry 16 transponders, with a typical total transmitted RF power of 2.6 kW, higher than for other commercial satellites. DBS-TV satellites are large and heavy; generally use a three axis stabilized design, and has a large area of solar cells to generate the power required by the transponders.

- Typical mass for a DBS-TV satellite is 6800 kg at launch, among the largest commercial GEO satellites.

- The flux density at the earth surface produced by a DBS-TV 160 W transponder is typically in the range $- 105$ to $- 115$ dBW/m^2, which allows small receiving antennas (dishes) to be used for DBS-TV reception, with diameters in the range $0.45 - 0.75$ m. The small dish required for DBS-TV reception played a critical part in the acceptance and success of DBS-TV in the united states.

- Previously, DBS-TV reception of cable television signals was only possible at C band and Ku band with 2.0 to 3.5 m dishes.

- The local governments of many cities and towns refused to permit these large dishes in residential areas, although they became popular in rural areas and an estimated 4 M systems were sold in the 1980s. Congress passed laws in the 1990s that prevented local governments from restricting the use of antennas less than 1 m in diameter, opening up a large market for Ku-band DBS-TV services.

- The high flux density created by powerful transponders makes sharing of the DBS-TV frequency bands impossible, so the 12 GHz DBS band, known as the Broadcast Satellite Service (BSS) band, is allocated exclusively for television broadcasting.

- The small home receiving antenna has a wide beam, typically 4° for a 0.45 m (18 inch) dish, which forces wide spacing of DBS-TV satellites to avoid interference by the signals from adjacent DBS-TV satellites. A 9° spacing in the GEO arc has been adopted in the United States, which restricts the number of DBS-TV satellites that can be placed in geostationary orbit to serve the United States.

- In the 1990s the U.S. FCC successfully auctioned spectrum and orbital locations for DBS-TV satellites, raising hundreds of millions of dollars from companies that foresaw a profitable commercial venture.

- The DBS-TV system must provide a received signal power at the small receiving antenna that has an adequate C/N margin in clear sky conditions.

- Heavy rain will cause attenuation that exceeds the link margin, so occasional outages will be experienced, especially during the summer months when thunderstorms and heavy rain are more frequent.

- The C/N margins used in DBS-TV systems are usually quite small to avoid the need for a large receiving antenna. The selection of a C/N margin is a design tradeoff between the outage level that customers can be expected to tolerate, the maximum allowable diameter of the receiving dish antenna, and the power output from the satellite transponders.

- Typical designs with receiving antennas in the 0.5 to 0.75 m range and 100-200 W satellite transponders yield rain attenuation margins of 3 to 8 dB depending on the location of the receiving terminal within the satellite antenna coverage, and outage times totaling 10 to 40h per year.

- These link margins are much lower than those found in high capacity communication systems. Availability of the link has been exchanged for a smaller earth terminal antenna and lower equipment costs to the user.

- Discussing rain attenuation in Ku-band, we will use statistics that are representative of many locations in the central and eastern parts of the United States, where typical path attenuation in rain exceeds 3 dB for 0.2 (15h) and 6 dB for 0.01 (52 min) of an average year.

- Such attenuation levels at the given time percentage are typical of many temperate latitude locations such as the west coast of the United States, central United States, Virginia, and other states north of Virginia on the east cost of the United States, Europe, Chile, Uruguay, and New Zealand.

- DIRECTV. claims that receiving systems designed for their DBS-TV transmissions have an average annual availability exceeding 99.7, which corresponds to an outage time of 0.3 of the year, or about 25h.

- For much of the United States, this corresponds to rain attenuation in the slant path of 3 dB and requires a link margin of 5.7 dB when allowance is made for the increase in antenna noise temperature that accompanies 3 dB of rain attenuation.

Table 6.5 : Link Budget for ku-band DBS-TV Receiver

DBS-TV Terminal Received Signal Power	
Transponder output power, 160 W	22.0 dBW
Antenna beam on-axis gain	34.3 dB
Path loss at 12.2 GHz, 38,000 m path	205.7 dB
Receiving antenna gain, on axis	33.5 dB
Edge of beam loss	– 3.0 dB
Clear sky atmospheric loss	– 0.4 dB
Miscellaneous losses	– 0.4 dB
Received power C	– 119.7 dBW
DBS-TV terminal receiver noise power	
Boltzmann's constant, k	–228.6 dBW/K/Hz
System noise temperature, clear sky, 145 K	21.6 dBK
Receiver noise bandwidth, 20 MHz	73.0 dBHz
Noise power, N	– 134.0 dBW
DBS-TV terminal C/N in clear sky	
Clear sky overall C/N	14.3 dB
Link margin over 8.6 dB threshold	5.7 dB
Link availability throughout United States	Better than 99.7

- A representative link budget for a GEO DBS-TV system serving the United States is shown in Table 6.5. The threshold C/N value is set at 8.6 dB, corresponding to a system using QPSK with an implementation margin of 0.8 dB, half rate forward error correction that produces 6 dB of coding gain, and a maximum BER of 10^{-5}.

- This requires a clear sky C/N ratio in the DBS-TV receiver of 8.6 + 5.7 = 14.3 dB. The link budget in table 6.5 shows the required clear sky C/N is achieved for a receiver located on the – 3 dB contour of the satellite antenna beam.

- A receiver located in the center of this beam would have a clear sky C/N 3 dB higher, and a corresponding fade margin of 8.7 dB, sufficient to ensure only a few outages each year.

- In table 6.5 a transponder output power of 160 W is used, with no backoff because a single QPSK signal is transmitted. The satellite antenna gain is 34.3 dB on axis, corresponding to a high efficiency antenna with a beam that is shaped to cover the land mass of the United States.

- The beam is approximately 5.5° wide in the E-W direction and 2.5° in the N-S direction. The resulting coverage zone, taking account of the earth's curvature is approximately 4000 km E-W and 2000 km N-S a maximum path length of 38,000 km is used in this example.

- The receiving antenna is a high efficiency design with a front fed offset parabolic reflector 0.45 m in diameter and a circularly polarized feed. The offset design ensures that the feed system does not block the aperture of the antenna, which increases its efficiency.

- The gain of this antenna is 33.4 dB at 12.0 GHz with aperture efficiency of 67. The receiver is located at the − 3 dB contour of the transmitting antenna, and miscellaneous losses of 0.4 dB for clear sky attenuation at 12 GHz and 0.4 dB for receive antenna mispointing and other losses are allowed. The result is a received carrier power of − 119.7 dBW in clear conditions.

- The noise power budget of the link is based on a receiver noise bandwidth of 20 MHz. The IF filters in the receiver must be designed to match the symbol rate of the transmitted signal, and to approximate a Root Raised Cosine (RRC) transfer function.

- The noise bandwidth of all RRC filters is always equal to the symbol rate of the digital transmission. In the DBS-TV system described in table 6.5, a QPSK signal with a symbol rate of 20 Mbps is assumed, which results in a receiver noise bandwidth of 20 MHz.

- The 20 Mbps QPSK transmission delivers a bit rate of 40 Mbps, but the half rate FEC coding reduces the data rate to 20 Mbps. A 20 Mbps data stream can carry three live compressed digital video signals using MPEG2 encoding, or up to 10 prerecorded and processed video signals.

- The antenna noise temperature is set at 35 K in clear sky conditions, and a 12 GHz LNA with 110 K noise temperature is used. The result is a noise power of − 134.0 dBW referred to the input of the LNA and a clear sky C/N ratio of 14.3 dB.

- This is a worst case result for clear sky conditions, since most of the DBS-TV receivers will lie inside the −3 dB contour of the satellite beam.

- DBS-TV receivers can be used outside the −3 dB contour of the satellite beam, but will have a lower link margin and consequently more outages per year, if heavy rain occurs frequently. For example, a receiver on the −5 dB contour of the satellite beam will have a link margin of 3.7 dB, which would allow about 2 dB of rain attenuation before the C/N reaches threshold.

- If the user is in a relatively dry area, for example, central Canada, the performance of the receiving system may be quite acceptable. The C/N ratio in the home receiver will fall when rain is in the path between the satellite and the receiving antenna. Much of the reduction in C/N ratio is caused by an increase in the sky noise temperature and $\left(\dfrac{C}{N}\right)_{dn}$ are determined when rain attenuation is present.

- The first step is to determine the total path attenuation, A in dB, which is the sum of the clear sky path attenuation due to atmospheric gaseous absorption, A_{ca} and attenuation due to rain, A_{rain}.

$$A = A_{ca} + A_{rain} \text{ dB} \qquad \text{... (6.29)}$$

- The sky noise temperature resulting from a path attenuation A_{total} dB is found from the output noise model using an assumed medium temperature of 270 K for the rain.

$$T_{sky} = 270 \times (1 - 10^{-A/10}) \text{ K} \qquad \text{... (6.30)}$$

- The antenna noise temperature may be assumed to be equal to the sky noise temperature, although practically not all of the incident noise energy from the sky is output by the antenna, and so a coupling coefficient, η_c of 90 to 95 is often used when calculating antenna noise temperature in rain. Thus antenna noise temperature may be calculated as

$$T_A = \eta_c \times T_{sky} \text{ K} \qquad \text{... (6.31)}$$

- Almost all satellite receivers use a high gain LNA as the first element in the receiver front end. This makes the contribution of all later parts of the receiver to the system noise temperature negligible. System noise temperature is then given by

$$T_{strain} = T_{LNA} + T_{AK} \qquad \text{... (6.32)}$$

- In equation (6.32), the LNA is assumed to be placed right at the feed horn so that there is no waveguide or coaxial run between the feed horn of the antenna and the LNA. We will assume that there are no feed losses. The increase in noise power, ΔN_{rain} dB, caused by the increase in sky noise temperature is given by

$$\Delta N_{rain} = 10 \log_{10}\left[\frac{kT_{srain}B_n}{kT_{sca}B_n}\right] = 10 \log_{10}\left[\frac{T_{srain}}{T_{sca}}\right] \text{ dB} \qquad \text{... (6.33)}$$

where T_{sca} is the system noise temperature in clear sky conditions.

- The received power is reduced by the attenuation caused by the rain in the slant path, so in rain the value of carrier power is C_{rain} where

$$C_{rain} = C_{ca} - A_{rain} \text{ dB} \qquad \qquad \text{... (6.34)}$$

the resulting $\left(\dfrac{C}{N}\right)_{dn\,rain}$ value when rain intersects the downlink is given by

$$\left(\dfrac{C}{N}\right)_{dnrain} = \left(\dfrac{C}{N}\right)_{dnca} - A_{rain} - \Delta N_{rain} \text{ dB} \qquad \qquad \text{... (6.35)}$$

where $\left(\dfrac{C}{N}\right)_{dnca}$ is the downlink C/N ratio in clear sky conditions.

- If a linear (bent pipe) transponder is used, the $\left(\dfrac{C}{N}\right)_{up}$ ratio must be combined with $\left(\dfrac{C}{N}\right)_{dnrain}$ to yield the overall $\left(\dfrac{C}{N}\right)_{0}$ ratio for the link. Many digital systems use regenerative transponders that provide constant output power regardless of uplink attenuation provided that the received C/N ratio at the satellite is above the threshold of the onboard processing demodulator. In this case the value of $\left(\dfrac{C}{N}\right)_{dnrain}$ will be used as the overall $\left(\dfrac{C}{N}\right)_{0}$ value in rain for the link.

6.6 UPLINK DESIGN

- The uplink design is easier than the downlink in many cases, since an accurately specified carrier power must be presented at the satellite transponder and it is often feasible to use much higher power transmitters at earth stations that can be used on a satellite.

- However, VSAT systems use earth stations with small antennas and transmitter powers below 5 W, giving low uplink EIRP.. Satellite telephone handsets are restricted to transmitting at power levels below 1 W because of the risk of EM radiation hazards. In mobile systems the uplink from the satellite telephone is usually the link with the lowest C/N ratio.

- The cost of transmitters tends to be high compared with the cost of receiving equipment in satellite communication systems.

- The major growth in satellite communications has been in point-to-multipoint transmission, as in cable TV distribution and direct broadcast satellite television.

- One high power transmit earth station provides service via a DBS satellite to many low cost receive only stations, and the high cost of the transmitting station is only a small part of the total network cost.

- The satellite transponder is a quasilinear amplifier and the received carrier level determines the output level. Where a traveling wave tube is used as the output High Power Amplifier (HPA) in the transponder, as is often the case, and FDMA is employed, the HPA must be run with a predetermined backoff to avoid intermodulation products appearing at the output.

- The output backoff is typically 1 to 3 dB when more than one signal is present in the transponder, and is determined by the uplink carrier power level received at the spacecraft.

- Accurate control of the power transmitted by the earth station is therefore essential, which is easily achieved in a fixed network of earth stations.

- Where a very large number of earth stations access a single transponder output backoff of 5 to 7 dB may be required to maintain intermodulation products at a sufficiently low level.

- Even with a single access to the transponder (i.e. only one carrier present) some backoff is normally applied to avoid the PM-AM conversion that occurs when modulated signals are transmitted through nonlinear devices.

- Each earth station transmitter power is set by the power level required at the input to the transponder. This can be done in one of two ways. Either a specific flux density is required at the satellite, or a specific power level is required at the input to the transponder.

- Early Intelsat C-band satellites required high flux densities to saturate their transponders, in the range -73.7 to -67.5 dBW/m^2, depending on the transponder gain setting. This is a high flux density which requires a large earth station and a powerful transmitter generating up to 3 kW. Domestic GEO satellites operating into North America generally require lower flux densities allowing the use of smaller earth station antennas. At C-band, a typical uplink earth station transmits 100 W with a 9-meter antenna, giving a flux density at the satellite of -100 W/m^2.

- Although flux density at the satellite is a convenient way to determine earth station transmit EIRP requirements, analysis of the uplink requires calculation of the power level at the input to the transponder so that the uplink C/N ratio can be found.

- The link equation is used to make this calculation, using either a specified transponder C/N ratio or a required transponder output power level. When a C/N ratio is specified for the transponder, the calculation of required transmit power is straightforward. Let $\left(\dfrac{C}{N}\right)_{up}$ be the specified C/N ratio in the transponder, measured in a noise bandwidth B_n Hz. The bandwidth B_n Hz is the bandwidth of the band pass filter in the IF stage of the earth station receiver for which the uplink signal is intended.

- Even if B_n is much less than the transponder bandwidth, it is important that the uplink C/N ratio be calculated in the bandwidth of the receiver, not the bandwidth of the transponder. The noise power referred to the transponder input is N_{xp}W where

$$N_{xp} = k + T_{xp} + B_n \text{ dBW} \qquad \qquad \dots (6.36)$$

where T_{xp} is the system noise temperature of the transponder in dBK and B_n is in units of dBHz.

The power received at the input to the transponder is P_{rxp}

$$P_{rxp} = P_t + G_t + G_r - L_p - L_{up} \text{ dBW} \qquad \qquad \dots (6.37)$$

- Where $P_t G_t$ is the uplink earth station EIRP in dBW, G_r is the satellite antenna gain in dB in the direction of the uplink earth station and L_p is the path loss in dB. The factor L_{up} dB accounts for all uplink losses other than path loss. The value of $\left(\dfrac{C}{N}\right)_{up}$ at the LNA input of the satellite receiver is given by,

$$C/N = 10 \log_{10} [P_r/(kT_s B_n)] = P_{rxp} - N_{xp} \text{ dB} \qquad \qquad \dots (6.38)$$

- The earth station transmitter output power P_t is calculated from Equation (6.23) using the given value of C/N in Eq.(6.38) and the noise power N_{xp} calculated from Equation (6.36). Note that the received power at the transponder input is also given by

$$P_{rxp} = N + C/N \text{ dBW} \qquad \qquad \dots (6.39)$$

- The earth station transmitter output power P_t can also be calculated from the output power of the transponder and transponder gain when these parameters are known and a bent pipe transponder is used. In general

$$P_{rxp} = P_{sat} - BO_0 - G_{xp} \text{ dBW} \qquad \qquad \dots (6.40)$$

- Where P_{sat} is the saturated power output of the transponder in dBW, BO_0 is the output backoff in dB and G_{xp} is the gain of the transponder in dB.

- With small diameter earth stations, a higher power earth station transmitter is required to achieve a similar satellite EIRP.

- This has the disadvantage that the interference level at adjacent satellites rises, since the small earth station antenna inevitably has a wider beam.

- Thus it is not always possible to trade off transmitter power against uplink antenna size.

- There is a specification for transmit station antenna patterns, designed to minimize interference from adjacent uplinks.

- It is the uplink interference problem that determines satellite spacing and limits the capacity of the geostationary orbit in any frequency band. Fig. 6.9 shows the ITU-R (formerly CCIR) specification, $G(\theta) = (32 - 25 \log_{10} \theta)$ dB, where θ is in degrees, for $\theta > 1$ degree off axis, for satellites spaced by 3°.

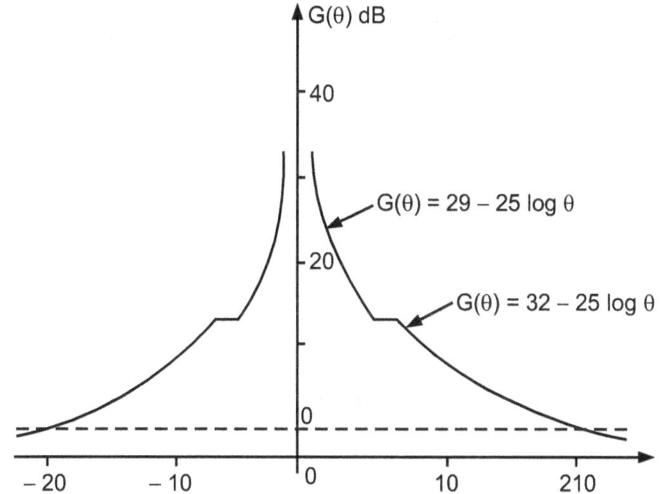

Fig. 6.8 : ITU-R specifications on the side-lobe envelope of transmit antenna patterns for 2° GEO satellite spacing.

- To increase the capacity of the crowded geostationary orbit arc south of the United States, the FCC introduced new regulations in 1983 requiring better control of 6 GHz earth station antenna transmit patterns so that intersatellite spacing could be reduced to 2°.

- The same specification has now been adopted by the ITU-R for the entire geostationary arc.

- The requirement is for the transmit antenna pattern to lie below $G(\theta) = (29 - 25 \log_{10} \theta)$ dB in the range $1° < \theta < 7°$ from the antenna boresight and $G(\theta) = (32 - 25 \log_{10} \theta)$ dB beyond 7°. The required antenna pattern envelope is shown in Fig.. 6.10.

- At frequencies above 10 GHz, for example, 14.6 GHz and 30 GHz, propagation disturbances in the form of fading in rain cause the received power level at the satellite to fall.

- This lowers the uplink C/N ratio in the transponder, which lowers the overall $\left(\dfrac{C}{N}\right)_0$ ratio in the earth station receiver when a linear (bent pipe) transponder is used on the satellite. Uplink Power Control (UPC) can be used to combat uplink rain attenuation.

- The transmitting earth station monitors a beacon signal from the satellite, and watches for reduction in power indicating rain fading on the downlink.

- Automatic monitoring and control of transmitted uplink power is used in 14 GHz uplink earth stations to maintain the uplink C/N ratio in the satellite transponder during periods of rain attenuation.

- New generations of Ka-band satellites employ uplink power level detection at the satellite. A control link to each uplink earth station closes the loop.

- The downlink is always at a different frequency from the uplink, so a downlink attenuation of AdB must be scaled to estimate uplink attenuation.

- The scaling factor used is typically $(f_{up}/d_{wodn})^u$ where a is typically between 2.0 and 2.4. For example, an uplink station transmitting at 14.10 GHz to a Ku-band satellite monitors the satellite beacon at 11.45 GHz.

- The uplink attenuation is therefore given by

$$A_{up} = A_{down} \times (f_{up}/f_{down})^a \text{ dB} \qquad \dots (6.41)$$

- Where A_{up} the estimated uplink is rain attenuation and A_{down} is the measured downlink rain attenuation.

- For a value of a = 2.2 ^ (f_{up}/f_{down}) 1.222 the factor $(f_{up}/f_{down})^a$ is 1.56. Hence a downlink rain attenuation of 3 dB would give an estimated uplink attenuation of 4.7 dB. This uplink attenuation value applies only to rain and does not include gaseous attenuation or scintillation, which require different scaling ratios.

- Unless a certain amount of attenuation is built up in the link we cannot apply Uplink power control. This is typically around 2 dB for the downlink due to measurement inaccuracies, corresponding to about 3 dB for a Ka-band uplink.

- As rain begins to affect the link between the earth station and satellite,the uplink C/N ratio in the transponder will fall until UPC starts to operate in the earth station transmitter.

- The transponder C/N ratio will then remain relatively constant until the UPC system reaches the maximum available transmit power. Further attenuation on the uplink will cause the C/N ratio in the transponder to fall.

Example 6.7 : A transponder of a Ku-band satellite has a linear gain of 127 dB and a nominal output power at saturation of 5 W. the satellite's 14 GHz receiving antenna has a gain of 26 dB on axis, and the beam covers western Europe.

Calculate the power output of an uplink transmitter that gives an output power of 1 W from the satellite transponder at a frequency of 14.45 GHz when the earth station antenna has a gain of 50 dB and there is a 1.5 dB loss in the waveguide run between the transmitter and antenna. Assume that the atmosphere introduces a loss of 0.5 dB under clear sky conditions and that the earth station is located on the – 2dB contour of the satellite's receiving antenna.

If rain in the path causes attenuation of 7 dB for 0.01 of the year, what output power rating is required for the transmitter to guarantee that a 1 W output can be obtained from the satellite transponder for 99.99 of the year if uplink power control is used?

Solution : The input power required by the transponder is simply the output power minus the transponder gain, so

$$P_{in} = 0 \text{ dBW} - 127 \text{ dB} = -127 \text{ dBW}$$

the uplink power budget is given by Equation (6.11)

$$P_r = EIRP + G_r - L_p - L_{at} - L_{ta} \text{ dBW}$$

Rearranging and putting in the appropriate losses

$$P_t = P_r - G_t - G_r + L_p + L_{ta} + L_{at} - L_{pt} \text{ dBW}$$

where L_{ta} is the waveguide loss, L_{at} is the atmospheric loss, and L_{pt} is the pointing loss (antenna pattern loss). Then assuming a path length of 38,500 km

$$P_t = -127.0 - 50 - 26 + 207.2 + 1.5 + 0.5 + 2.0 \text{ dBW}$$

that is

$$P_t = 7.2 \text{ dBW} \vee 5.2 \text{ W}$$

if we provide an extra 7 dB of output power to compensate for fading on the path due to rain, the transmitter output power will be

$$P_{train} = 7.2 + 7 = 14.2 \text{ dBW} \vee 26.3 \text{ W}$$

6.7 DESIGN FOR SPECIFIED C/N : COMBINING C/N AND C/I VALUES IN SATELLITE LINKS

- The BER or S/N ratio in the baseband channel of an earth station receiver is determined by the ratio of the carrier power to the noise power in the IF amplifier at the input to the demodulator.

- The noise present in the IF amplifier comes from many sources.

- So far in our analysis of uplinks and downlinks we have considered only the receiver thermal noise and noise radiated by atmospheric gases and rain in the slant path.

- When a complete satellite link is engineered, the noise in the earth station IF amplifier will have contributions from the receiver itself, the receiving antenna, sky noise, the satellite transponder from which it receives the signal, and adjacent satellites and terrestrial transmitters which share the same frequency band.

- The method presented for adding these noise contributions together in a hypothetical reference circuit. This was the standard technique used in CCIR (now ITU-R).

- More recently, addition of C/N and C/I (carrier-to-interface) ratios has been widely used, and is easier to apply than the reference circuit approach, although both methods will lead to the same result.

- The latter method using C/N values is presented here.

- When more than one C/N ratio is present in the link, we can add the individual C/N ratios reciprocally to obtain an overall C/N ratio, which we will denote here as $(C/N)_0$.

- The overall $(C/N)_0$ ratio is what would be measured in the earth station at the output of the IF amplifier

$$(C/N)_0 = 1 / \left[\frac{1}{\left(\dfrac{C}{N}\right)_1} + \frac{1}{\left(\dfrac{C}{N}\right)_2} + \frac{1}{\left(\dfrac{C}{N}\right)_3} + \dots \right] \qquad \dots (6.42)$$

- This is sometimes referred to as the reciprocal C/N formula. The C/N values must be linear ratios, NOT decibel values. Since the noise power in the individual C/N ratios is referenced to the carrier power at that point, all the C values in Equation (6.42) are the same.

- Expanding the formula by cross multiplying gives the overall $(C/N)_0$ as a power ratio, not in decibels

$$(C/N)_0 = \frac{1}{\dfrac{N_1}{C} + \dfrac{N_2}{C} + \dfrac{N_3}{C} + \dots} = C/(N_1 + N_2 + N_3 + \dots) \qquad \dots (6.43)$$

In decibel units: $\qquad (C/N)_0 = C dBW - 10 \log_{10} (N_1 + N_2 + N_3) \dots W) \, dB \qquad \dots (6.44)$

- Note that $(C/n)_{dn}$ cannot be measured at the receiving earth station. The satellite always transmits noise as well as signal, so a C/N ratio measurement at the receiver will always yield $(C/N)_0$, the combination of transponder and earth station C/N ratios.

- To calculate the performance of a satellite link the uplink $(C/N)_{up}$ ratio in the transponder and the downlink $(C/N)_{dn}$ in the earth station receiver need to be determined.

- Any interference present, either in the satellite receiver or the earth station receiver must be considered. One case of importance is where the transponder is operated in a FDMA mode and intermodulation products ($\Im$) are generated by the transponder's nonlinear input-output characteristic. If the IM power level in the transponder is known, a C/I value can be found and included in the calculation of $(C/N)_0$ ratio.

- Interference from adjacent satellites is likely whenever small receiving antennas are used, as with VSATs (very small aperture terminals) and DBS-TV receivers.

- Since C/N values are usually calculated from power and noise budgets, their values are typically in decibels. There are some useful rules of thumb for estimating $(C/N)_0$ from two C/N values :

  - If the C/N values are equal, as in the example above, $(C/N)_0$ is 3 dB lower than either value.

  - If one C/N value is 10 dB smaller than the other value, $(C/N)_0$ is 0.4 dB lower than the smaller of the C/N values.

- If one C/N value is 20 dB or more greater than the other C/N value, the overall $(C/N)_0$ is equal to the smaller of the two C/N values within the accuracy of decibel calculations ($\pm$ 0.1 dB).

Example 6.8 : Thermal noise in an earth station receiver results in a $(C/N)_{dn}$ ratio of 20.0 dB. A signal is received from a bent pipe transponder with a carrier to noise ratio $(C/N)_{up}$ 20.0 dB. What is the value of overall $(C/N)_0$ at the earth station? If the transponder introduces intermodulation products with (C/I) ratio 24 dB, what is the overall $(C/N)_0$ ratio at the receiving earth station?

Solution: Using Equation (6.42) and noting down that (C/N) = 20.0 dB corresponds to a (C/N) ratio of 100

$$\left(\frac{C}{N}\right)_0 = \left[\frac{1}{\dfrac{1}{\left(\dfrac{C}{N}\right)_{up}} + 1/(C/N)_{dn}}\right] = \left[\frac{1}{0.01 + 0.01}\right] = 50 \text{ V } 17.0 \text{ dB}$$

The intermodulation (C/I) value of 24.0 dB corresponds to a ratio of 0.004. The overall $(C/N)_0$ value is then

$$\left(\frac{C}{N}\right)_0 = \left[\frac{1}{0.01 + 0.01 + 0.004}\right] = 41.7 \text{ V } 16.2 \text{ dB}$$

6.7.1 Overall $(C/N)_0$ with Uplink and Downlink Attenuation

- Most satellite links are designed with link margins to allow for attenuation that may occur in the link or increases in noise power caused by interference. (Interference is almost always treated as though it were white noise, regardless of whether the interfering signal actually has a uniform spectral power distribution or Gaussian stastics.

- When the interference has known characteristics, such as a depolarized cochannel or a jamming signal, cancellation techniques can be used to reduce the level of interference).

- The effect of a change in the uplink C/N ratio has a different impact on overall $(C/N)_0$ depending on the operating mode and gain of the transponder.

- There are three different transponder types or operating modes:

Linear transponder:	$P_{out} = P + G_{xp}$	dBW
Nonlinear transponder:	$P_{out} = P + G_{xp} - \Delta G$	dBW
Regenerative transponder:	$P_{out} = $ constant	dBW

- Where P_{in} is the power delivered by the satellite's receiving antenna to the input of the transponder, P_{out} is the power delivered by the transponder HPA to the input of the satellite's transmitting antenna, G_{xp} is the gain of the transponder, and all parameters are in decibel units.

- The parameter ΔG is dependent on P_{in} and accounts for the loss of gain caused by the nonlinear saturation characteristics of a transponder which is driven hard to obtain close to its maximum power output the gain is effectively falling as the input power level increases.

- The maximum output power from a transponder is called the saturated output power and is the nominal transponder power output rating that is usually quoted.

- The transponder input-output characteristic is highly nonlinear when operated at this output power level.

- When a transponder is operated close to its saturated output power level, digital waveforms are changed, resulting in intersymbol interference (ISI), and FDMA operation results in the generation of intermodulation products by multiplication of the individual signals.

- Transponders are usually operated with output backoff, to make the characteristic more nearly linear.

- The exact amount of output backoff required in any given application depends on the specific characteristics of the transponder and the signals it carries. Typical values of output backoff are 1 dB for a single FM or PSK carrier to 3 dB for FDMA operation with several carriers.

- The corresponding input backoff values might be 3 dB and 5 dB, but the individual transponder characteristics must be known to make an accurate assessment. For convinence in this text, we will frequently assume linear transponder operation when calculating the overall $\left(\dfrac{C}{N}\right)_0$ ratio, even if this may not, in fact, be the case.

6.7.2 Uplink and Downlink Attenuation in Rain

- Rain attenuation affects uplinks and downlinks differently. We usually assume that rain attenuation is occurring on either the uplink or the downlink, but not on both at the same time.

- This is usually true for earth stations that are well separated geographically, but not if they are close together (< 20 km). Heavy rain occurs with a somewhat random geographic distribution for less than 1 of the time, so the probability of significant attenuation occurring on both the uplink and downlink simultaneously is small. In the following analysis of uplink and downlink attenuation effects, it will be assumed that one link is attenuated and the other is operating in clear air.

6.7.3 Uplink Attenuation and (C/N)up

- The transponder receiver noise temperature does not change significantly when rain is present in the uplink path to the satellite.

- The satellite receiving antenna beam is always sufficiently wide that it sees a large area of the (warm) earth's surface and local noise temperature variations are insignificant.

- The noise temperature of the earth seen by a GEO satellite varies from a maximum of 270 K for a satellite antenna beam over Africa and northern Europe, to a minimum of 250 K over the Pacific Ocean.

- The corresponding system noise temperature for the transponders on a GEO satellites is in the range 400 to 500 K there is effectively no increase in uplink noise power when heavy rain is present in the link between an earth station and a satellite because the satellite antenna beam sees the tops of cumulonimbus clouds above the rain, which are always colder than 270 K, instead of the earth's surface.

- Rain attenuation on the uplink path to the satellite reduces the power at the satellite receiver input, and thus reduces $(C/N)_{up}$ in direct proportion to the attenuation on the slant path. If the transponder is operating in a linear mode, the output power will be reduced by the same amount, which will cause $\left(\dfrac{C}{N}\right)_{dn}$ to fall by an amount equal to the attenuation on the uplink. When both $(C/N)_{up}$ and $\left(\dfrac{C}{N}\right)_{dn}$ are reduced by A_{up}dB, the value of $\left(\dfrac{C}{N}\right)_{0}$ is reduced by exactly the same amount, A_{up}dB. Hence for the case of a linear transponder and rain attenuation in the uplink of A_{up}dB.

$$\left(\frac{C}{N}\right)_{up\ link\ rain} = \left(\frac{C}{N}\right)_{0\ clear\ air} - A_{up}\ dB \quad \text{Linear transponder} \qquad \text{... (6.45)}$$

- If the transponder is nonlinear, the reduction in input power caused by uplink attenuation of A_{up} dB results in a smaller reduction in output power, by an amount ΔG.

$$\left(\frac{C}{N}\right)_{up\ link\ rain} = \left(\frac{C}{N}\right)_{0\ clear\ air} - A_{up}\ \Delta G dB \quad \text{Non-linear transponder} \qquad \text{... (6.46)}$$

- If the transponder is digital and regenerative, or incorporates an Automatic Gain Control (AGC) system to maintain a constant output power level.

$$\left(\frac{C}{N}\right)_{up\ link\ rain} = \left(\frac{C}{N}\right)_{0\ clear\ air} \quad \text{dB Regenerative transponder or AGC} \qquad \text{... (6.47)}$$

- The above equation will hold only if the received signal is above threshold and the BER of the recovered digital signal in the transponder is small.

- If the signal falls below threshold, the uplink will contribute significantly to the BER of the digital signal at the receiving earth station.

6.7.4 Downlink Attenuation and $(C/N)_{dn}$

- During rain the earth station receiver noise temperature can change very significantly in the downlink path from the satellite.

- Particularly in heavy rain, the sky noise temperature can increase to close to the physical temperature of the individual raindrops.

- A reasonable temperature to assume for temperate latitudes in a variety of rainfall rates is $270K$ will increase the receiving antenna temperature markedly above its clear air value. The result is that the received power level, C, is reduced and the noise power, N, in the receiver increases. The result for downlink C/N is given by Equation (6.48)

$$(C/N)_{dnrain} = (C/N)_{dnclearair} - A_{rain} - \Delta N_{rain} \text{ dB} \qquad \dots (6.48)$$

the overall C/N is then given by

$$(C/N)_0 = 1/[1/(C/N)_{dnrain} + 1/(C/N)_{up}] \text{ dB} \qquad \dots (6.49)$$

- As noted earlier, unless we are making a loop-back test, we will assume that the value of $(C/N)_{up}$ is for clear air, and remains constant regardless of the attenuation on the downlink.

6.7.5 System Design for Specific Performance

- A typical two way satellite communication link consists of four separate paths: an outbound uplink path from one terminal to the satellite and an outbound downlink to the second terminal; and an inbound uplink from the second terminal to the satellite and an inbound downlink to the first terminal.

- The links in the two directions are independent and can be designed separately, unless they share a single transponder using FDMA.

- A broadcast link, like the DBS-TV system is a one way system, with just one uplink and one downlink.

6.7.6 Satellite Communication Link Design Procedure

In short the design procedure for a one way satellite communication link can be summarized into following 10 steps. The return link design follows the same procedure.

- To determine the frequency band in which the system must operate. Comparative designs may be required to help make the selection.

- To determine the communications parameters of the satellite. Estimate values that are not known.

- To determine the parameters of the transmitting and receiving earth stations.

- Start at the transmitting earth station. Establish an uplink budget and a transponder noise power budget to find $\left(\dfrac{C}{N}\right)_{up}$ in the transponder.

- Based on transponder gain or output backoff, find the output power of the transponder.

- Establish a downlink power and noise budget for the receiving earth station. Calculate $\left(\dfrac{C}{N}\right)_{dn}$ and $\left(\dfrac{C}{N}\right)_{0}$ for a station at the edge of the coverage zone(worst case).

- Calculate S/N or BER in the baseband channel. Find the link margins.

- Evaluate the result and compare with the specification requirements. Change parameters of the system as required to obtain acceptable $\left(\dfrac{C}{N}\right)_{0}$ or S/N or BER values. This may require several trial designs.

- Determine the propagation conditions under which the link must operate. Calculate outage times for the uplinks and downlinks.

- Redesign the system by changing some parameters if the link margins are in adequate. Check that all parameters are reasonable, and that the design can be implemented within the expected budget.

6.8 SYSTEM DESIGN EXAMPLES

The following sample system designs demonstrate how the ideas developed in this unit can be applied to the design of satellite communication systems.

Table 6.7 : System and Satellite Specification

Ku-band Satellite Parameters	
Geostationary at 73°W longitude, 28 Ku-band transponders	
Total RF output power	2.24 kW
Antenna gain, on axis (transmit and receive)	31 dB
Receive system noise temperature	500 K
Transponder saturated output power: Ku band	80 W
Transponder bandwidth: Ku-band	54 MHz
Signal Compressed digital video signals with transmitted symbol rate of 43.2 Mspa Minimum permitted overall $\left(\dfrac{C}{N}\right)_{0}$ in receiver	9.5 dB

Transmitting Ku-Band Earth Station	
Antenna diameter	5 m
Aperture efficiency	68
Uplink frequency	14.15 GHz
Required C/N in Ku-band transponder	30 dB
Transponder HPA output backoff	1 dB
Miscellaneous uplink losses	0.3 dB
Location: −2 dB contour of satellite receiving antenna	
Receiving Ku-Band Earth Station	
Downlink frequency	11.45 GHz
Receiver IF noise bandwidth	43.2 MHz
Antenna noise temperature	30 K
LNA noise temperature	110 K
Required overall $\left(\dfrac{C}{N}\right)_0$ in clear air	17 dB
Miscellaneous downlink losses	0.2 dB
Location: − 3 dB contour of satellite transmitting antenna	
Rain Attenuation and Propagation Factors	
Ku-Band Clear Air Attenuation	
Uplink 14.15 GHz	0.7 dB
Downlink 11.45 GHz	0.5 dB
Rain attenuation	
Uplink 0.01 of year	6.0 dB
Downlink 0.01 of year	5.0 dB

6.8.1 System Design Example

- This example examines the design of a satellite communication link using a Ku-band geostationary satellite with bent pipe transponders to distribute digital TV signals from an earth station to many receiving stations throughout the United States.

- The design requires that an overall C/N ratio of 9.5 dB be met in the TV receiver to ensure that the video signal on the TV screen is held to an acceptable level.

- The uplink transmitter power and the receiving antenna gain and diameter are determined for each system.

- The available link margins for each of the systems are found and the performance of the systems is analyzed when rain attenuation occurs in the satellite-earth paths. The advantages and disadvantages of implementing uplink power control are considered.

- In this example, the satellite is located at 73°W. However, for international registration of this satellite location, the location would be denoted as 287°E. The link budgets developed in the examples below use decibel notation throughout.

- The satellite and earth stations are specified in Table 6.6, and Fig. 6.11 shows an illustration of the satellite television distribution system.

6.8.2 Ku-band Uplink Design

- We must find the uplink transmitter power require to achieve $(C/N)_{up}$ = 30 dB in clear air atmospheric conditions.

- We will first find the noise power in the transponder for 43.2 MHz bandwidth, and then add 30 dB to find the transponder input power level.

Uplink Noise Power Budget	
k = Boltzmann's constant	228.6 dBW/K/Hz
T_s = 500 K	27.0 dBK
B = 43.2 MHz	76.4 dBHz
N = transponder noise power	125.2 dBW

- The received power level at the transponder input must be $30dB$ greater than the noise power.

    P_r = Power at transponder input = − 95.2 dBW.

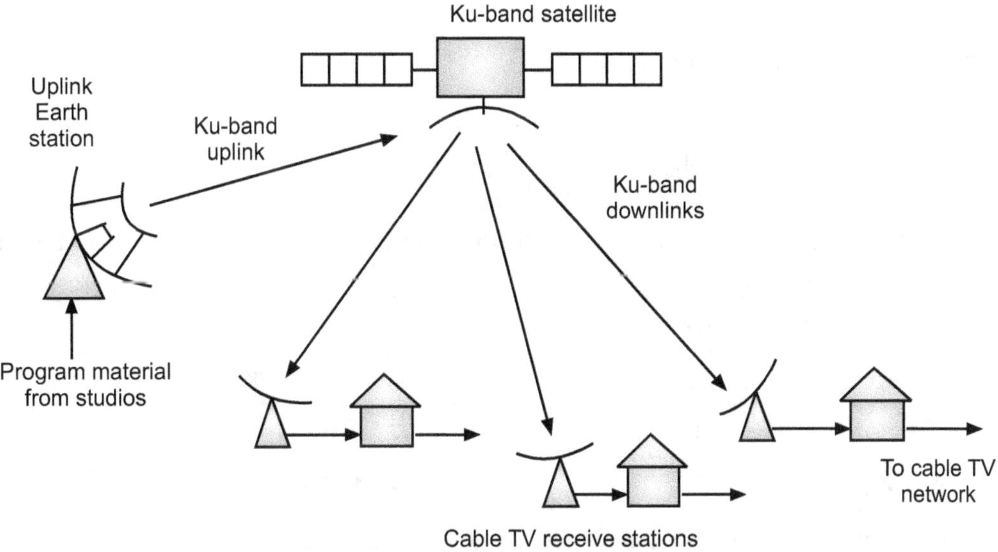

Fig. 6.9 : Satellite television distribution systems

- The uplink antenna has a diameter of 5 m and an aperture efficiency of 68. At 14.15 GHz the wavelength is 2.120 cm = 0.0212 m the antenna gain is :

$$G_t = 10 \log [0.68 \times (\pi D/\lambda)^2] = 55.7 \text{ dB}$$

The free space path loss is $L_p = 10 \log [(4\pi R/\lambda)^2] = 207.2$ dB

Uplink Power Budget	
P_t = Earth station transmitter power	P_t dBW
G_t = Earth station antenna gain	55.7 dB
G_r = Satellite antenna gain	31.0 dB
L_p = Free space path loss	−207.2 dB
L_{ant} = E/S on 2 dB contour	−2.0 dB
L_m = Other losses	−1.0 dB
P_r = Received power at transponder	P_t − 123.5 dB

- The required power at the transponder input to meet the $\left(\dfrac{C}{N}\right)_{up}$ = 30 objective is −95.2 dBW. Hence

$$P_t - 123.5 \text{ dB} = -95.2 \text{ dBW}$$
$$P_t = 28.3 \text{ dBW} \vee 675 \text{ W}$$

- This is a relatively high transmit power so we need to increase the transmitting antenna diameter to increase its gain, allowing a reduction in transmit power.

6.8.3 Ku-Band Downlink Design

- The first step is to calculate the downlink $\left(\dfrac{C}{N}\right)_{dn}$ that will provide $(C/N)_0$ = 17 dB when $\left(\dfrac{C}{N}\right)_{up}$ 30 dB. From Equation (6.43)

$$1(C/N)_{dn} = 1/(C/N)_0 - 1/(C/N)_{up} \qquad \text{(not in dB)}$$

Thus
$$1/(C/N)_{dn} = 1/50 - 1/1000 = 0.019$$
$$(C/N)_{dn} = 52.6 \ldots 17.2 \text{ dB}$$

- We must find the required receiver input power to give $(C/N)_{dn}$ = 17.2 dB and then find the receiving antenna gain, G_r.

Downlink Noise Power Budget	
K = Boltzmann's constant	228.6 dBW/K/Hz
T_s = 30 + 110 K = 140 K	21.5 dBK
B_n = 43.2 MHz	76.4 dBHz
N = transponder noise power	130.7 dBW

- The power level at the earth station receiver input must be 17.2 dB greater than the noise power in clear air.

P_r = power at earth station receiver input = $- 130.7$ dBW + 17.2 dB = $- 113.5$ dBW

- We need to calculate the path loss at 11.45 GHz. At 14.15 GHz path loss was 207.2 dB . At 11.45 GHz path loss is

$$L_p = 207.2 - 20 \log_{10} (14.15/11.45) = 205.4 \text{ dB}$$

- The transponder is operated with 1 dB output backoff, so the output power is 1 dB below 80 W (80 W ... 19.0 dBW)

$$P_t = 19 \text{ dBW} - 1 \text{ dB} = 18 \text{ dBW}$$

Downlink Power Budget	
P_t = Satellite transponder output power	18.0 dBW
G_t = Satellite antenna gain	31.0 dB
G_r = Earth station antenna gain	G_r dB
L_p = Free space path loss	−205.4 dB
L_a = E/S on −3 dB contour of satellite antenna	−3.0 dB
L_m = Other losses	−0.8 dB
P_r = Received power at transponder	G_r − 160.2 dB

- The required power into the earth station receiver to meet the $(C/N)_{dn}$ = 17.2 dB objective is P_r = −120.1 dBW. Hence the receiving antenna must have a gain G_t where

$$G_t - 160.2 \text{ dB} = -113.5 \text{ dBW}$$

$$G_t = 46.7 \text{ dB} \vee 4677.4 \text{ as a ratio}$$

- The earth station antenna diameter, D, is calculated from the formula for antenna gain, G, with a circular aperture

$$G_r = 0.65 \times (\pi D/\lambda)^2 = 46{,}774$$

- At 11.45 GHz, the wavelength is 2.62 cm = 0.0262 m. Evaluating the above equation to find D gives the required receiving antenna diameter as D = 2.14 m.

6.8.4 Rain Effects at Ku Band

- **Uplink :** Under conditions of heavy rain, the Ku band path to the satellite station suffers an attenuation of 6 dB for 0.01 of the year. We must find the uplink attenuation margin and decide whether uplink power control would improve system performance at Ku band.

- The uplink C/N was 30 dB in clear air. With 6 dB uplink path attenuation, the C/N in the transponder falls to 24 dB and assuming a linear transponder characteristic and no uplink power control, the transponder output power falls to 18 − 8 = 12 dBW.

- The downlink C/N falls by 6 dB from 17.2 dB to 11.2 dB and the overall $\left(\dfrac{C}{N}\right)_0$ falls by 6 dB to 11 dB. With the minimum overall C/N set at 9.5 dB, the additional margin for uplink attenuation is 1.5 dB. Hence the link margin available on the uplink is 8.5 dB without uplink power control.

- This is an adequate uplink rain attenuation margin for many parts of the United States, and would typically lead to rain outages of less than $1h$ total time per year.

- Uplink Power Control (UPC) could be implemented so that the earth station transmitter output power is increased when the uplink attenuation is estimated to have reached 3 dB. This would hold the value of overall $\left(\dfrac{C}{N}\right)_0$ in the receiver at 14 dB.

- If the UPC system has a dynamic range of 6 dB, the uplink rain attenuation margin is increased to 12 dB and the maximum Ku-band transmitter power is increased to 34.3 dBW (2690 W).

- Rain attenuation can exceed 12 dB at 14 GHz for a few minutes at a time in very heavy thunderstorms, but there would only be a handful of such occurrences in an average year.

- UPC definitely improves the ability of the uplink to resist rain attenuation, but at the expense of a considerably more powerful, and expensive, uplink transmitter.

  The extra expense can be justified in a television distribution system with many receiving stations. There is also an increased risk that the additional power radiated by the uplink station when UPC is active will cause interference at an unacceptable level into other satellite links using the same frequencies.

- It would be advisable to increase the earth station antenna diameter to increase its gain, and thus reduce the maximum transmit power required.

Downlink attenuation and Sky Noise Increase :

- The 11.45 GHz path between the satellite and the receiving station suffers rain attenuation exceeding 5 dB or 0.01 of the year.

- Assuming 100 coupling of sky noise into antenna noise, and 0.5 dB clear air gaseous attenuation, calculate the overall C/N under these conditions. Assume that the uplink station is operating in clear air. We need to calculate the available downlink fade margin.

- We need to find the sky noise temperature that results from a total excess path attenuation of 5.5 dB (clear air attenuation plus rain attenuation); this is the new antenna temperature in rain, because we assumed 100 coupling between sky noise temperature and antenna temperature.

- We must evaluate the change in received power and increase in system noise temperature in order to calculate the change in C/N ratio for the downlink.

- In clear air, the atmospheric attenuation on the downlink is 0.5 dB. The corresponding sky noise temperature is $270 (1 - 10^{0.05}) = 29$ K, which leads to the antenna temperature of 30 K given in the Ku band system specification.

- When the rain causes 5 dB attenuation, the total path attenuation from the atmosphere and the rain is 5.5 dB.

- The corresponding sky noise temperature is given by

$$T_{skyrain} = T_0 (1 - G) \text{ where } G = 10^{-A/10} = 2.82$$

$$T_{skyrain} = 270 (1 - 0.282) = 194 \text{ K}$$

- Thus the antenna temperature has increased from 30 K in clear air to 194 K in rain. The system noise temperature in rain, T_{srain}, is increased from the clear air value of 140 K (30 K sky noise temperature plus 110 KLNA temperature)

$$T_{skyrain} = 194 + 110 = 304 \text{ K} \vee 24.8 \text{ dBK}$$

The increase in noise power is

$$\Delta N = 10 \log (304/140) = 3.4 \text{ dB}$$

- The signal is attenuated by 5 dB in the rain, so the total reduction in downlink C/N ratio is 8.4 dB, which yield a new value

$$(C/N)_{dnrain} = 17.2 - 8.4 = 8.8 \text{ dB}$$

- The overall C/N is then found by combining the clear air uplink $(C/N)_{up}$ of 30 dB with the rain faded downlink $(C/N)_{dnrain}$ of 8.8 dB, giving

$$(C/N)_{0rain} = 8.8 \text{ dB}$$

- The overall $(C/N)_0$ is below the minimum acceptable value of 9.5 dB. The downlink link margin is

Downlink fade margin $(C/N)_{dn} - (C/N)_{min} = 17.2 - 9.5 = 7.7$ dB

- Since downlink rain attenuation of 5 dB causes the overall $(C/N)_0$ to go below the minimum permitted value of 9.5 dB, we should recalculate the maximum attenuation that the downlink can sustain.

- This involves an iterative process, since changing the attenuation changes both C and N values in $(C/N)_{dn}$. At an attenuation level of 5 dB, the increase in noise power is 3.4 dB, so a starting guess would be that decreasing the attenuation by 0.3 dB will decrease the noise power by 0.2 dB. The rain attenuation will then be a little less than 5 dB.

Recalculating $(C/N)_{dn}$ for a rain attenuation value of 4.7 dB gives

$$T_{skyrain} = T_0 (1 - G) \text{ where } G = 10^{-A/10} = 0.339$$
$$T_{skyrain} = 270 (1 - 0.339) = 178 \text{ K}$$
$$\Delta N = 10 \log (288/140) = 3.1 \text{ dB}$$
$$(C/N)_{dnrain} = 17.2 - 4.7 - 3.1 = 9.4 \text{ dB}$$
$$(C/N)_{0rain} = 9.36 \approx 9.4 \text{ dB}$$

- The result is close enough to the required value of $(C/N)_{0rain}$ = 9.5 dB to conclude that we can tolerate about 4.7 dB of rain attenuation on the downlink.

- If better availability is required less outage time the diameter of the receiving antenna can be increased.

- For example, if the receiving antenna diameter is increased to 2.4 m, (about 8 ft) the increase in antenna gain is 20 $\log_{10}$ (2.40/2.14) = 1.0 dB, which increases the downlink margin to 8.7 dB.

- Repeating the iterative calculation outlined above, the corresponding rain attenuation on the downlink is 5.5 dB with a noise power increase of 3.2 dB.

- The downlink C/N with 5.5 dB rain attenuation is 17.2 − 8.7 = 9.5 dB and the overall $(C/N)_0 \approx 9.5$ dB.

- The extra antenna gain now ensures that the link meets the required specification, which will keep outages to a total of about 50 min in an average year in the eastern United States.

- However, an increase in antenna diameter will reduce the beamwidth of the antenna and may require an upgrade in the tracking requirements. With a fixed pointing antenna,diurnal motion of the satellite may cause a variation in received signal strength as the satellite moves through the antenna beam.

6.8.5 Summary of Ku-Band Link Performance

- The Ku-band link with a 2.4 m earth station antenna will suffer rain outages because attenuation exceeding 5.5 dB will occur occasionally on the downlinks, affecting individual customers. Outages will rarely occur on the uplink. With uplink power control (UPC) and a more powerful transmitter, uplink outages can be restricted to a few minutes per year.

- A 2.4 m receiving antenna is needed to ensure that the Ku-band downlink will be out for no more than 0.01 of an average year with the given attenuation statistics.

- The threshold value for overall C/N was set at 9.5 dB because we can use QPSK and half error rate correction coding to obtain an equivalent (C/N) ratio of about 15.5 dB without coding. Allowing a 1 dB implementation margin, the BER on the downlink will remain below 10^{-7} except when very heavy rain affects the downlink.

- In clear sky conditions there will be no errors on the link. The 43.2 Msps QPSK signal with half rate EFC can deliver a data rate of 43.2 Mbps, which can support seven MPEG-2 video channels.

- The video distribution system described here is designed to deliver multiple video channels to cable TV stations with low risk of outages. Direct broadcast satellite television delivers video signals directly to the customer's location using a much smaller 0.5 m receiving antenna. The smaller antenna can be used because the DBS-TV satellites transmit at a higher power level (160 W), the symbol rate is lower (20 Mbps) and availability of the signal at the receiving antenna is guaranteed for only 99.7 of the year.

6.8.6 System Design

Personal Communication System Using Low Earth Orbit Satellites

- Low Earth Orbit (LEO) satellite systems are designed to provide personal communication service similar to a cellular telephone, but over a much wider area.

- LEO satellite systems can cover sparsely populated regions of a country, or the world, where there are no terrestrial cellular telephone systems.

- The user has a handset similar to a cellular telephone handset that provides two way voice communication through a gateway station,usually to a conventional telephone in a home or office connected to the Public Switched Telephone Network (PSTN).

- Satellite telephones can equally well connect to another satellite handset, or to a terrestrial cellular telephone.

- Most LEO satellite systems operate in L band ,in the 1500 and 1600 MHz bands, and in the lower part of S band around 2460 MHz, frequency bands that are allocated for mobile satellite communications.

- Some LEO systems use intersatellite links so user can connect to any point in the world without an intermediate return to earth. However, the signals invariably pass through a gateway station at each end of the link to facilitate control of the call and to ensure that users can be charged for using the system.

- Connections between the gateway earth stations and the satellites use S band, C band, Ku band or Ka band frequencies, depending on the system requirements.

- Only a small portion of the radio spectrum at L band is allocated to LEO and MEO satellite systems, so L band frequencies are reserved for the critical links between the user and the satellite.

- A handoff process is required for LEO satellites similar to that used in cellular telephone networks, but the handoff between the satellites should not be apparent to the user.

- Most LEO satellites have multiple beam antennas, and the beam pattern moves across the earths surface at the speed of the satellite typically about 7.7 km/sec or 17200 mph.

- A single beam is typically 500 km in diameter, so an individual user is in any one beam for less than a minute.

- The system provides automatic switching from beam to beam within the same satellite antenna coverage, much like a cellular telephone system switches user from cell to cell, which nearly always requires a change in the link frequencies, but as with satellite to satellite handsoffs, the process must be transparent to the user.

- The example below analyses the links between a user and a gateway station. LEO satellite systems uses digital transmission so that advantage can be taken of forward error correction coding (FEC) and speech compression techniques.

- The bit rate of digital voice in LEO satellite link is typically 4800 bps and thus needs powerful compression algorithms.

- The low bit rate allows more signals to be sent in the available bandwidth and also helps maintain the C/N ratio in the receivers.

- When FEC is applied to a digital bit stream, carrier to noise ratios down to 5 dB can be used.

- Personal communication via LEO satellite is possible due to the low bit rate and the operation of the receivers at low C/N ratios are essential.

- The link between the gateway station and the mobile terminal is defined as the outbound link, and the link from the mobile terminal to the gateway as inbound link.

- There are four satellite paths, just as in all other two way satellite communication systems: outbound uplink, outbound downlink, inbound uplink, inbound downlink.

- Each has its own unique frequency, and in most LEO satellite systems, one of the links will be weaker than the other three links and will thus limits the system performance.

- One of the objective in the example below is to identify the weakest path and to then attempt to improve that part of the system.

- Fig. 6.10 illustrates the two way link between the gateway station and the handset. Note that separate transponders are used for the inbound and outbound paths.

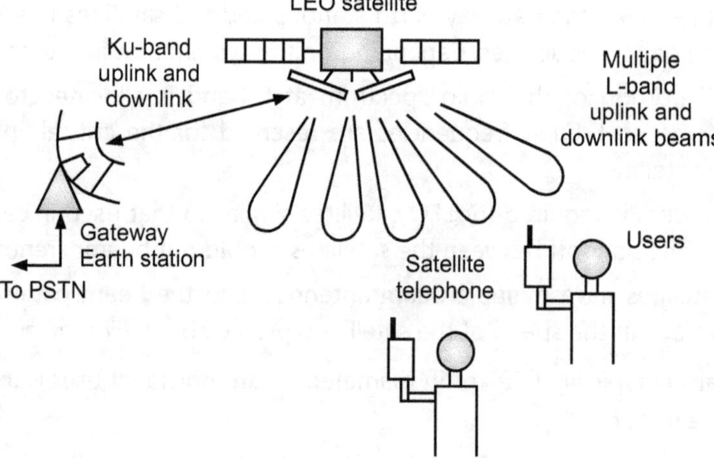

Fig. 6.10: two way personal communication system using L band LEO satellite links

- In this example, the mobile terminals transmits to a transponder on the satellite using frequency division multiple access (FDMA) and single channel per carrier (SCPC) techniques.
- The principle here is simple, each transmitter is allocated its own frequency, just like broadcast stations.
- The available frequencies are shared among active user on demand, as in a cellular telephone system, so a call begins with a start up sequence that establishes communication between the mobile terminal and a local gateway station via the nearest LEO satellite.
- The gateway station than allocates frequencies for the call. At the end of the call, the frequencies are released and become available for another user. This is called demand assignment(DA), and the multiple access technique is identified by the acronym SCPC-FDMA-DA or alternatively, SCPC-FDMA-DAMA where DAMA stands for demand assignment multiple access.
- A common set of control channels at preassigned frequencies enable call setup and teardown.
- The link from the gateway station via the satellite to the mobile terminal uses Time Division Multiplexing (TDM).
- A TDM signal consists of a sequence of packets with addresses that repeat every 20 to 100 ms.
- The addresses identify which terminal should each packet. The TDM bit stream rate must exceed the total bit rate of all active terminals in a two-way telephone system.
- So that there is sufficient capacity available for each terminal within the TDM bit stream.
- In this example we begin by assuming that 50 active users share one common TDM channel we will also assume that the gateway earth stations operates at Ku band to and from the satellite, and that the satellite employs a linear transponder (bent pipe) rather than having onboard processing.
- The parameters of the satellite transponder, the mobile terminal, and a gateway station are given in table 6.8. The table gives the maximum path length for any satellite-earth link.

Table 6.8 : LEO Satellite Personal Communication System Parameters

Satellite Parameters	
Saturated output power	10 W
Transponder bandwidth	1 MHz
Uplink frequency for mobile terminal	1650 MHz
Downlink frequency for mobile terminal	1550 MHz

Antenna gain 1650 MHz uplink (one beam)	23 dB
Antenna gain 1550 MHz downlink (One Beam)	23 dB
Uplink frequency for gateway station	14 GHz
Downlink frequency for gateway station	11.5 GHz
Antenna gain 14 GHz uplink	3 dB
Antenna gain 11.5 GHz downlink	3 dB
Satellite receiver system noise temperature	500 K
Maximum range to edge of coverage zone	2200 km
Mobile Terminal Parameters	
Transmitter output power	0.5 W
Antenna gain (Transmit and receive)	0 dB
Receiver system noise temperature	300 K
Transmit bit rate	4800 bps
Receive bit rate	96 kbps
Required maximum bit error rate	10^{-4}
Gateway Station Parameters	
Transmitter output power (Maximum per transponder)	10 W
Antenna gain (Transmit, 14.0 GHz)	55 dB
Antenna gain (Receive 11.5 GHz)	53.5 dB
Receive system noise temperature (Clear Air)	140 K
Transmit Bit rate (before FEC encoder)	300 kbps
Receive bit rate (After FEC decoder)	4800 bps
Required maximum bit error rate	10^{-4}

- The User's transmitter and receiver is called a mobile terminal. It could be a handheld device like a cellular telephone, sometimes called a satellite telephone or handset, or the terminal could be mounted in a vehicle.

- The satellite has multiple L band beams serving different parts of its instanteneous coverage zone because a single beam from an LEO satellite serving different parts of its instantaneous coverage zone would have both low gain and limited capacity. For an antenna with a gain of 23 dB, G = 200 and the beamwidth is $\theta_{3\,dB}$ where

$$\theta_{3\,dB} = (33{,}000/200)^{1/2} = 12.8°$$

- The use of a multiple beam antenna on the satellite increases the antenna gain toward the mobile terminal, which increases the C/N ratio of the signals in the mobile terminals and gateway station receivers.

- The Ku band antennas that link the satellite to the gateway station have broad beams and low gain. The C/N on these links is high through the use of a relatively large antenna and a high transmitter power at the gateway earth station, allowing the use of a small and simple Ku band antennas on the satellite.

- The antenna gain at the mobile terminal is low, with a value of 0 dB used for calculation, because the antenna coverage of the terminal must be very broad.

- If the terminal is a satellite telephone, an omnidirectional antenna allows the user to move around freely.

- If the mobile terminal antenna gain were to be increased, its beam would be correspondingly narrower, and the user would have to point the handset at the satellite.

- In a LEO satellite system, the user does not know which satellite is being used nor where it is in the sky, so requiring the user to point the handset antenna at the satellite is not a feasible option. When the mobile terminal is mounted in a vehicle with the antenna on the roof, pointing the antenna at the satellite is not possible unless a sophisticated (and expensive) steered antenna is used.

- In this example, we will begin by assuming that there are 50 users sharing a single transponder on the satellite, and that one transponder serves one of the L band beams within the LEO satellite coverage, operating within a given set of frequencies.

- A large number of users can share an LEO satellites through the provision of many transponders, each of which is connected to one of the individual beams in the multiple L-band antenna coverage of the satellite.

- The signal received by a mobile terminal from the gateway is a TDM sequence of packets carrying 50 digital voice channels, each at 4800 bps.

- The bit rate of the TDM signal would be 240 kbps if it carried only the voice signals, but will be higher in practice because additional bits must be sent with each packet; a TDM bit rate of 300 kbps is used in this example.

- Individual mobile terminals pull off their assigned packets from within the TDM stream and ignore the rest. Initially, the links will be analyzed without forward error correction.

- All digital links are designed with ideal (Nyquist) filters which have noise bandwidth, B_n Hz, equal to the symbol rate of the digital signal in symbols per second. In this example, handheld transceivers send and receive binary phase shift keyed (BPSK) modulation. The maximum permitted bit error rate of the digital signal of 10^{-4} leads to a S/N ratio in the speech channel of 34 dB. (S/N = 1/4 P_e, where P_e is the BER)

6.8.7 Inbound Link : Mobile Terminal to Gateway Station

- Each terminal transmits a BPSK signal at 4800 bps at an allocated frequency. The satellite transponder shifts all received L-band signals in frequency before retransmission at Ku band to the gateway station, and also amplifies the signal with a linear transponder.

- At the gateway station, the antenna and RF receiver are connected to many identical IF receivers tuned to the individual frequencies of the handheld transmitters. Each IF receiver has a noise bandwidth of 4800 Hz, set by a square root raised cosine filter with $\alpha = 0.5$, giving an occupied channel bandwidth of 7.2 kHz.

- At the receiving end of the link, the C/N at the input to the BPSK demodulator must be high enough to provide an acceptable bit error rate. Here, we require a maximum BER of 10^{-4} which provides a minimum S/N or 34 dB in the spee h channel.

- In a practical digital digital communication system, we always need a higher C/N than theory suggests because we do not have ideal Nyquist filters, and other parts of the system are also not identical, so we must add an implementation margin to account for the nonideal nature of the system.

- In this example, the implementation margin is set at 0.6 dB, we need a minimum C/N = 9.0 dB to meet the BER and S/N specifications.

- We can now design the satellite link to achieve the minimum C/N.

6.8.8 Mobile Terminal to Satellite Link

- We will establish power and noise link budgets for each of the four paths, beginning with the uplink from the mobile terminal to the satellite.

- The received power at the output of the uplink antenna on the satellite from Equation (6.11) is

$$P_r = EIRP + G_e - L_p - L_m \text{ dBW}$$

- Where EIRP is the product of transmitter output power and transmitting antenna gain, P_tG_t in dBW, G_r is the satellite receive antenna gain, L_p is the path loss of the link, and L_m accounts for all other losses. The noise power, N, at the input to the satellite receiving system from Equation (6.13) is

$$N = P_n = kT_sB_n \text{ watts}$$

$$k + T_s + B_n \text{ dBW}$$

Path loss L_p is found from Equation (6.12)

$$L_p = [4\pi R/\lambda]^2 \text{ or } 20 \log_{10} (4\pi R/\lambda) \text{ dB}$$

Where R is the distance in meters between the transmitting and receiving antennas in the link and λ is the wavelength in meters.

- The uplink frequency is 1650 MHz, giving $\lambda = 0.1818$ m. The maximum range is 2200 km so maximum path loss is

$$L_p = 20 \log_{10} (4\pi \times 2.2 \times 10^6/0.1818) = 163.6 \text{ dB}$$

- We will assume that there are miscellaneous losses in the 1550 MHz link of 0.5 dB, caused by polarization misalignments, gaseous absorption in the atmosphere, etc. the calculation of the C/N ratio is made for the worst case of an earth station located on the −3dB contour of the satellite antenna beam.

- So a 3 dB reduction in satellite antenna gain is applied, making the value of $L_m = -3.5$ dB. We can now set out the link power and noise budgets for clear line of sight conditions, where there is no attenuation caused by obstructions in the path.

Uplink Power Budget		
Parameter	**Symbol**	**Value Units**
EIRP of handheld unit	$P_t G_t$	− 3 dBW
Gain of receiving antenna	G_r	23 dB
Path loss at 1650 MHz	L_p	− 163.6 dB
Miscellaneous losses	L_m	− 3.5 dB
Received power at satellite	P_r	− 147.1 dBW

Transponder Noise Power Budget		
Parameter	**Symbol**	**Value Units**
Boltzmann's constant	k	−228.6 dBW/K/Hz
System noise temperature	T_s	27.0 dBK
Noise bandwidth	B_n	36.8 dBHz
Noise power	N	− 164.8 dBW

- The inbound uplink C/N ratio in the transponder can now be calculated from the power and noise budgets:

$$(C/N)_{up} = \frac{P_r}{N} = -147.1 \text{ dBW} - (-164.8 \text{ dBW}) = 17.7 \text{ dB}$$

Note : This is the lowest C/N ratio that should occur in the transponder in clear air conditions, since the calculation was made for a mobile terminal at the longest range from the satellite and at the edge of a satellite antenna beam. The mobile terminal antenna gain has also been set to its minimum value of 0 dB. If the satellite were directly overhead the range would be 1000 km instead of 2200 km, making the path loss lower by 6.8 dB and the miscellaneous losses would be 3 dB lower at the center of the satellite antenna beam, making the power received at the transponder 10.8 dB greater , and then $(C/N)_{up}$ = 28.5 dB. However, we cannot use this figure for the system design, otherwise there would be only one user who could make calls, and then only for a brief moment as the satellite passes directly overhead. We must ensure that all users within the satellite's coverage zone have adequate C/N ratios in their links for successful communication.

6.8.9 Satellite to Gateway Station Link

- The next step in calculating the C/N ratio for the inbound link is to calculate $(C/N)_{dn}$ in the gateway receiver. We are operating the transponder in FDMA, so the individual mobile terminal signals must share the output power of a transponder.

- We will assume that 50 active terminal signals share the 1 MHz transponder bandwidth and that 3 dB backoff is used at the transponder output to obtain quasi-linear operation of the transponder HPA (remembering that we have assumed linear transponder operation in this example).

- The transponder output power is therefore 10 dBW – 3 dB = 7 dBW (5 W). The 5 W transponder output power must be shared equally between the 50 signals in the transponder, giving 0.1 W = – 10 dBW per signal at the transponder output for the downlink to the gateway station.

- We can now establish a link budget for a single channel downlink from the satellite to the gateway station.

- We will use the same worst-case conditions as for the uplink maximum path length and minimum satellite antenna gain, with miscellaneous losses of 3.5 dB, including the edge of satellite beam effect.

Downlink Power Budget		
Parameter	**Symbol**	**Value Units**
EIRP per channel	P_tG_t	– 10.0 dBW
Gain of receiving antenna	G_r	53.5 dB
Path loss at 11.5 GHz	L_p	– 180.5 dB
Miscellaneous losses	L_m	– 3.5 dB
Received power at satellite	P_r	140.5 dBW
Gateway Station Noise Power Budget		

Parameter	Symbol	Value Units
Boltzmann's constant	k	-228.6 dBW/K/Hz
System noise temperature	T_s	21.5 dBK
Noise bandwidth	B_n	36.8 dBHz
Noise power	N	-170.3 dBW

- The C/N ratio in the 4.8 kHz noise bandwidth of a gateway station IF receiver is given by :

$$(C/N)_{dn} = P_r/N = -14.05 - (-170.3) = 29.8 \text{ dB}$$

- $(C/N)_{dn}$ for the inbound downlink is higher than $(C/N)_{up}$ for the inbound uplink because of the high gain of the gateway station antenna. Because the gain of the antenna is high, 53.5 dB, which corresponds to an antenna diameter of 5 m and an aperture efficiency of 60, its beamwidth is narrow, about 0.4° and the gateway station must track the satellite as it crosses the sky.

- The overall $(C/N)_0$ at the gateway is calculated by combining the uplink C/N and downlink C/N values using Equation (6.43), since both the transponder and the gateway station receiver add noise to the signal. The values used in the formula are ratios, that is, C/N values are not in decibels.

$$1/(C/N)_0 = 1/(C/N)_{up} + 1/(C/N)_{dn}$$

- For the inbound uplink, $(C/N)_{up} = 17.7$ dB $\rightarrow$ 58.9 as a ratio. For the inbound downlink, $(C/N)_{dn} = 29.8$ dB $\rightarrow$ 955.0 as a ratio.

$$(C/N)_0 = 1/(1/58.9 + 1/955.0) = 55.5 \vee 17.4 \text{ dB}$$

- The overall C/N ratio of 17.4 dB at the gateway station receiver guarantees that with BPSK and a bit rate of 4800 bps there will be extremely few bit errors and the S/N of the speech channel will be set by quantization noise in the analog to digital converters.

- The maximum permitted BER is 10^{-4}, which occurs with $(C/N)_0 = 9.0$ dB. We therefore have an inbound link margin of $(17.4 - 9.0) = 8.4$ dB. However, we must calculate the individual link margins for the uplink and downlink in order to be able to use the margins for fading analysis. This will be done at the end of the example.

6.8.10 Outbound Link

- The outbound link from the gateway station to the mobile terminal sends a continuous 300 kbps TDM bit stream using EPSK modulation and a separate transponder with 1 MHz bandwidth. The bit stream is a series of packets addresses to all 50 active terminals.

- The noise bandwidth of the terminal receiver is 300 kHz, assuming ideal Nyquist filters.

- The outbound uplink and downlink C/N values are calculated in exactly the same way as for the inbound link, and the power and noise budgets are combined to give C/N ratios directly from a single table.

- At the uplink frequency of 14 GHz, clear atmospheric attenuation of 1.0 dB is included in the miscellaneous losses, together with the usual 3 dB loss for the user at the edge of the satellite antenna beam.

Uplink C/N Budget

Parameter	Symbol	Value Units
Gateway station EIRP	$P_t G_t$	65.0 dBW
Gain of receiving antenna	G_r	3.0 dB
Path loss at 14.0 GHz	L_p	− 182.2 dB
Miscellaneous losses	L_m	− 4.0 dB
Received power at satellite	P_r	− 118.2 dBW
Boltzmann's constant	k	− 228.6 dBW/K/Hz
System noise temperature	T_s	27.0 dBk
Noise bandwidth	B_n	54.8 dBHz
Noise power	N	− 146.8 dBW
Uplink C/N	$(C/N)_{up} = -118.2 - (-146.8) = 28.6$ dB	

6.8.11 Downlink C/N Budget

- The satellite transponder carrying the single 300 kbps TDM outbound signal can be operated close to saturation because there is only one signal in the transponder, thus eliminating intermodulation problems. We will allow 1.0 dB backoff at the transponder output to avoid suturing the transponder, giving a transmitted power P_t = 9.0 dBW. Miscellaneous losses on the downlink are 0.5 dB atmospheric loss and 3 dB for the edge of the antenna beam.

Downlink C/N Budget

Parameter	Symbol	Value Units
EIRP of satellite	$P_t G_t$	32.0 dBW
Gain of receiving antenna	G_r	0 dB
Path loss at 1550 MHz	L_p	163.1 dB
Miscellaneous losses	L_m	3.5 dB
Received power at mobile	P_r	− 134.6 dBW
Boltzmann's constant	k	− 228.6 dBW/K/Hz

System noise temperature	T_s	24.8 dBK
Noise bandwidth	B_n	54.8 dBHz
Noise power	N	-149.0 dBW
Downlink C/N	$(C/N)_{dn} = -134.6 - (-149.0) = 14.4$ dB	

- Combining the C/N values for the uplink and downlink gives the overall $(C/N)_0$ ratio at the mobile terminal receiver. Converting the C/N values from decibels gives $(C/N)_{up}$ = 28.6 dB = 724.4, $(C/N)_{dn}$ = 14.4 dB = 27.6. Hence, the overall $(C/N)_0$ for the outbound link is

$$(C/N)_0 = 1/[1/(C/N)_{up} + 1/(C/N)_{dn}] = 1/[0.00139 + 0.0364] = 26.5 \vee 14.2 \text{ dB}$$

Note : The downlink C/N ratio is so much lower than the uplink C/N ratio that the overall C/N ratio is almost equal to the downlink C/N ratio.

- The clear air $(C/N)_0$ value is 5.2 dB above the minimum allowed for BER = 10^{-4} on the outbound link, leaving 15.2 dB margin for blockage by buildings, the user's head, multipath effects, the ionosphere, or vegetative shadowing on the downlink. The link margins for the outbound link are much lower than for the inbound link, and it is therefore the weakest part of the system.

- Attenuation exceeding 5.2 dB in the downlink from the satellite to the mobile terminal will cause the BER to exceed 10^{-4} and the S/N in the speech channel will fall below 30 dB. A S/N ratio of 30 dB in a speech channel is regarded as the minimum acceptable value for intelligible communication. Because of the very steep characteristics of the BER vs C/N ratio curve for BPSK, the speech channel will be unusable if downlink attenuation exceeds 5.2 dB.

- The link margins are quite small for a mobile system in which the line of sight between the satellite and the user can easily be blocked by trees, or by the user's body. It is the link between the mobile terminal and the satellite that sets the overall C/N value for both the inbound and the outbound links, but there is little room to change the system parameters to yield higher margins.

- When the mobile terminal is a satellite telephone handset, the transmitter power is limited by FCC regulations to ensure that there is no short term biological hazard to the user when the handset is transmitting. The power from the satellite is limited by the transponder HPA output power and the low gain of the handset antenna.

- However, a higher gain antenna would have a narrower beam and would have to track the satellite automatically a smart antenna could be built to do this, but the small size of most mobile telephone handsets limits the available improvement to no more than 3 or 4 dB.

6.8.12 Optimizing System Performance

- The preceeding calculations show that the LEO satellite system can support two way digital speech with 50 active users per transponder, and provides a link margin of 8.4 dB in the inbound link and a margin of 5.3 dB in the outbound link. The RF bandwidth used by the inbound and outbound links is found from the symbol rates and α values of the filters. For the outbound link using $\alpha = 0.5$, the symbol rate is 300 kbaud, giving

$$B_{outbound} = 300 \times (1 + \alpha) = 450 \text{ kHz}$$

- For the inbound link using $\alpha = 0.5$, the symbol rate for one speech channel is 4800 baud, giving

$$B_{inbound} = 4.8 \times (1 + \alpha) = 7.2 \text{ kHz}$$

- The inbound channels access the satellite transponder using SCPC-FDMA, so the RF signals are distributed across the transponder bandwidth. We must space the channels more than 7.2 kHz apart in the transponder so that the narrow bandpass filters in the gateway station receiver can extract each speech channel without interference from adjacent channels. If we use 10 kHz channel spacing, there will be a frequency gap, called a guard band of 2.8 kHz between each channel; which will ensure minimal interference from adjacent channels. With 50 channels sharing one transponder, the total bandwidth occupied in the inbound link transponder will be 500 kHz.

- Neither the inbound nor the outbound transponder bandwidth is fully utilized; in fact only half of the available 1 MHz is used in each case. However, we cannot add additional speech channels to the system because the C/N values are already low, indicating that the system is power limited with the given link margins. We can incorporate FEC coding, however, which lowers the C/N threshold for the minimum BER. Half rate convolution coding would be a good choice in this system because the threshold C/N value can be much lower.

- This allows a wider noise bandwidth to be used and thus better utilization of the available transponder bandwidth. Using constraint length eight and soft decision coding, the C/N ratio for BER = 10^{-4} an be lowered to 3.5 dB; alternatively Turbo coding could be used. However, the bit rate of the signal is now doubled, since a half rate code adds as many coding bits as there are data bits in the bit stream.

- The new outbound bit rate with FEC is 600 kbps and each inbound speech channel has a bit rate of 9600 bps. The corresponding RF bandwidths for $\alpha = 0.5$ Nyquist filters are 900 kHz outbound and 14.4 kHz per channel inbound. With 50 active users, the RF signal bandwidths are within the available 1 MHz bandwidth of the satellite transponders.

- Lowering the threshold value of C/N for the maximum permitted BER of 10^{-4} improves the link margins by a factor called coding gain.

- Coding gain is typically quoted as the difference between the C/N value required for a given BER without coding and the C/N required to obtain the same BeR with coding. In this example, the coding gain is $8.4 - 3.5 = 4.9$ dB. However, the coding gain cannot simply be added to the system margin, because the half rate FEC code doubles the bit rate of the signals and also doubles the noise bandwidth of the filters in the receivers.

- Thus noise power increases by 3 dB in every link receiver when FEC is added, and the C/N values all fall by 3 dB. This results in the overall values of $(C/N)_0$ for both the inbound and the outbound links falling by 3 dB. There is no need to recalculate all the link noise budgets and C/N values, since all of the values change by the same amount. With half rate FEC added to the system, the new C/N values are all 3 dB lower than for the system without FEC.

Inbound Link
$(C/N)_{up} = 14.7$ dB
$(C/N)_{dn} = 26.8$ dB
$(C/N)_0 = 14.4$ dB
Outbound Link
$(C/N)_{up} = 25.6$ dB
$(C/N)_{dn} = 11.4$ dB
$(C/N)_0 = 11.2$ dB

- The new link margins with a threshold overall $(C/N)_0$ of 3.5 dB are: inbound 10.9 dB, outbound 7.7 dB.

- Although the improvement over the earlier values without FEC is only 2 dB, the increased link margins are valuable, so FEC is invariably used in satellite personal communication systems, as it is in almost all digital wireless applications, whether satellite or terrestrial. FEC can be implemented by inserting a coding IC in the terminal, and identical ICs in the gateway station, in the baseband bit streams. The 2 dB advantage that FEC brings to the system's link margins cannot easily be obtained any other way.

6.8.13 Link Margins with FEC

- Rain attenuation affects the Ku-band links between the gateway station and the satellite, and blockage affects the link between the mobile terminal and the satellite. Individual link margins must be calculated to determine the amount of fading or blockage that can be tolerated in each link. Excessive rain attenuation in the Ku-band links could cause the links to fail, which affects all 50 users.

- We must therefore ensure that the Ku-band link margins are sufficiently large to make a rain outage unlikely. Blockage of the line of sight to a mobile terminal may cause that one terminal to lose its link, but this is less serious than losing all 50 links simultaneously. The margin available for overcoming blockage should be as large as possible, but is set by the system design and cannot be improved beyond the values given above without a reduction in the number of users in the system.

- It should be remembered that all the calculations are for a worst case: the user is at the edge of the satellite coverage zone where the satellite is at maximum range, and also at the edge of one of the satellite's multiple L-band beams. Most of the users have higher C/N ratios on their links than the calculated worst case values most of the time, allowing greater margins for blockage of the path to the handset.

- In commercial satellite system design, the fact that most users are not at the edge of the coverage zone most of the time is used in developing a coverage advantage factor that increases the average link margin available per user and thus optimizes traffic capacity.

6.8.14 Rain Attenuation at Ku Band

- Rain causes attenuation at Ku band as we discussed. We must calculate the rain attenuation margins for the inbound downlink and the outbound uplink and determine the probability of an outage.

- The link margin is the number of decibels by which the C/N ratio on an uplink or a downlink can be reduced before the overall $(C/N)_0$ for that link falls to the threshold value. We will use 3.5 dB as the threshold value for overall C/N in each case, assuming that half rate FEC is used. We will also assume that clear sky conditions prevail on the uplink when extreme attenuation occurs on the downlink and vice versa.

- For the inbound Ku-band downlink, using half rate FEC, the clear air C/N ratio is 26.9 dB (ratio 478.6) and the L-band clear uplink C/N ratio is 14.7 dB (ratio 29.5). with a threshold at 3.5 dB (ratio 2.24), the minimum downlink C/N will be given by (using ratios, not dB)

$$1/(C/N)_{dnmin} \; = \; 1/(C/N)_0 - 1/(C/N)_{up}$$

$$\tfrac{1}{2}.24 - 1/478.6 \; = \; 0.444$$

- Hence the minimum permitted value for $(C/N)_{dn} = 2.5 \rightarrow 3.5$ dB. The downlink margin is $26.8 - 3.5 = 23.3$ dB. Rain attenuation at 11.5 GHz very rarely exceeds this value in the United States, so for a U.S. system, the Ku-band downlink margin is adequate.

- The Ku-band uplink has a clear sky $(C/N)_{up}$ ratio of 25.6 dB, but attenuation of the uplink signal causes a reduction in received power at the transponder input. If the satellite transponders are linear (bent pipe), the output power will fall when the input power is reduced by uplink rain attenuation. Because the transponder is operated close to saturation, there will not be a one-to-one correspondence in the changes in power level at the input and output, but exact analysis is beyond the scope of this example; a linear relationship will be assumed here.

- The transponder nonlinearity actually increases the uplink rain attenuation margin, because the output signal from the satellite will fall less than the input signal to the satellite, so the results that follow represent a pessimistic estimate of the margin available. A regenerative repeater always transmits at constant output power and is very desirable in a digital system. It avoids the difficulty of attenuation on the uplink causing a reduction in transponder output power.

- Applying the same analysis as used for the Ku-band downlink, with $(C/N)_{dn}$ = 11.4 dB (ratio 13.8) in clear sky conditions and $(C/N)_{0min}$ = 3.5 dB (ratio 2.24)

$$C/N$$

$$1/$$

$$1/2.24 - 1/13.8 = 0.374$$

- Thus the minimum $(C/N)_{up}$ ratio is 10 log (1/0.374) = 4.3 dB, ignoring the effects of coupling between input and output power in the transponder. When the latter effect is considered with a linear transponder characteristic, the limit is set by the $(C/N)_{dn}$ ratio falling to 3.5 dB. This will occur with 11.4 − 3.5 = 7.9 dB uplink attenuation, which is the limiting value.

- Uplink power control (UPC) can be used to prevent the input power level of the transponder from falling when rain affects the uplink. It would be straightforward to use uplink power control in this case.

- Attenuation on the downlink at 11.5 GHz is measured using the satellite beacon, scaled to 14.4 GHz and used to set the gateway station transmit power level. If a 10 dB dynamic range of UPC is available, and attenuation is allowed to reach 2 dB at 14.4 GHz before the UPC comes in, the downlink C/N ratio will not fall below 9.4 dB in an uplink fade, leaving a downlink margin of 5.9 dB during uplink rain fades. This gives the 14.4 GHz uplink a rain attenuation margin of 12 dB, which would maintain the link for better than 99.99 of a year throughout the United States. The open loop UPC system discussed here would probably have a margin of error of at least ± 1 db in estimating uplink attenuation under low fading conditions. Uncertainties in identifying the propagation mechanism that is causing the fading and the difficulty of accurately setting the clear sky baseline for the signal make greater accuracy unlikely.

- If two mobile terminals are located within the same satellite beam coverage, and are therefore operating through the same gateway earth station, the assumption of nonsimultaneous outage of the two links would not be valid. Such situations are expected to be rare occurrences.

- The gateway station would typically be sited in a dry region, such as Wyoming or Idaho in the United States, to minimize the number and severity of rain attenuation events. Thus rain attenuation at Ku band can be overcome by a large link margin for the downlink and implementation of uplink power control in the uplink, and by intelligent siting of the station. All 50 channels can be guaranteed to be unaffected by rain at the gateway station.

6.8.15 Path Blockage at L-band

- Trees, buildings, and people are the most likely causes of blockage that affect the performance of the mobile terminal at L band. Blockage by buildings is too severe to allow the L-band link to operate, and most LEO satellite telephones will not work indoors. Some systems like Iridium incorporate a cellular telephone into the handset. The cellular telephone is used in preference to the satellite phone to reduce loading on the LEO satellite system, and also whenever the satellite signal is unavailable, such as indoors. Paging options have been designed into some mobile satellite systems which permit users to be alerted that there is an incoming call. The user still has to run outdoors to be able to receive the call, and this has evidently been a factor deterring the use of a satellite telephone by business people.

- The link margins for the L-band links are calculated in the same way as the Ku-band margins. Repeating the calculations with a minimum overall C/N ratio of 3.5 dB and no rain attenuation in the Ku-band links gives

  L-band uplink margin = 11.4 dB

  L-band downlink margin = 7.8 dB

- The downlink from the satellite to the mobile terminal is therefore the most vulnerable of the links, and cannot be made robust without reducing the number of users per transponder. However, the value of 7.8 dB for the downlink margin is a worst case value and most of the users will have a margin several decibels higher. A margin of 7.8 dB can be exceeded by attenuation through a stand of trees.

- For example, if the user is in a vehicle traveling along a road cut through a forest, and the satellite has a low elevation angle, the 7.8 dB attenuation margin may be exceeded from time to time, causing repeated break up of the downlink signal. Transmission protocols and signal buffering can be designed to reduce the impact of this type of intermittent loss of signal.

- Multipath effects when the satellite is at a low elevation angle can also cause variations in signal level leading to lower performance and occasional outages in extreme cases, such as an overwater path.

REVIEW QUESTIONS

April 2015

1. Derive the link power budget equation.

2. Diagrammatically explain the combined uplink and downlink carrier to noise ratio.   [8]

3. Discuss the significance of system noise temperature and G/T ratio in calculation for link budget.   [6]

4. Discuss various sources of interferences between two satellite circuits. Also discuss how it affects link design calculations.   [6]

5. Comment on the following :

   (i) Uplink budget.

   (ii) Downlink Budget.

   (iii) Overall link budget.

Oct. 2014

1. A SCPC-FM satellite link has an RF channel bandwidth of 45 kHz and a base band maximum frequency of 3.4 kHz. De-emphasis provides a subjective improvement in base band S/N ratio of 7 dB. Calculate base band S/N ratio for the voice channel for a receiver C/N ratio of 13 dB. If the FM demodulator has an FM threshold at 6 dB, what is the link margin for this system.

2. Derive the expression for Link Budget of Satellite communication system.   [8]

3. Derive step by step, the power received by an earth station P_r, from a satellite transmitter in terms of P_t-Power transmitted, G_r, G_t-gain of transmitting and receiving antenna, respectively, losses associated with transmitting and receiving antenna and attenuation in atmosphere.

April 2013

1. The antenna on the satellite transmits at a frequency of 3875 MHz to an earth station at a distance of 39,000 km. The antenna has a 6° E-W beamwidth and a 3° N-S beamwidth. The receiving earth station has an antenna with a gain of 53 dB and a system noise temperature of 100 K and is located at the edge of the coverage zone of the satellite antenna. (Assume antenna gain is 3 dB lower than in the center of the beam). Transponder carrier power is 10 W at the input port of the transmit antenna on the satellite.

   (a) Calculate the gain of the satellite antenna in the direction of the receiving earth station.

   (b) Calculate the carrier power received by the earth station in dBW.

(c) Calculate the noise power of the earth station in 36 MHz bandwidth

(d) Hence find the C/N in dB for the earth station.

2. Discuss the importance of G/T ratio for earth station. How does it affect C/N ratio for satellite communication system?

3. Consider that the satellite communication receiver operating at 4 GHz has the following gains and noise temperatures :

$$T_{in} = 30 \text{ K}, \ G_{RF} = 24 \text{ dB}, \ T_{RF} = 45 \text{ K}, \ F_{IF} = 30 \text{ dB}, \ T_{IF} = 1000 \text{ K}, \ T_m = 500 \text{ K}.$$

Calculate the system Noise temperature assuming that the mixer has a gain $G_m = 0$ dB. Recalculate the system noise temperature when the mixer has a 10 dB loss. How can the noise Temperature of the receiver be minimized when the mixer has a loss of 10 dB?

4. What are the various considerations and assumptions while designing the uplink and downlink budget?

5. Geostationary satellites use L, C, Ku and Ka bands. The path length from an earth station to the GEO satellite is 38,500 km. For this range calculate the path loss in decibels for the following frequencies.

(i) 1.6 GHz, 1.5 GHz.

(ii) 6.2 GHz, 4.0 GHz.

(iii) 14.2 GHz, 12.0 GHz.

(iv) 30.0 GHz, 20.0 GHz.

April 2012

1. Explain the meaning of Noise temperature of receiver. With the help of overall noise model of the receiver derive the expression for effective system noise temperature T_s for the receiving earth stations.   [10]

2. Calculate the Noise Temperature (T_s) of a 8 GHz receiver, which has different gains and noise temperatures as given below.   [6]

$$T_{in} = 50 \text{ K}, \ T_{RF} = 50 \text{ K}, \ G_{RF} = 23 \text{ dB}, \ T_M = 500 \text{ K}, \ G_M = 0 \text{ dB}, \ T_{IF} = 1000 \text{ K}, \ G_{IF} = 30 \text{ dB}.$$

3. Explain the terms :   [8]

(i) C/N ratio.

(ii) G/T ratio.

BROADBAND COMMUNICATION SYSTEM

1. (a) Describe with the aid of a neat diagram the basic principle of total internal reflection that enables the fiber to work as a light conduit. [4]

(b) What is dispersion? Explain intermodal dispersion and intramodal dispersion. [3]

(c) Explain the conditions necessary to attain lasing action in LASERs. Also state the advantages of laser diodes over LEDs, for use in context of fiber-optic communication. [3]

OR

2. (a) An optical fiber has core refractive index of 1.5 and cladding refractive index 1.45. Calculate the following :

(i) Critical angle.

(ii) Numerical Aperture.

(iii) Acceptance angle. [3]

(b) Describe the important linear and nonlinear scattering losses in optical fibers. [4]

(c) The radiative and nonradiative recombination lifetime of majority carriers in active region of double heterojunction InGaAsP LED are 30 ns and 100 ns respectively. Determine bulk recombination life time and power internally generated within the device when peak emission wavelength is 1310 nm at a LED drive current of 40 mA. [3]

3. (a) Explain in detail the importance of budgets. What are different system considerations for rise time budget? [5]

(b) Describe the system design considerations involved in establishing point-to-point optical fiber link. [5]

OR

4. (a) Explain the concept of link power budget and rise time budget in optical fiber communication system. [4]

(b) Components are chosen for a digital optical link of overall length of 6 km. LED chosen is capable of launching – 10 dBm into a graded index fiber, which has an attenuation of 3 dbkm^{-1}. It requires splicing every kilometer with a loss of 0.5 dB per splice. The connector loss at the receiver is 1.5 dB. The receiver requires mean optical power of – 41 dBm in order to give necessary BER of 10^{-10}. It is also predicted that a safety margin of 6 dB will be required. Write down the optical power budget for the system and hence determine its viability. [6]

5. (a) Explain the principle of operation of Febry-parot amplifier. State the advantages and disadvantages of SOA. [6]

   (b) Draw neat diagrams of SOA and EDFA. Compare SOA and EDFA. [4]

OR

6. (a) Describe the concept of Wavelength Division Multiplexing and state the key system features of WDM. [4]

   (b) Describe and differentiate between active and passive WDM couplers. [4]

   (c) A 2×2 biconical tapered fiber coupler data sheet with a 40/60 splitting ratio states that the insertion losses are 2.7 dB for the 60% channel and 4.7 dB for the 40% channel

   (i) If the input power is 200 µW , find the output levels P_1 and P_2.

   (ii) find the excess loss of the coupler. [2]

•••

MODEL END-SEMESTER QUESTION PAPER
BROADBAND COMMUNICATION SYSTEM

1. (a) Using ray theory, derive an expression for the Numerical Aperture and the solid acceptance angle in terms of the physical parameters of a step index fiber and explain their importance in the propagation of optical signal through the fiber. Why do we need cladding? **[7]**

  (b) Describe the system design considerations involved in establishing point-to-point optical fiber link. **[6]**

  (c) Explain the principle of operation of Erbium Doped Fiber Amplifiers (EDFA) with a neat diagram. Comment on the gain and noise in EDFA. **[7]**

OR

2. (a) Write short note on : WDM Couplers/ Splitters and explain its Excess loss, Insertion loss Coupling ratio, Isolation and Uniformity properties.

  (b) Explain the design procedure with graphical representation for link loss budget analysis. **[8]**

  (c) Calculate the pulse spreading caused by material dispersion for a graded index multimode fiber working at λ = 850 nm if the fiber's length is 100 km and the light source is an LED whose rms spectral width is 70 nm. The given parameters are :

  Dispersion slope, S_0 = 0.097 ps/nm^2.km and λ_0 = 1343 nm.

3. (a) Why is there a need for satellite communication? Explain various advantages and limitations of satellite communication. **[8]**

  (b) Define Kepler's laws of orbiting bodies and derive an equation to show that the third law is true for any orbiting satellite. **[8]**

OR

4. (a) Explain following terms : **[8]**

  (i) Apogee and Perigee.

  (ii) Ascending and Descending nodes.

  (iii) Arguement of perigee.

  (iv) Mean and True anomaly.

  (b) Explain the effect of solar eclipse on the performance of a geostationary satellite. In what way it is related to fixing the parking place of a satellite? **[8]**

5. (a) Discuss the TT and C system of a communication satellite.   [8]

    (b) What are the characteristics that are most important in satellite antenna?

OR

6. (a) Explain how attitude and orbit control is achieved from an earth station?   [8]

    (b) Explain briefly antenna tracking systems.   [8]

7. (a) Diagrammatically explain the combined Uplink and Downlink carrier to noise ratio.   [8]

    (b) Discuss the significance of system noise temperature and G/T ratio in calculation of link budget.   [8]

OR

8. (a) Derive the Link-Power Budget equation.   [10]

    (b) Comment on the following :   [6]

       (i) Uplink Budget.

       (ii) Downlink Budget.

       (iii) Overall link Budget.

●●●

SOLVED UNIVERSITY QUESTION PAPERS

IN SEM. EXAM. FEBRUARY 2016

Time : 1 Hour   **Max. Marks : 30**

Instruction to the candidates:

(1) Answer Q.1 or Q.2, Q.3 or Q.4, Q.5 or Q.6.

(2) Neat diagrams must be drawn wherever necessary.

(3) Figures to the right indicate full marks.

(4) Use of electronic pocket calculator is allowed.

(5) Assume suitable data if necessary.

1. (a) Compare and contrast single mode step index fiber, Multi mode step index fiber and multi mode graded index fiber sketch index profile for each of the above fiber. **[6]**

Ans. Please Refer Article No. 1.8 on Page No. 1.18 to 1.23.

(b) A multi mode step index fiber with core diameter of 80 µm and relative index difference of 1.5% is operating at a wavelength of 0.85 µm. If the core refractive index is 1.48. Estimate the normalized frequency for the fiber and the number of modes guided. **[4]**

Ans. Please Refer Example No. 1.5. on Page No. 1.20.

OR

2. (a) Describe the following terms with respect to optical fiber. **[6]**

    (i)   Attenuation

    (ii)   Absorption

    (iii) Scattering

    (iv) Dispersion

Ans.   **(i)**   **Attenuation :** Please Refer Article No. 1.12.1. on Page No. 1.63.

      (ii) **Absorption :** Please Refer Article No. 1.12.2. on Page No. 1.64.

      (iii) **Scattering :** Please Refer Article No. 1.12.3. on Page No. 1.66.

      (iv) **Dispersion :** Please Refer Article No. 1.13. on Page No. 1.73

(b) A multimode silica fiber has core refractive index 1.48 and cladding refractive index 1.46. Calculate critical angle and numerical aperture. **[4]**

Ans. The critical angle ϕ_c at the core – cladding interface is given by

$$\phi_c = \sin^{-1}\left(\frac{n_2}{n_1}\right) = \sin^{-1}\left(\frac{1.46}{1.48}\right) = 80.40$$

$$NA = \left(n_1^2 - n_2^2\right)^{1/2} = (2.1904 - 2.1316)^{1/2}$$

$$= (0.0588)^{1/2} = 0.2424$$

P.1

3. (a) An optical fiber link of length 4 km comprises a fiber cable with an attenuation of 5 dB/km. The splice losses for the link are estimated at 2dB/km, and the connector losses at the source and detector are 3.5 and 2.5 dB respectively. Ignoring the effects of dispersion on the link determine the total channel loss.   **[3]**

Ans. The total channel loss is given by

$$C_L = \alpha_f L + \alpha_{con} + \alpha_{splice}$$

Where,

$$\alpha_f = \text{fiber loss in dB/km}$$

$$L = \text{length of fiber link}$$

$$\alpha_{con} = \text{connector loss}$$

$$\alpha_{splice} = \text{splice loss}$$

$$C_L = 5 \times 4 + 3.5 + 2.5$$

$$= 20 + 3.5 + 2.5$$

$$= 26 \text{ dB.}$$

(b) For a digital link using optical fiber, LED with its driver circuit has rise time of 15ns, Taking a typical LED spectral width of 40nm, a material dispersion related rise – time degradation of 21 ns over the 6 km link. Model dispersion induced fiber rise – time is 3.9 nsec. Assuming that receiver has 25 MHz bandwidth, the contribution to the rise – time degradation from receiver is 14 nsec. Calculate link – time. Hence find which data format is supported NRZ or RZ?   **[3]**

Ans.

$$t_{tx} = 15 \text{ nsec}$$

$$t_{mat} = 21 \text{ nsec}$$

$$t_{mod} = 3.9 \text{ nsec}$$

Now,

$$t_{rx} = \frac{350}{B_{rx}}$$

$\therefore$

$$t_{rx} = \frac{350}{25}$$

$\therefore$

$$t_{rx} = 14 \text{ nsec}$$

Since

$$t_{sys} = \left(\sum_{i=1}^{N} t_{ri}^2 \right)^{1/2}$$

$$t_{sys} = [15^2 + 21^2 + 3.9^2 + 14^2]^{1/2}$$

$$t_{sys} = 29.61 \text{ nsec}$$

(c) Enlist the components contributing to system rise – time for a digital link. Write the formula for total system rise – time.   **[4]**

Ans. Please Refer Article No. 2.5. on Page No. 2.14.

OR

4. **(a)** Explain key system requirements to establish point to point link.   **[6]**

Ans.   Please Refer Article No. 2.2.1. on Page No. 2.1.

   (b) Enlist and Explain different fiber misalignment losses.   **[4]**

Ans.   Different Fiber Mislignment Losses are

   (1)   Material Absorption Losses

      (a) Intrinsic Absorption

      (b) Extrinsic Absorption

   (2)   Linear Scattering Losses

      (a) Rayleigh Scattering

      (b) Mie Scattering

   (3)   Nonlinear Scattering Losses

      (a) Stimulated Brillouin Scattering

      (b) Stimulated Raman Scattering

   (4)   Fiber bend loss

5. **(a)** Explain operational principle of WDM. Support your answer with suitable diagram. **[4]**

Ans.   Please Refer Article No. 3.2.1 on Page No. 3.2.

   (b) A 2×2 biconical tapered fiber coupler has an i/p optical power level of $P_0 = 200\mu W$. The output powers at the other three ports are $P_1 = 90\mu W$, $P_2 = 85\mu W$ and $P_3 = 63\mu W$. Calculate coupling ratio (splitting ratio), excess loss, insertion loss and cross talk for the coupler.   **[6]**

Ans.   Please Refer Example No. 3.1 on Page No. 3.9.

OR

6. **(a)** Write short note on semiconductor optical amplifier.   **[4]**

Ans.   Please Refer Article No. 3.9 on Page No. 3.24

   (b) Explain application of FBG as demultiplexer for WDM system.   **[6]**

Ans.   Please Refer Article No. 3.5.3 on Page No. 3.19.

END SEM. EXAM. MAY 2016

Time : $2\frac{1}{2}$ Hours   **Max. Marks : 70**

Instructions to the candidates :

(1)   Answer Q. 1 or Q. 2, Q. 3 or Q. 4, Q. 5 or Q. 6, Q. 7 or Q. 8, Q. 9 or Q. 10.

(2)   Neat diagrams must be drawn wherever necessary.

(3)   Figures to the right indicate full marks.

(4)   Assume suitable data, if necessary.

1. (a) Explain advantages of optical fibers as communication media. Also state its drawbacks if any.   **[6]**

Ans.   Please Refer Article No. 1.5.1 on Page No 1.10.

Advantages [4M]

Drawbacks [2M]

(b) Define cut off wavelength of a single mode fiber. Determine the cutoff wavelength for a step index fiber to exhibit single-mode operation when the core refractive index and radius are 1.46 and 4.5 μm, respectively, with the relative index difference being 0.25%. Assume $V_c = 2.405$.   **[4]**

Ans.   Please Refer Example No. 1.4 on Page No 1.15.

OR

2. (a) A multimode step index fiber has a relative refractive index difference of 1% and a core refractive index of 1.5. The number of modes propagating at a wavelength of 1.3 μm is 1100. Estimate the diameter of the fiber core.   **[6]**

Ans.   Relative refractive index = 1% = 0.01

$$n_1 = 1.5$$

$$mg = 1100, \lambda = 1.3\ \mu m$$

$$mg = \frac{V^2}{2} = 1100 \qquad \dots [1M]$$

$$\therefore \quad V = 46.9$$

Now,
$$V = \frac{2\pi}{\lambda}\, a\, n_1\, (2\Delta)^{1/2} \qquad \dots [1M]$$

$$46.9 = \frac{2\pi \times a \times 1.5 \times (0.02)^{1/2}}{1.3 \times 10^{-6}} \qquad \left.\right\}\ \dots [2M]$$

$$\therefore \quad a = \frac{46.9 \times 103 \times 10^{-6}}{2\pi \times 1.5 \times (0.02)^{1/2}}$$

P.4

$\therefore$ $a = 45.74\ \mu m$

$\therefore$ Diameter $= 45.74 \times 2 = 91.48\ \mu m$ ... [2M]

(b) Describe working principle with the aid of simple ray diagram

    (i)   Multimode Step Index Fiber

    (ii)   Graded Index Fiber

Compare advantages and drawbacks of these fibers.

Draw a diagram indicating major possible fiber refractive index profiles for the profile parameter $\alpha = 1, 2$ and ∞.   **[4]**

Ans.   Please Refer Article No. 1.8.1 on Page No. 1.18.

         For Comparison : Please Refer Page No. 1.23.

---

3. (a) An optical fiber system is to be designed to operate over an 8 km length without repeaters. The rise times of the chosen components are: **[6]**

Source (LED) : 8 ns

Fiber: Intermodal 5 ns km^{-1}

(pulse broadening) intra-modal : 1 ns km^{-1}

Detector (*p-i-n* photodiode) : 6 ns

From system rise time considerations, estimate the maximum bit rate that may be achived on the link when using an NRZ format.

Ans.   8 Km length without repeaters

         Rise times = 8 ns = LED   = 5 ns/Km fiber cable (intra)

                               = 1 ns/Km (inter)

PIN detector 6 ns.

$$t_{sys} = \left(t_{tx}^2 + t_{GVD}^2 + t_{mod}^2 + t_{rx}^2\right)^{1/2} \qquad ... [2M]$$

$$= \left[(8ns)^2 + [5ns/km \times 8]^2 + [1\ ns/km \times 8]^2 + [6\ ns]^2\right]^{1/2}$$

$$= \left[(8ns)^2 + (4ons)^2 + (8ns)^2 + (6ns)^2\right]^{1/2}$$

$\therefore$ $t_{sys} = 42\ ns$ ... [2M]

Now $t_{sys} = \dfrac{0.70}{\text{bit rate of NRZ}}$ ... [1M]

$$BT_{max} = \frac{0.7}{t_{sys}} = \frac{0.7}{42\ ns}$$

$$= 0.0166 \times 10^9$$

$$= 16.6\ Mbit/s \qquad ... [1M]$$

(b) Compare and contrast p-i-n and avalanche photo detectors as optical detector for optical fiber communication. **[4]**

Ans.

Sr. No.	PIN Photodiode	Avalanche Photodiode
1.	Intrinsic layer is placed between two highly doped p and n regions.	Here Π layer is placed between two highly doped p and n regions.
2.	Response time is less.	Greater response time.
3.	Small output current.	Large output current.
4.	Sensitivity is less.	More sensitive.
5.	Amplifier is used to connect externally.	No need of external amplifier.

OR

4. (a) Compare the following optical amplifiers based on working principle, amplification gain and drawbacks. **[6]**

(i) SOA

(ii) EDFA

Ans. Please Refer Article Nos. 3.9 and 3.11 on Page Nos 3.24 and 3.33 respectively.

(b) Compare and contrast LED and ILD as optical source for optical fiber communication. **[4]**

Ans. Please Refer Article No. 1.28 on Page No. 1.153.

5. (a) Which orbital parameter completely specify the orbit? Briefly describe each one of these. **[6]**

Ans. Minimum three parameters expected with one line explanation out of the following. [Equation or diagram]

(i) Ascending and descending nodes (ii) Equinoxes (iii) Solstics (iv) Apogee (v) Perigee (vi) Eccentricity (vii) semi-major axis (viii) Right ascension and Ascending node (ix) Inclination

Please Refer Article No. 4.6 on Page No. 4.13.

(b) Verify that geostationary satellite needs to be at a height of about 35780 km above the surface of the Earth. Assume radius of earth to be 6380 km and $\mu = 39.8 \times 10^{13}$ Nm^2/kg. **[6]**

Ans. The orbital radius a is given by

$$T^2 = \frac{4\pi^2 a^3}{\mu}$$

… [2M]

Rearranging the equation, we get

$$a^3 = T^2\mu / (4\pi)^2 \qquad \text{... [2M]}$$

Consider $\qquad T$ = in seconds $\qquad\qquad$ ... [1M]

$\qquad\qquad\qquad a$ = 35780 Km $\qquad\qquad$ ... [1M]

(c) Explain briefly various look angles for satellite earth station. **[6]**

Ans. Please Refer Article No. 4.8 on Page No. 4.30.

OR

6. (a) How does solar eclipse affect satellite communication? **[6]**

Ans. Please Refer Article No. 4.12.3 on Page No. 4.51

(b) Determine the maximum possible line of sight distance between two geostationary satellites orbiting the earth at a height of 36000 km above the surface of the Earth. Assume radius of earth to be 6380 km. **[6]**

Ans. The maximum possible line of sight distance between two geostationary satellites is given by,

$$d = 2(R+H)\sin\left[\cos^{-1}\left(\frac{R}{R+H}\right)\right] \qquad \text{... [2M]}$$

$$= 2(6380 + 36000)\sin\left[\cos^{-1}\left(\frac{R}{6380 + 36000}\right)\right]$$

$$\left.\begin{array}{l} \\ \\ \\ \end{array}\right\} \quad \text{... [2M]}$$

$$= 2(42380)\sin\left[\cos^{-1}\left(\frac{6380}{42380}\right)\right]$$

$$= 2 \times 42380 \times 0.9886$$

$$= 83793.73\ \text{Km} \qquad \text{... [2M]}$$

(c) Describe the launch sequence used to inject satellite. **[6]**

Ans. Please Refer Article No. 4.11.2 on Page No. 4.48.

Possible geostationary launch sequence diagram [2M], Explanation [4M].

7. (a) What are the different components of satellite's power supply subsystem? Briefly describe the role of each component. **[8]**

Ans. Please Refer Article No. 5.5 on Page No. 5.15.

(b) Explain in detail any two of the following for orbital satellite **[8]**

(i) Communication Subsystem

(ii) Antenna Subsystem.

Ans. Please Refer Article Nos. 5.6 and 5.7 on Page Nos. 5.17 and 5.27 respectively.

OR

8. (a) Explain double conversion transponder for 14/11 GHz band. Support your answer with suitable diagram and specify frequencies of local oscillators and IF amplifiers. **[8]**

Ans. Please Refer Article No. 5.6 on Page No. 5.24 last points onwards upto Page No. 5.26.

(b) Explain Bath-tub curve for probability of failure with reference to satellite. Hence define MTBF. State relation of MTBF with probability of device failure. Explain various redundancy connections used to mitigate device failure. **[8]**

Ans. Please Refer Article No. 5.8, in that reliability upto redundancy, on Page Nos. 5.36 5.37 and 5.38.

---

9. (a) A 4 GHz receiver has the following gains and noise temperatures

T_{in} = 25K, T_{RF} = 50 K, T_{IF} = 1000 K, T_m = 500 K, G_{RF} = 23 dB, G_{IF} = 30 dB. **[8]**

(i) Calculate the system noise temperature assuming that the mixer has a gain G_m = 0 dB.

(ii) Recalculate the system noise temperature when the mixer has a 10 dB loss.

(iii) How can the noise temperature of the receiver be minimized when the mixer has a loss of 10 dB?

(iv) The system has an LNA with a gain of 50 dB. A section of lossy waveguide with an attenuation of 2 dB is inserted between the antenna and the RF amplifier. Find the new system noise temperature for a waveguide temperature of 300° K.

Ans. Please Refer Example Nos. 6.3 and 6.4 on Page Nos. 6.18.

(b) What do you understand by link budget of a satellite communication link? What type of information do you get from such an analysis? **[8]**

Ans. Please Refer Article No. 6.4.1 Link budgets on Page No. 6.21.

OR

10. (a) Explain various losses in downlink analysis. **[8]**

Ans. Please Refer Article No. 6.4 on Page No. 6.21.

(b) A transponder of a Ku-band satellite has a linear gain of 127 dB and a nominal output power at saturation of 5 W. The satellite's 14 GHz receiving antenna has a gain of 26 dB on axis.

Calculate the power output of an uplink transmitter that gives an output power of 1 W from the satellite transponder at a frequency of 14.45 GHz when the earth station antenna has a gain of 50 dB and there is a 1.5 dB loss in the waveguide run between the transmitter and antenna. Assume that the atmosphere introduces a loss of 0.5 dB under clear sky conditions and that the earth station is located on the -2dB contour of the satellite's receiving antenna. If the rain in the path causes attenuation

---

P.8

of 7 dB for 0.01% of the year, what output power rating is required for the transmitter to guarantee that a 1 W output can be obtained from the satellite transponder for 99.99% of the year if uplink power control is used?   **[8]**

Ans.   Please Refer Example No. 6.7 on Page No. 6.38.

END SEM. EXAM. NOVEMBER 2016

Time : $2\frac{1}{2}$ Hours   **Max. Marks : 70**

Instructions to the candidates :

(1)   Answer Q.1 or Q.2, Q.3 or Q.4, Q.5 or Q.6, Q.7 or Q.8, Q.9 or Q.10.

(2)   Neat diagrams must be drawn wherever necessary.

(3)   Figures to the right indicate full marks.

(4)   Assume suitable data, if necessary.

1.   (a) Compare and contrast LED and ILD as light source for optical fiber communication.**[6]**

Ans.   Please Refer Article No. 1.28. on Page No. 1.153.

(b) A multimode step index fiber with a core diameter of 80 µm and a relative index difference of 1.5% is operating at a wavelength of 0.85 µm. If the core refractive index is 1.48, estimate :   **[4]**

(i)   The normalized frequency for the fiber

(ii)   The number of guided modes.

Ans.   Please Refer Example No. 1.5. on Page No. 1.20.

OR

2.   (a) Define the following terms with respect to single mode fiber   **[6]**

(i)   Cut off Wavelength

(ii)   Mode field diameter

Ans.   **(i)   Cut off Wavelength:** Please Refer Article No. 1.6.3. on Page No. 1.14.

(ii)   Mode field diameter: Please Refer Article No. 1.10.1. on Page No. 1.59.

(b) A multimode step index fiber has a relative refractive index difference of 1% and a core refractive index of 1.5. The number of modes propagating at a wavelength of 1.3 µm is 1100. Estimate the diameter of the fiber core.   **[4]**

Ans.   Please Refer Q. 2 (a) in May 2016.

3.   (a) The following parameters are established for a long-haul single-mode optical fiber system operating at a wavelength of 1.3 µm :

Mean power launched from the laser transmitter:- –3 dBm

Cabled fiber loss: 0.4 dB km^{-1}

Splice loss: 0.1 dB km^{-1}

Connector losses at the transmitter and receiver: 1 dB each

Mean power required at the APD receiver:

When operating at 35 Mbit s^{-1} (BER 10^{-9}): $-$ 55 dBm

Required safety margin: 7 dB

Estimate the maximum possible link length without repeaters when operating at 35 Mbit s^{-1} (BER 10^{-9}). It may be assumed that there is no dispersion-equalization penalty at this bit rate. **[6]**

Ans.   Refer Article no. 1.20.2 on Page No. 1.116.

(b) Write a short note on (Any one) **[4]**

   (i)   SOA

   (ii)   EDFA

Ans.   **(i)**   **SOA:** Please Refer Article 3.9. on Page No. 3.24.

   (ii)   **EDFA:** Please Refer Article 3.11. on Page No. 3.33.

OR

4.   **(a)** Explain working principle of FBG and explain its usage as WDM de-multiplexer.   **[6]**

Ans.   Please Refer Article Nos. 3.5.2 and 3.5.3. on Page No. 3.16 and 3.19.

(b) What is need of WDM? Hence compare Dense WDM and Coarse WDM.   **[4]**

Ans.   Please Refer Article Nos. 3.2 and 3.2.2. on Page No. 3.2 and 3.4

---

5.   **(a)** State and explain Kepler's three laws of planetary motion.   **[6]**

Ans.   Please Refer Article No. 4.6.1. on Page No. 4.17.

(b) The apogee and perigee distance of a satellite orbiting in an elliptical orbit are, respectively, 45000 km and 7000 km. Determine the following   **[6]**

   (i)   Semi-major axis of the elliptical orbit

   (ii)   Orbital eccentricity

   (iii)   Distance between the center of Earth and the center of elliptical orbit.

Ans.

(i)   The major axis of an elliptical orbit is a straight line between the apogee and perigee. Hence, for a semi-major axis length a, earth radius r_e, perigee eight hp and apogee height h_a.

$$2a = 2r_e + h_p + h_a$$

Using a mean earth radius of 6378.14 km.

$$2a = 2 \times 6378.14 + 45000.0 + 7000.0$$

$$2a = 64756.28$$

$$a = 32378.14.$$

Thus the semi-major axis of the orbit has a length

$$a = 32378.14 \text{ km.}$$

(ii) The eccentricity of the orbit is given by e and is calculated using the following formula:

$$r_e + h_p = a.(1 - e)$$

$$e = 1 - \frac{(r_e + h_p)}{a}$$

$$= 1 - \frac{13378.14}{32378.14}$$

$$= 0.586$$

The semilaters rectum is

$$P = a (1 - e^2)$$

$$= 32378 (1 - (0.586)^2)$$

$$= 21259.61 \text{ km.}$$

$$\text{Now latus rectum} = 2P = 2 \times 21259.61 = 42519.23 \text{ km}$$

(iii) The distance between foci = ae

$$= 0.586 \times 32378.14$$

$$= 18973.59 \text{ km.}$$

(c) A satellite is in an elliptical orbit with a perigee of 1000 km and an apogee of 4000 km. Using a mean earth radius of 6378 km, find the period of the orbit in hours, minutes and seconds, and the eccentricity of the orbit. **[6]**

Ans. Please Refer Example No. 4.2. on Page No. 4.29.

OR

6. (a) Compare and contrast use of LEO, MEO and GEO satellite earth orbits for the purpose of communication. **[6]**

Ans. Please Refer Article No. 4.3. on Page No. 4.3.

(b) The difference between the farthest and the closest points in a satellite's elliptical orbit from the surface of the Earth is 30000 km and the sum of the distances is 50000 km. If the mean radius of the earth is considered to be 6378 km, determine the orbit eccentricity. **[6]**

Ans. Farthest point is Apogee, and closet point is perigee

$$40000 - 30000 = hp$$

$$hp = 10000$$

$$
\begin{array}{rcrcll}
& ha & - & hp & = & 30000 \quad Km \\
+ & ha & + & hp & = & 50000 \quad Km \\
\hline
& 2ha & & & = & 80000 \quad Km \\
& ha & & & = & \dfrac{80000}{2} = 4000
\end{array}
$$

The semi-major axis a $= \dfrac{2r_e + hp + ha}{2}$

$$= \dfrac{2 \times 6378 + 40000 + 10000}{2} = 31378 \text{ km.}$$

The eccentricity e is given by

$$e = 1 - \dfrac{r_e + hp}{a}$$

$$= 1 - \dfrac{6378 + 10000}{31378}$$

$$= 1 - \dfrac{16378}{31378}$$

$$= 0.478.$$

(c) An earth station is located at 30°W longitude and 60°N latitude. Determine the earth station's azimuth and elevation angles with respect to a geostationary satellite located at 50°W longitude. The orbital radius is 42164 km. Assume radius of earth to be 6378 km.   **[6]**

Ans.   From the data given

$\lambda = \lambda_\in - \lambda s = 30° - 50° = -20°\in$ of Earth station.

$$\xi = \tan^{-1}\left[\dfrac{\cos \lambda_{AE} \cos \lambda - 0.151}{\sqrt{1 - \cos^2 \lambda_{A\in} \cos^2\lambda}}\right]$$

$$= \tan^{-1}\left[\dfrac{\cos 60 \cos 20 - 0.151}{\sqrt{1 - \cos^2 60 \cos^2 20}}\right]$$

$$= \tan\left[\dfrac{0.5 \times 0.939 - 0.151}{\sqrt{1 - 0.5 \times 0.5 \times 0.939 \times 0.939}}\right]$$

$$= \tan^{-1}\left[\dfrac{0.4695 - 0.151}{\sqrt{1 - 0.25 \times 0.8817}}\right]$$

$$= \tan^{-1}\left[\dfrac{0.3185}{\sqrt{0.7795}}\right]$$

$$= \tan^{-1}\left[\frac{0.3185}{0.8828}\right]$$

$$= \tan^{-1}[0.36]$$

$$= 19.79°$$

$$A_z(cal) = \tan^{-1}\left[\frac{\tan \lambda}{\sin \lambda_{AE}}\right]$$

$$= \tan^{-1}\left[\frac{\tan 20}{\sin 60}\right]$$

$$= \tan^{-1}\left[\frac{0.3639}{0.8660}\right]$$

$$= \tan^{-1}[0.420] = 22.78°$$

Since the sub-satellite point (sat. itself) is SE of earth station.

$$Az = 180° - Az\,(cal) = 180° - 22.78° = 157.22°$$

---

7. (a) Explain with help of block diagram typical tracking, telemetry command and monitoring system. **[8]**

Ans. Please Refer Article No. 5.4. on Page No. 5.12.

(b) What are different types of antennas used in satellite systems? Explain importance of each. **[8]**

Ans. Please Refer Article No. 5.7. on Page No. 5.27.

OR

8. (a) Explain the following with respect to satellite **[8]**

    (i)   Attitude Control System

    (ii) Orbit Control System

Ans. **(i) Attitude Control System:** Please Refer Article No. 5.3.1. on Page No. 5.5.

    (ii) Orbit Control System: Please Refer Article No. 5.3.2. on Page No. 5.10.

(b) Explain double conversion transponder for 14/11 GHz band. Support your answer with suitable diagram and specify frequencies of local oscillators and IF amplifiers. **[8]**

Ans. Please Refer Article 5.6. on Page No. 5.17. With Answer on Page No. 5.24 last paragraph on words upto page. No. 5.26.

---

9. (a) A satellite at a distance of 40,000 km from a point on the earth's surface radiates a power of 10 W from an antenna with a gain of 17 dB in the direction of the observer. Find the flux density at the receiving point, and the power received by an antenna at this point with an effective area of 10 m^2. **[8]**

Ans. Please Refer Example No. 6.1. on Page No. 6.11.

(b) Explain the following terms and hence explain their significance in satellite communication. **[8]**

(i)   G/T Ratio for the Earth station

(ii) Antenna Noise Temperature for the Earth station antenna.

Ans.   **(i)   G/T Ratio for the Earth station:** Please Refer Article No. 6.3.4. on Page No. 6.20.

(ii) Antenna Noise Temperature for the Earth station antenna: Please Refer Article No. 6.3.1. on Page No. 6.12.

OR

10. (a) Explain procedure for satellite Communication link design. **[8]**

Ans.   Please Refer Article No. 6.7.6. on Page No. 6.44.

(b) A C-band earth station has an antenna with a transmit gain of 54 dB. The transmitter output power is set to 100 W at a frequency of 6.100 GHz. The signal is received by a satellite at a distance of 37,500 km by an antenna with a gain of 26 dB. The signal is then routed to a transponder with a noise temperature of 500 k, a bandwidth of 36 MHz and a gain of 110 dB. **[8]**

(i)   Calculate the path loss at 6.1 GHz

(ii) Calculate the power at the output port (output waveguide flange) at the satellite antenna in dBw.

(iii) Calculate the noise power at the transponder input, in dBw, in a bandwidth of 36 MHz.

(iv) Calculate the C/N ratio in the transponder.

Ans.

(i)
$$\text{Path loss} = 20 \log (4\pi R/\lambda)$$
$$= 20 \log (4\pi \times 37500 \times 10^3/0.04918)\text{dB}$$
$$L_P = 199.6 \text{ dB}$$

(ii) Uplink power budget given
$$P_r = P_t + G_t + G_r - L_P \text{ dbw}$$
$$= 20 + 54 + 26 - 199.6 = -99.6 \text{ dBw}$$

(iii)
$$N = KT_S B_N$$
$$= -228.6 + 27 + 75.6 = -126.0 \text{ dBw}$$

(iv)
$$C/M = P_r - N = -99.6 + 126.0 = 26.4 \text{ dB}$$